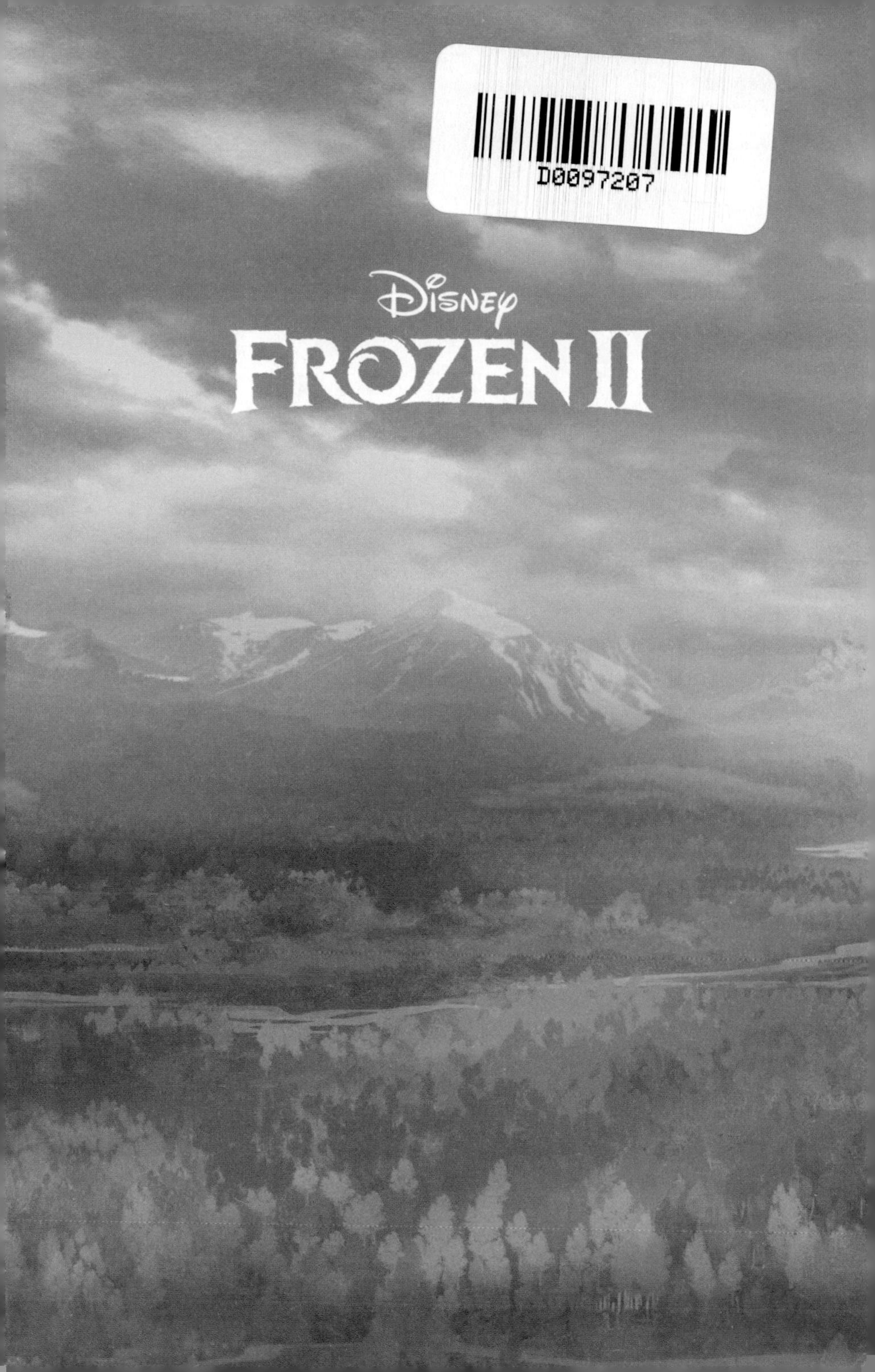

Disney

FROZEN II

Disney

FROZEN II

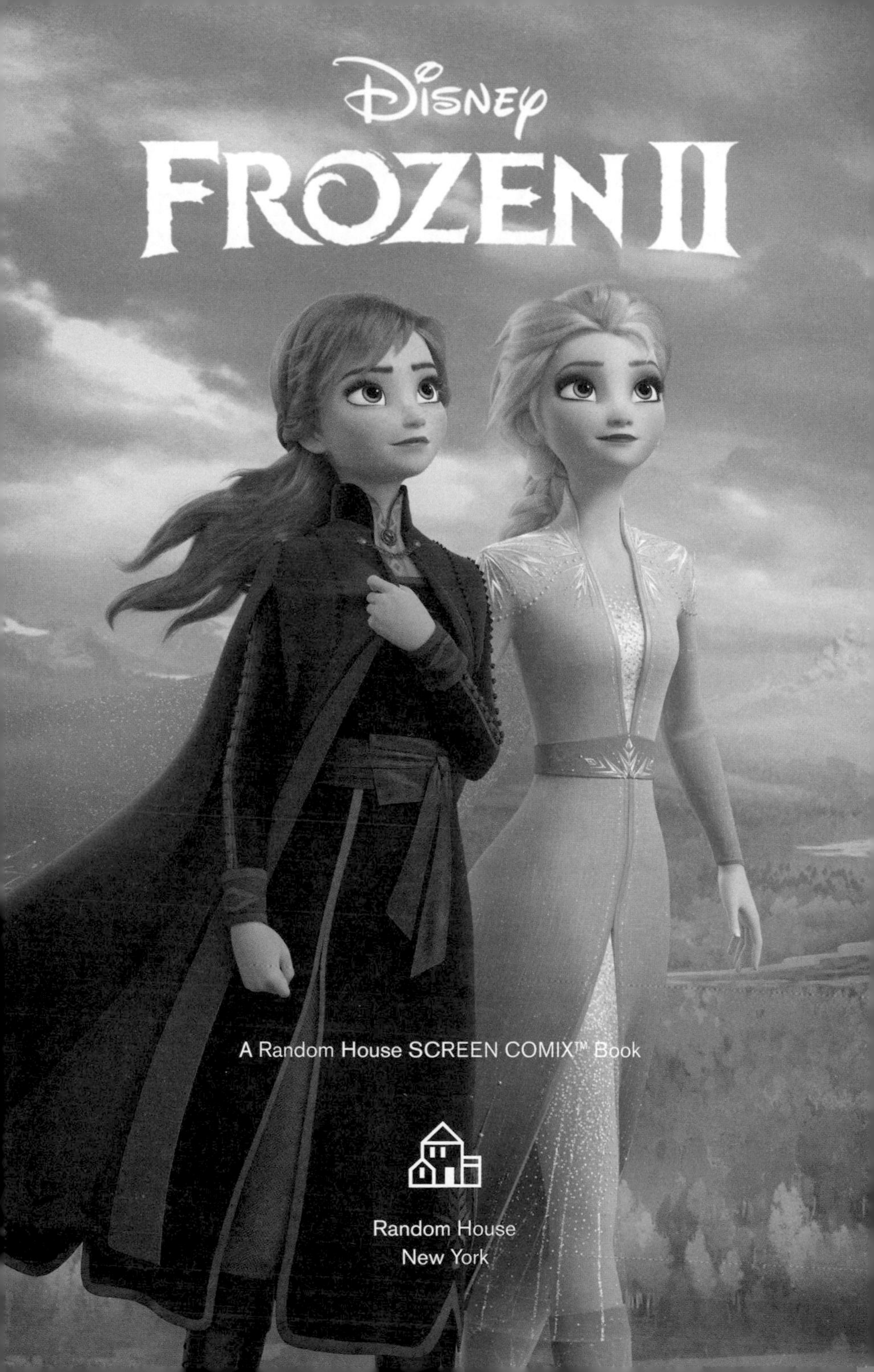

A Random House SCREEN COMIX™ Book

Random House
New York

FROZEN 2

Directed by

Chris Buck

Jennifer Lee

Produced by

Peter Del Vecho, p.g.a.

Screenplay by

Jennifer Lee

Executive Producer

Byron Howard

ISBN 978-0-7364-4138-4
rhcbooks.com
Printed in the United States of America
10 9 8 7 6 5 4 3 2 1

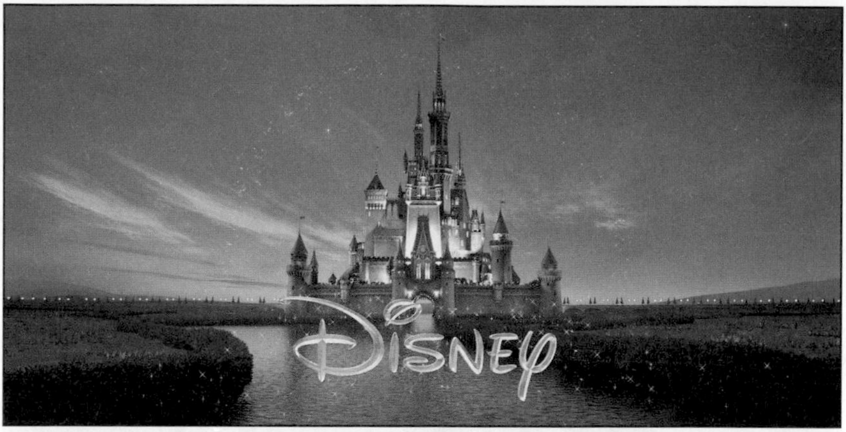
DISNEY

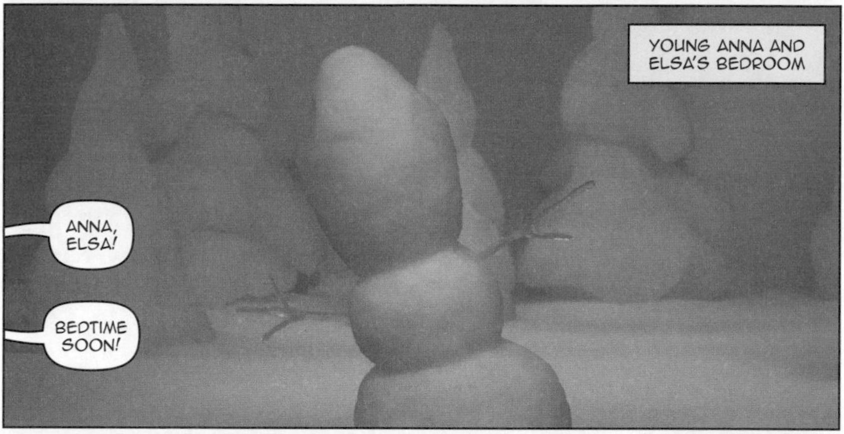
YOUNG ANNA AND ELSA'S BEDROOM
ANNA, ELSA!
BEDTIME SOON!

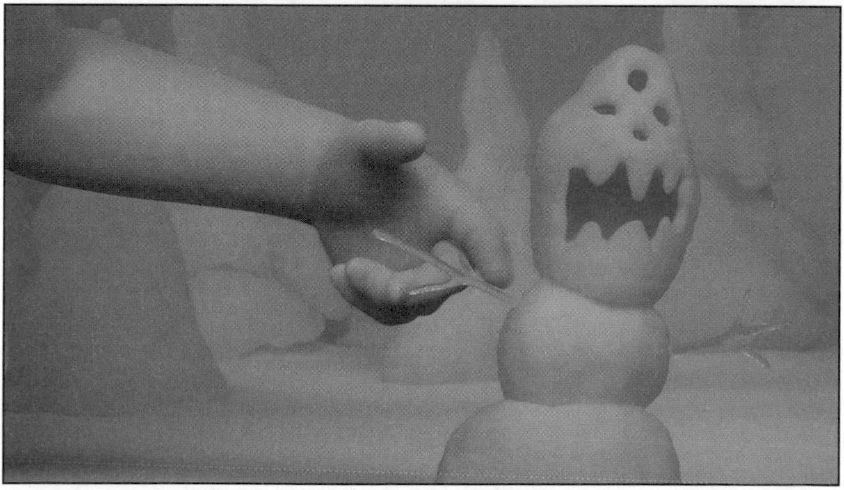

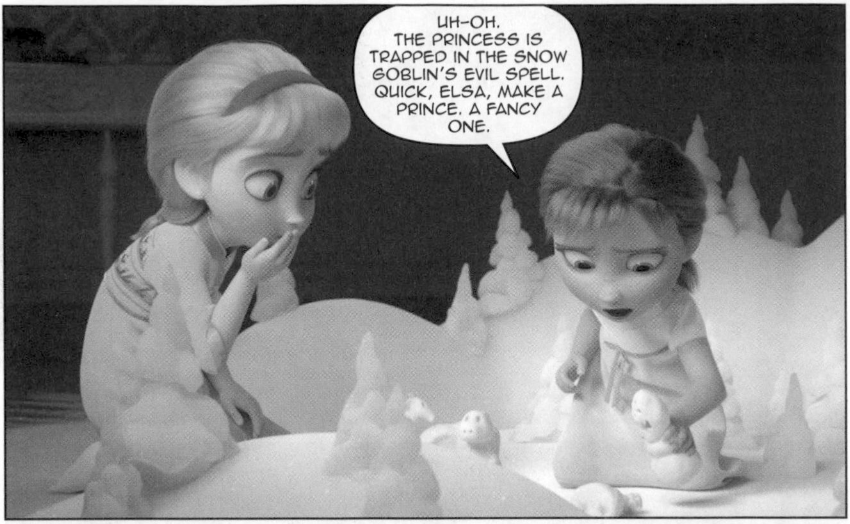
UH-OH. THE PRINCESS IS TRAPPED IN THE SNOW GOBLIN'S EVIL SPELL. QUICK, ELSA, MAKE A PRINCE. A FANCY ONE.

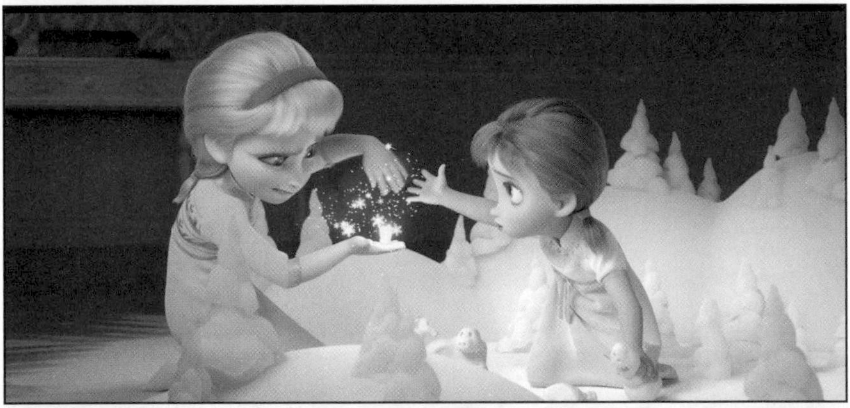

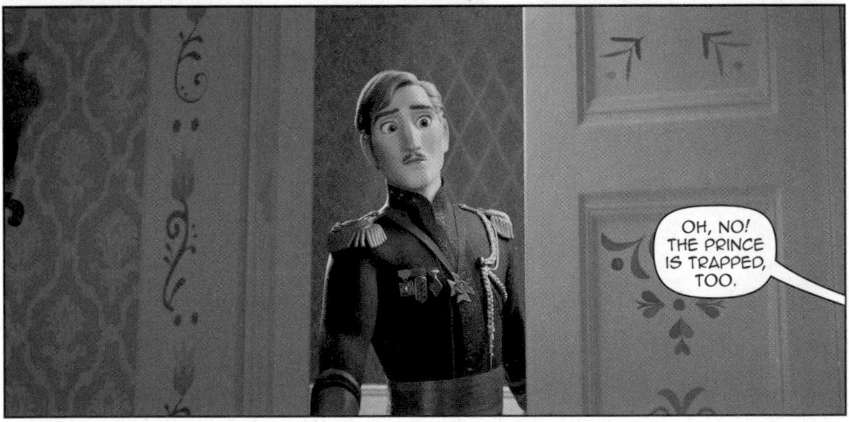
OH, NO! THE PRINCE IS TRAPPED, TOO.

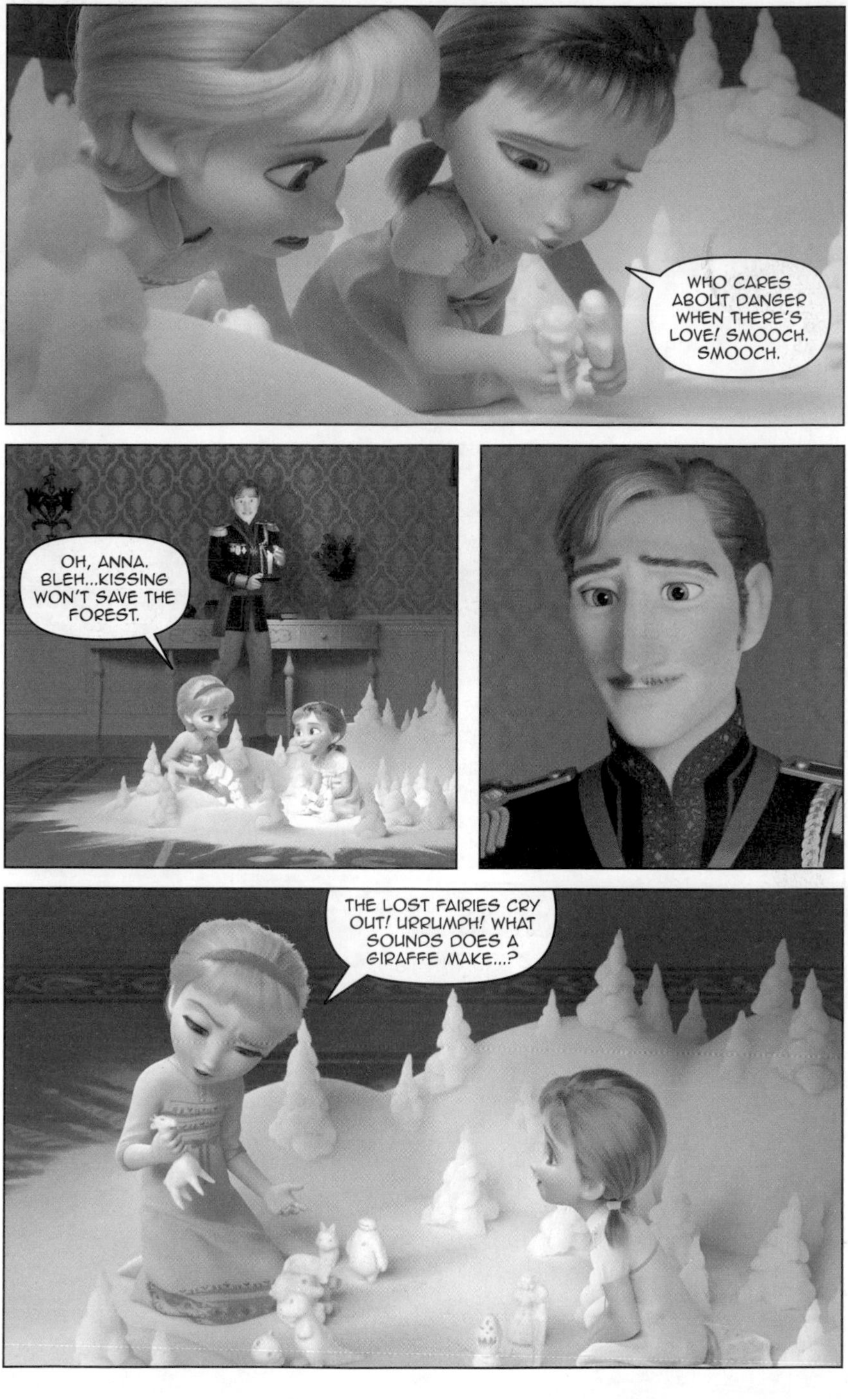
WHO CARES ABOUT DANGER WHEN THERE'S LOVE! SMOOCH. SMOOCH.
OH, ANNA. BLEH...KISSING WON'T SAVE THE FOREST.
THE LOST FAIRIES CRY OUT! URRUMPH! WHAT SOUNDS DOES A GIRAFFE MAKE...?

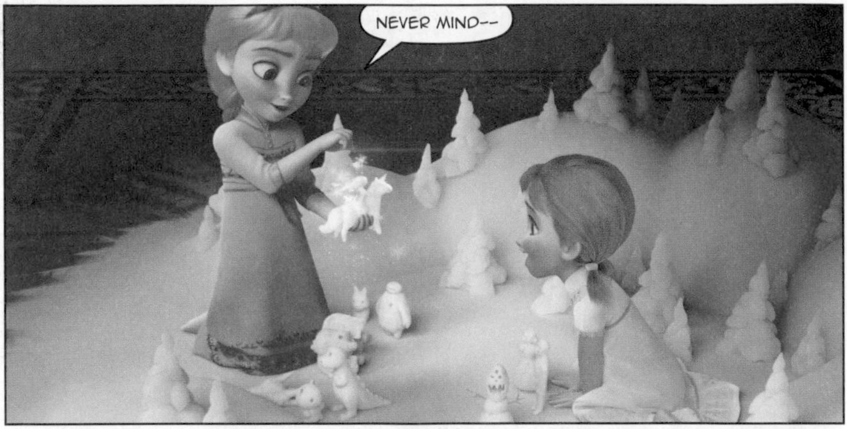
NEVER MIND--

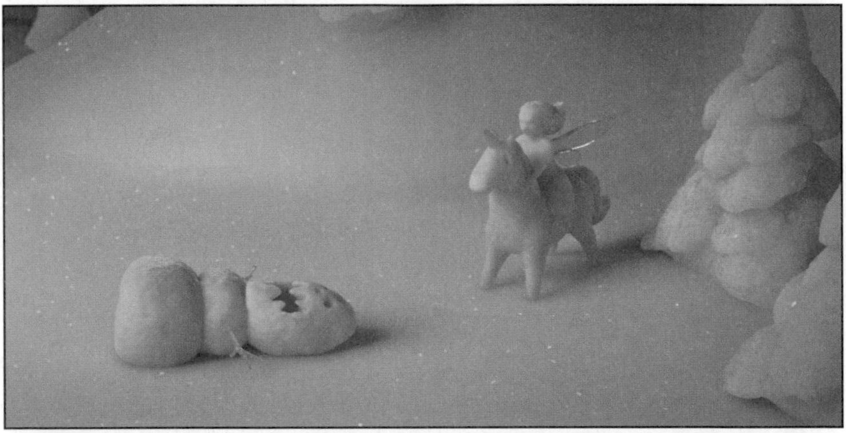

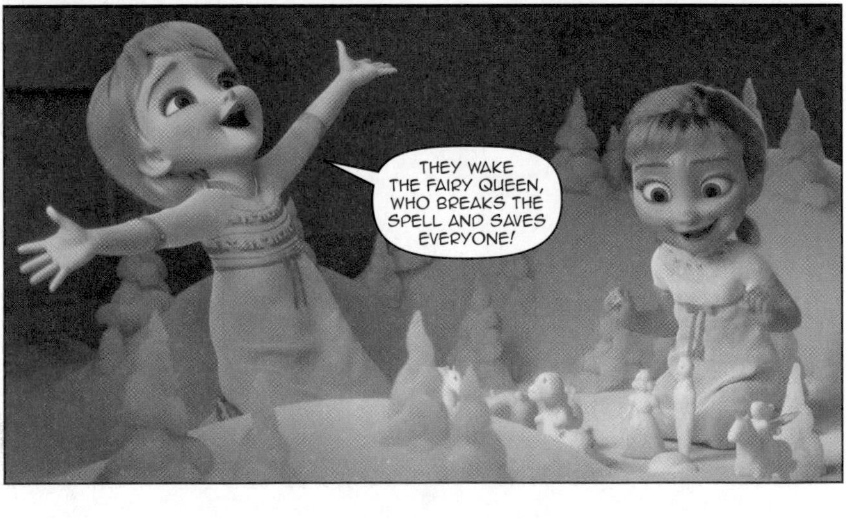
THEY WAKE THE FAIRY QUEEN, WHO BREAKS THE SPELL AND SAVES EVERYONE!

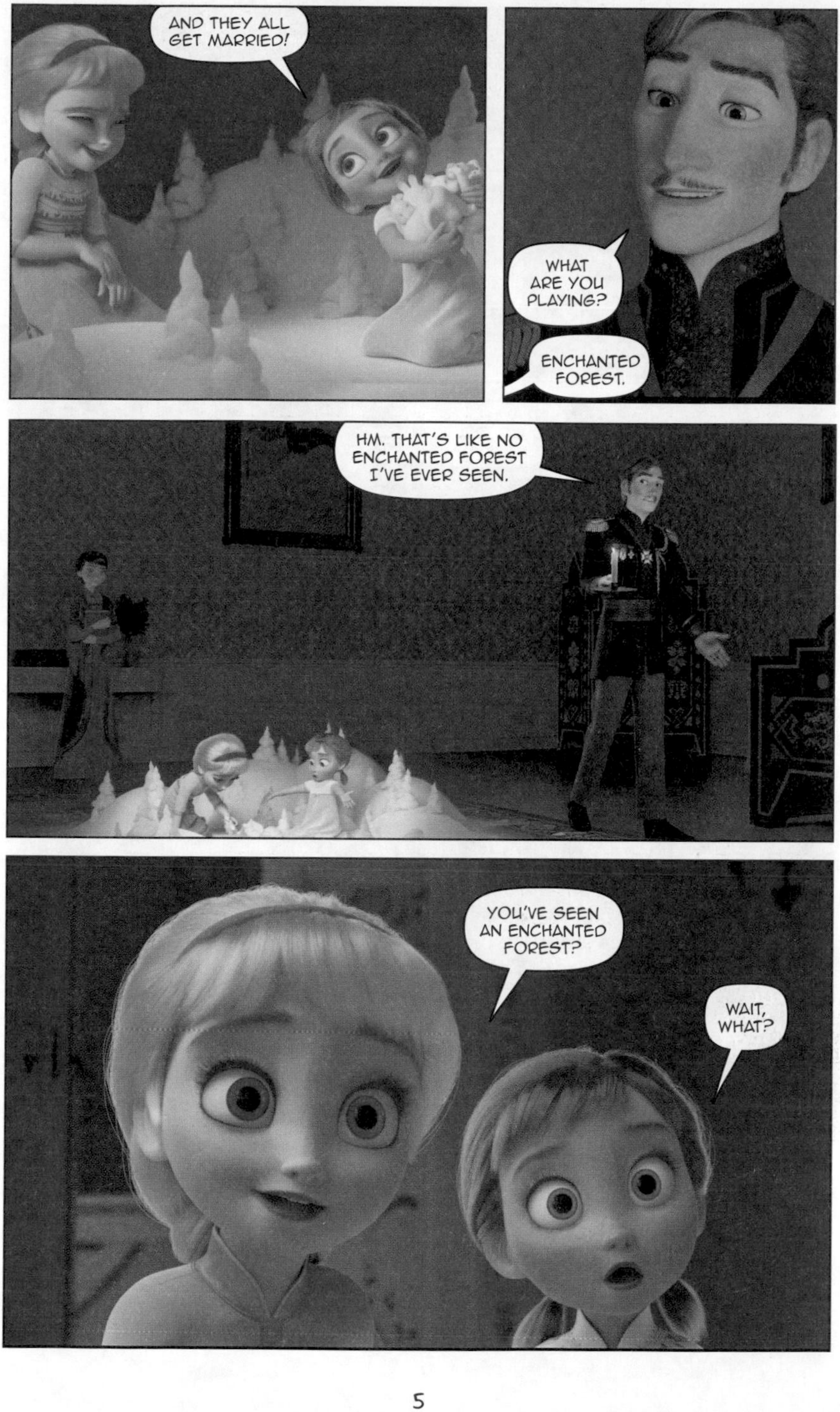
AND THEY ALL GET MARRIED!
WHAT ARE YOU PLAYING?
ENCHANTED FOREST.
HM. THAT'S LIKE NO ENCHANTED FOREST I'VE EVER SEEN.
YOU'VE SEEN AN ENCHANTED FOREST?
WAIT, WHAT?

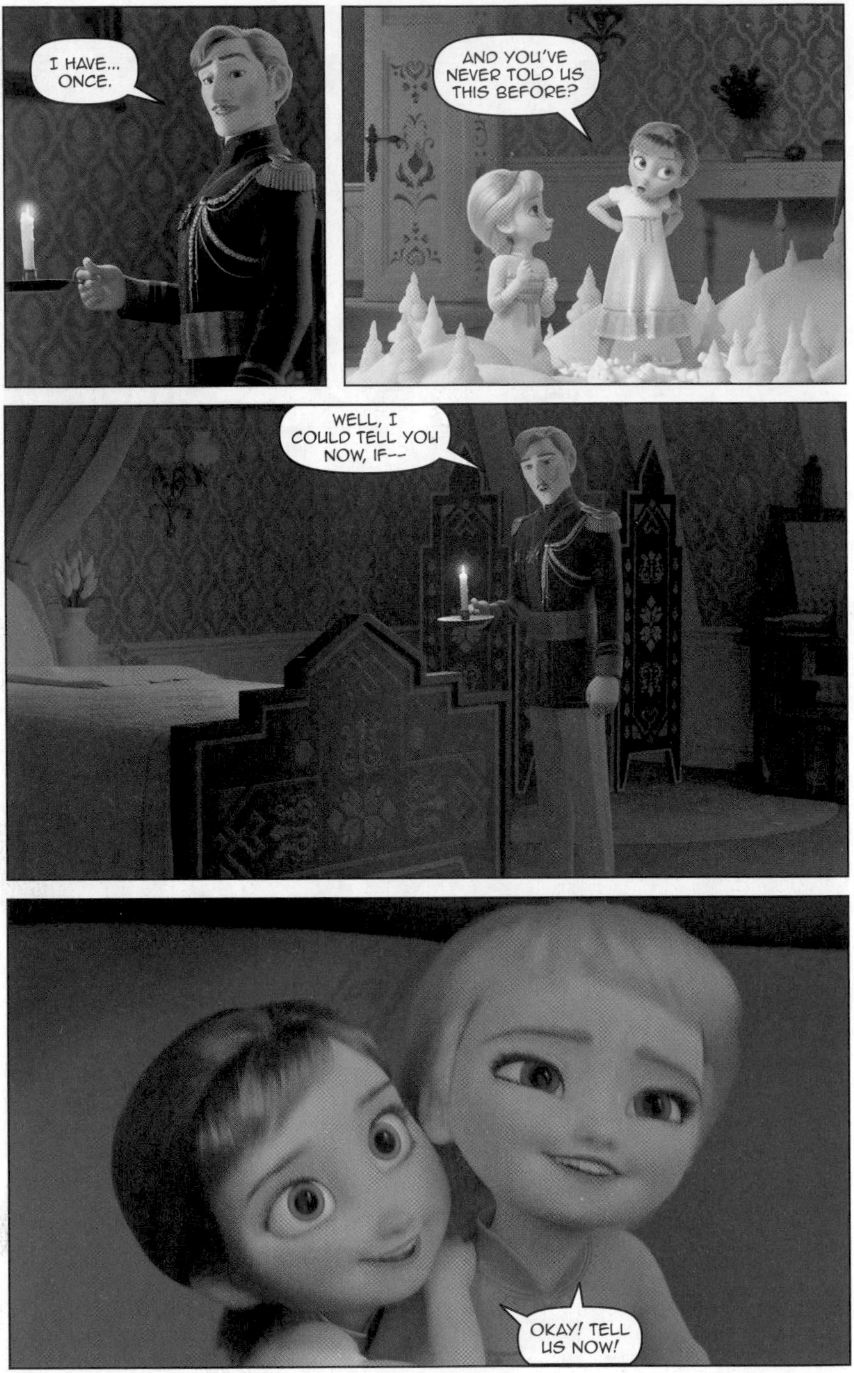
I HAVE... ONCE.
AND YOU'VE NEVER TOLD US THIS BEFORE?
WELL, I COULD TELL YOU NOW, IF--
OKAY! TELL US NOW!

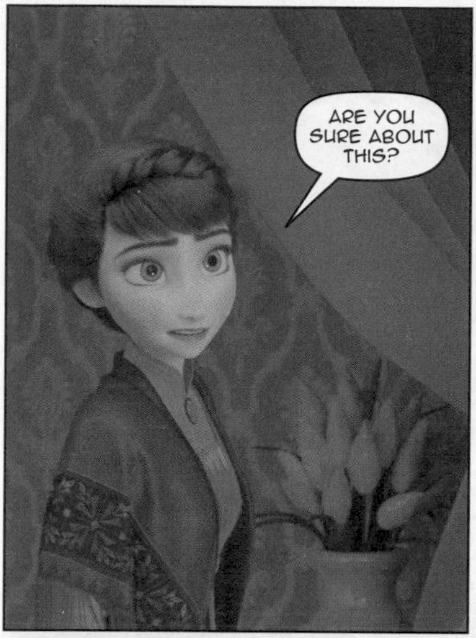
ARE YOU SURE ABOUT THIS?

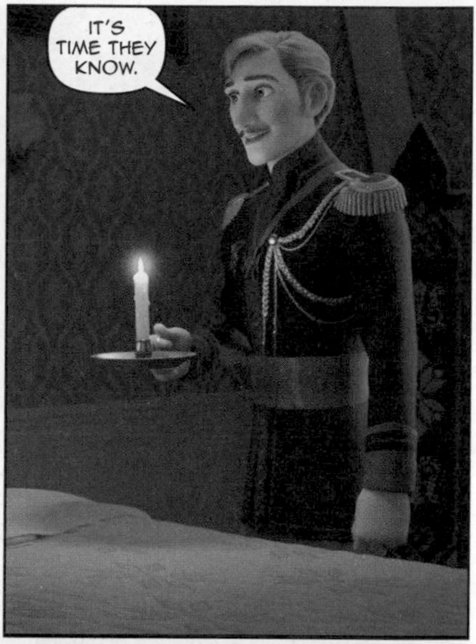
IT'S TIME THEY KNOW.

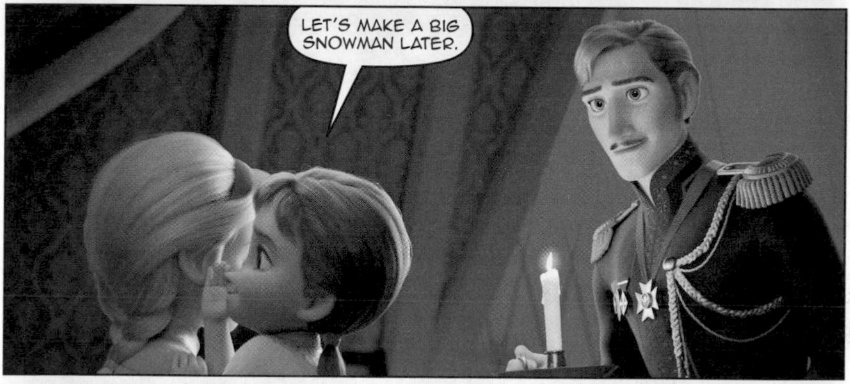
LET'S MAKE A BIG SNOWMAN LATER.

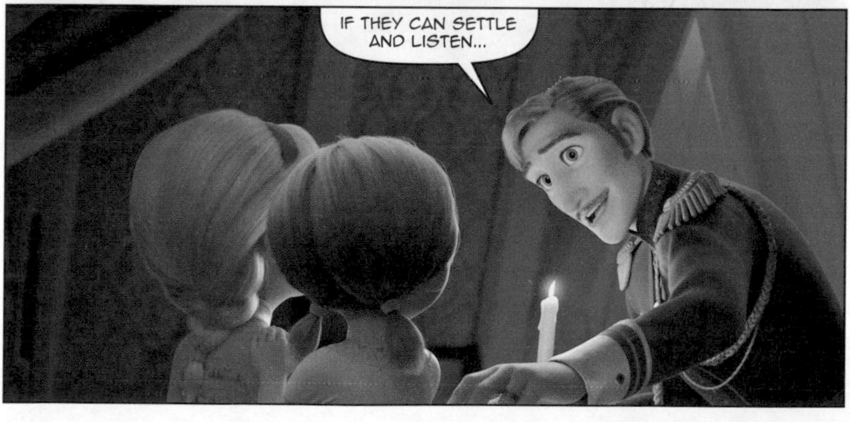
IF THEY CAN SETTLE AND LISTEN...

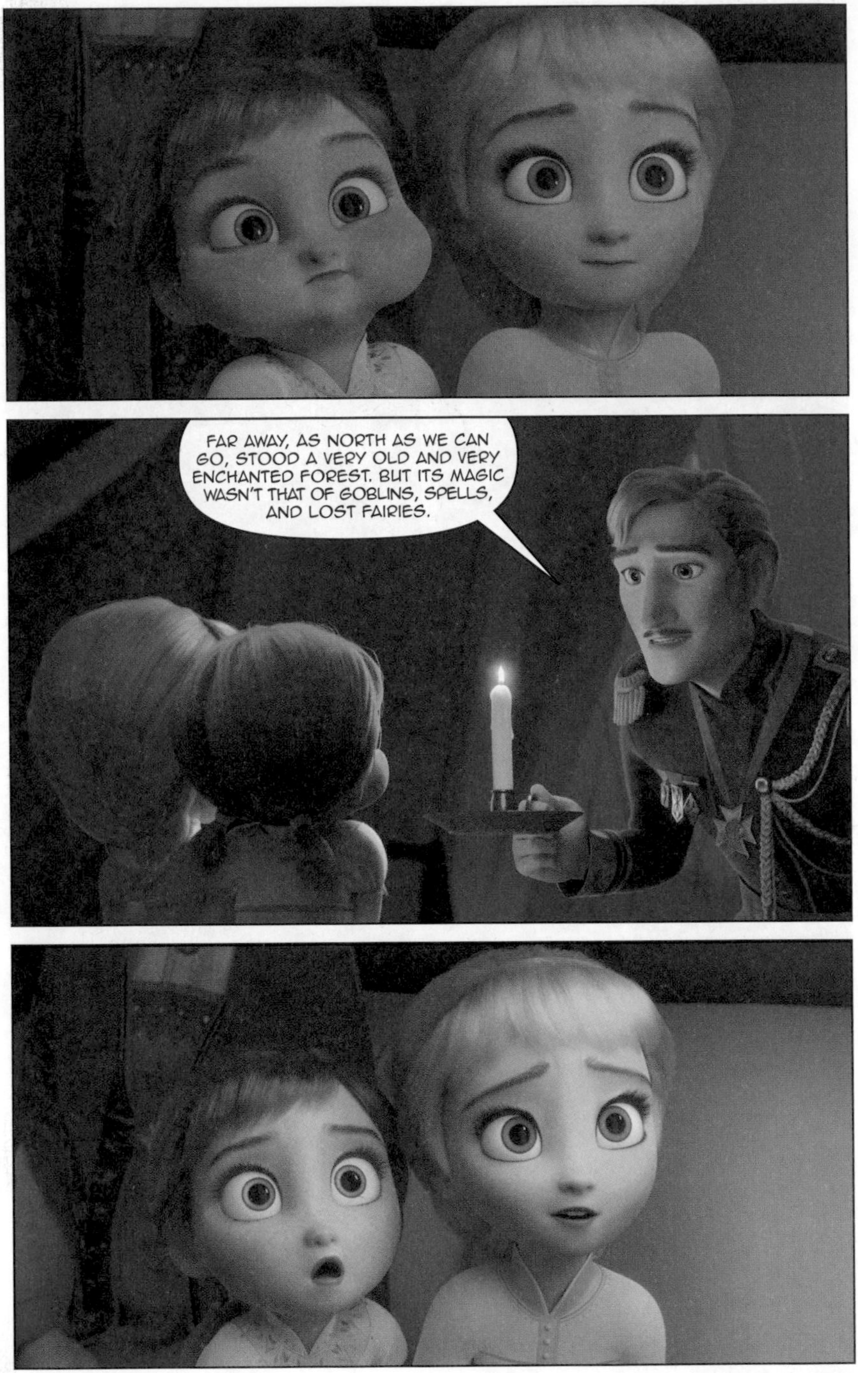
FAR AWAY, AS NORTH AS WE CAN GO, STOOD A VERY OLD AND VERY ENCHANTED FOREST. BUT ITS MAGIC WASN'T THAT OF GOBLINS, SPELLS, AND LOST FAIRIES.

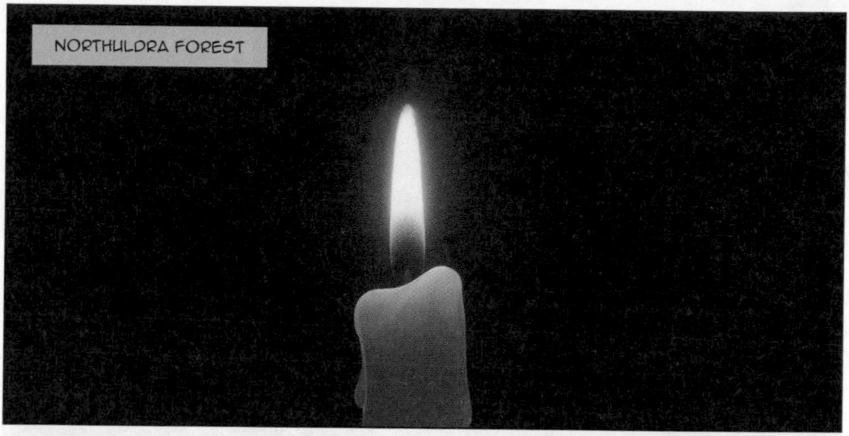
NORTHULDRA FOREST

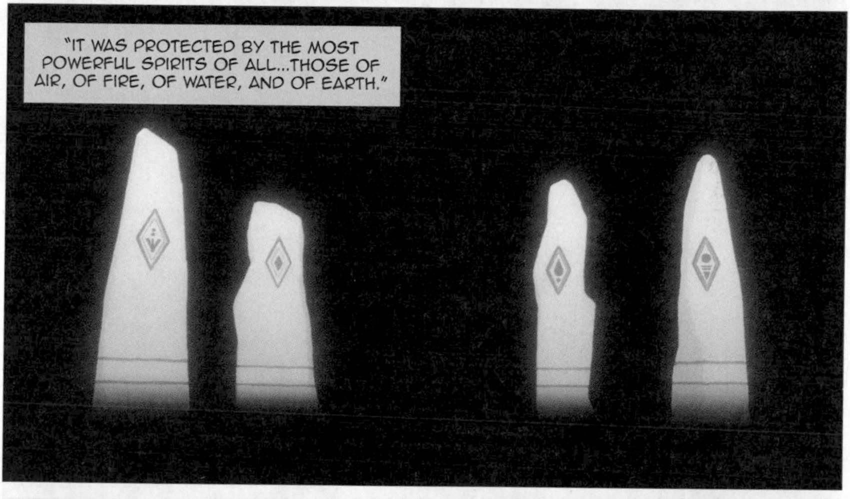
"IT WAS PROTECTED BY THE MOST POWERFUL SPIRITS OF ALL...THOSE OF AIR, OF FIRE, OF WATER, AND OF EARTH."

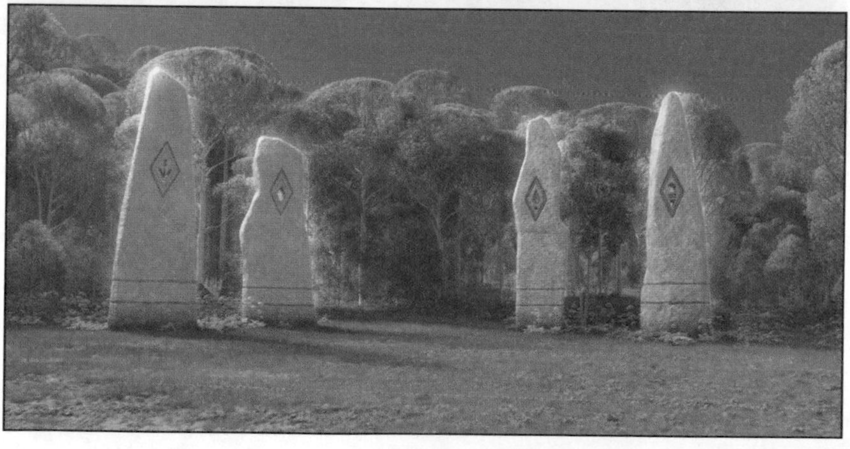

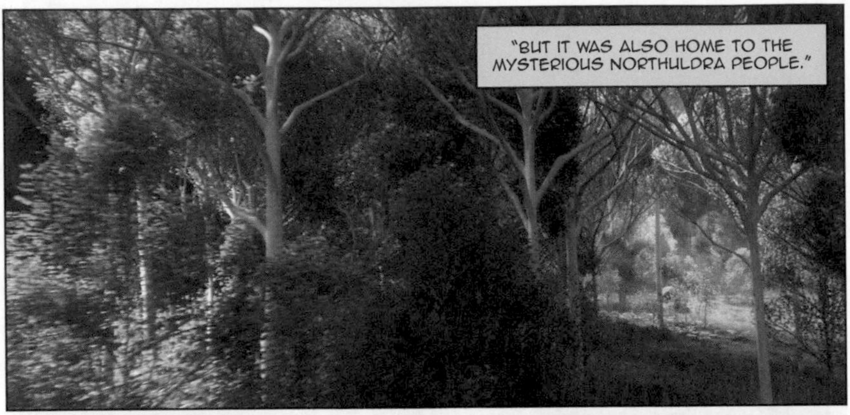
"BUT IT WAS ALSO HOME TO THE MYSTERIOUS NORTHULDRA PEOPLE."

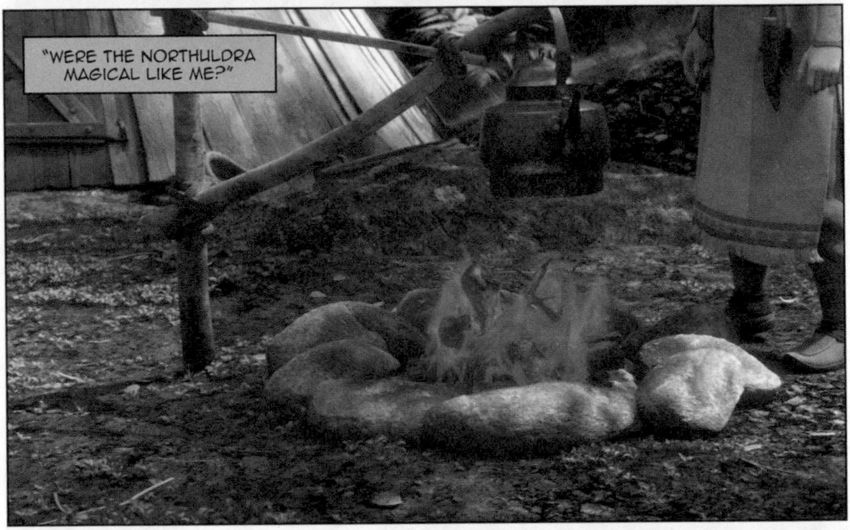
"WERE THE NORTHULDRA MAGICAL LIKE ME?"

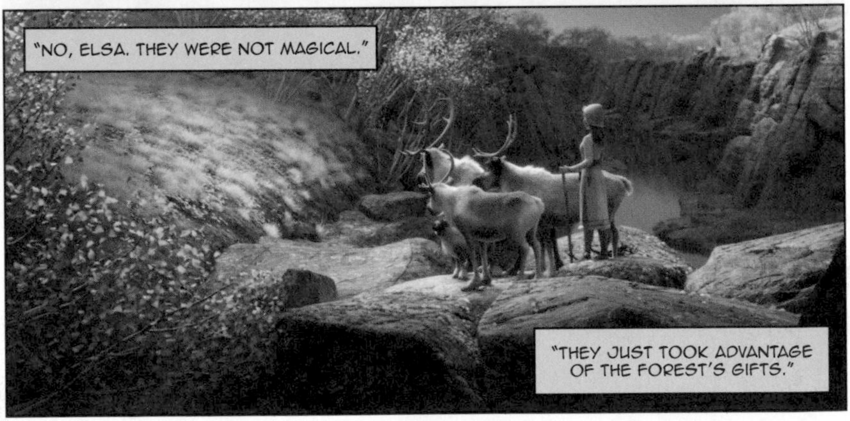
"NO, ELSA. THEY WERE NOT MAGICAL."
"THEY JUST TOOK ADVANTAGE OF THE FOREST'S GIFTS."

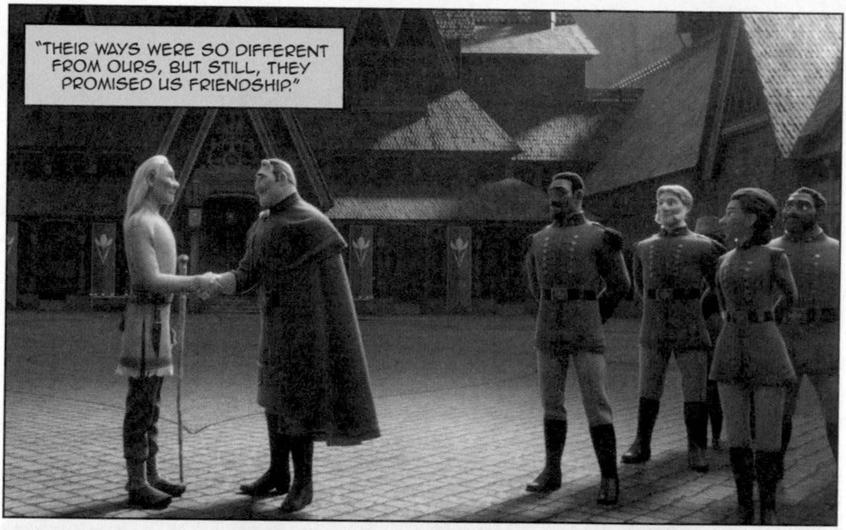
"THEIR WAYS WERE SO DIFFERENT FROM OURS, BUT STILL, THEY PROMISED US FRIENDSHIP."

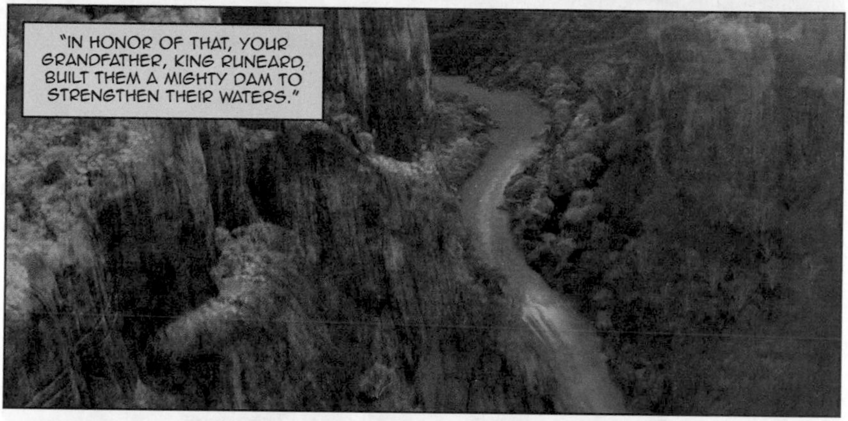
"IN HONOR OF THAT, YOUR GRANDFATHER, KING RUNEARD, BUILT THEM A MIGHTY DAM TO STRENGTHEN THEIR WATERS."

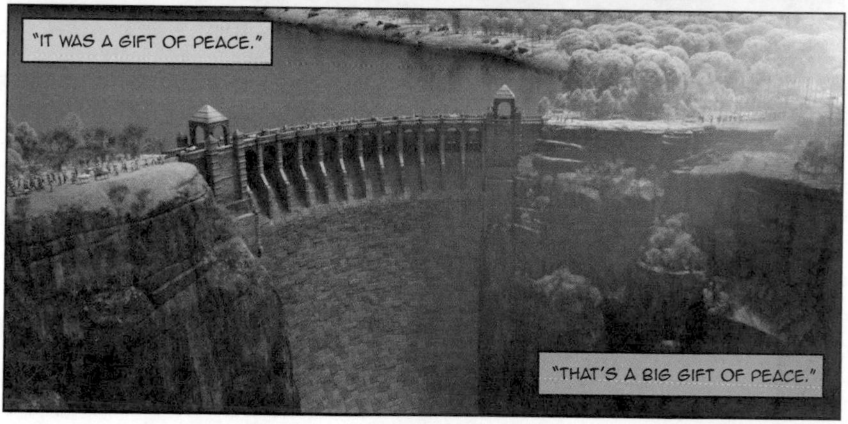
"IT WAS A GIFT OF PEACE."
"THAT'S A BIG GIFT OF PEACE."

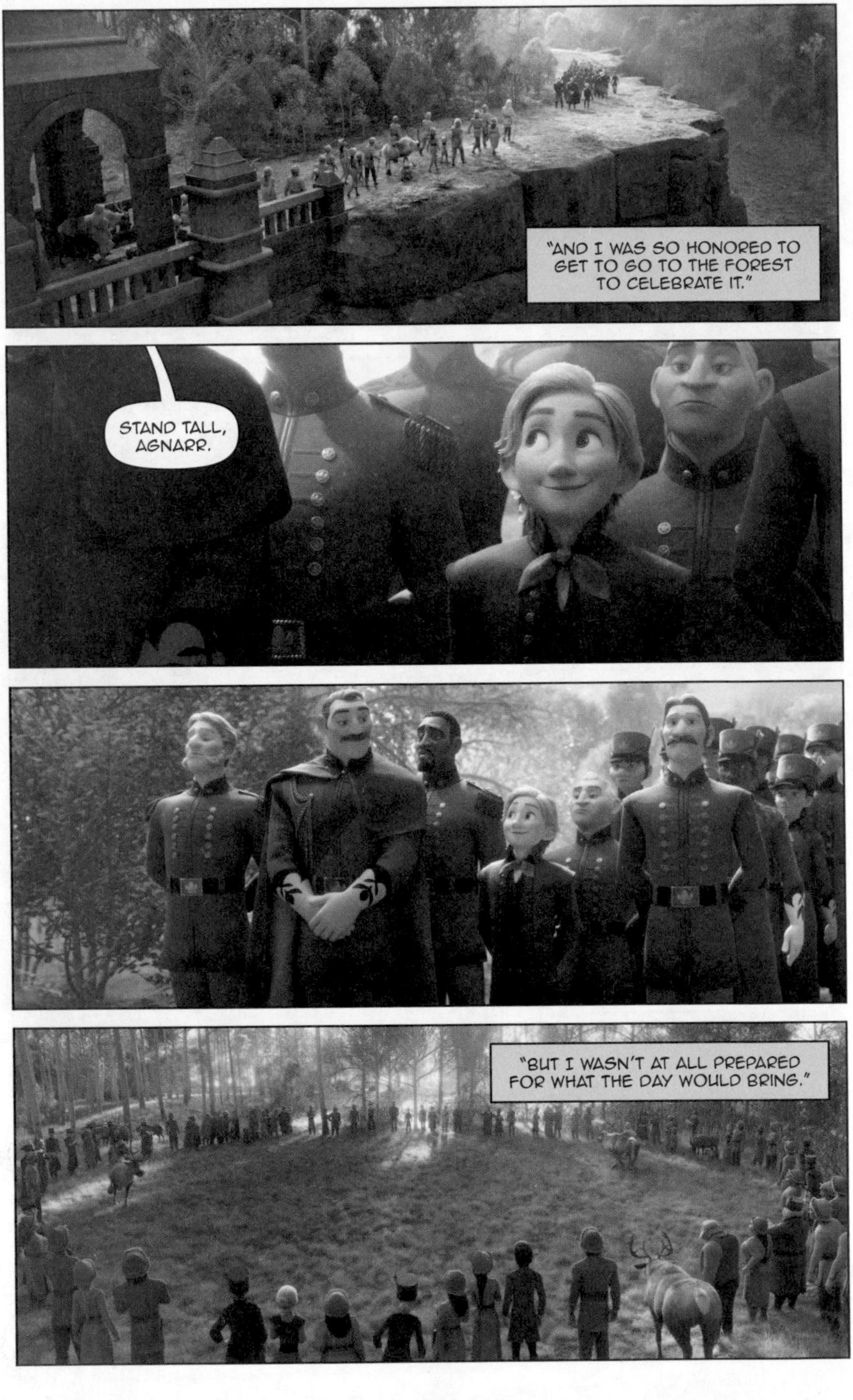
"AND I WAS SO HONORED TO GET TO GO TO THE FOREST TO CELEBRATE IT."
STAND TALL, AGNARR.
"BUT I WASN'T AT ALL PREPARED FOR WHAT THE DAY WOULD BRING."

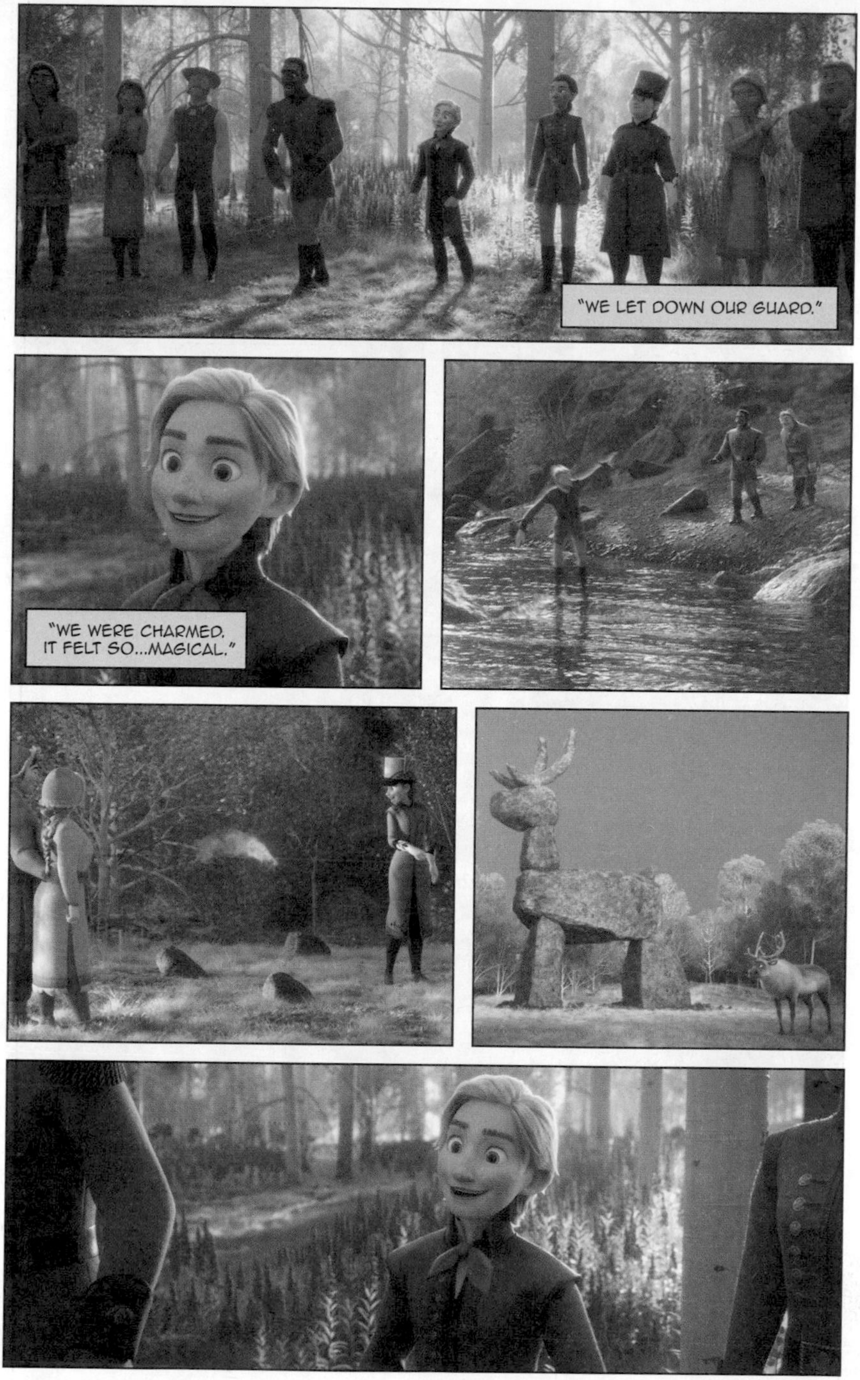
"WE LET DOWN OUR GUARD."
"WE WERE CHARMED. IT FELT SO...MAGICAL."

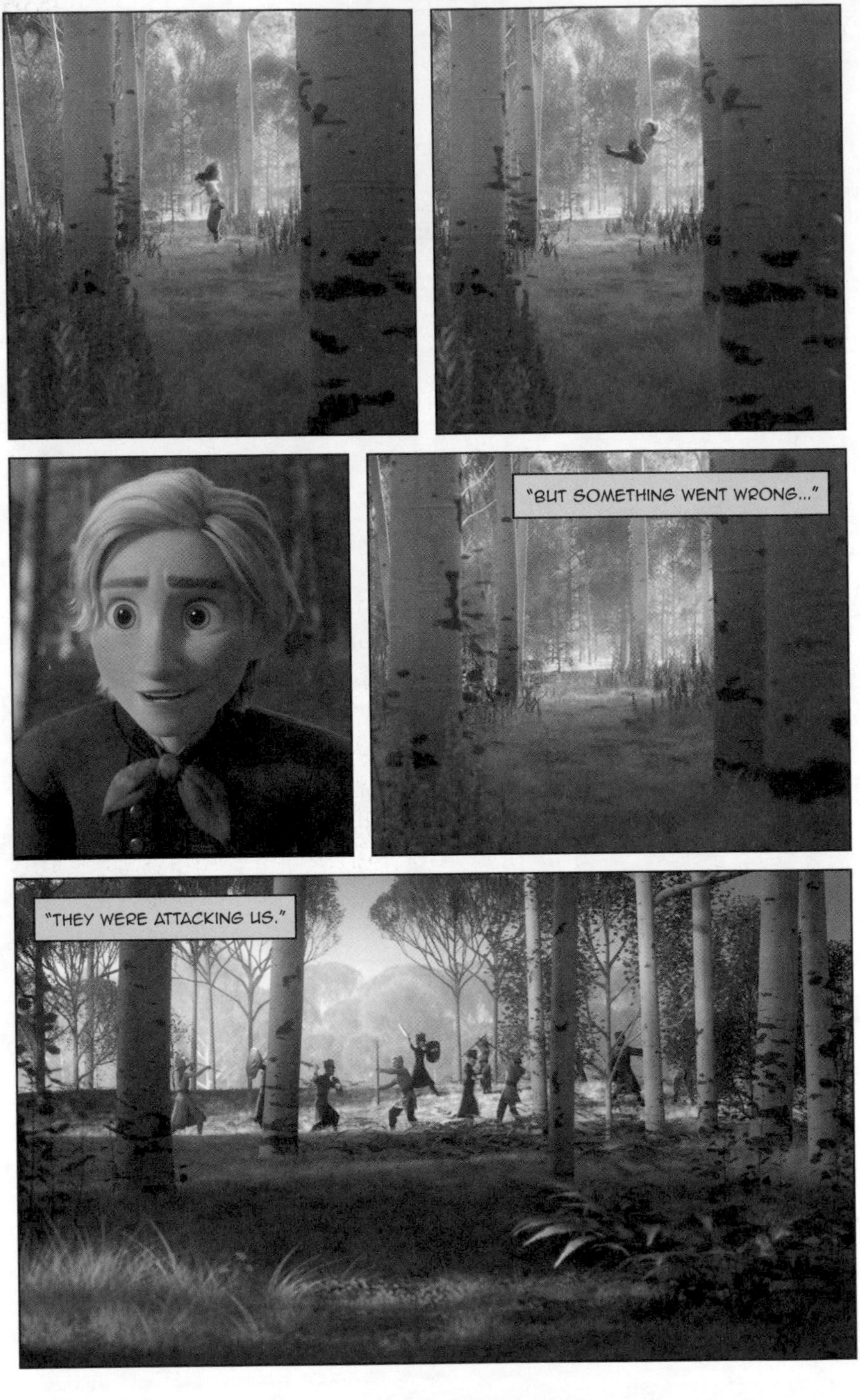
"BUT SOMETHING WENT WRONG..."
"THEY WERE ATTACKING US."

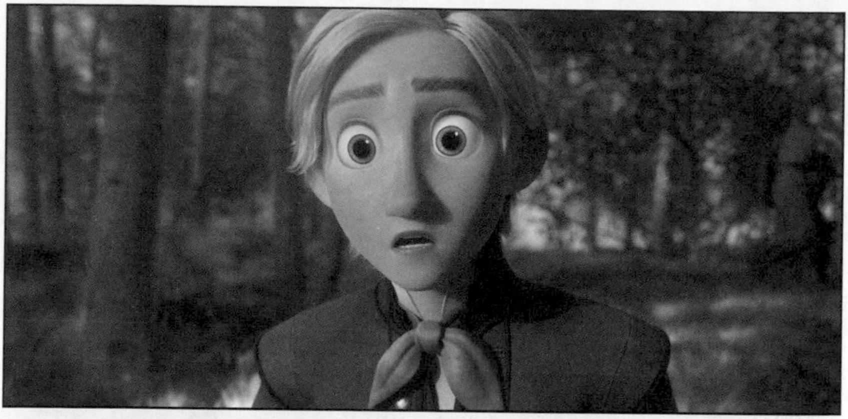

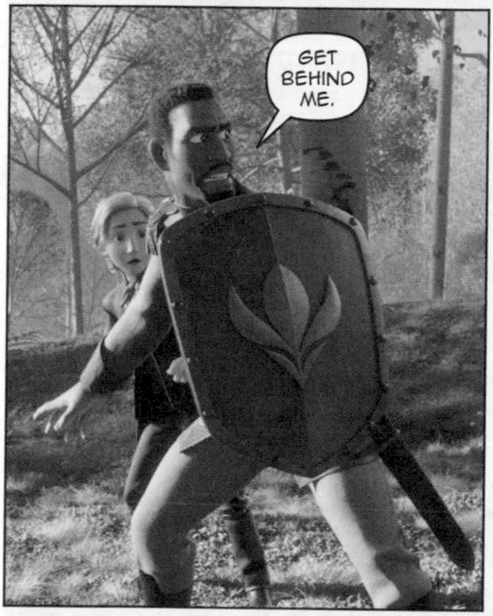
GET BEHIND ME.

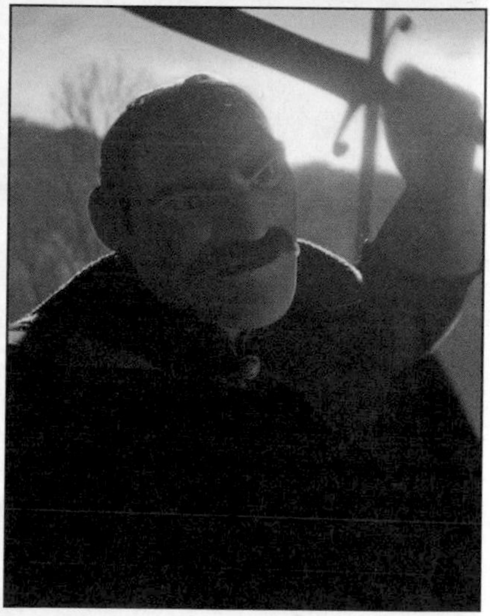

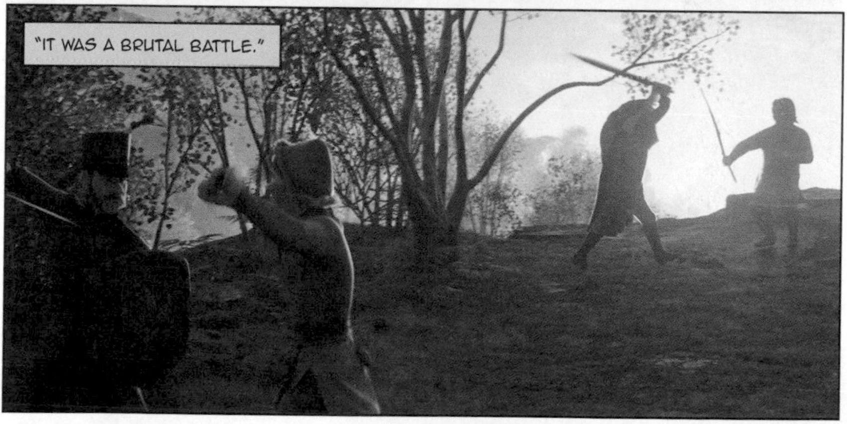
"IT WAS A BRUTAL BATTLE."

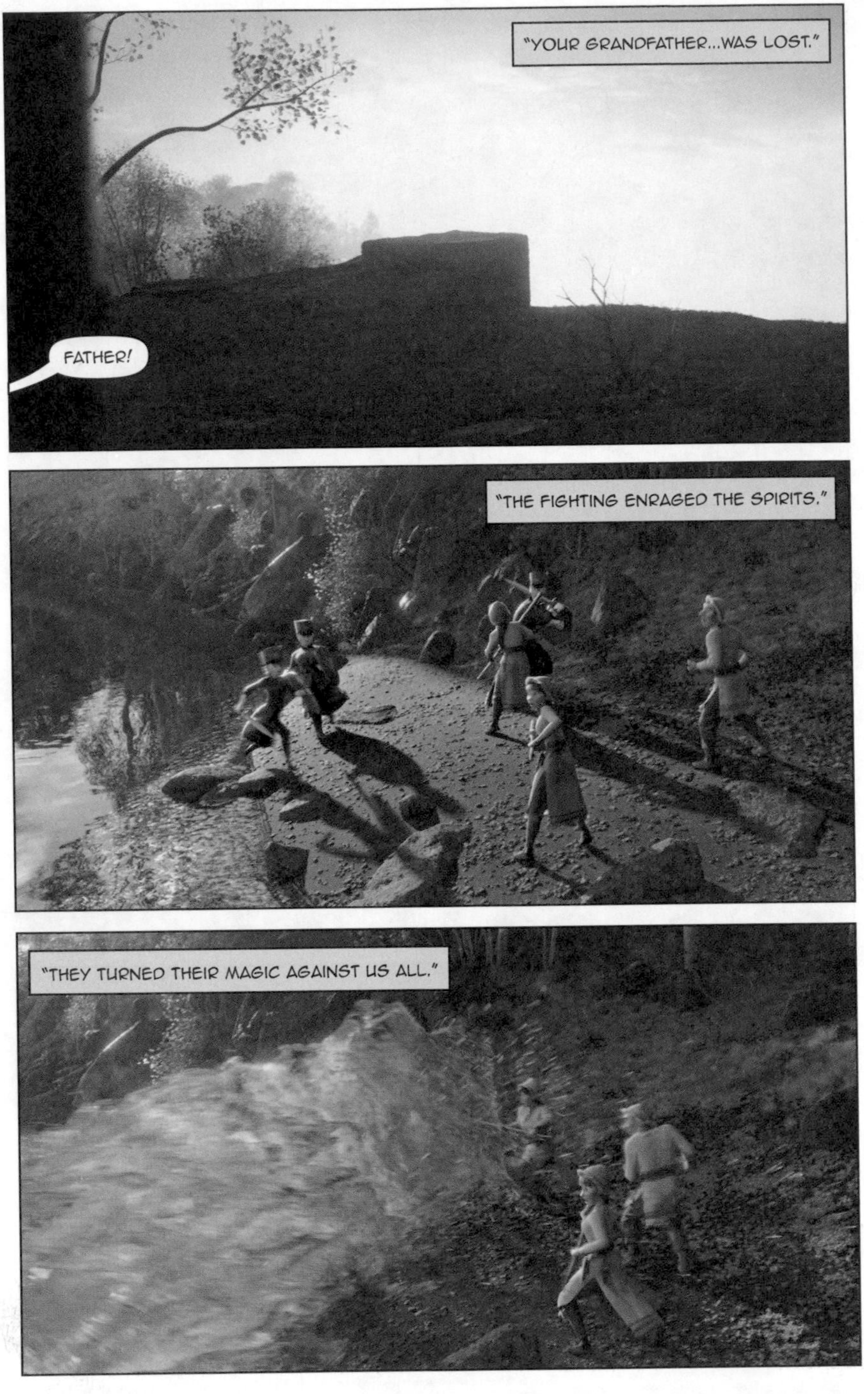
"YOUR GRANDFATHER...WAS LOST."
FATHER!
"THE FIGHTING ENRAGED THE SPIRITS."
"THEY TURNED THEIR MAGIC AGAINST US ALL."

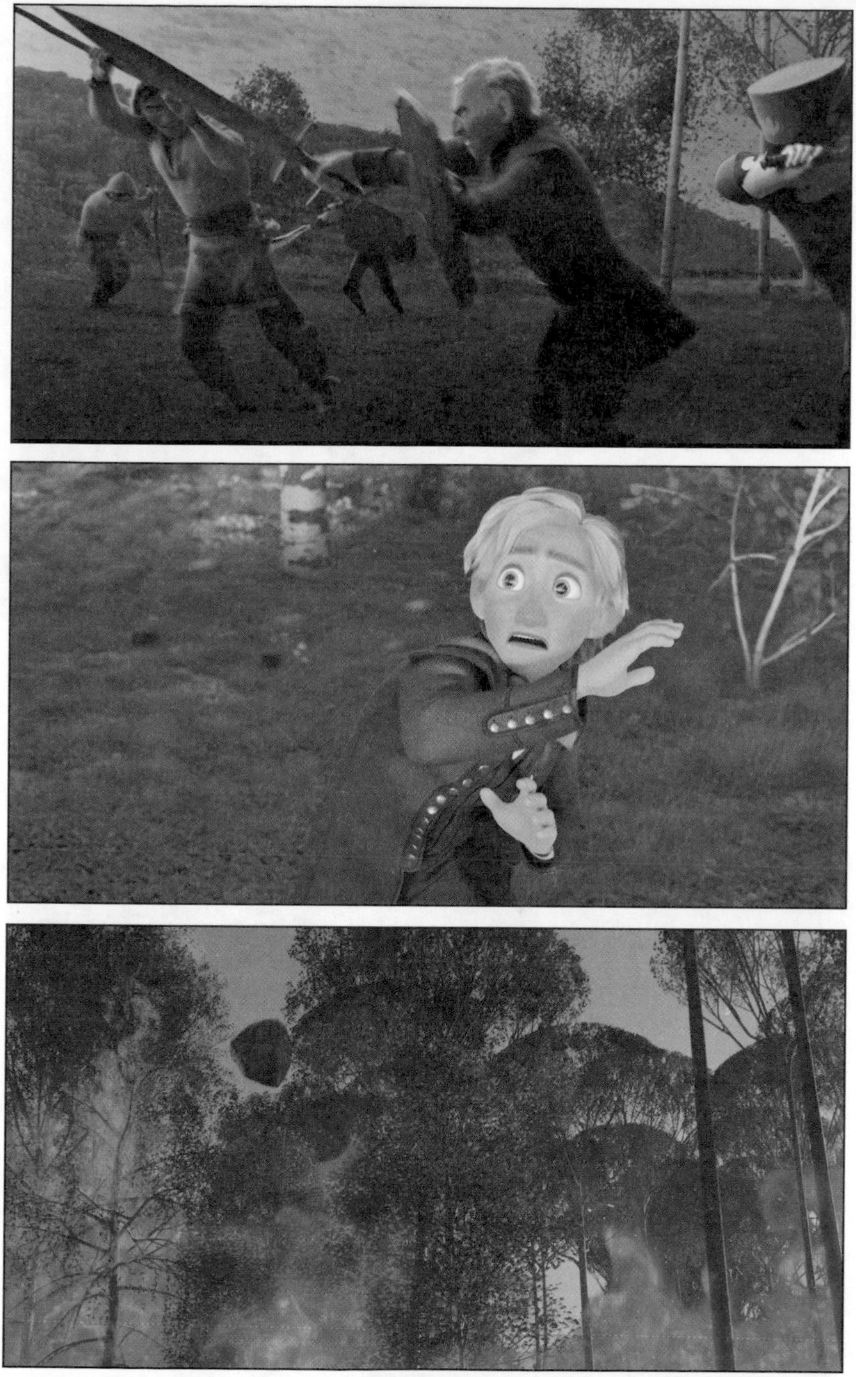

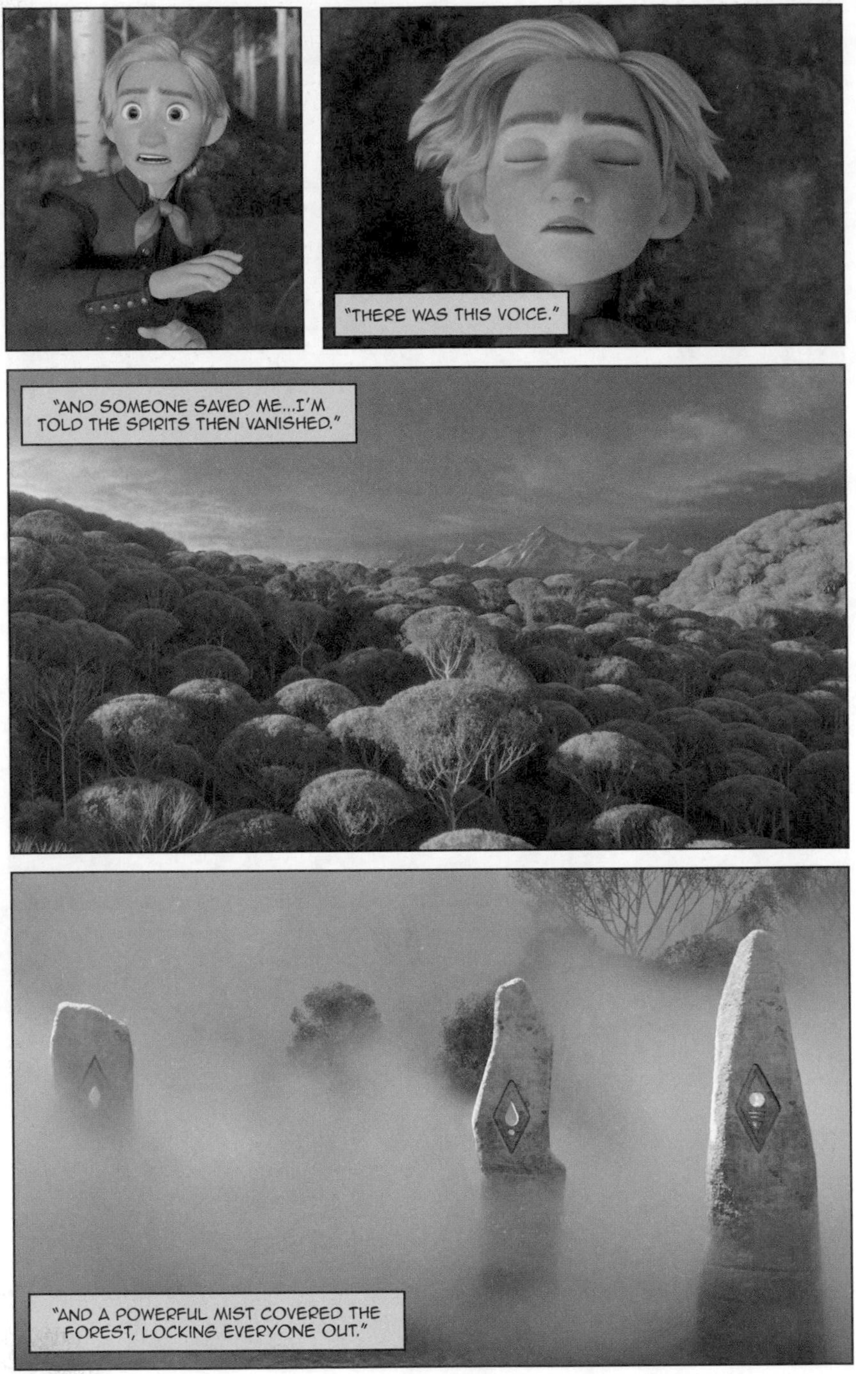
"THERE WAS THIS VOICE."
"AND SOMEONE SAVED ME...I'M TOLD THE SPIRITS THEN VANISHED."
"AND A POWERFUL MIST COVERED THE FOREST, LOCKING EVERYONE OUT."

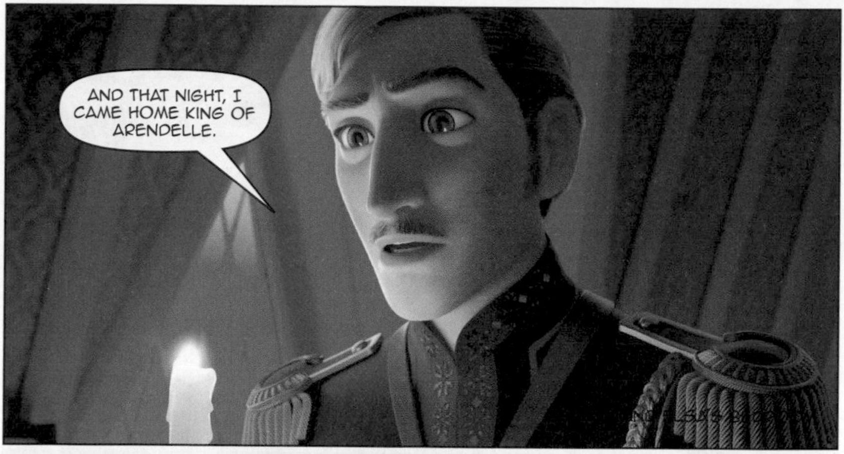
AND THAT NIGHT, I CAME HOME KING OF ARENDELLE.

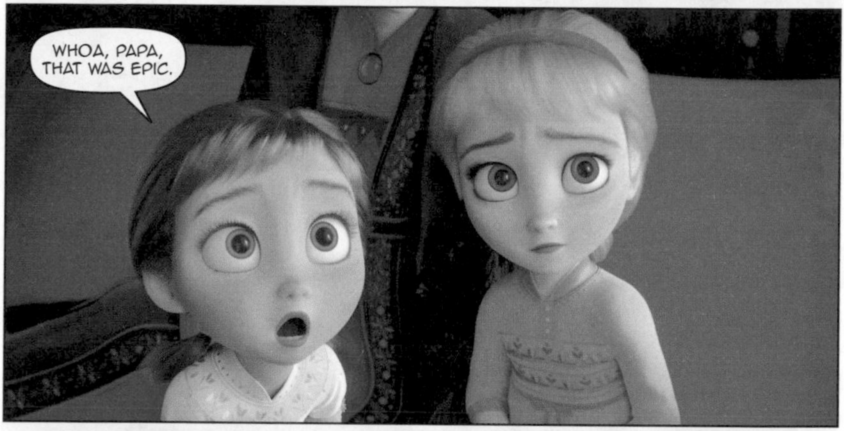
WHOA, PAPA, THAT WAS EPIC.

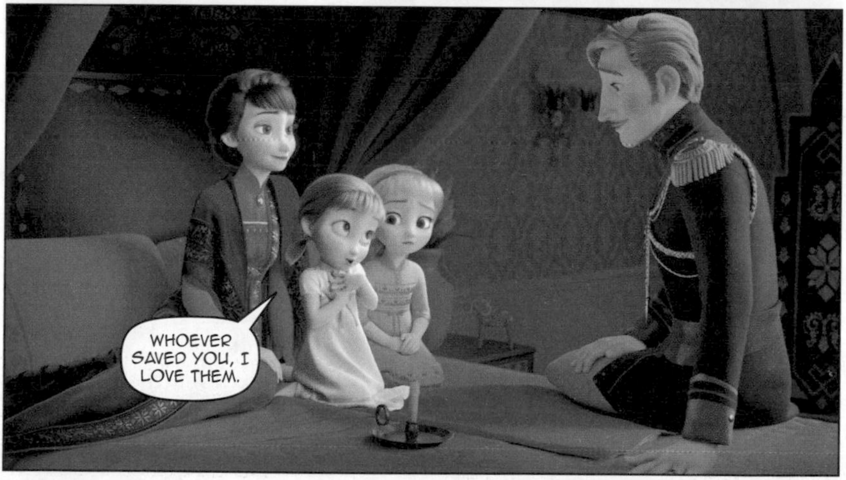
WHOEVER SAVED YOU, I LOVE THEM.

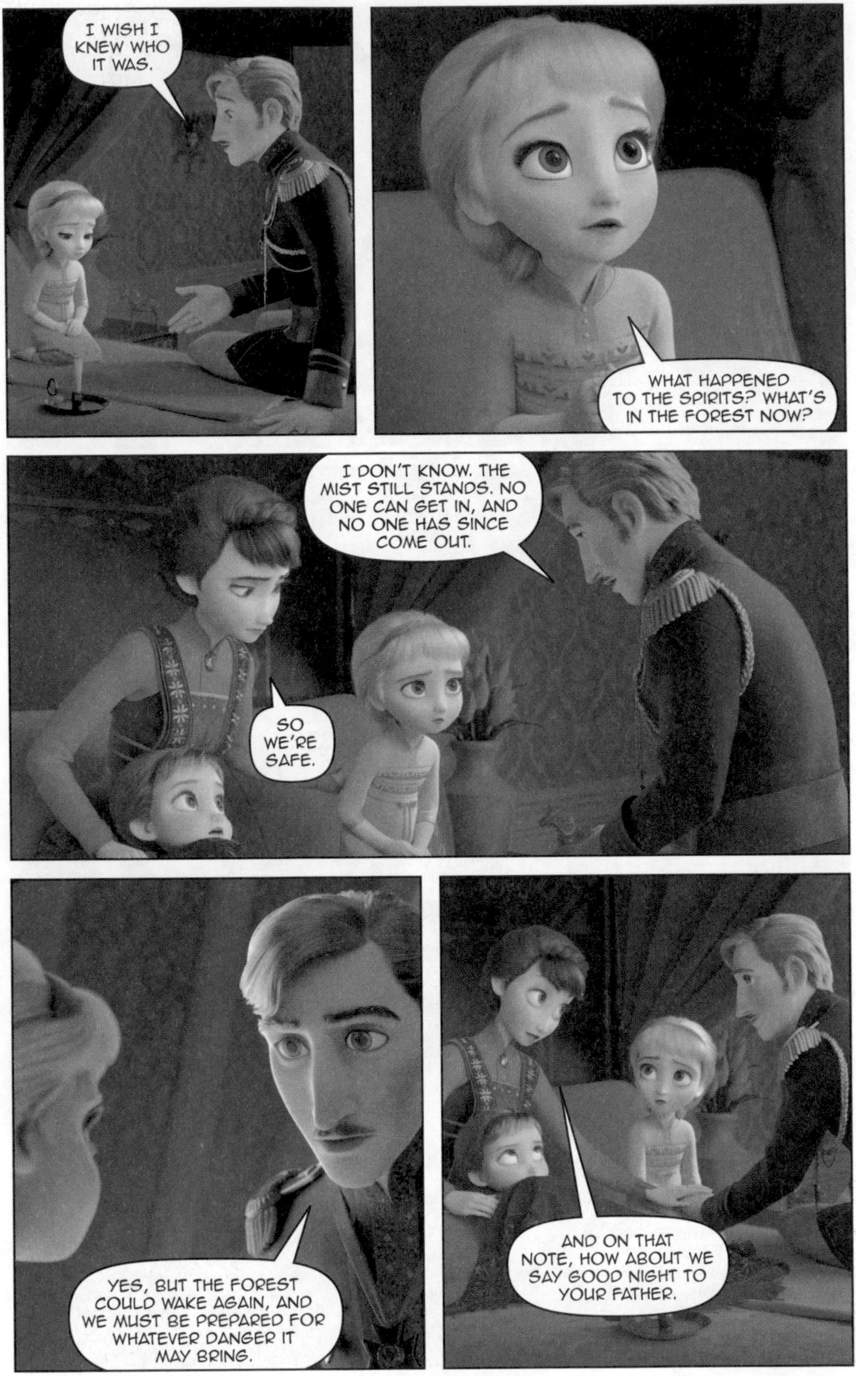
I WISH I KNEW WHO IT WAS.
WHAT HAPPENED TO THE SPIRITS? WHAT'S IN THE FOREST NOW?
I DON'T KNOW. THE MIST STILL STANDS. NO ONE CAN GET IN, AND NO ONE HAS SINCE COME OUT.
SO WE'RE SAFE.
YES, BUT THE FOREST COULD WAKE AGAIN, AND WE MUST BE PREPARED FOR WHATEVER DANGER IT MAY BRING.
AND ON THAT NOTE, HOW ABOUT WE SAY GOOD NIGHT TO YOUR FATHER.

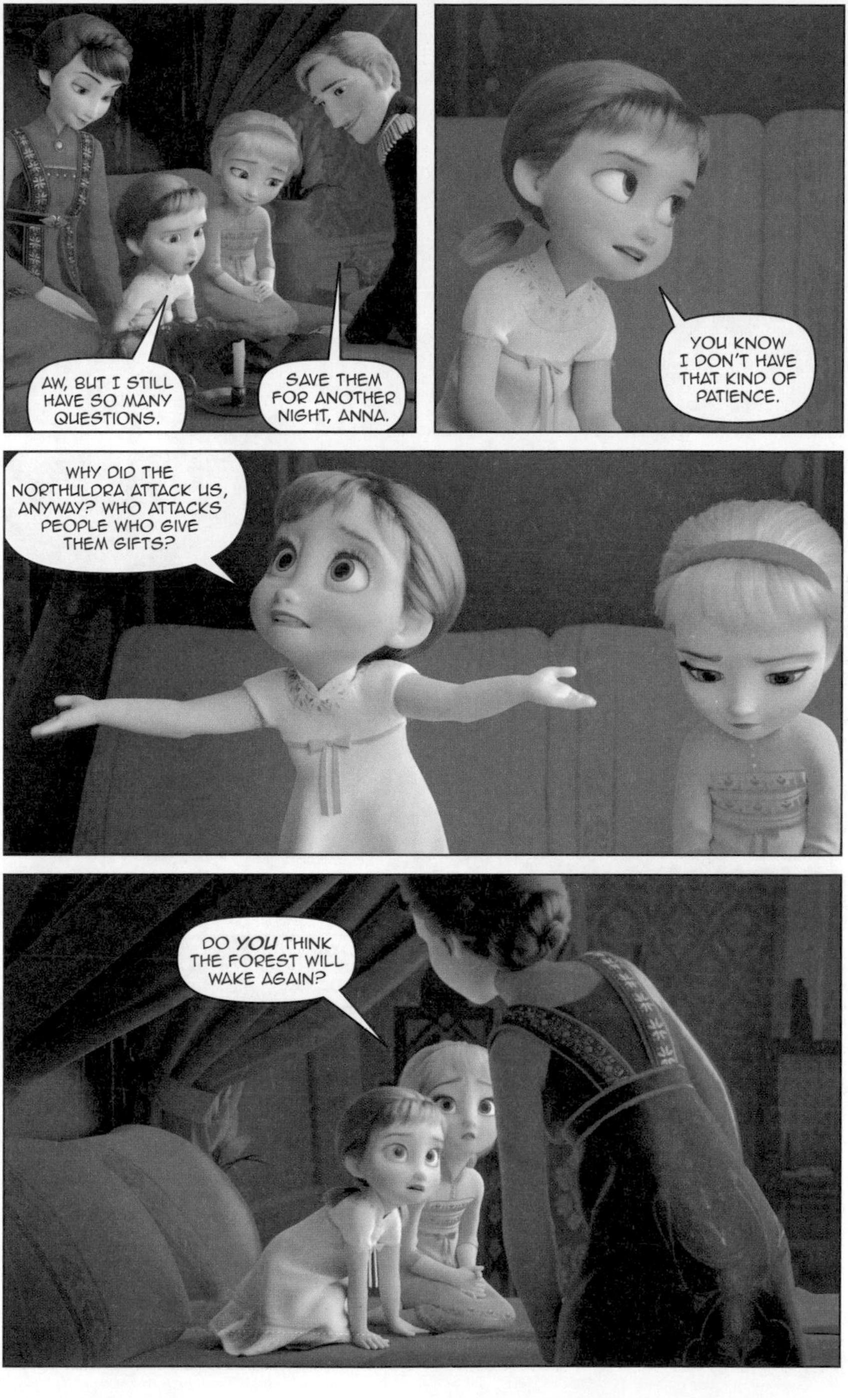
AW, BUT I STILL HAVE SO MANY QUESTIONS.
SAVE THEM FOR ANOTHER NIGHT, ANNA.
YOU KNOW I DON'T HAVE THAT KIND OF PATIENCE.
WHY DID THE NORTHULDRA ATTACK US, ANYWAY? WHO ATTACKS PEOPLE WHO GIVE THEM GIFTS?
DO *YOU* THINK THE FOREST WILL WAKE AGAIN?

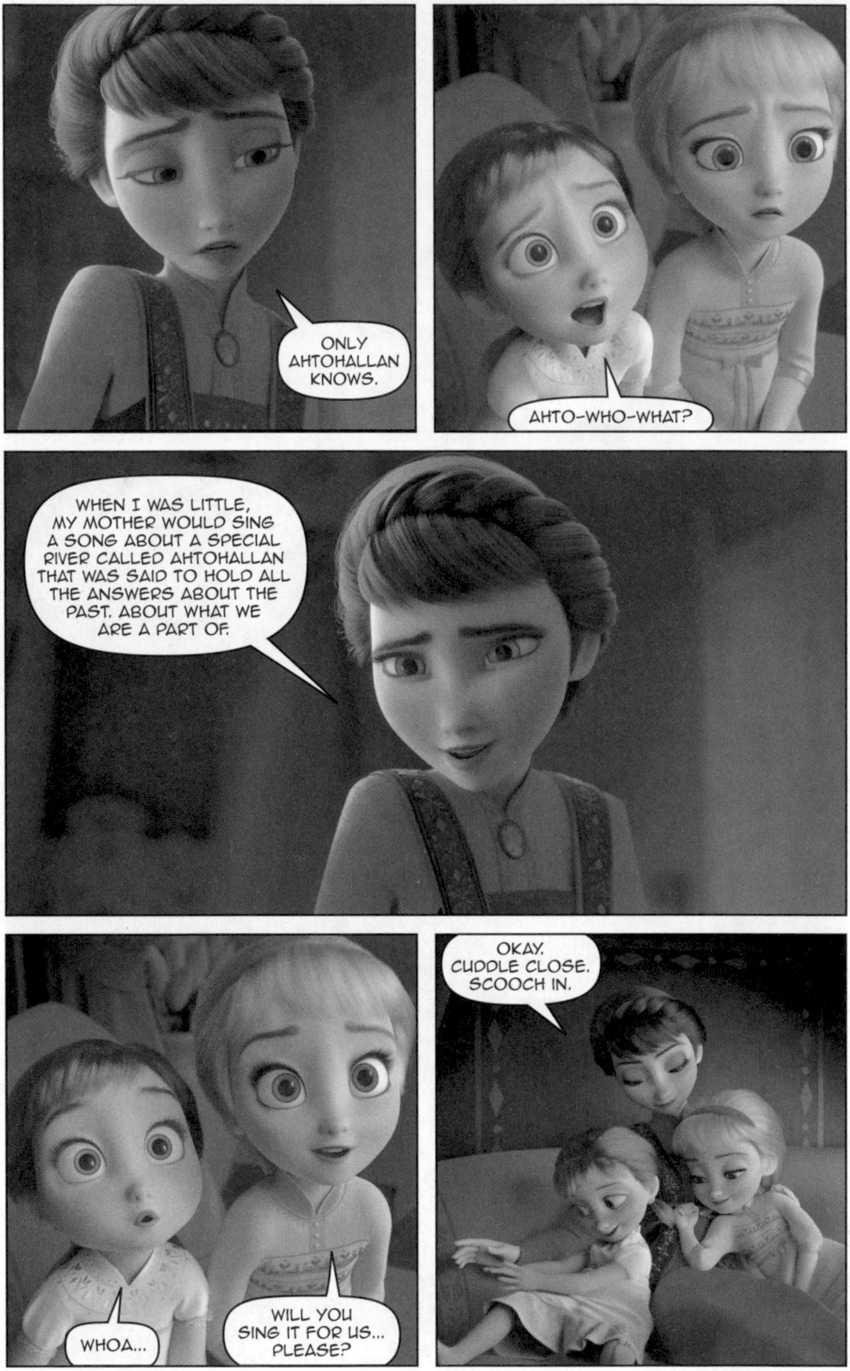
ONLY AHTOHALLAN KNOWS.
AHTO-WHO-WHAT?
WHEN I WAS LITTLE, MY MOTHER WOULD SING A SONG ABOUT A SPECIAL RIVER CALLED AHTOHALLAN THAT WAS SAID TO HOLD ALL THE ANSWERS ABOUT THE PAST. ABOUT WHAT WE ARE A PART OF.
WHOA...
WILL YOU SING IT FOR US... PLEASE?
OKAY. CUDDLE CLOSE. SCOOCH IN.

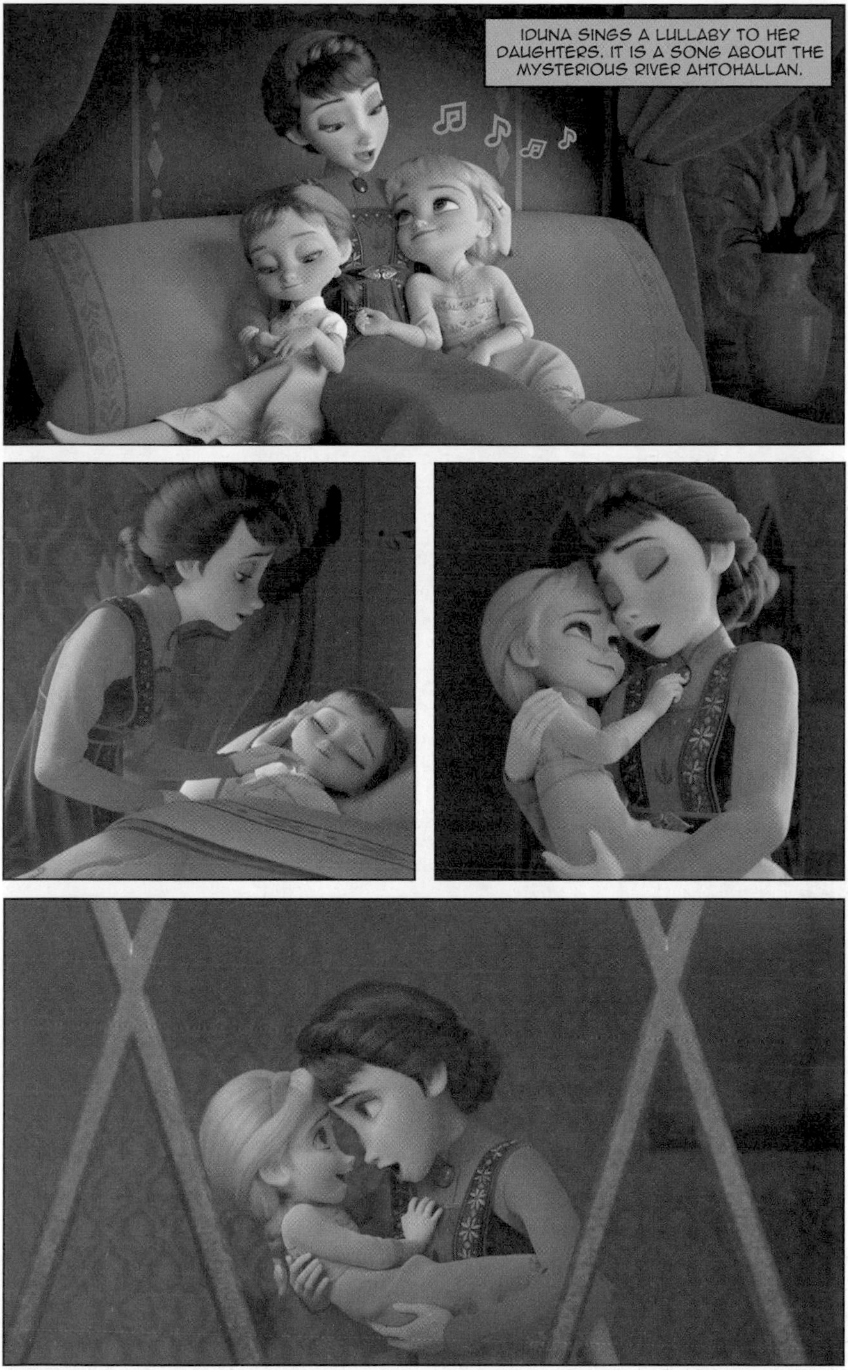
IDUNA SINGS A LULLABY TO HER DAUGHTERS. IT IS A SONG ABOUT THE MYSTERIOUS RIVER AHTOHALLAN.

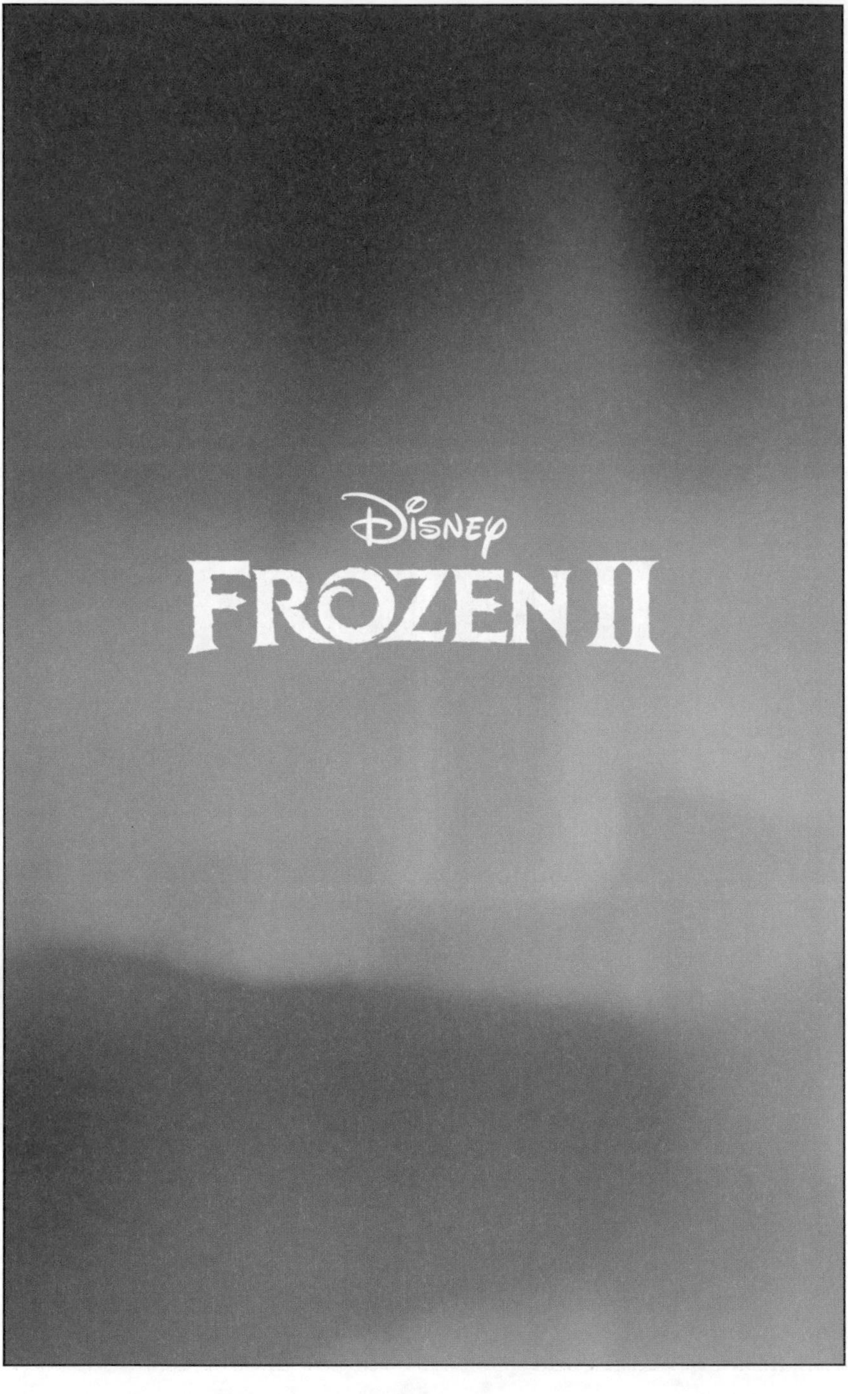
Disney
FROZEN II

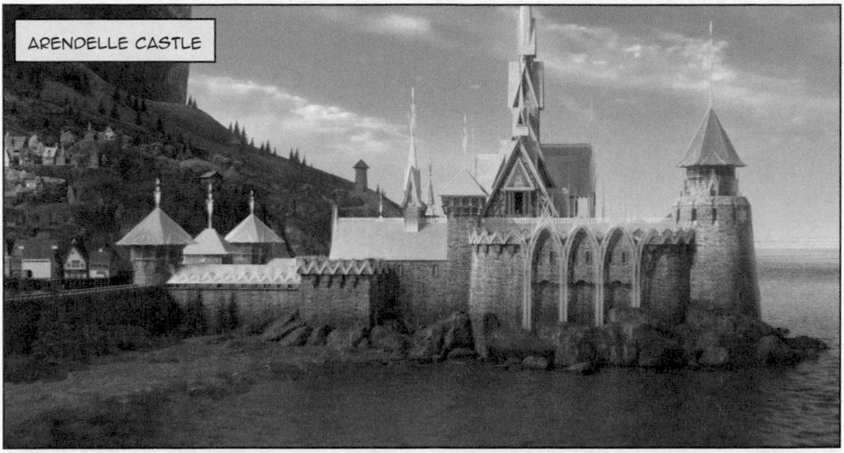
ARENDELLE CASTLE

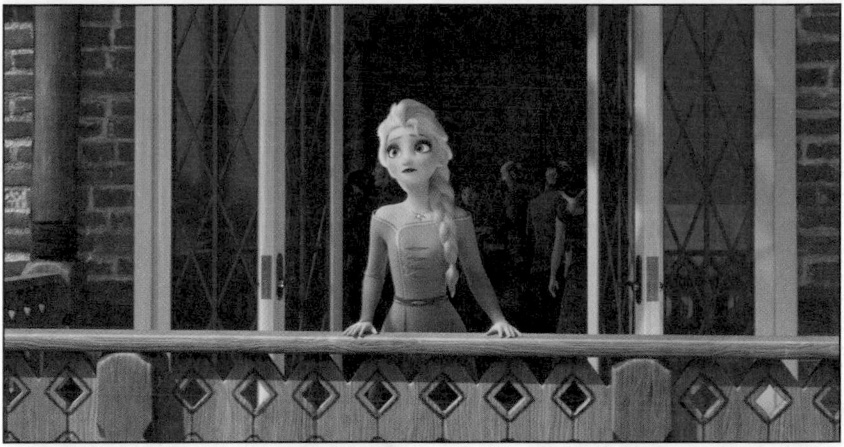

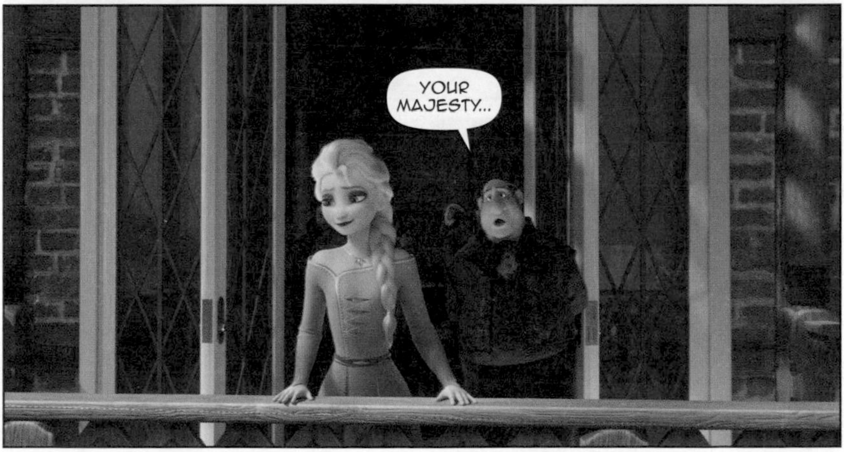
YOUR MAJESTY...

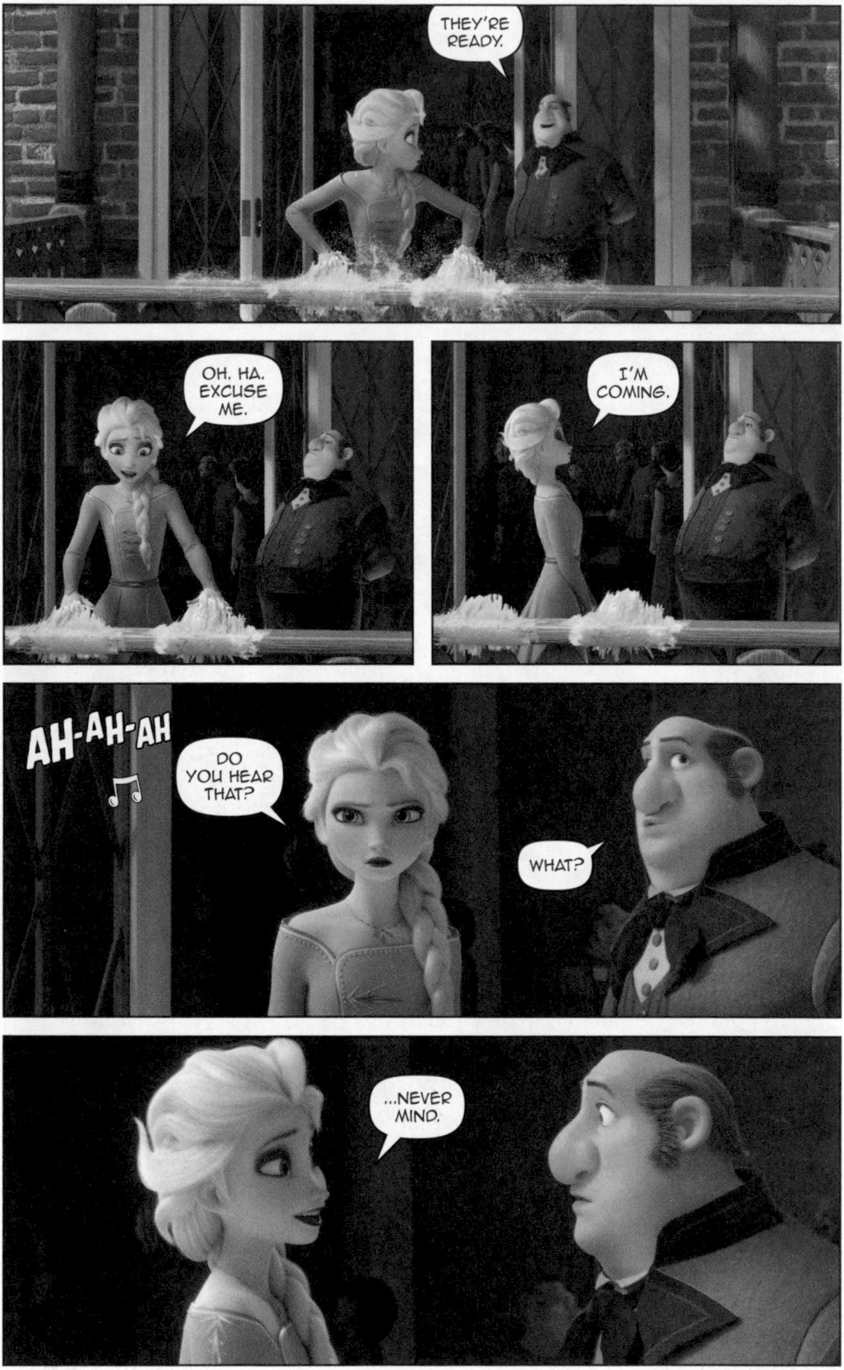

THEY'RE READY.
OH. HA. EXCUSE ME.
I'M COMING.
AH-AH-AH
DO YOU HEAR THAT?
WHAT?
...NEVER MIND.

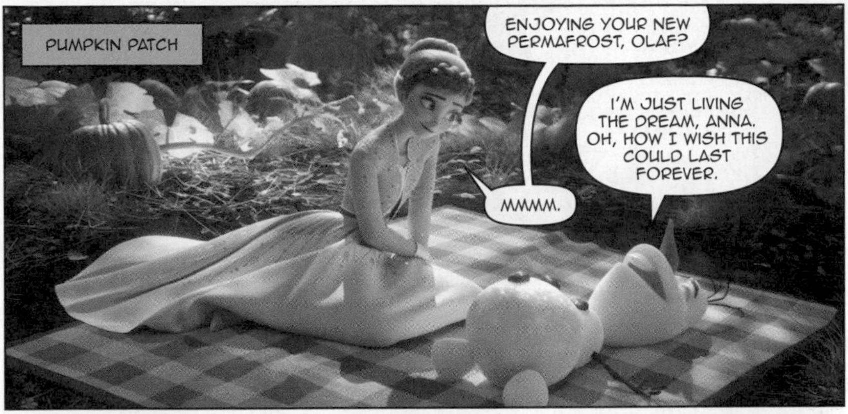
PUMPKIN PATCH
ENJOYING YOUR NEW PERMAFROST, OLAF?
MMMM.
I'M JUST LIVING THE DREAM, ANNA. OH, HOW I WISH THIS COULD LAST FOREVER.

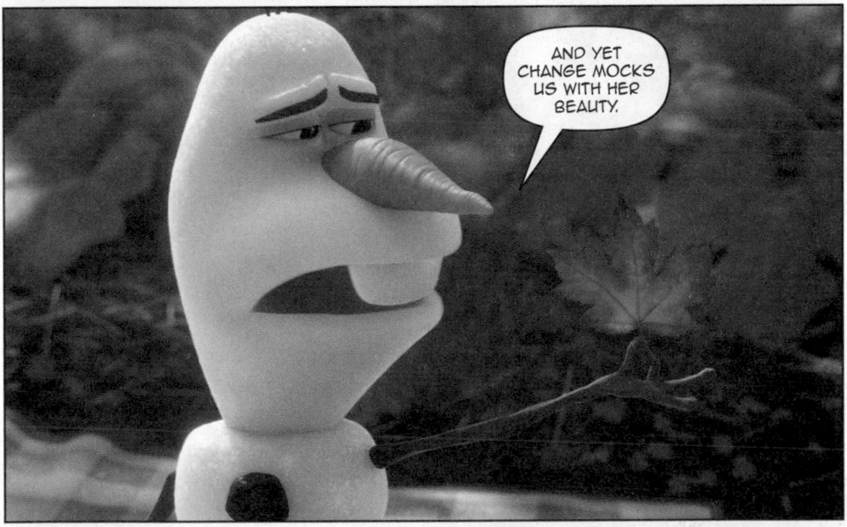
AND YET CHANGE MOCKS US WITH HER BEAUTY.

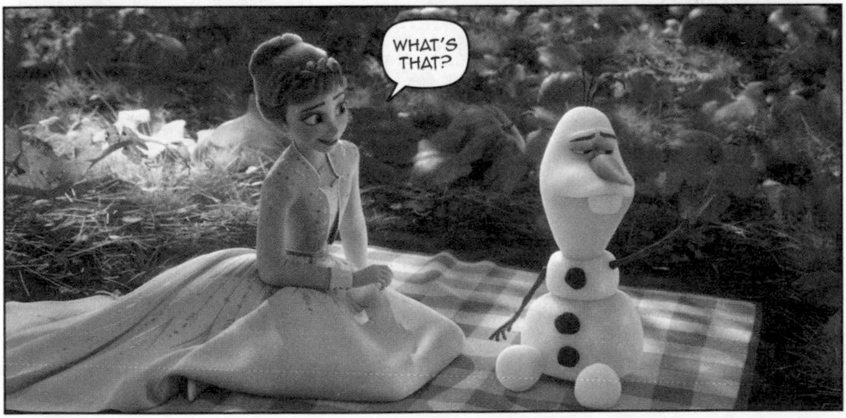
WHAT'S THAT?

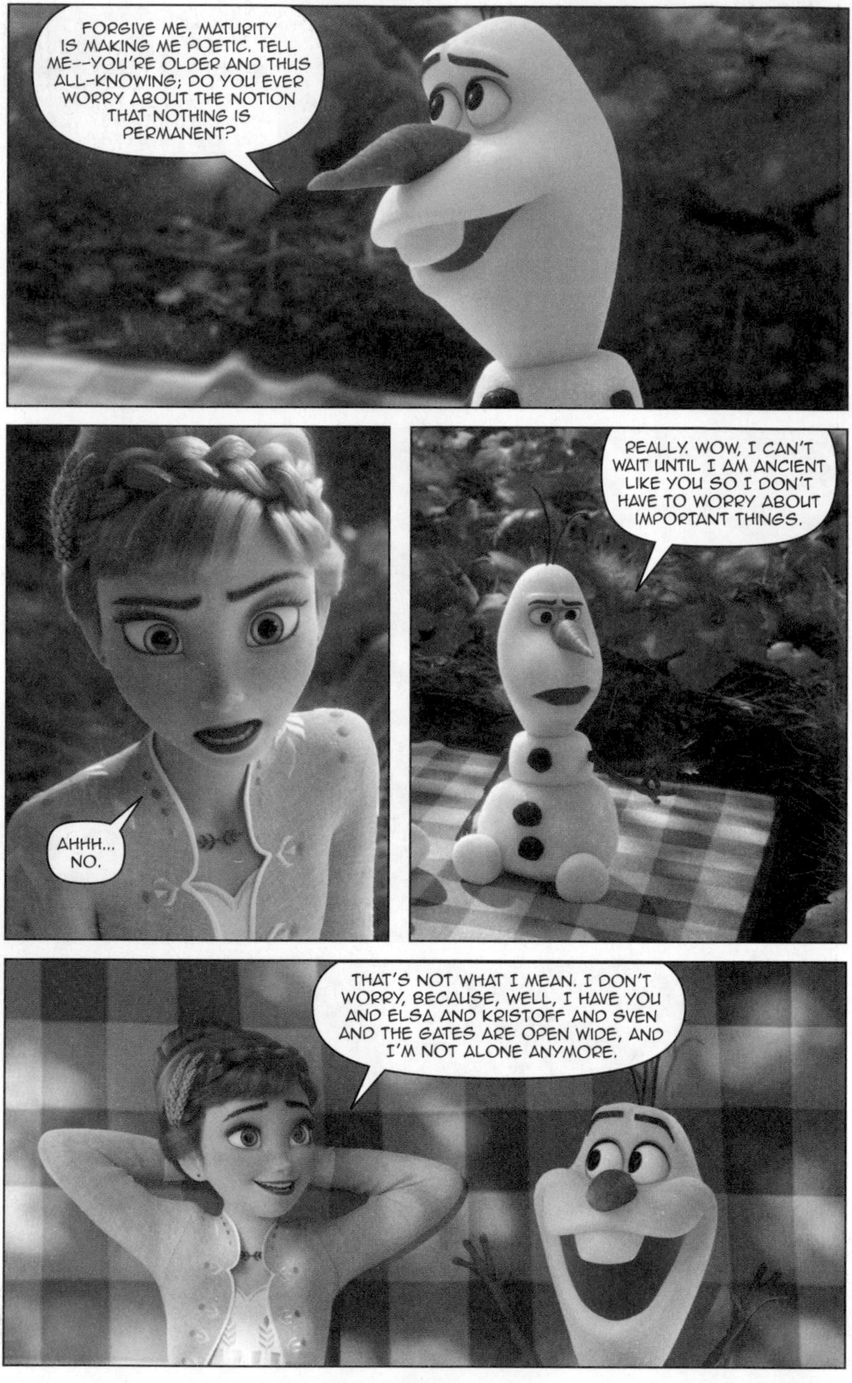
FORGIVE ME, MATURITY IS MAKING ME POETIC. TELL ME--YOU'RE OLDER AND THUS ALL-KNOWING; DO YOU EVER WORRY ABOUT THE NOTION THAT NOTHING IS PERMANENT?
AHHH... NO.
REALLY. WOW, I CAN'T WAIT UNTIL I AM ANCIENT LIKE YOU SO I DON'T HAVE TO WORRY ABOUT IMPORTANT THINGS.
THAT'S NOT WHAT I MEAN. I DON'T WORRY, BECAUSE, WELL, I HAVE YOU AND ELSA AND KRISTOFF AND SVEN AND THE GATES ARE OPEN WIDE, AND I'M NOT ALONE ANYMORE.

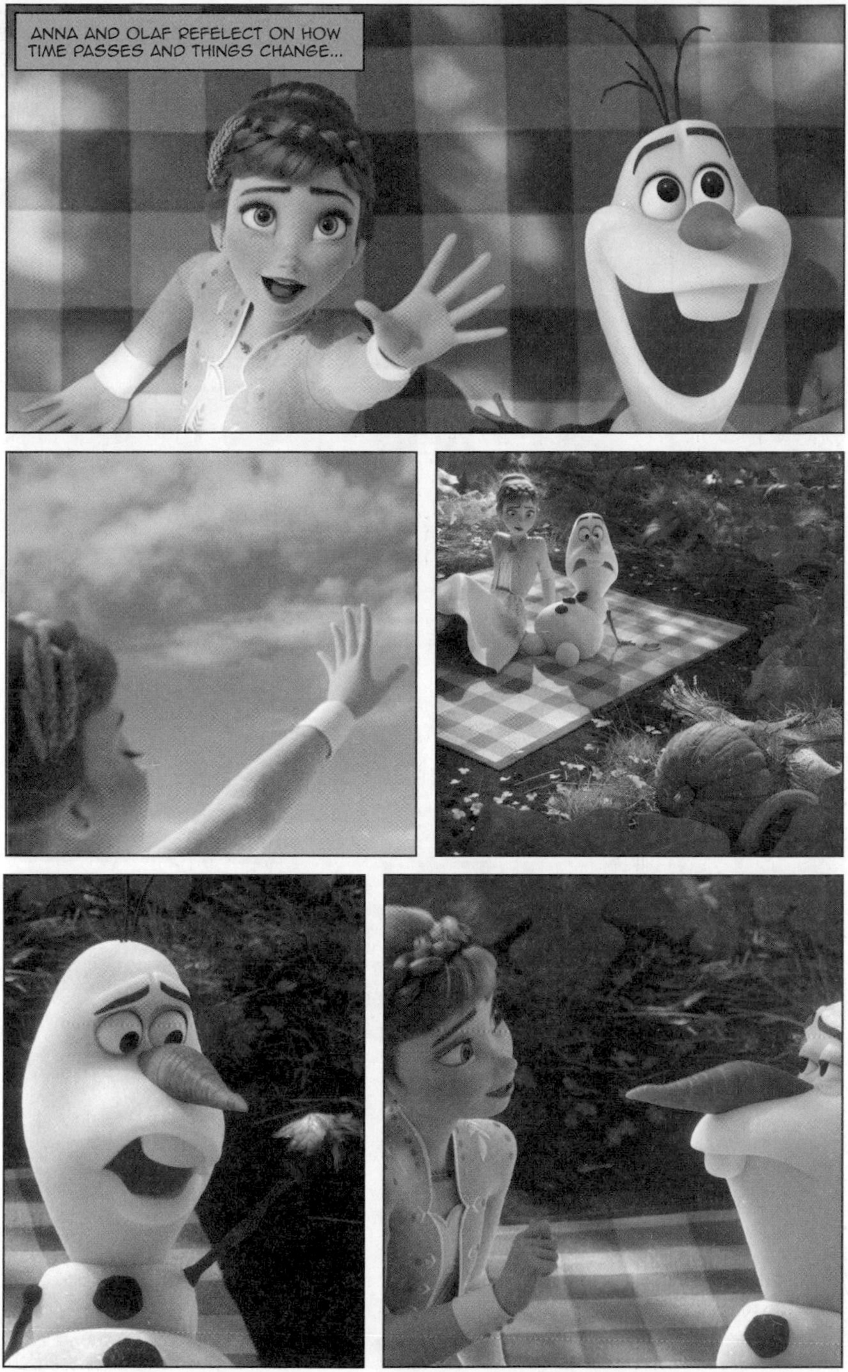
ANNA AND OLAF REFELECT ON HOW TIME PASSES AND THINGS CHANGE...

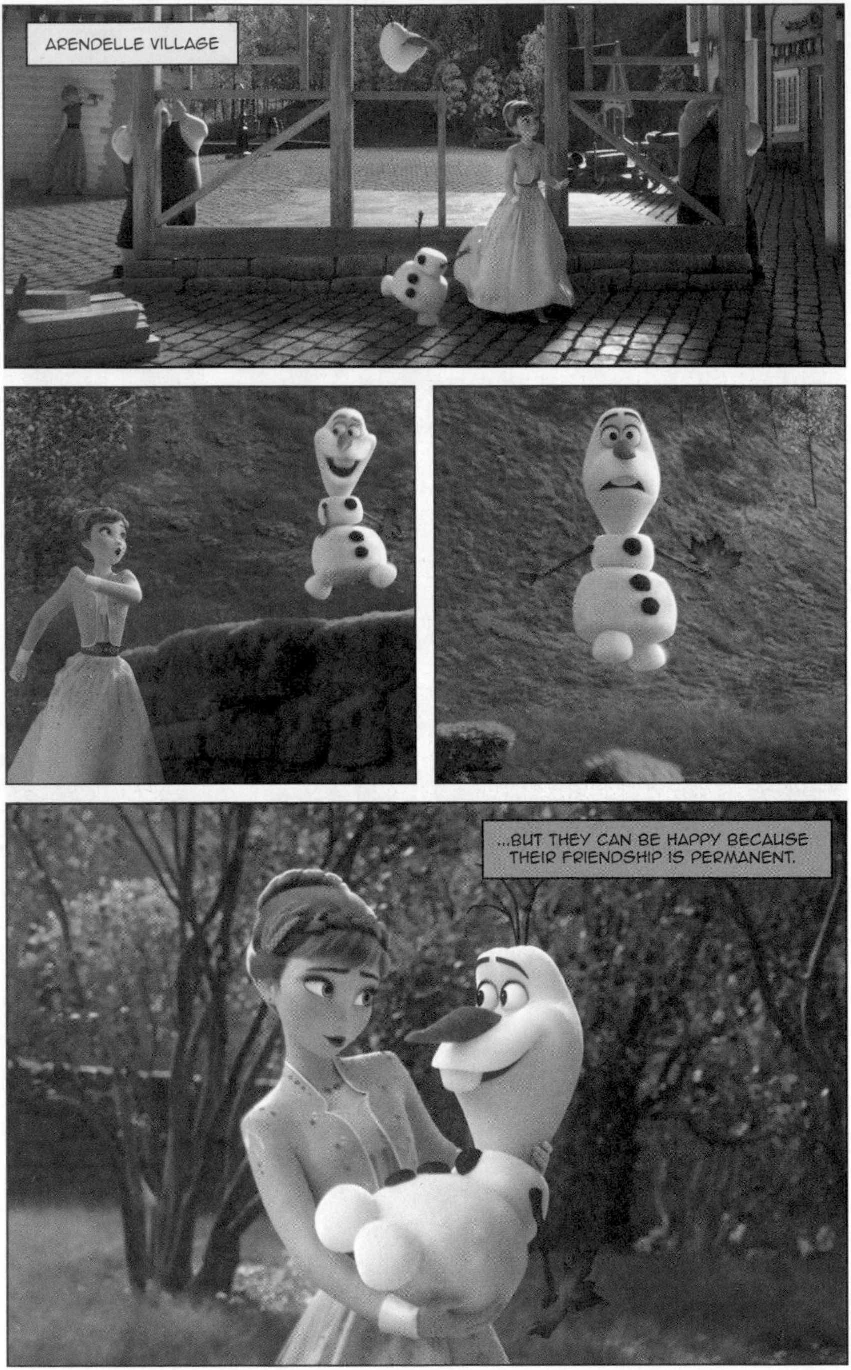
ARENDELLE VILLAGE
...BUT THEY CAN BE HAPPY BECAUSE THEIR FRIENDSHIP IS PERMANENT.

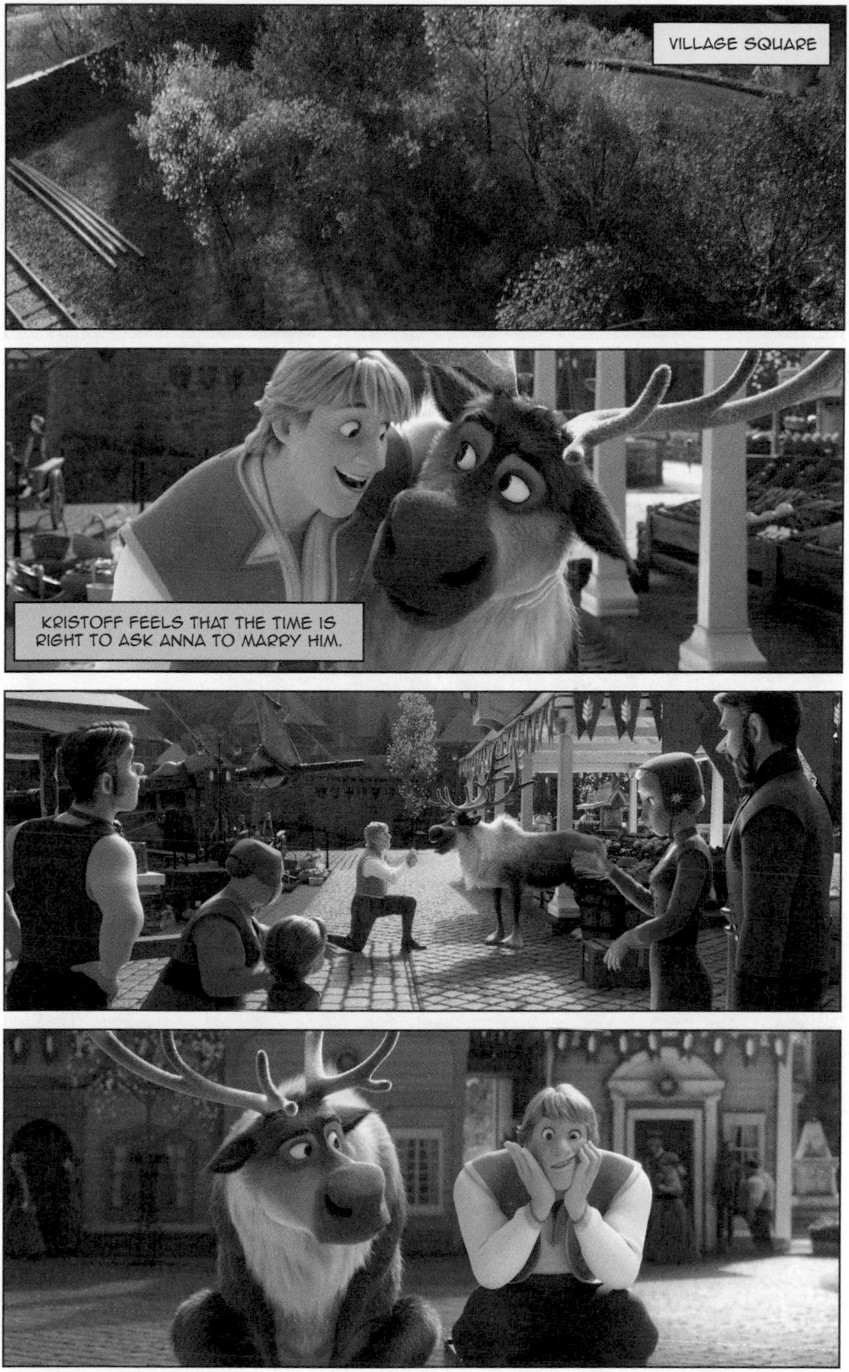
VILLAGE SQUARE
KRISTOFF FEELS THAT THE TIME IS RIGHT TO ASK ANNA TO MARRY HIM.

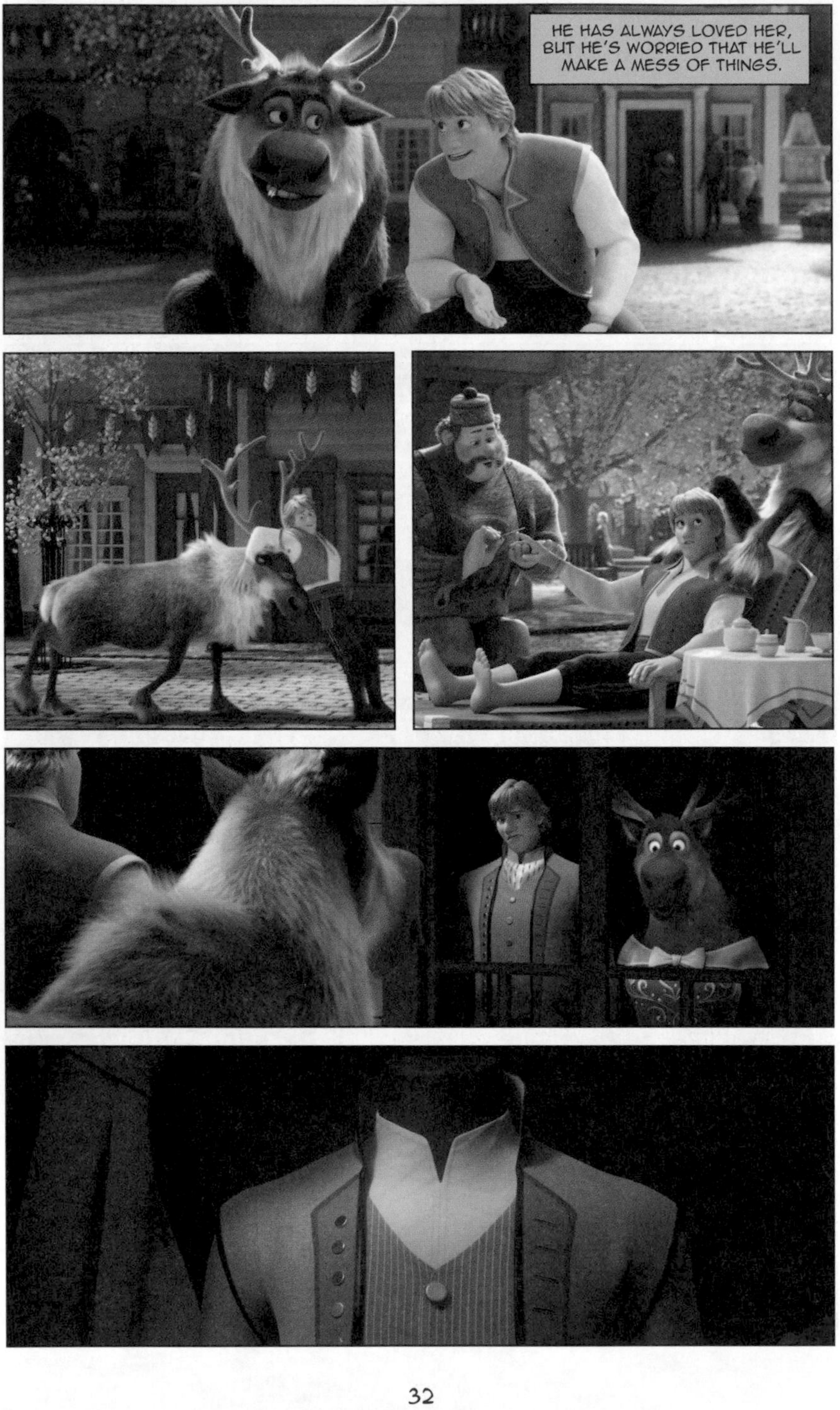
HE HAS ALWAYS LOVED HER, BUT HE'S WORRIED THAT HE'LL MAKE A MESS OF THINGS.

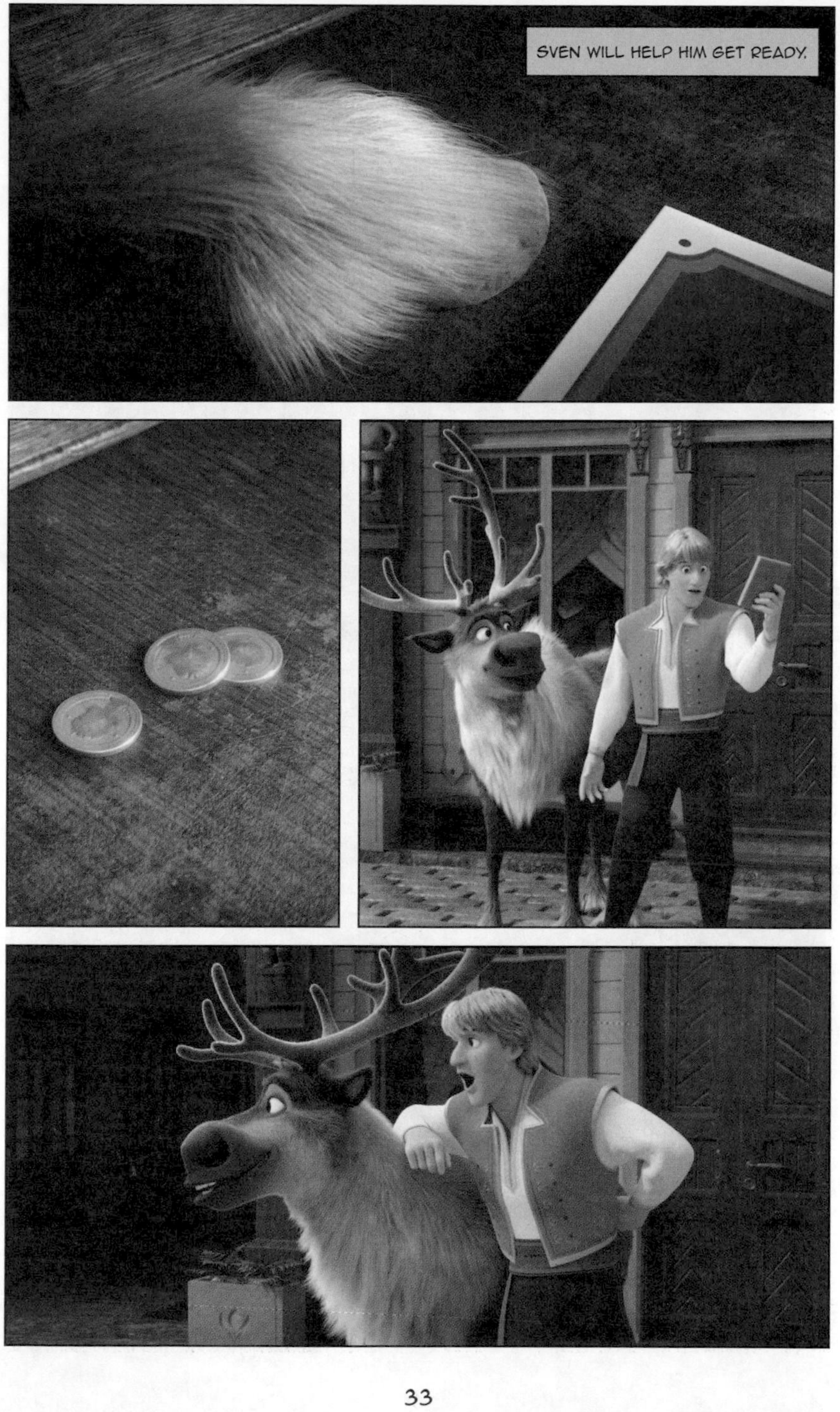
SVEN WILL HELP HIM GET READY.

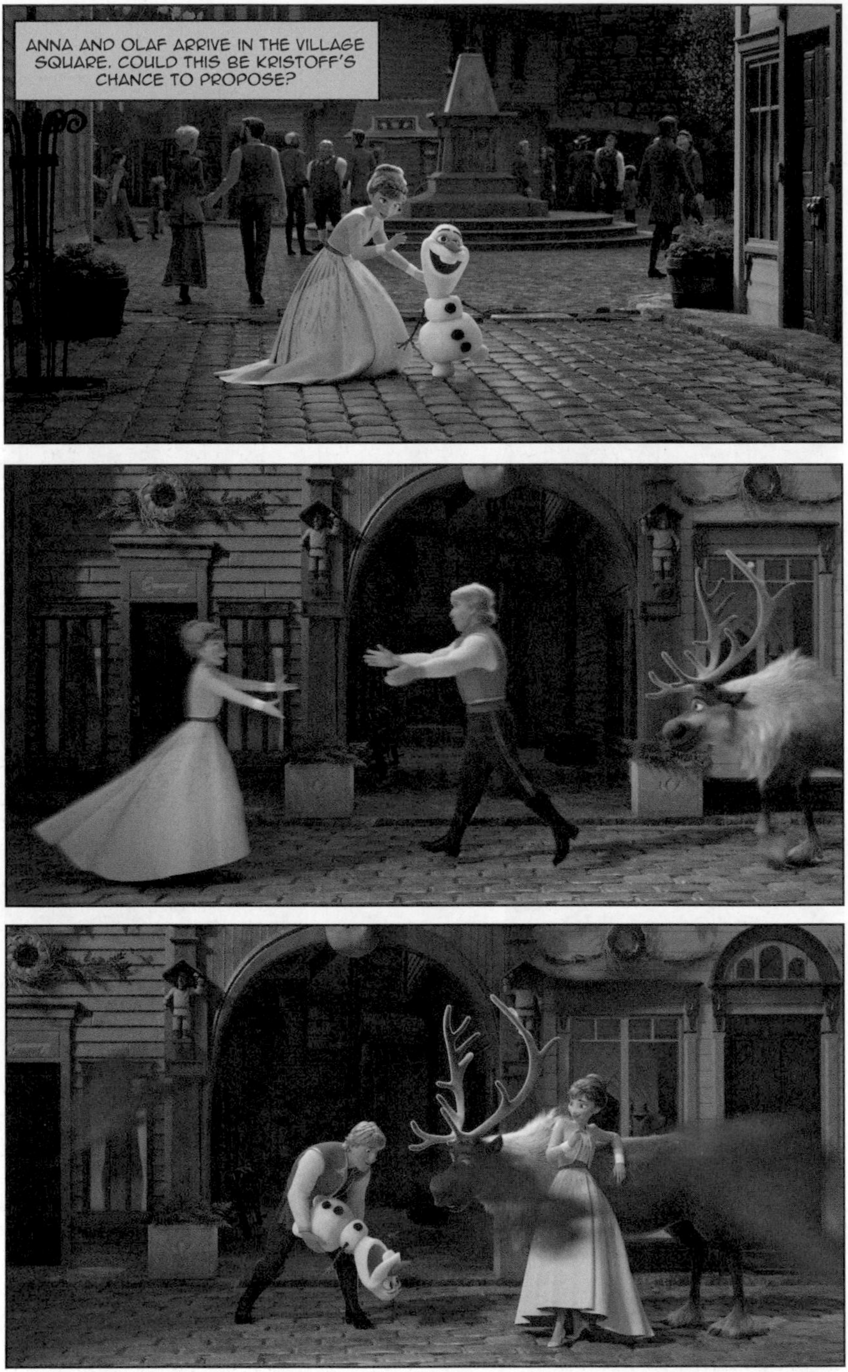
ANNA AND OLAF ARRIVE IN THE VILLAGE SQUARE. COULD THIS BE KRISTOFF'S CHANCE TO PROPOSE?

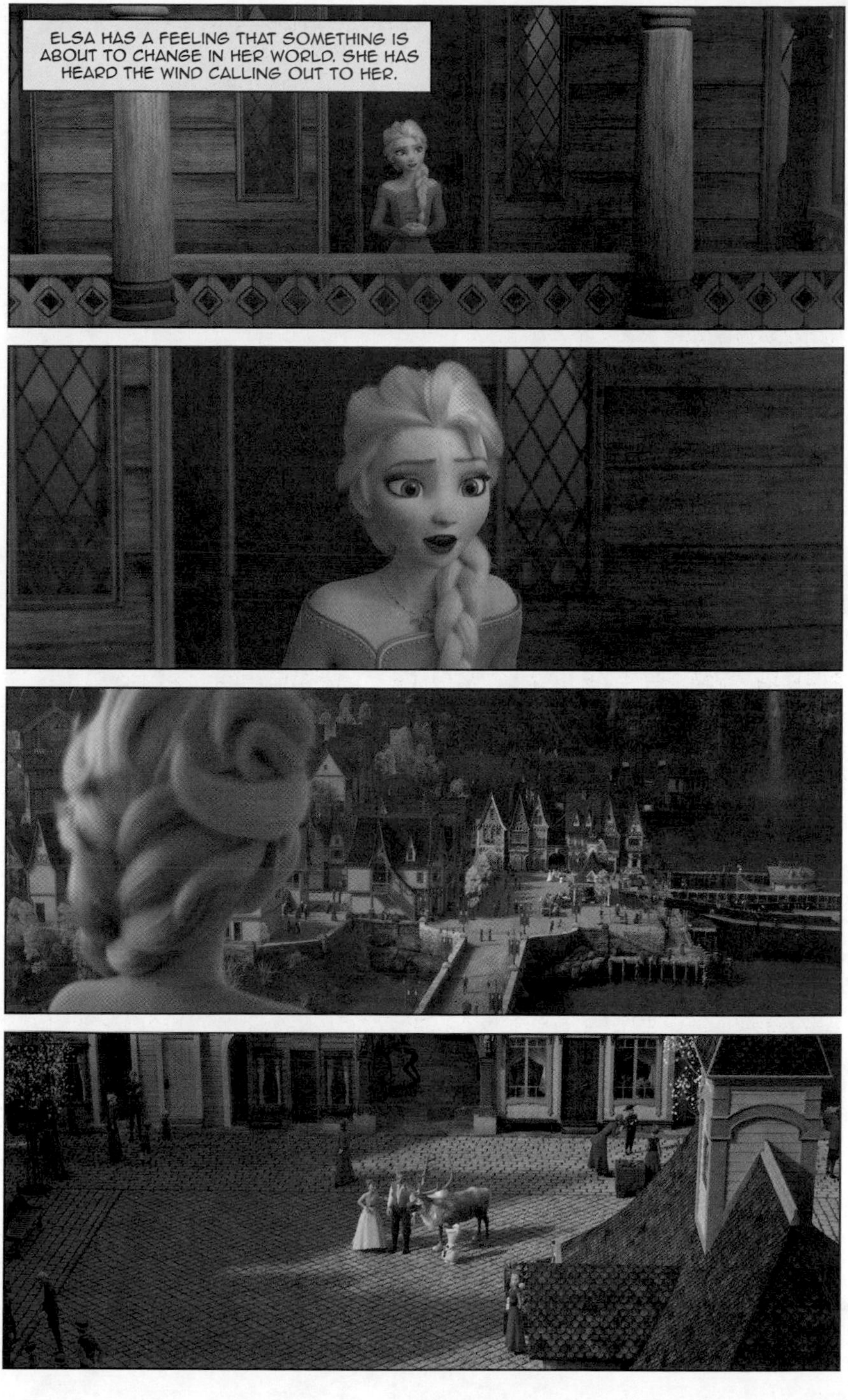
ELSA HAS A FEELING THAT SOMETHING IS ABOUT TO CHANGE IN HER WORLD. SHE HAS HEARD THE WIND CALLING OUT TO HER.

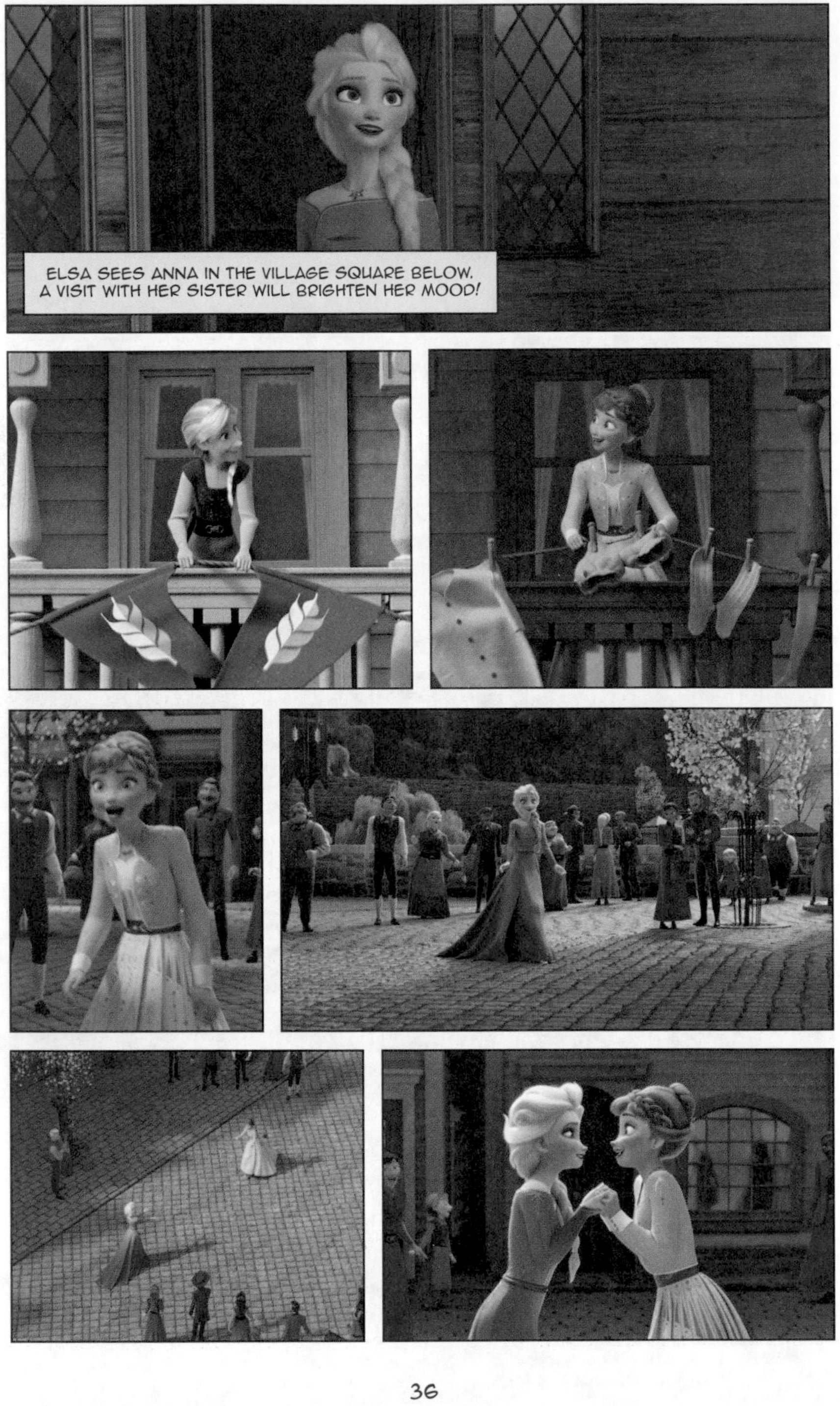
ELSA SEES ANNA IN THE VILLAGE SQUARE BELOW.
A VISIT WITH HER SISTER WILL BRIGHTEN HER MOOD!

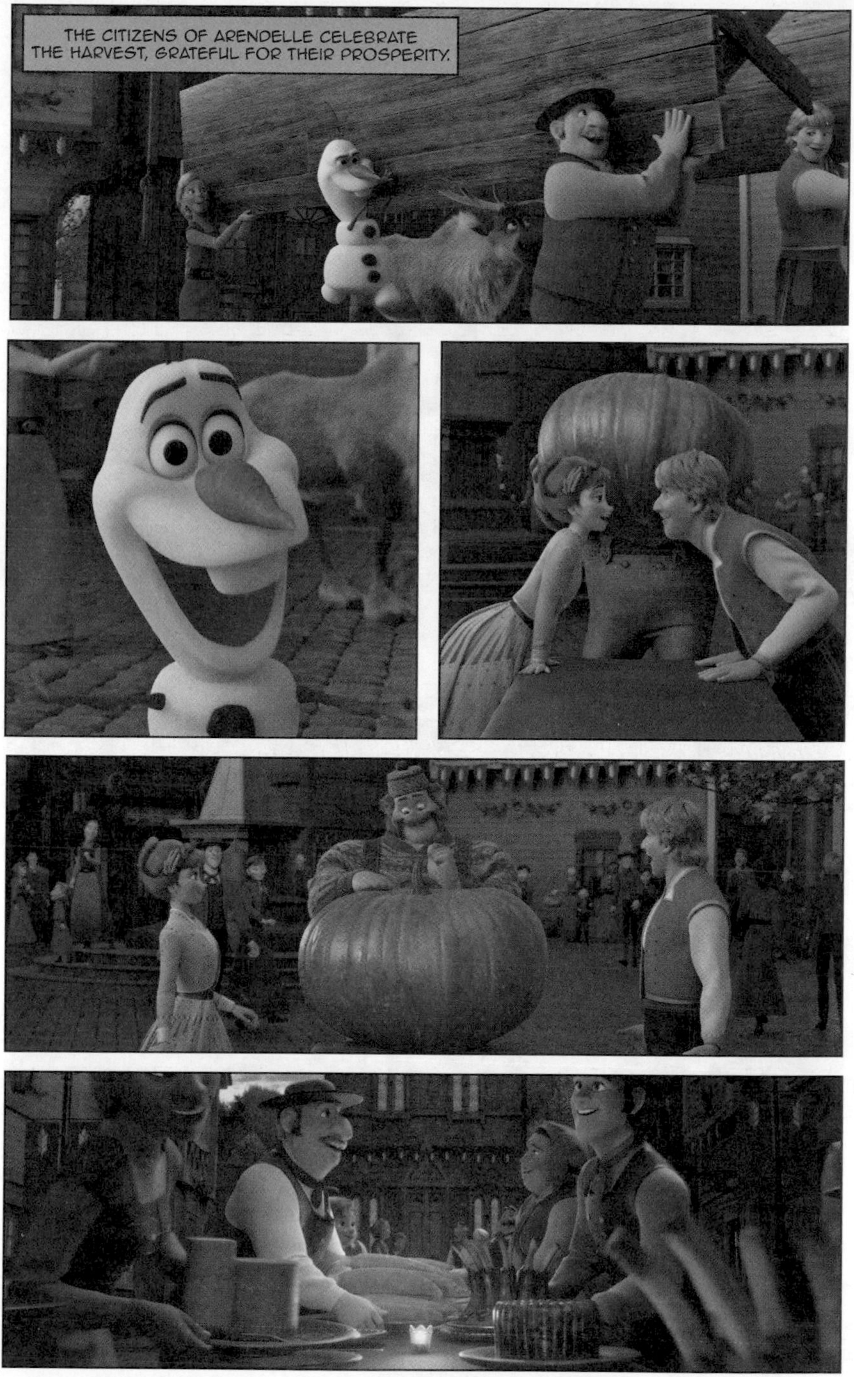
THE CITIZENS OF ARENDELLE CELEBRATE THE HARVEST, GRATEFUL FOR THEIR PROSPERITY.

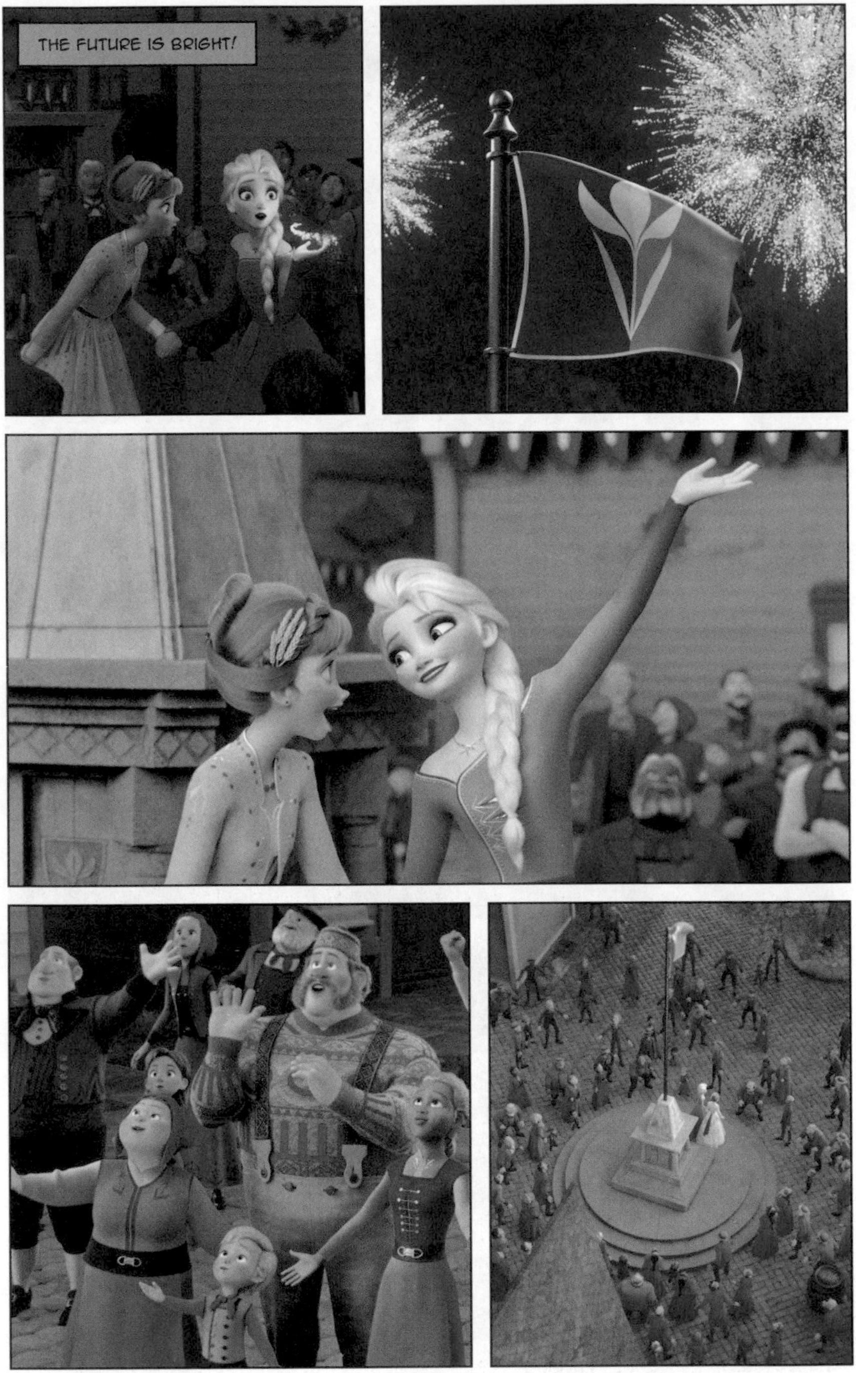
THE FUTURE IS BRIGHT!

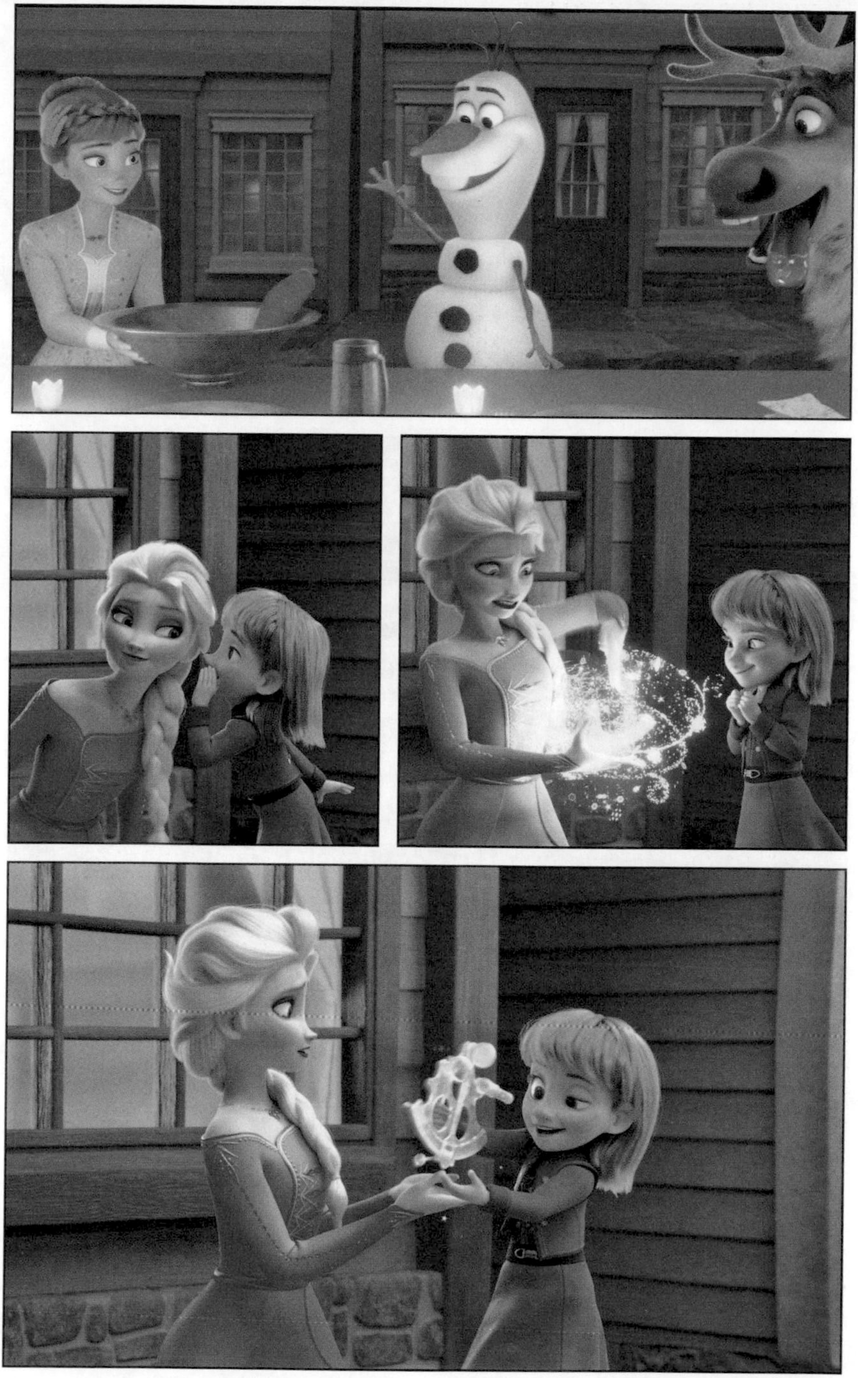

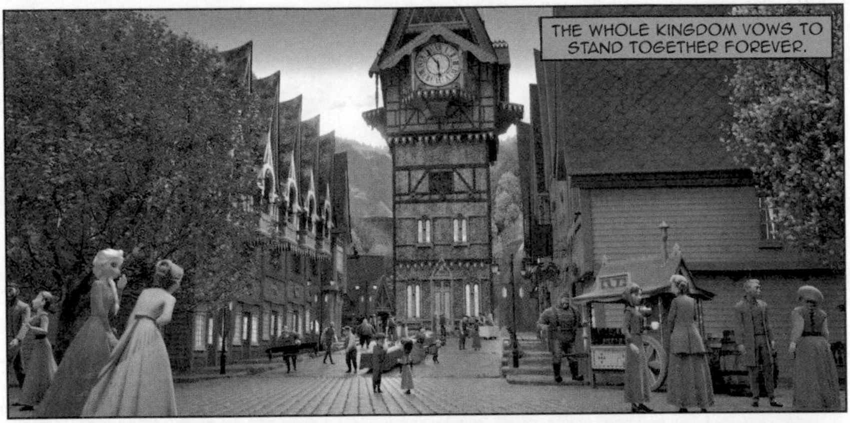
THE WHOLE KINGDOM VOWS TO STAND TOGETHER FOREVER.

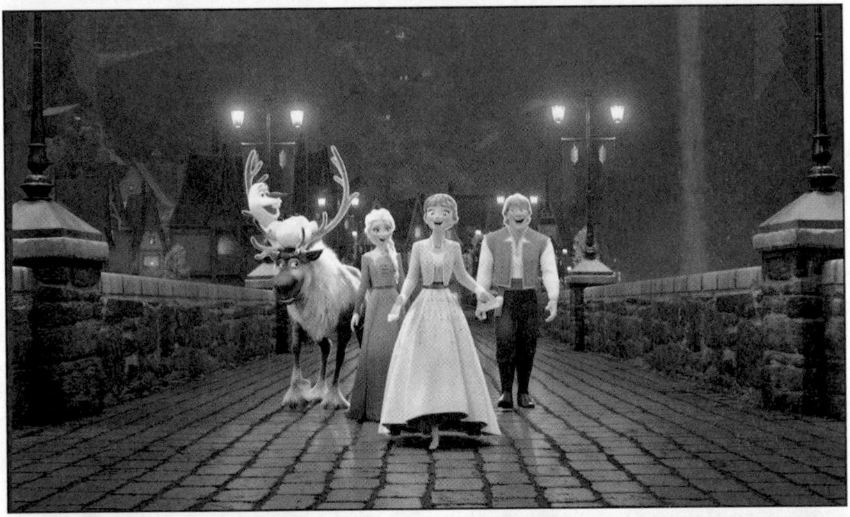

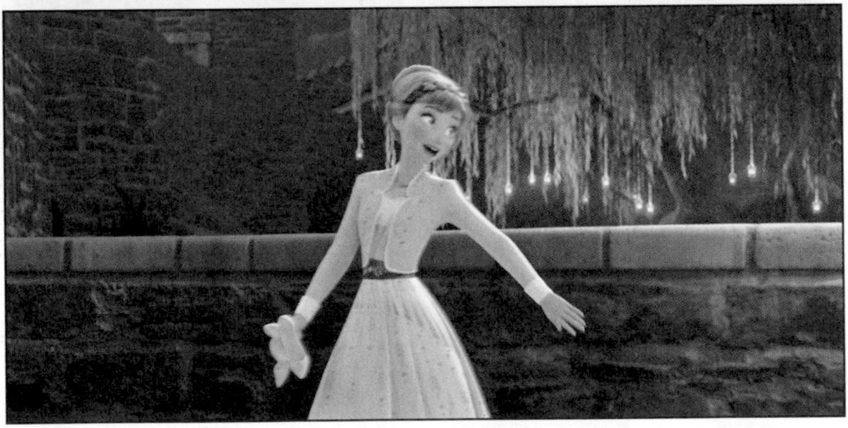

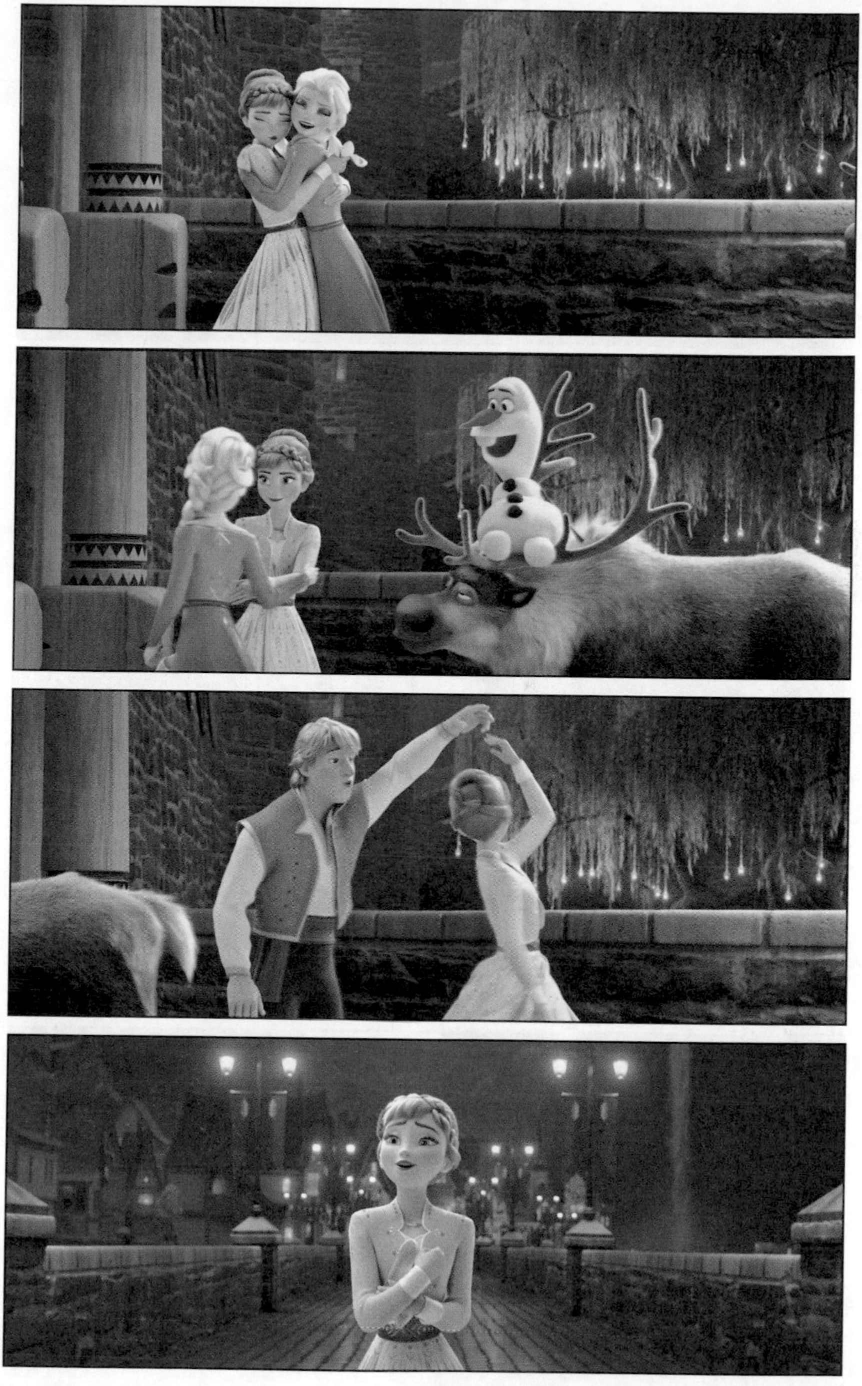

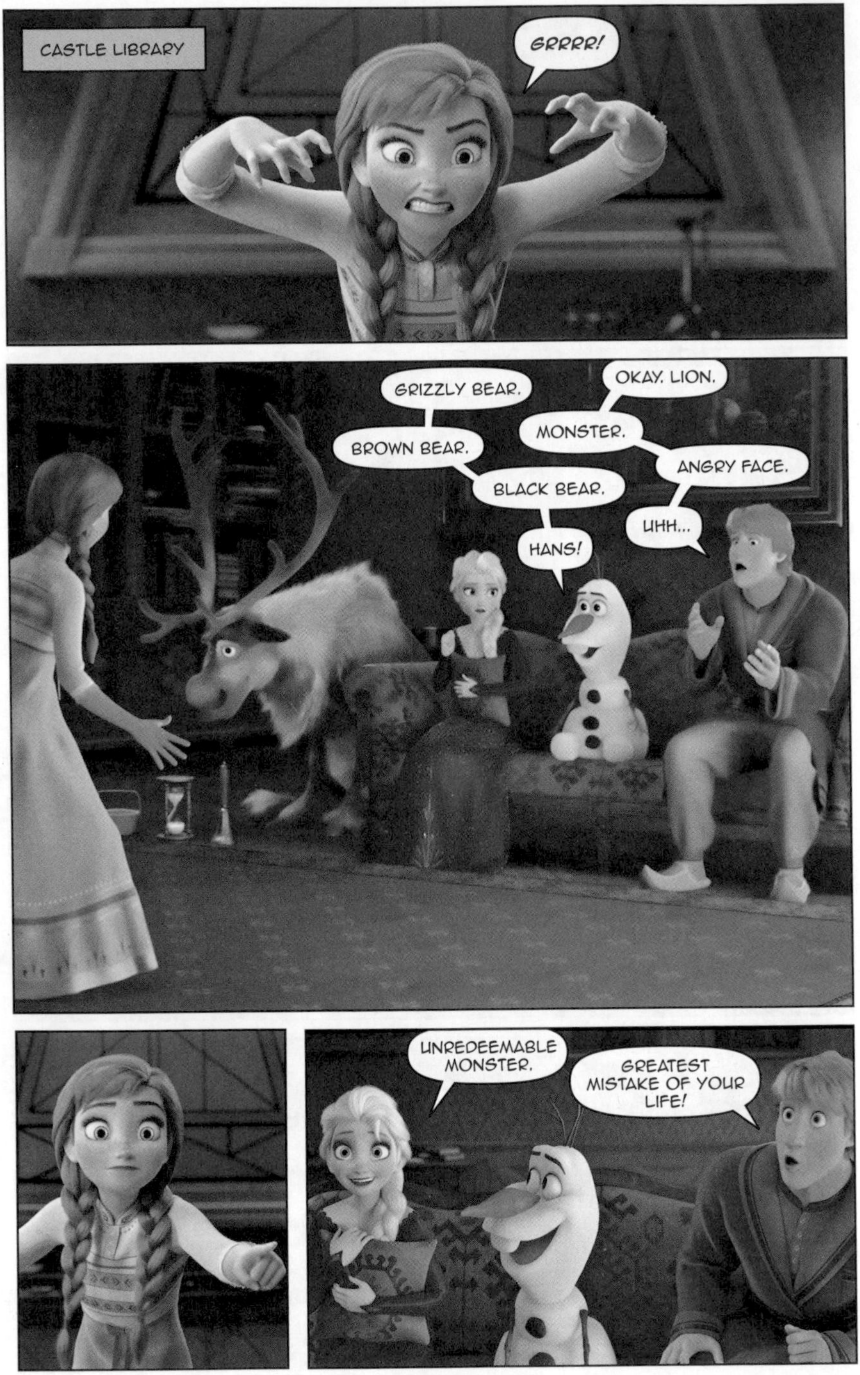
CASTLE LIBRARY
GRRRR!
OKAY. LION.
GRIZZLY BEAR.
MONSTER.
BROWN BEAR.
ANGRY FACE.
BLACK BEAR.
UHH...
HANS!
UNREDEEMABLE MONSTER.
GREATEST MISTAKE OF YOUR LIFE!

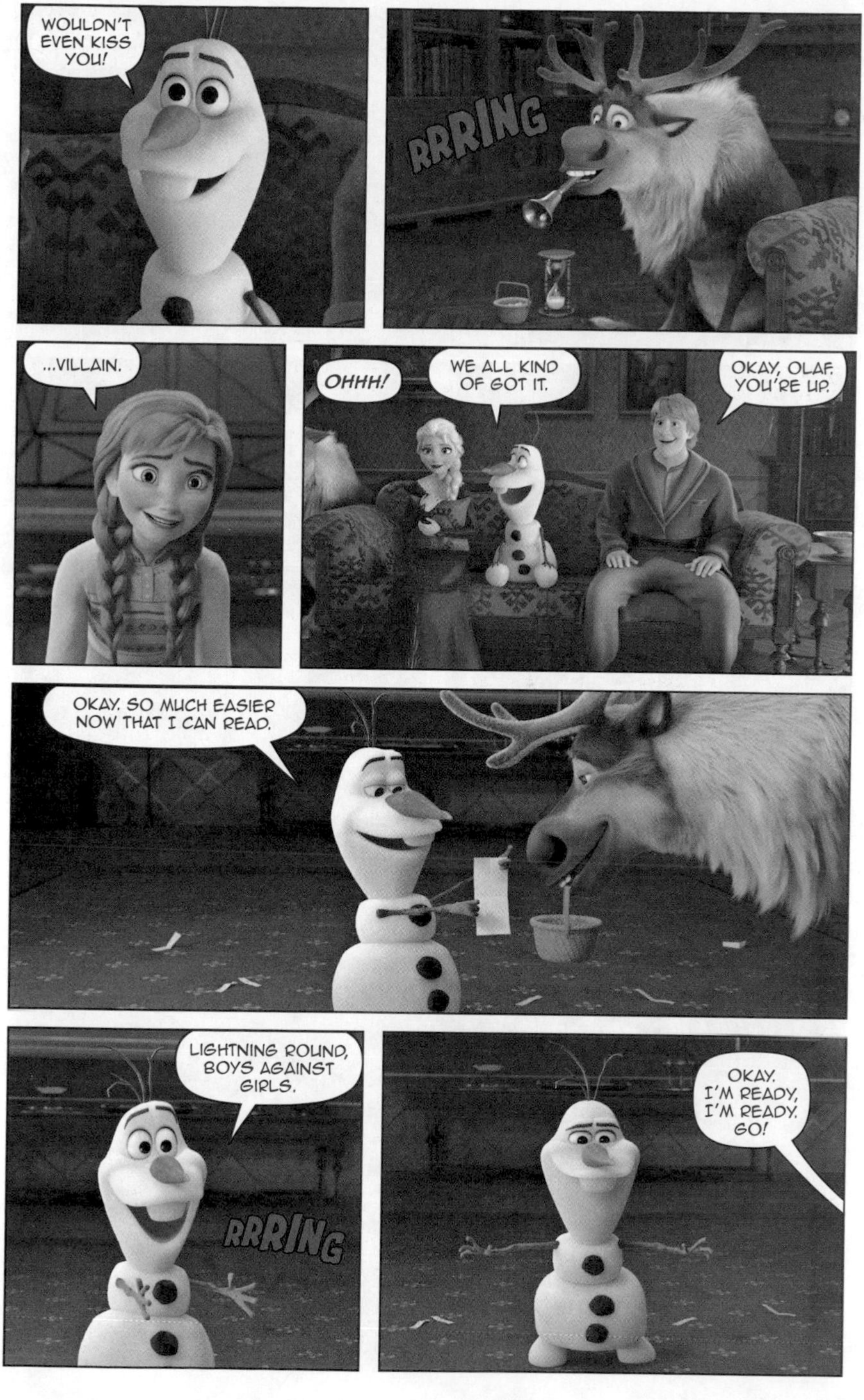
WOULDN'T EVEN KISS YOU!
RRRING
...VILLAIN.
OHHH!
WE ALL KIND OF GOT IT.
OKAY, OLAF. YOU'RE UP.
OKAY. SO MUCH EASIER NOW THAT I CAN READ.
LIGHTNING ROUND, BOYS AGAINST GIRLS.
RRRING
OKAY. I'M READY, I'M READY. GO!

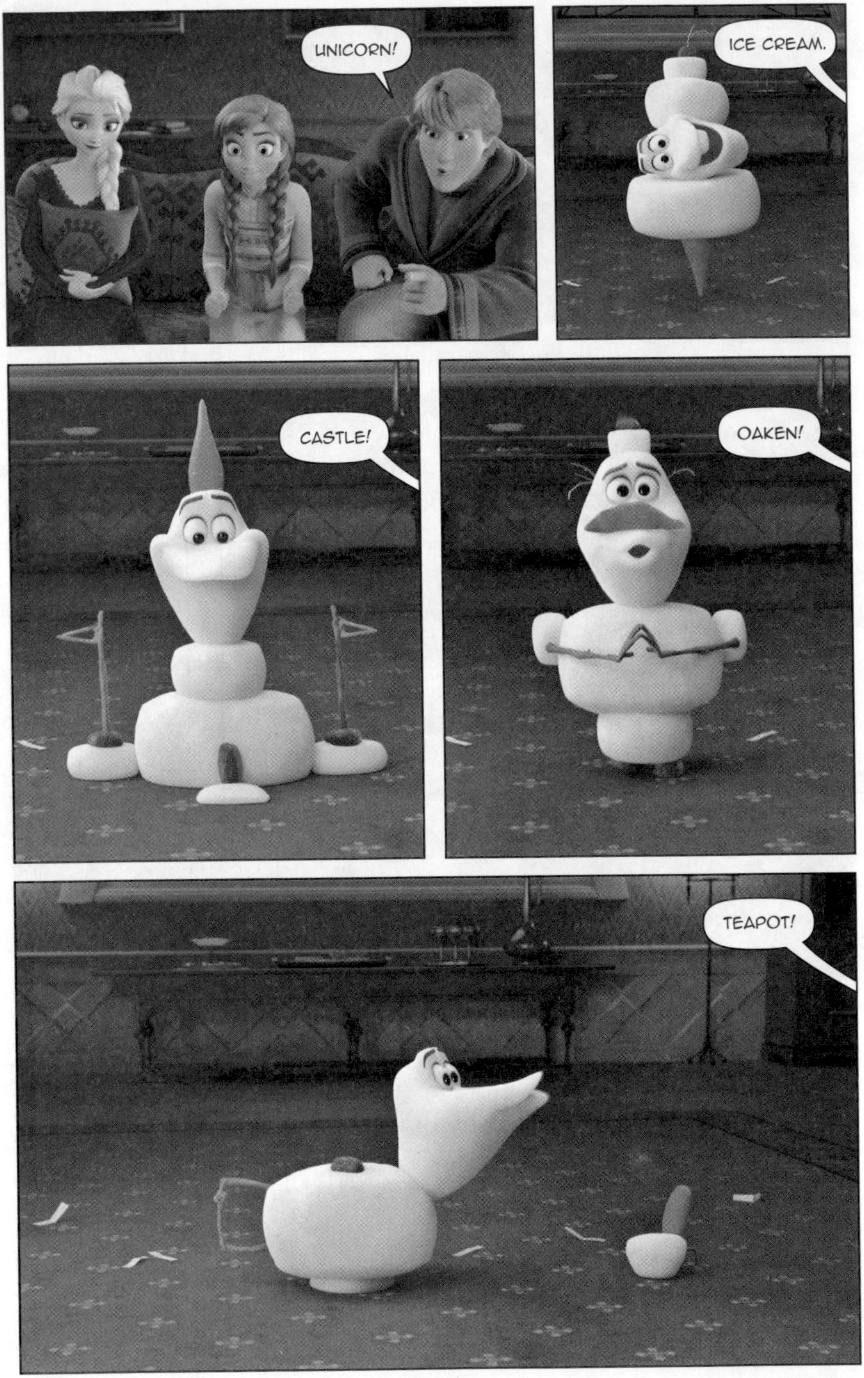
UNICORN!
ICE CREAM.
CASTLE!
OAKEN!
TEAPOT!

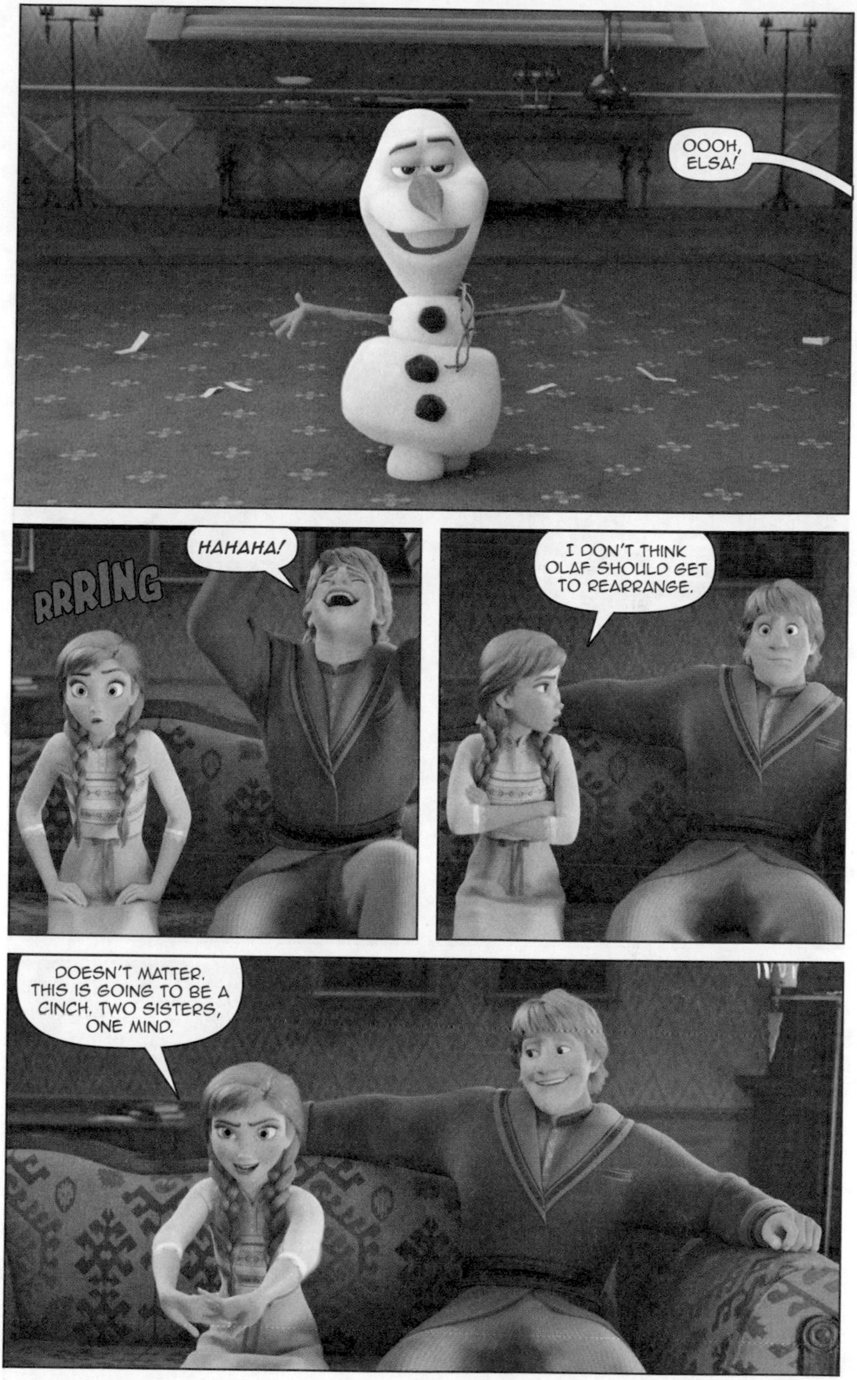
OOOH, ELSA!
RRRING
HAHAHA!
I DON'T THINK OLAF SHOULD GET TO REARRANGE.
DOESN'T MATTER. THIS IS GOING TO BE A CINCH. TWO SISTERS, ONE MIND.

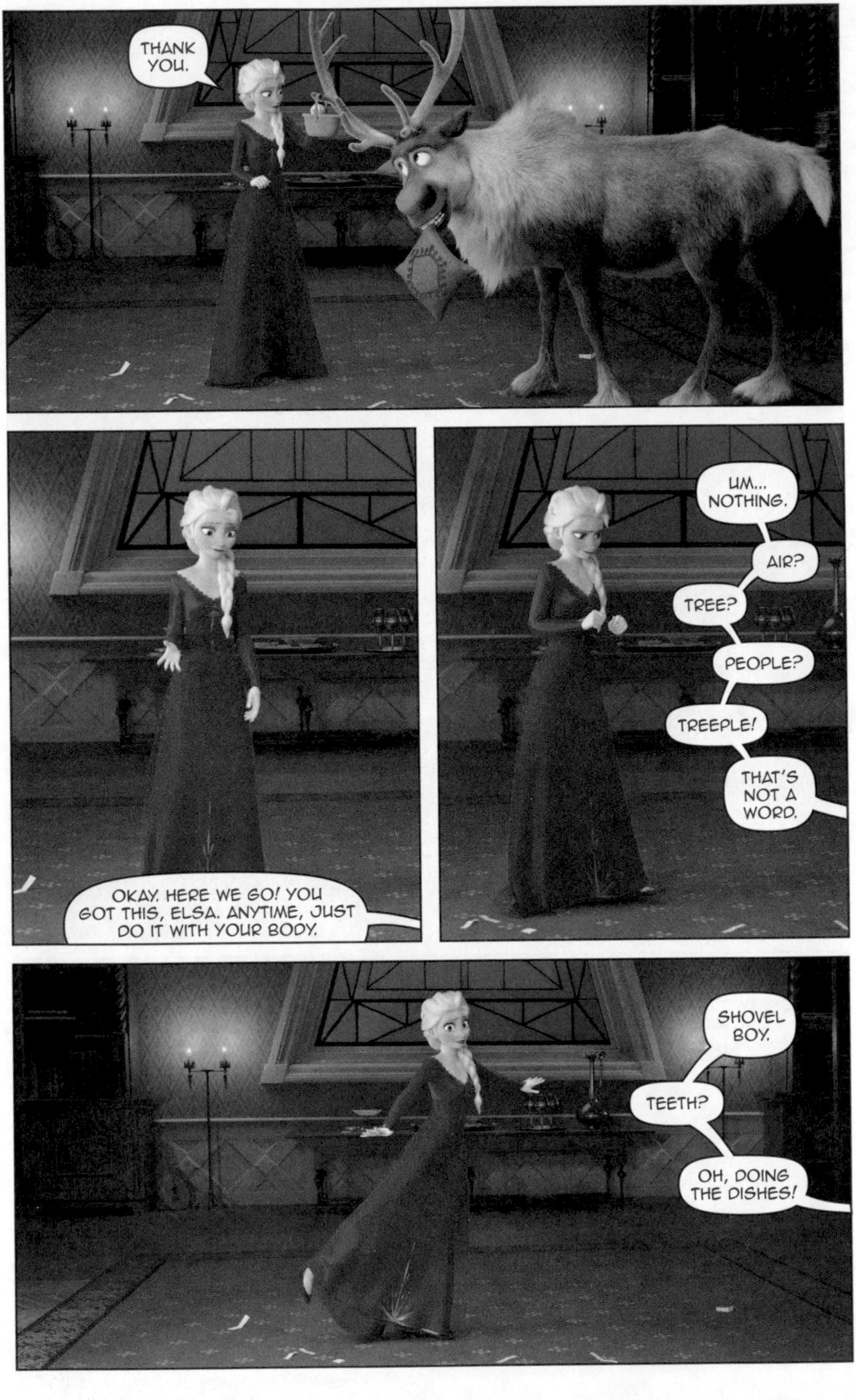
THANK YOU.
OKAY. HERE WE GO! YOU GOT THIS, ELSA. ANYTIME, JUST DO IT WITH YOUR BODY.
UM... NOTHING.
AIR?
TREE?
PEOPLE?
TREEPLE!
THAT'S NOT A WORD.
SHOVEL BOY.
TEETH?
OH, DOING THE DISHES!

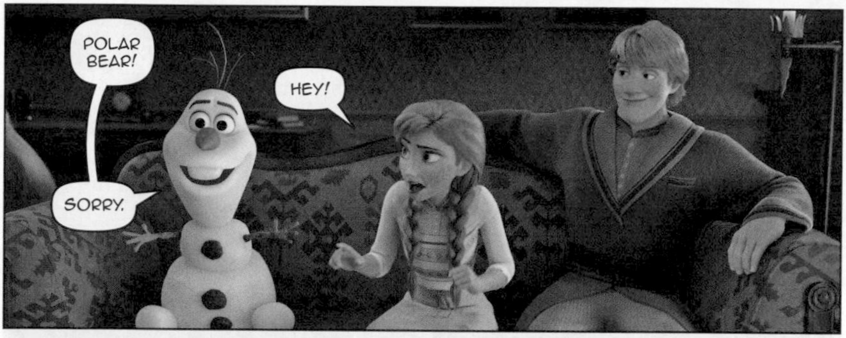
POLAR BEAR!
SORRY.
HEY!

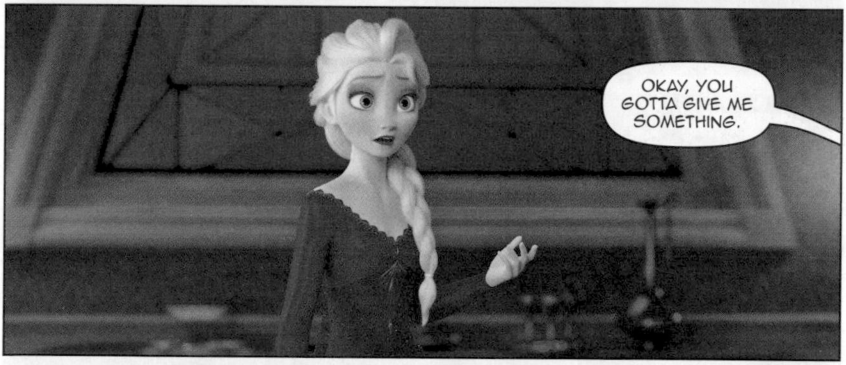
OKAY, YOU GOTTA GIVE ME SOMETHING.

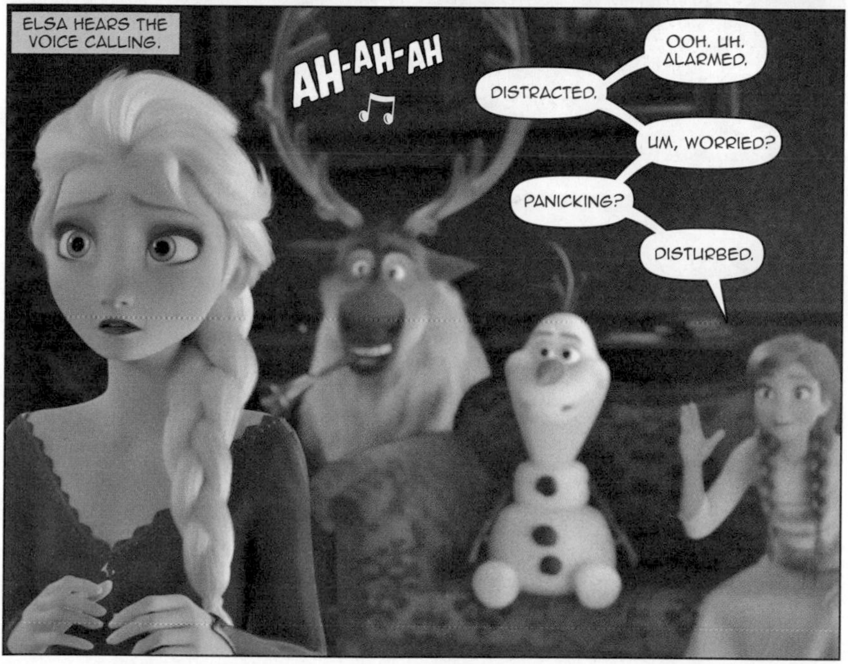
ELSA HEARS THE VOICE CALLING.
AH-AH-AH
DISTRACTED.
OOH. UH. ALARMED.
UM, WORRIED?
PANICKING?
DISTURBED.

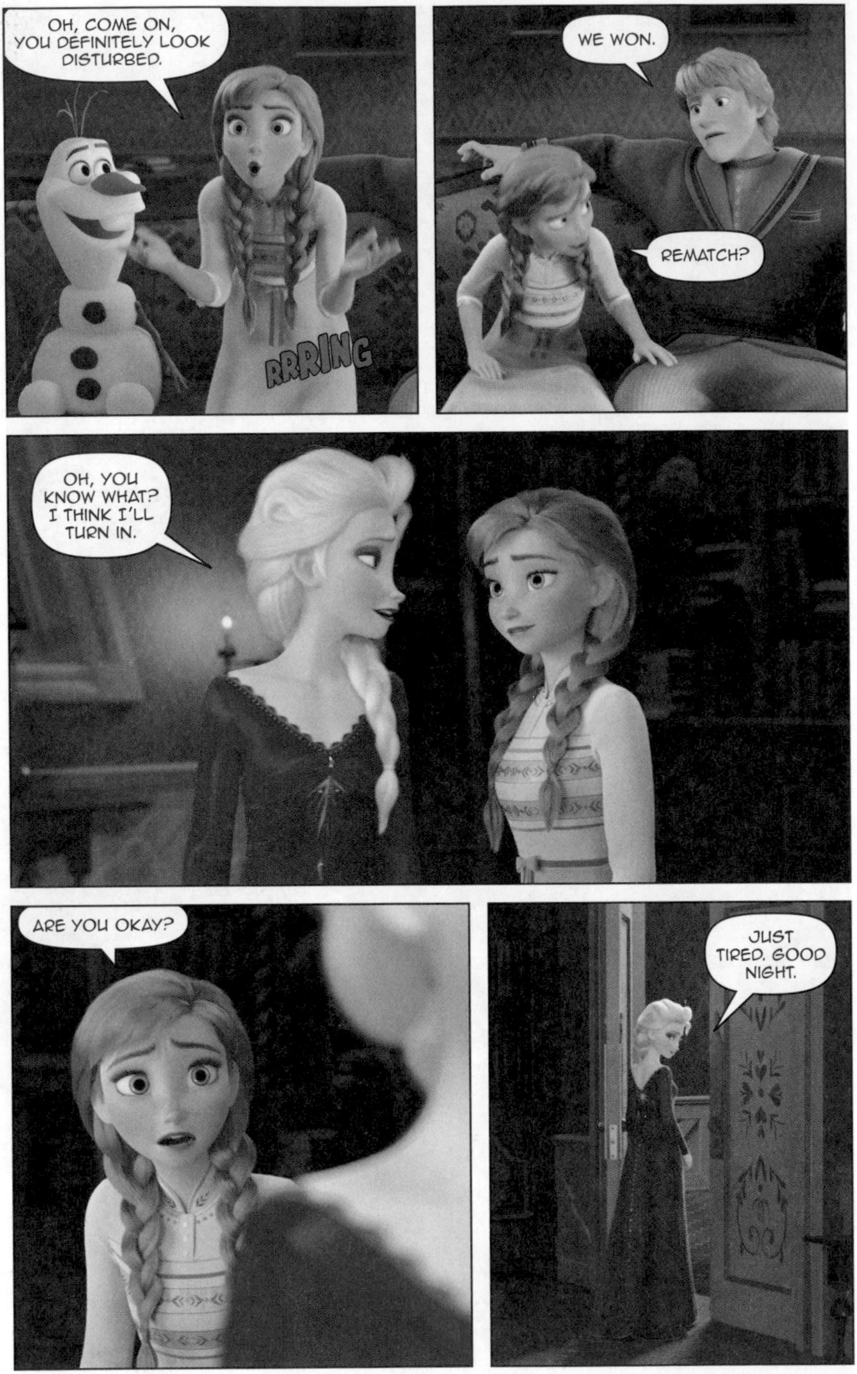
OH, COME ON, YOU DEFINITELY LOOK DISTURBED.
RRRING
WE WON.
REMATCH?
OH, YOU KNOW WHAT? I THINK I'LL TURN IN.
ARE YOU OKAY?
JUST TIRED. GOOD NIGHT.

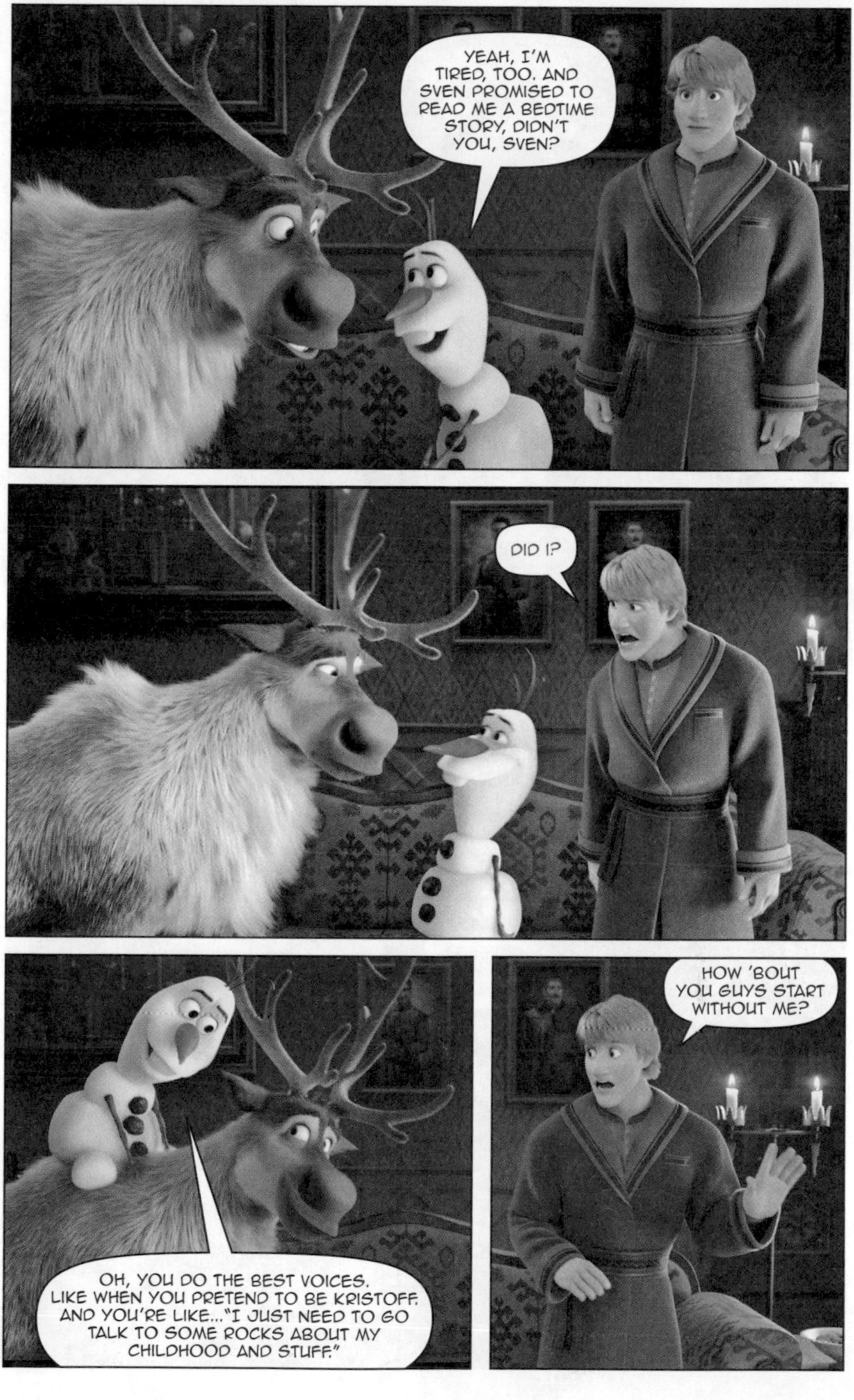
YEAH, I'M TIRED, TOO. AND SVEN PROMISED TO READ ME A BEDTIME STORY, DIDN'T YOU, SVEN?
DID I?
OH, YOU DO THE BEST VOICES. LIKE WHEN YOU PRETEND TO BE KRISTOFF. AND YOU'RE LIKE..."I JUST NEED TO GO TALK TO SOME ROCKS ABOUT MY CHILDHOOD AND STUFF."
HOW 'BOUT YOU GUYS START WITHOUT ME?

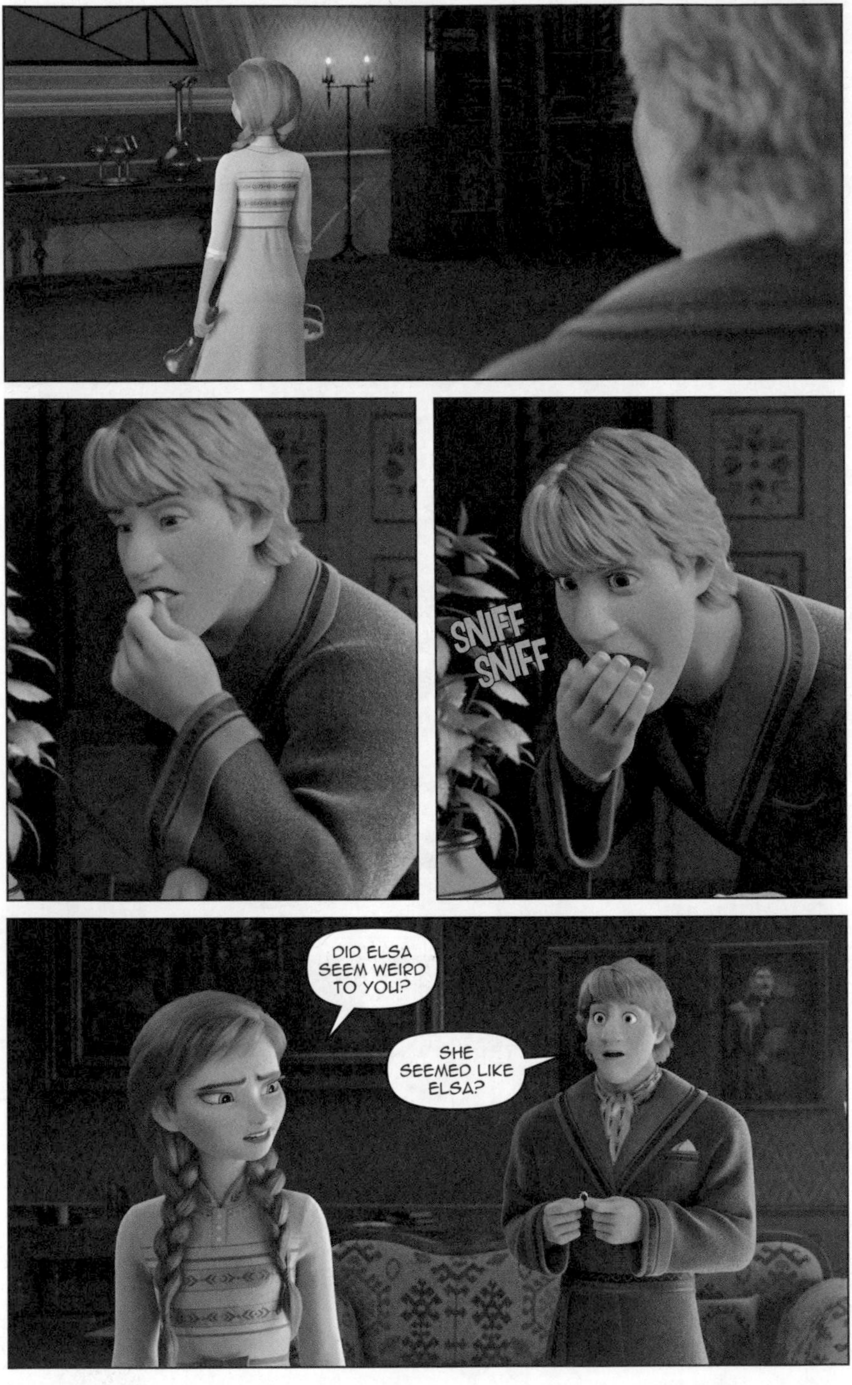
SNIFF
SNIFF
DID ELSA SEEM WEIRD TO YOU?
SHE SEEMED LIKE ELSA?

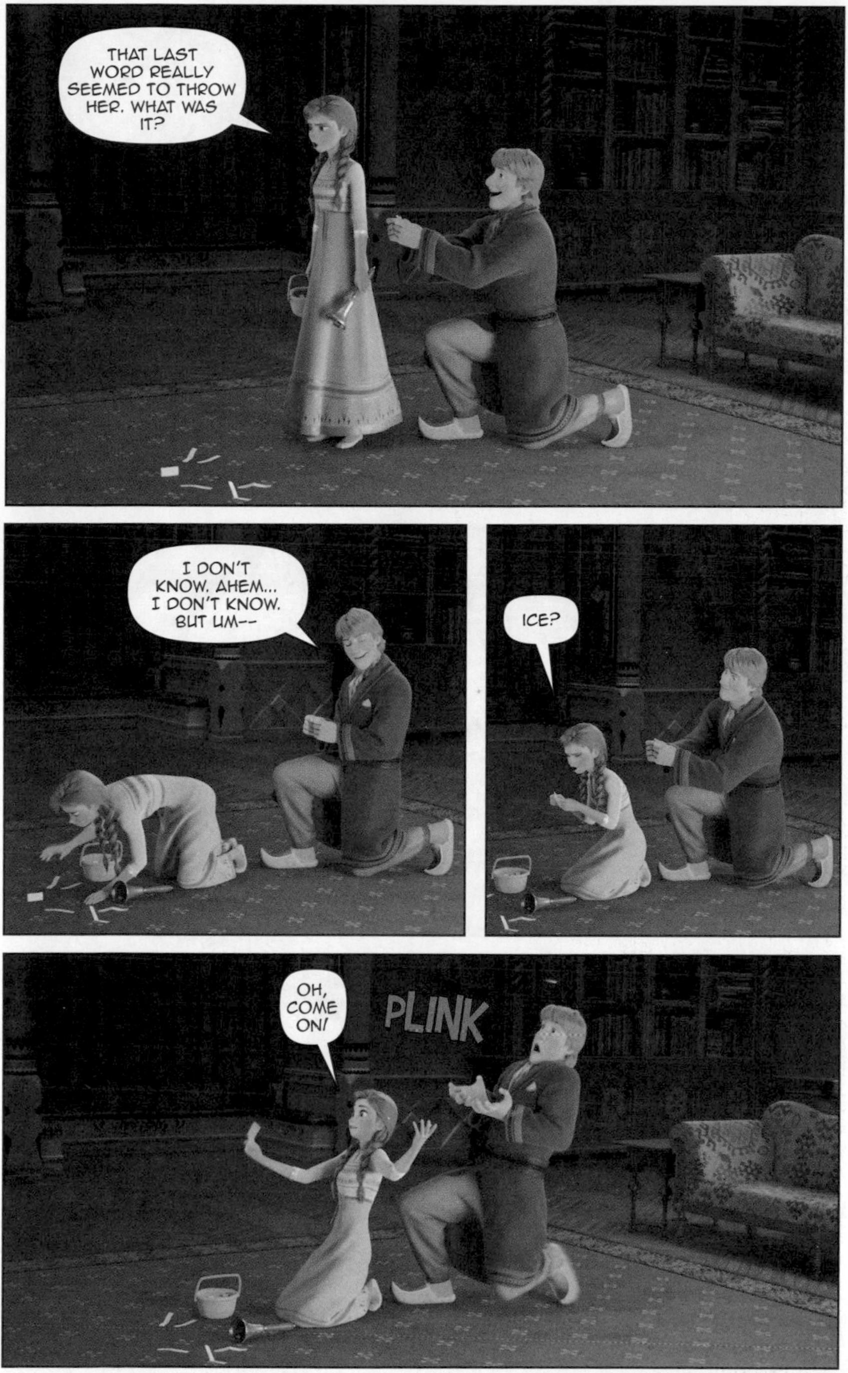
THAT LAST WORD REALLY SEEMED TO THROW HER. WHAT WAS IT?
I DON'T KNOW. AHEM... I DON'T KNOW. BUT UM--
ICE?
OH, COME ON!
PLINK

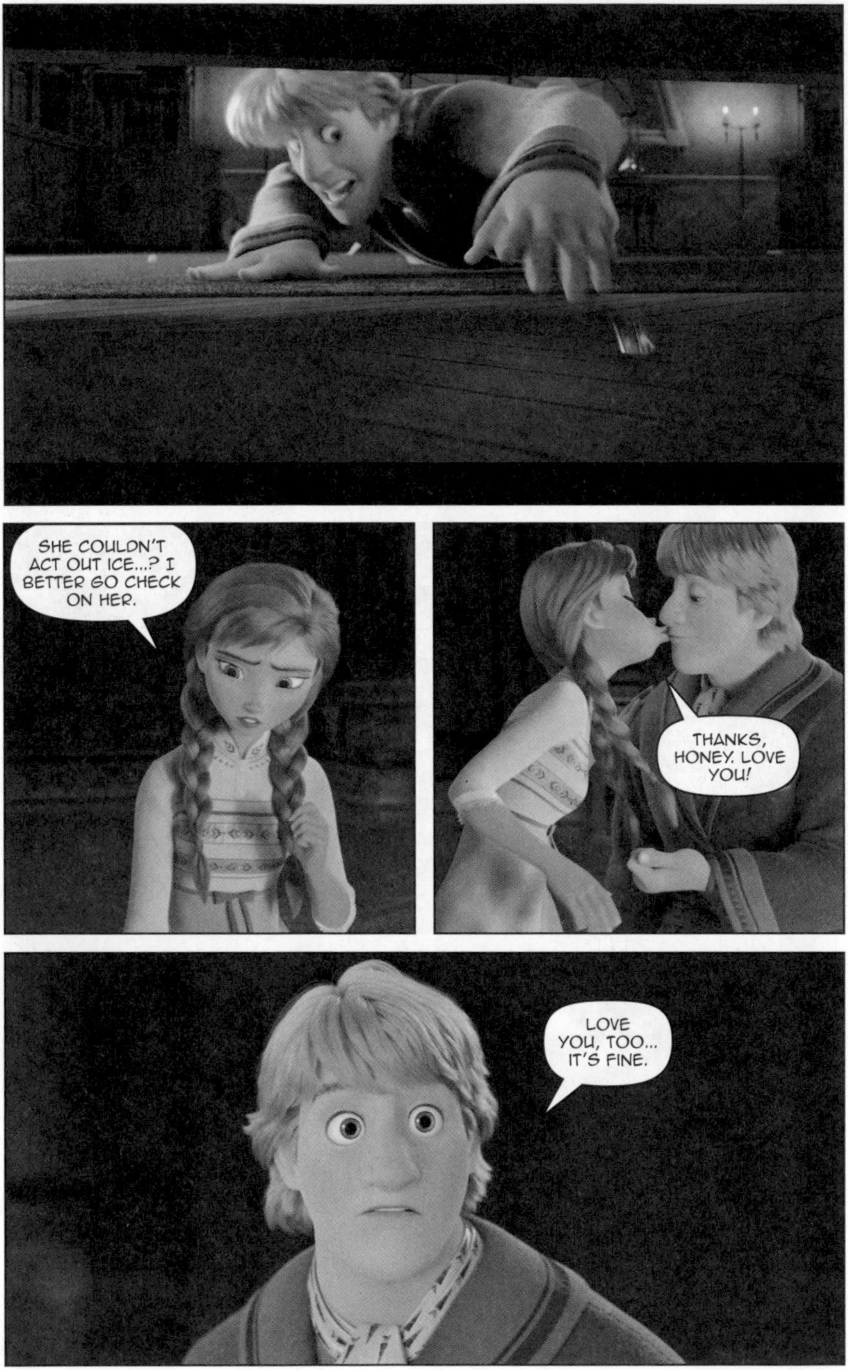
SHE COULDN'T ACT OUT ICE...? I BETTER GO CHECK ON HER.
THANKS, HONEY. LOVE YOU!
LOVE YOU, TOO... IT'S FINE.

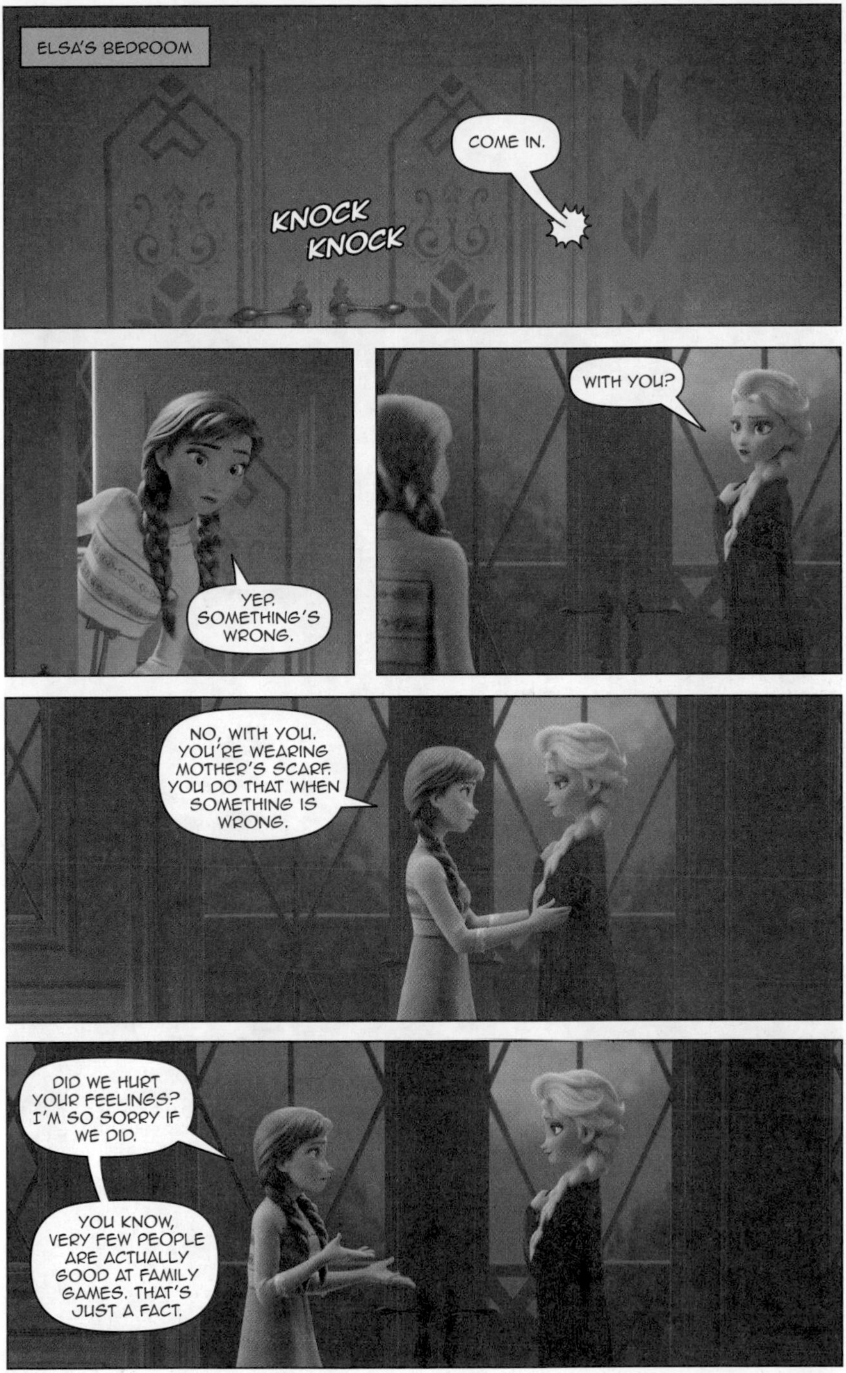
ELSA'S BEDROOM
KNOCK KNOCK
COME IN.
YEP. SOMETHING'S WRONG.
WITH YOU?
NO, WITH YOU. YOU'RE WEARING MOTHER'S SCARF. YOU DO THAT WHEN SOMETHING IS WRONG.
DID WE HURT YOUR FEELINGS? I'M SO SORRY IF WE DID.
YOU KNOW, VERY FEW PEOPLE ARE ACTUALLY GOOD AT FAMILY GAMES. THAT'S JUST A FACT.

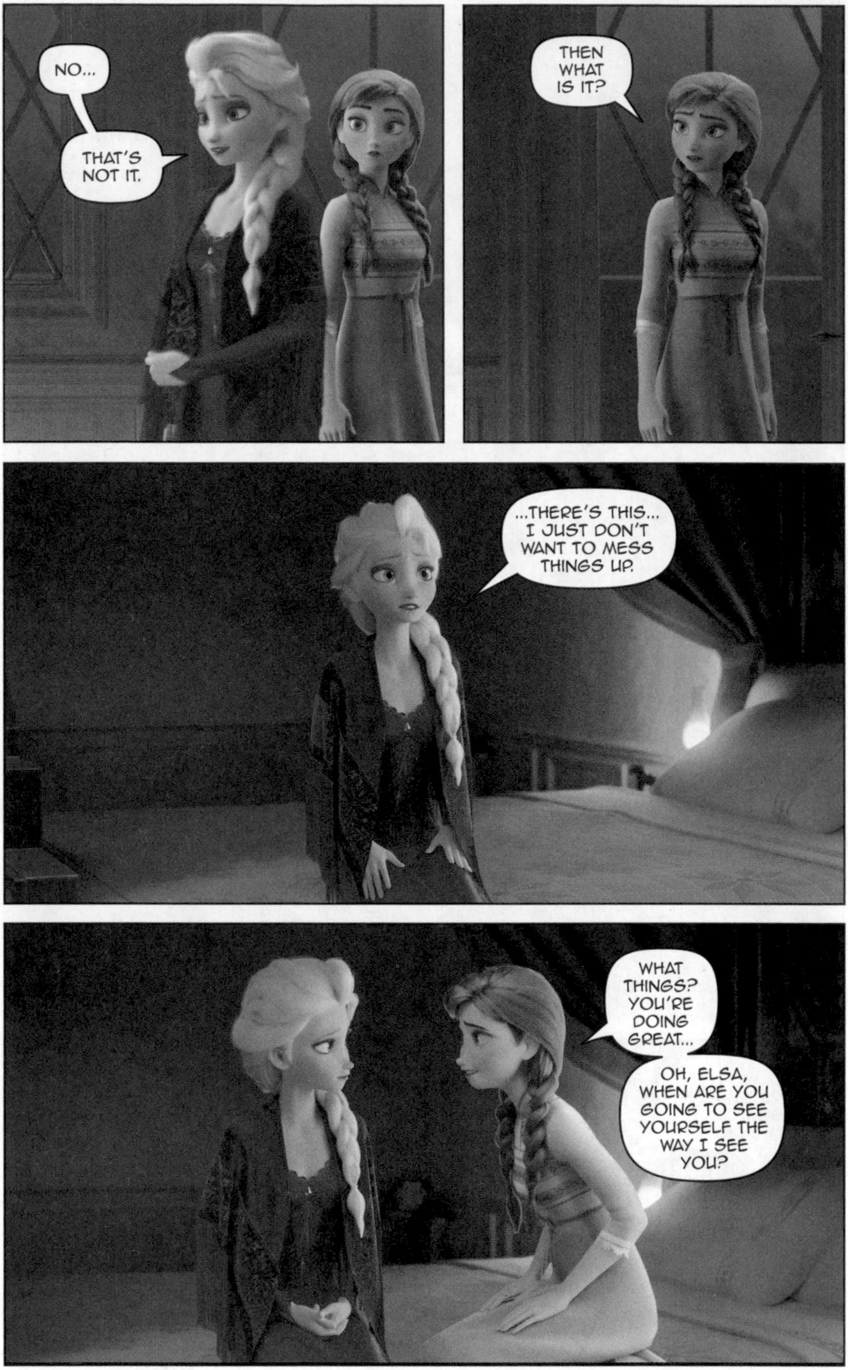
NO...
THAT'S NOT IT.
THEN WHAT IS IT?
...THERE'S THIS... I JUST DON'T WANT TO MESS THINGS UP.
WHAT THINGS? YOU'RE DOING GREAT...
OH, ELSA, WHEN ARE YOU GOING TO SEE YOURSELF THE WAY I SEE YOU?

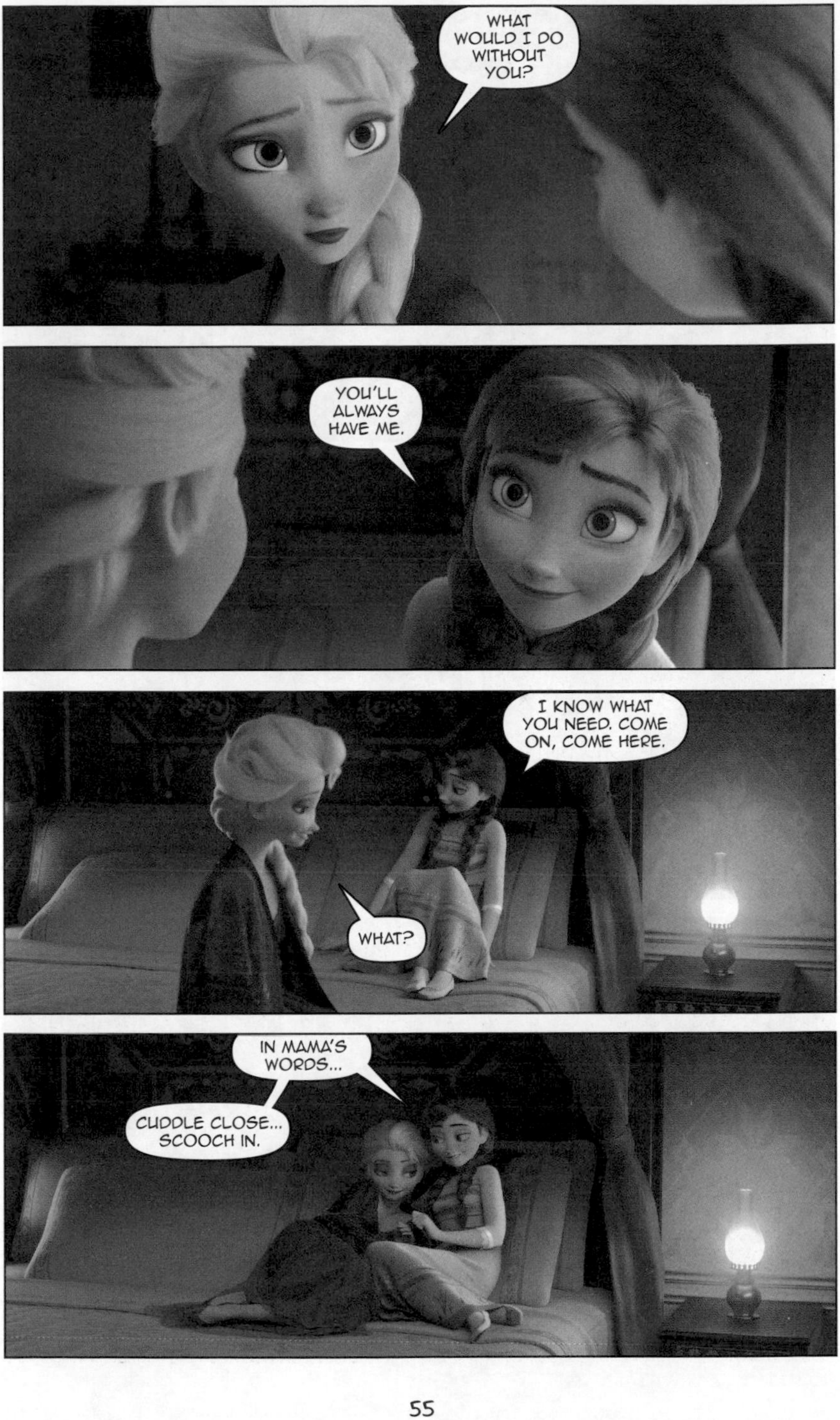
WHAT WOULD I DO WITHOUT YOU?
YOU'LL ALWAYS HAVE ME.
I KNOW WHAT YOU NEED. COME ON, COME HERE.
WHAT?
IN MAMA'S WORDS...
CUDDLE CLOSE... SCOOCH IN.

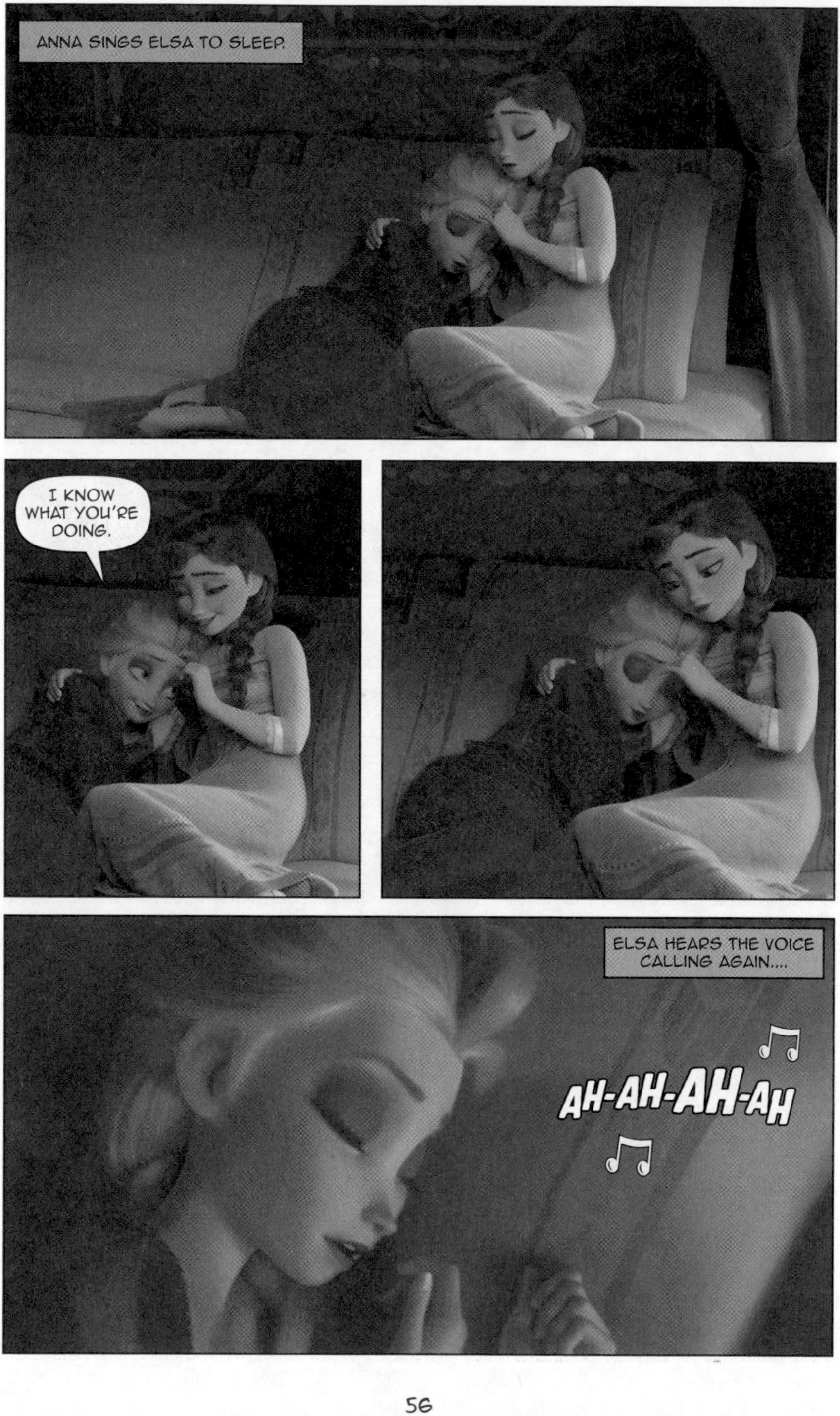
ANNA SINGS ELSA TO SLEEP.
I KNOW WHAT YOU'RE DOING.
ELSA HEARS THE VOICE CALLING AGAIN....
AH-AH-AH-AH

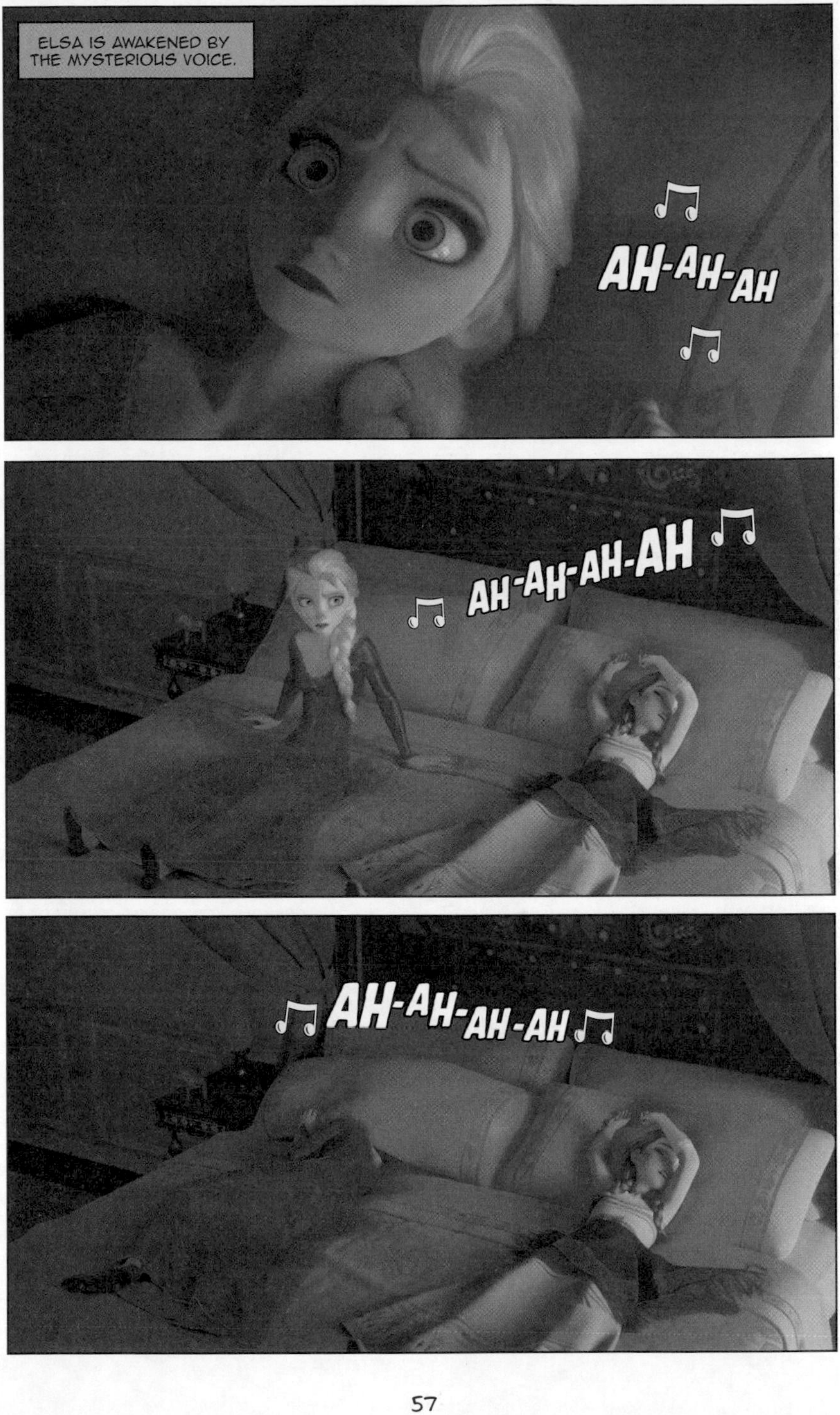
ELSA IS AWAKENED BY THE MYSTERIOUS VOICE.
AH-AH-AH
AH-AH-AH-AH
AH-AH-AH-AH

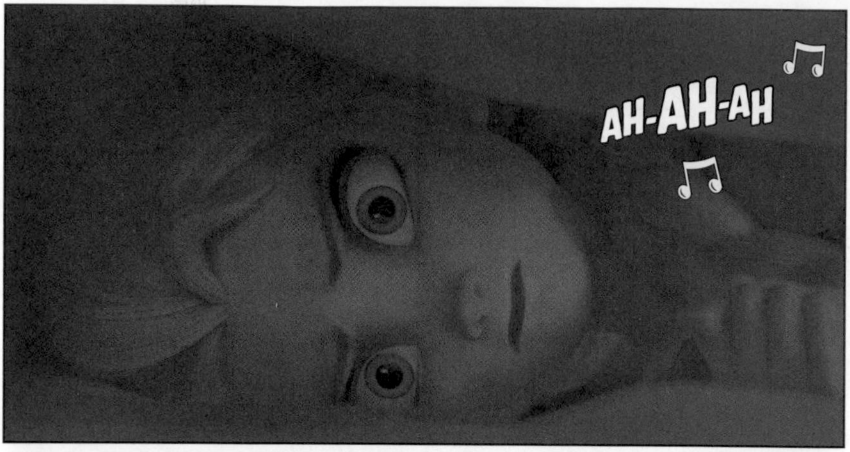
AH-AH-AH

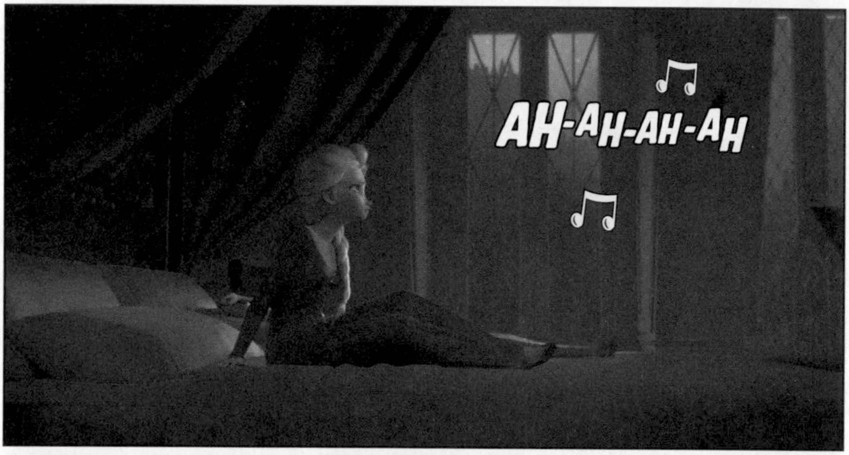
AH-AH-AH-AH

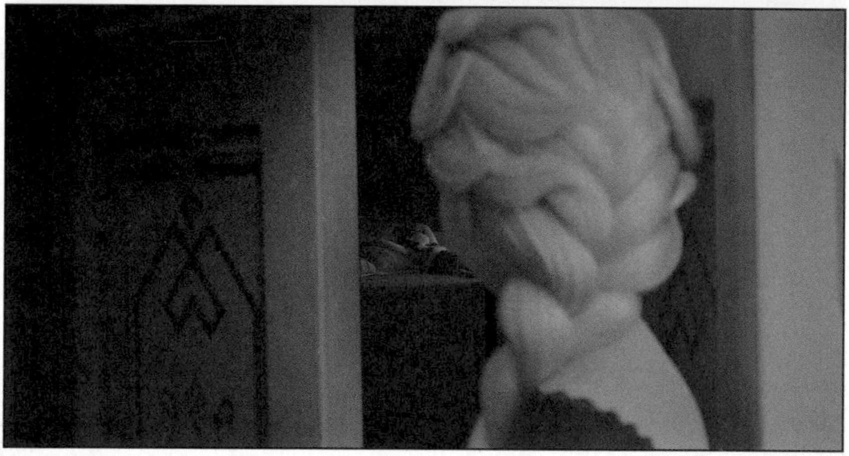

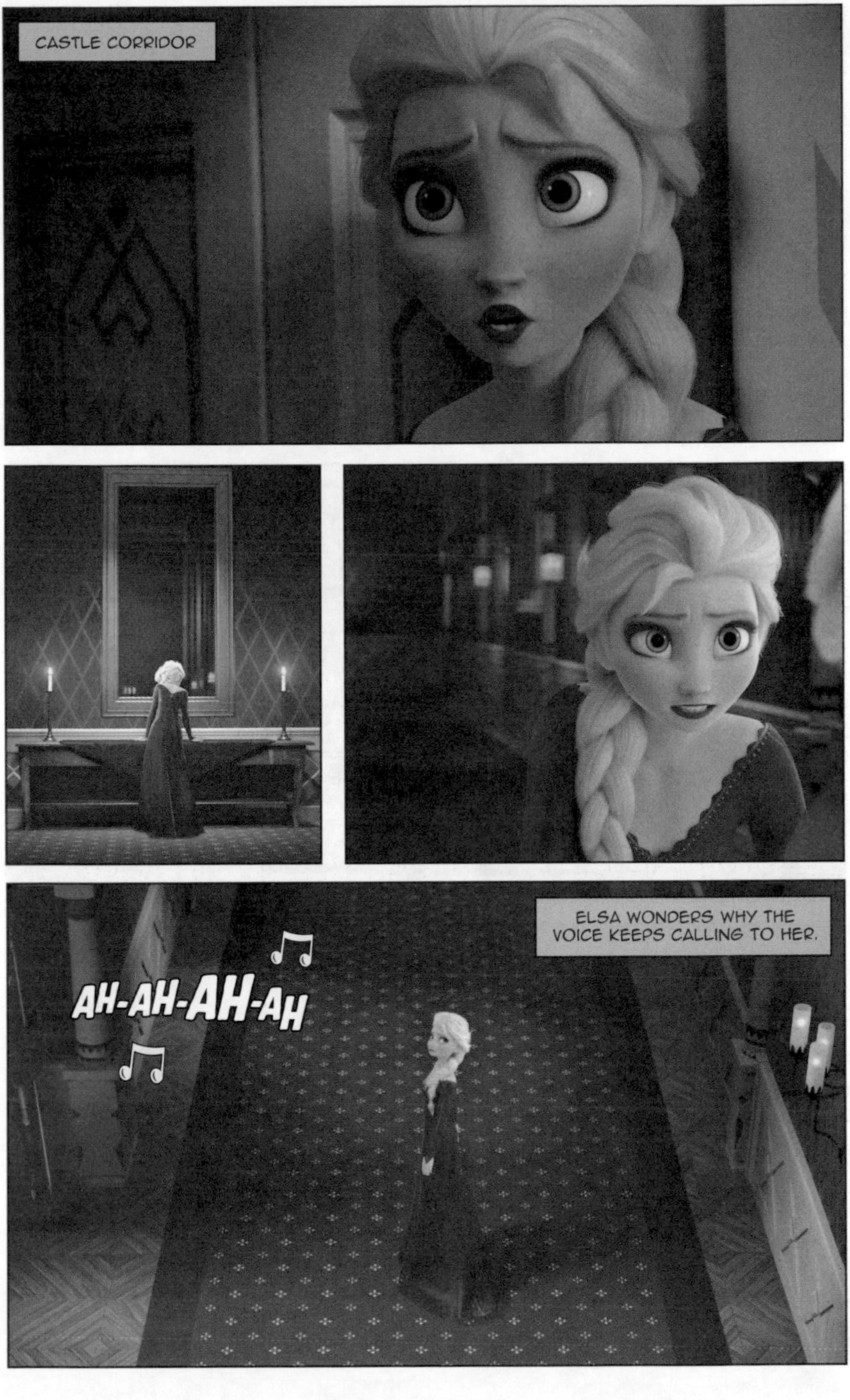
CASTLE CORRIDOR
ELSA WONDERS WHY THE VOICE KEEPS CALLING TO HER.
AH-AH-AH-AH

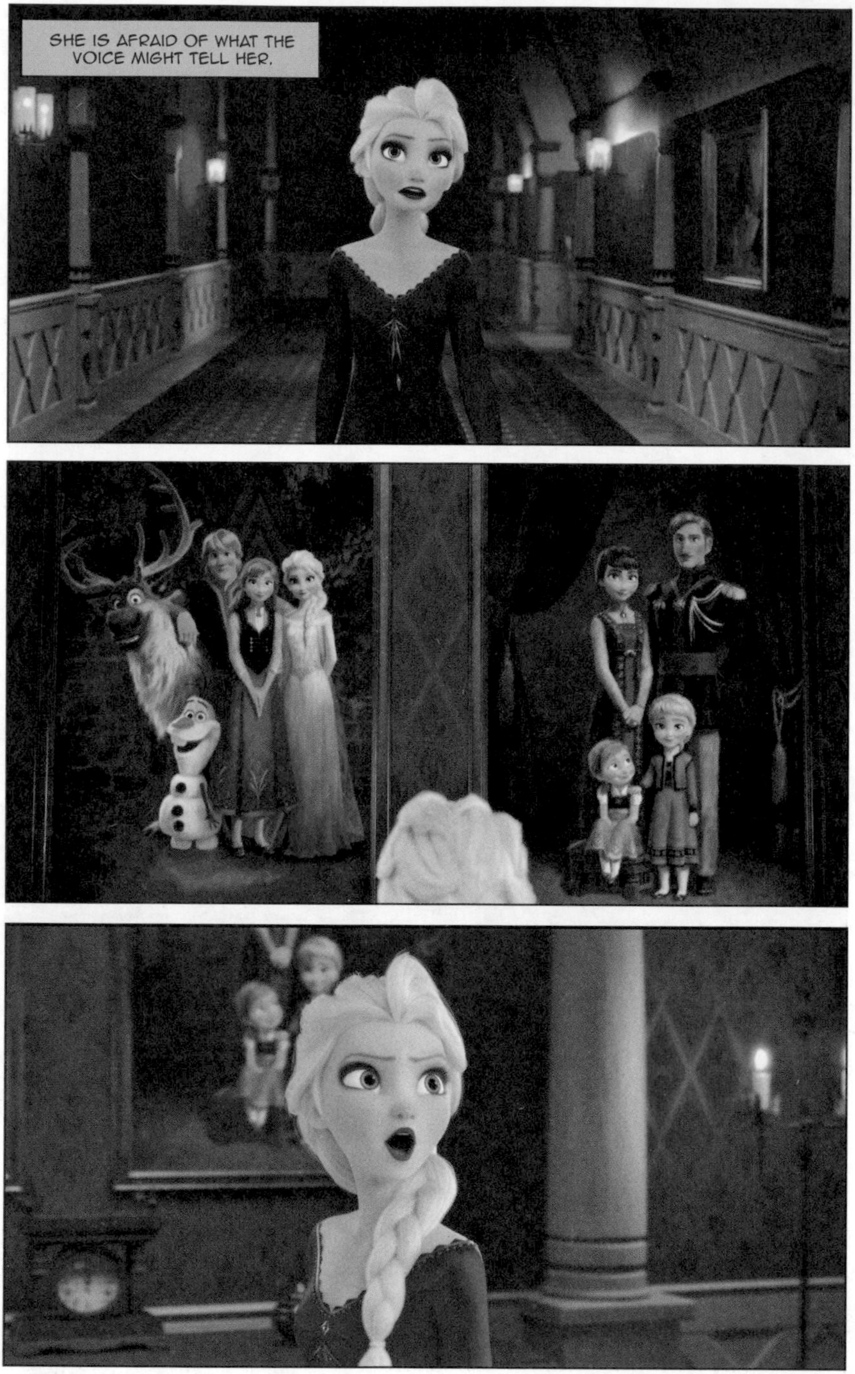
SHE IS AFRAID OF WHAT THE VOICE MIGHT TELL HER.

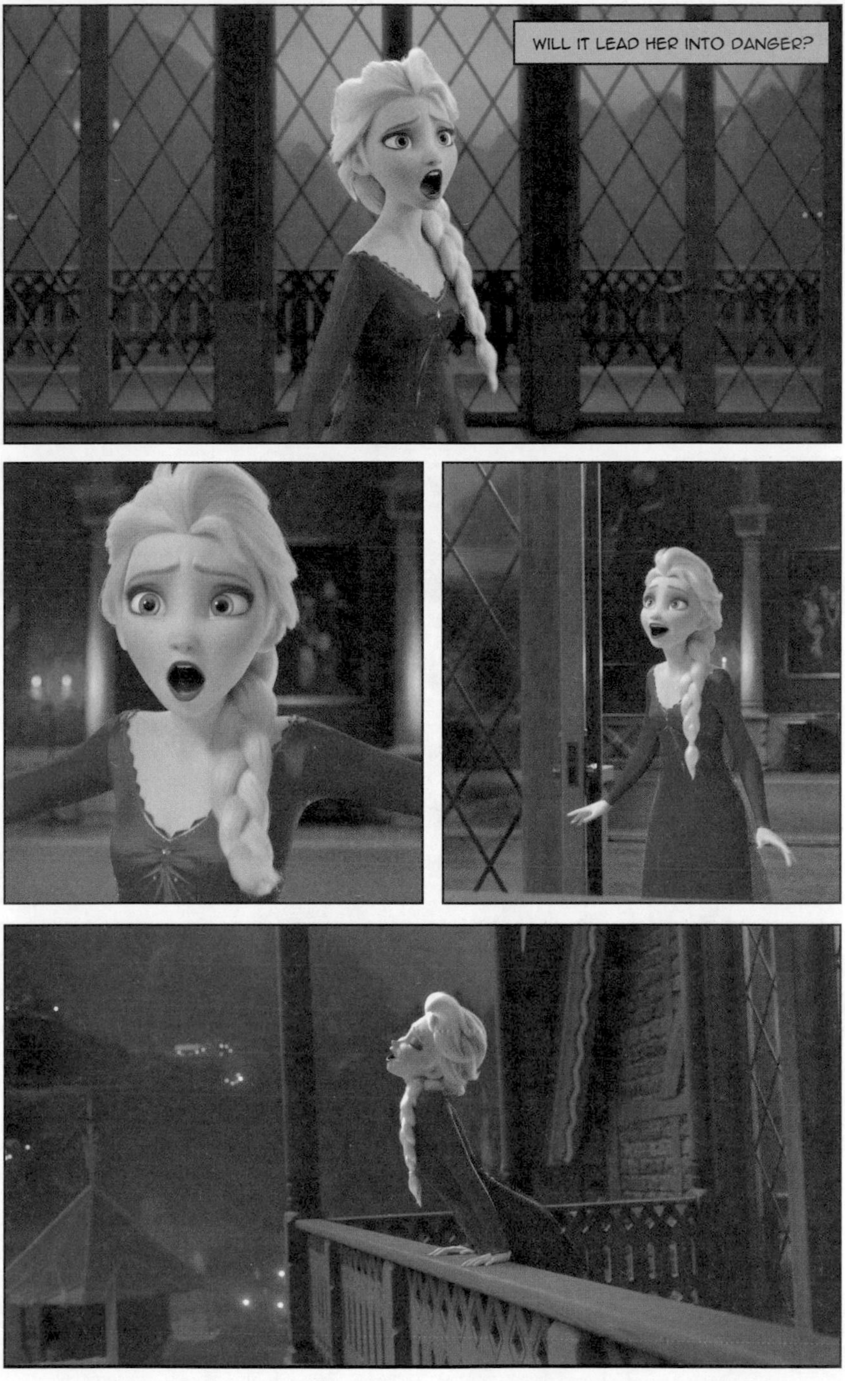
WILL IT LEAD HER INTO DANGER?

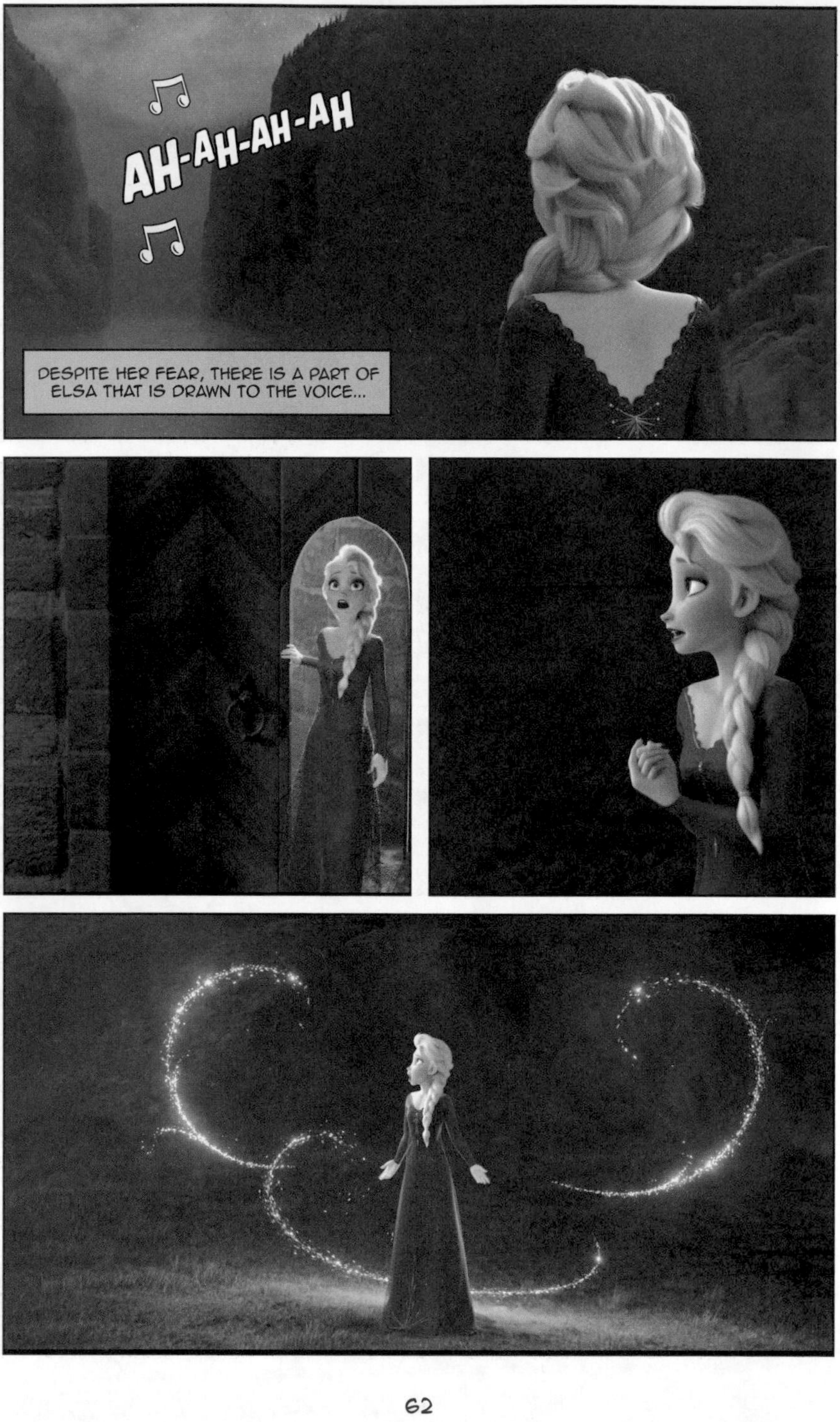
AH-AH-AH-AH
DESPITE HER FEAR, THERE IS A PART OF ELSA THAT IS DRAWN TO THE VOICE...

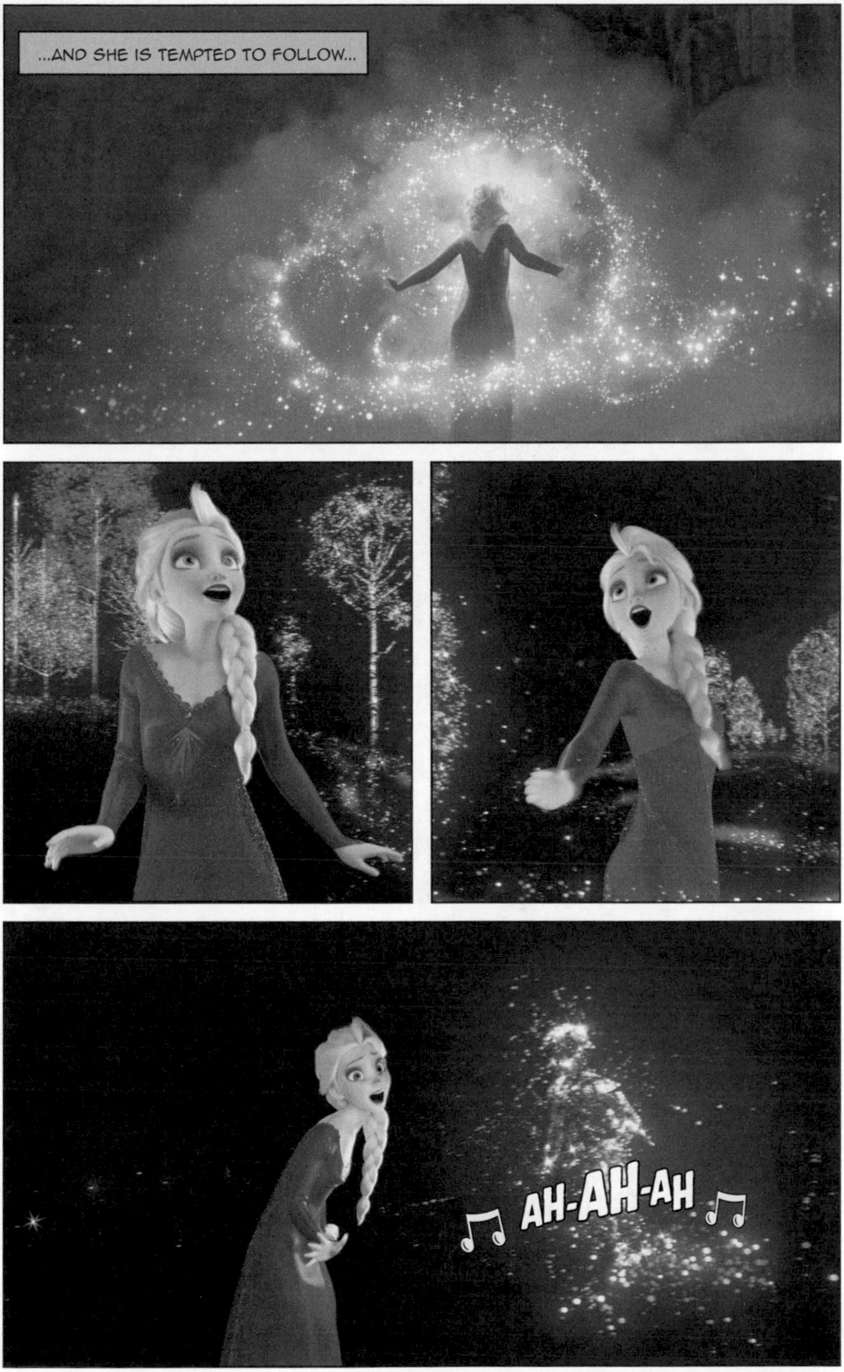
...AND SHE IS TEMPTED TO FOLLOW...
AH-AH-AH

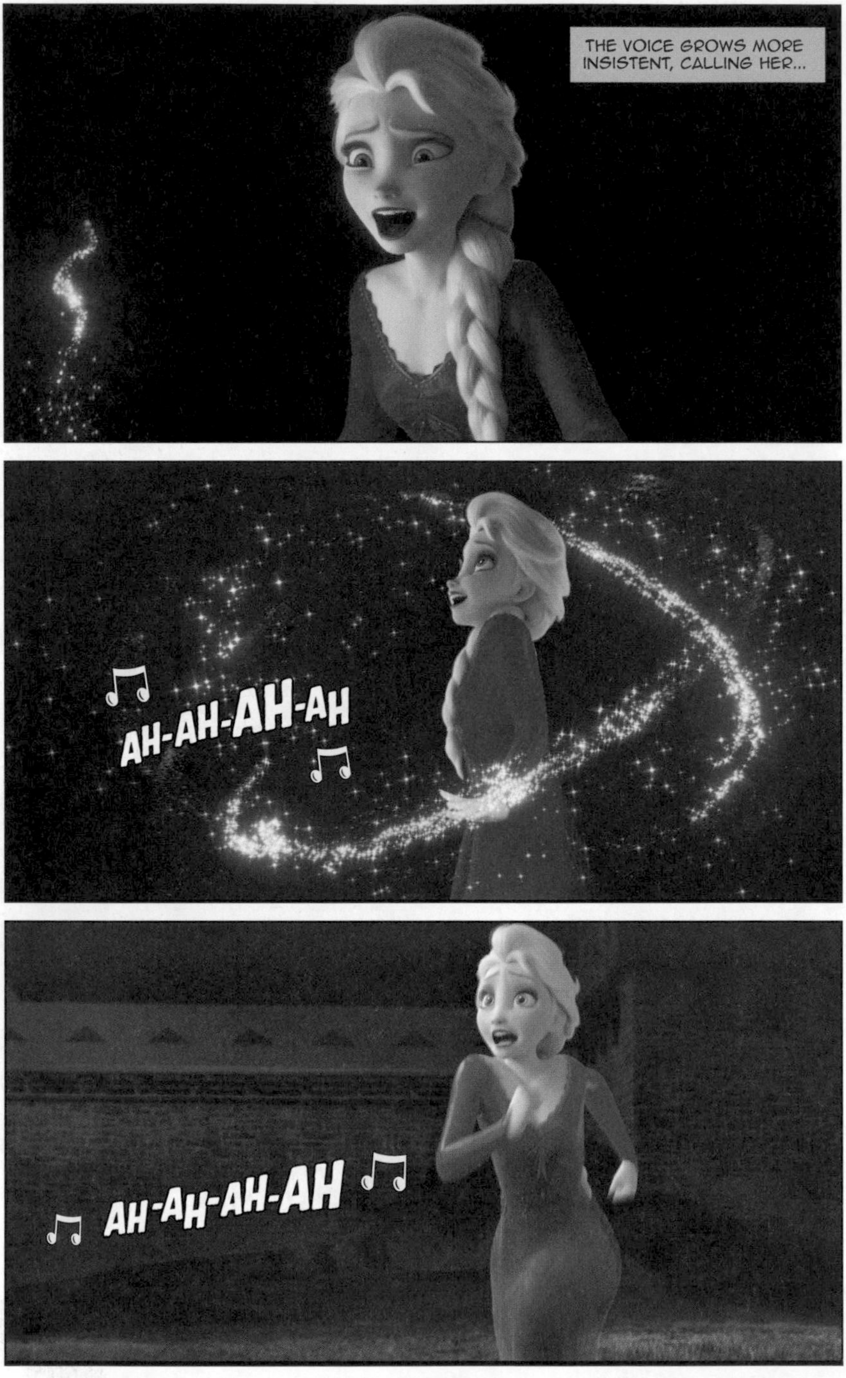
THE VOICE GROWS MORE INSISTENT, CALLING HER...
AH-AH-AH-AH
AH-AH-AH-AH

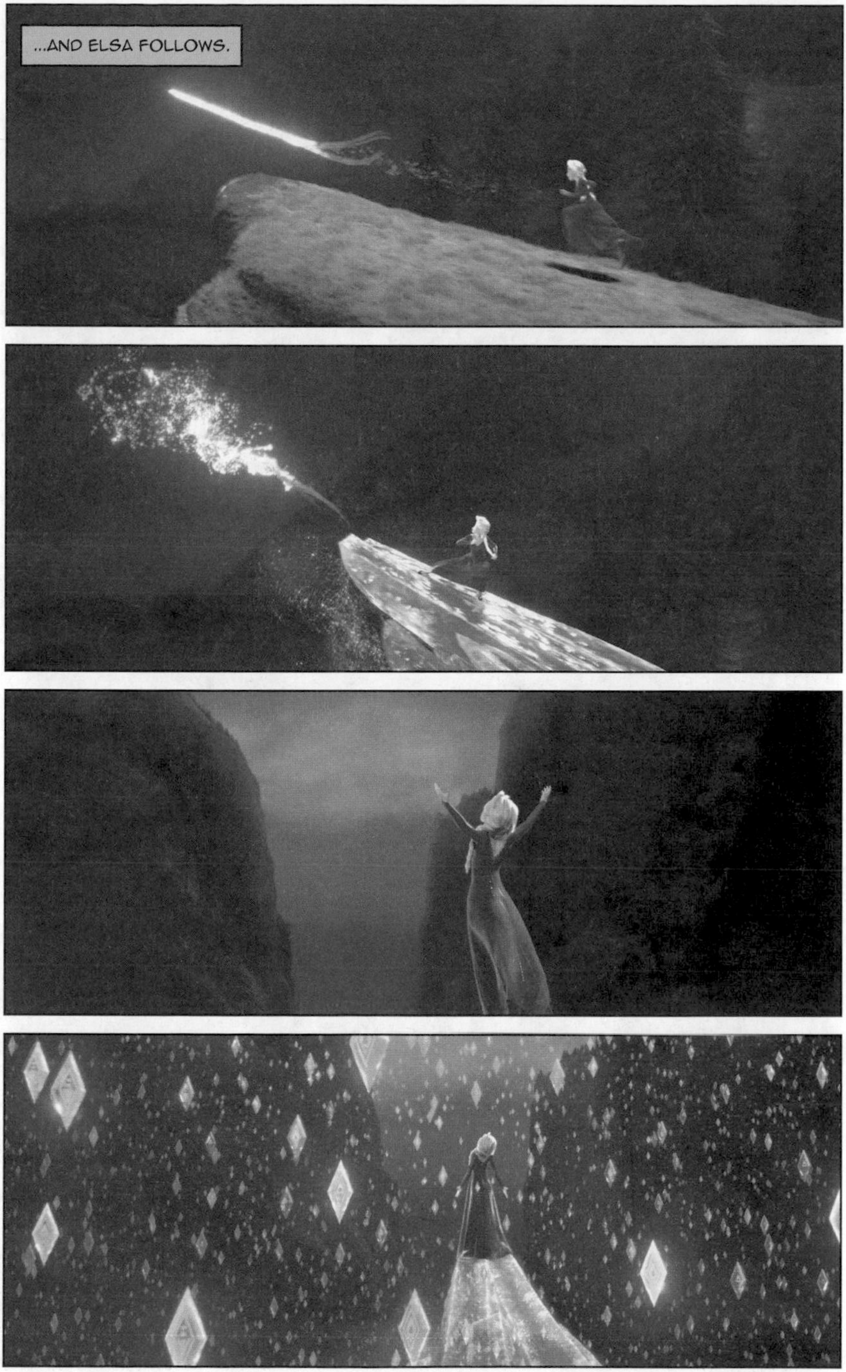
...AND ELSA FOLLOWS.

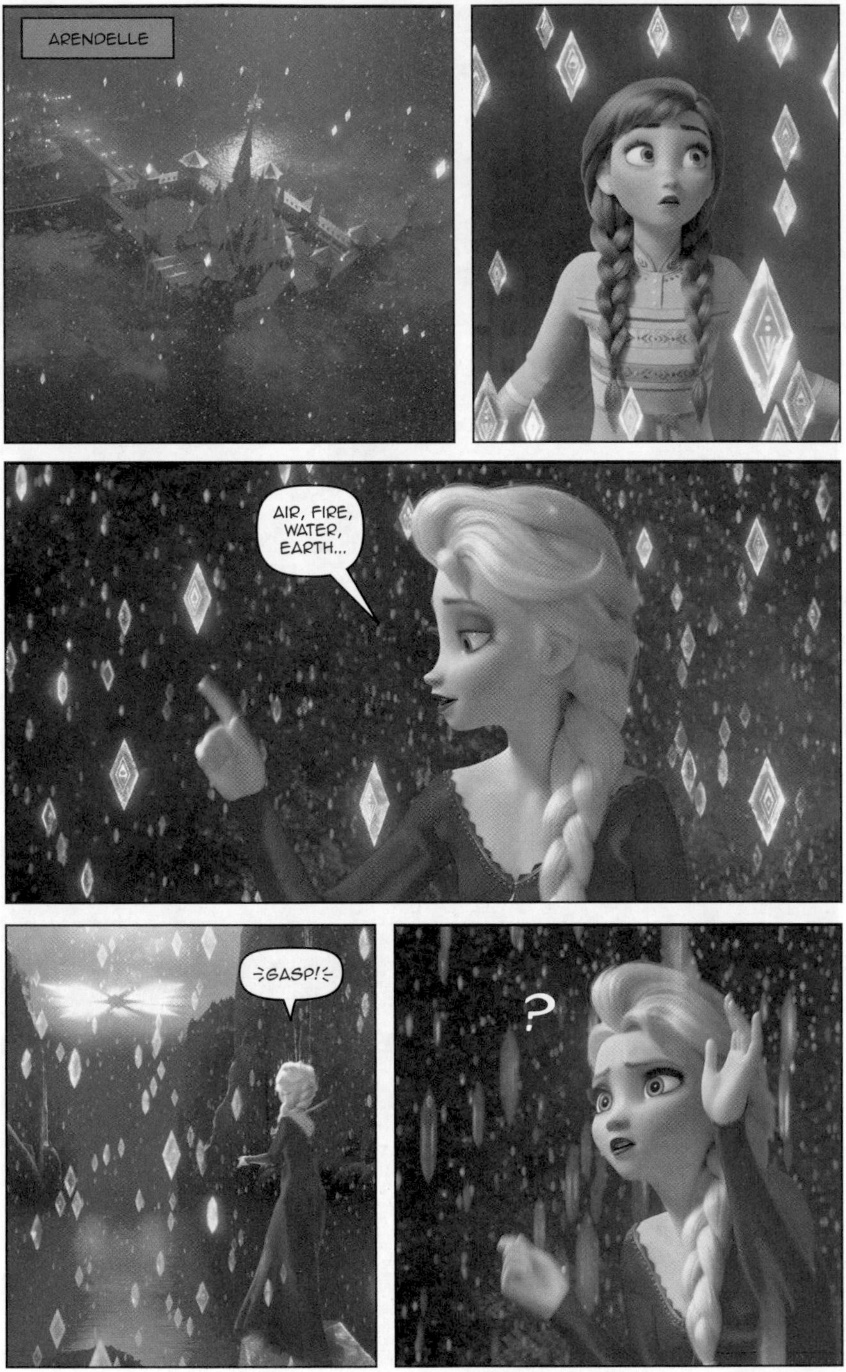
ARENDELLE
AIR, FIRE, WATER, EARTH...
GASP!
?

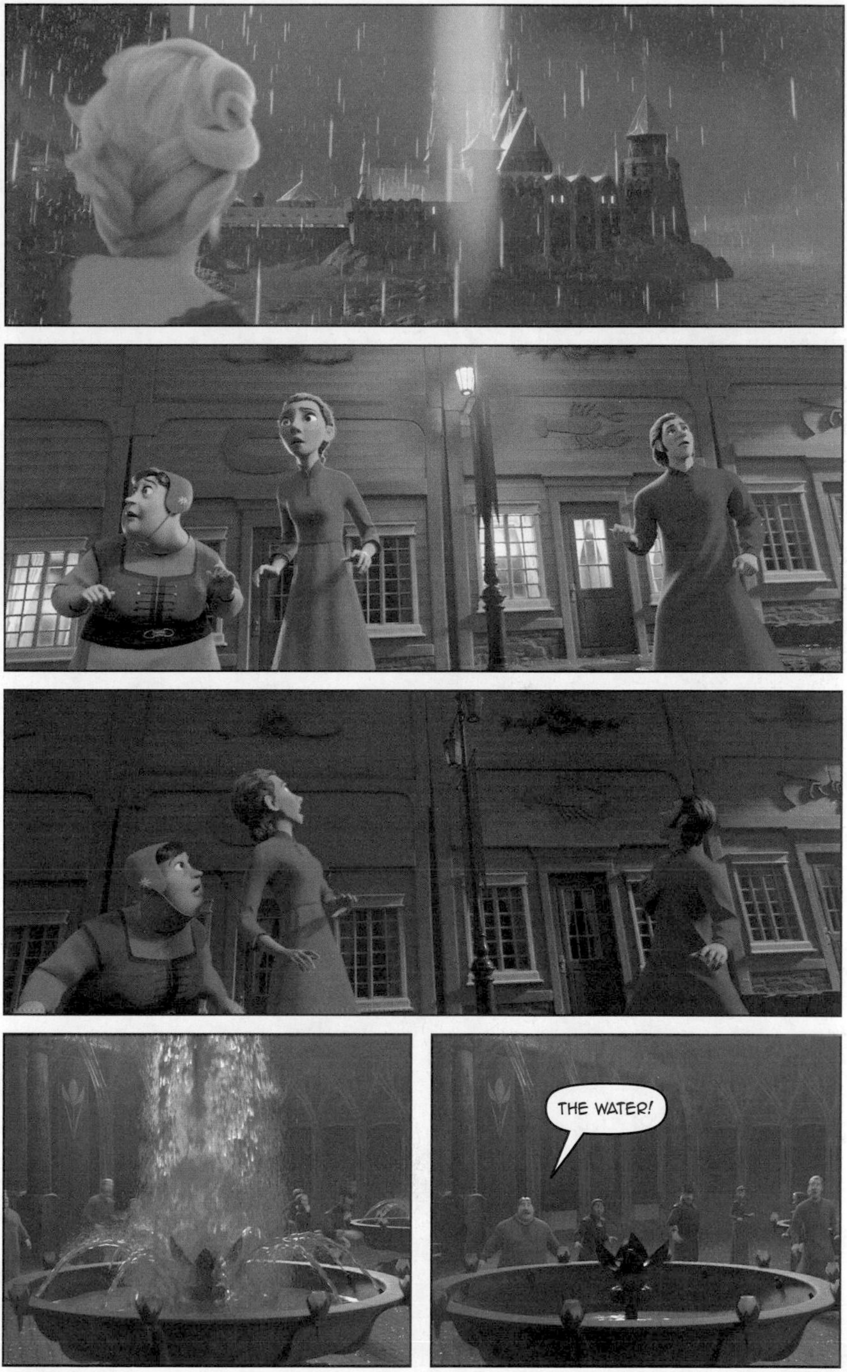
THE WATER!

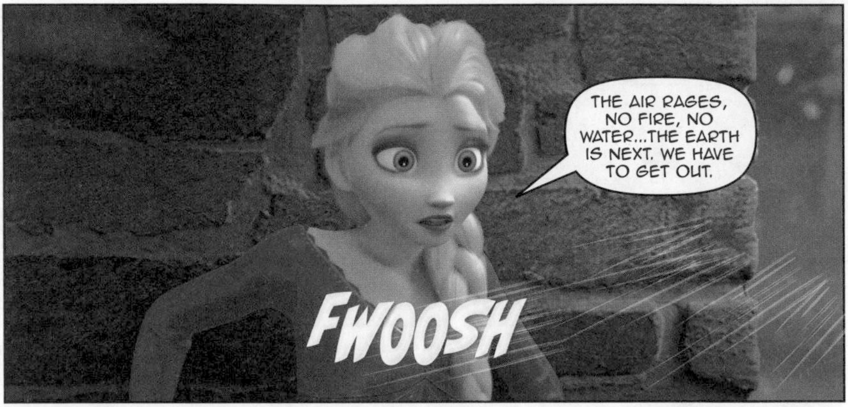
THE AIR RAGES, NO FIRE, NO WATER...THE EARTH IS NEXT. WE HAVE TO GET OUT.
FWOOSH

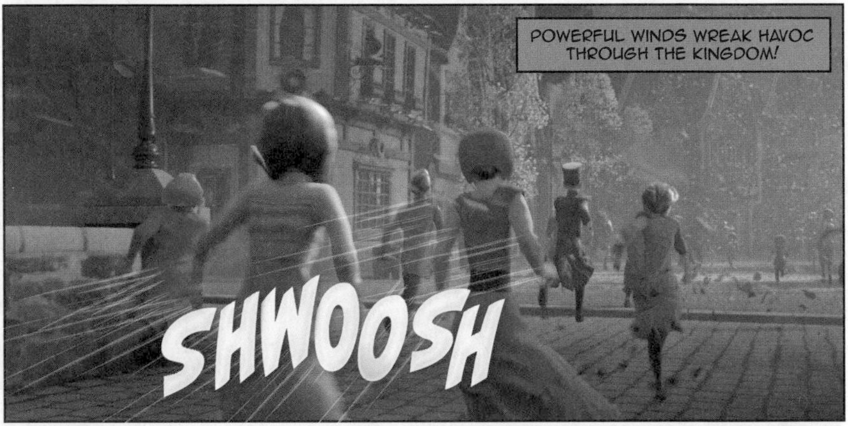
POWERFUL WINDS WREAK HAVOC THROUGH THE KINGDOM!
SHWOOSH

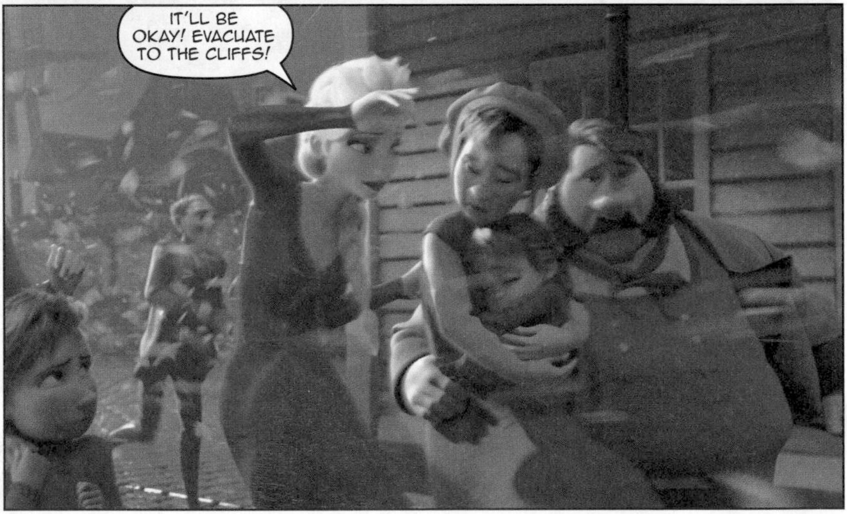
IT'LL BE OKAY! EVACUATE TO THE CLIFFS!

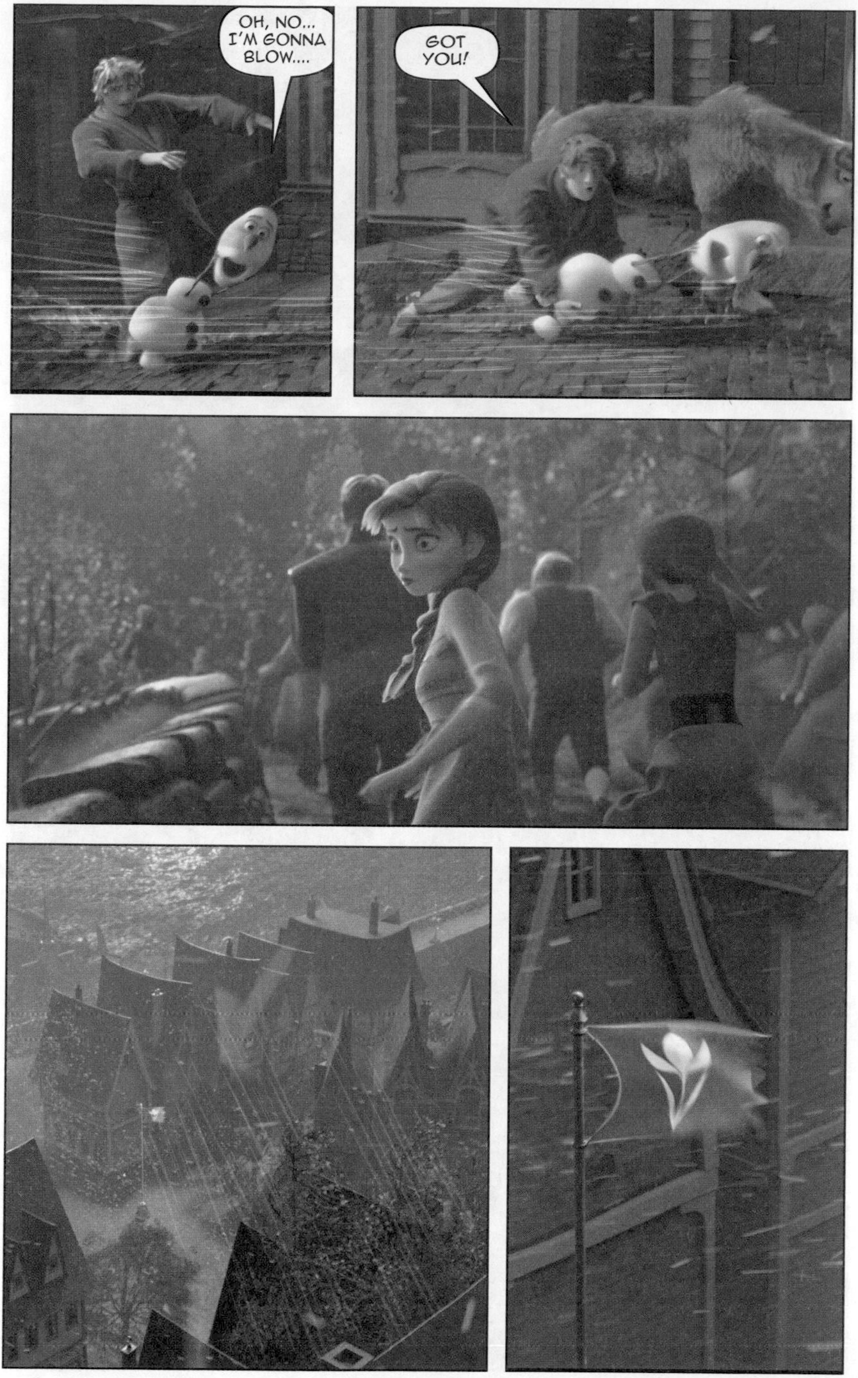
OH, NO... I'M GONNA BLOW....
GOT YOU!

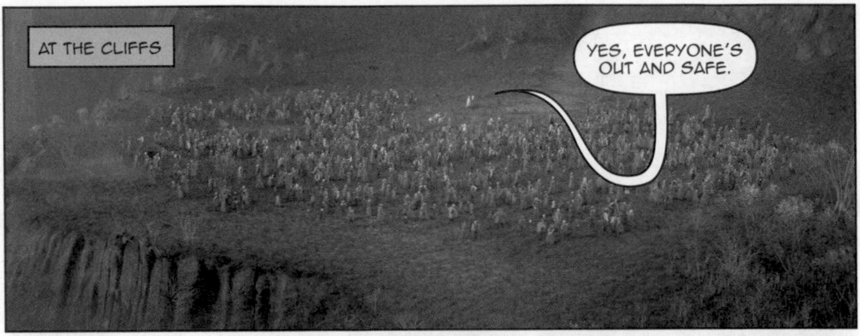
AT THE CLIFFS
YES, EVERYONE'S OUT AND SAFE.

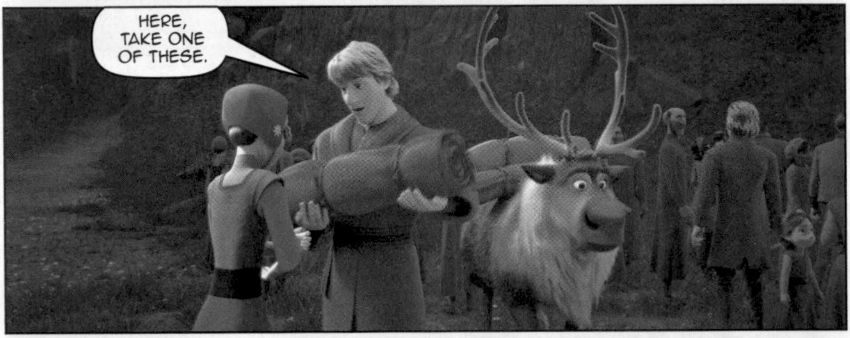
HERE, TAKE ONE OF THESE.

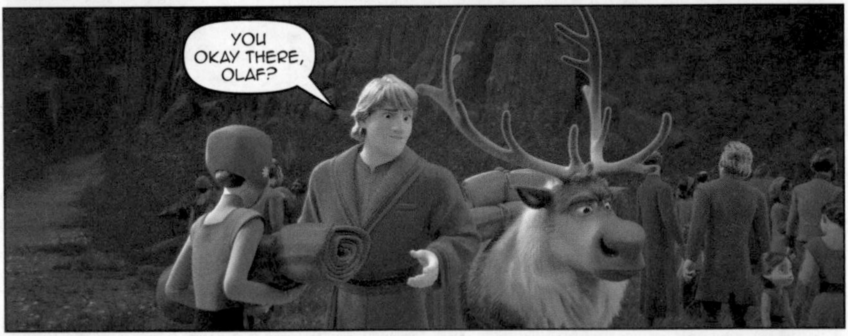
YOU OKAY THERE, OLAF?

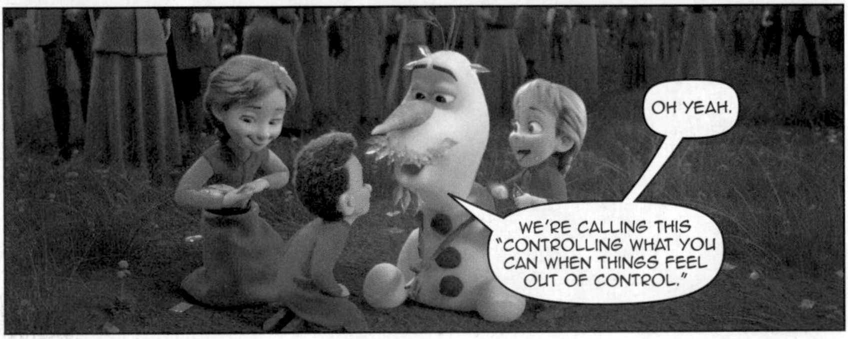
OH YEAH.
WE'RE CALLING THIS "CONTROLLING WHAT YOU CAN WHEN THINGS FEEL OUT OF CONTROL."

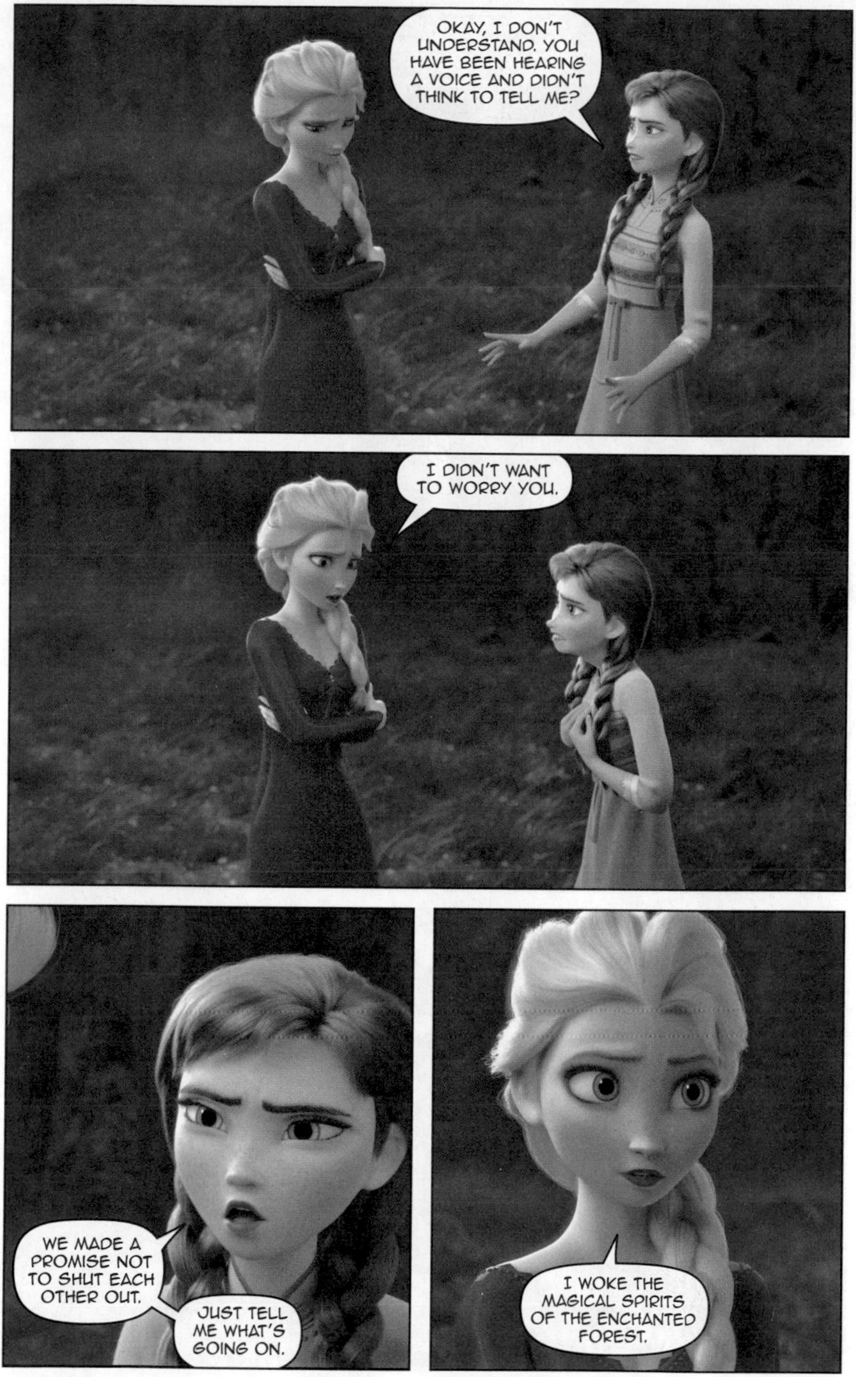
OKAY, I DON'T UNDERSTAND. YOU HAVE BEEN HEARING A VOICE AND DIDN'T THINK TO TELL ME?
I DIDN'T WANT TO WORRY YOU.
WE MADE A PROMISE NOT TO SHUT EACH OTHER OUT.
JUST TELL ME WHAT'S GOING ON.
I WOKE THE MAGICAL SPIRITS OF THE ENCHANTED FOREST.

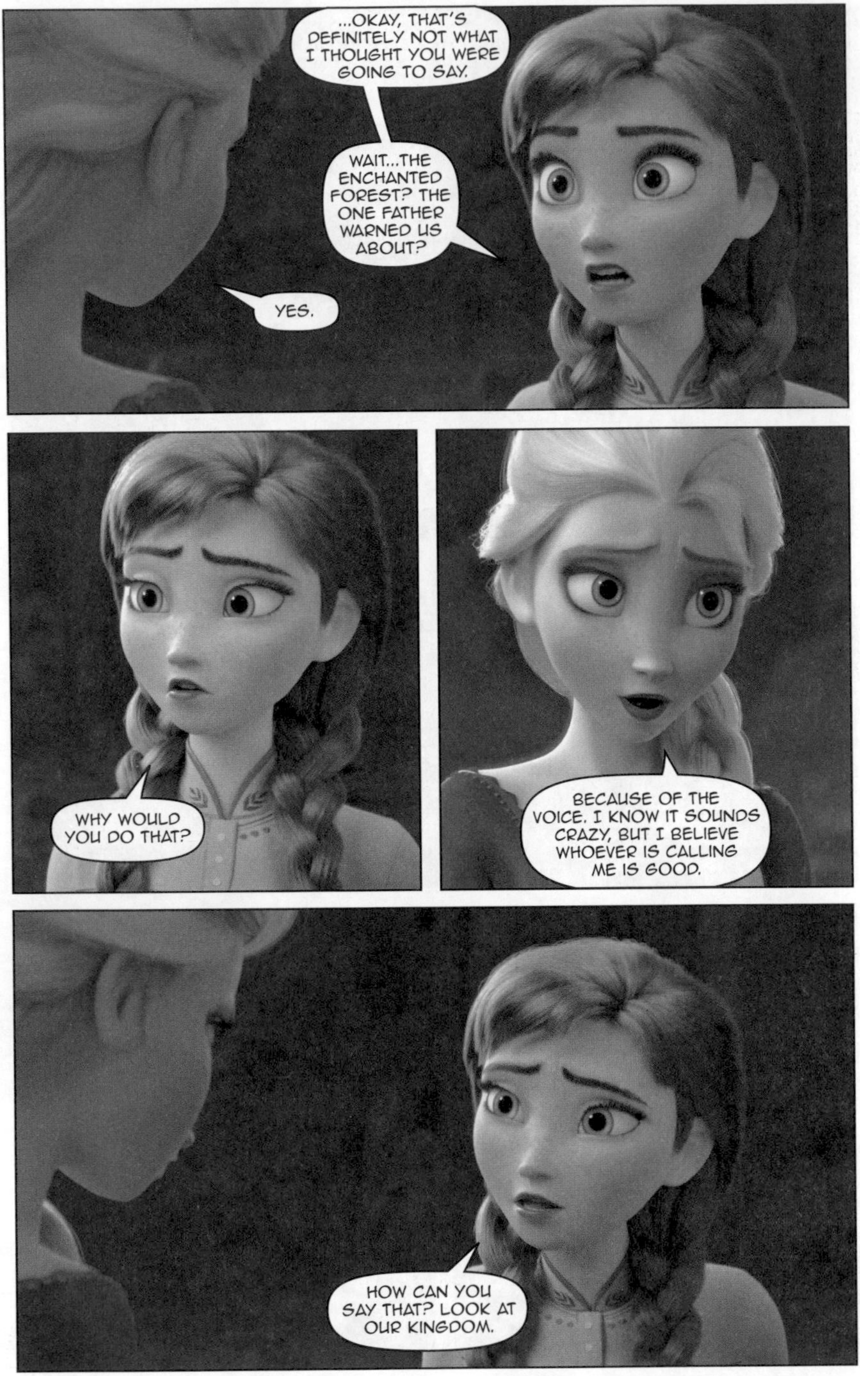
...OKAY, THAT'S DEFINITELY NOT WHAT I THOUGHT YOU WERE GOING TO SAY.
WAIT...THE ENCHANTED FOREST? THE ONE FATHER WARNED US ABOUT?
YES.
WHY WOULD YOU DO THAT?
BECAUSE OF THE VOICE. I KNOW IT SOUNDS CRAZY, BUT I BELIEVE WHOEVER IS CALLING ME IS GOOD.
HOW CAN YOU SAY THAT? LOOK AT OUR KINGDOM.

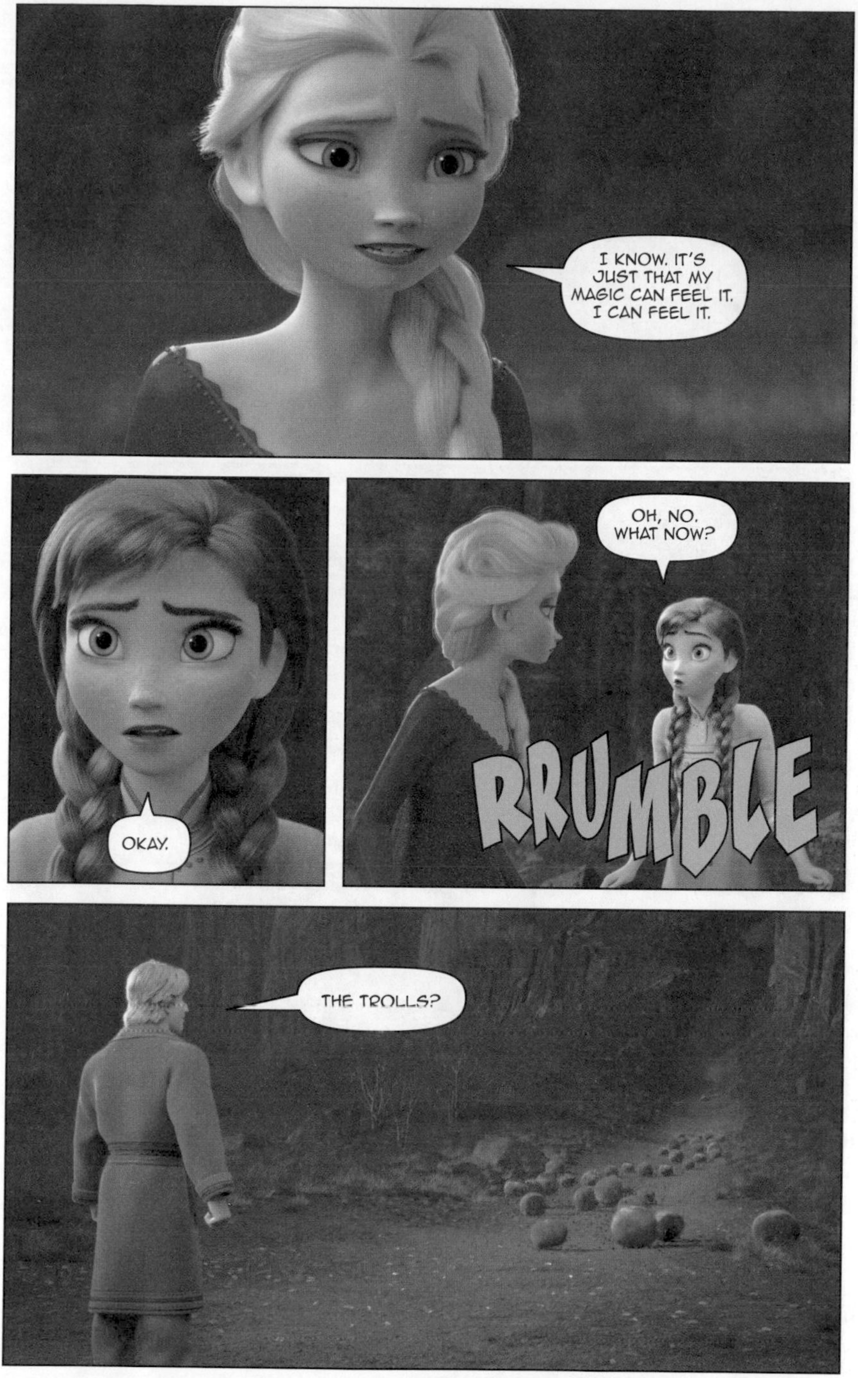
I KNOW. IT'S JUST THAT MY MAGIC CAN FEEL IT. I CAN FEEL IT.
OKAY.
OH, NO. WHAT NOW?
RRUMBLE
THE TROLLS?

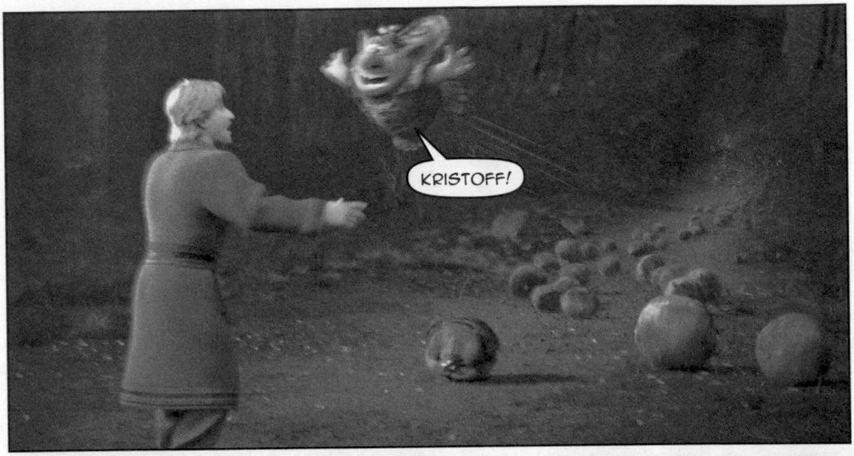
KRISTOFF!

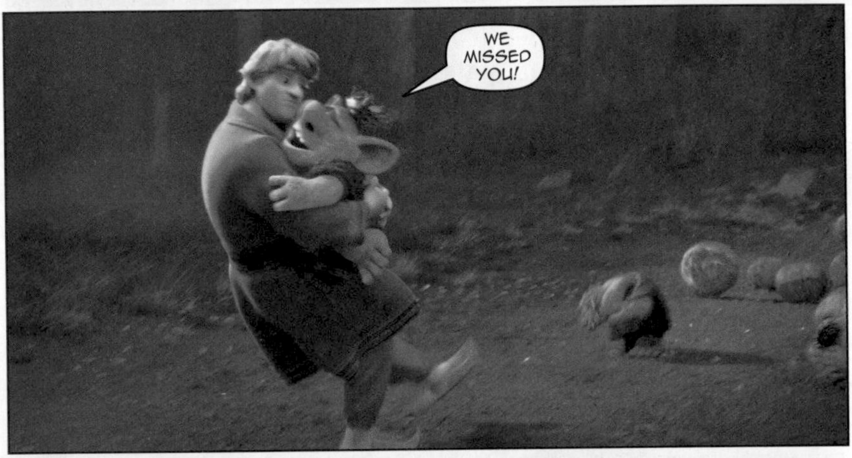
WE MISSED YOU!

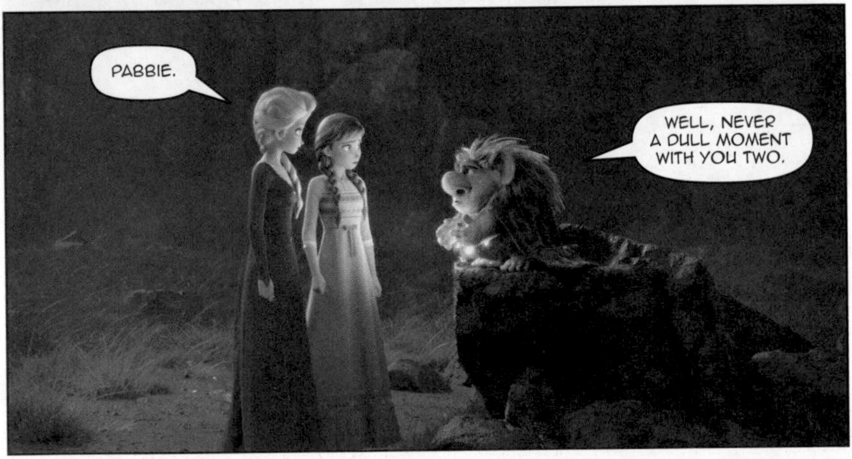
PABBIE.
WELL, NEVER A DULL MOMENT WITH YOU TWO.

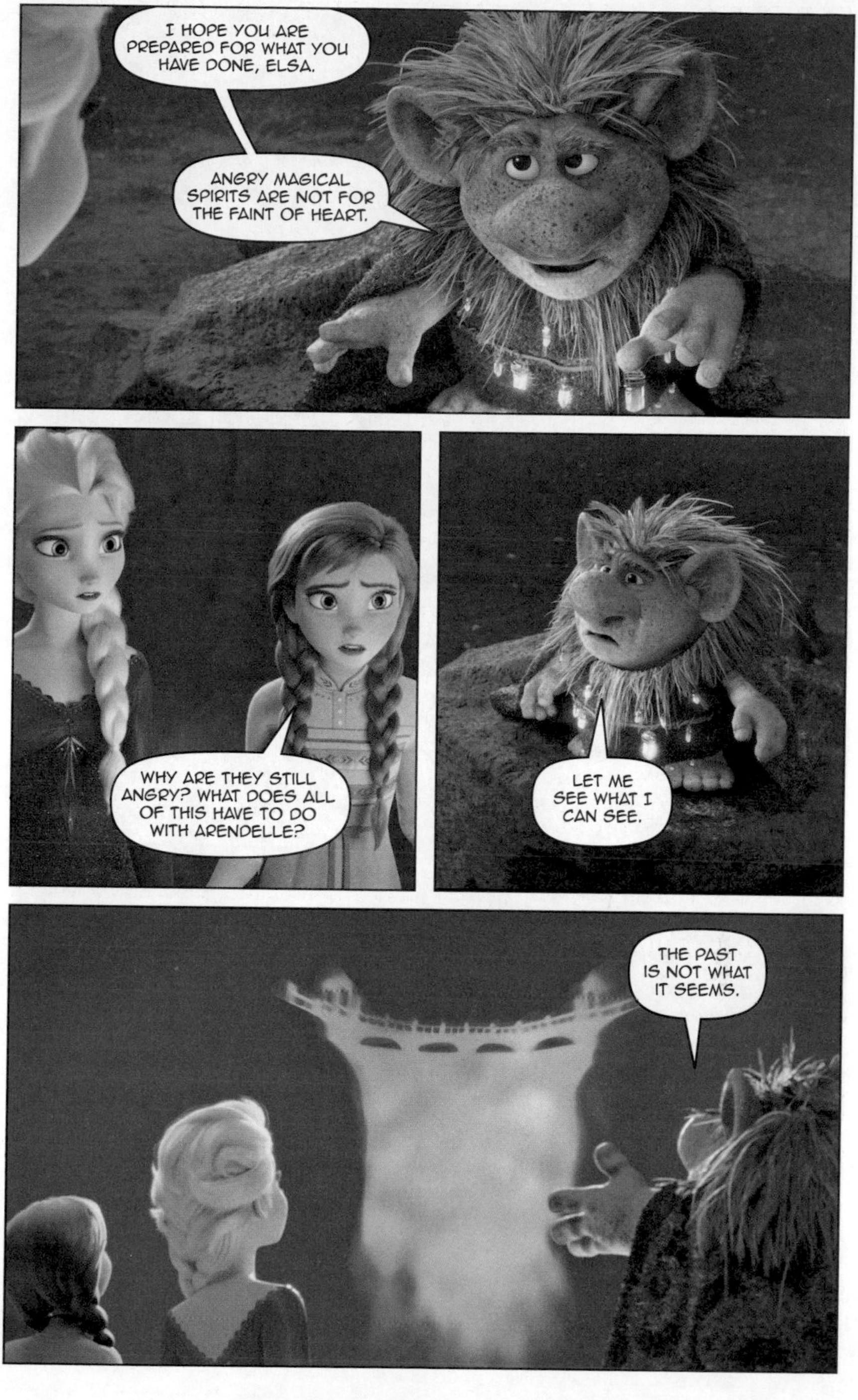
I HOPE YOU ARE PREPARED FOR WHAT YOU HAVE DONE, ELSA.
ANGRY MAGICAL SPIRITS ARE NOT FOR THE FAINT OF HEART.
WHY ARE THEY STILL ANGRY? WHAT DOES ALL OF THIS HAVE TO DO WITH ARENDELLE?
LET ME SEE WHAT I CAN SEE.
THE PAST IS NOT WHAT IT SEEMS.

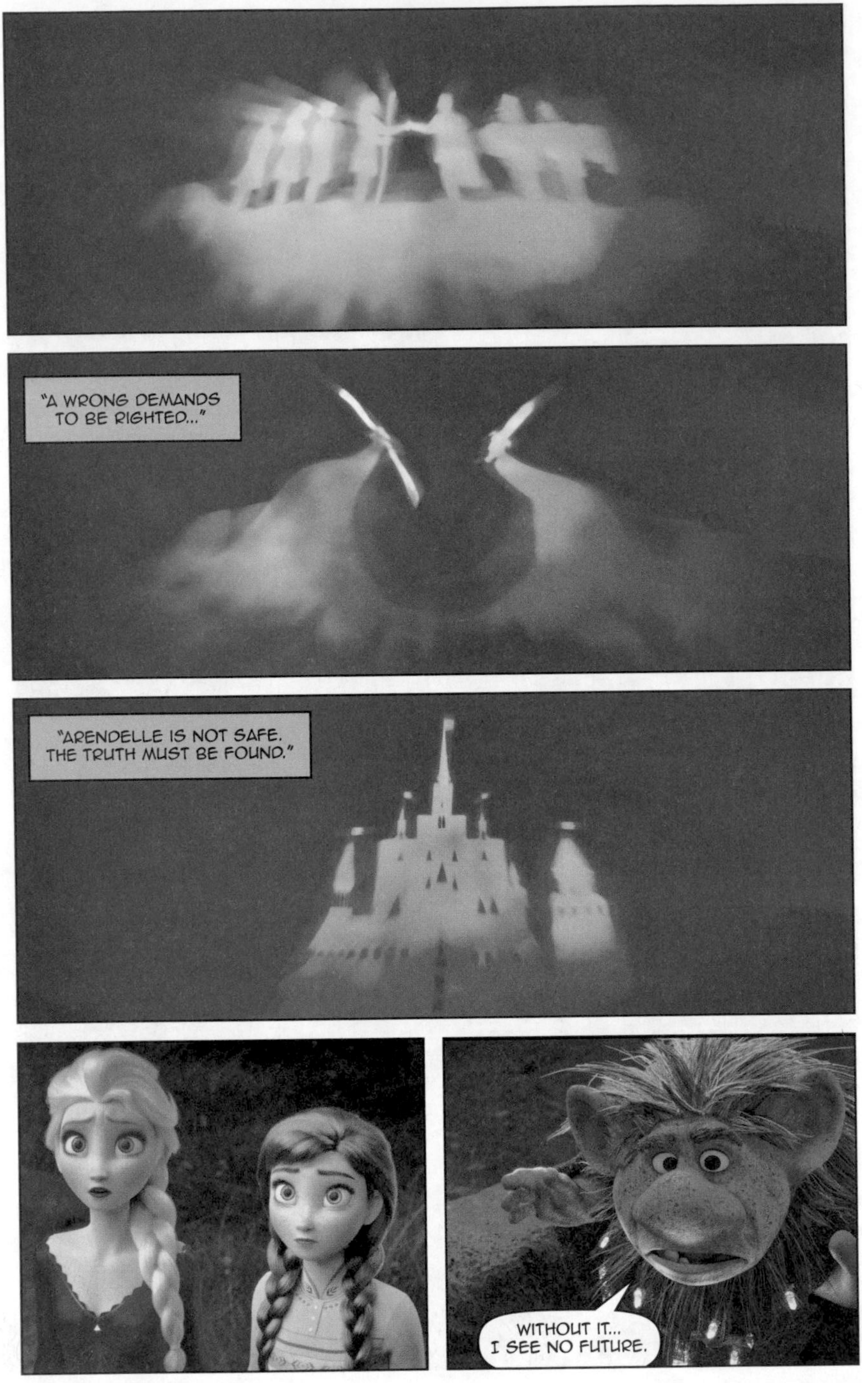
"A WRONG DEMANDS TO BE RIGHTED..."
"ARENDELLE IS NOT SAFE. THE TRUTH MUST BE FOUND."
WITHOUT IT... I SEE NO FUTURE.

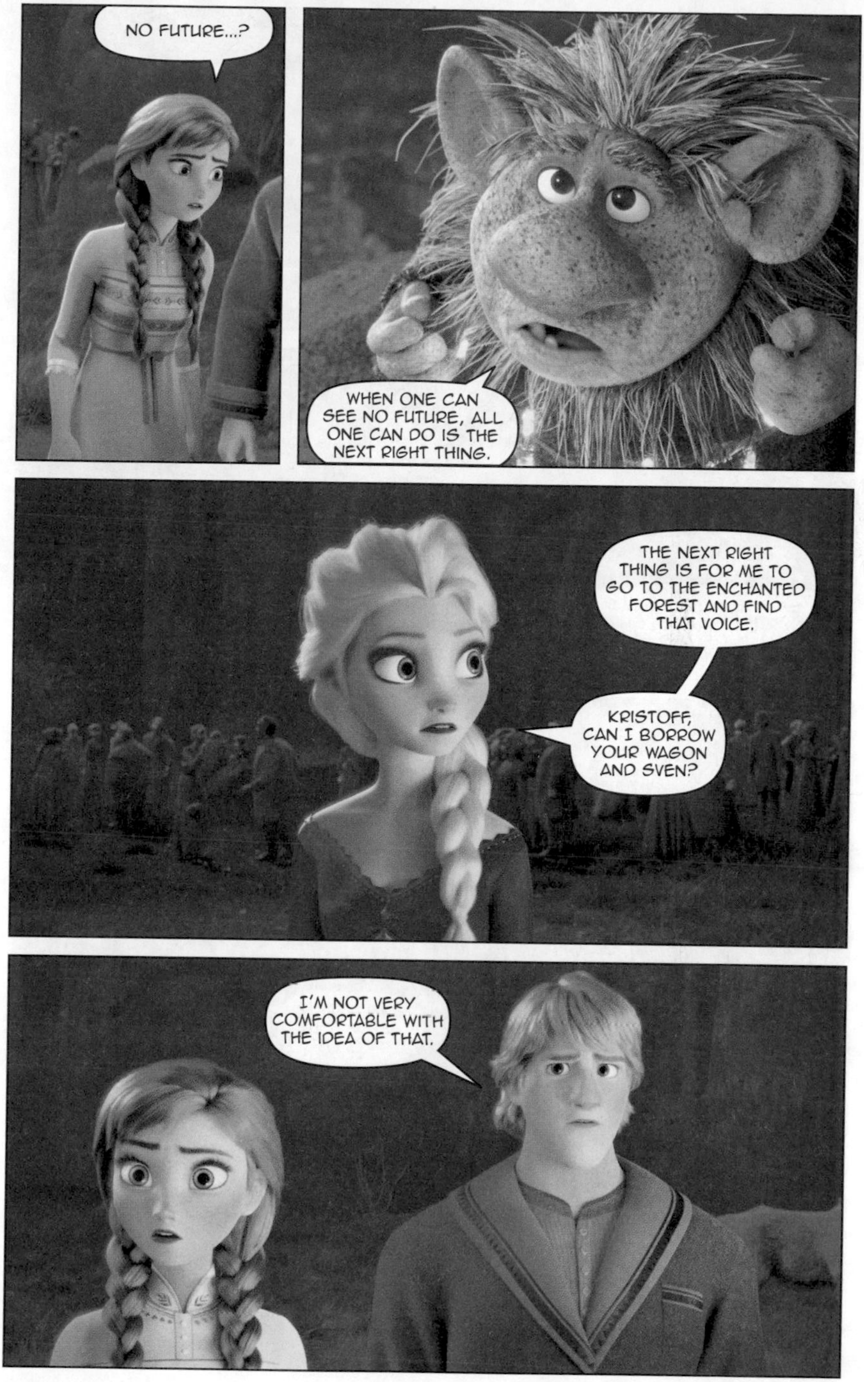
NO FUTURE...?
WHEN ONE CAN SEE NO FUTURE, ALL ONE CAN DO IS THE NEXT RIGHT THING.
THE NEXT RIGHT THING IS FOR ME TO GO TO THE ENCHANTED FOREST AND FIND THAT VOICE.
KRISTOFF, CAN I BORROW YOUR WAGON AND SVEN?
I'M NOT VERY COMFORTABLE WITH THE IDEA OF THAT.

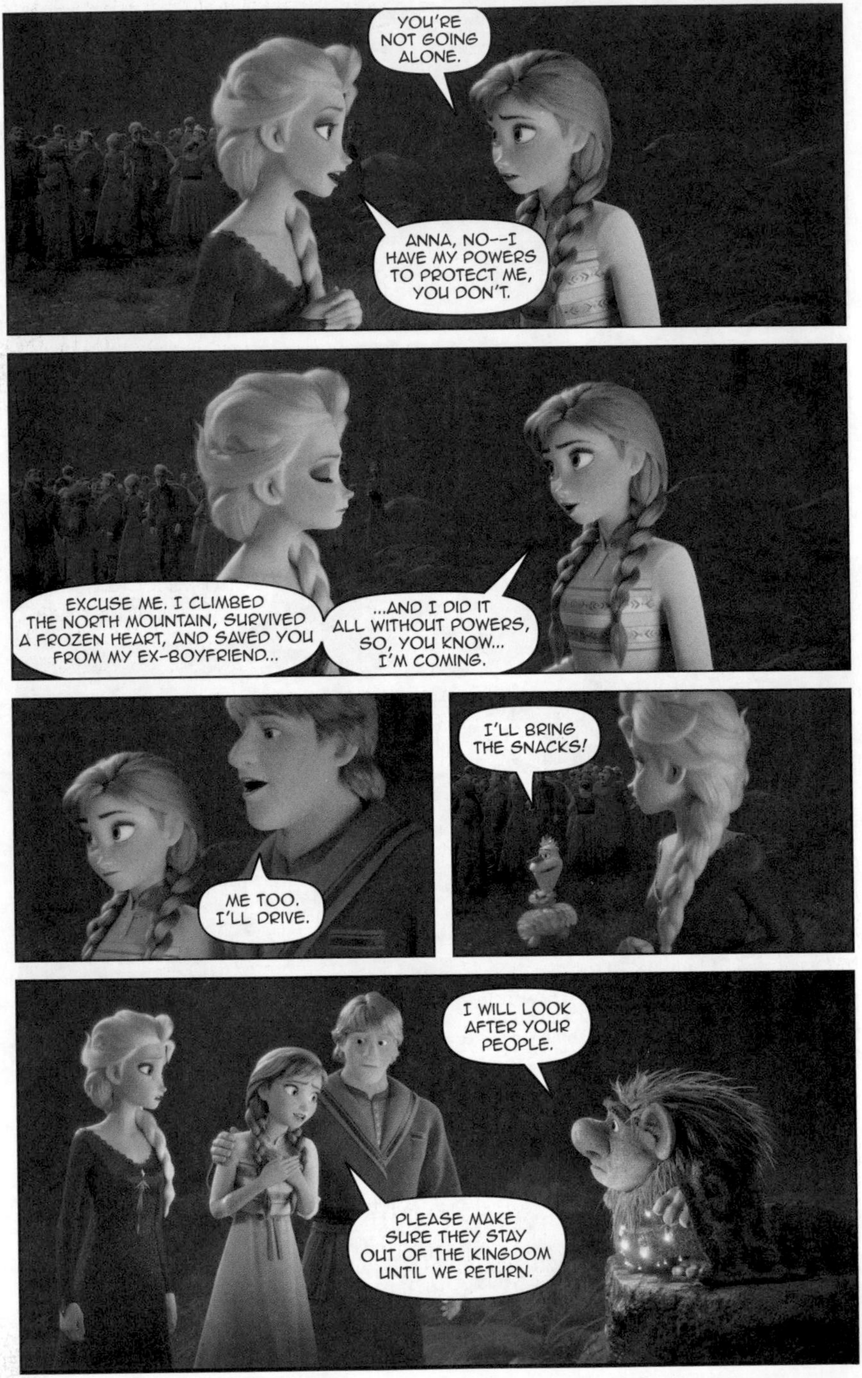
YOU'RE NOT GOING ALONE.
ANNA, NO--I HAVE MY POWERS TO PROTECT ME, YOU DON'T.
EXCUSE ME. I CLIMBED THE NORTH MOUNTAIN, SURVIVED A FROZEN HEART, AND SAVED YOU FROM MY EX-BOYFRIEND...
...AND I DID IT ALL WITHOUT POWERS, SO, YOU KNOW... I'M COMING.
ME TOO. I'LL DRIVE.
I'LL BRING THE SNACKS!
I WILL LOOK AFTER YOUR PEOPLE.
PLEASE MAKE SURE THEY STAY OUT OF THE KINGDOM UNTIL WE RETURN.

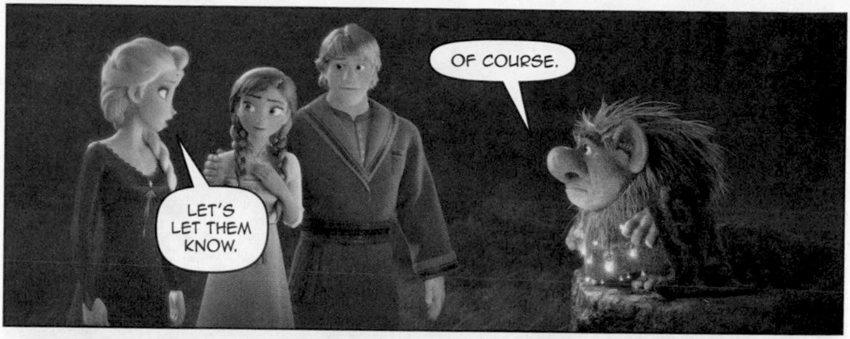
OF COURSE.
LET'S LET THEM KNOW.

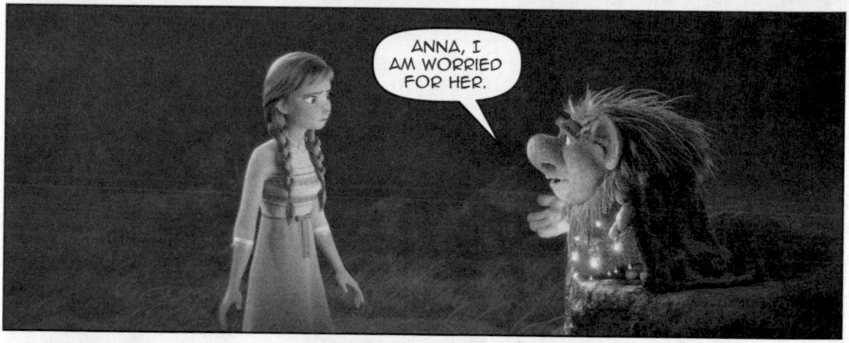
ANNA, I AM WORRIED FOR HER.

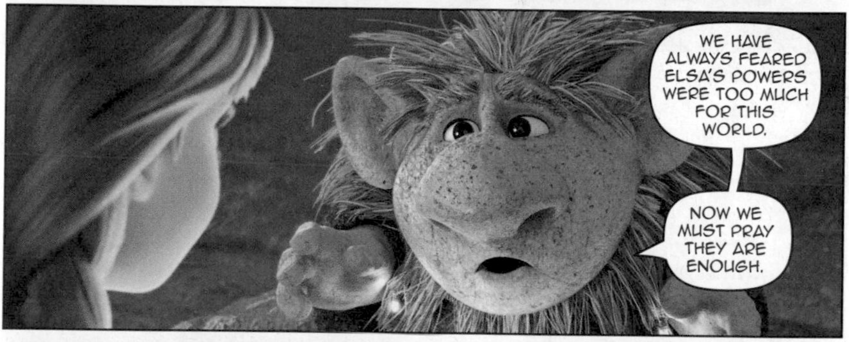
WE HAVE ALWAYS FEARED ELSA'S POWERS WERE TOO MUCH FOR THIS WORLD.
NOW WE MUST PRAY THEY ARE ENOUGH.

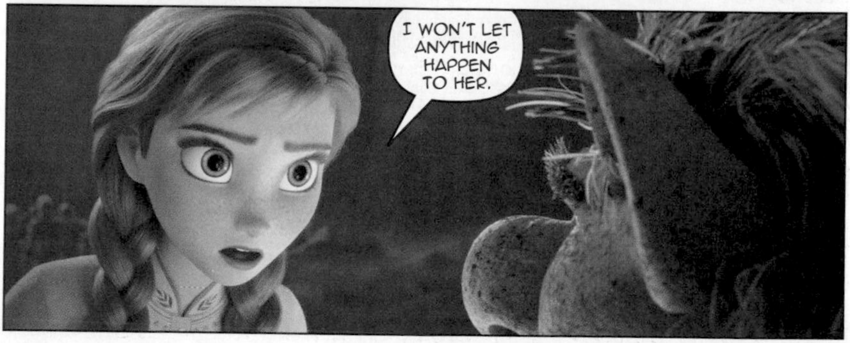
I WON'T LET ANYTHING HAPPEN TO HER.

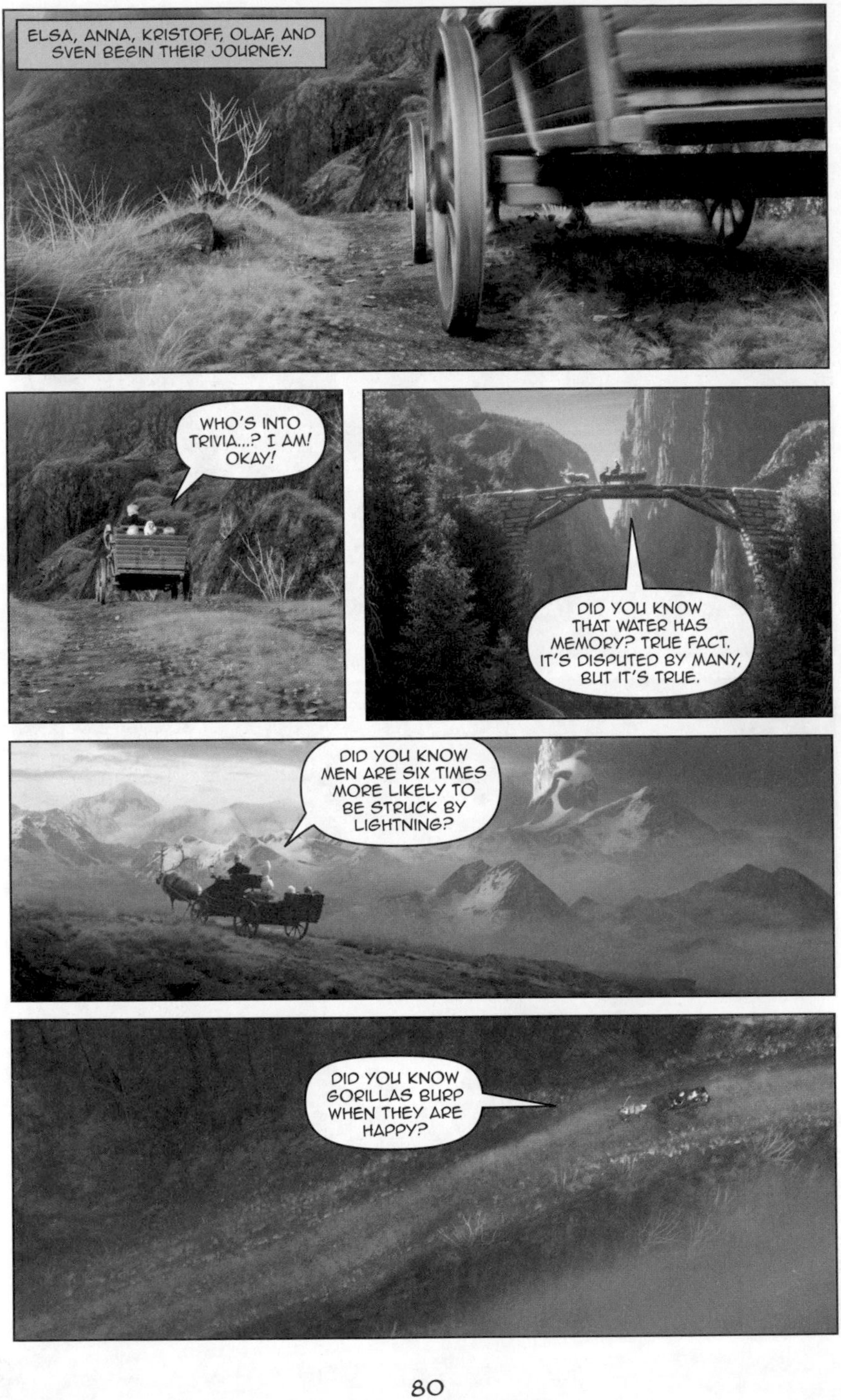
ELSA, ANNA, KRISTOFF, OLAF, AND SVEN BEGIN THEIR JOURNEY.
WHO'S INTO TRIVIA...? I AM! OKAY!
DID YOU KNOW THAT WATER HAS MEMORY? TRUE FACT. IT'S DISPUTED BY MANY, BUT IT'S TRUE.
DID YOU KNOW MEN ARE SIX TIMES MORE LIKELY TO BE STRUCK BY LIGHTNING?
DID YOU KNOW GORILLAS BURP WHEN THEY ARE HAPPY?

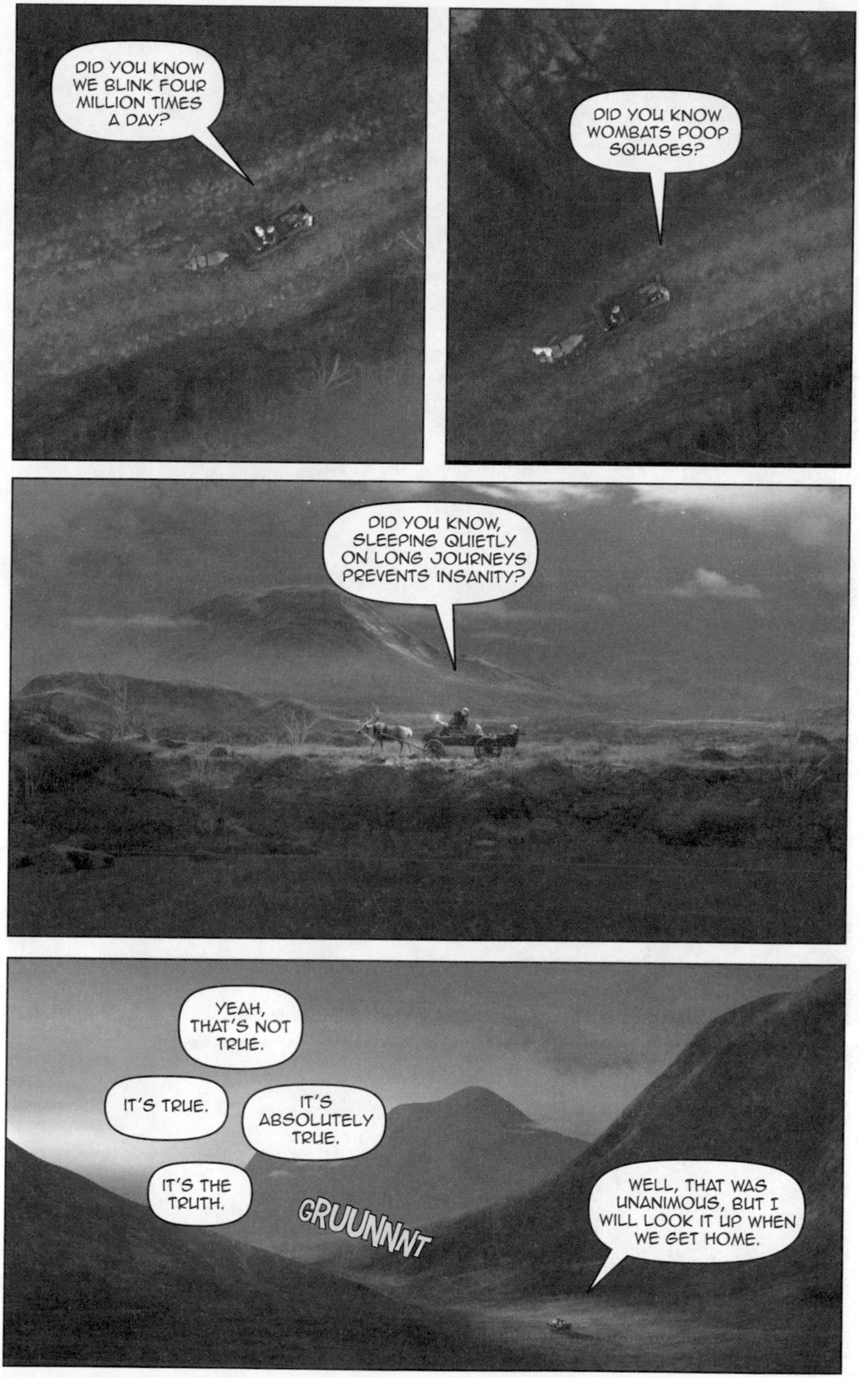
DID YOU KNOW WE BLINK FOUR MILLION TIMES A DAY?
DID YOU KNOW WOMBATS POOP SQUARES?
DID YOU KNOW, SLEEPING QUIETLY ON LONG JOURNEYS PREVENTS INSANITY?
YEAH, THAT'S NOT TRUE.
IT'S TRUE.
IT'S ABSOLUTELY TRUE.
IT'S THE TRUTH.
GRUUNNNT
WELL, THAT WAS UNANIMOUS, BUT I WILL LOOK IT UP WHEN WE GET HOME.

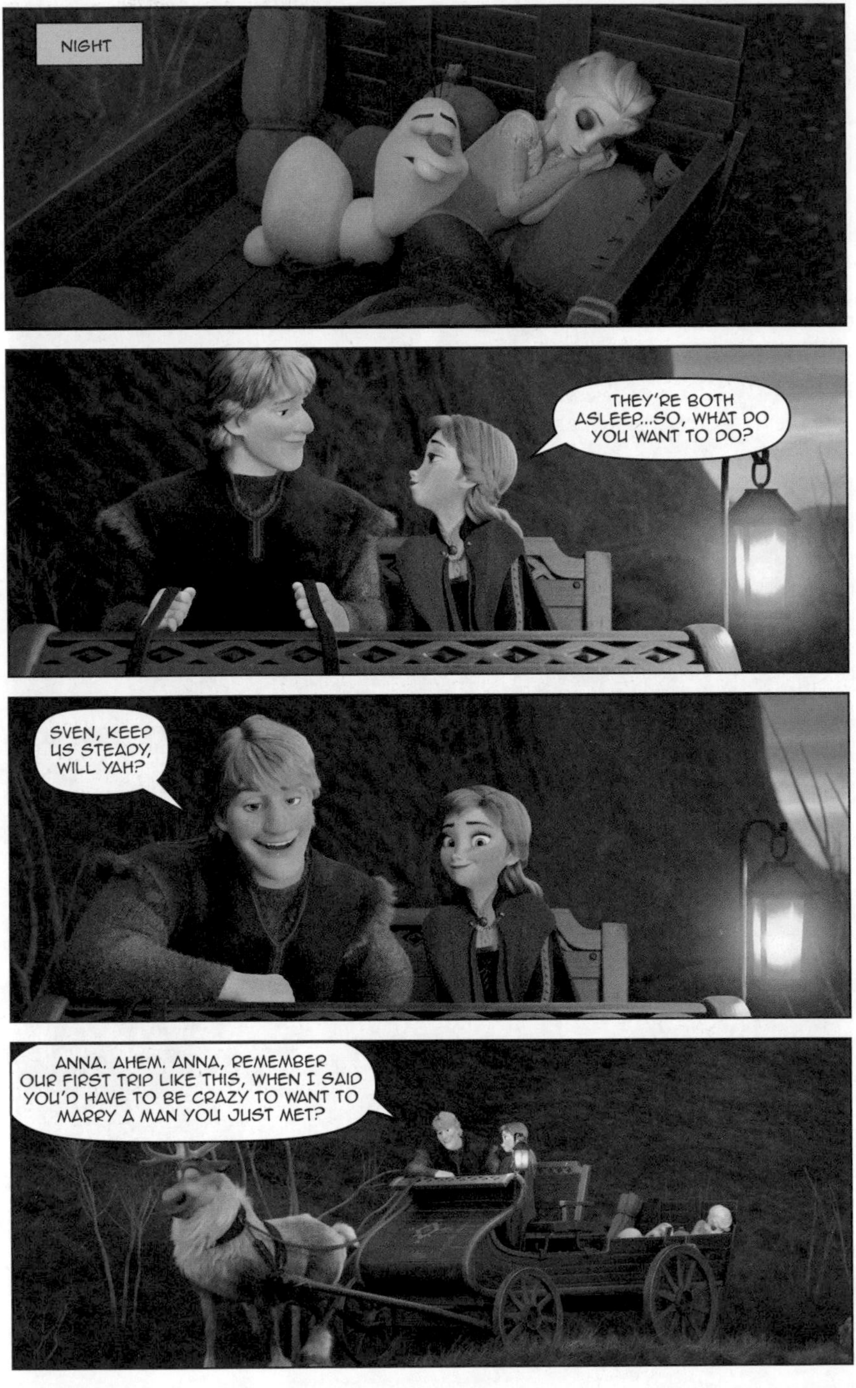
NIGHT
THEY'RE BOTH ASLEEP...SO, WHAT DO YOU WANT TO DO?
SVEN, KEEP US STEADY, WILL YAH?
ANNA. AHEM. ANNA, REMEMBER OUR FIRST TRIP LIKE THIS, WHEN I SAID YOU'D HAVE TO BE CRAZY TO WANT TO MARRY A MAN YOU JUST MET?

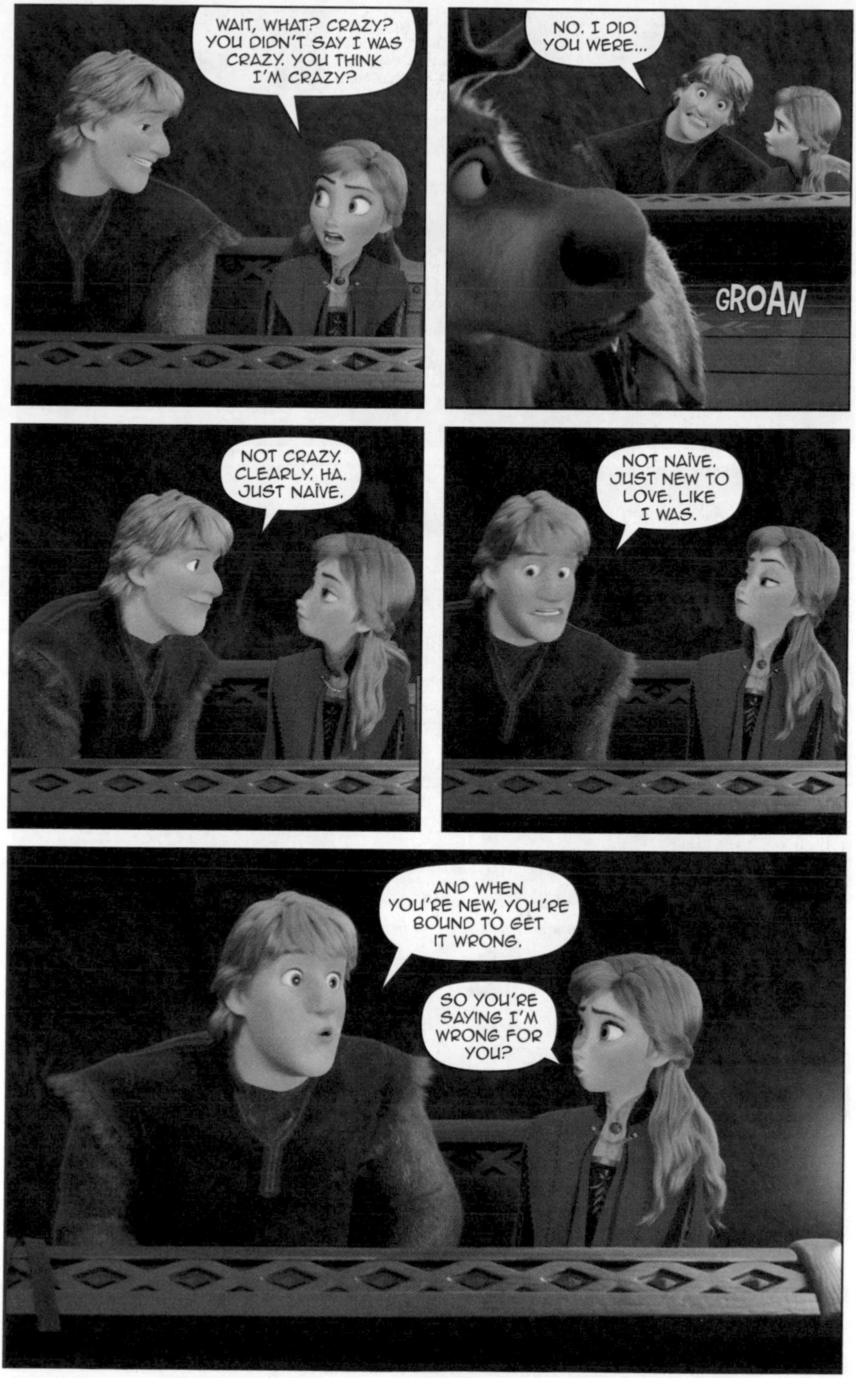
WAIT, WHAT? CRAZY? YOU DIDN'T SAY I WAS CRAZY. YOU THINK I'M CRAZY?
NO. I DID. YOU WERE...
GROAN
NOT CRAZY. CLEARLY. HA. JUST NAÏVE.
NOT NAÏVE. JUST NEW TO LOVE. LIKE I WAS.
AND WHEN YOU'RE NEW, YOU'RE BOUND TO GET IT WRONG.
SO YOU'RE SAYING I'M WRONG FOR YOU?

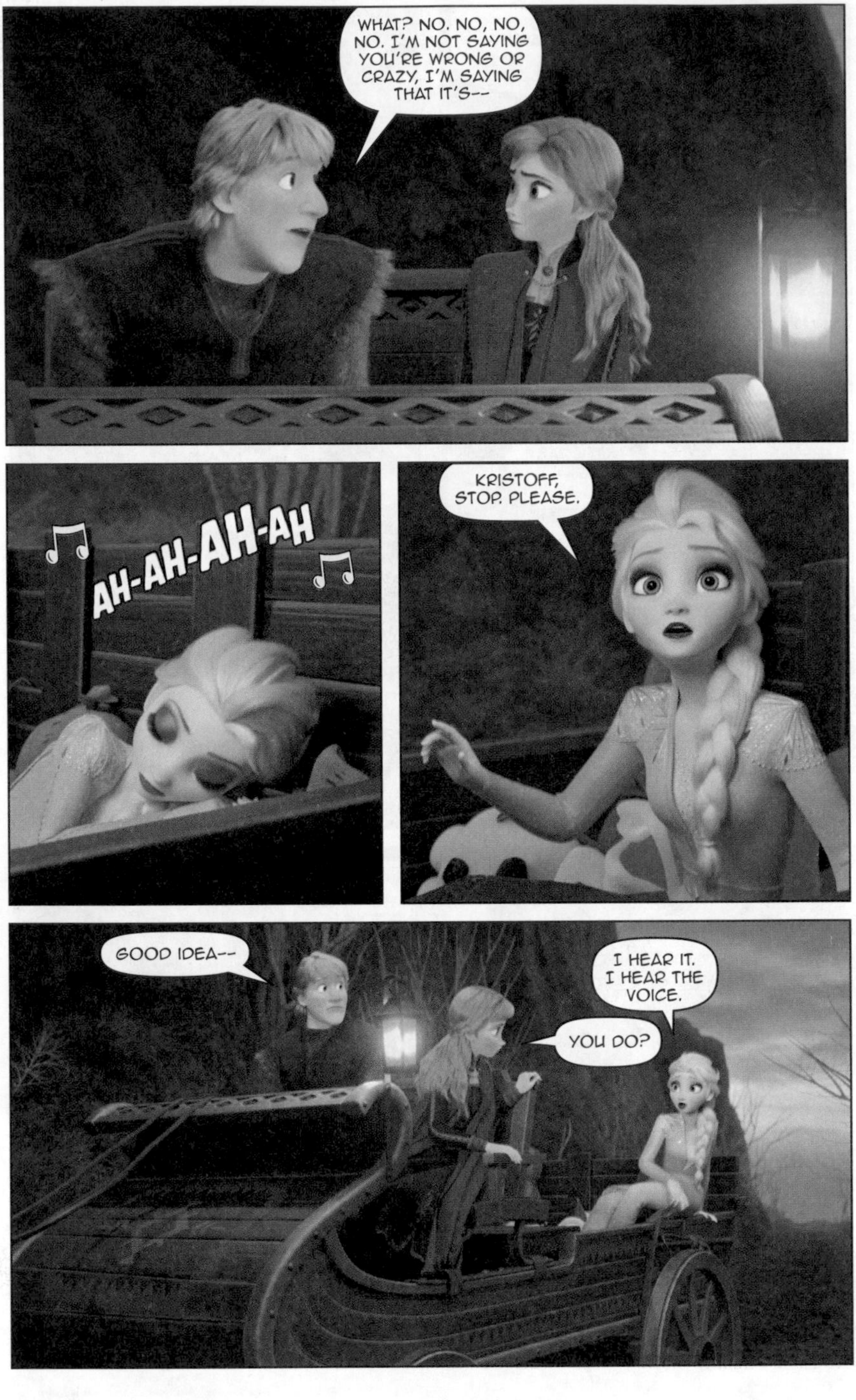
WHAT? NO. NO, NO, NO. I'M NOT SAYING YOU'RE WRONG OR CRAZY, I'M SAYING THAT IT'S--
AH-AH-AH-AH
KRISTOFF, STOP. PLEASE.
GOOD IDEA--
I HEAR IT. I HEAR THE VOICE.
YOU DO?

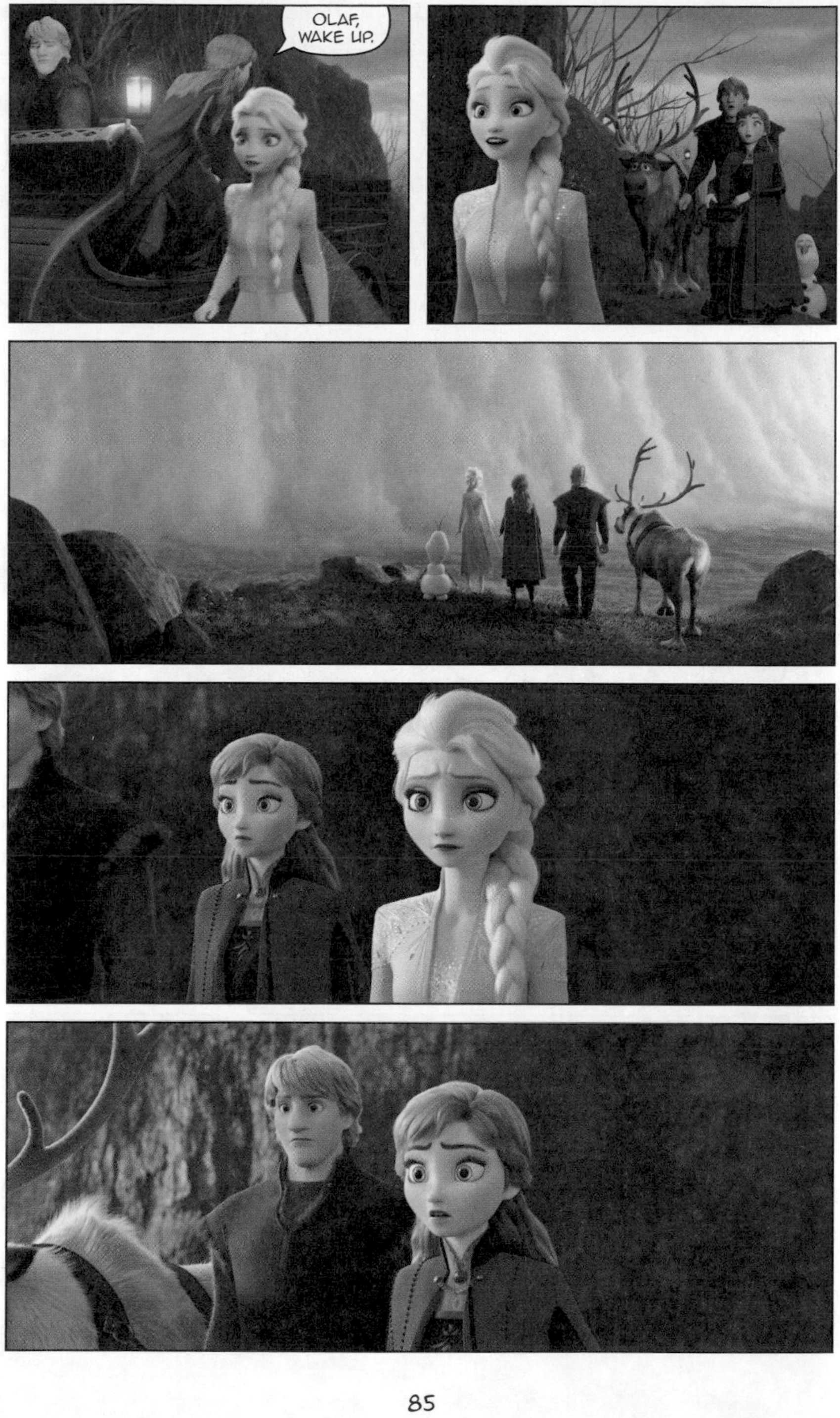
OLAF, WAKE UP.

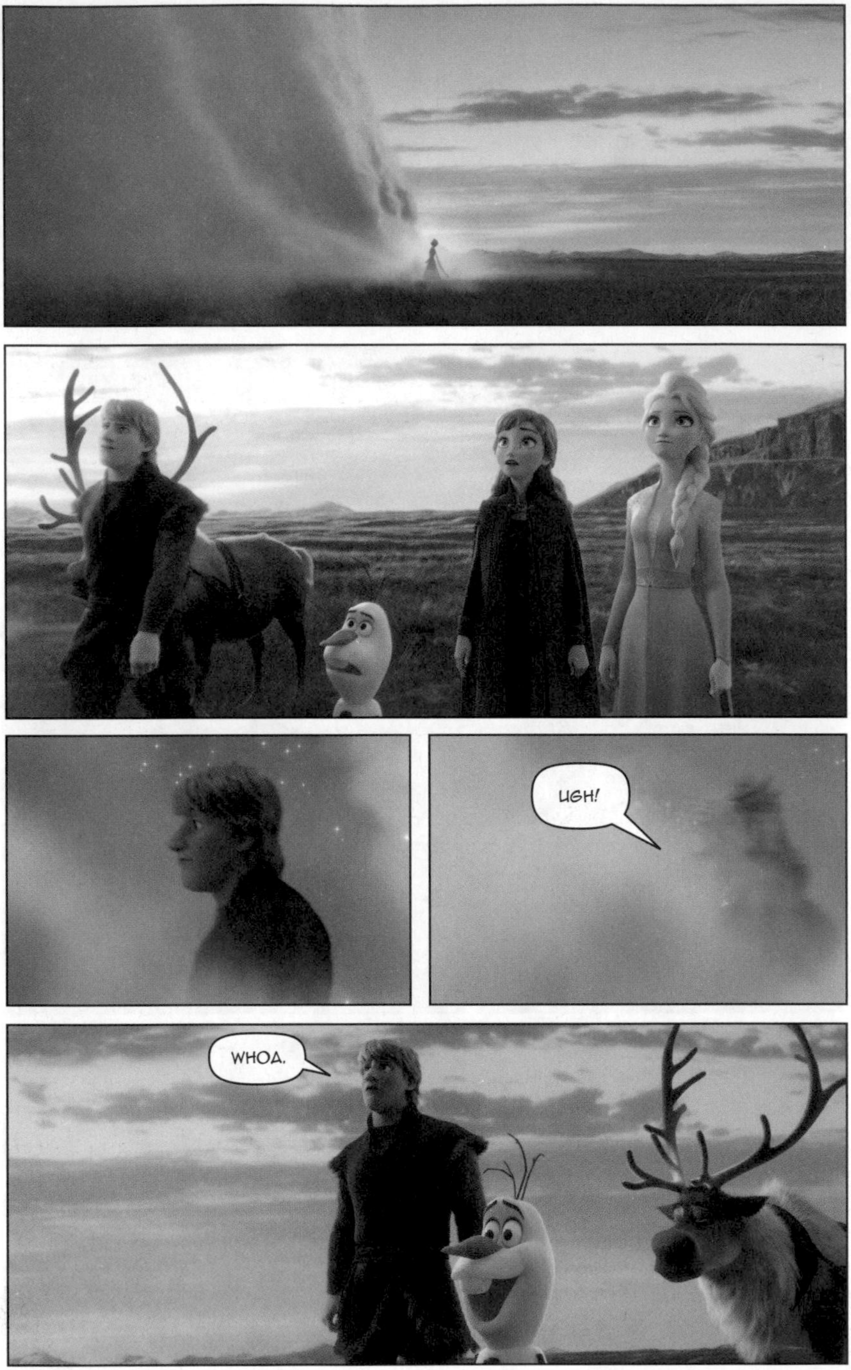
UGH!
WHOA.

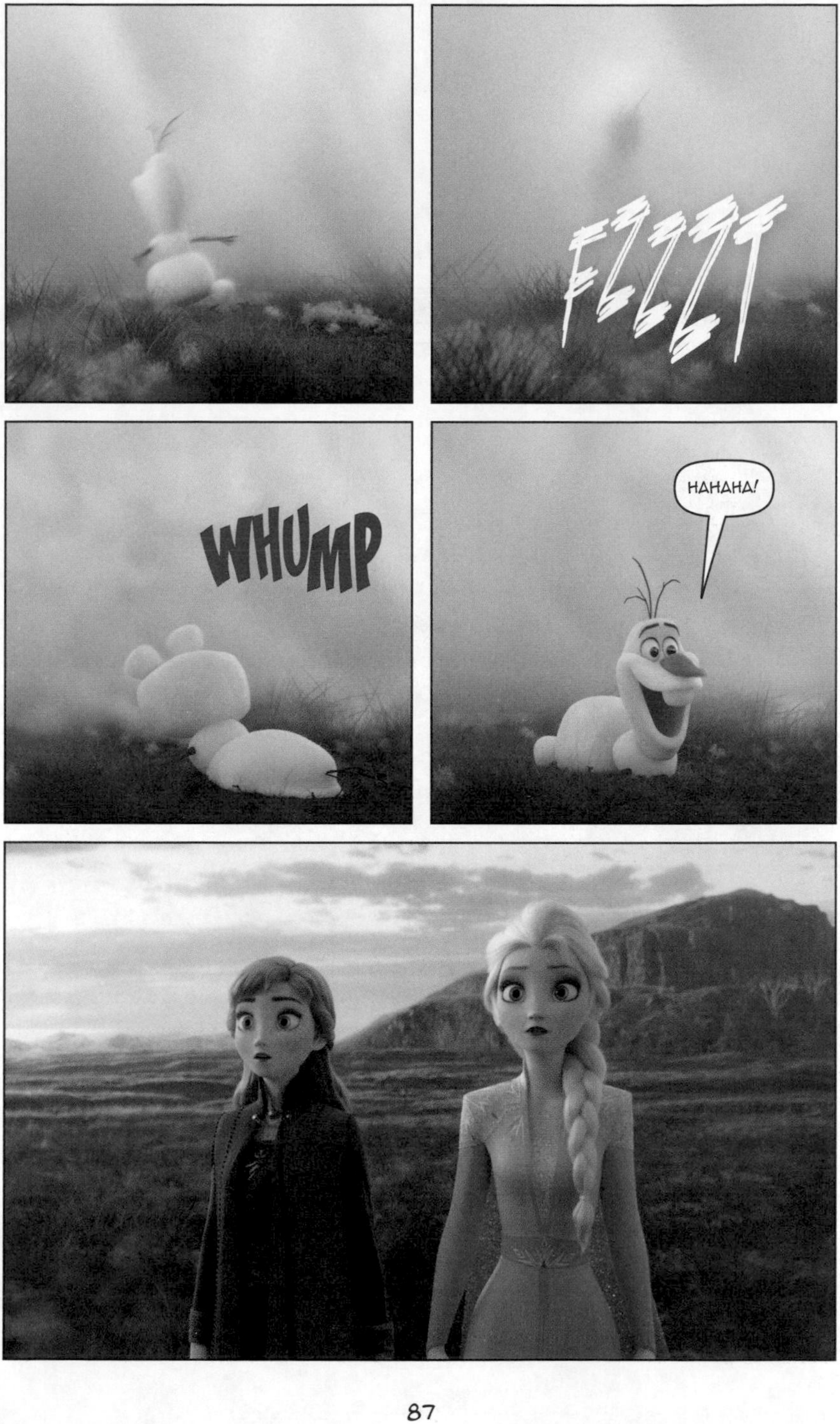
FZZZZT
WHUMP
HAHAHA!

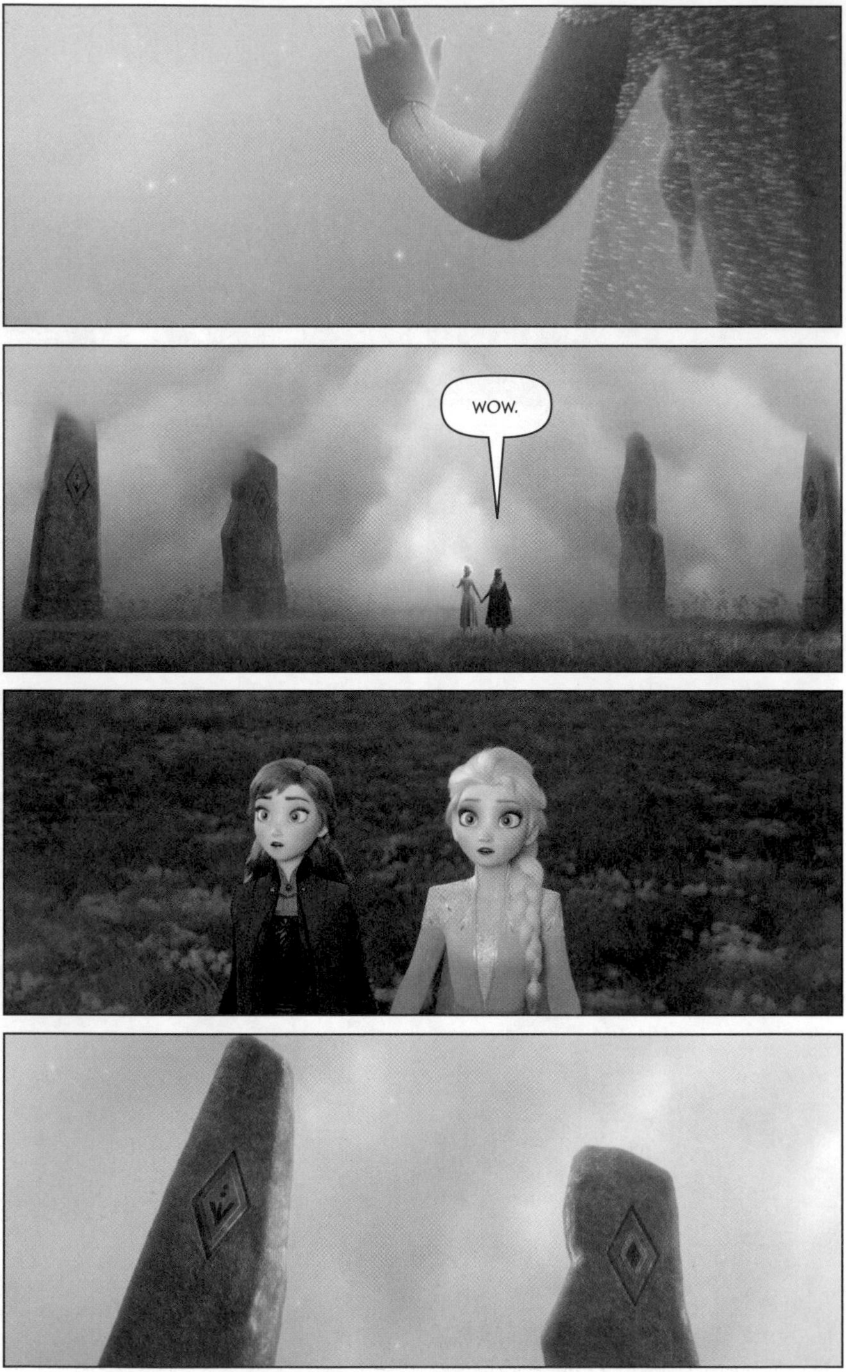
WOW.

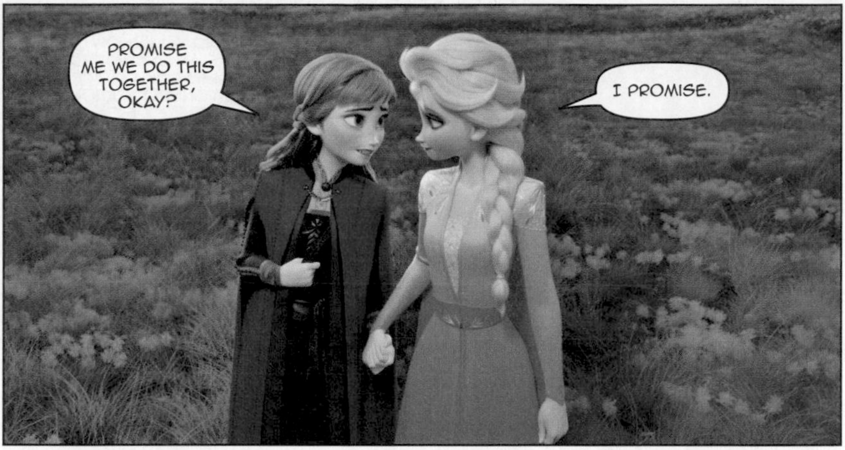
PROMISE ME WE DO THIS TOGETHER, OKAY?
I PROMISE.

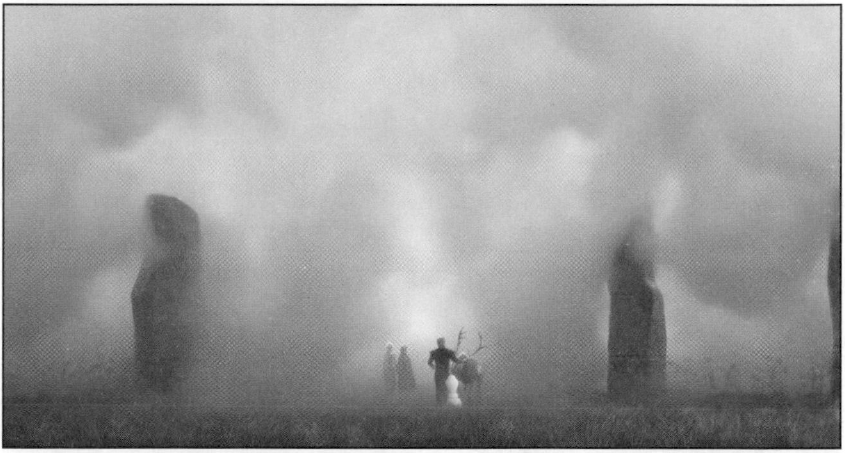

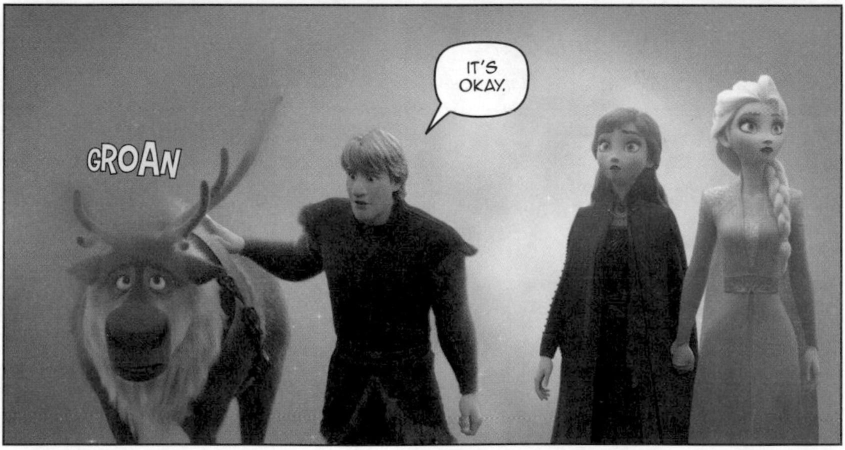
IT'S OKAY.
GROAN

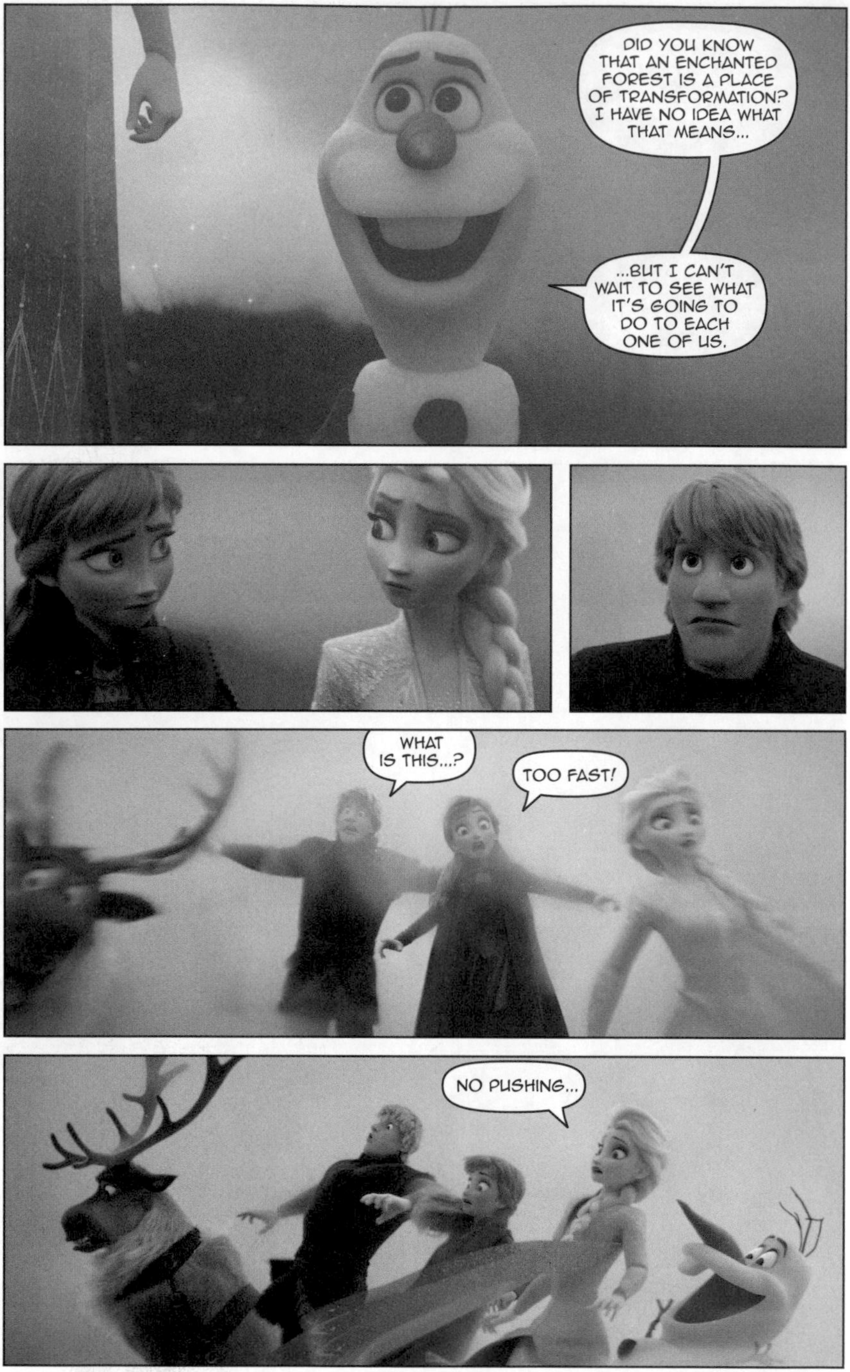
DID YOU KNOW THAT AN ENCHANTED FOREST IS A PLACE OF TRANSFORMATION? I HAVE NO IDEA WHAT THAT MEANS...
...BUT I CAN'T WAIT TO SEE WHAT IT'S GOING TO DO TO EACH ONE OF US.
WHAT IS THIS...?
TOO FAST!
NO PUSHING...

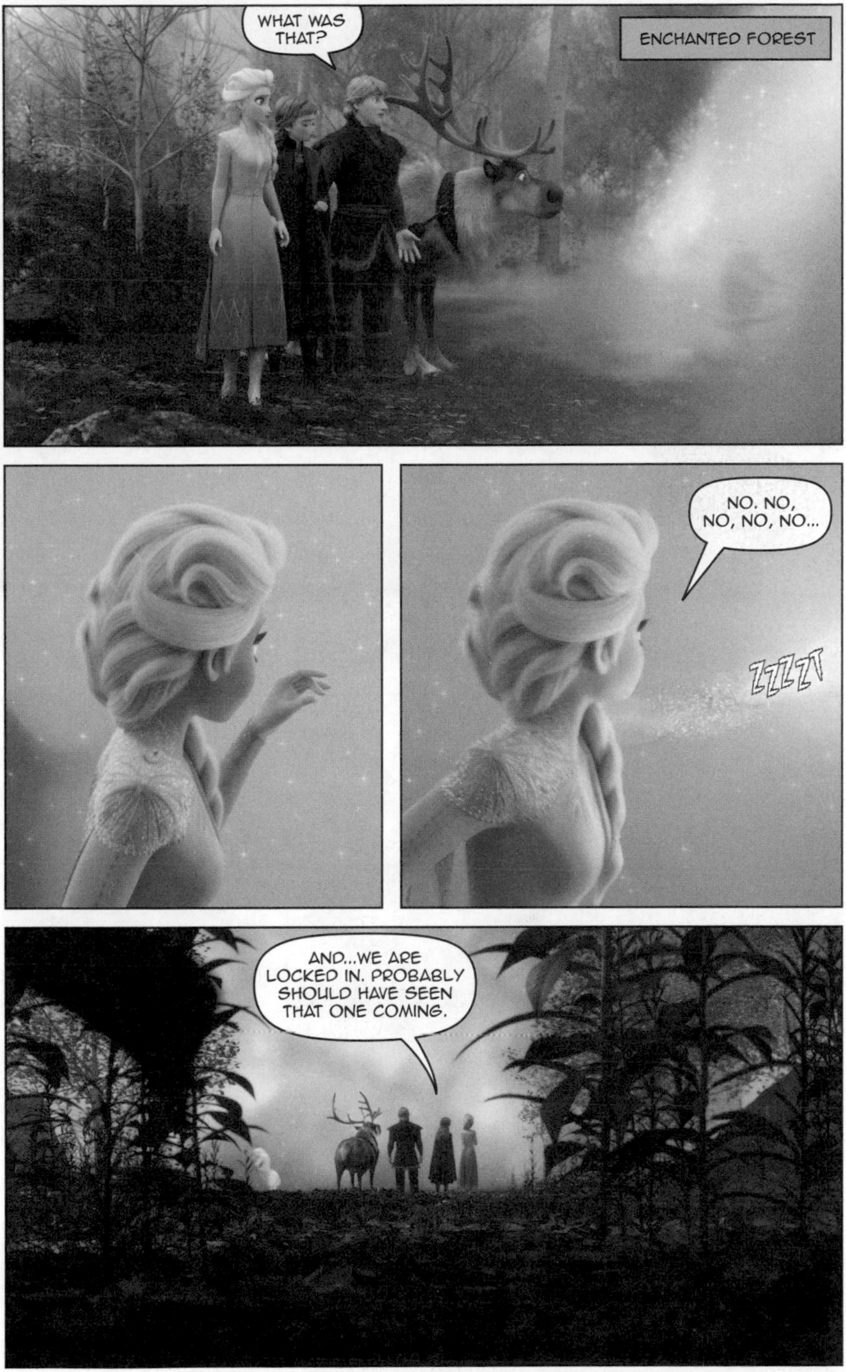
WHAT WAS THAT?
ENCHANTED FOREST
NO. NO, NO, NO, NO...
ZZZZT
AND...WE ARE LOCKED IN. PROBABLY SHOULD HAVE SEEN THAT ONE COMING.

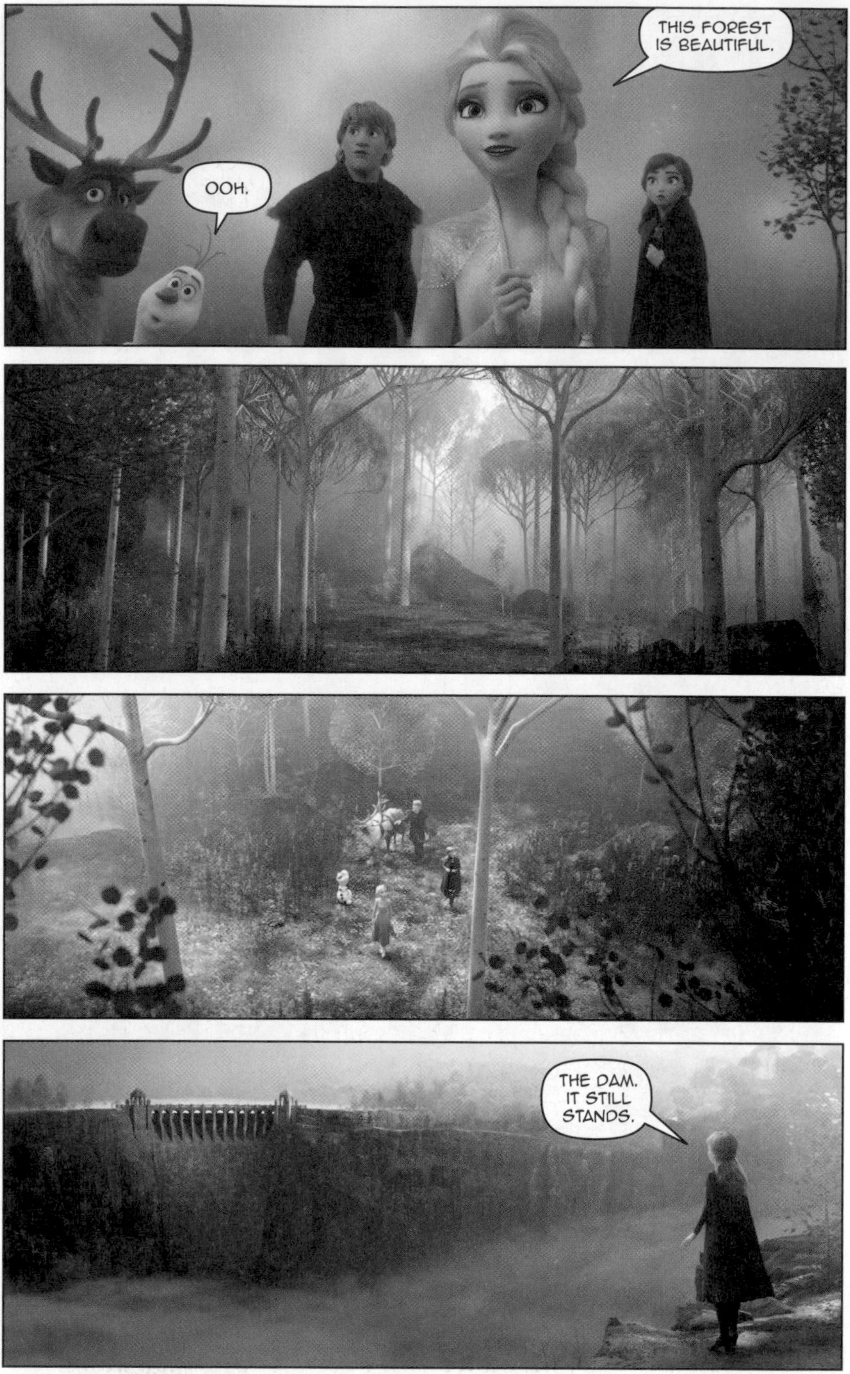
THIS FOREST IS BEAUTIFUL.
OOH.
THE DAM. IT STILL STANDS.

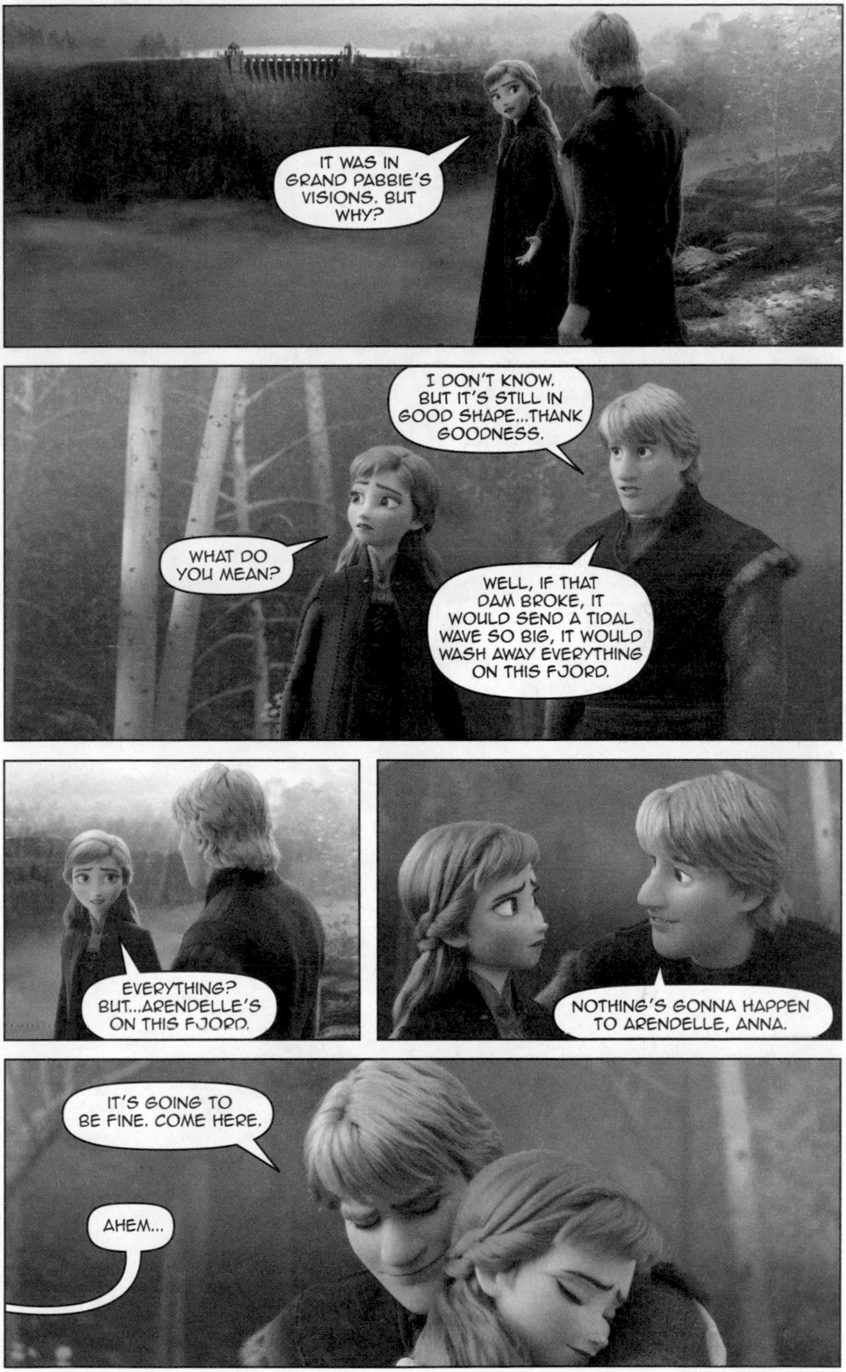
IT WAS IN GRAND PABBIE'S VISIONS. BUT WHY?
I DON'T KNOW. BUT IT'S STILL IN GOOD SHAPE...THANK GOODNESS.
WHAT DO YOU MEAN?
WELL, IF THAT DAM BROKE, IT WOULD SEND A TIDAL WAVE SO BIG, IT WOULD WASH AWAY EVERYTHING ON THIS FJORD.
EVERYTHING? BUT...ARENDELLE'S ON THIS FJORD.
NOTHING'S GONNA HAPPEN TO ARENDELLE, ANNA.
IT'S GOING TO BE FINE. COME HERE.
AHEM...

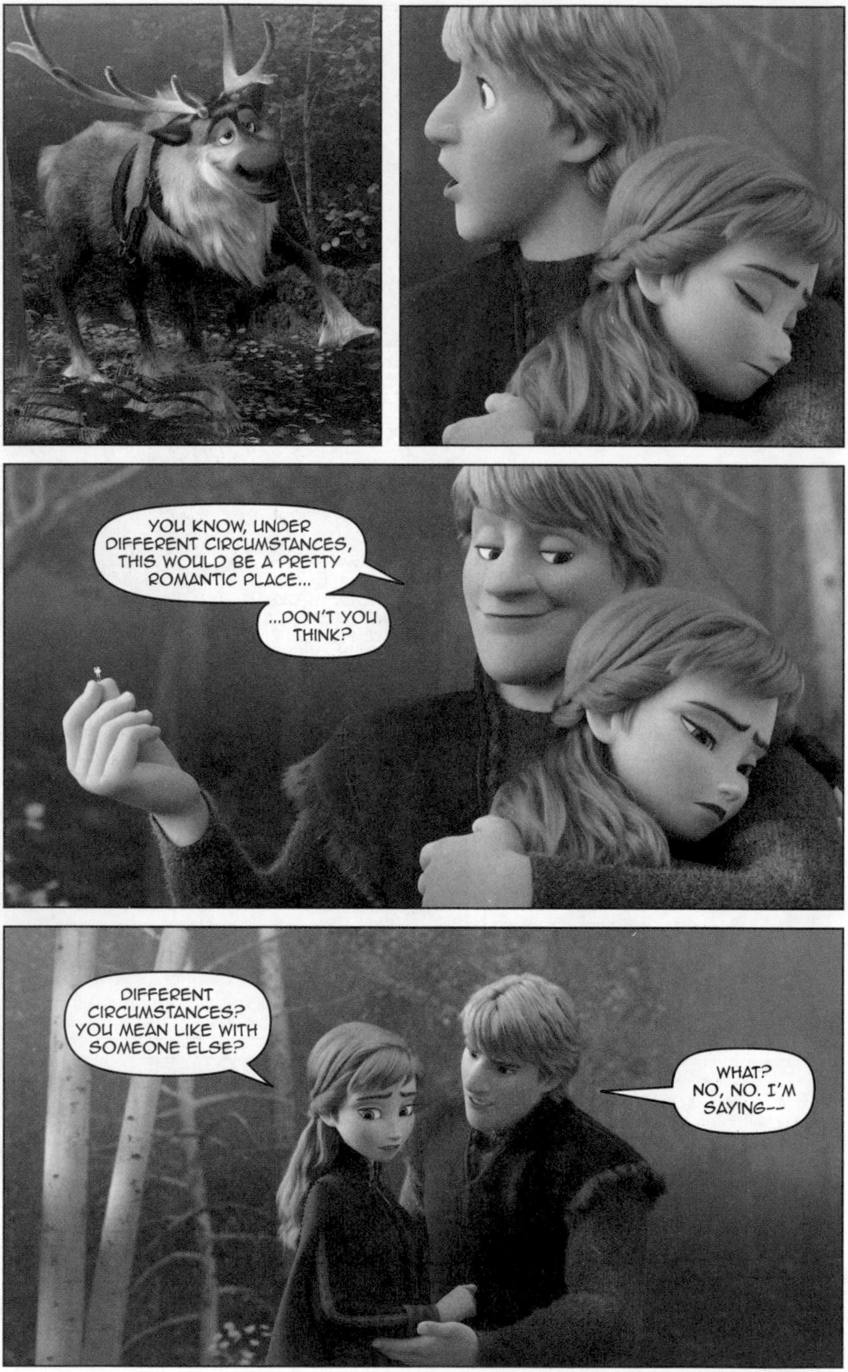
YOU KNOW, UNDER DIFFERENT CIRCUMSTANCES, THIS WOULD BE A PRETTY ROMANTIC PLACE...
...DON'T YOU THINK?
DIFFERENT CIRCUMSTANCES? YOU MEAN LIKE WITH SOMEONE ELSE?
WHAT? NO, NO. I'M SAYING--

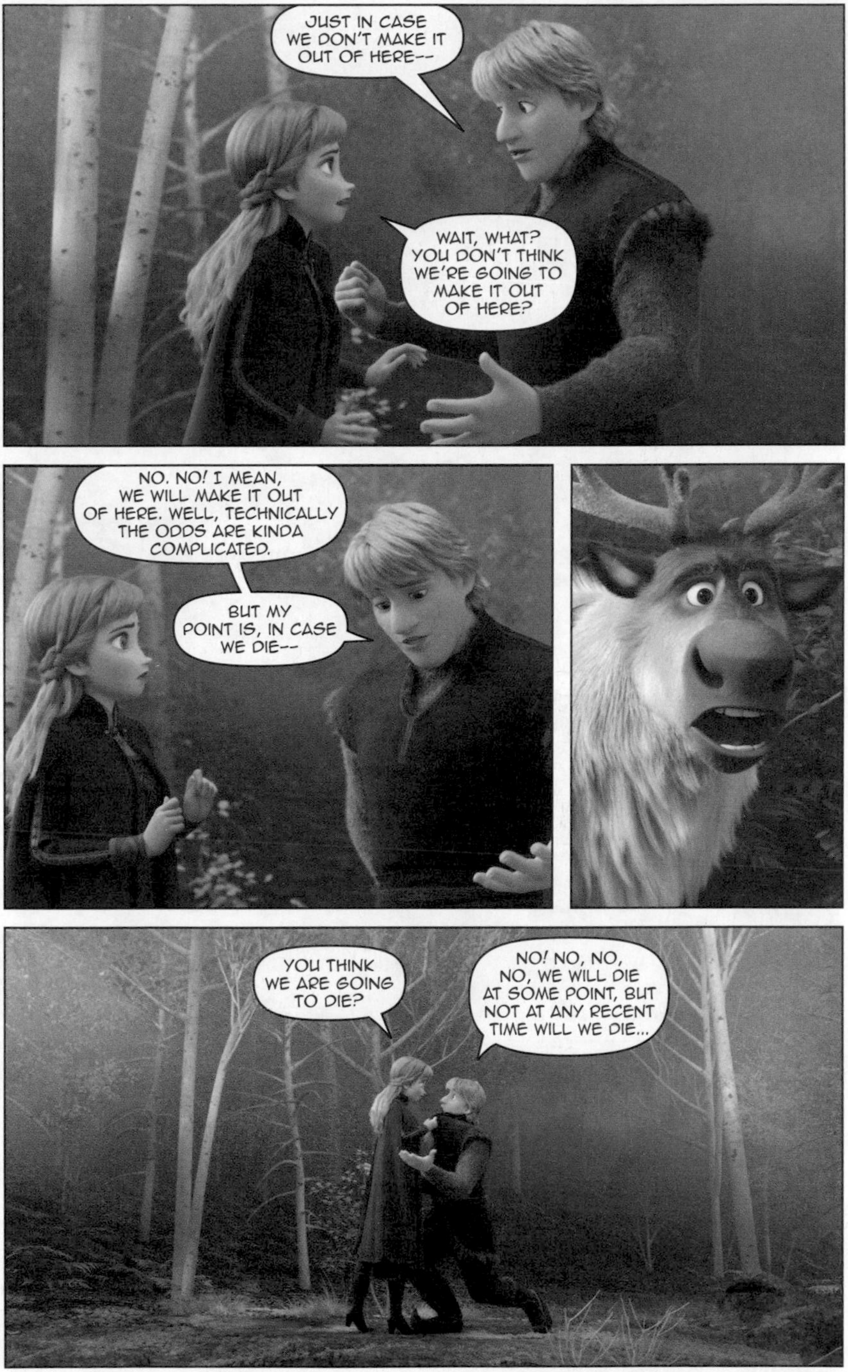
JUST IN CASE WE DON'T MAKE IT OUT OF HERE--
WAIT, WHAT? YOU DON'T THINK WE'RE GOING TO MAKE IT OUT OF HERE?
NO. NO! I MEAN, WE WILL MAKE IT OUT OF HERE. WELL, TECHNICALLY THE ODDS ARE KINDA COMPLICATED.
BUT MY POINT IS, IN CASE WE DIE--
YOU THINK WE ARE GOING TO DIE?
NO! NO, NO, NO, WE WILL DIE AT SOME POINT, BUT NOT AT ANY RECENT TIME WILL WE DIE...

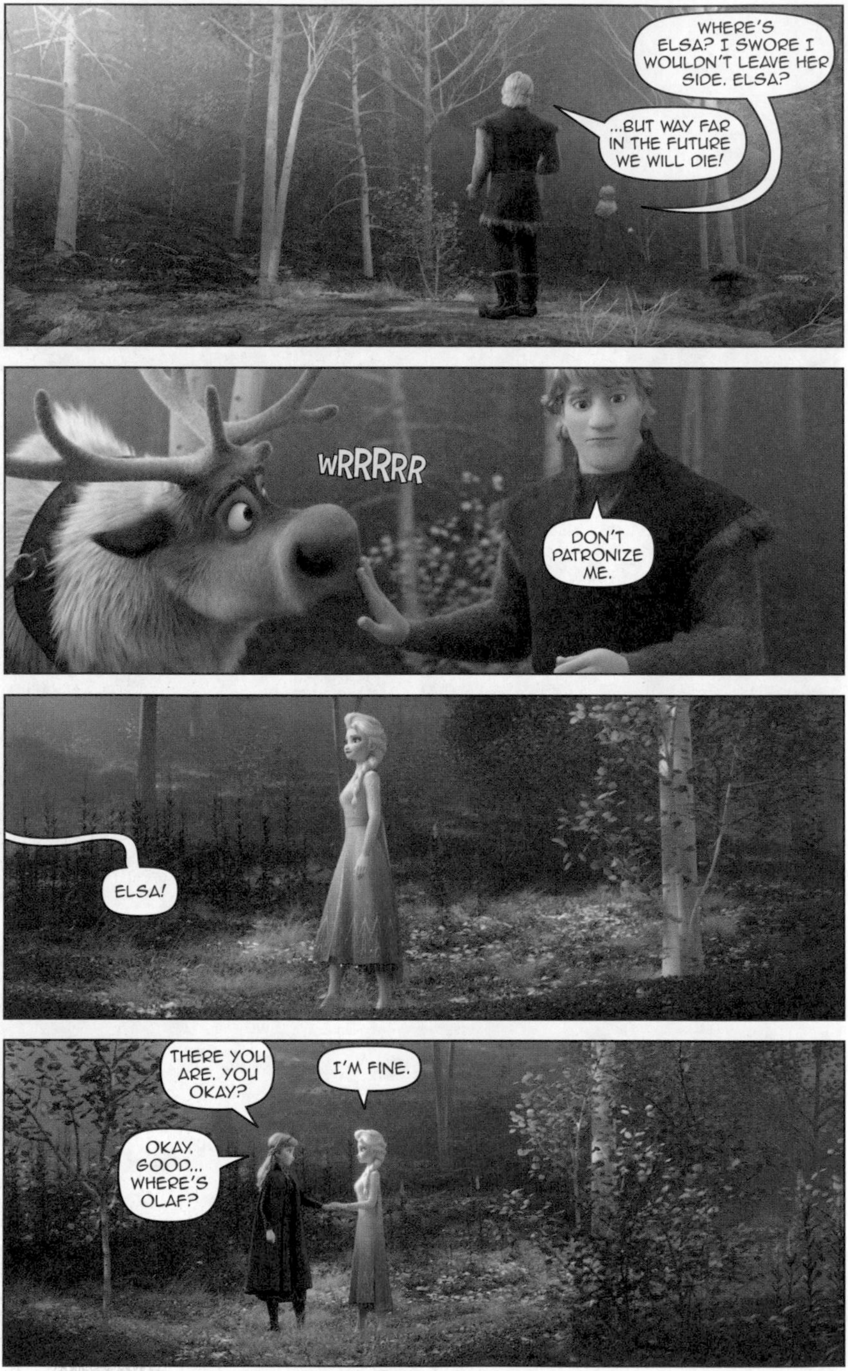
WHERE'S ELSA? I SWORE I WOULDN'T LEAVE HER SIDE. ELSA?
...BUT WAY FAR IN THE FUTURE WE WILL DIE!
WRRRRR
DON'T PATRONIZE ME.
ELSA!
THERE YOU ARE. YOU OKAY?
I'M FINE.
OKAY. GOOD... WHERE'S OLAF?

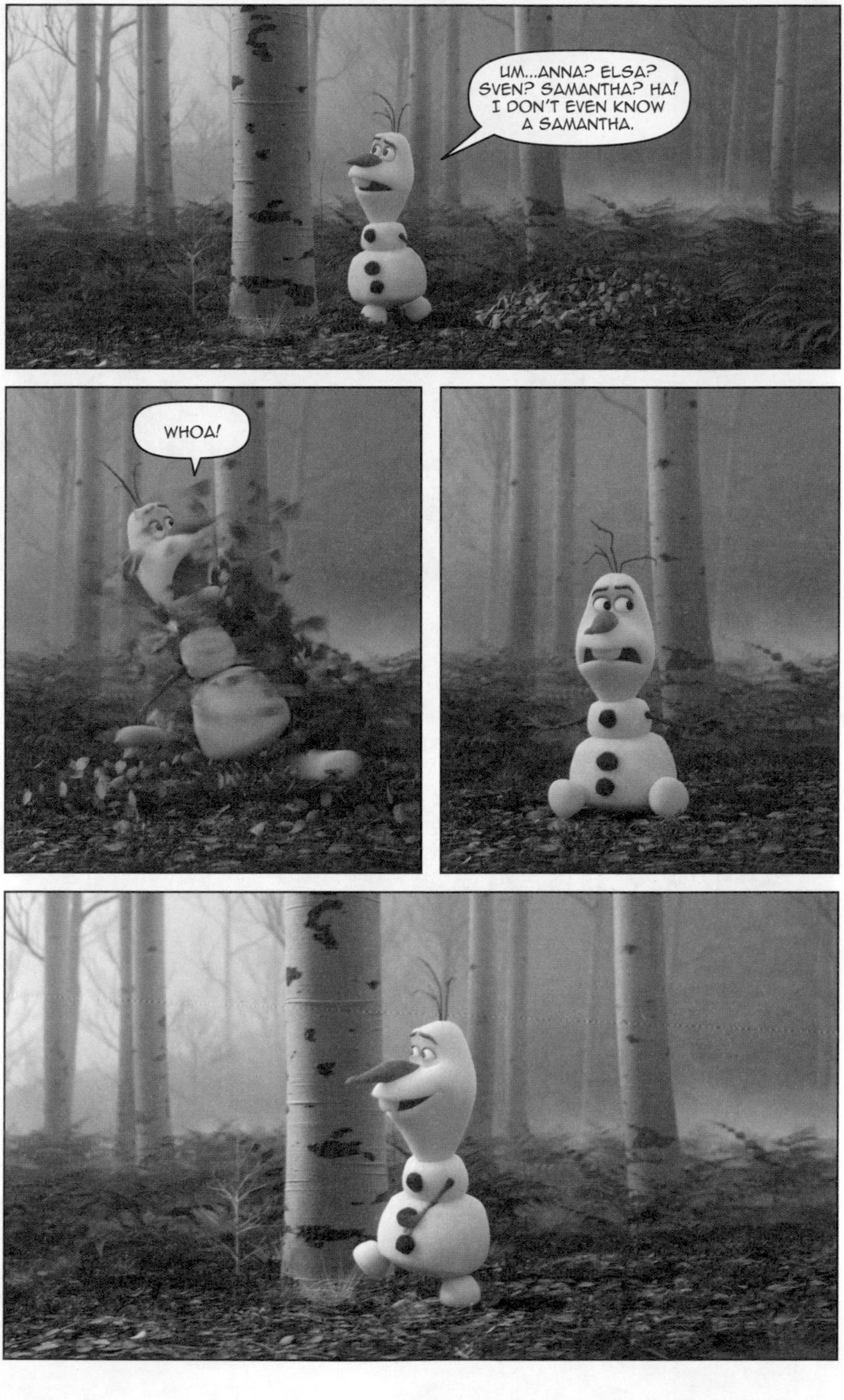
UM...ANNA? ELSA? SVEN? SAMANTHA? HA! I DON'T EVEN KNOW A SAMANTHA.
WHOA!

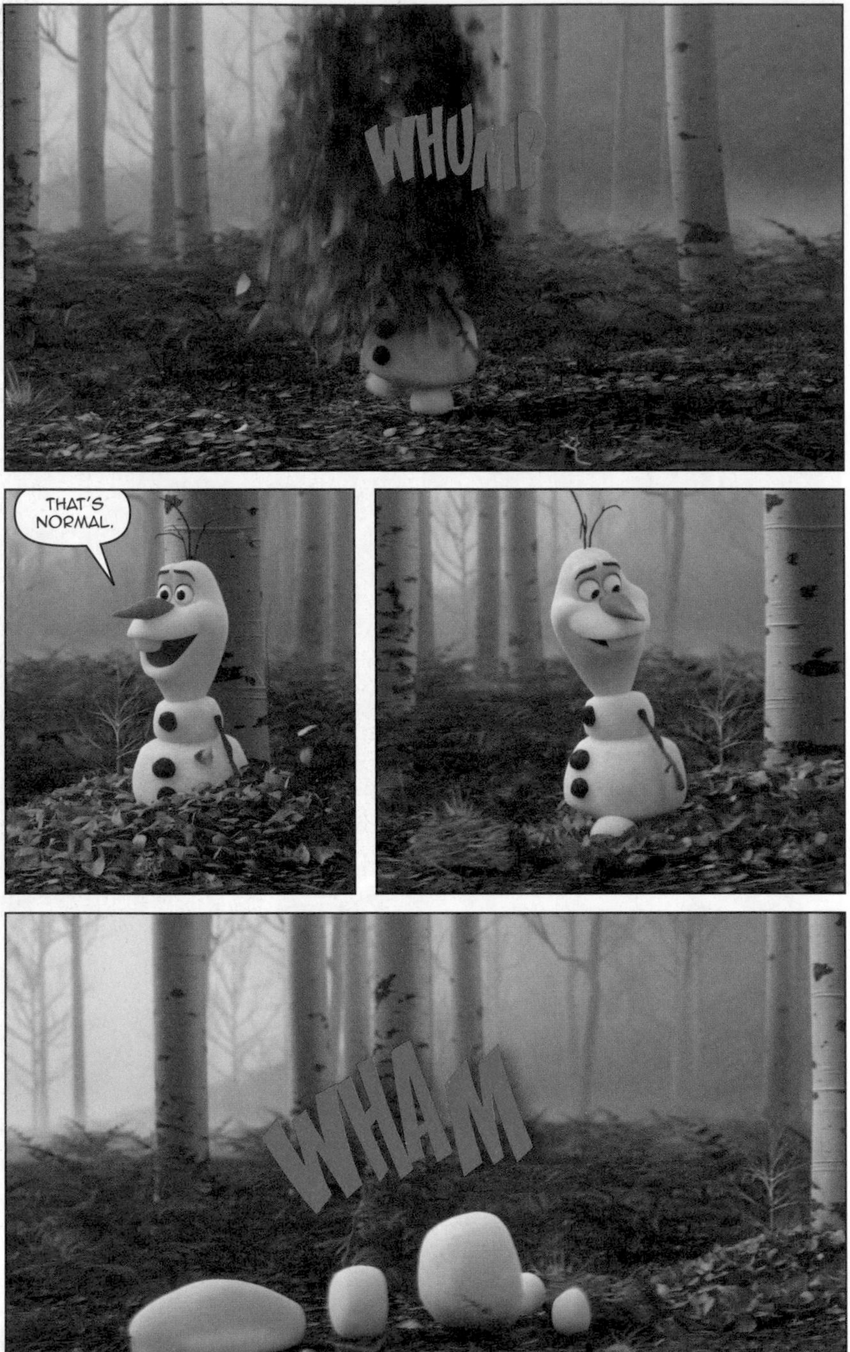
WHUMP
THAT'S NORMAL.
WHAM

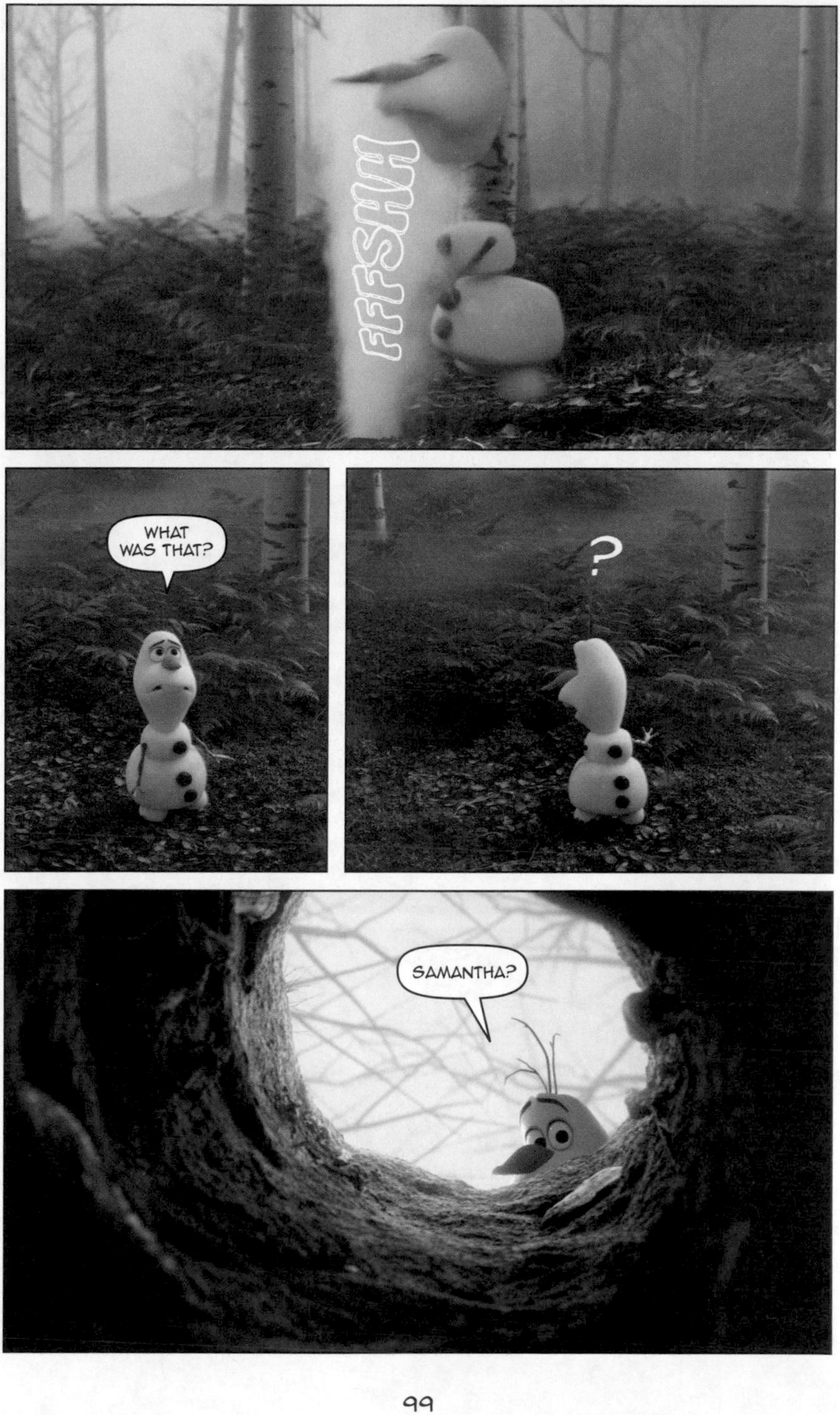
FFFSHH
WHAT WAS THAT?
?
SAMANTHA?

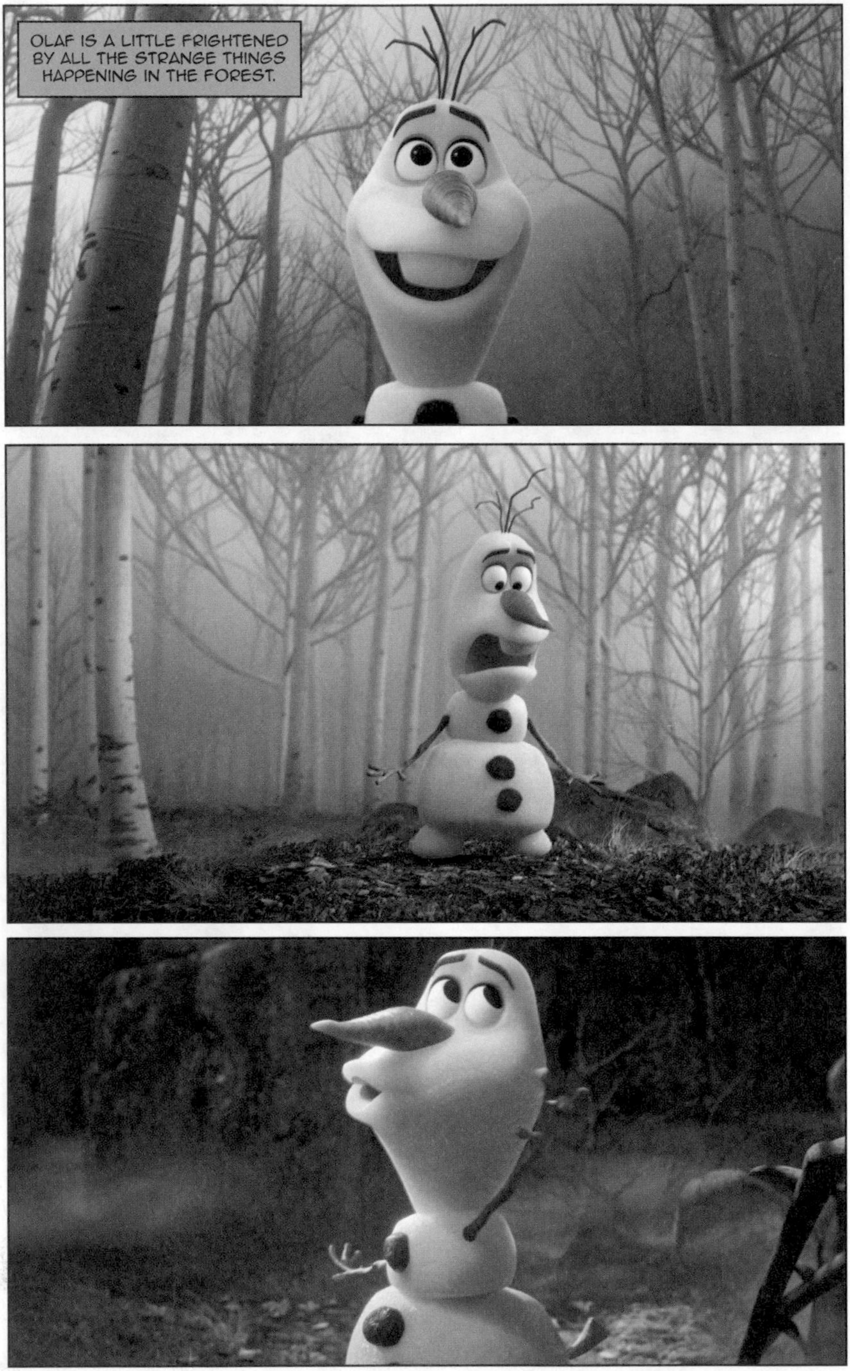
OLAF IS A LITTLE FRIGHTENED BY ALL THE STRANGE THINGS HAPPENING IN THE FOREST.

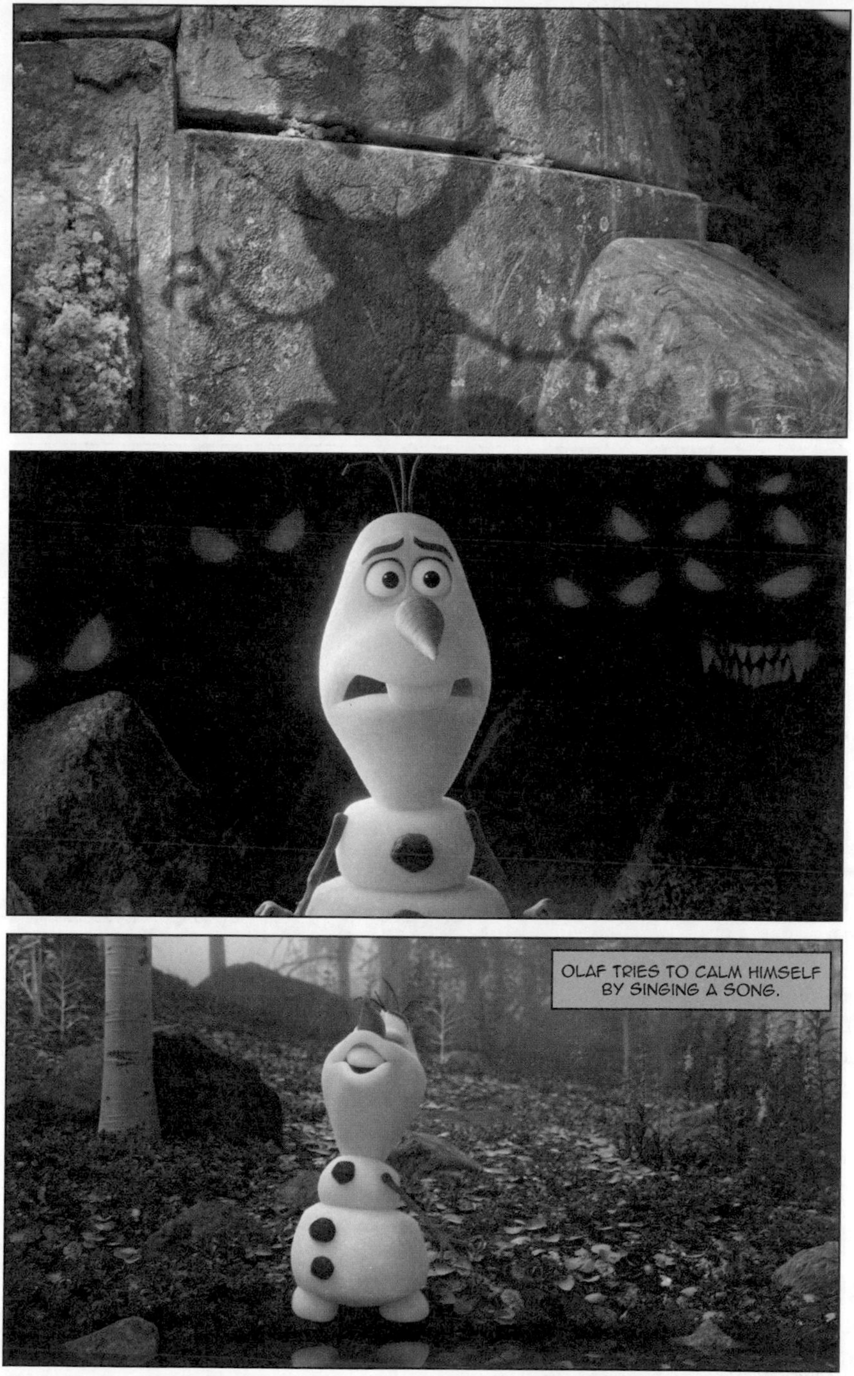
OLAF TRIES TO CALM HIMSELF BY SINGING A SONG.

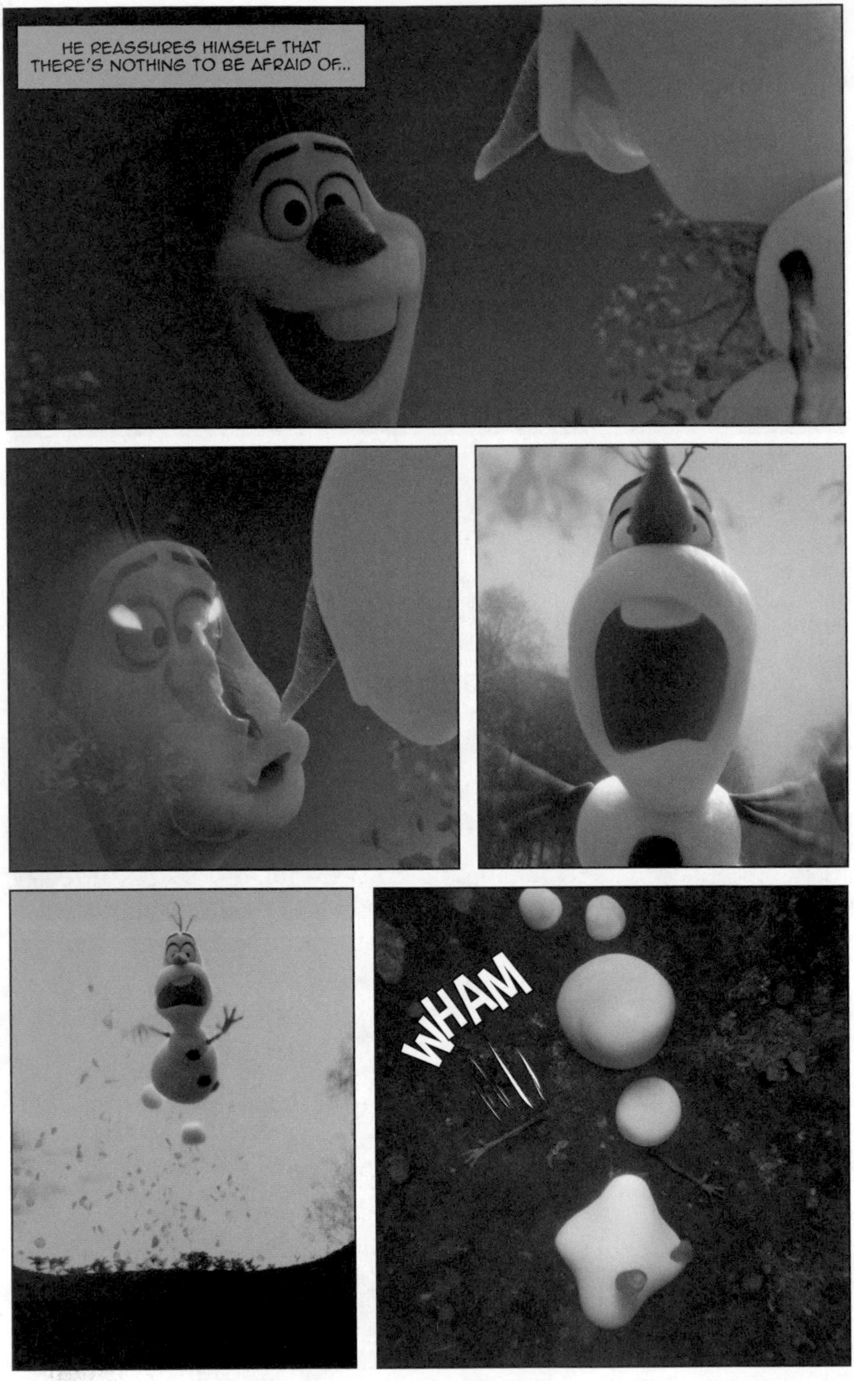
HE REASSURES HIMSELF THAT THERE'S NOTHING TO BE AFRAID OF...
WHAM

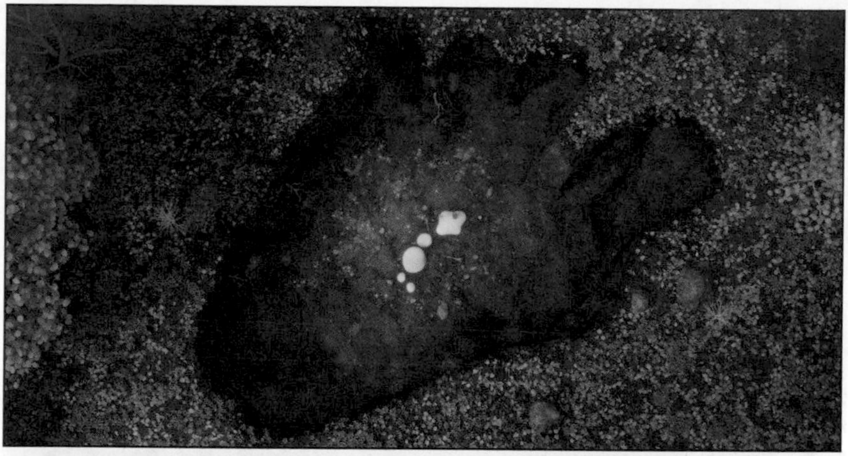

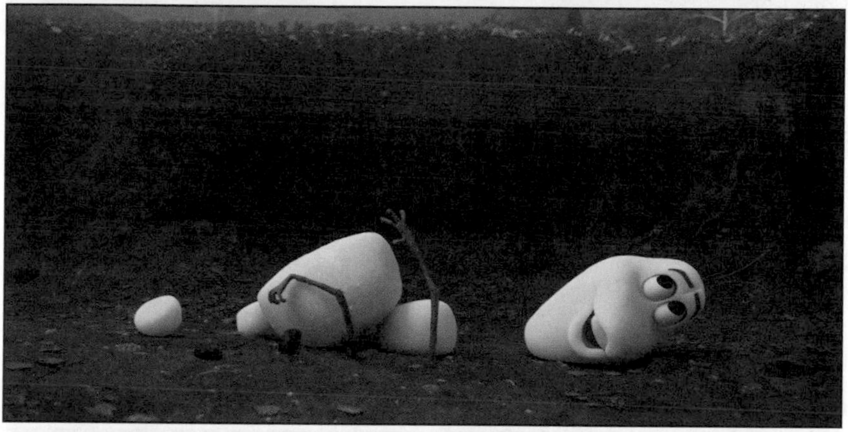

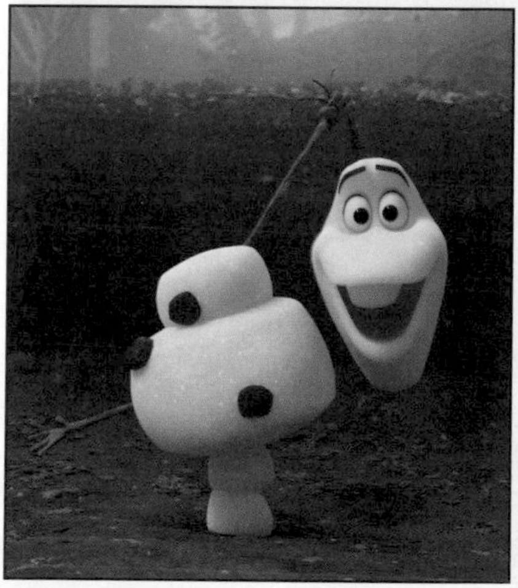

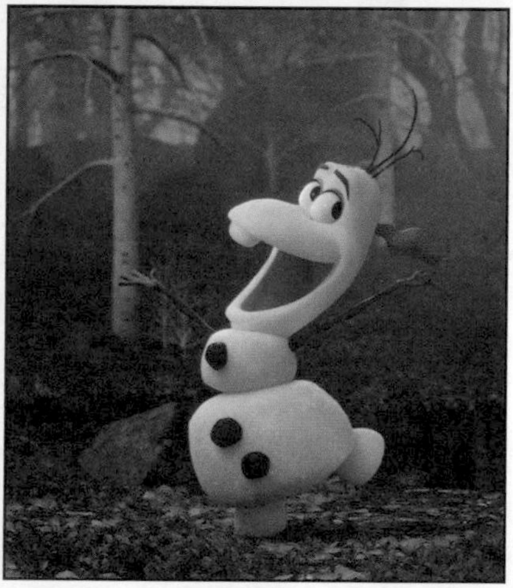

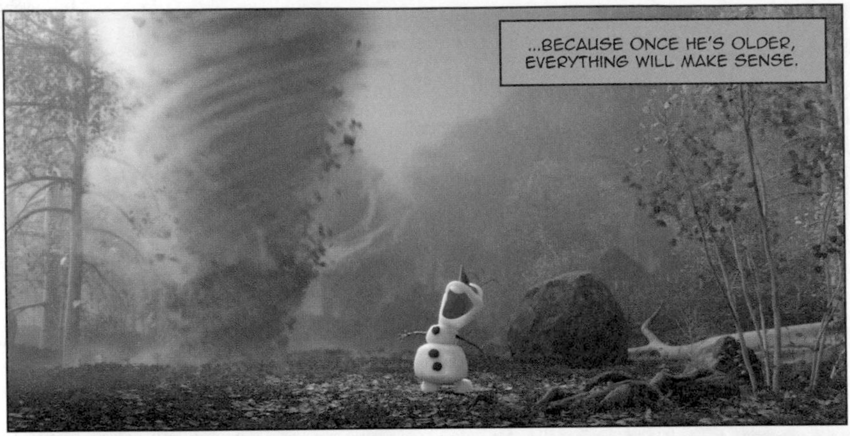
...BECAUSE ONCE HE'S OLDER,
EVERYTHING WILL MAKE SENSE.

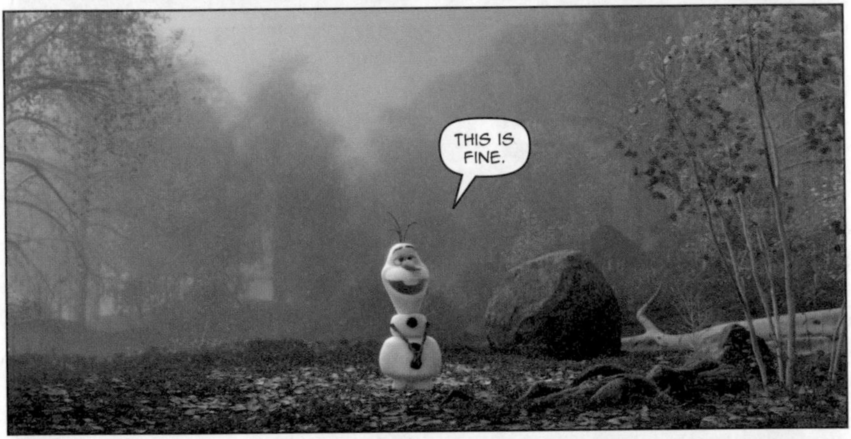
THIS IS
FINE.

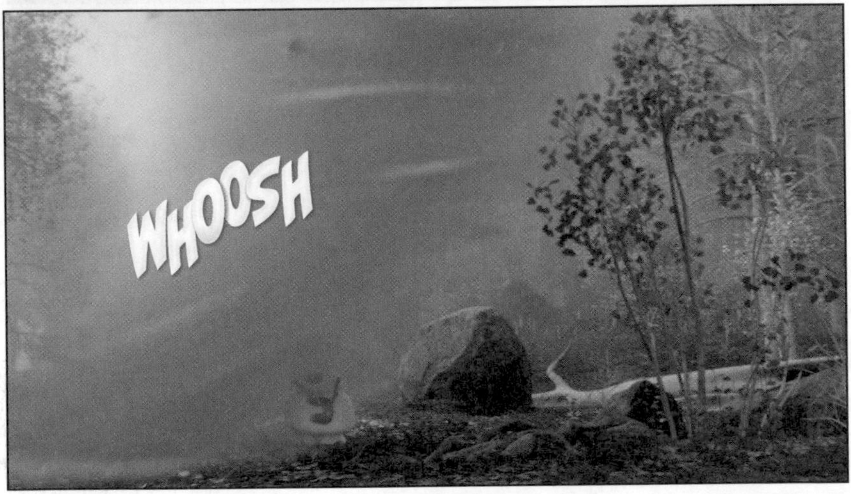
WHOOSH

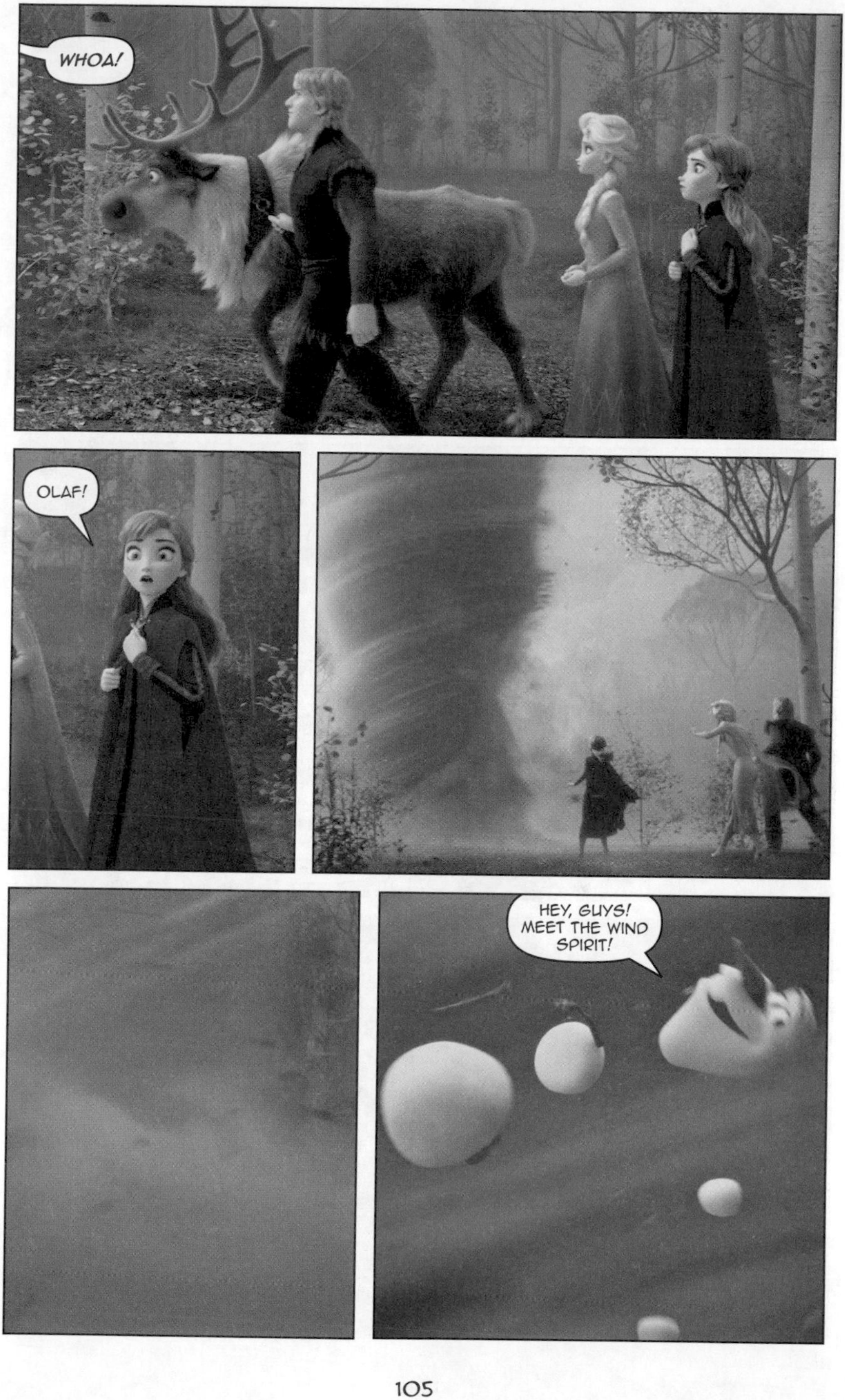
WHOA!
OLAF!
HEY, GUYS! MEET THE WIND SPIRIT!

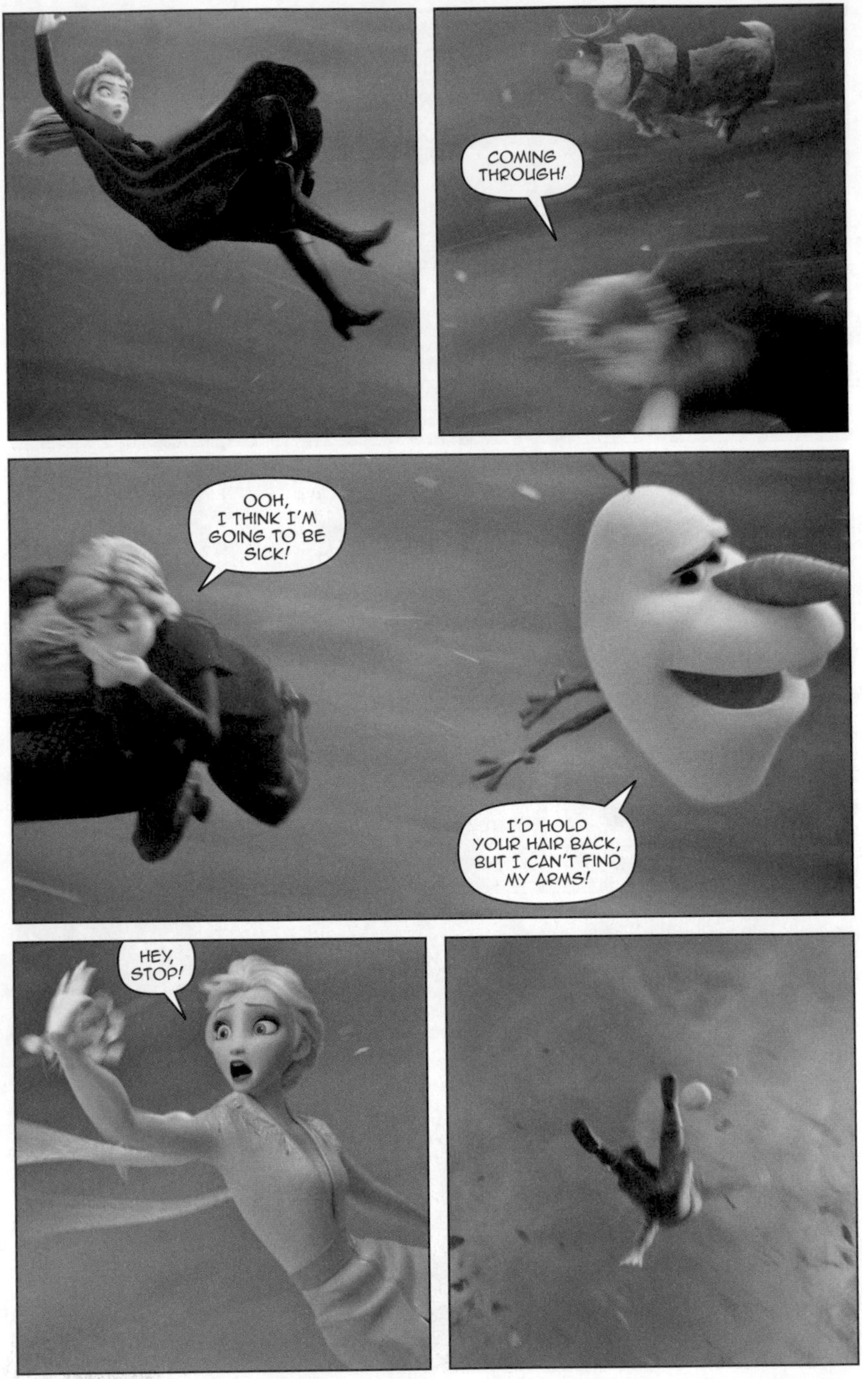
COMING THROUGH!
OOH, I THINK I'M GOING TO BE SICK!
I'D HOLD YOUR HAIR BACK, BUT I CAN'T FIND MY ARMS!
HEY, STOP!

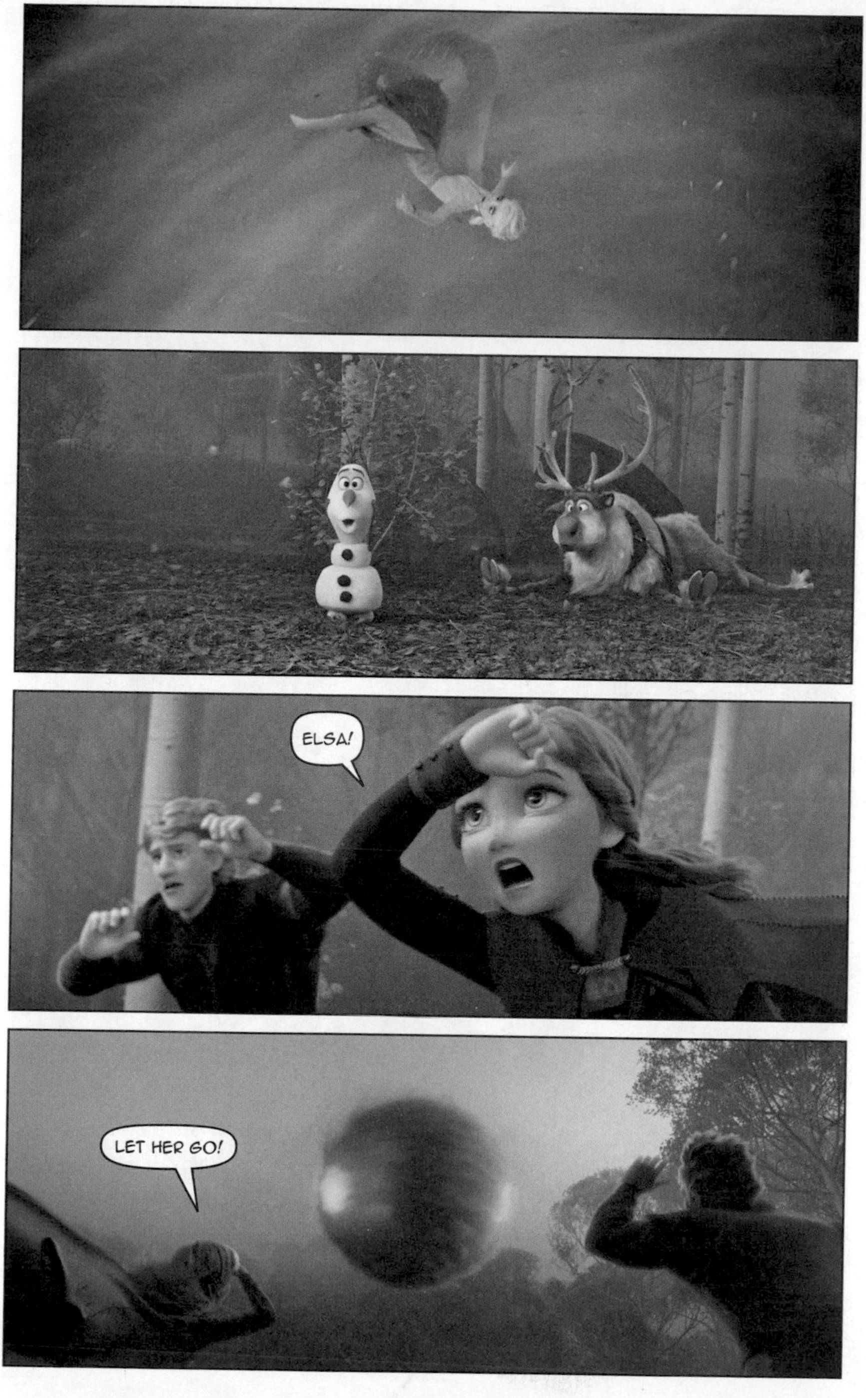
ELSA!
LET HER GO!

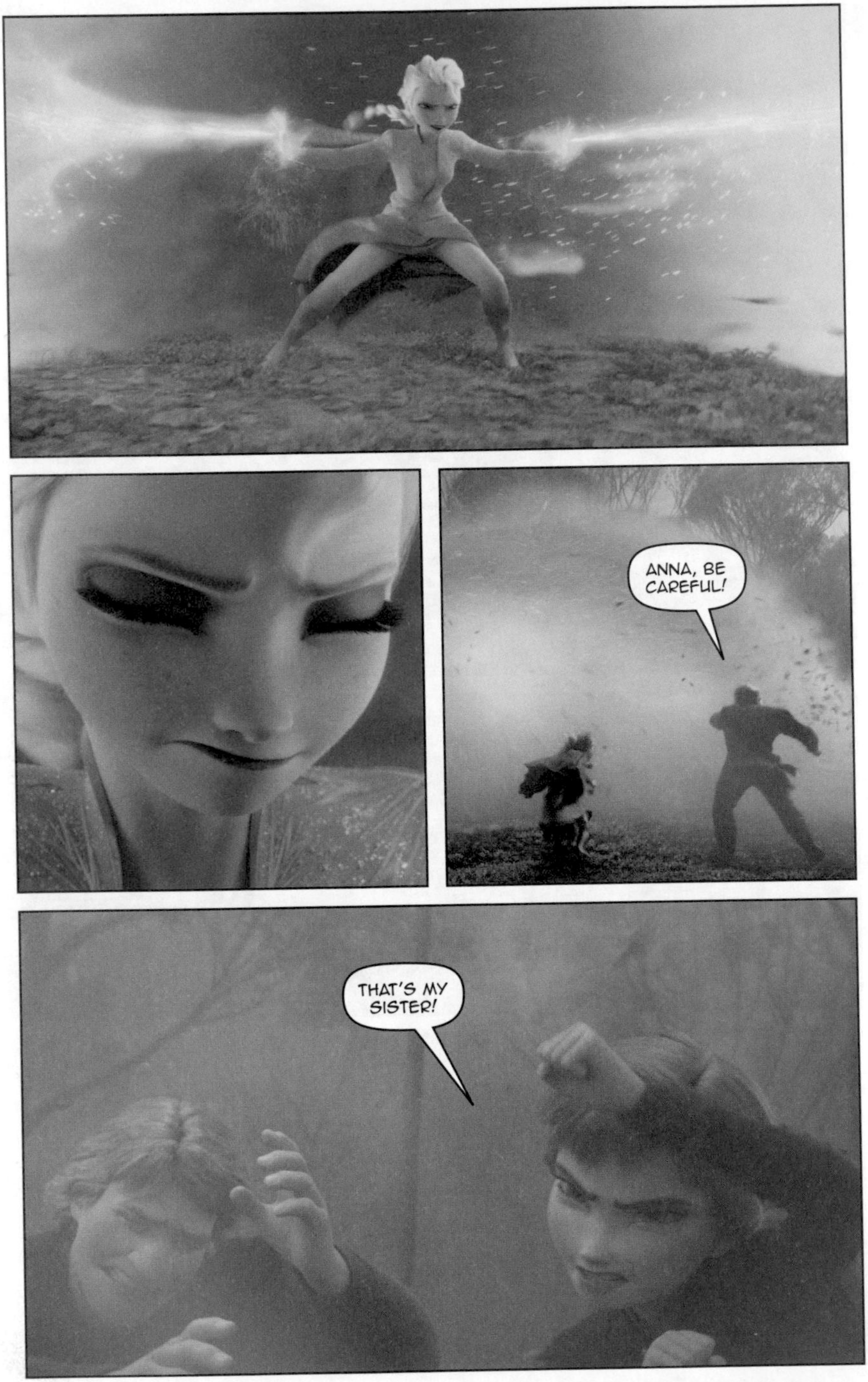
ANNA, BE CAREFUL!
THAT'S MY SISTER!

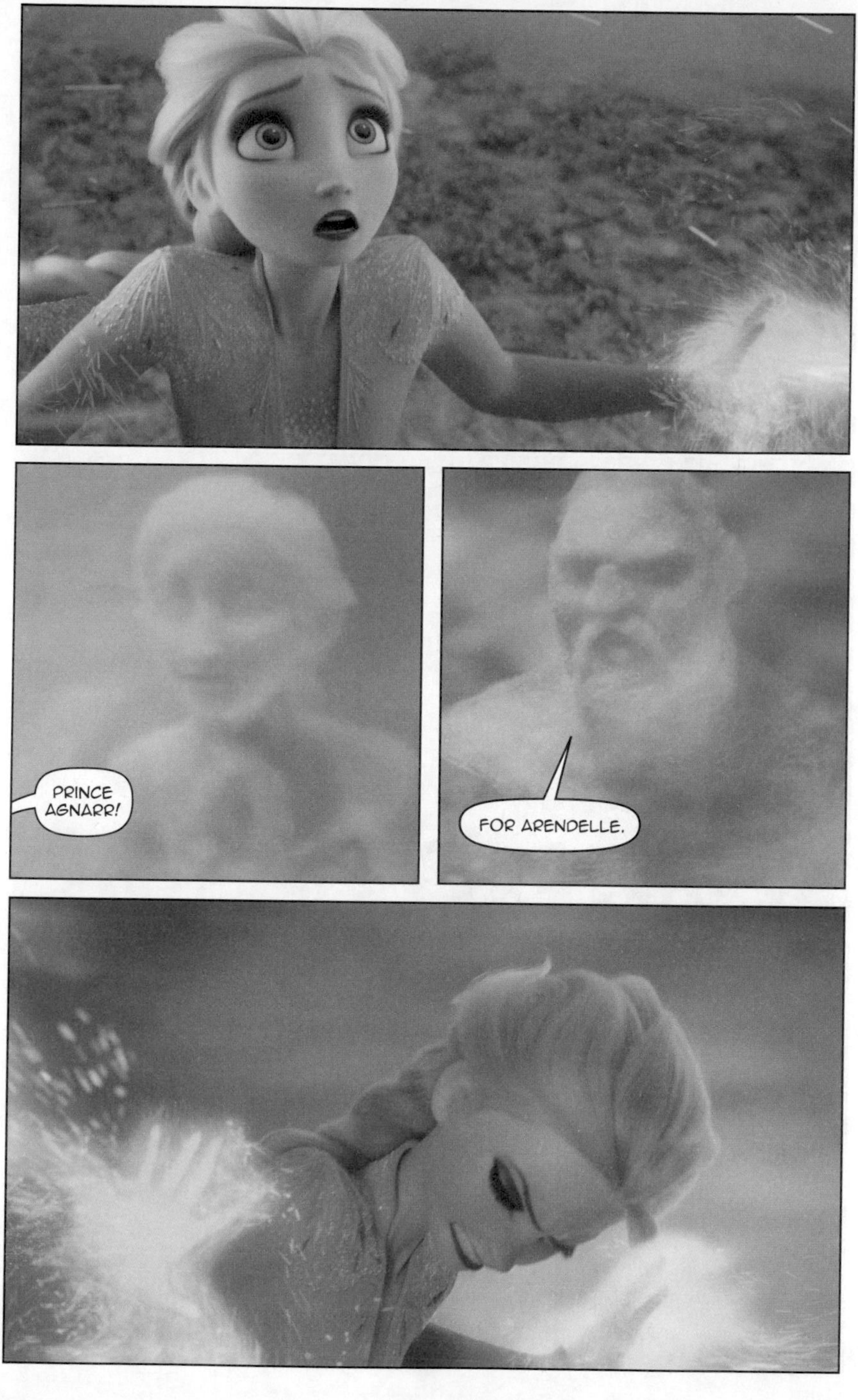
PRINCE AGNARR!
FOR ARENDELLE.

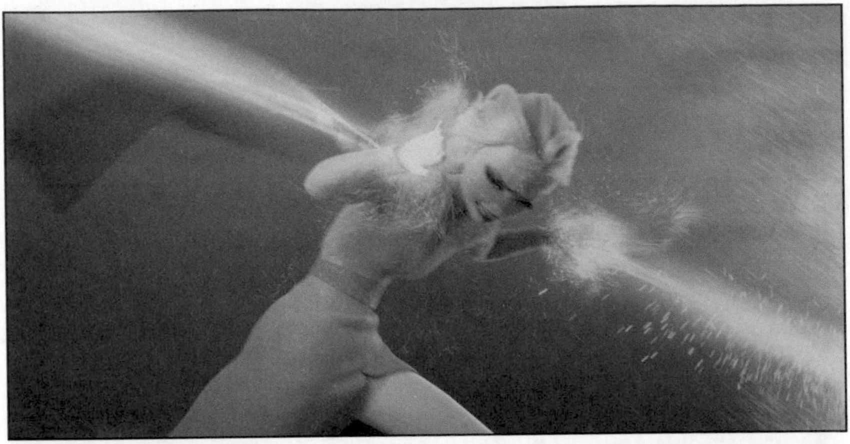

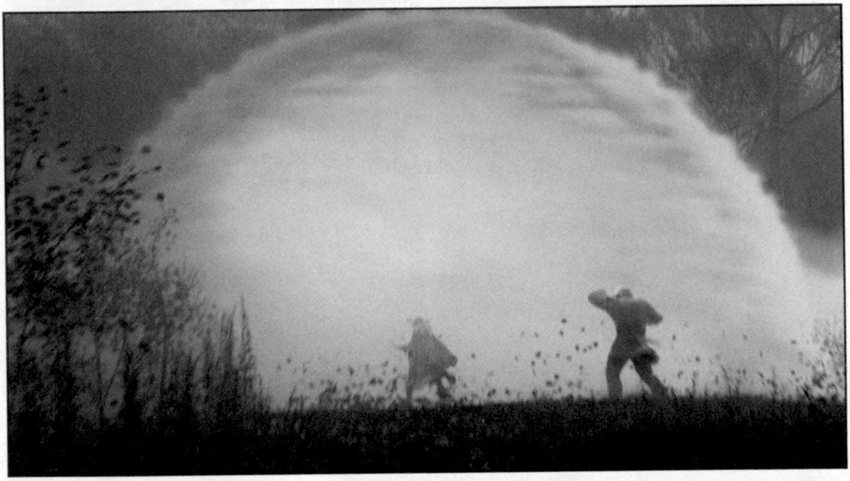

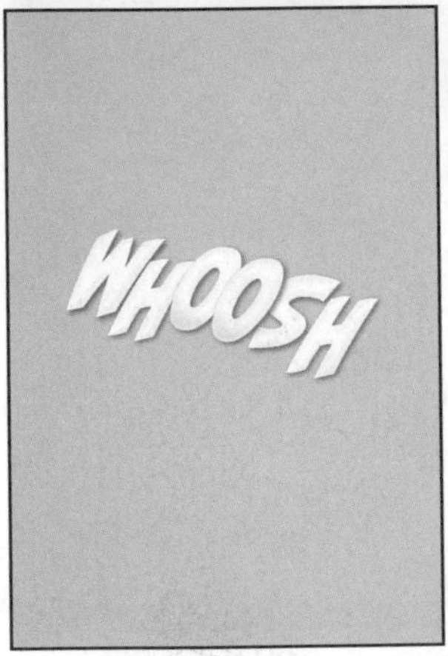
WHOOSH

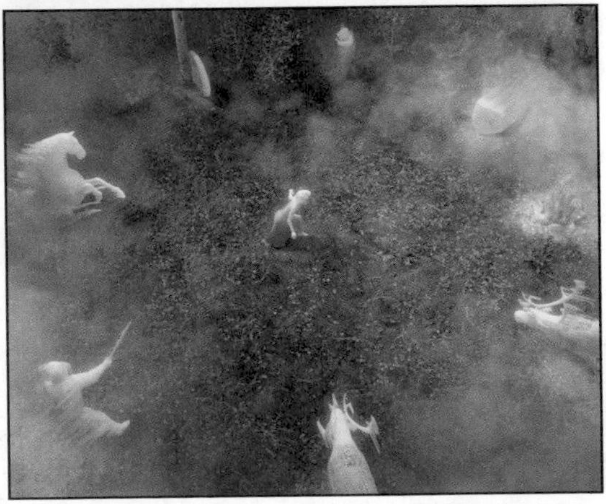

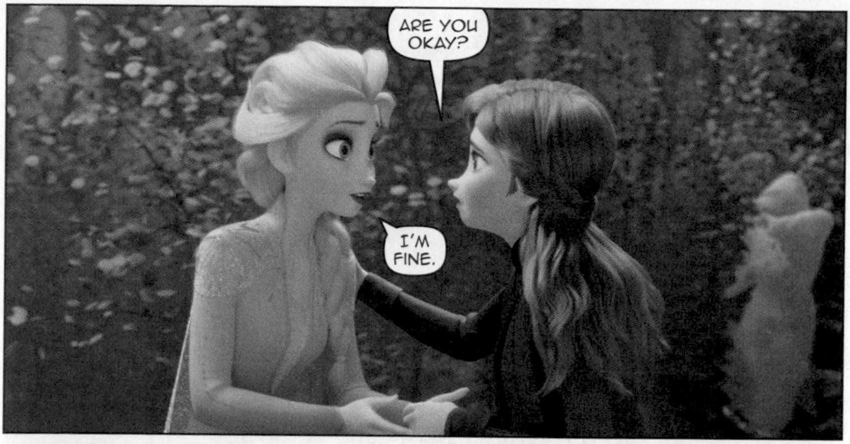
ARE YOU OKAY?
I'M FINE.

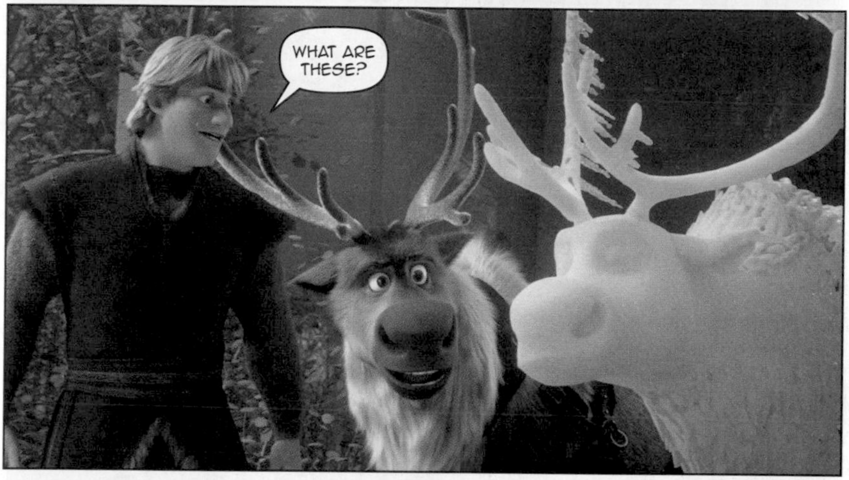
WHAT ARE THESE?

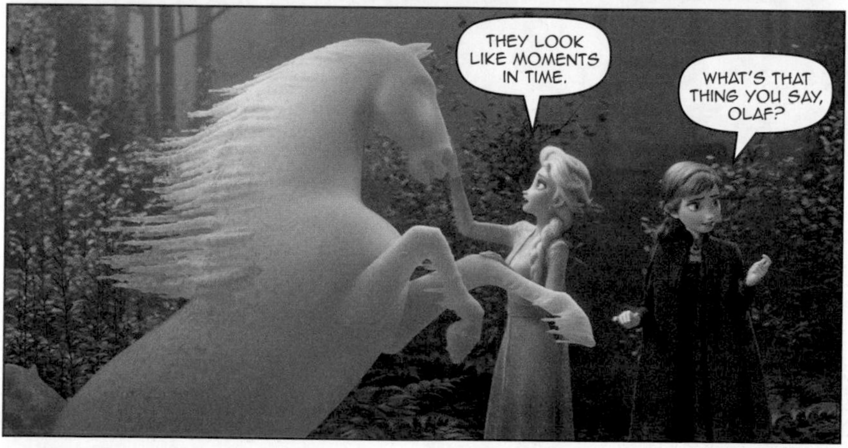
THEY LOOK LIKE MOMENTS IN TIME.
WHAT'S THAT THING YOU SAY, OLAF?

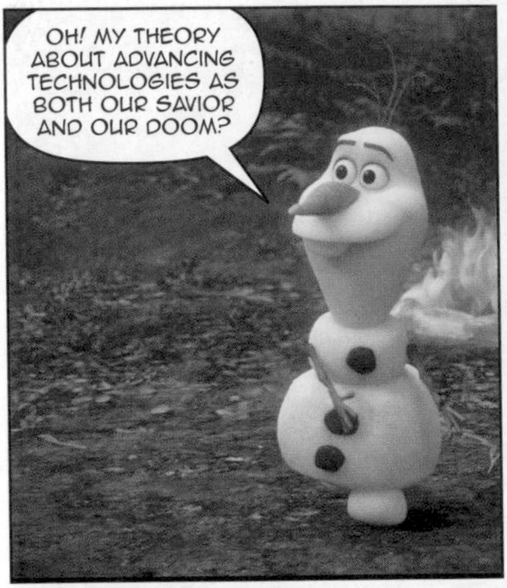
OH! MY THEORY ABOUT ADVANCING TECHNOLOGIES AS BOTH OUR SAVIOR AND OUR DOOM?

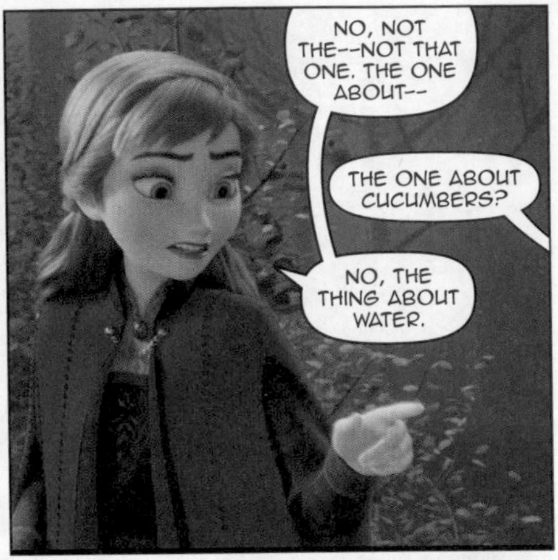
NO, NOT THE--NOT THAT ONE. THE ONE ABOUT--
THE ONE ABOUT CUCUMBERS?
NO, THE THING ABOUT WATER.

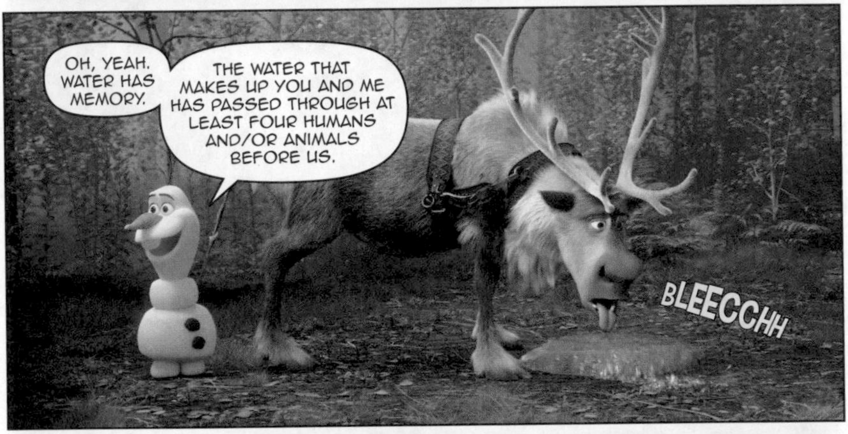
OH, YEAH. WATER HAS MEMORY.
THE WATER THAT MAKES UP YOU AND ME HAS PASSED THROUGH AT LEAST FOUR HUMANS AND/OR ANIMALS BEFORE US.
BLEECCHH

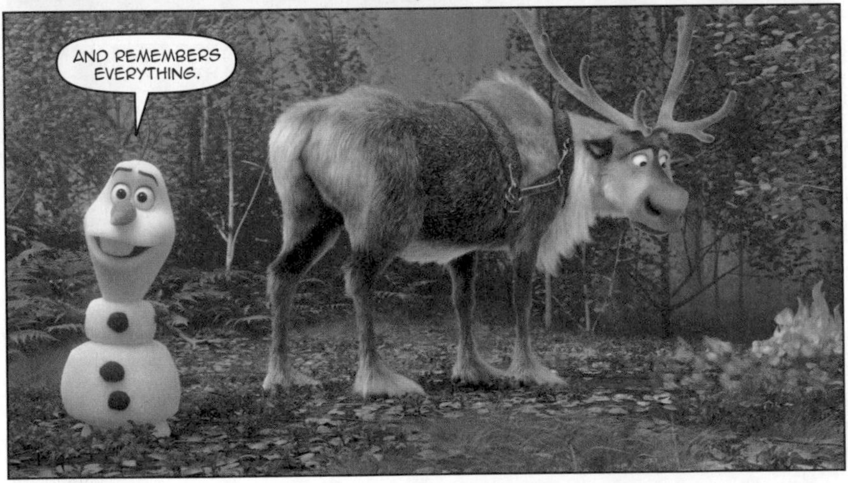
AND REMEMBERS EVERYTHING.

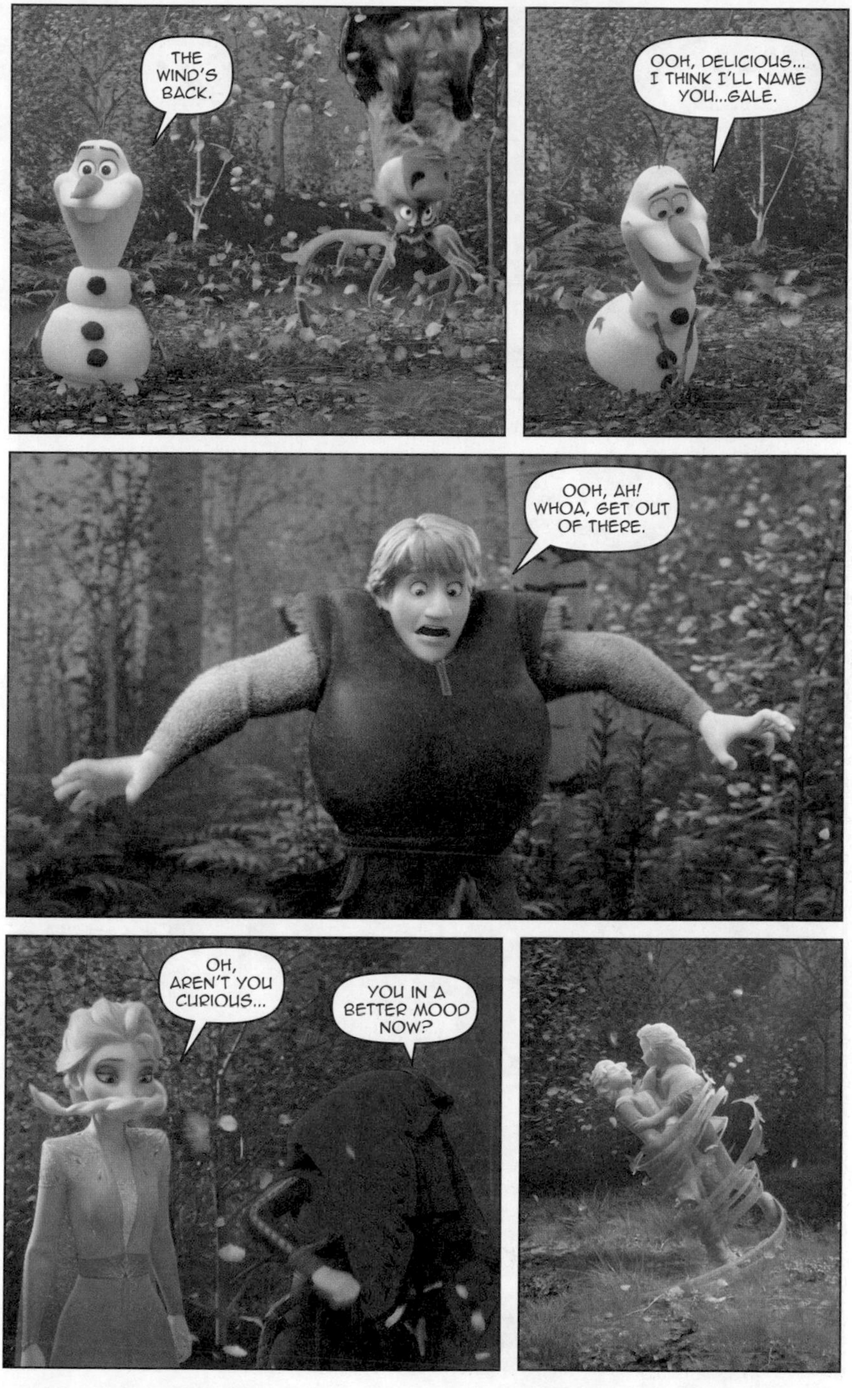
THE WIND'S BACK.
OOH, DELICIOUS... I THINK I'LL NAME YOU...GALE.
OOH, AH! WHOA, GET OUT OF THERE.
OH, AREN'T YOU CURIOUS...
YOU IN A BETTER MOOD NOW?

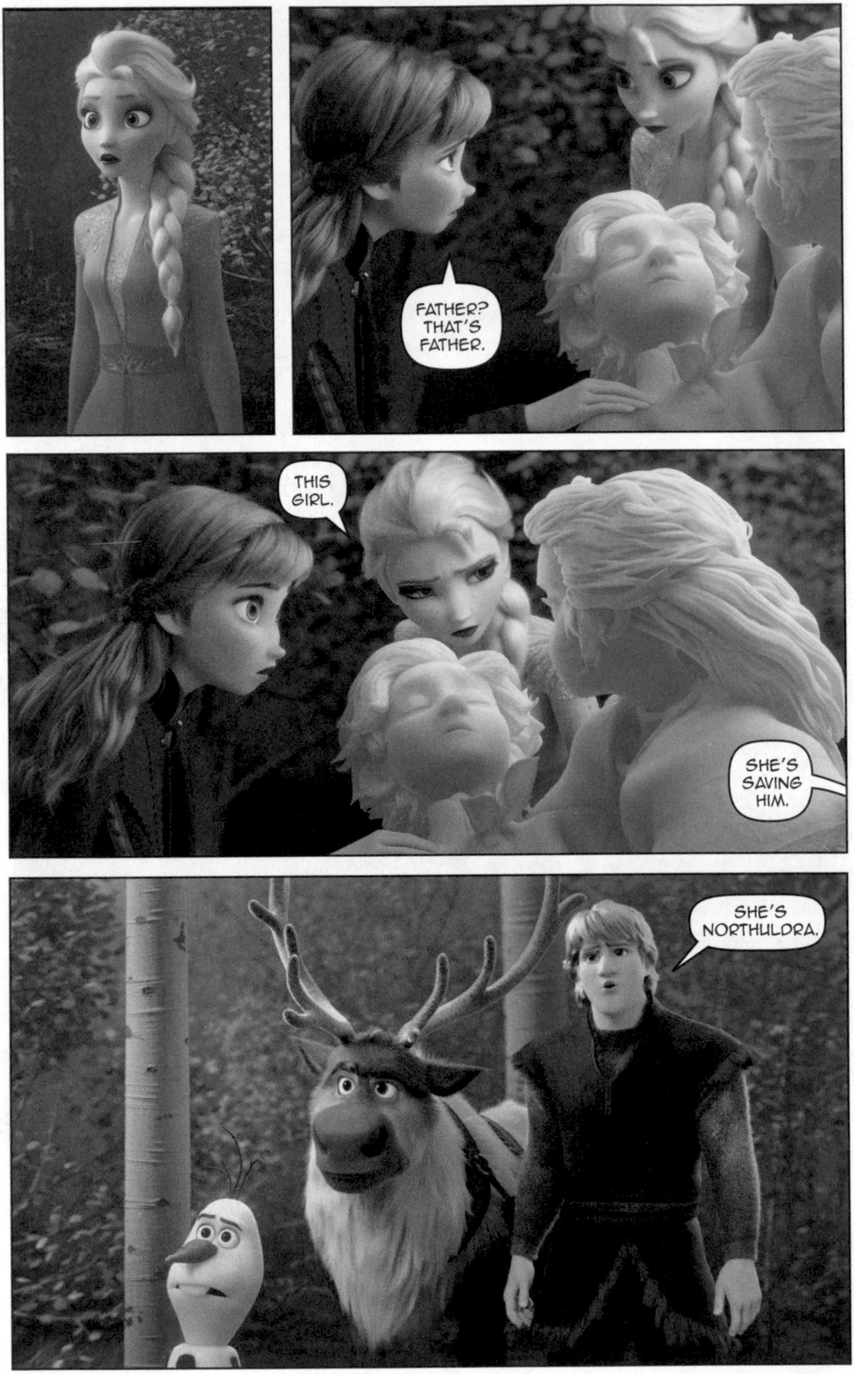
FATHER? THAT'S FATHER.
THIS GIRL.
SHE'S SAVING HIM.
SHE'S NORTHULDRA.

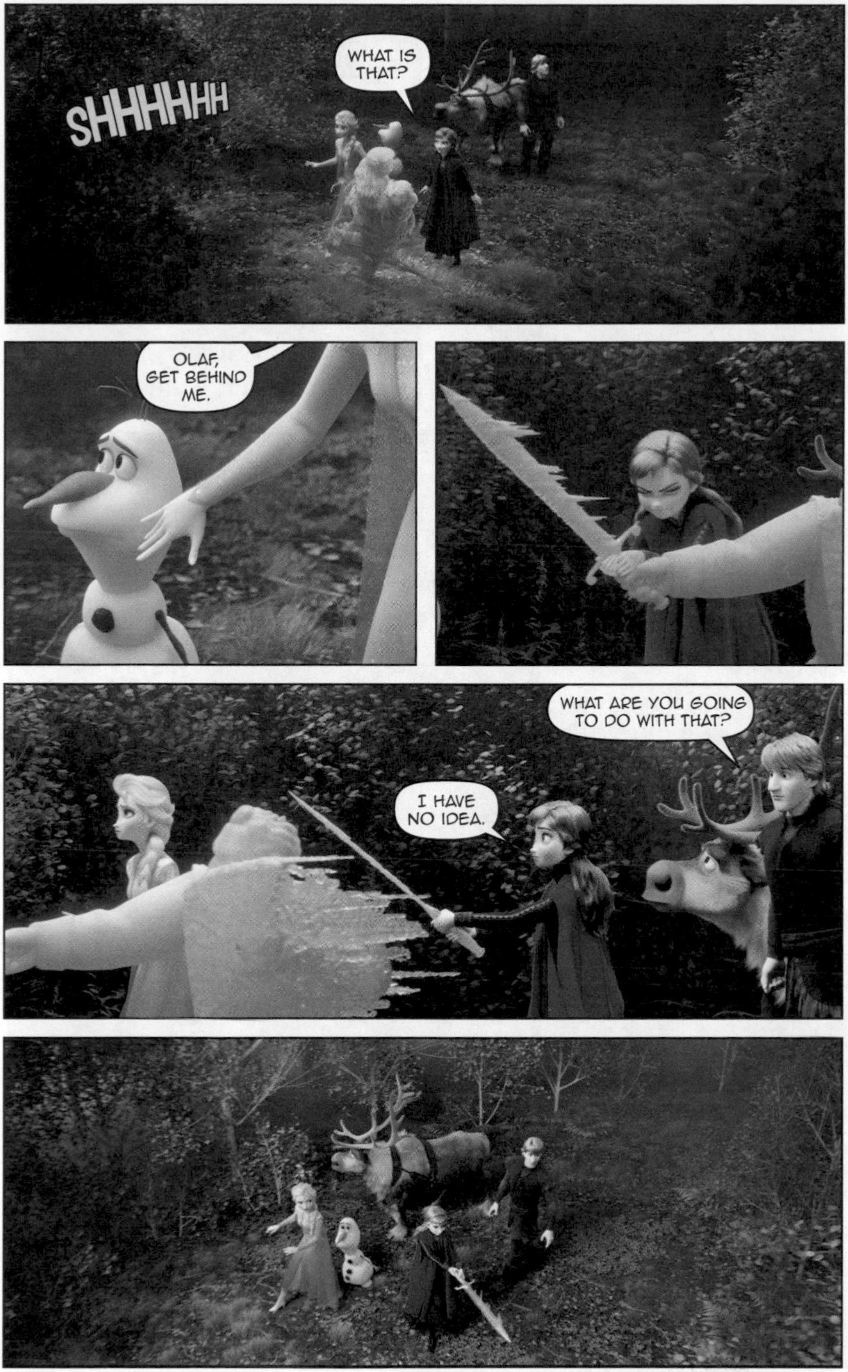
SHHHHHH
WHAT IS THAT?
OLAF, GET BEHIND ME.
WHAT ARE YOU GOING TO DO WITH THAT?
I HAVE NO IDEA.

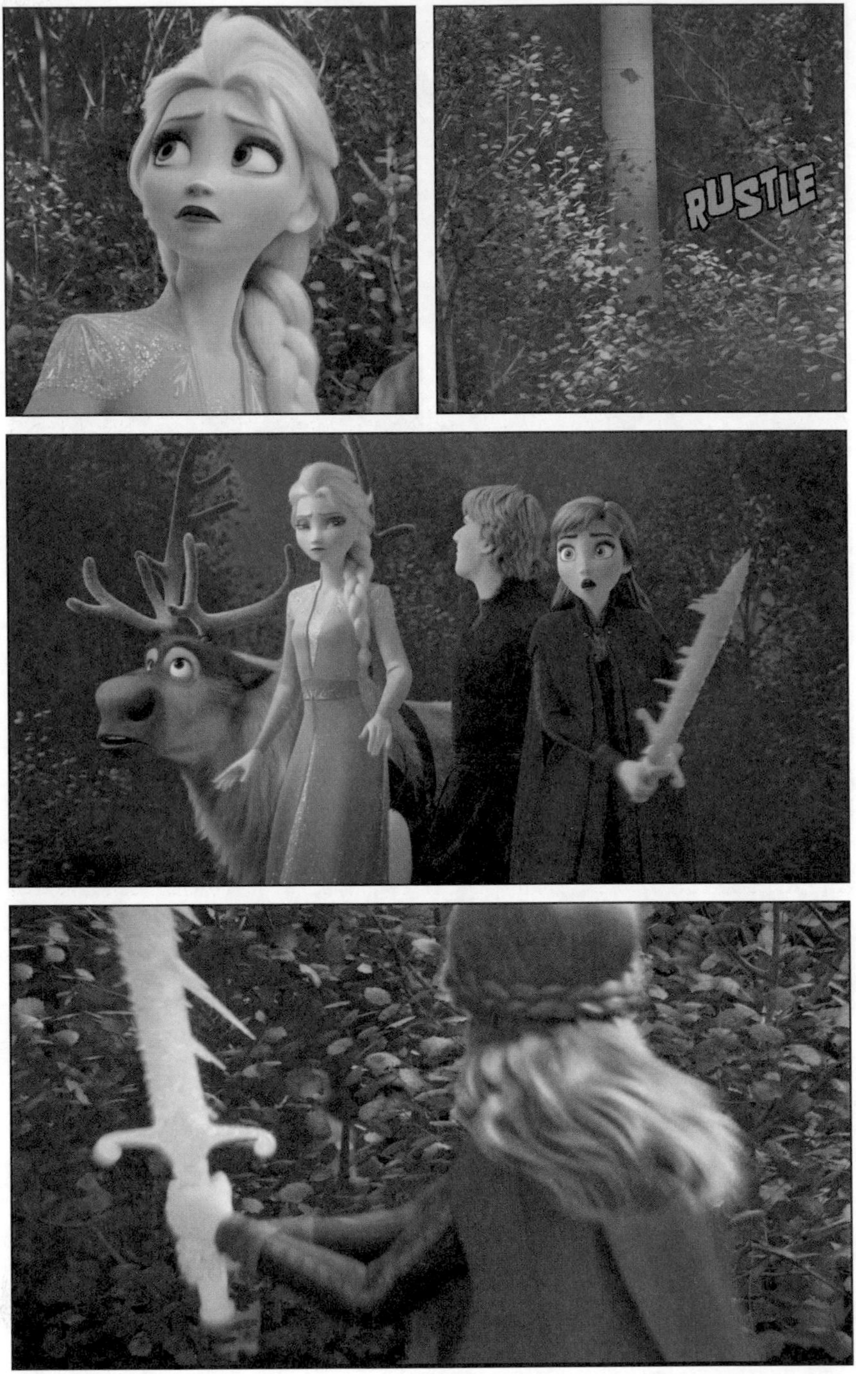
RUSTLE

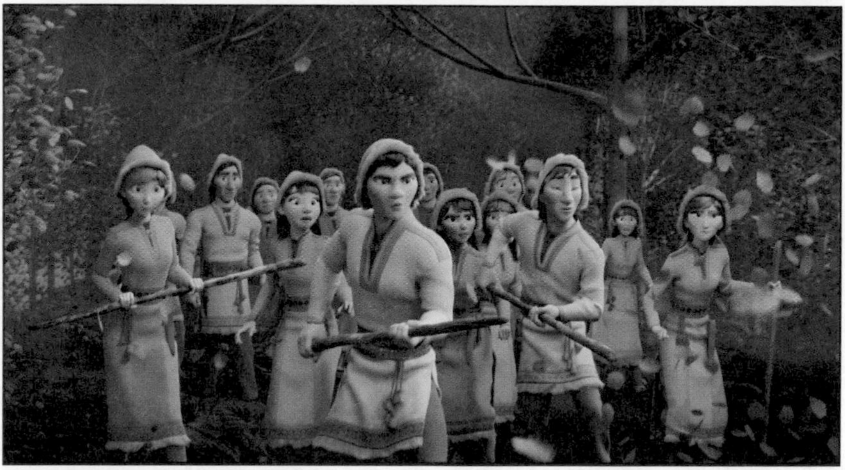

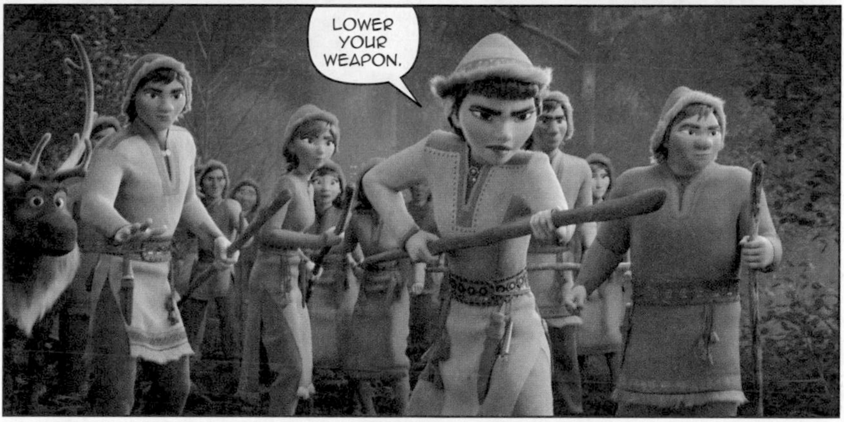
LOWER YOUR WEAPON.

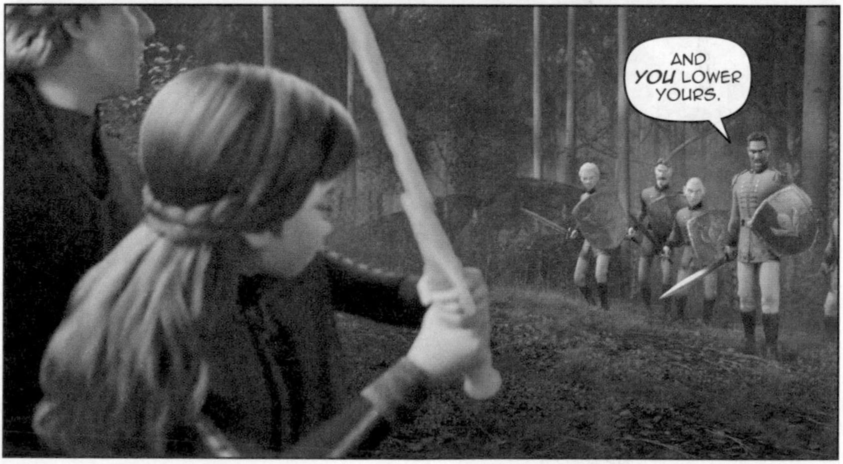
AND *YOU* LOWER YOURS.

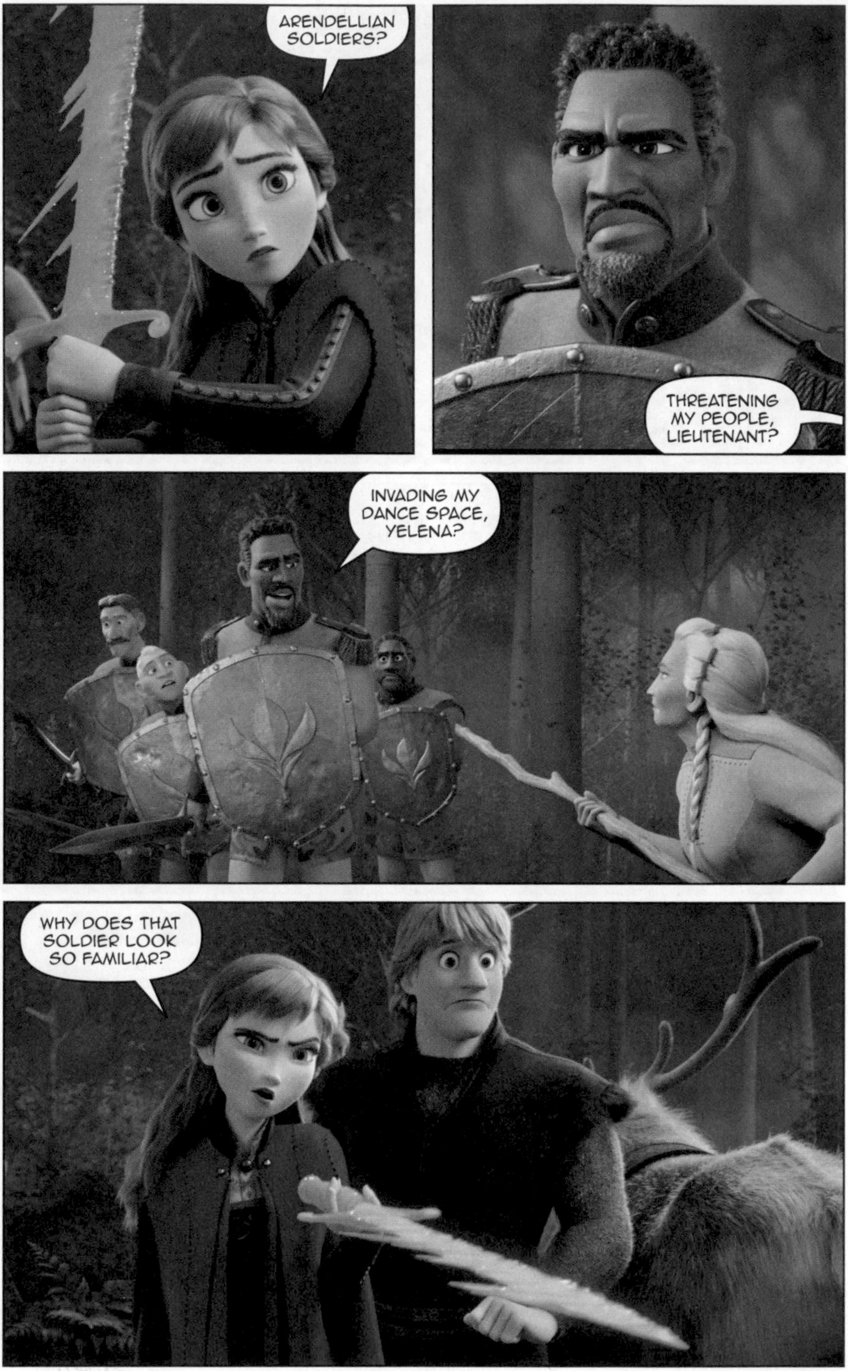
ARENDELLIAN SOLDIERS?
THREATENING MY PEOPLE, LIEUTENANT?
INVADING MY DANCE SPACE, YELENA?
WHY DOES THAT SOLDIER LOOK SO FAMILIAR?

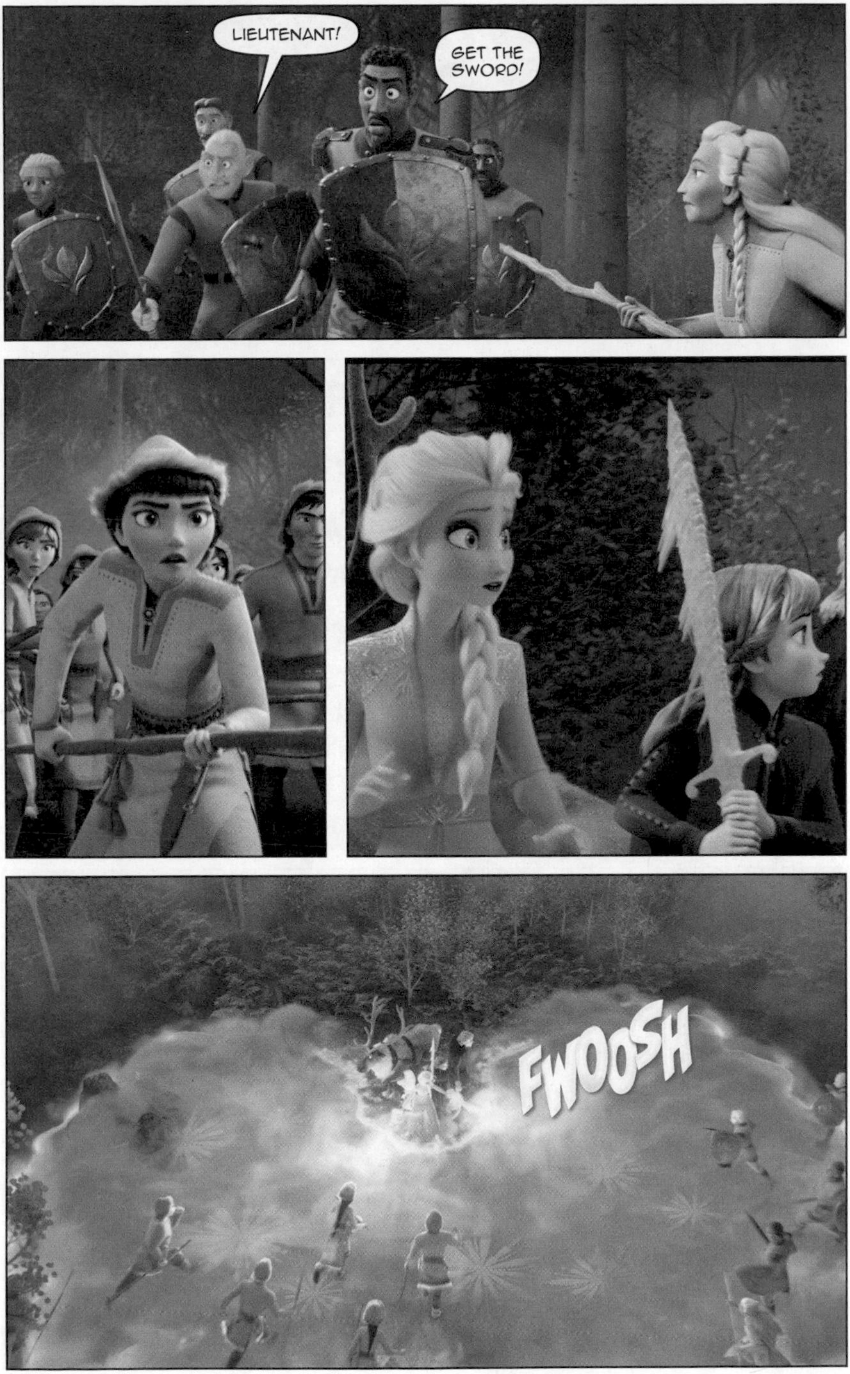
LIEUTENANT!
GET THE SWORD!
FWOOSH

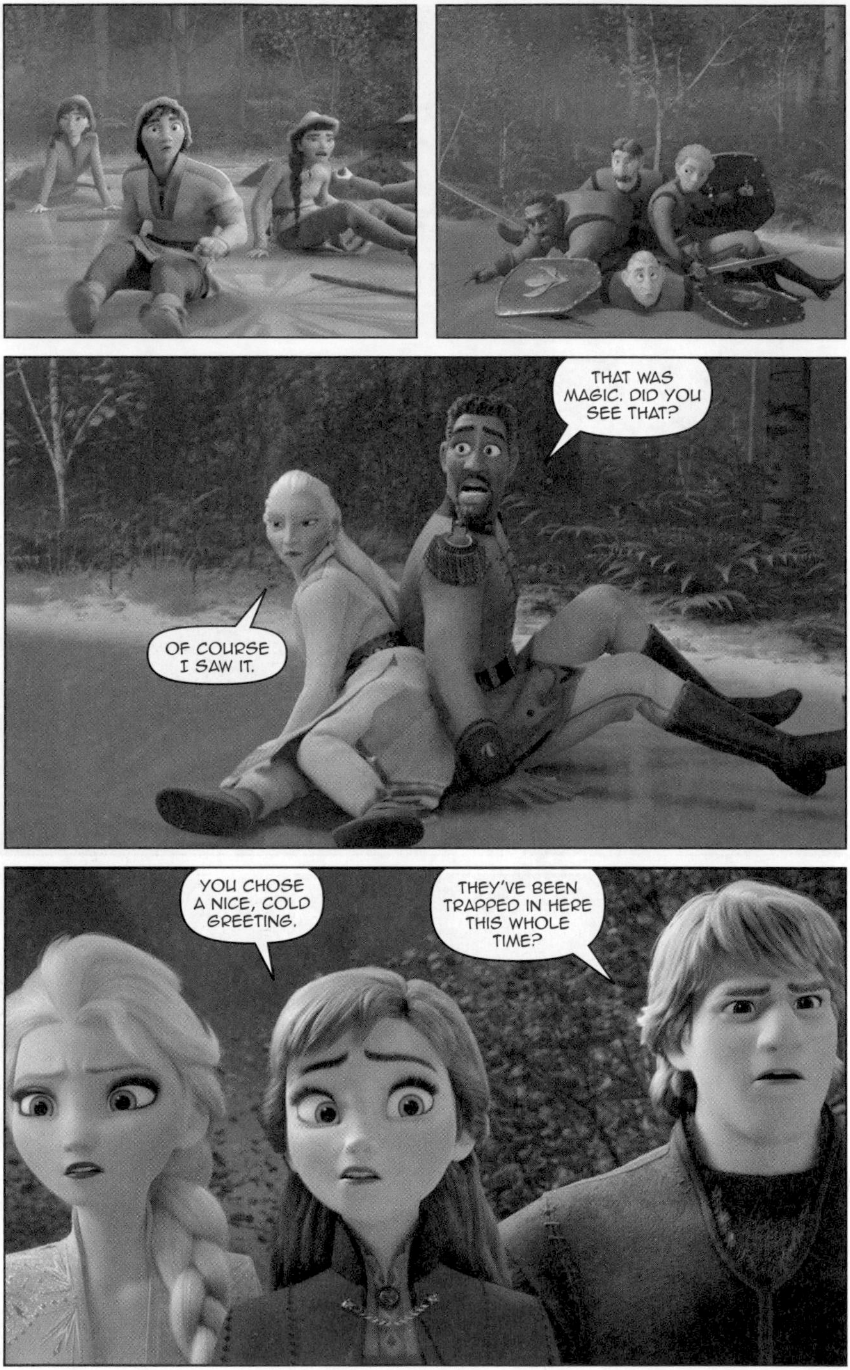
THAT WAS MAGIC. DID YOU SEE THAT?
OF COURSE I SAW IT.
YOU CHOSE A NICE, COLD GREETING.
THEY'VE BEEN TRAPPED IN HERE THIS WHOLE TIME?

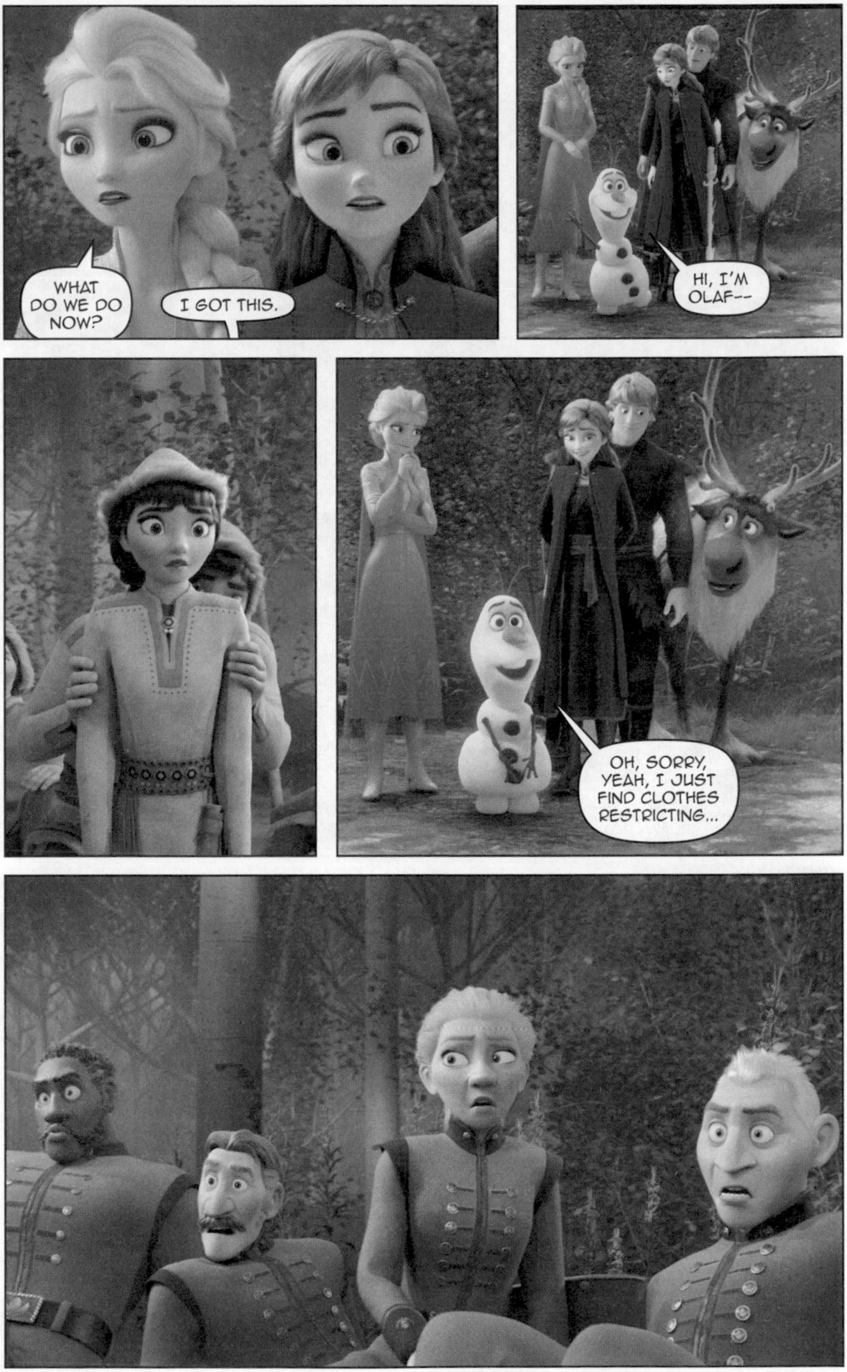
WHAT DO WE DO NOW?
I GOT THIS.
HI, I'M OLAF--
OH, SORRY, YEAH, I JUST FIND CLOTHES RESTRICTING...

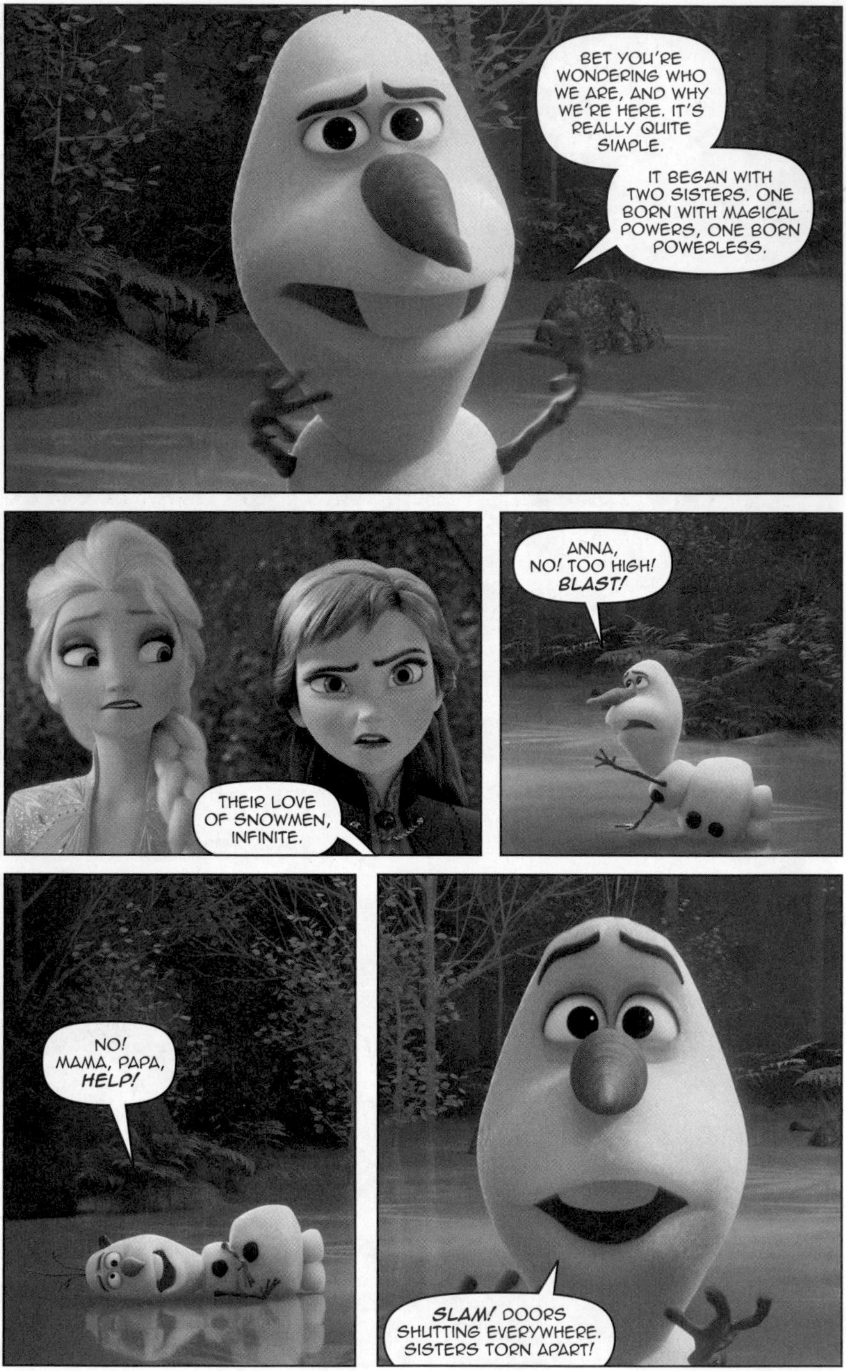
BET YOU'RE WONDERING WHO WE ARE, AND WHY WE'RE HERE. IT'S REALLY QUITE SIMPLE.
IT BEGAN WITH TWO SISTERS. ONE BORN WITH MAGICAL POWERS, ONE BORN POWERLESS.
THEIR LOVE OF SNOWMEN, INFINITE.
ANNA, NO! TOO HIGH! BLAST!
NO! MAMA, PAPA, HELP!
SLAM! DOORS SHUTTING EVERYWHERE. SISTERS TORN APART!

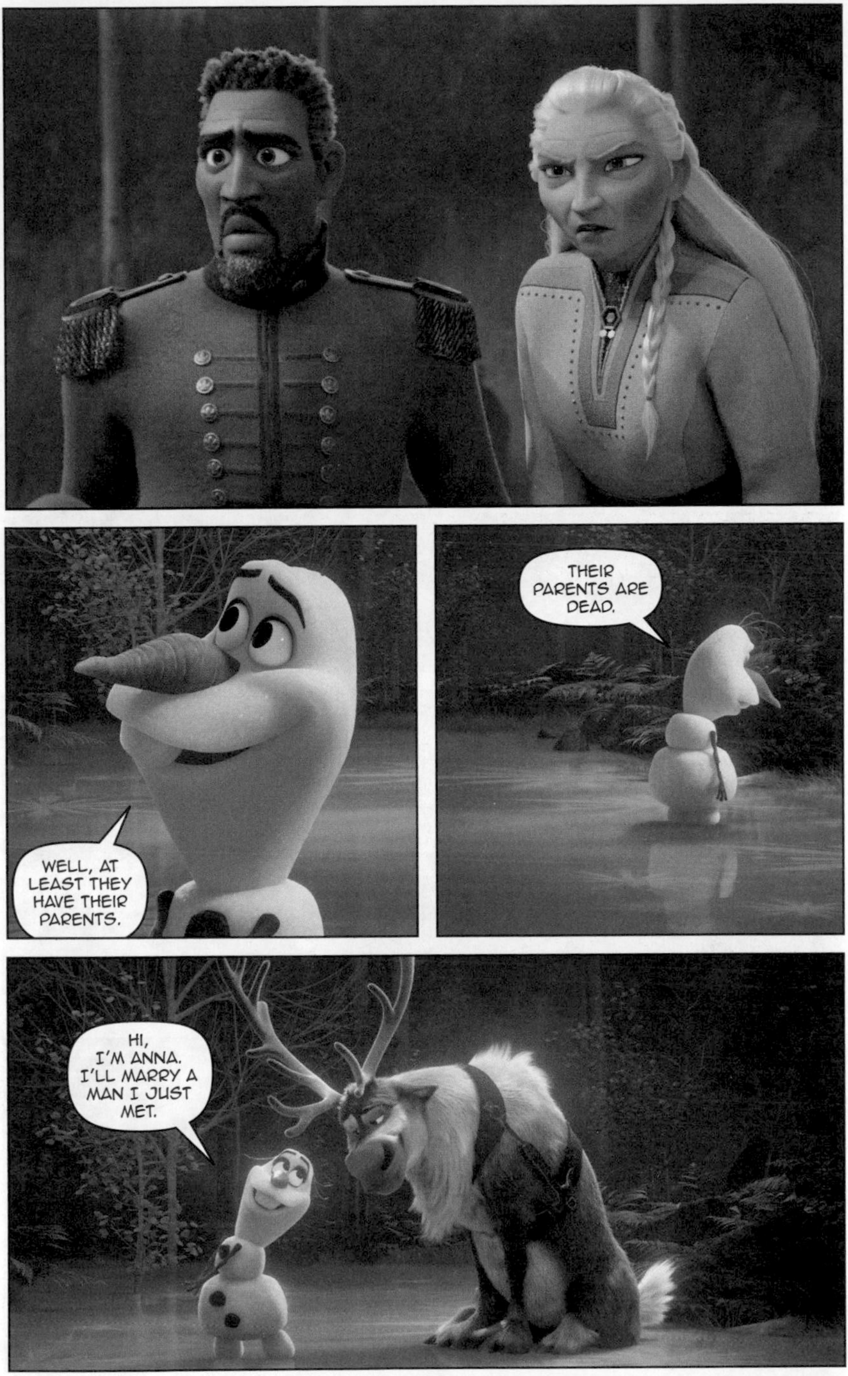
WELL, AT LEAST THEY HAVE THEIR PARENTS.
THEIR PARENTS ARE DEAD.
HI, I'M ANNA. I'LL MARRY A MAN I JUST MET.

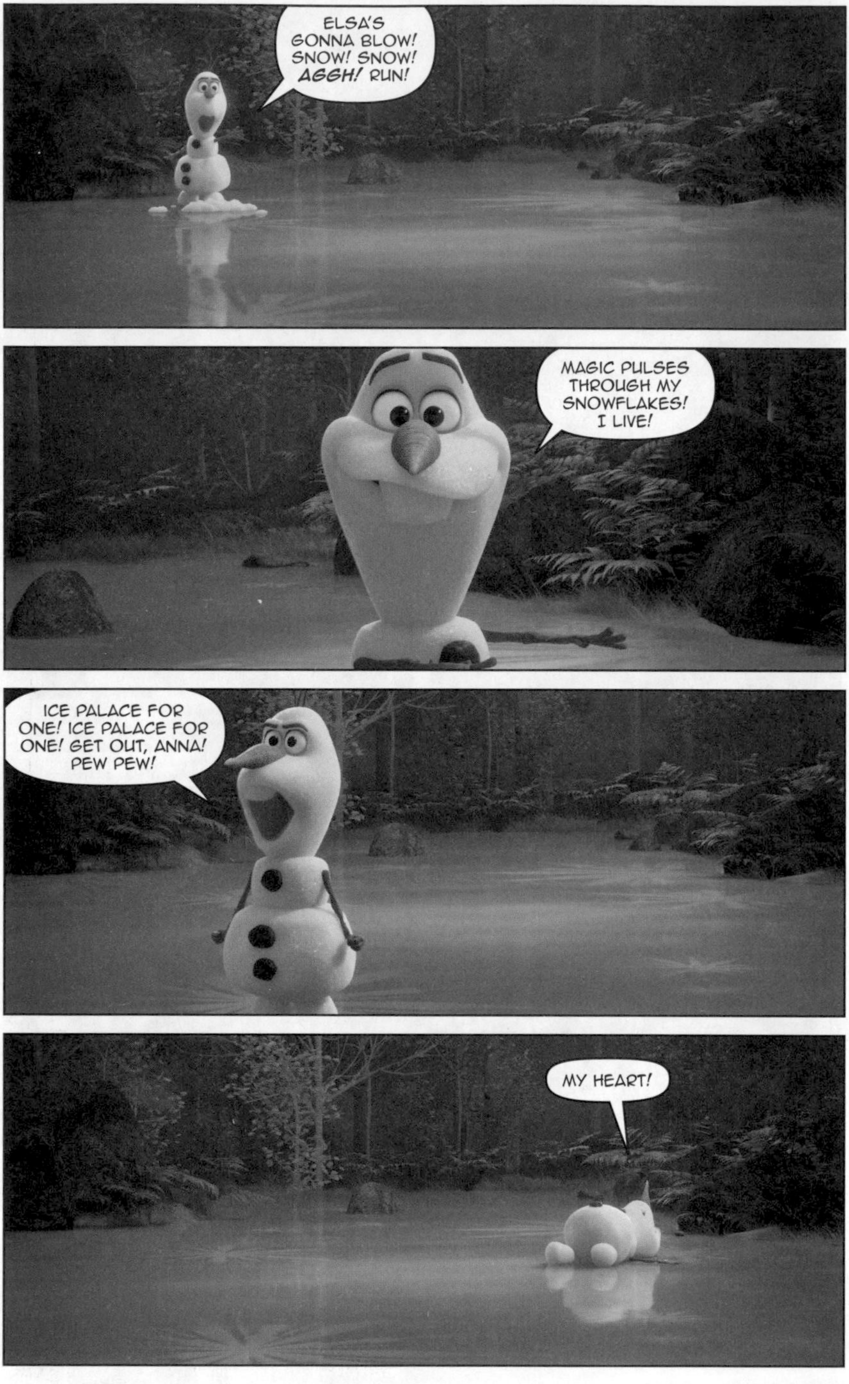
ELSA'S GONNA BLOW! SNOW! SNOW! AGGH! RUN!
MAGIC PULSES THROUGH MY SNOWFLAKES! I LIVE!
ICE PALACE FOR ONE! ICE PALACE FOR ONE! GET OUT, ANNA! PEW PEW!
MY HEART!

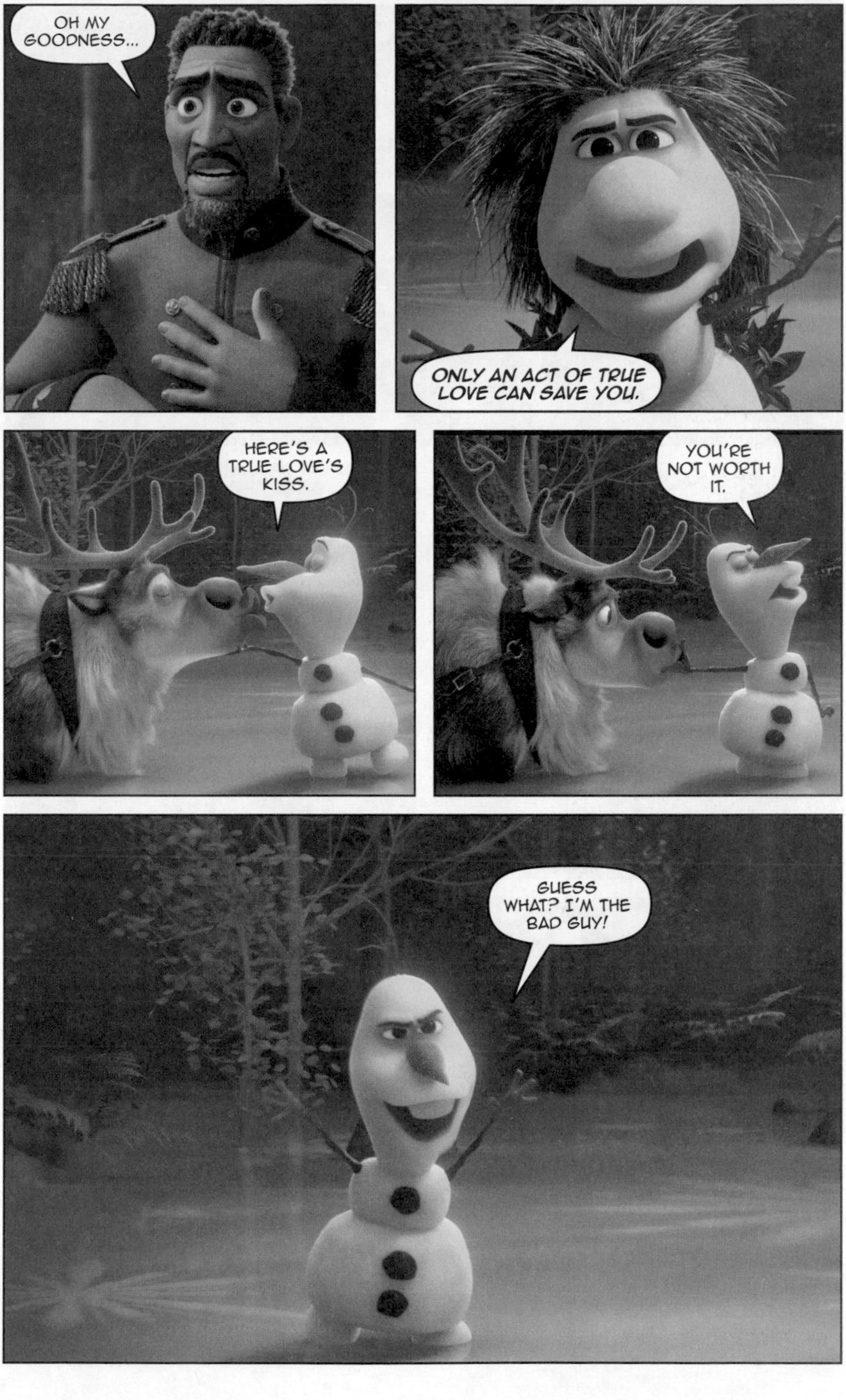
OH MY GOODNESS...
ONLY AN ACT OF TRUE LOVE CAN SAVE YOU.
HERE'S A TRUE LOVE'S KISS.
YOU'RE NOT WORTH IT.
GUESS WHAT? I'M THE BAD GUY!

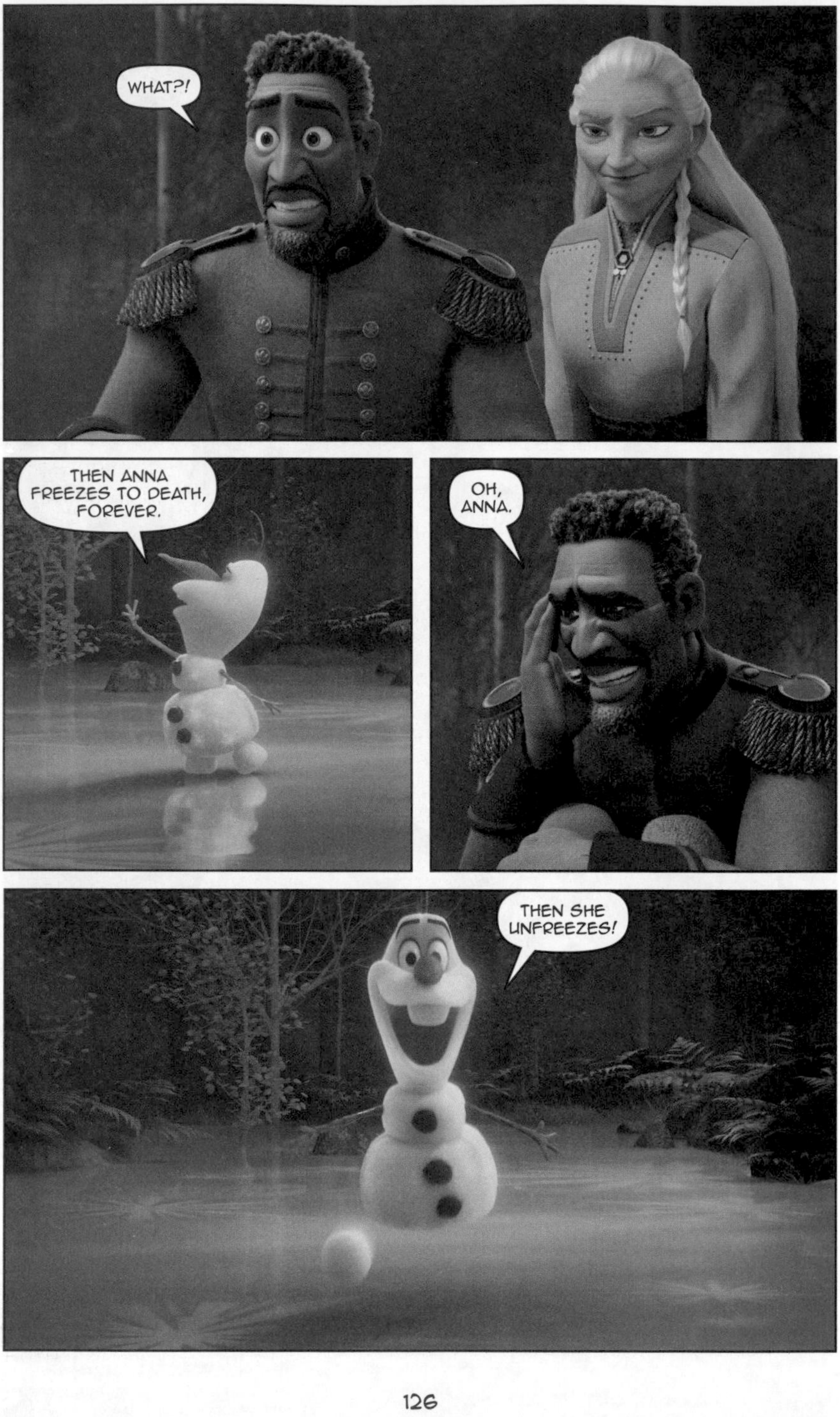
WHAT?!
THEN ANNA FREEZES TO DEATH, FOREVER.
OH, ANNA.
THEN SHE UNFREEZES!

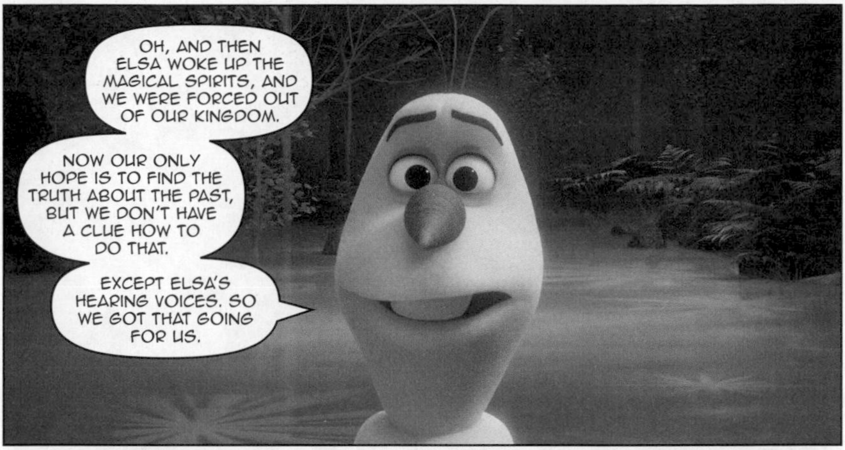
OH, AND THEN ELSA WOKE UP THE MAGICAL SPIRITS, AND WE WERE FORCED OUT OF OUR KINGDOM.
NOW OUR ONLY HOPE IS TO FIND THE TRUTH ABOUT THE PAST, BUT WE DON'T HAVE A CLUE HOW TO DO THAT.
EXCEPT ELSA'S HEARING VOICES. SO WE GOT THAT GOING FOR US.

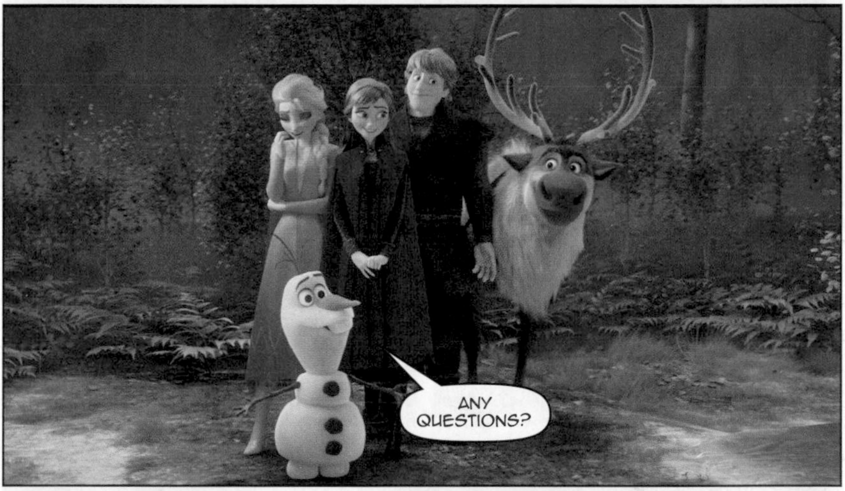
ANY QUESTIONS?

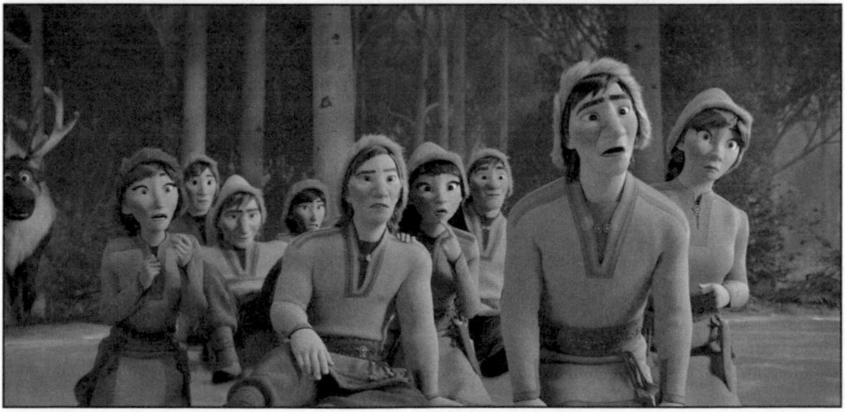

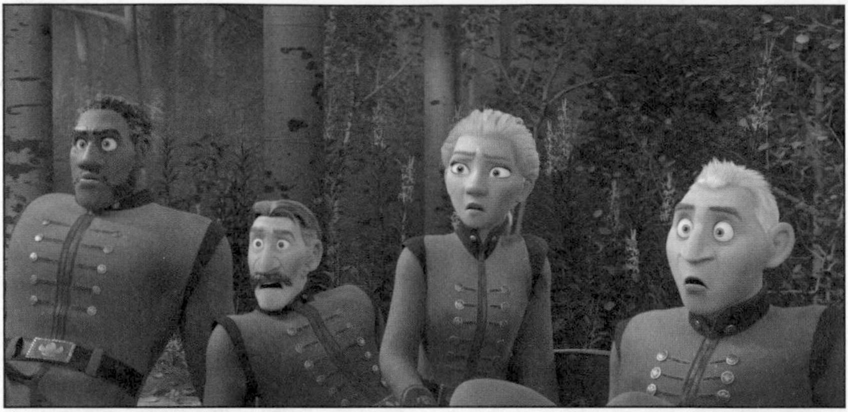

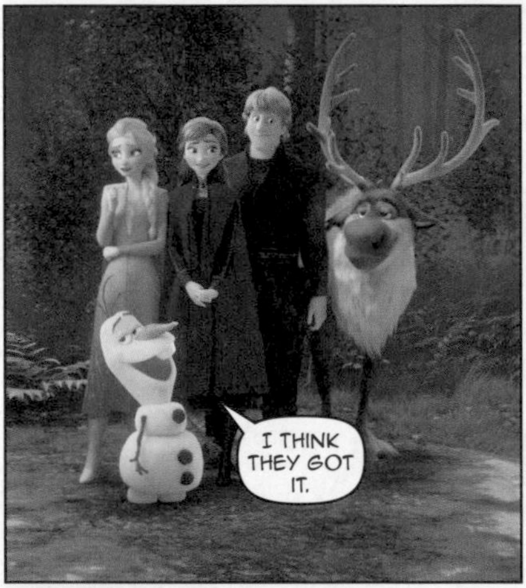
I THINK THEY GOT IT.

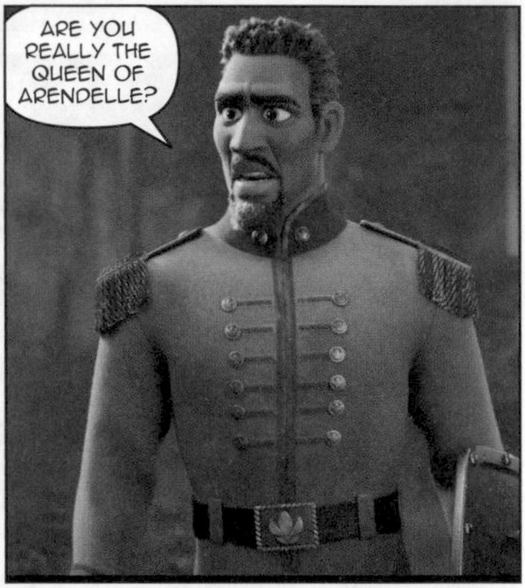
ARE YOU REALLY THE QUEEN OF ARENDELLE?

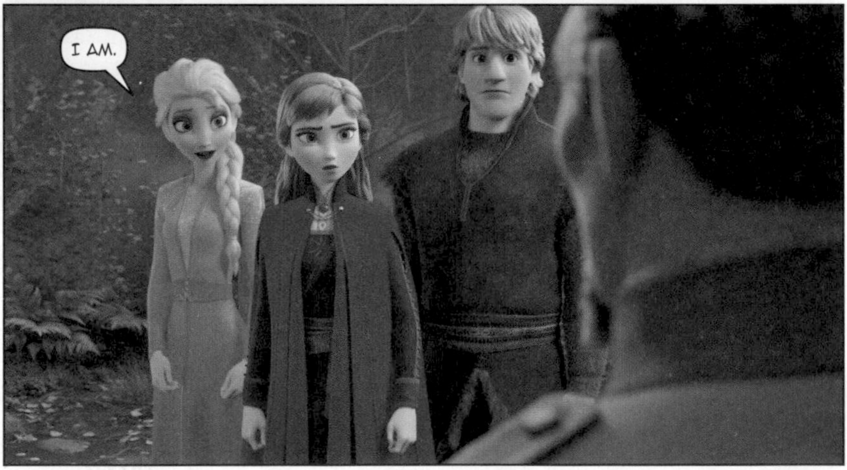
I AM.

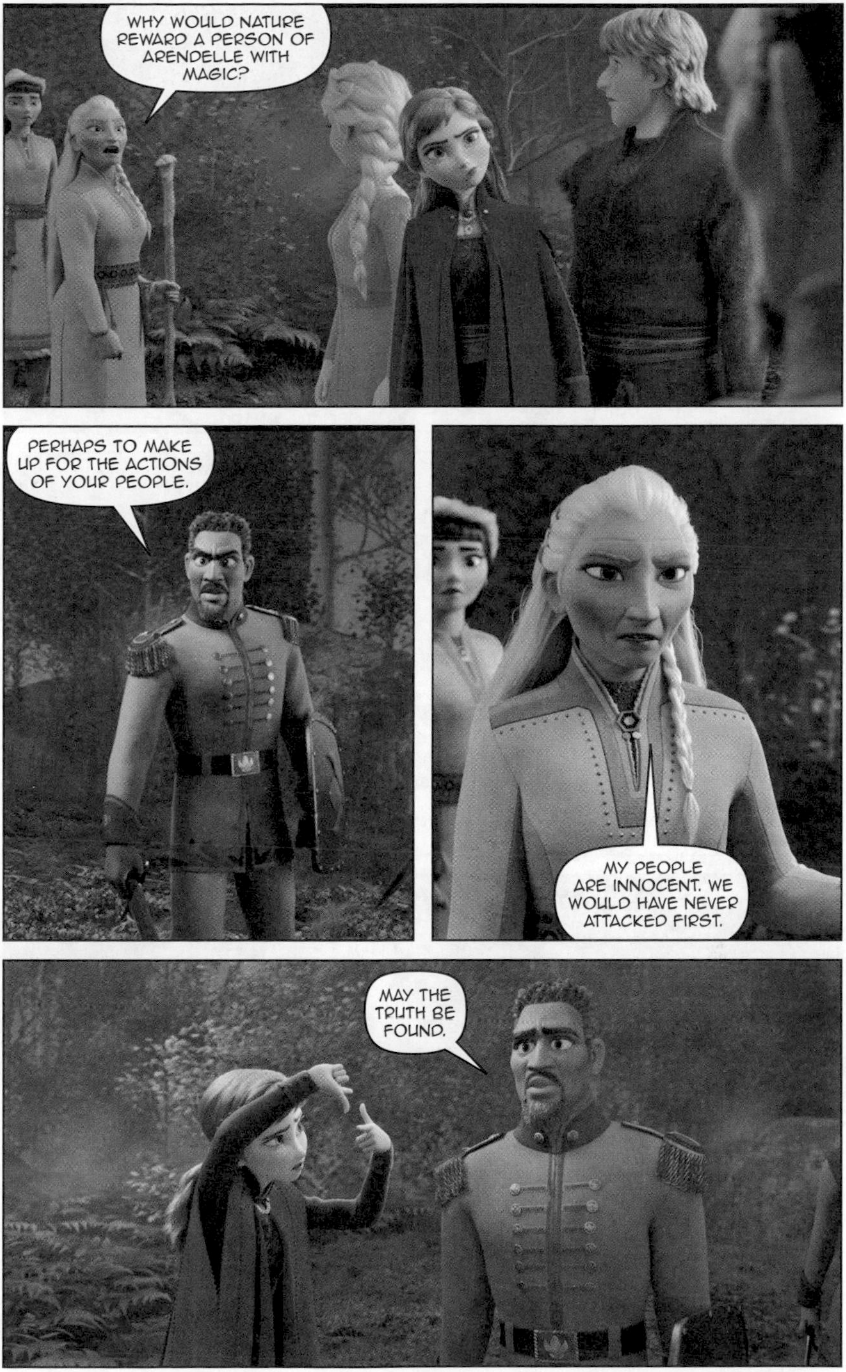
WHY WOULD NATURE REWARD A PERSON OF ARENDELLE WITH MAGIC?
PERHAPS TO MAKE UP FOR THE ACTIONS OF YOUR PEOPLE.
MY PEOPLE ARE INNOCENT. WE WOULD HAVE NEVER ATTACKED FIRST.
MAY THE TRUTH BE FOUND.

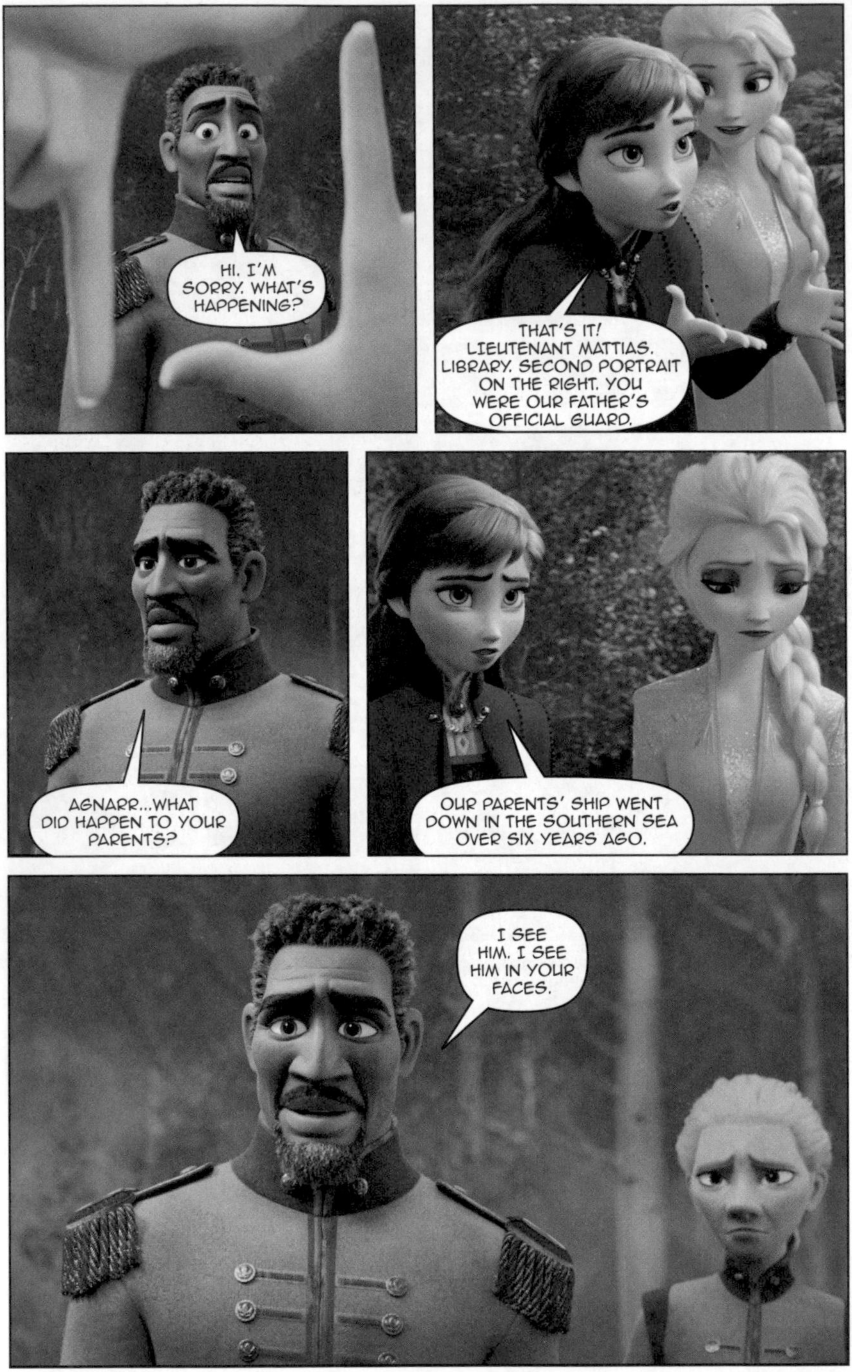
HI. I'M SORRY. WHAT'S HAPPENING?
THAT'S IT! LIEUTENANT MATTIAS. LIBRARY. SECOND PORTRAIT ON THE RIGHT. YOU WERE OUR FATHER'S OFFICIAL GUARD.
AGNARR...WHAT DID HAPPEN TO YOUR PARENTS?
OUR PARENTS' SHIP WENT DOWN IN THE SOUTHERN SEA OVER SIX YEARS AGO.
I SEE HIM. I SEE HIM IN YOUR FACES.

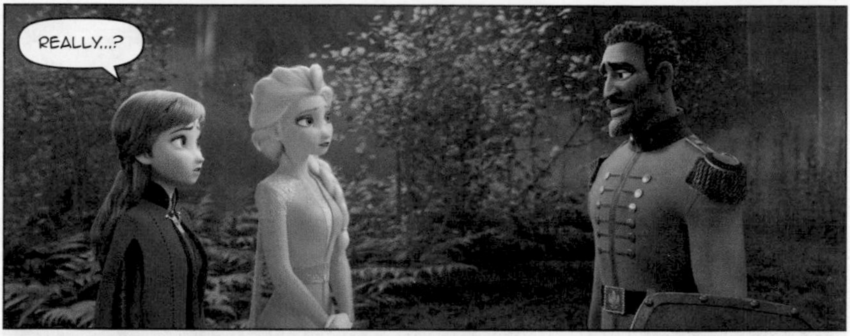
REALLY...?

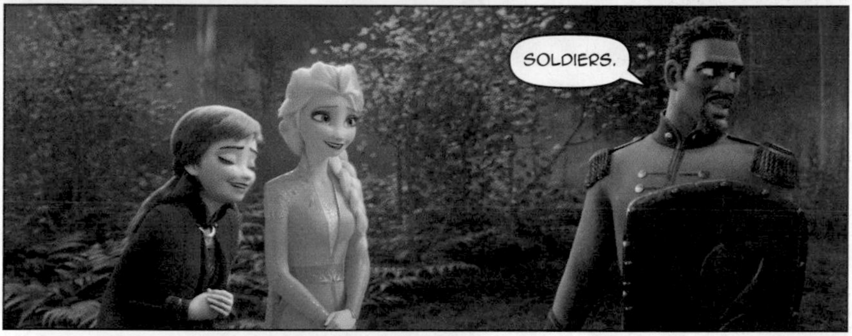
SOLDIERS.

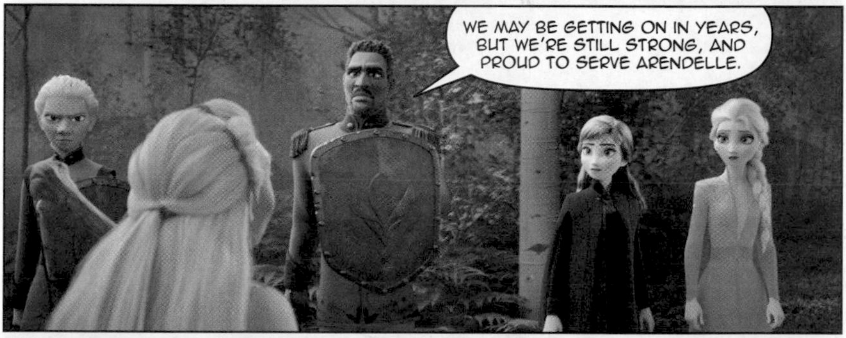
WE MAY BE GETTING ON IN YEARS, BUT WE'RE STILL STRONG, AND PROUD TO SERVE ARENDELLE.

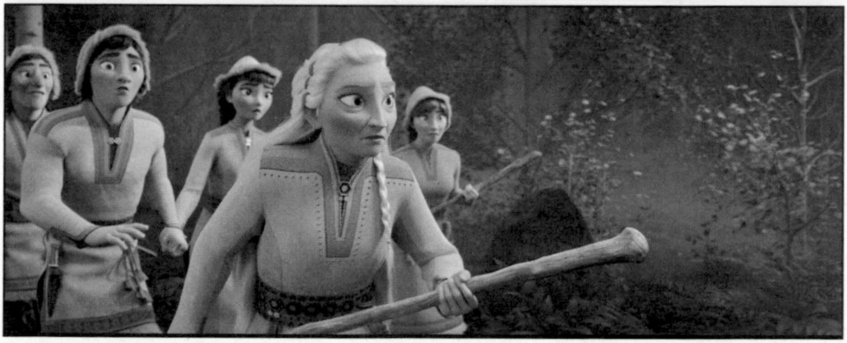

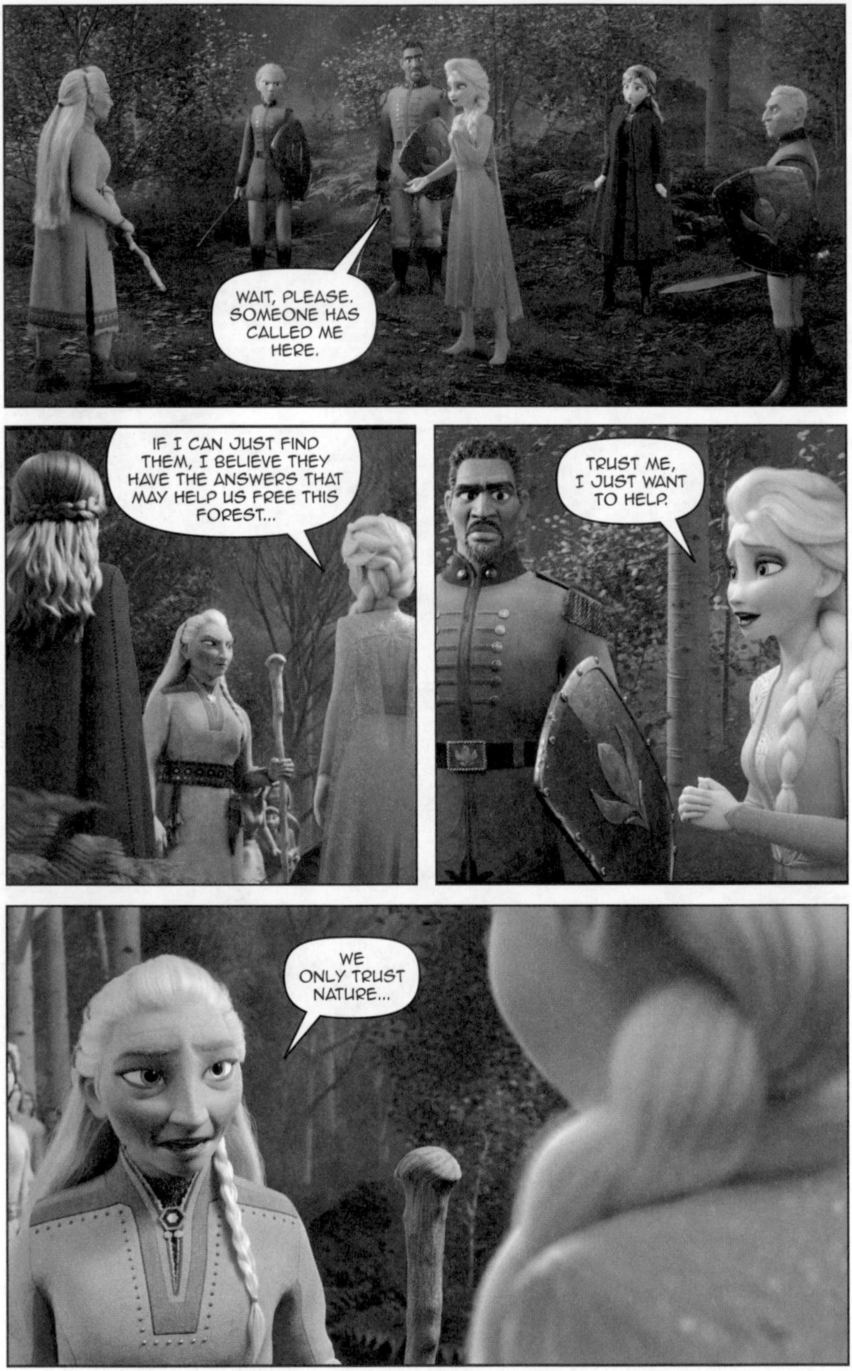
WAIT, PLEASE. SOMEONE HAS CALLED ME HERE.
IF I CAN JUST FIND THEM, I BELIEVE THEY HAVE THE ANSWERS THAT MAY HELP US FREE THIS FOREST...
TRUST ME, I JUST WANT TO HELP.
WE ONLY TRUST NATURE...

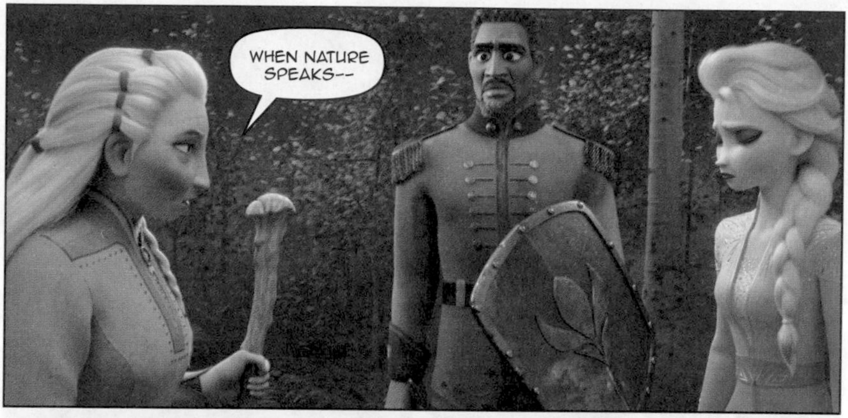
WHEN NATURE SPEAKS--

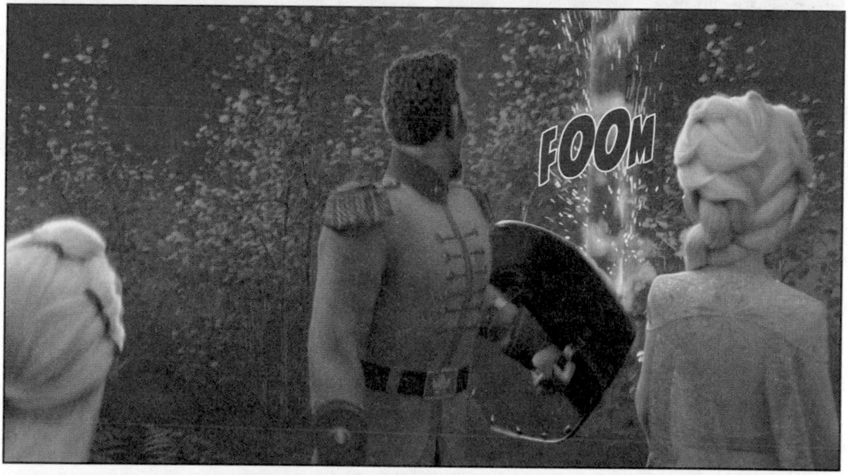
FOOM

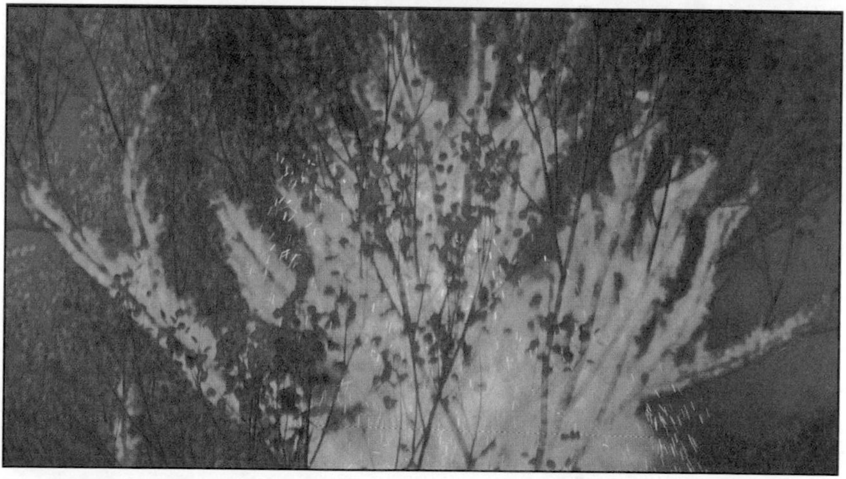

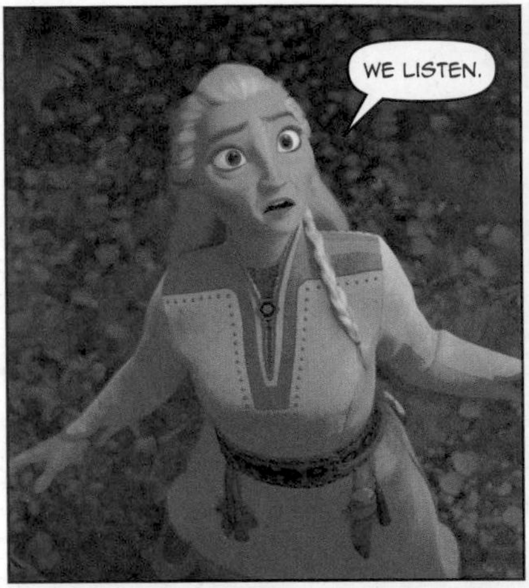
WE LISTEN.

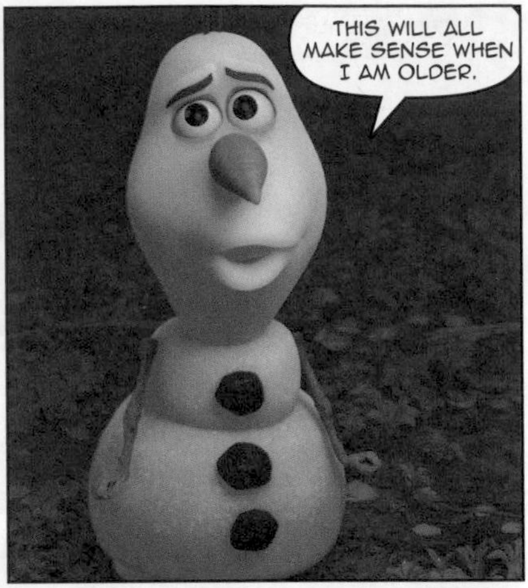
THIS WILL ALL MAKE SENSE WHEN I AM OLDER.

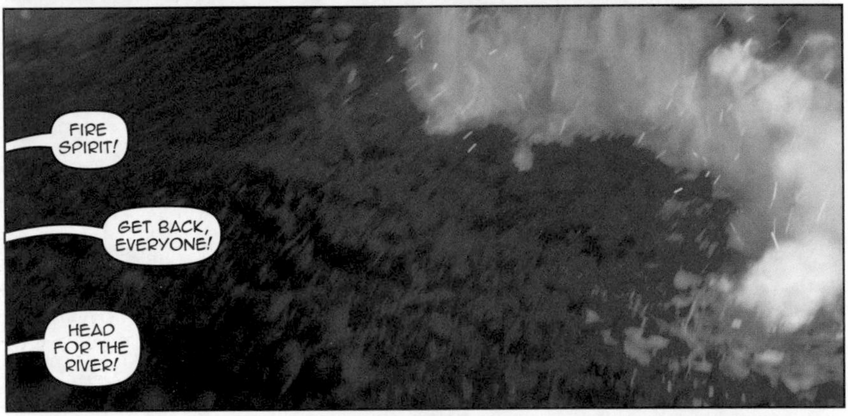
FIRE SPIRIT!
GET BACK, EVERYONE!
HEAD FOR THE RIVER!

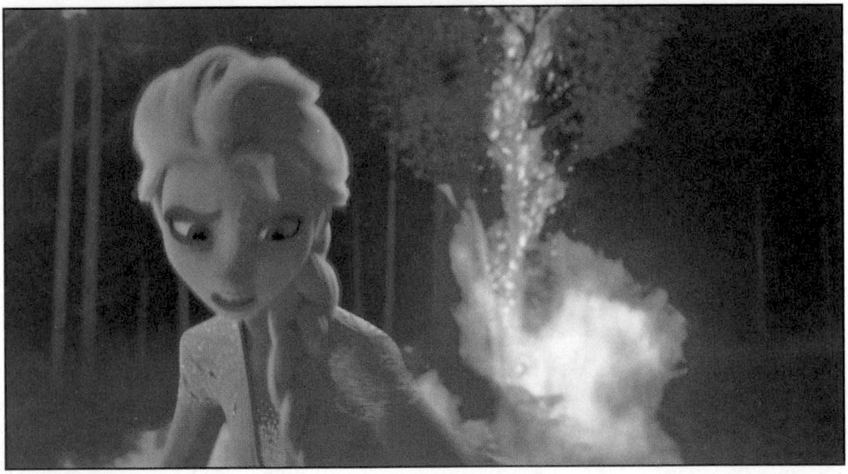

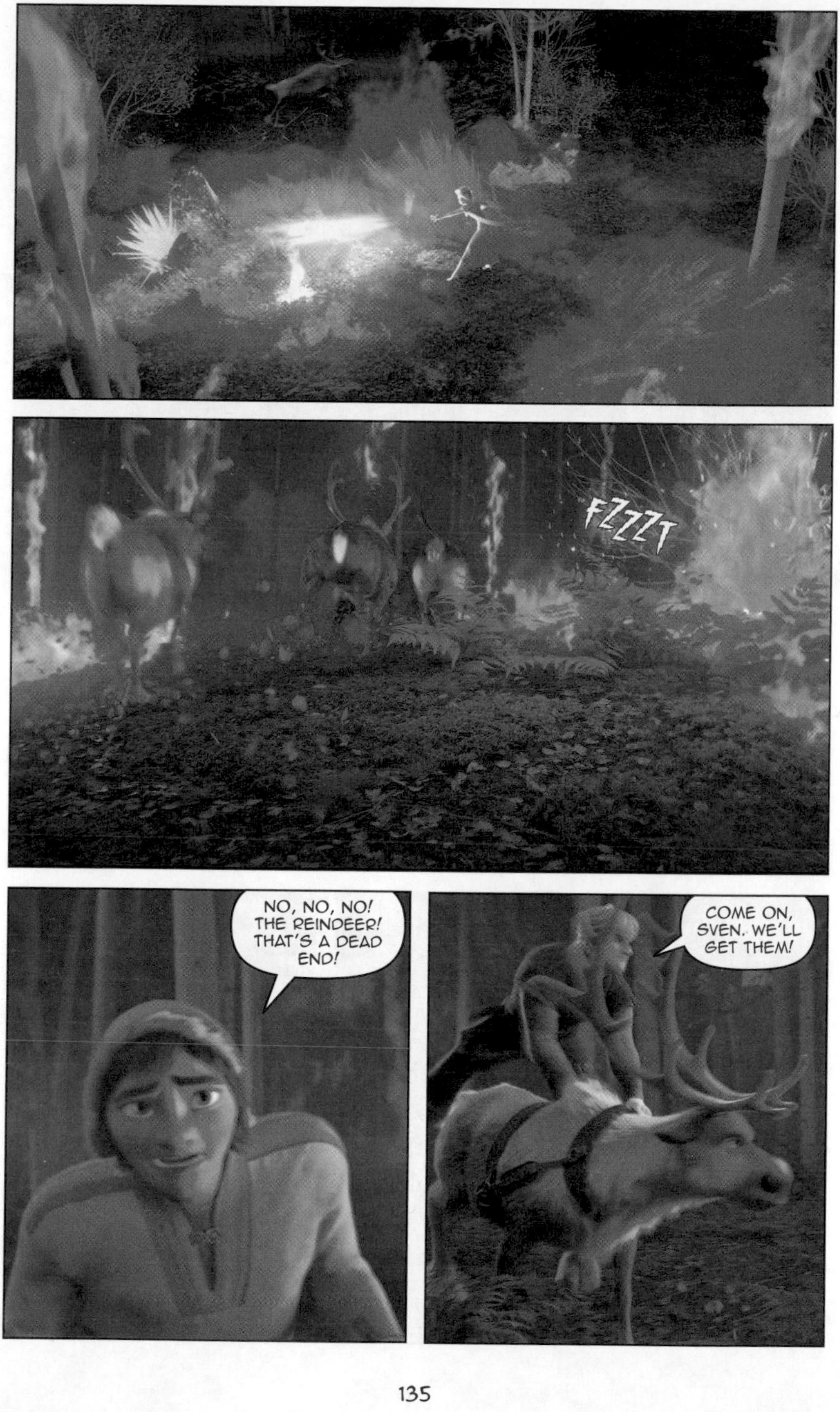
FZZZT
NO, NO, NO! THE REINDEER! THAT'S A DEAD END!
COME ON, SVEN. WE'LL GET THEM!

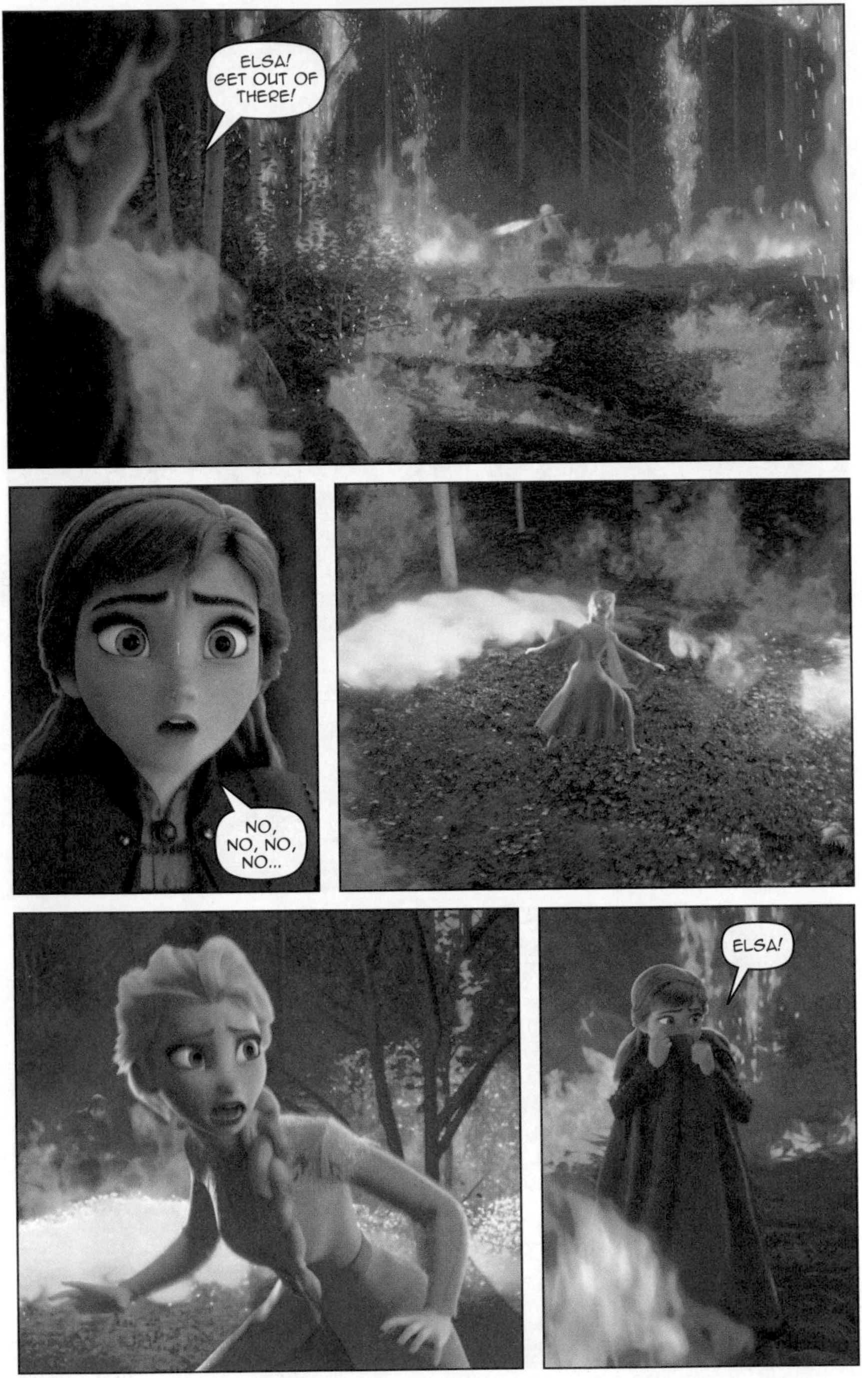
ELSA! GET OUT OF THERE!
NO, NO, NO, NO...
ELSA!

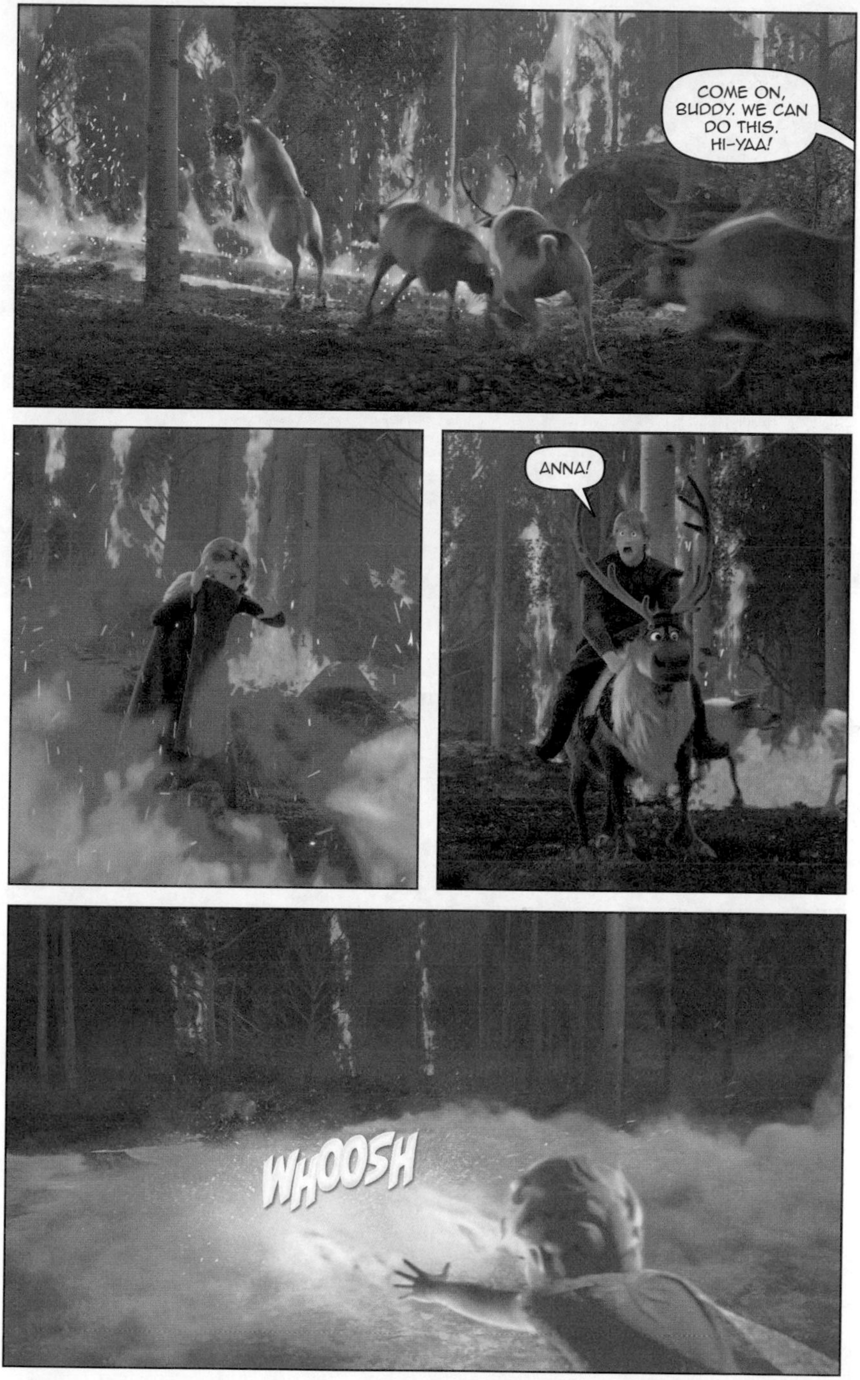
COME ON, BUDDY. WE CAN DO THIS. HI-YAA!
ANNA!
WHOOSH

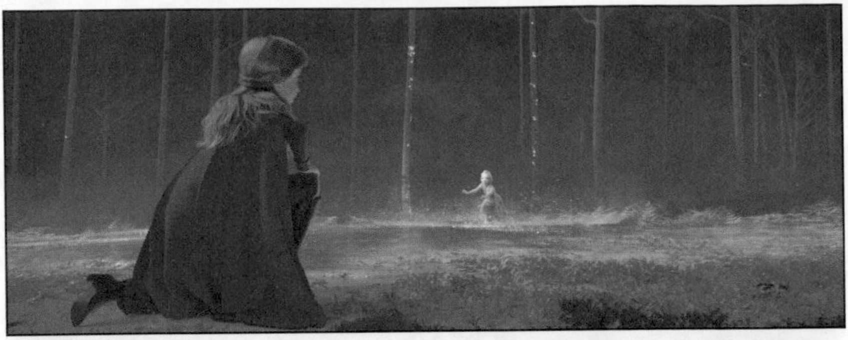

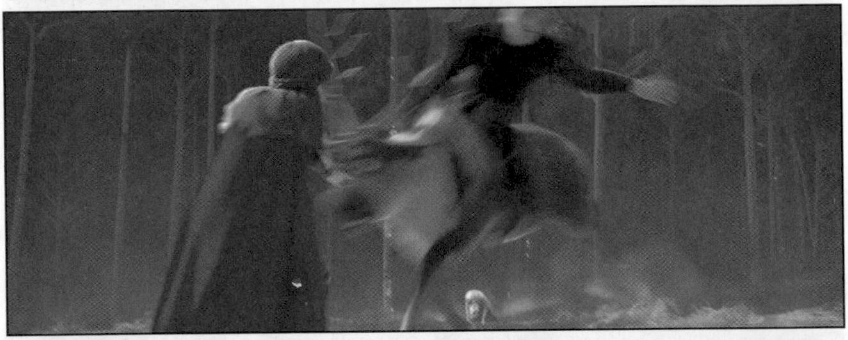

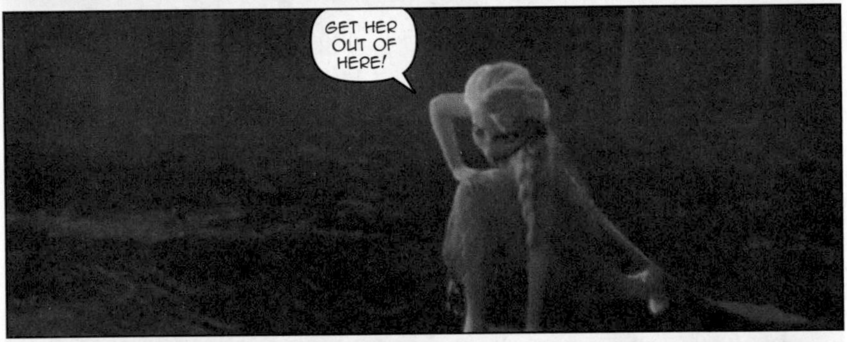
GET HER OUT OF HERE!

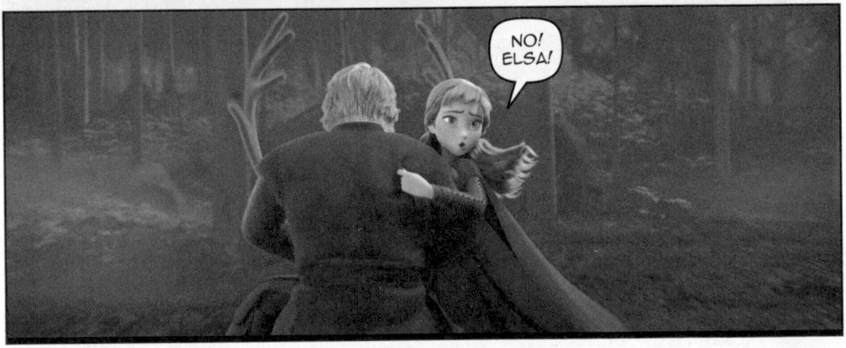
NO! ELSA!

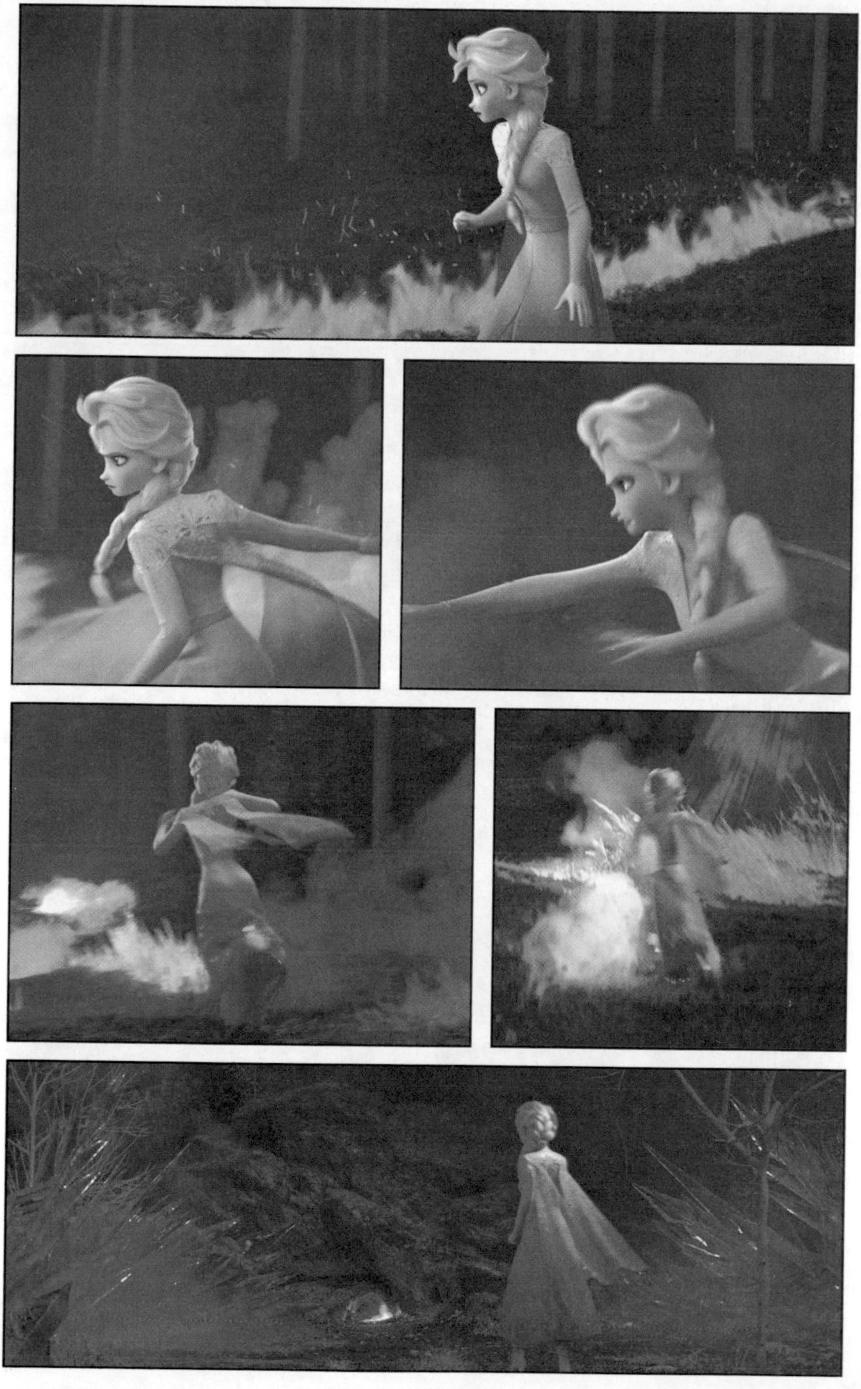

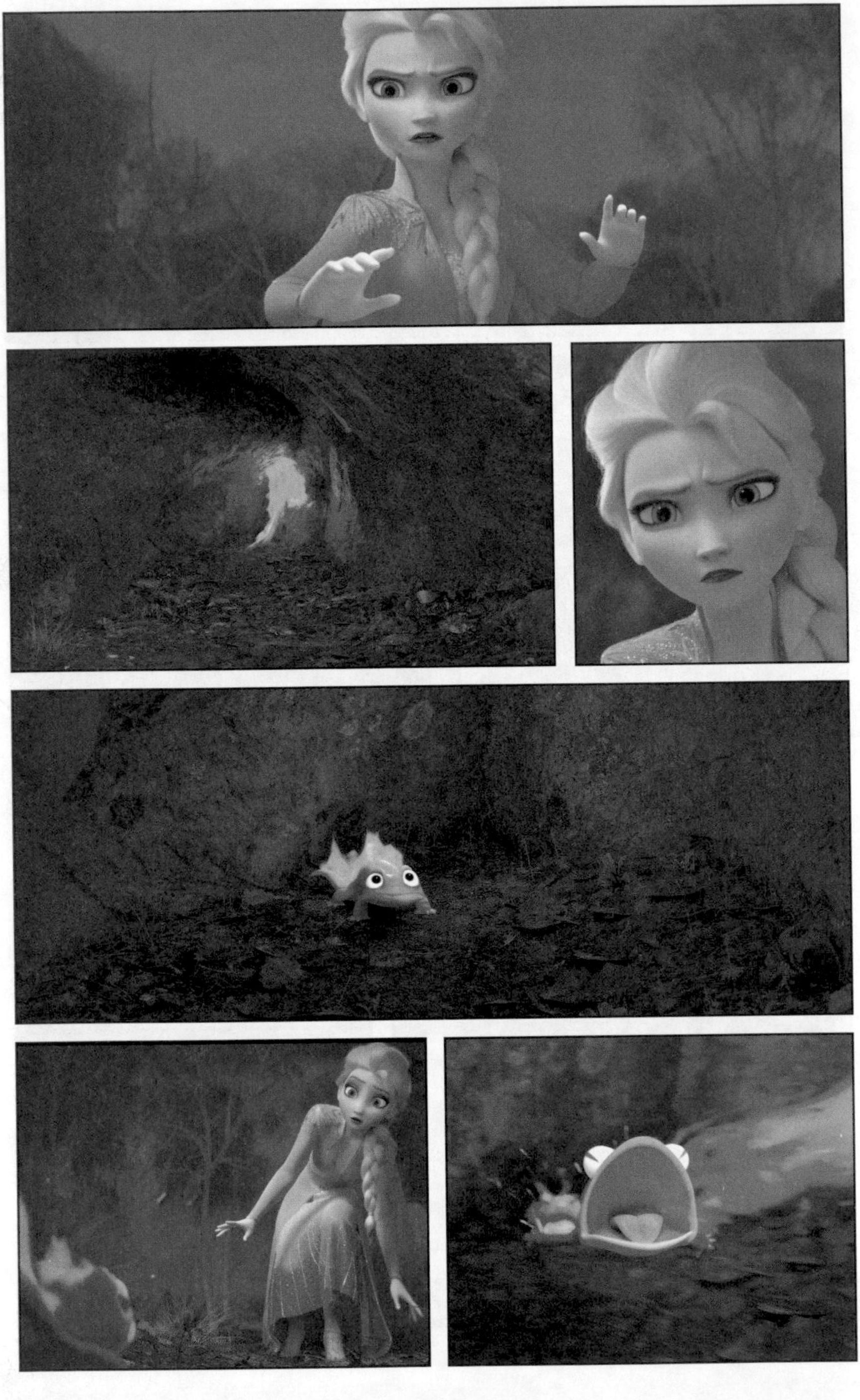

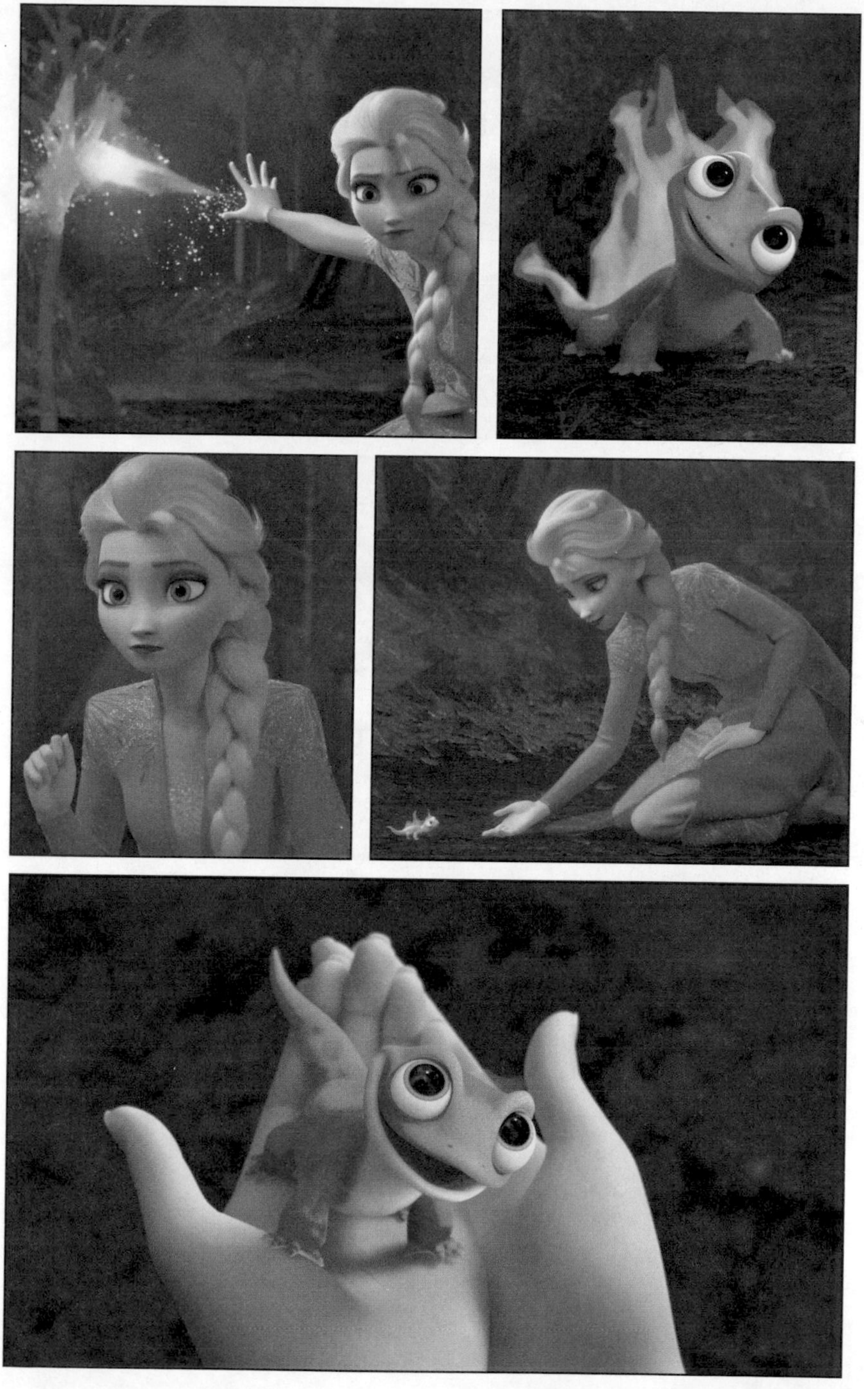

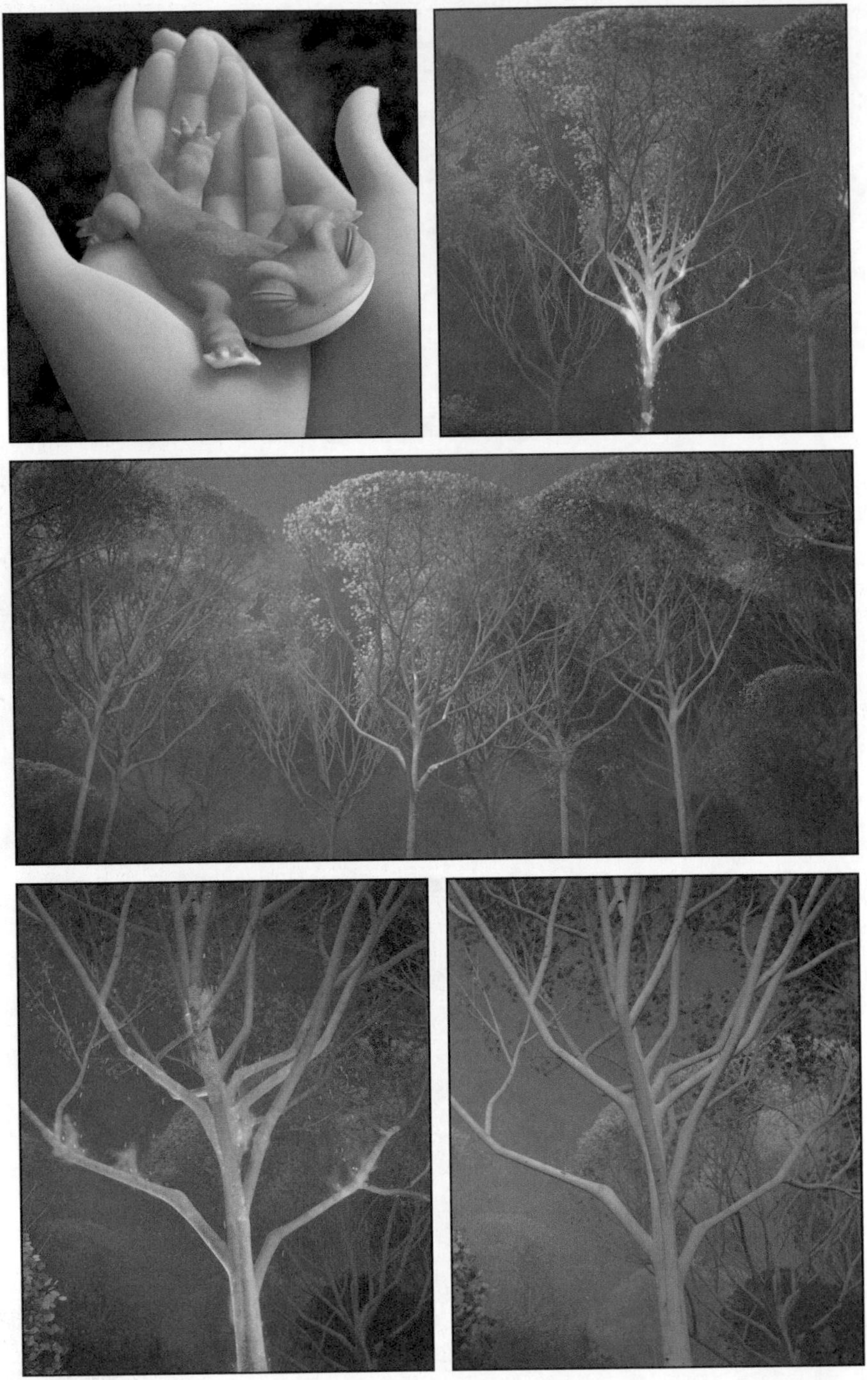

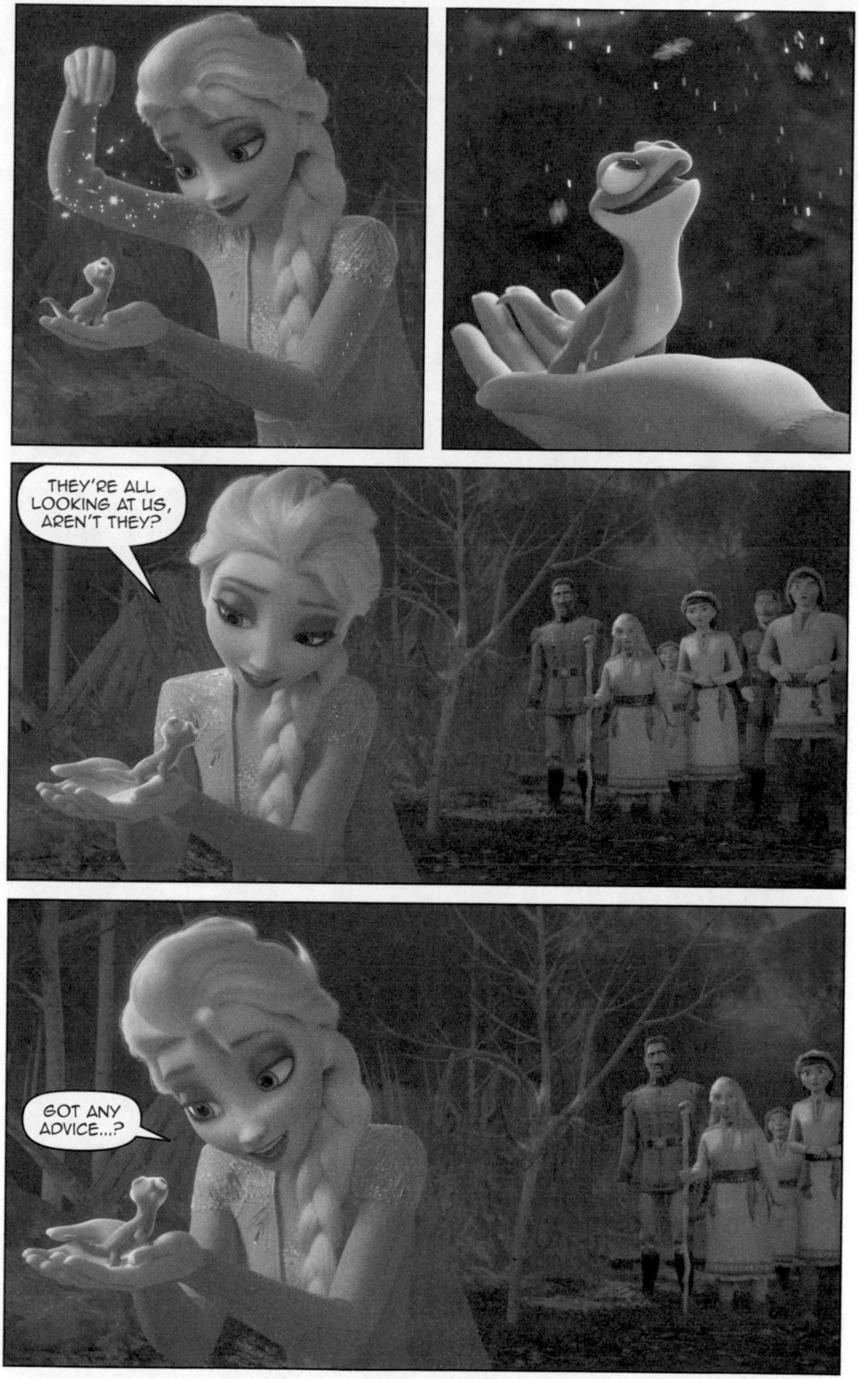
THEY'RE ALL LOOKING AT US, AREN'T THEY?
GOT ANY ADVICE...?

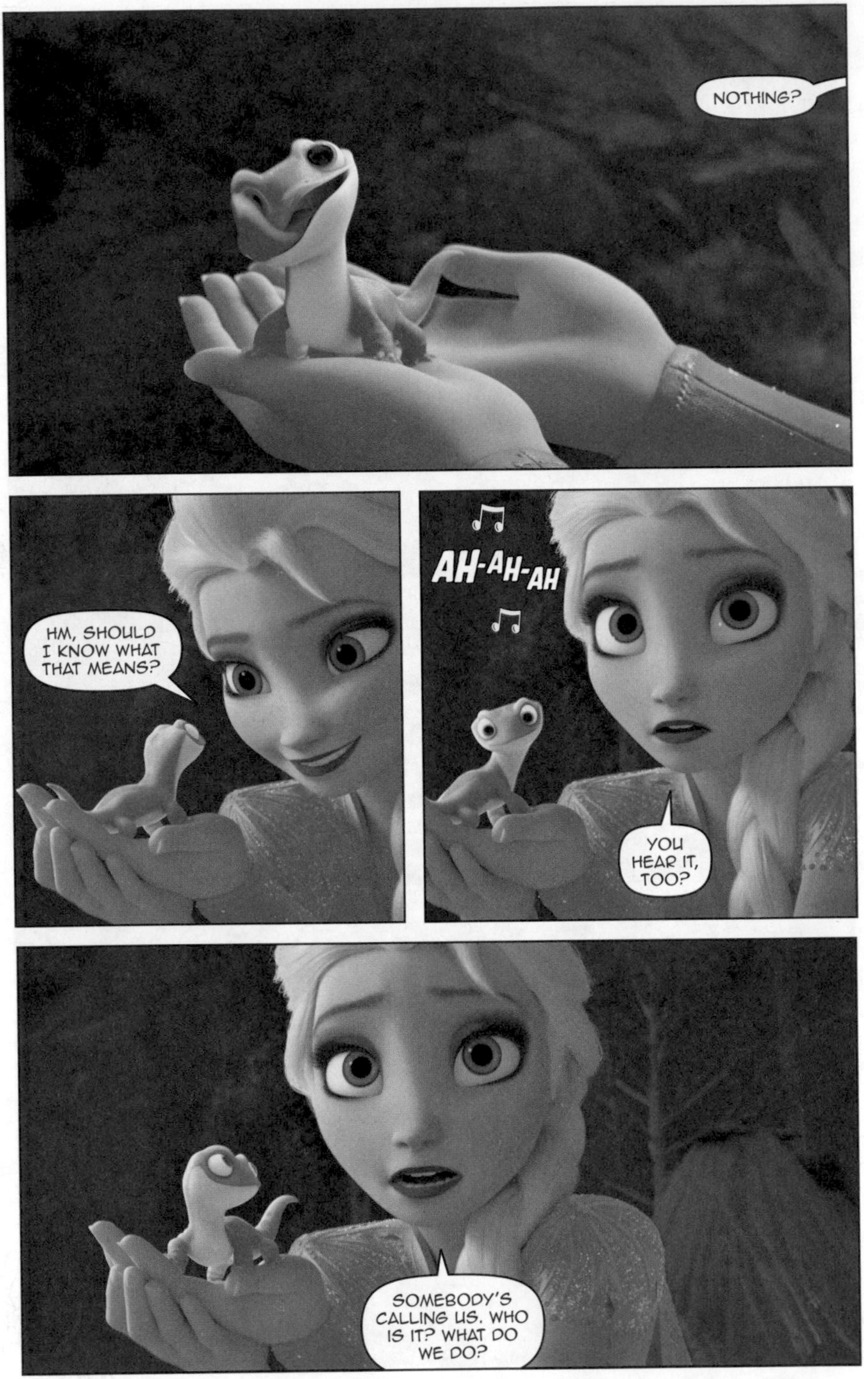
NOTHING?
HM, SHOULD I KNOW WHAT THAT MEANS?
AH-AH-AH
YOU HEAR IT, TOO?
SOMEBODY'S CALLING US. WHO IS IT? WHAT DO WE DO?

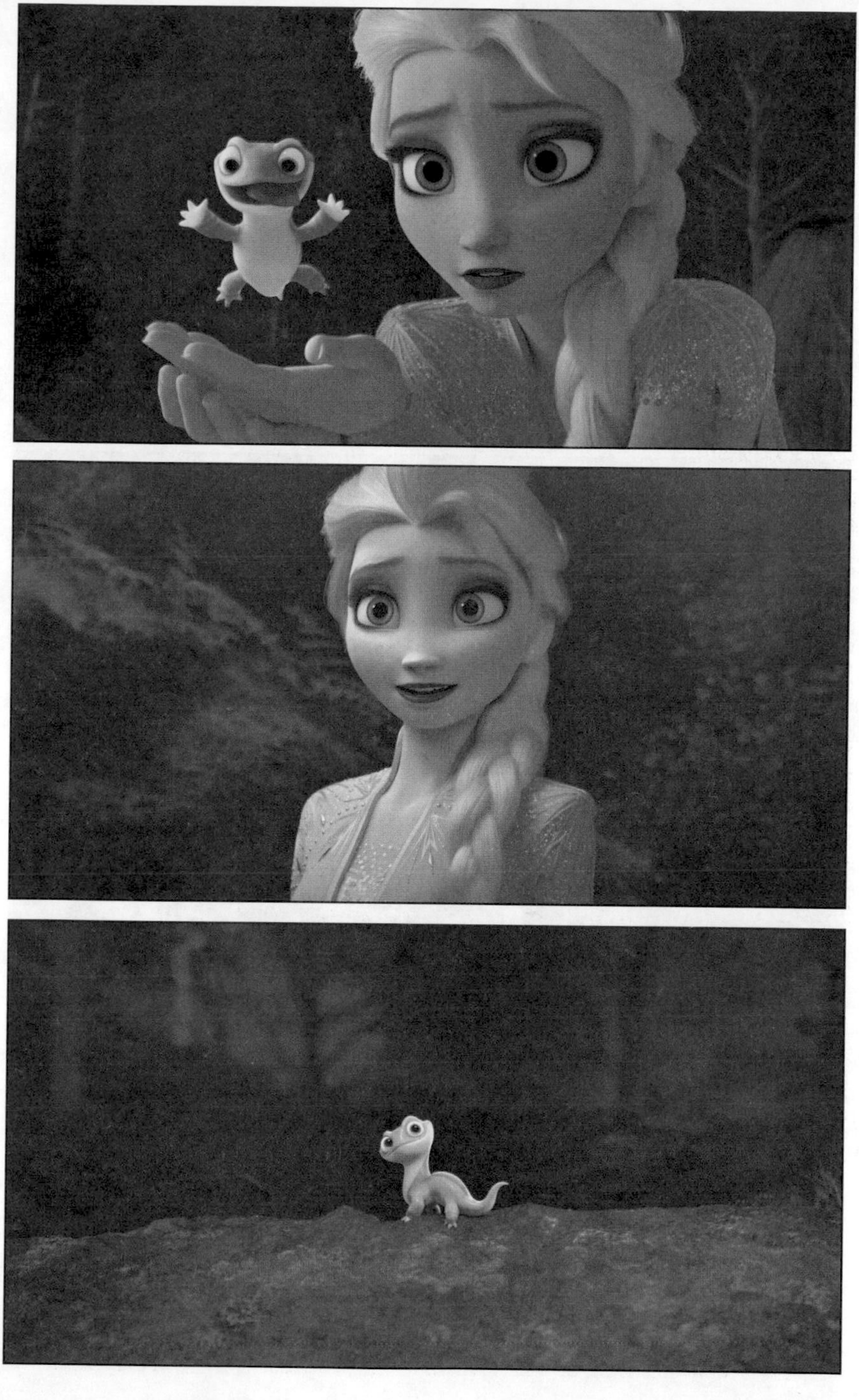

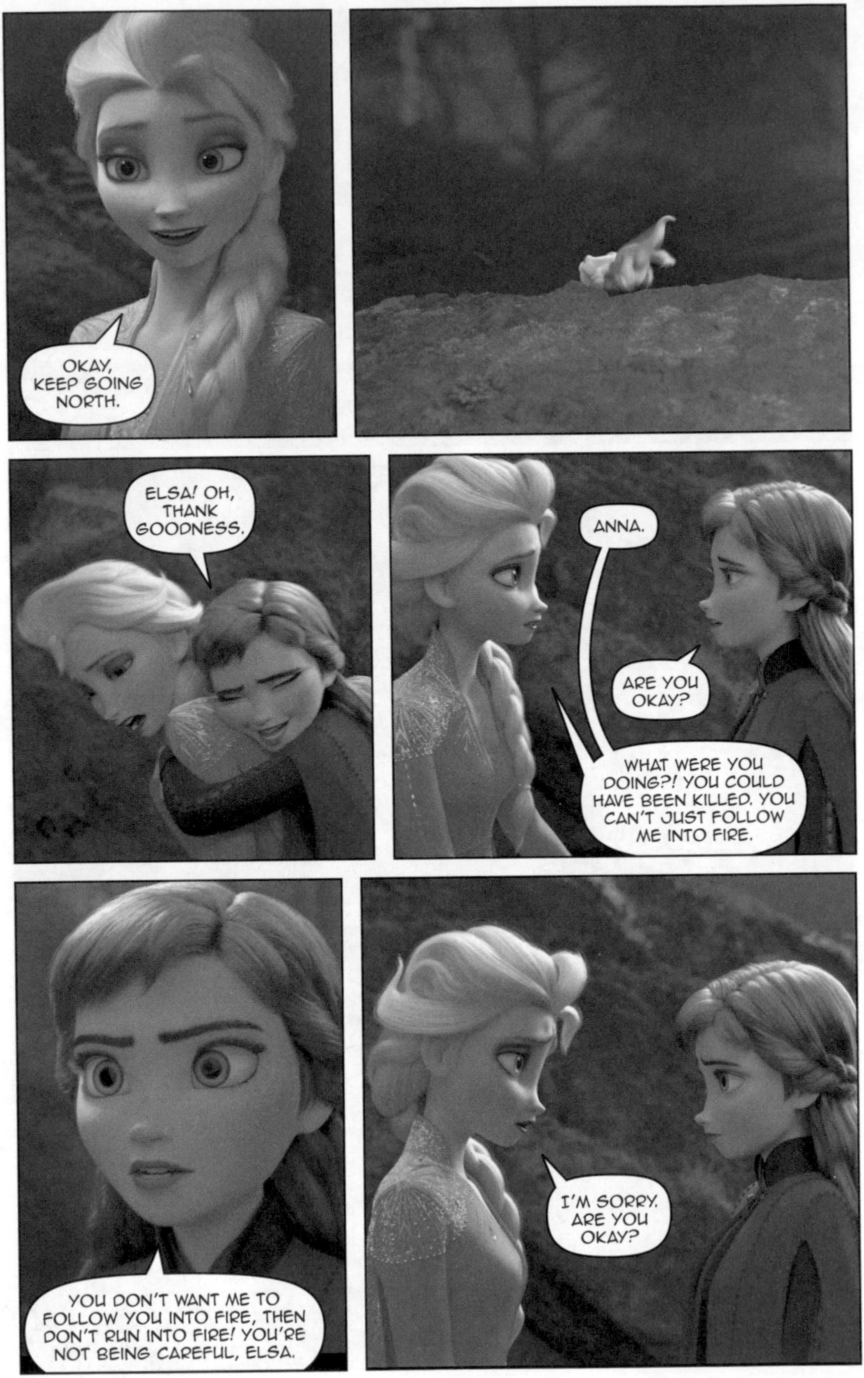
OKAY, KEEP GOING NORTH.
ELSA! OH, THANK GOODNESS.
ANNA.
ARE YOU OKAY?
WHAT WERE YOU DOING?! YOU COULD HAVE BEEN KILLED. YOU CAN'T JUST FOLLOW ME INTO FIRE.
YOU DON'T WANT ME TO FOLLOW YOU INTO FIRE, THEN DON'T RUN INTO FIRE! YOU'RE NOT BEING CAREFUL, ELSA.
I'M SORRY. ARE YOU OKAY?

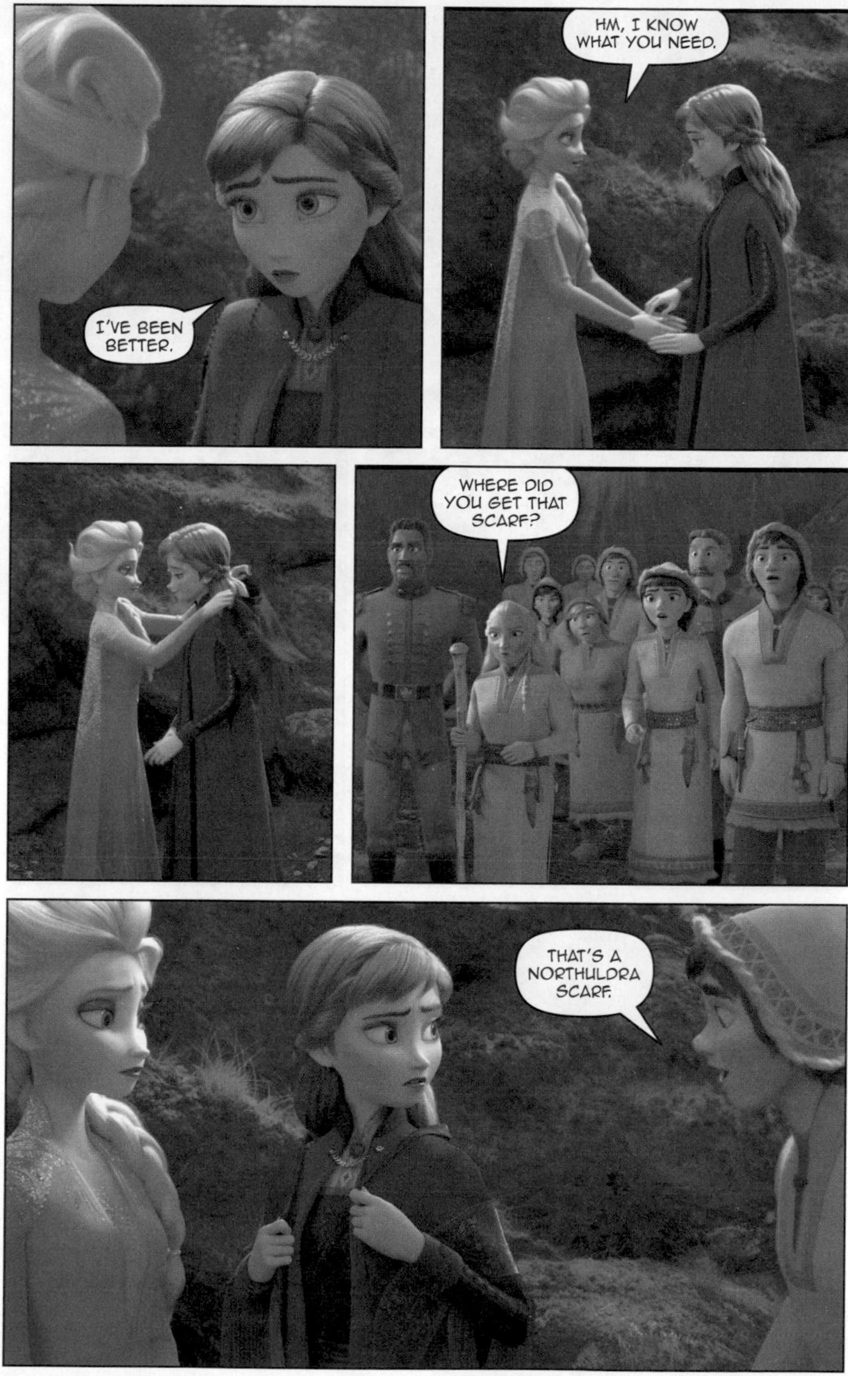
I'VE BEEN BETTER.
HM, I KNOW WHAT YOU NEED.
WHERE DID YOU GET THAT SCARF?
THAT'S A NORTHULDRA SCARF.

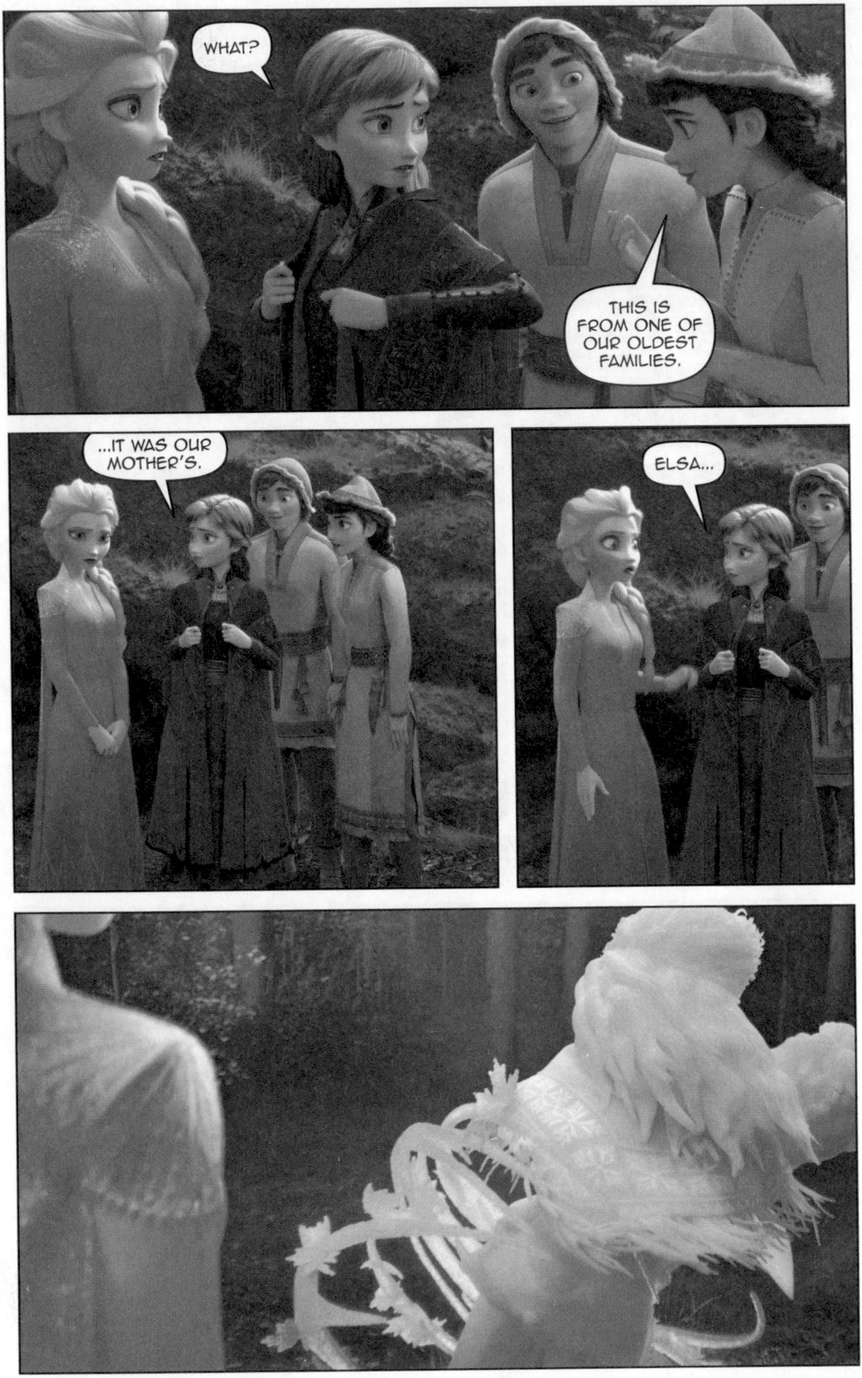
WHAT?
THIS IS FROM ONE OF OUR OLDEST FAMILIES.
...IT WAS OUR MOTHER'S.
ELSA...

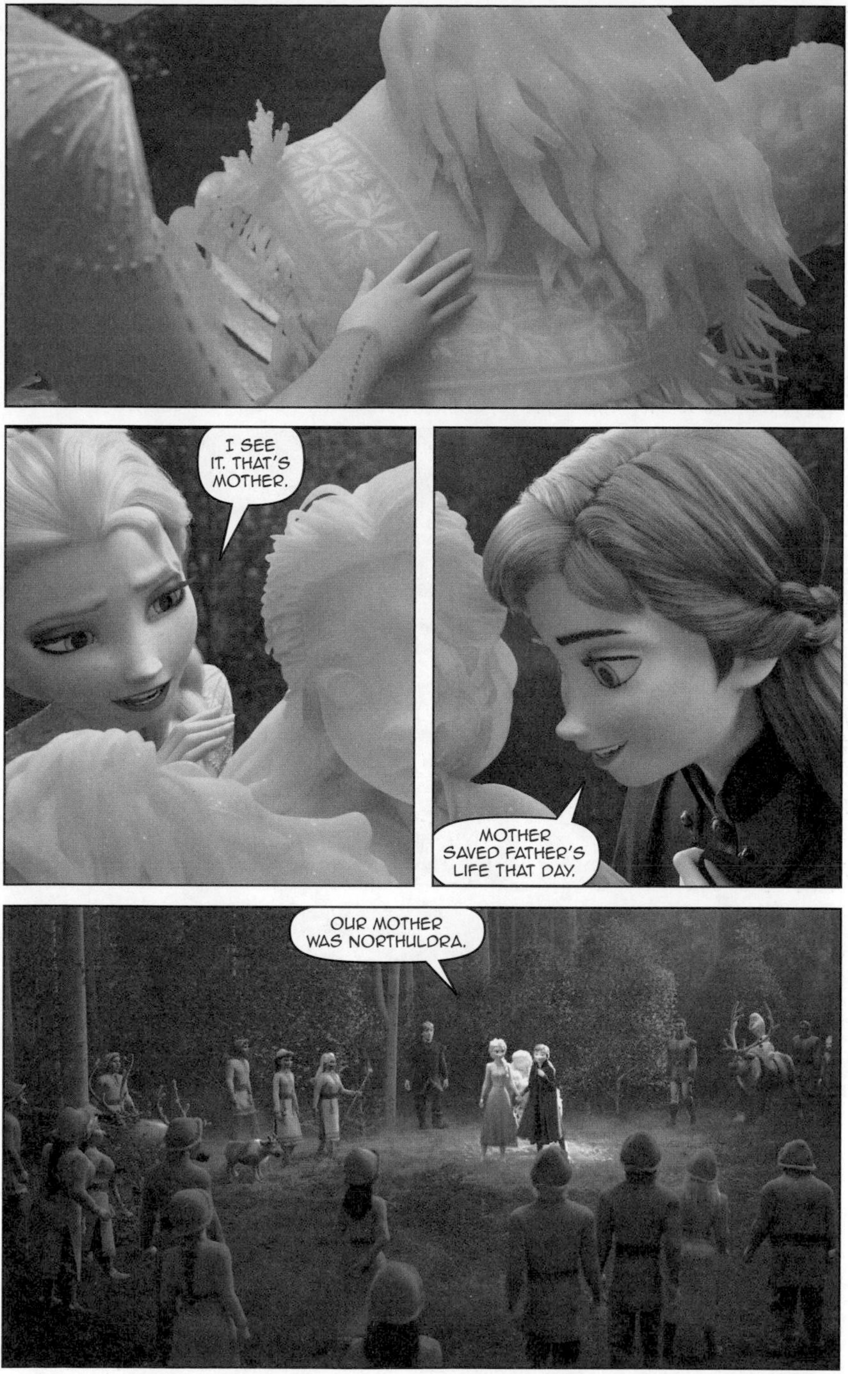
I SEE IT. THAT'S MOTHER.
MOTHER SAVED FATHER'S LIFE THAT DAY.
OUR MOTHER WAS NORTHULDRA.

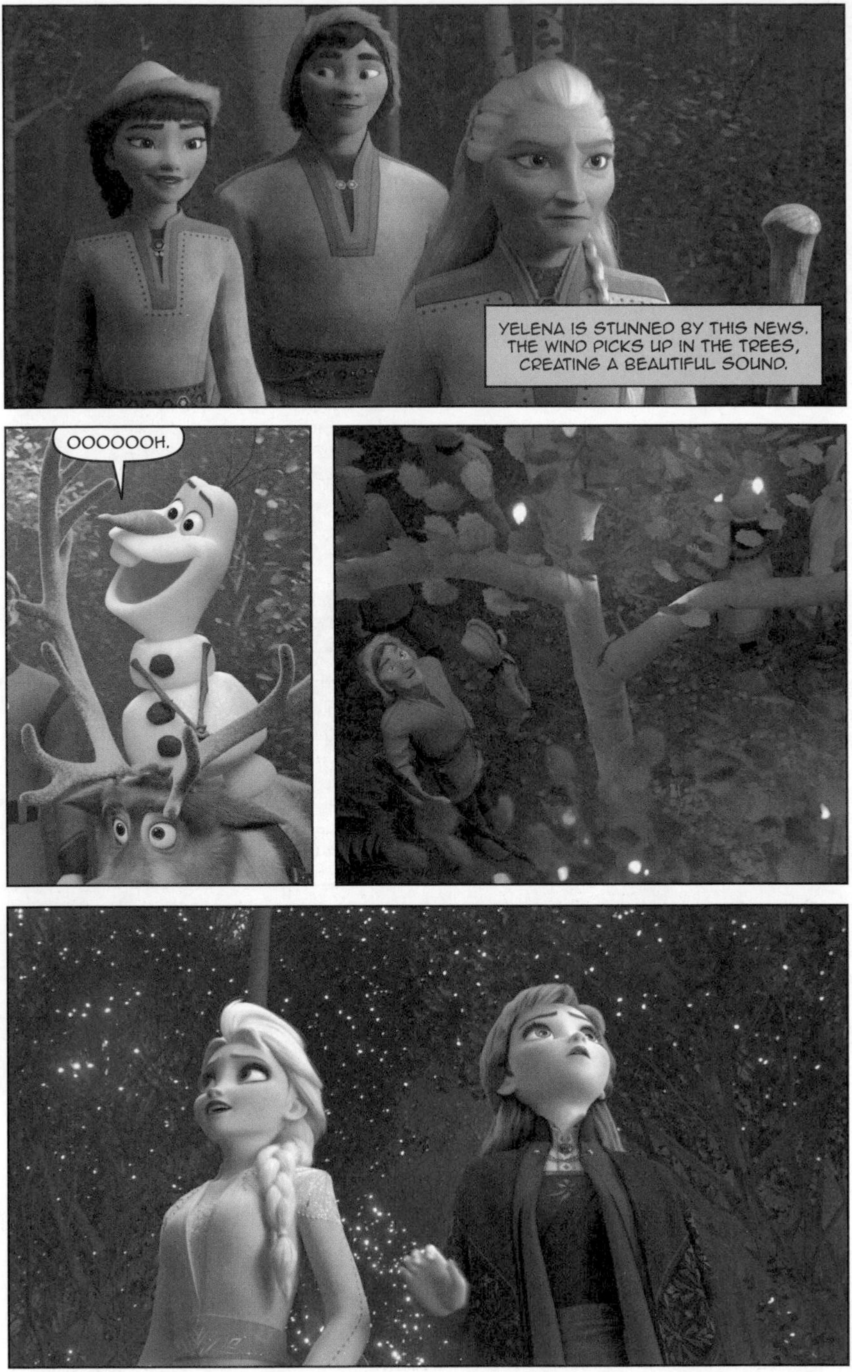
YELENA IS STUNNED BY THIS NEWS. THE WIND PICKS UP IN THE TREES, CREATING A BEAUTIFUL SOUND.
OOOOOOH.

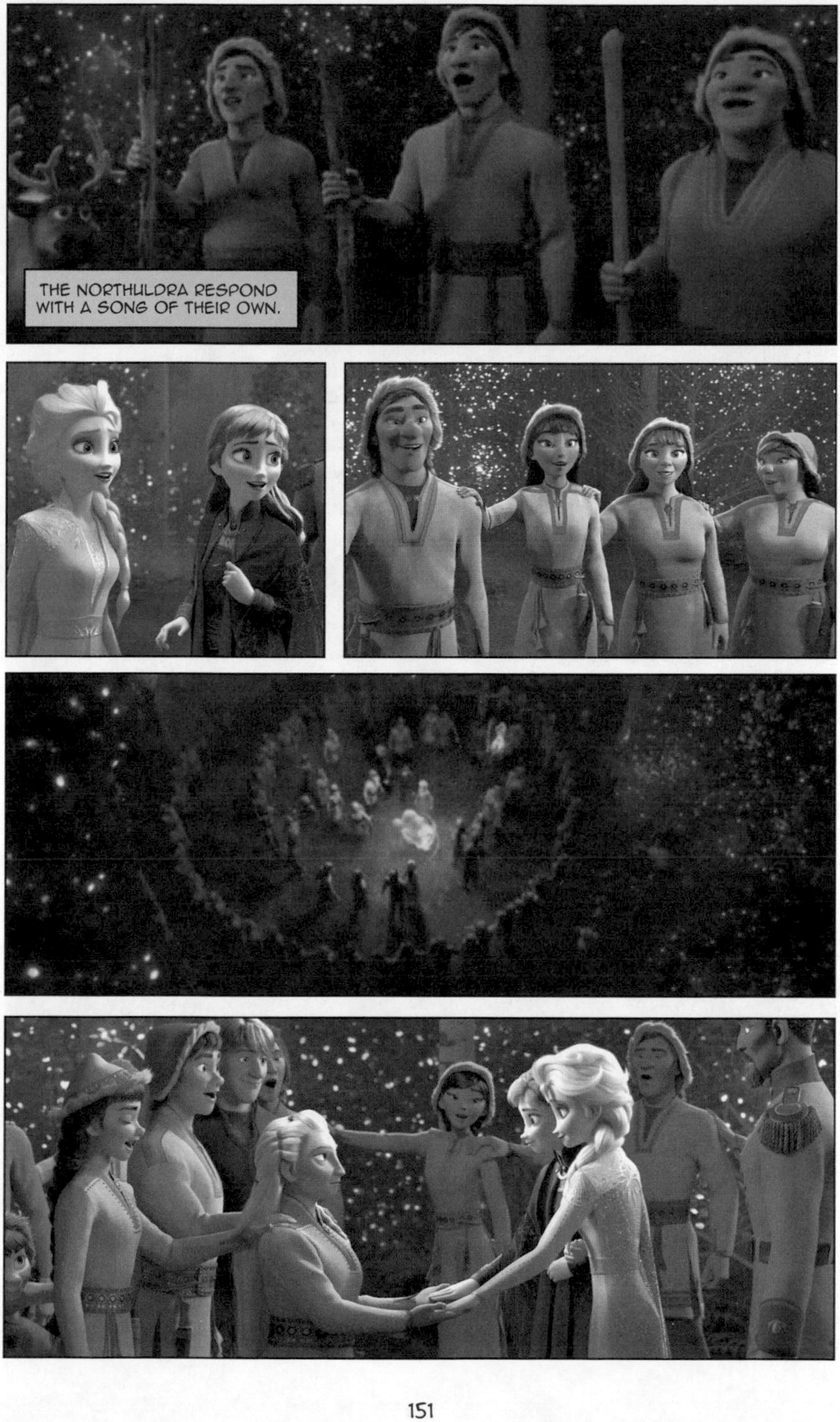
THE NORTHULDRA RESPOND WITH A SONG OF THEIR OWN.

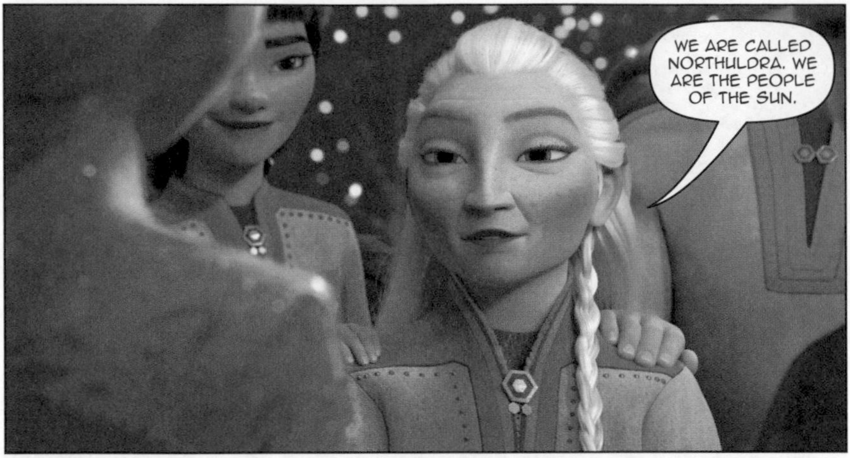
WE ARE CALLED NORTHULDRA. WE ARE THE PEOPLE OF THE SUN.

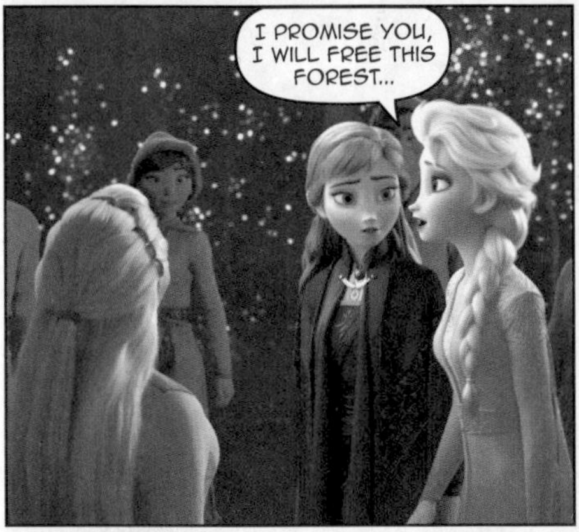
I PROMISE YOU, I WILL FREE THIS FOREST...

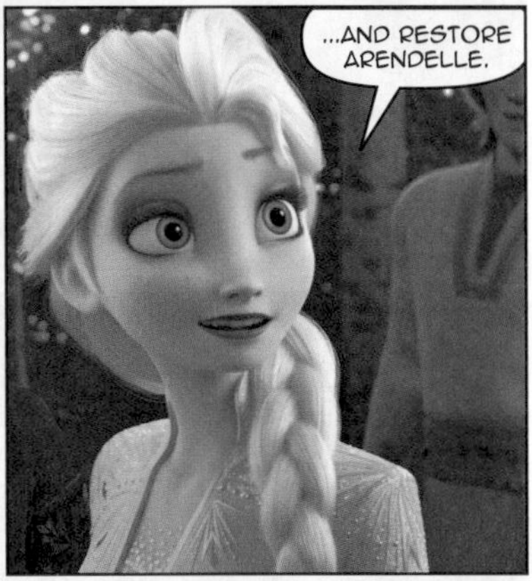
...AND RESTORE ARENDELLE.

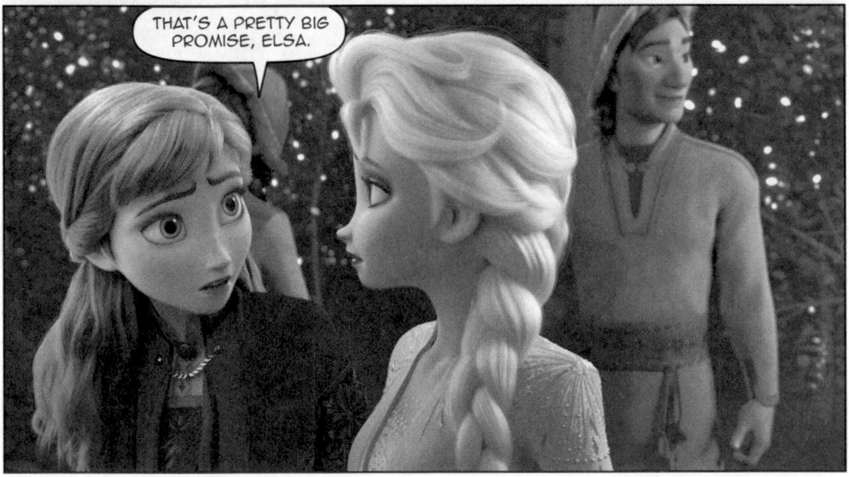
THAT'S A PRETTY BIG PROMISE, ELSA.

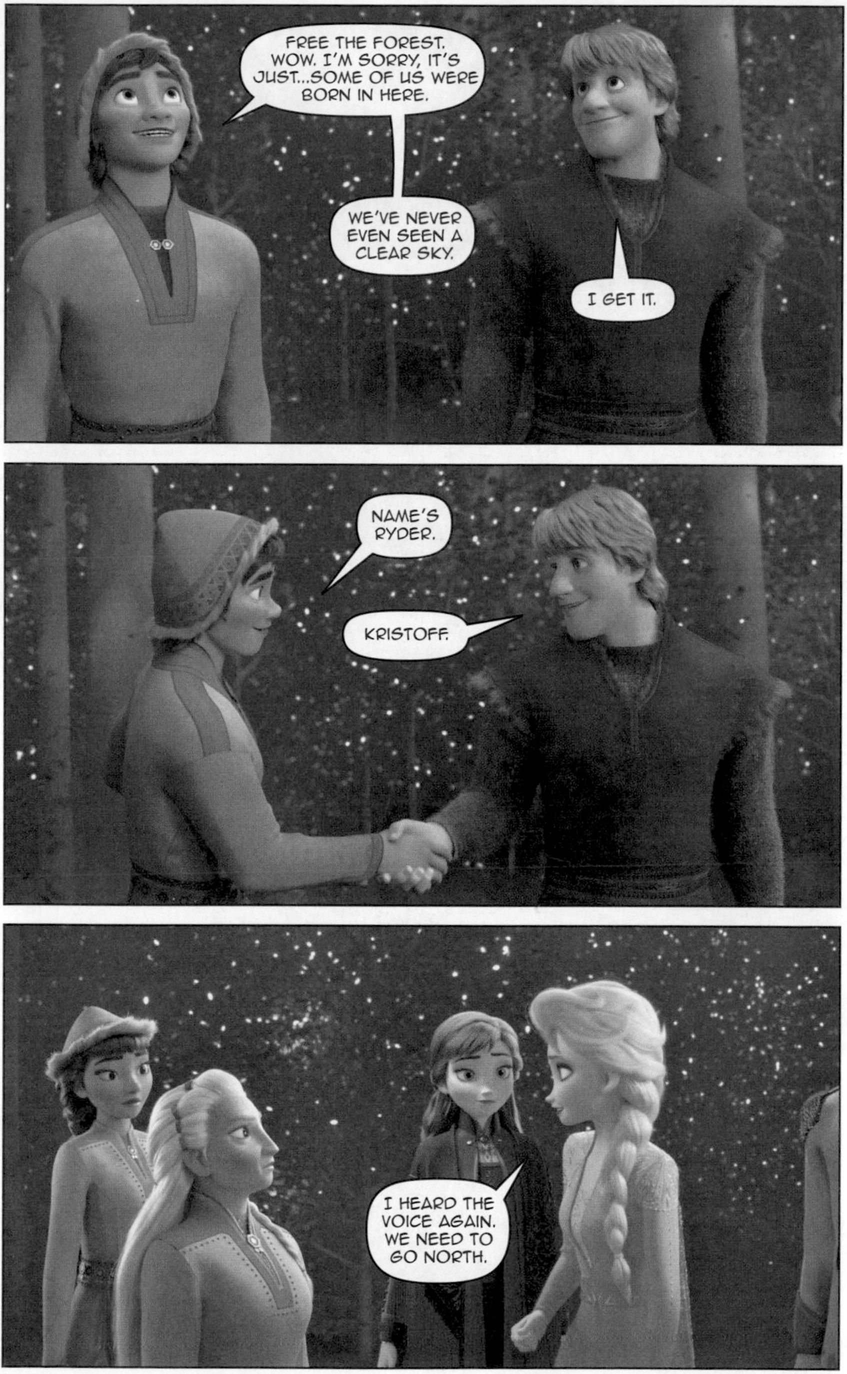
FREE THE FOREST. WOW. I'M SORRY, IT'S JUST...SOME OF US WERE BORN IN HERE.
WE'VE NEVER EVEN SEEN A CLEAR SKY.
I GET IT.
NAME'S RYDER.
KRISTOFF.
I HEARD THE VOICE AGAIN. WE NEED TO GO NORTH.

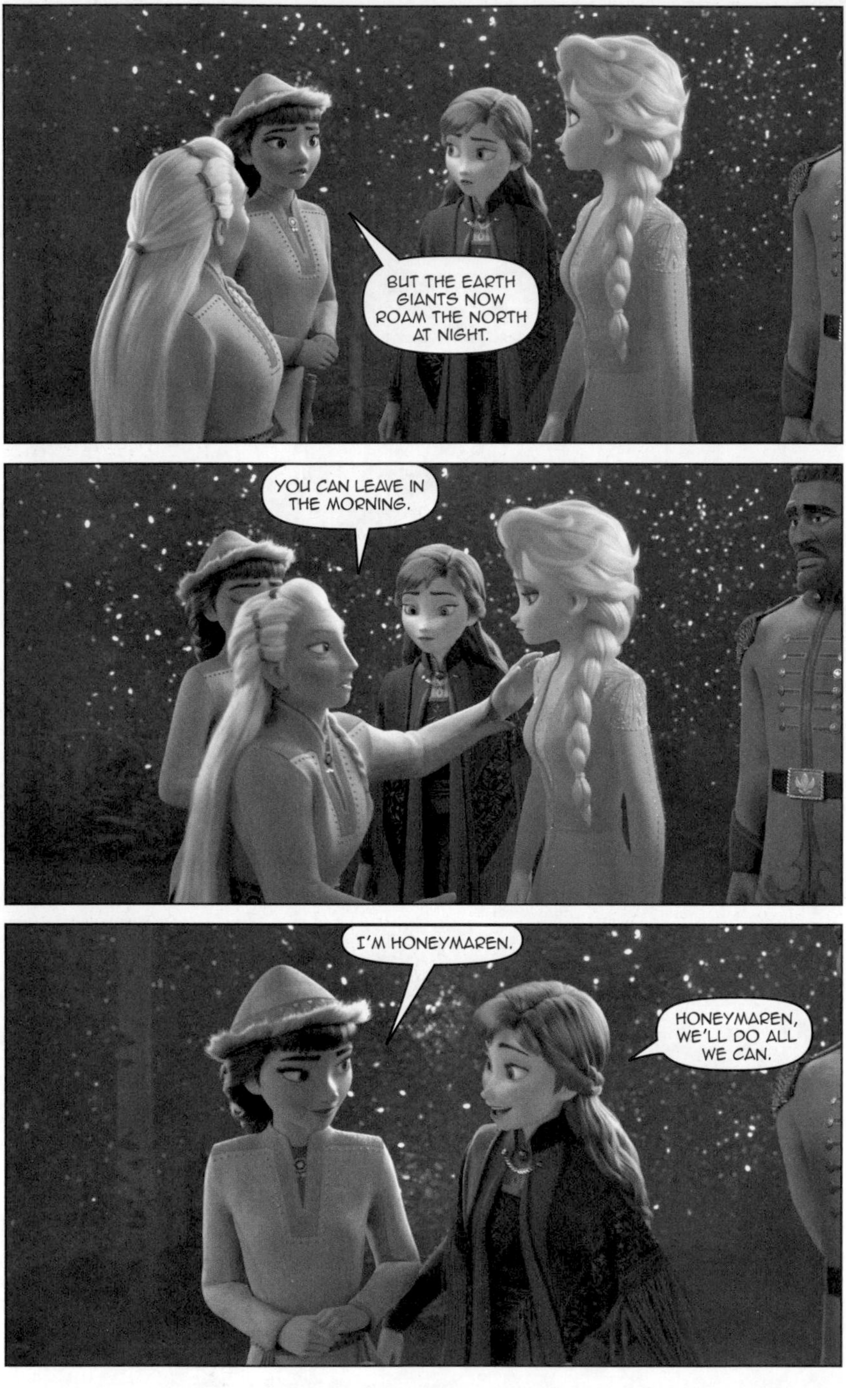
BUT THE EARTH GIANTS NOW ROAM THE NORTH AT NIGHT.
YOU CAN LEAVE IN THE MORNING.
I'M HONEYMAREN.
HONEYMAREN, WE'LL DO ALL WE CAN.

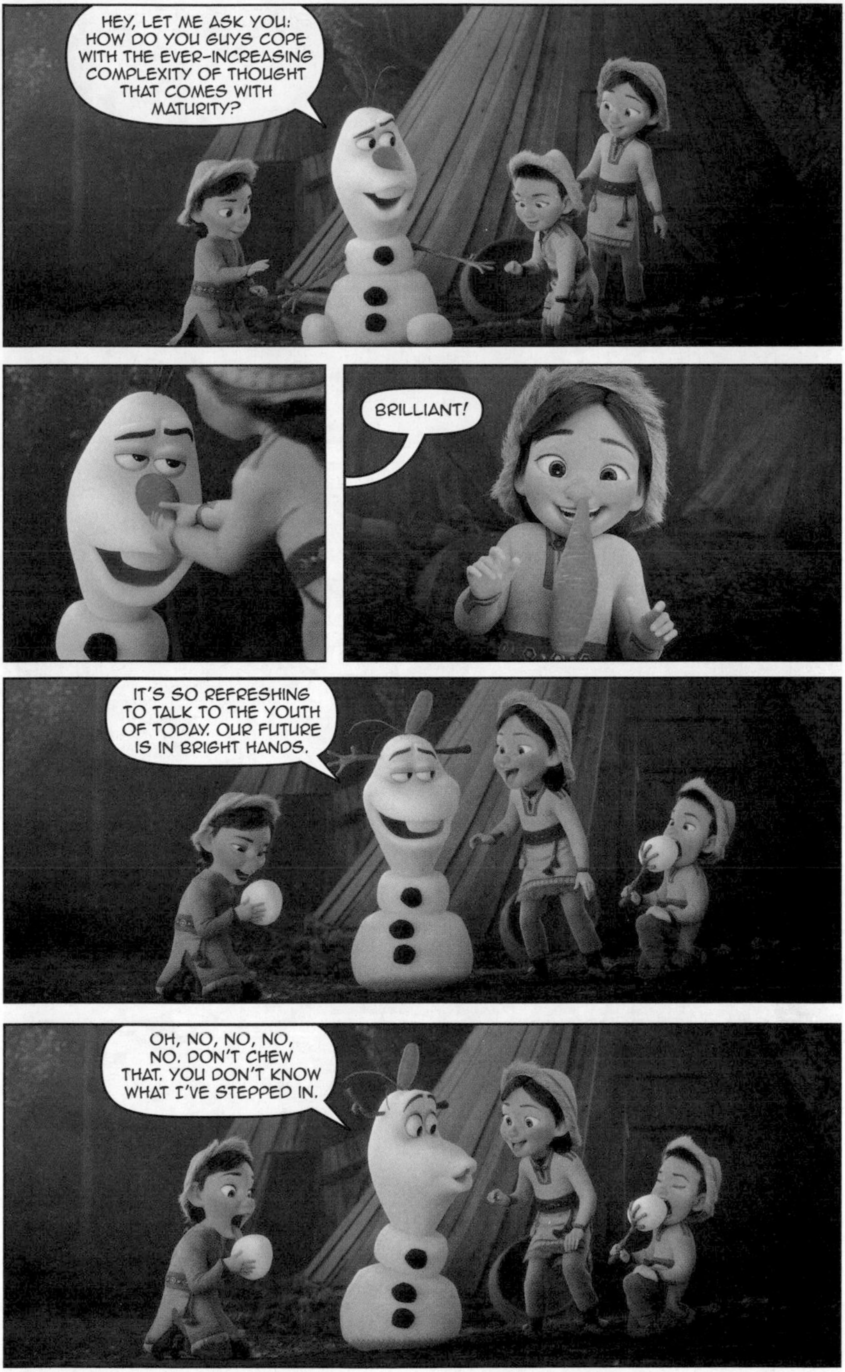
HEY, LET ME ASK YOU: HOW DO YOU GUYS COPE WITH THE EVER-INCREASING COMPLEXITY OF THOUGHT THAT COMES WITH MATURITY?
BRILLIANT!
IT'S SO REFRESHING TO TALK TO THE YOUTH OF TODAY. OUR FUTURE IS IN BRIGHT HANDS.
OH, NO, NO, NO, NO. DON'T CHEW THAT. YOU DON'T KNOW WHAT I'VE STEPPED IN.

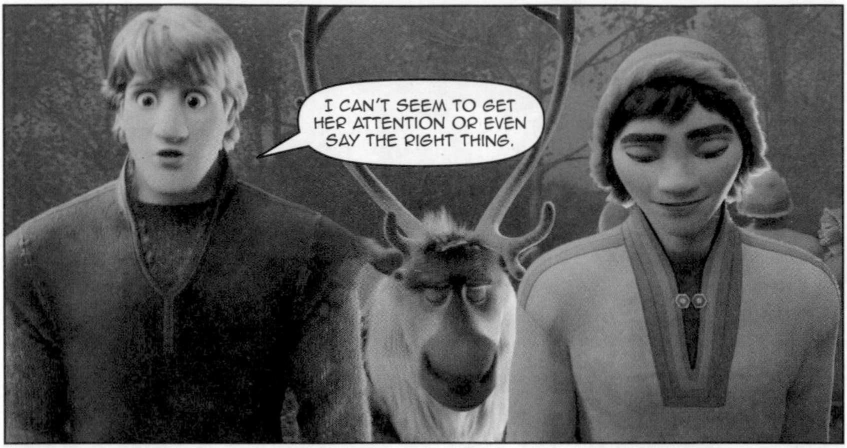
I CAN'T SEEM TO GET HER ATTENTION OR EVEN SAY THE RIGHT THING.

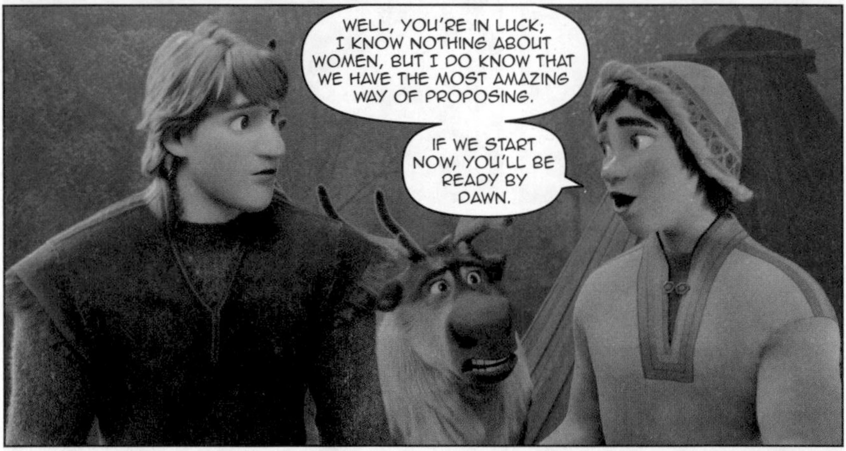
WELL, YOU'RE IN LUCK; I KNOW NOTHING ABOUT WOMEN, BUT I DO KNOW THAT WE HAVE THE MOST AMAZING WAY OF PROPOSING.
IF WE START NOW, YOU'LL BE READY BY DAWN.

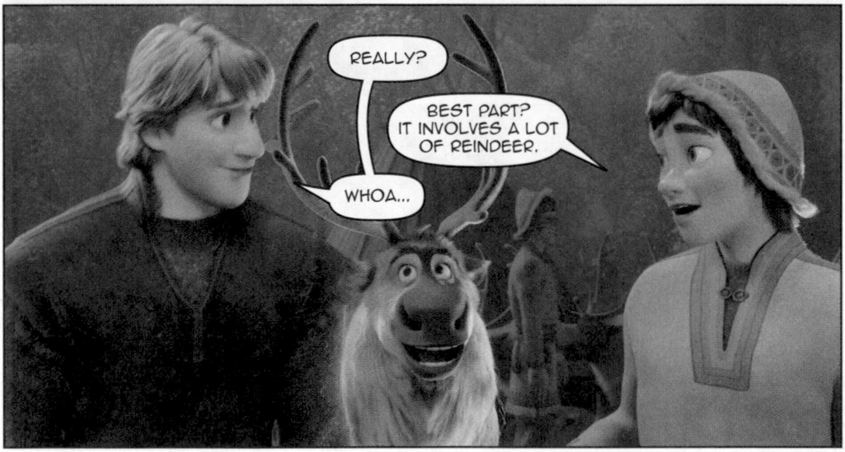
REALLY?
BEST PART? IT INVOLVES A LOT OF REINDEER.
WHOA...

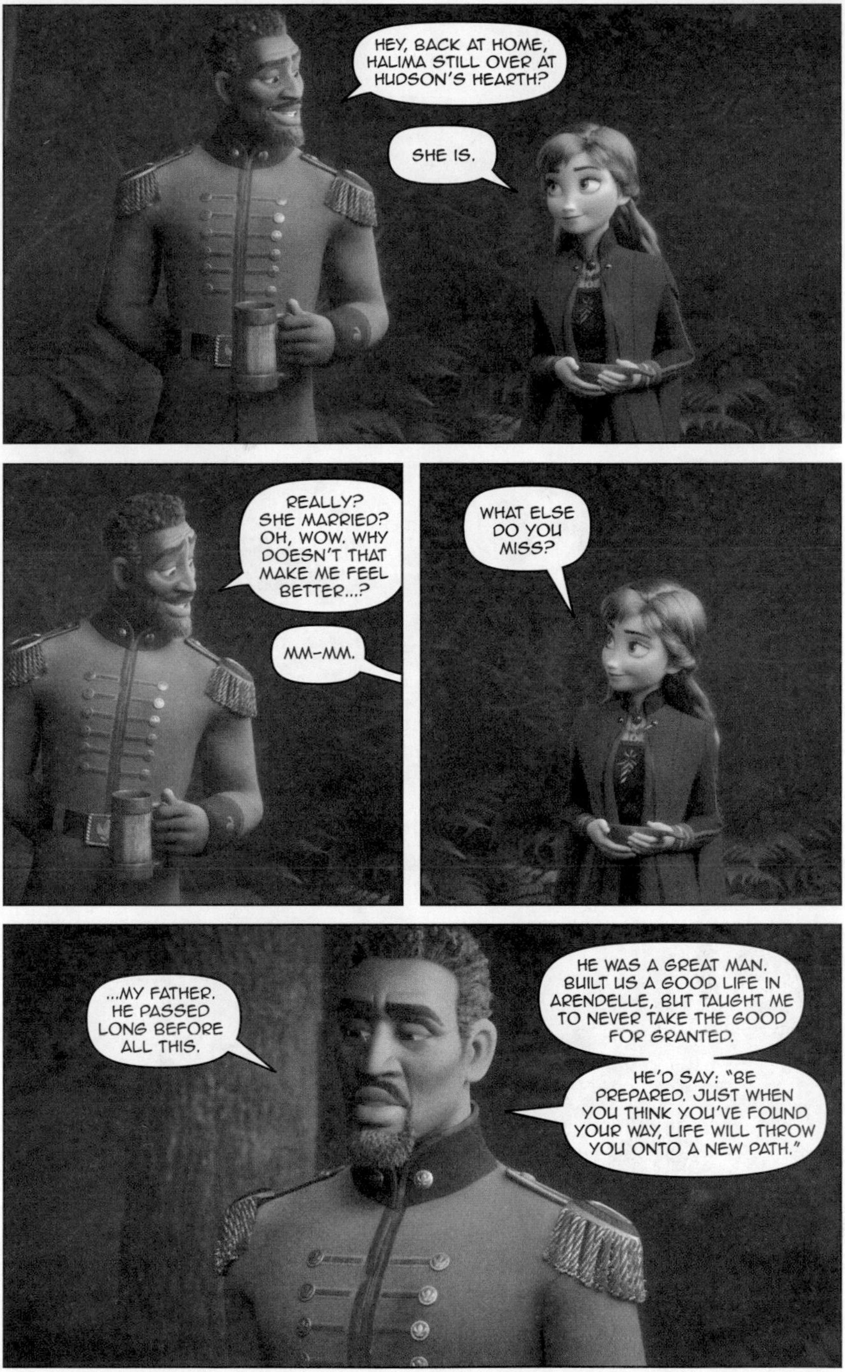
HEY, BACK AT HOME, HALIMA STILL OVER AT HUDSON'S HEARTH?
SHE IS.
REALLY? SHE MARRIED? OH, WOW. WHY DOESN'T THAT MAKE ME FEEL BETTER...?
MM-MM.
WHAT ELSE DO YOU MISS?
...MY FATHER. HE PASSED LONG BEFORE ALL THIS.
HE WAS A GREAT MAN. BUILT US A GOOD LIFE IN ARENDELLE, BUT TAUGHT ME TO NEVER TAKE THE GOOD FOR GRANTED.
HE'D SAY: "BE PREPARED. JUST WHEN YOU THINK YOU'VE FOUND YOUR WAY, LIFE WILL THROW YOU ONTO A NEW PATH."

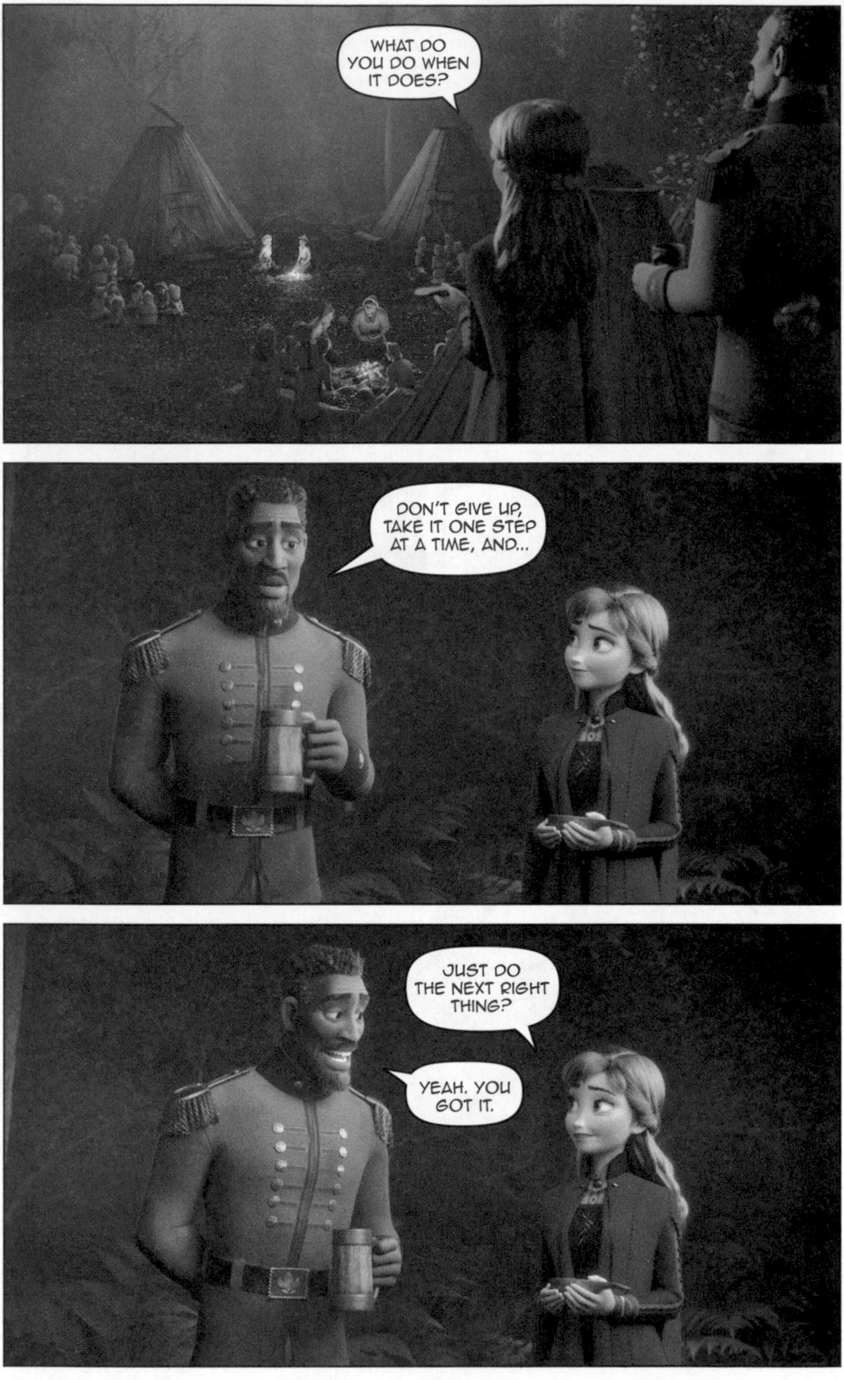
WHAT DO YOU DO WHEN IT DOES?
DON'T GIVE UP, TAKE IT ONE STEP AT A TIME, AND...
JUST DO THE NEXT RIGHT THING?
YEAH. YOU GOT IT.

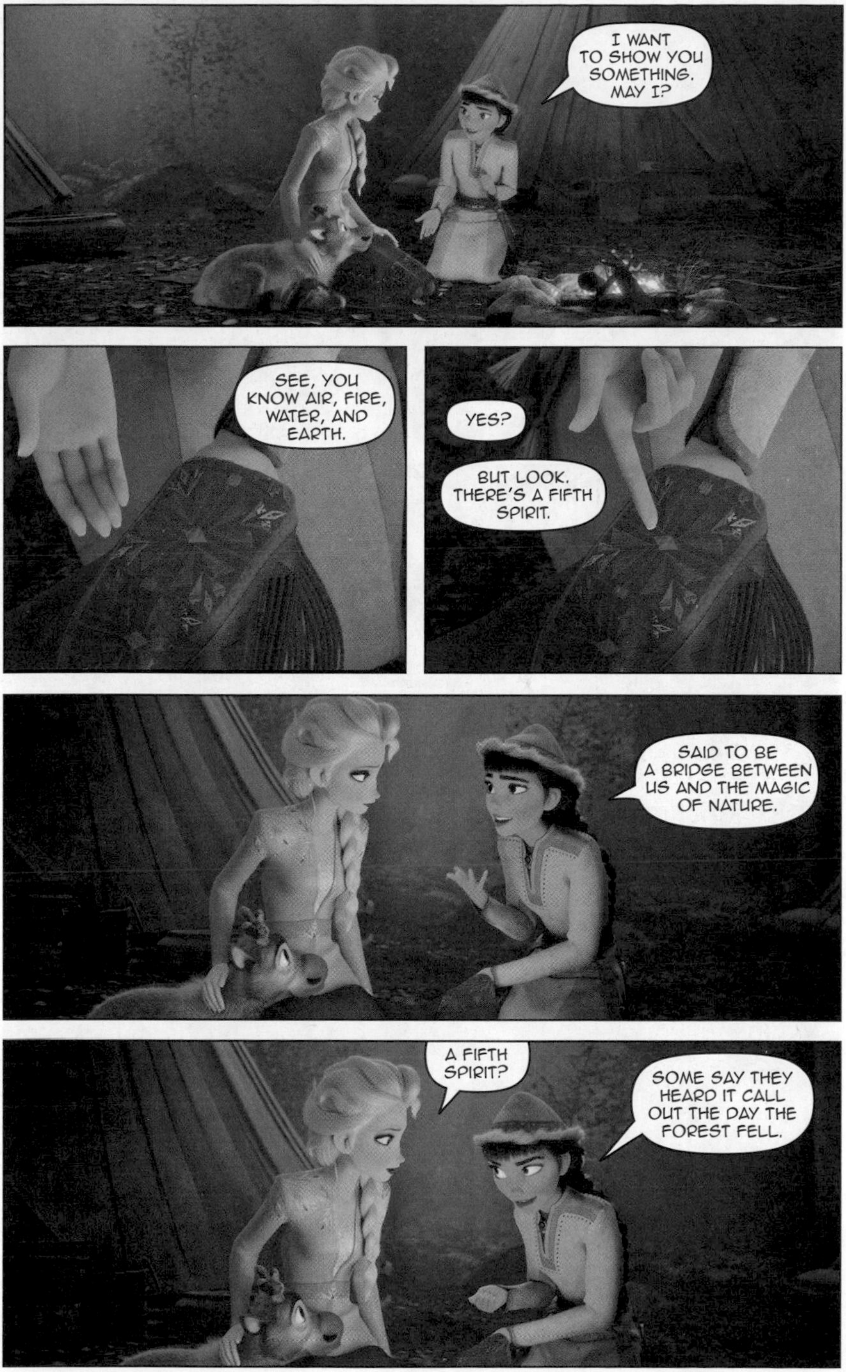
I WANT TO SHOW YOU SOMETHING. MAY I?
SEE, YOU KNOW AIR, FIRE, WATER, AND EARTH.
YES?
BUT LOOK. THERE'S A FIFTH SPIRIT.
SAID TO BE A BRIDGE BETWEEN US AND THE MAGIC OF NATURE.
A FIFTH SPIRIT?
SOME SAY THEY HEARD IT CALL OUT THE DAY THE FOREST FELL.

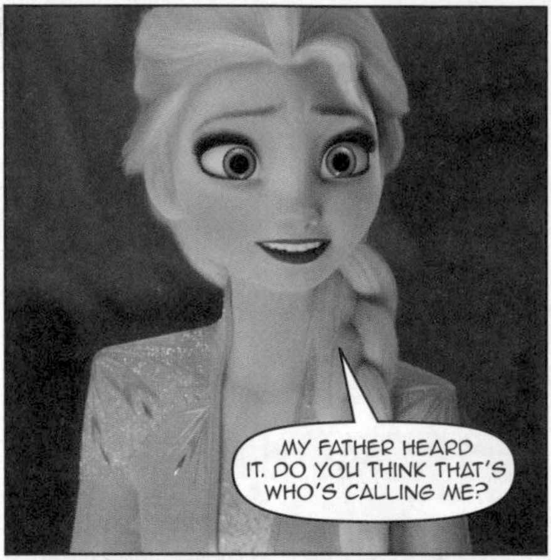
MY FATHER HEARD IT. DO YOU THINK THAT'S WHO'S CALLING ME?

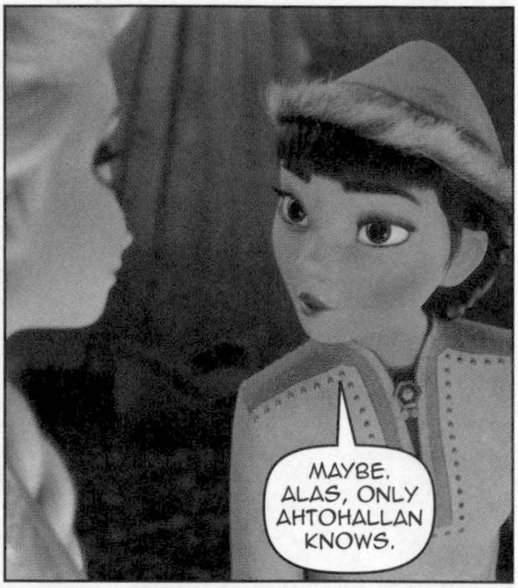
MAYBE. ALAS, ONLY AHTOHALLAN KNOWS.

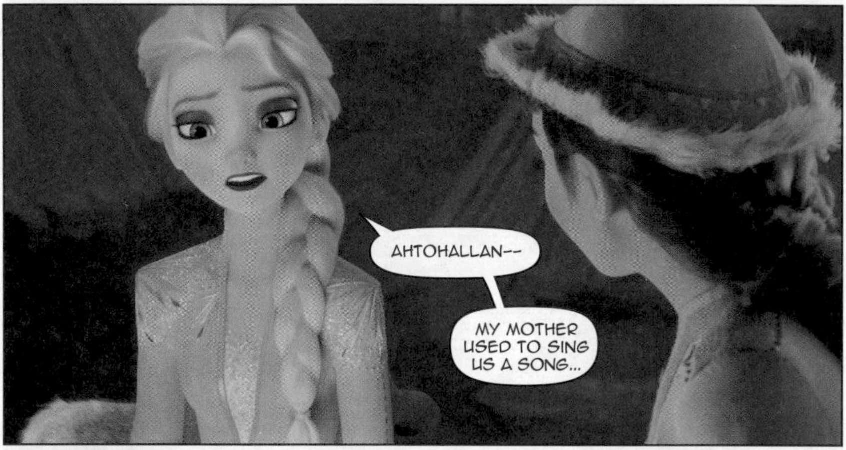
AHTOHALLAN--
MY MOTHER USED TO SING US A SONG...

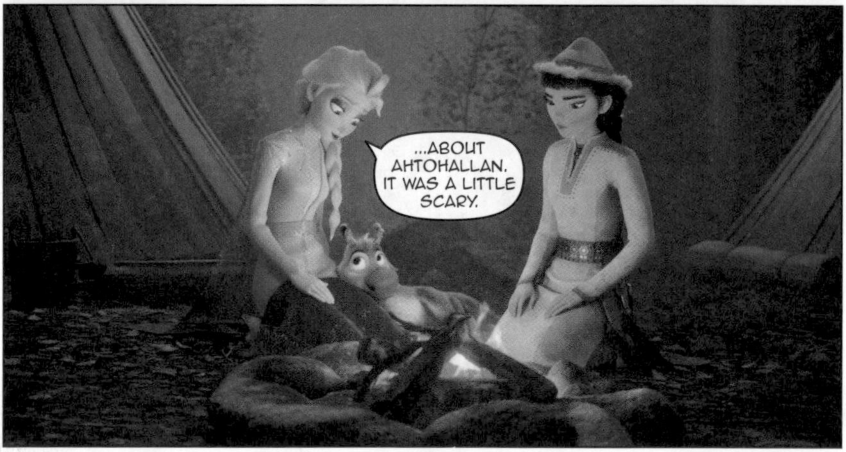
...ABOUT AHTOHALLAN. IT WAS A LITTLE SCARY.

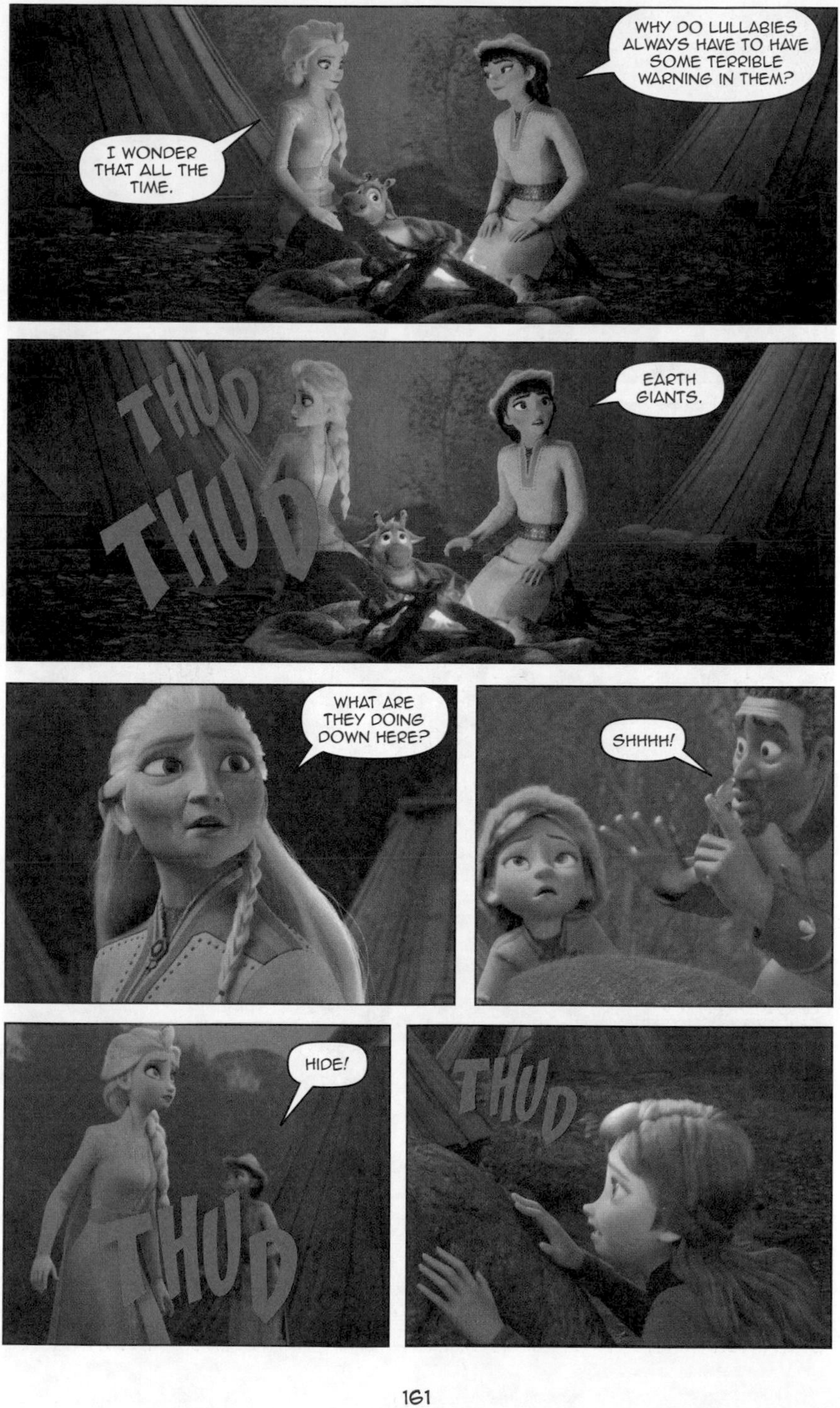
WHY DO LULLABIES ALWAYS HAVE TO HAVE SOME TERRIBLE WARNING IN THEM?
I WONDER THAT ALL THE TIME.
THUD
THUD
EARTH GIANTS.
WHAT ARE THEY DOING DOWN HERE?
SHHHH!
HIDE!
THUD
THUD

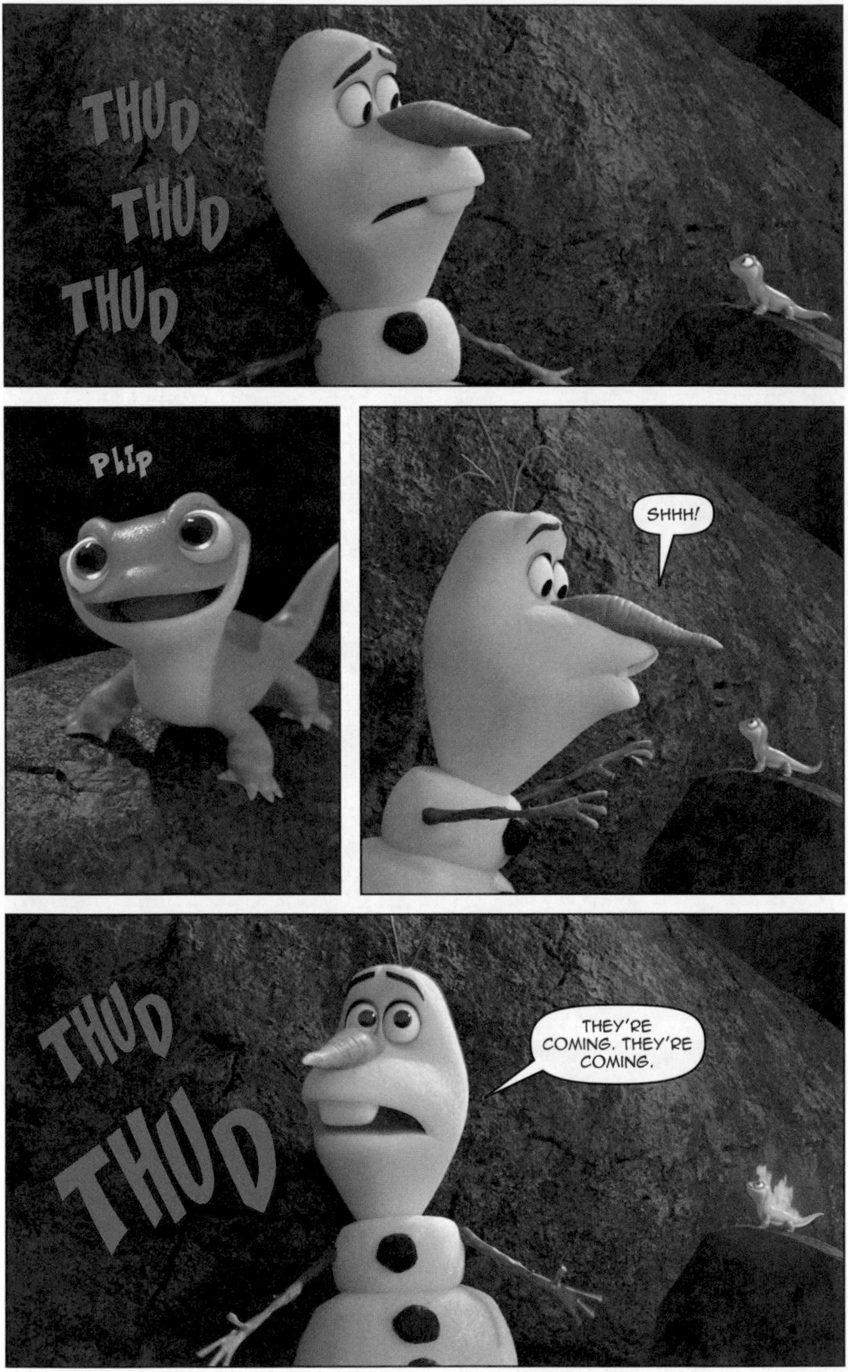
THUD
THUD
THUD
PLIP
SHHH!
THEY'RE COMING. THEY'RE COMING.
THUD
THUD

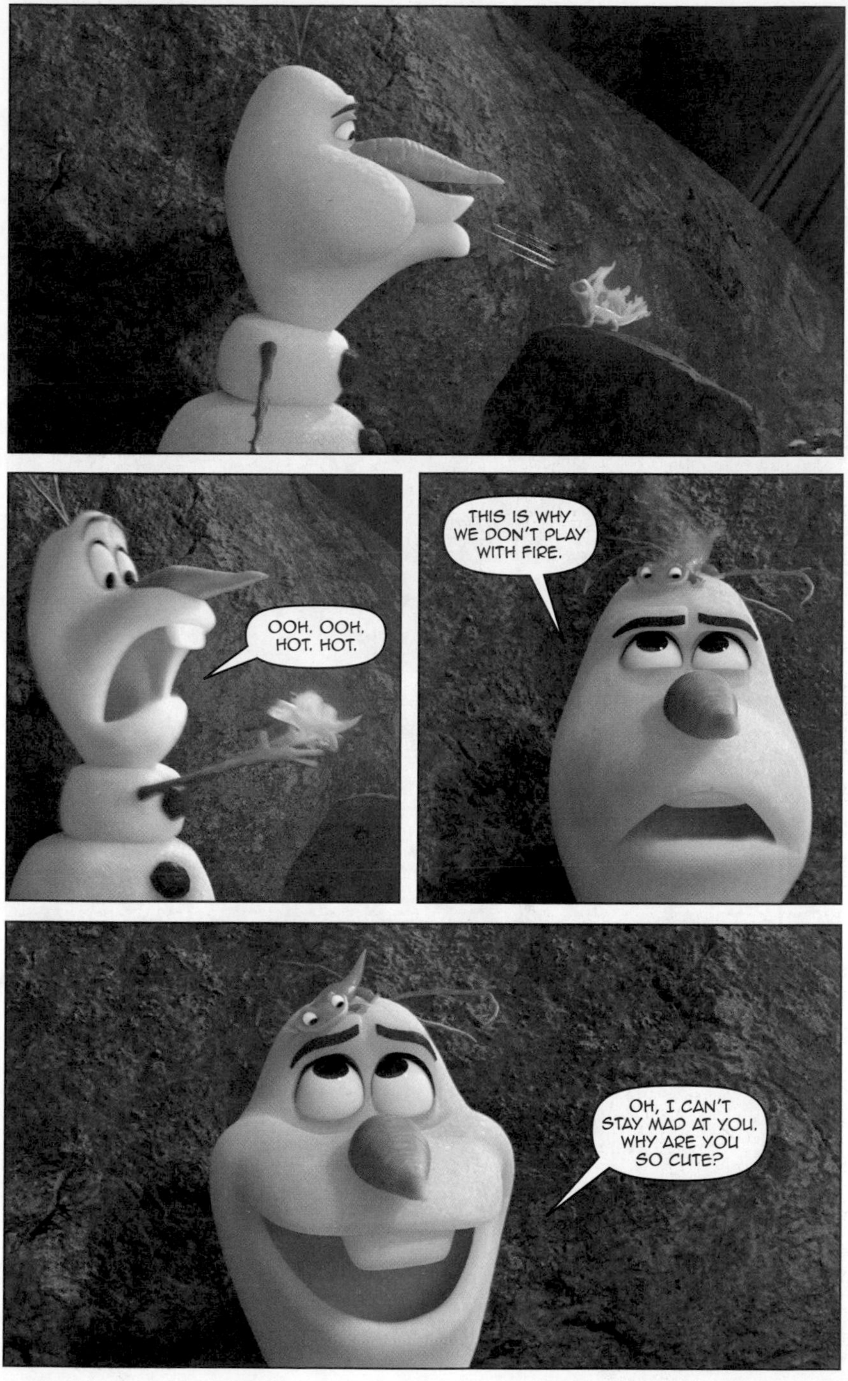
OOH. OOH. HOT. HOT.
THIS IS WHY WE DON'T PLAY WITH FIRE.
OH, I CAN'T STAY MAD AT YOU. WHY ARE YOU SO CUTE?

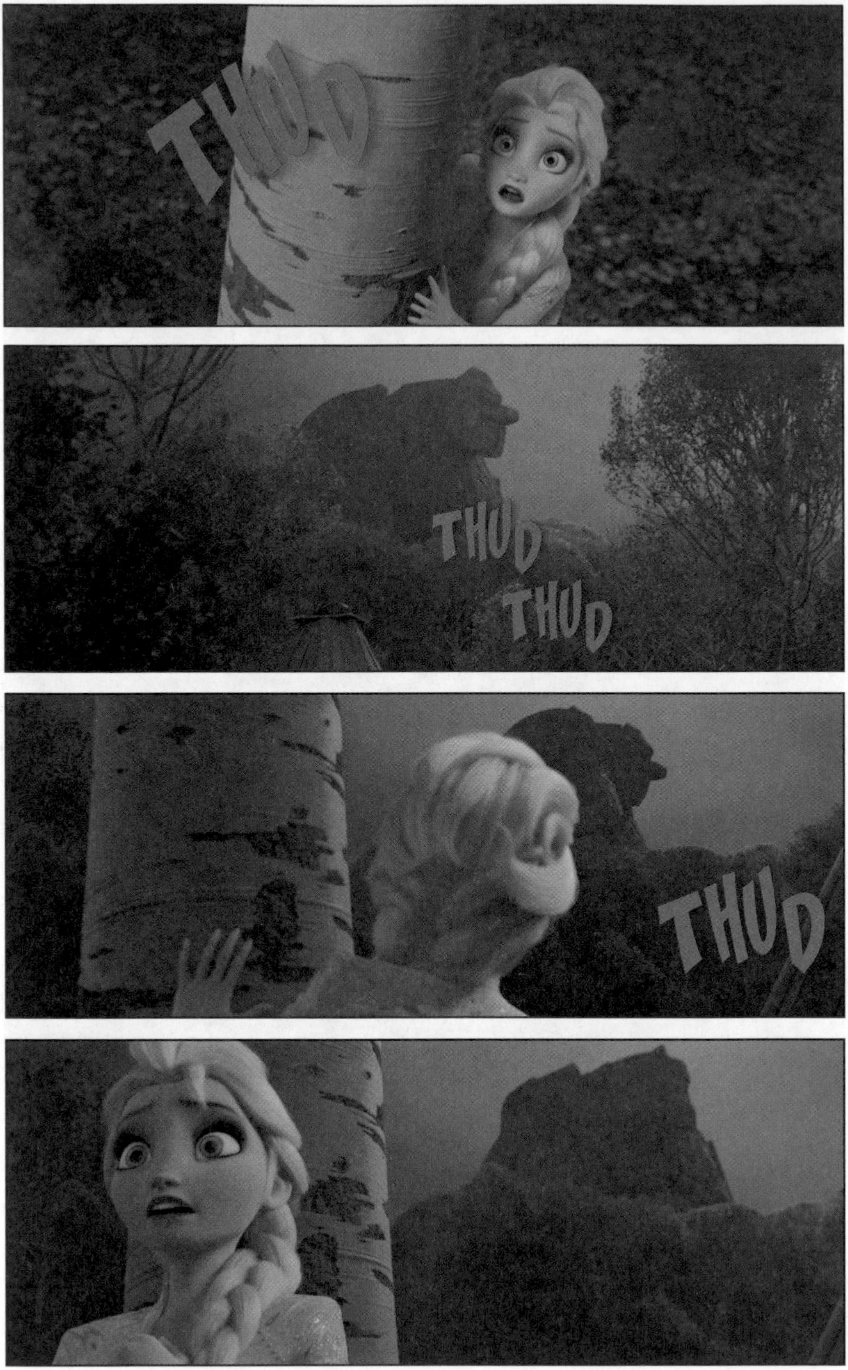
THUD
THUD
THUD
THUD

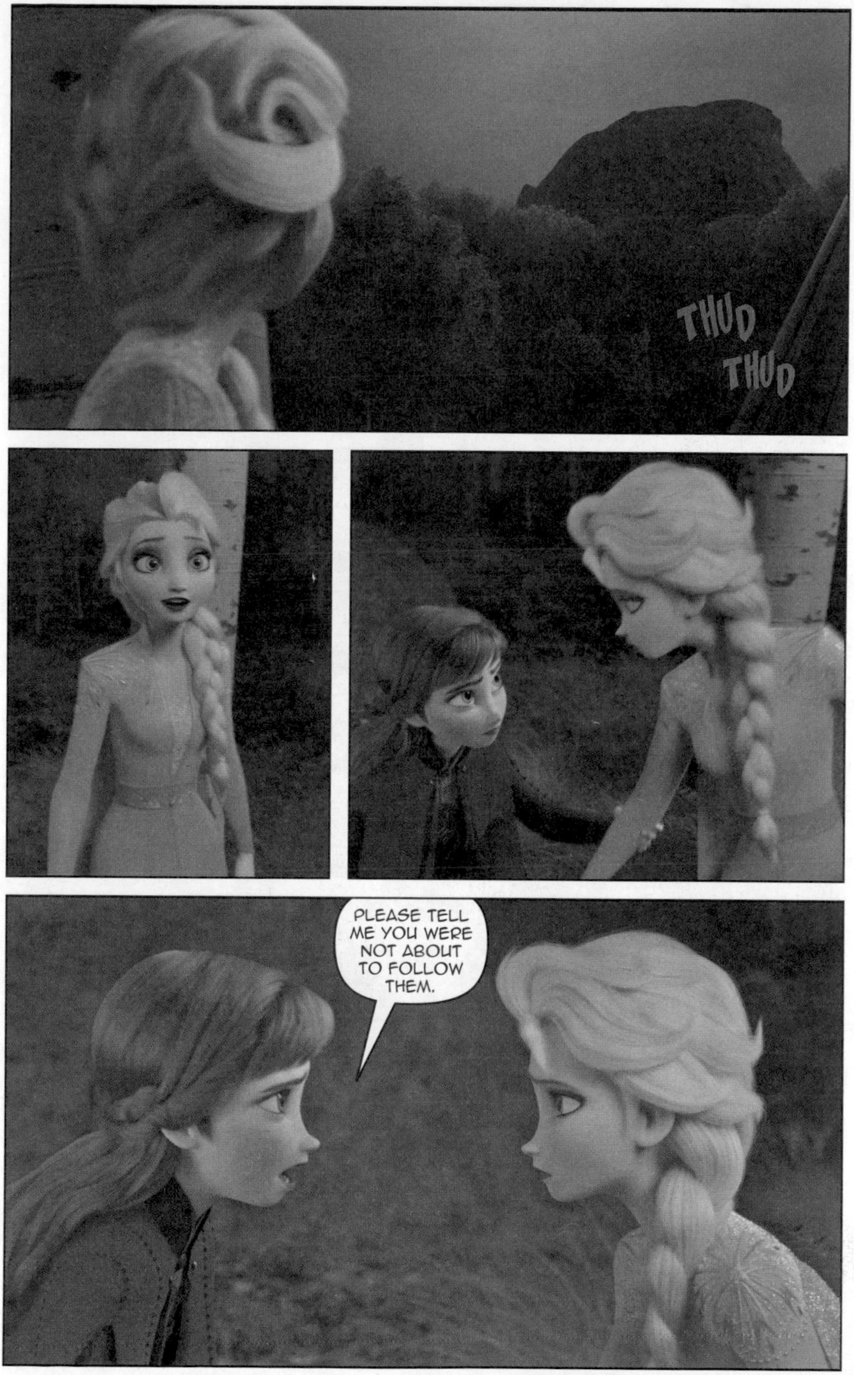
THUD THUD
PLEASE TELL ME YOU WERE NOT ABOUT TO FOLLOW THEM.

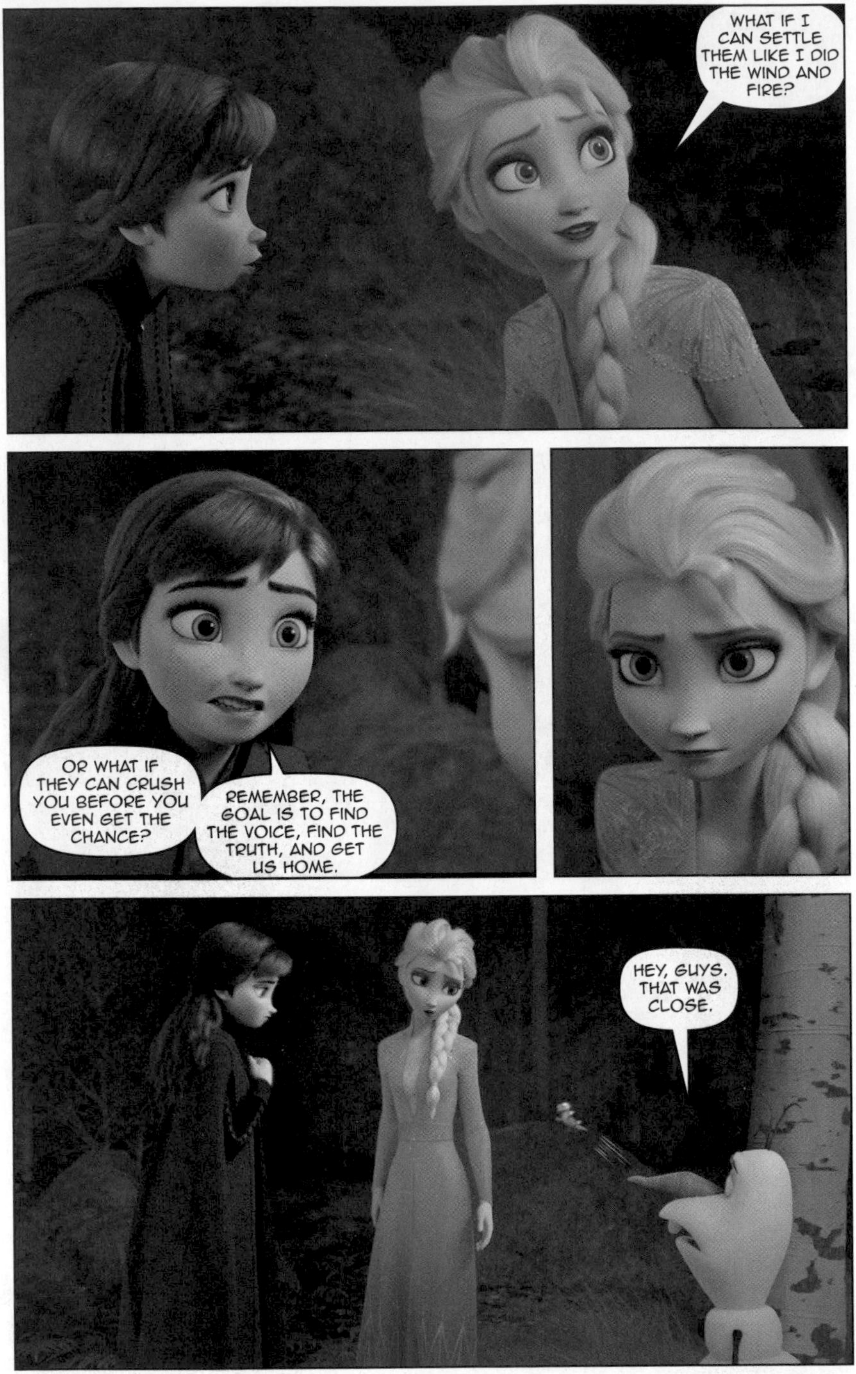
WHAT IF I CAN SETTLE THEM LIKE I DID THE WIND AND FIRE?
OR WHAT IF THEY CAN CRUSH YOU BEFORE YOU EVEN GET THE CHANCE?
REMEMBER, THE GOAL IS TO FIND THE VOICE, FIND THE TRUTH, AND GET US HOME.
HEY, GUYS. THAT WAS CLOSE.

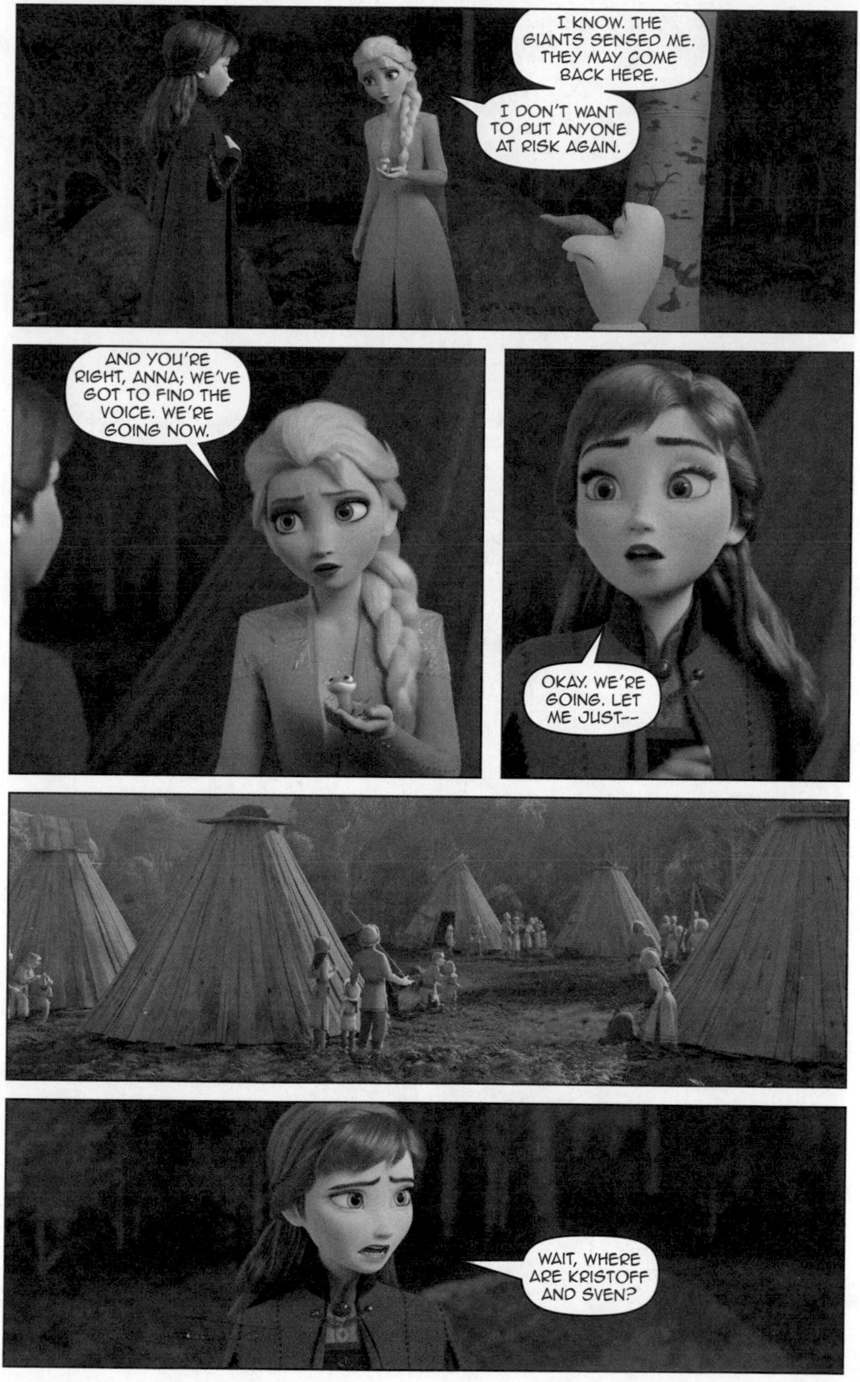
I KNOW. THE GIANTS SENSED ME. THEY MAY COME BACK HERE.
I DON'T WANT TO PUT ANYONE AT RISK AGAIN.
AND YOU'RE RIGHT, ANNA; WE'VE GOT TO FIND THE VOICE. WE'RE GOING NOW.
OKAY. WE'RE GOING. LET ME JUST--
WAIT, WHERE ARE KRISTOFF AND SVEN?

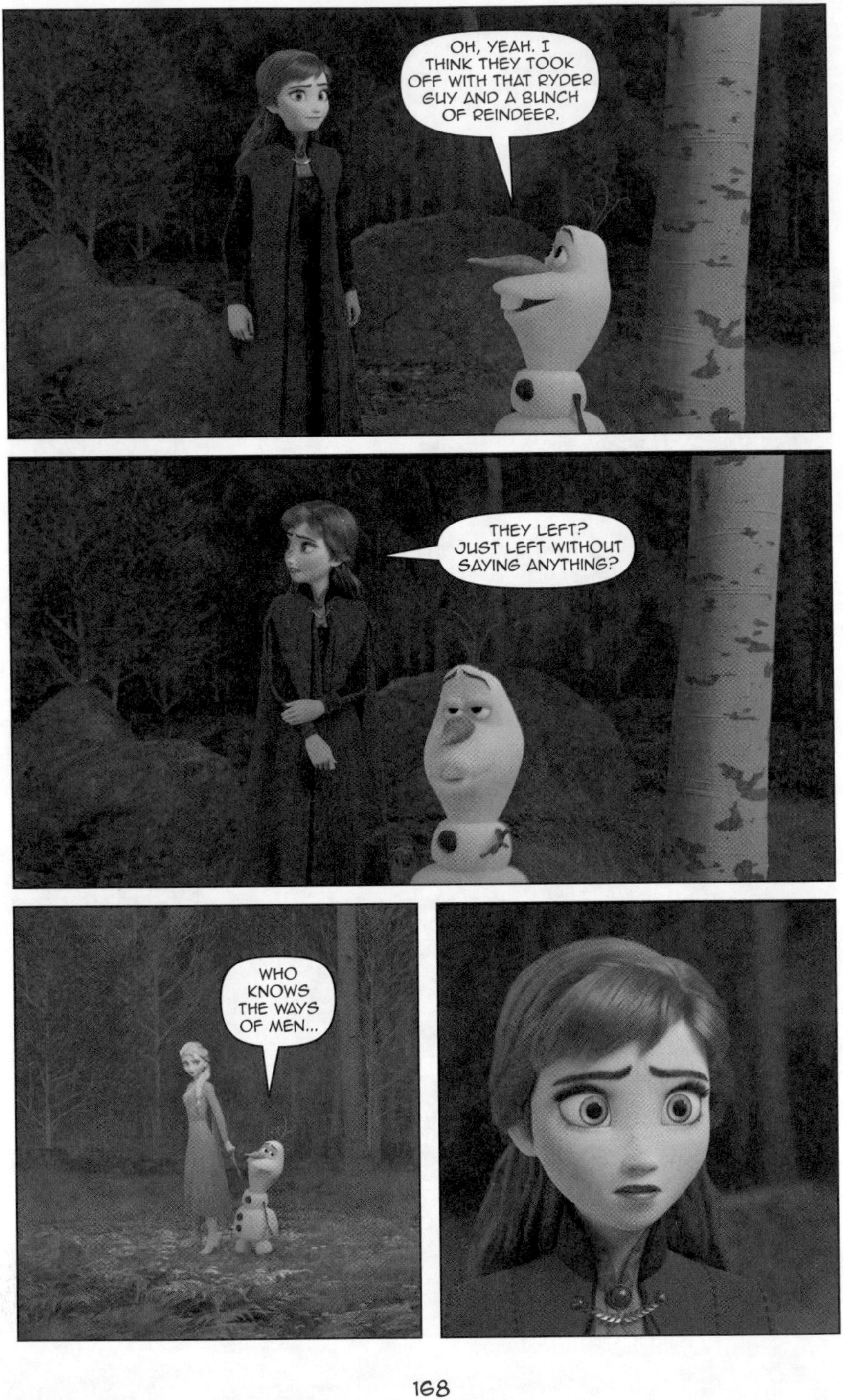
OH, YEAH. I THINK THEY TOOK OFF WITH THAT RYDER GUY AND A BUNCH OF REINDEER.
THEY LEFT? JUST LEFT WITHOUT SAYING ANYTHING?
WHO KNOWS THE WAYS OF MEN...

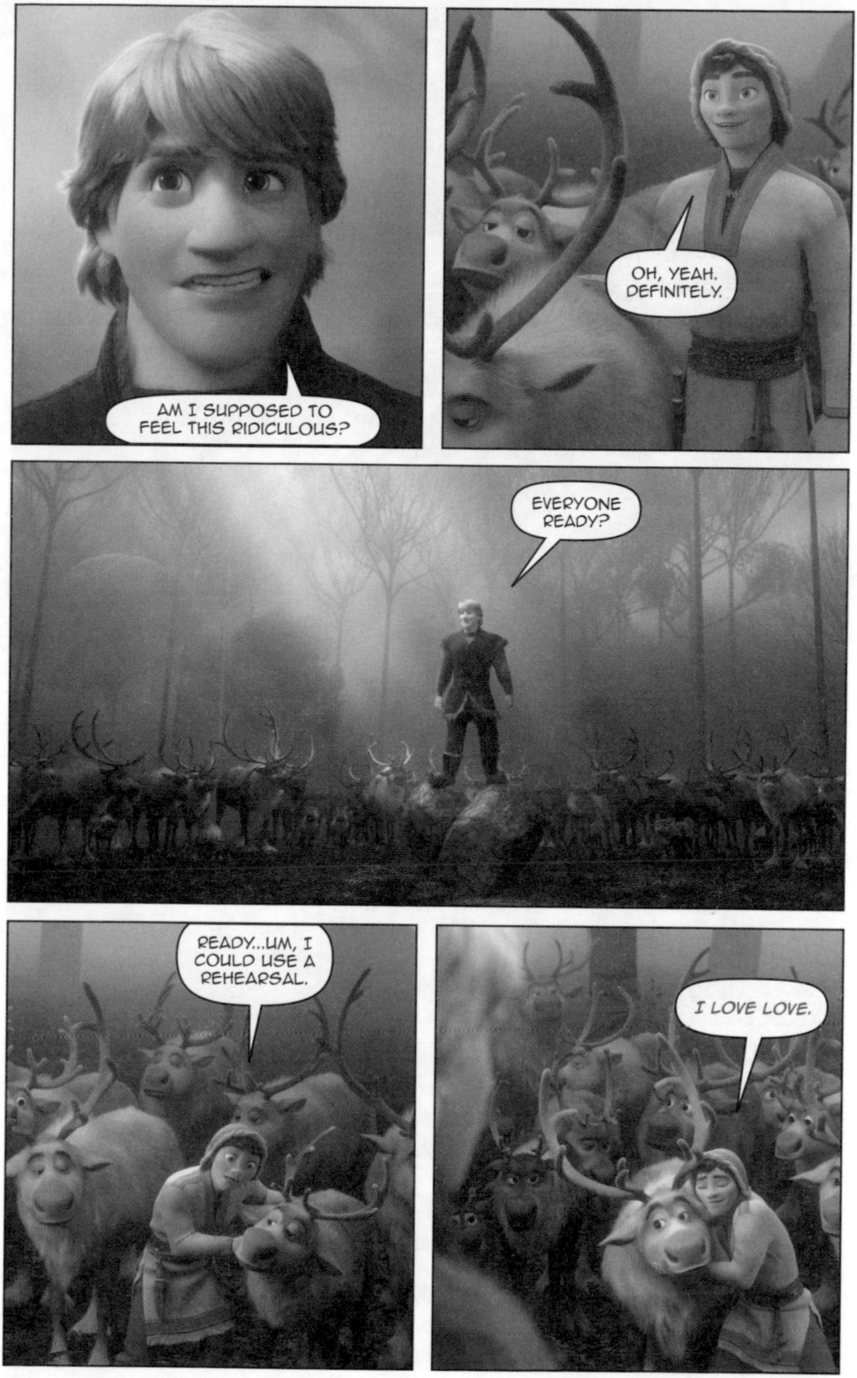
AM I SUPPOSED TO FEEL THIS RIDICULOUS?
OH, YEAH. DEFINITELY.
EVERYONE READY?
READY...UM, I COULD USE A REHEARSAL.
I LOVE LOVE.

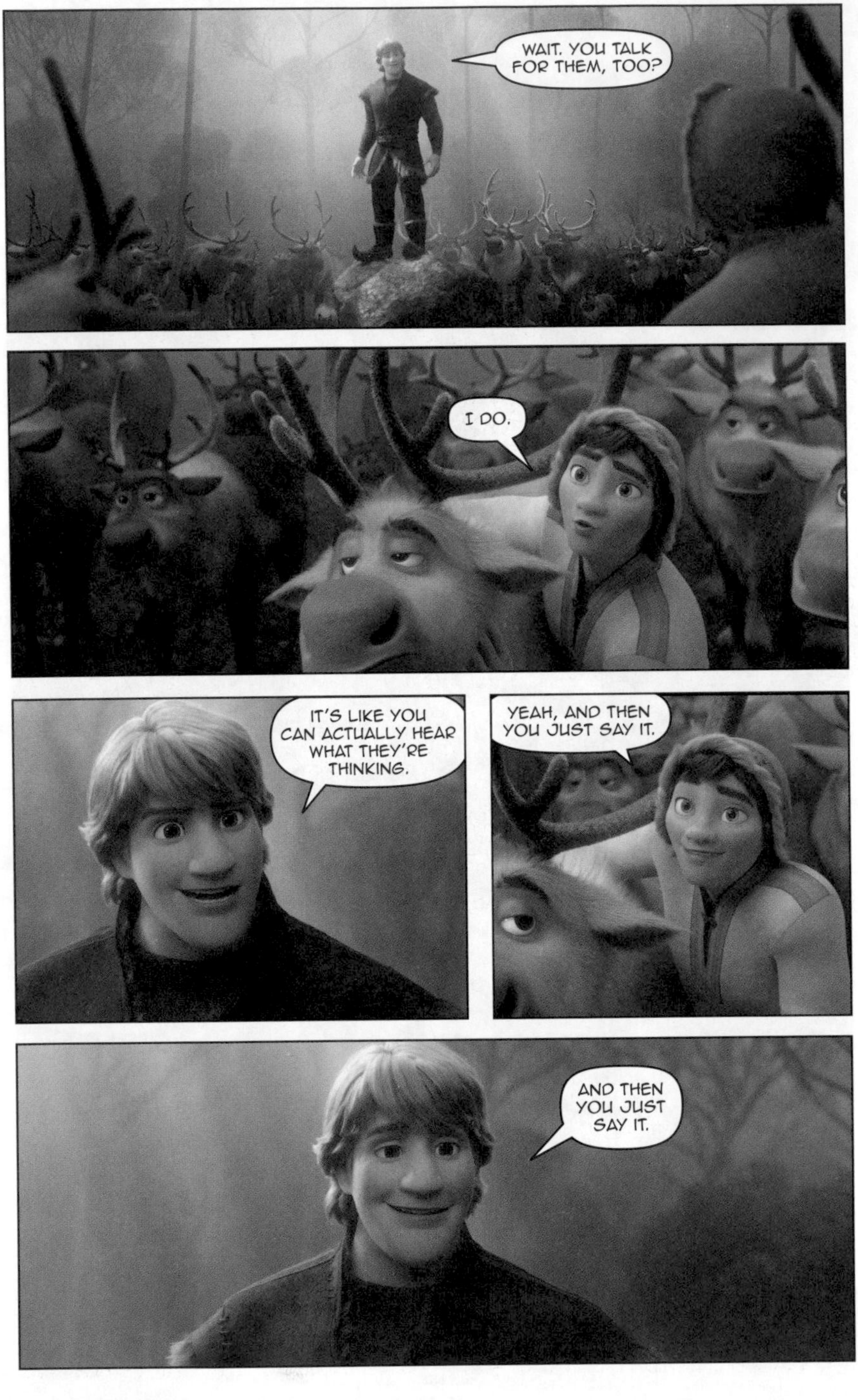
WAIT. YOU TALK FOR THEM, TOO?
I DO.
IT'S LIKE YOU CAN ACTUALLY HEAR WHAT THEY'RE THINKING.
YEAH, AND THEN YOU JUST SAY IT.
AND THEN YOU JUST SAY IT.

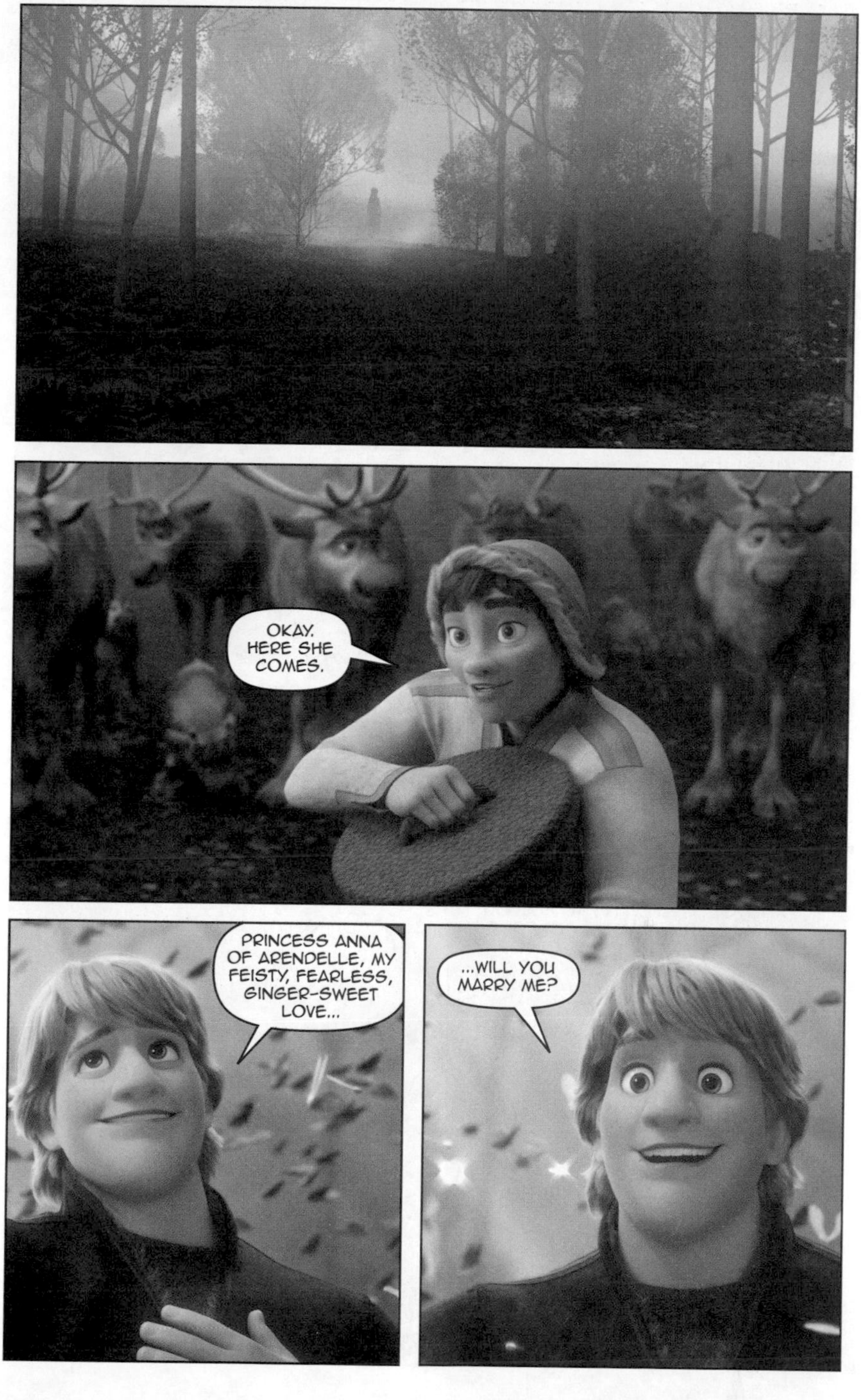
OKAY. HERE SHE COMES.
PRINCESS ANNA OF ARENDELLE, MY FEISTY, FEARLESS, GINGER-SWEET LOVE...
...WILL YOU MARRY ME?

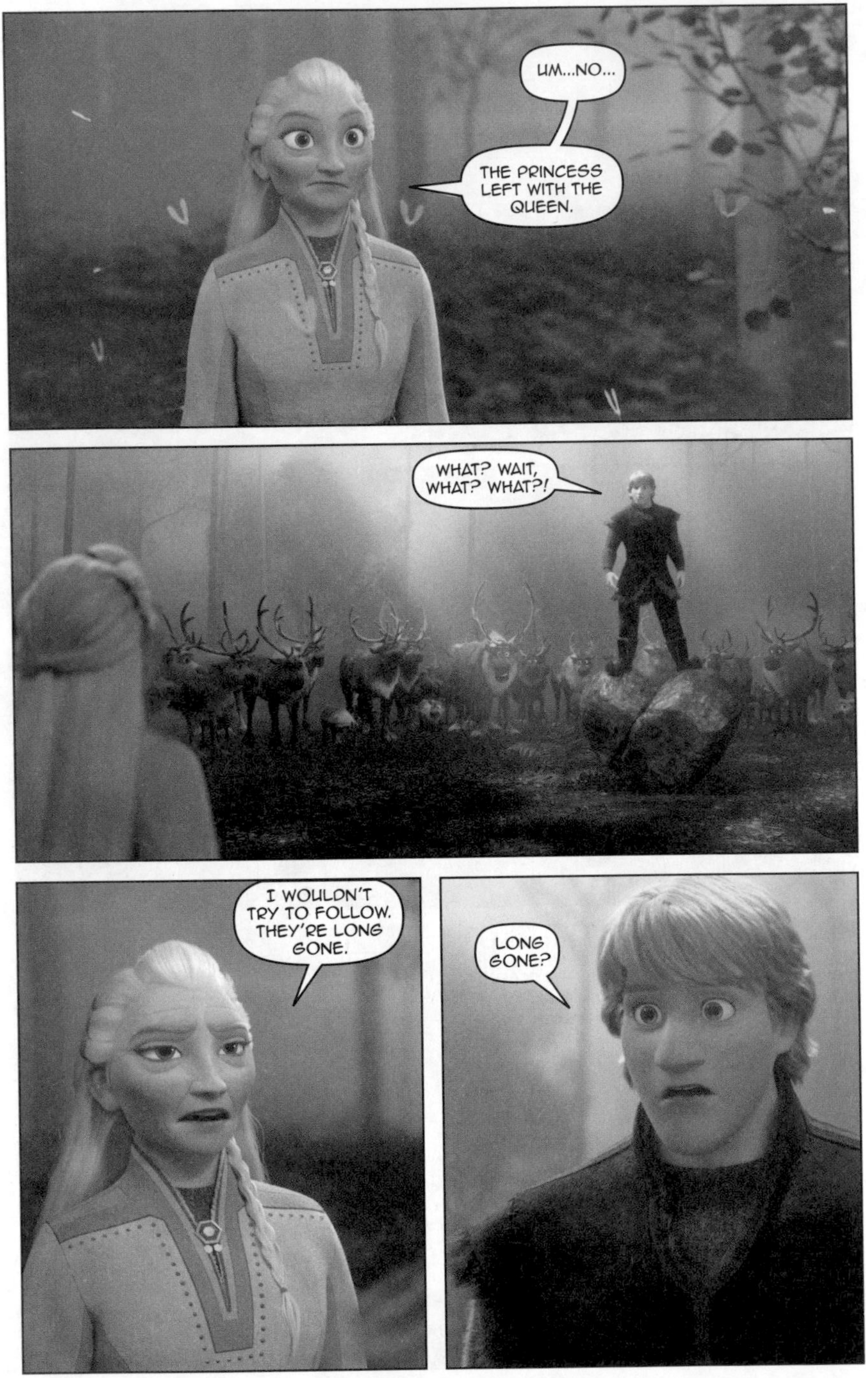
UM...NO...
THE PRINCESS LEFT WITH THE QUEEN.
WHAT? WAIT, WHAT? WHAT?!
I WOULDN'T TRY TO FOLLOW. THEY'RE LONG GONE.
LONG GONE?

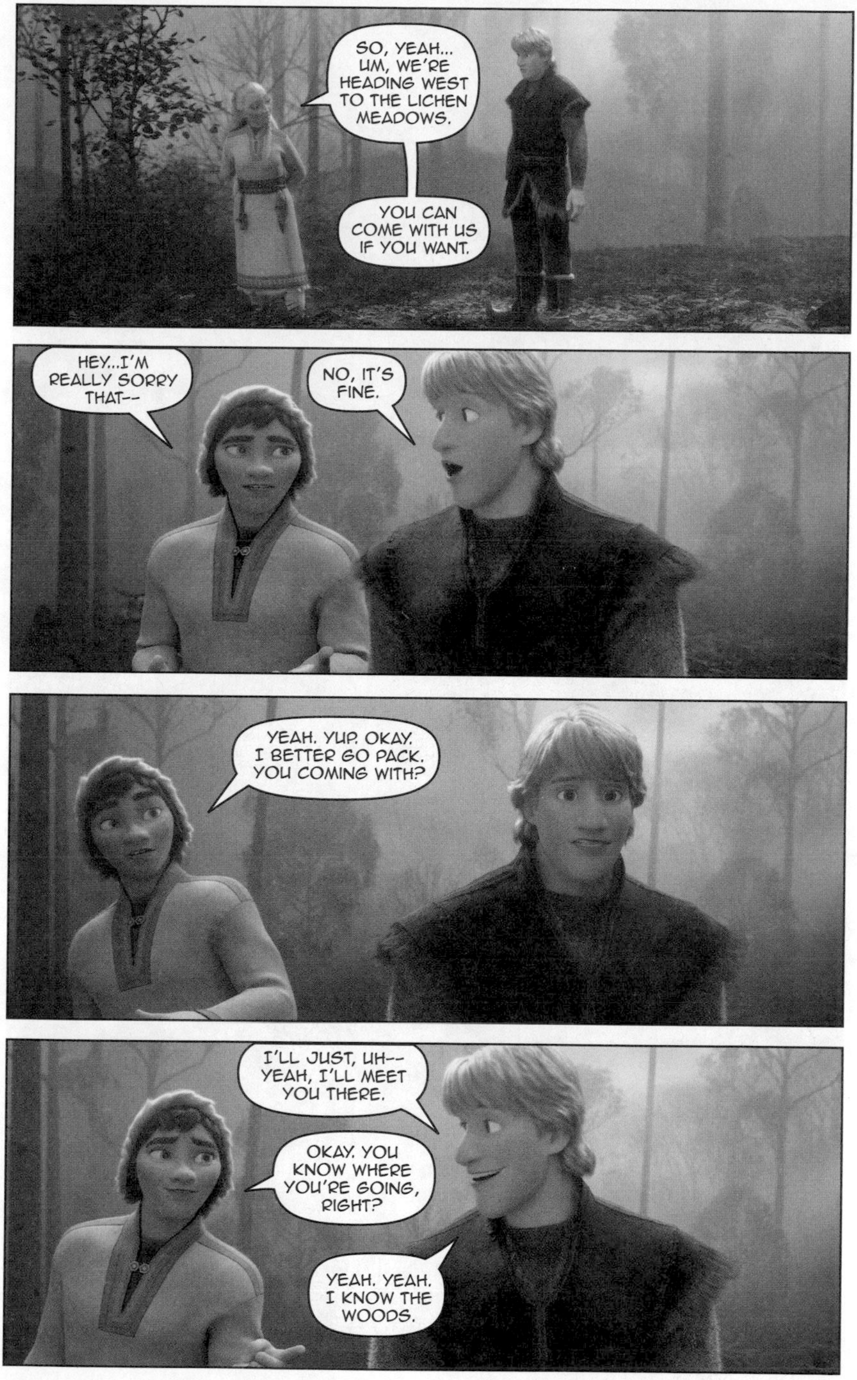
SO, YEAH... UM, WE'RE HEADING WEST TO THE LICHEN MEADOWS.
YOU CAN COME WITH US IF YOU WANT.
HEY...I'M REALLY SORRY THAT--
NO, IT'S FINE.
YEAH. YUP. OKAY. I BETTER GO PACK. YOU COMING WITH?
I'LL JUST, UH-- YEAH, I'LL MEET YOU THERE.
OKAY. YOU KNOW WHERE YOU'RE GOING, RIGHT?
YEAH. YEAH. I KNOW THE WOODS.

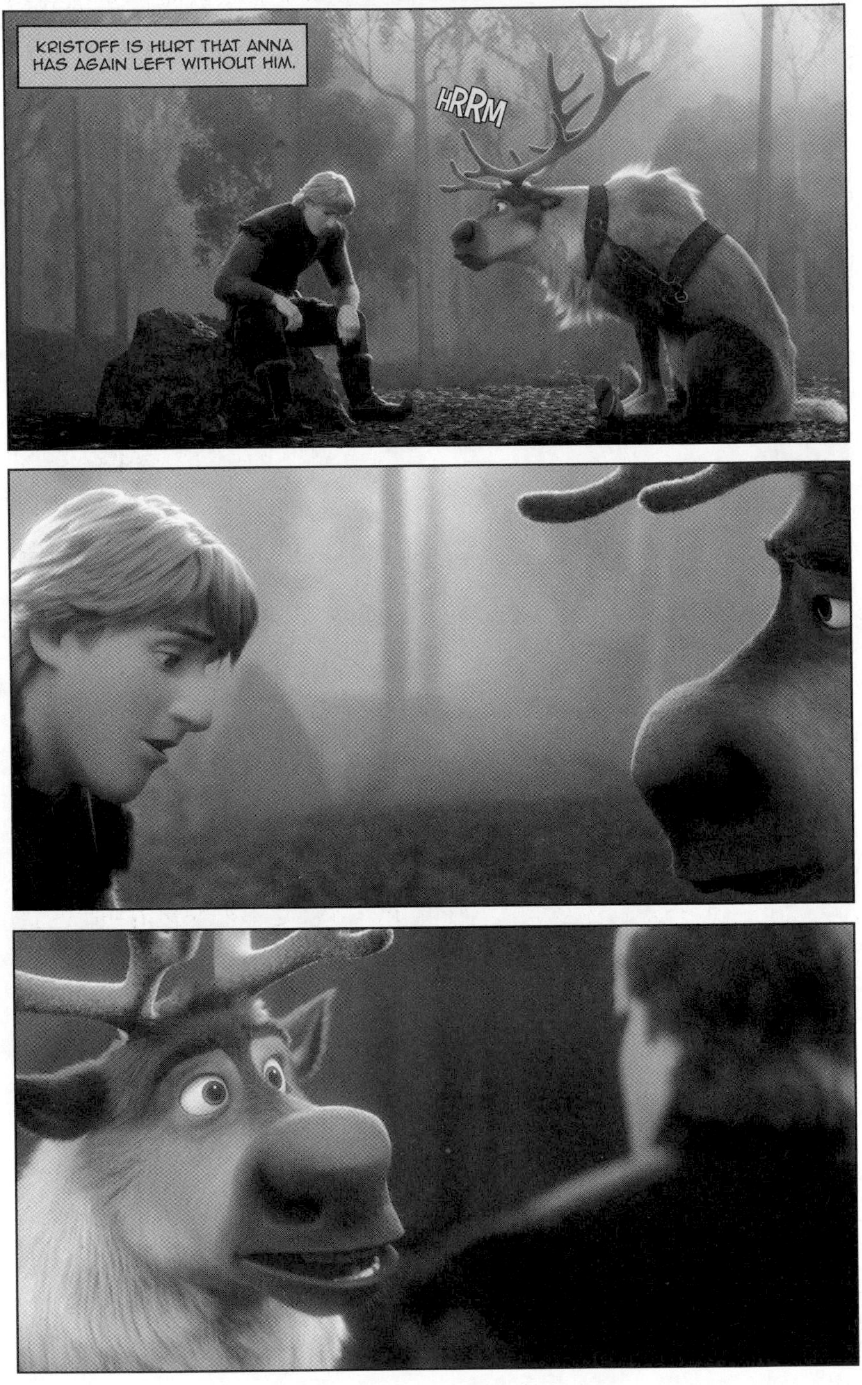
KRISTOFF IS HURT THAT ANNA HAS AGAIN LEFT WITHOUT HIM.
HRRM

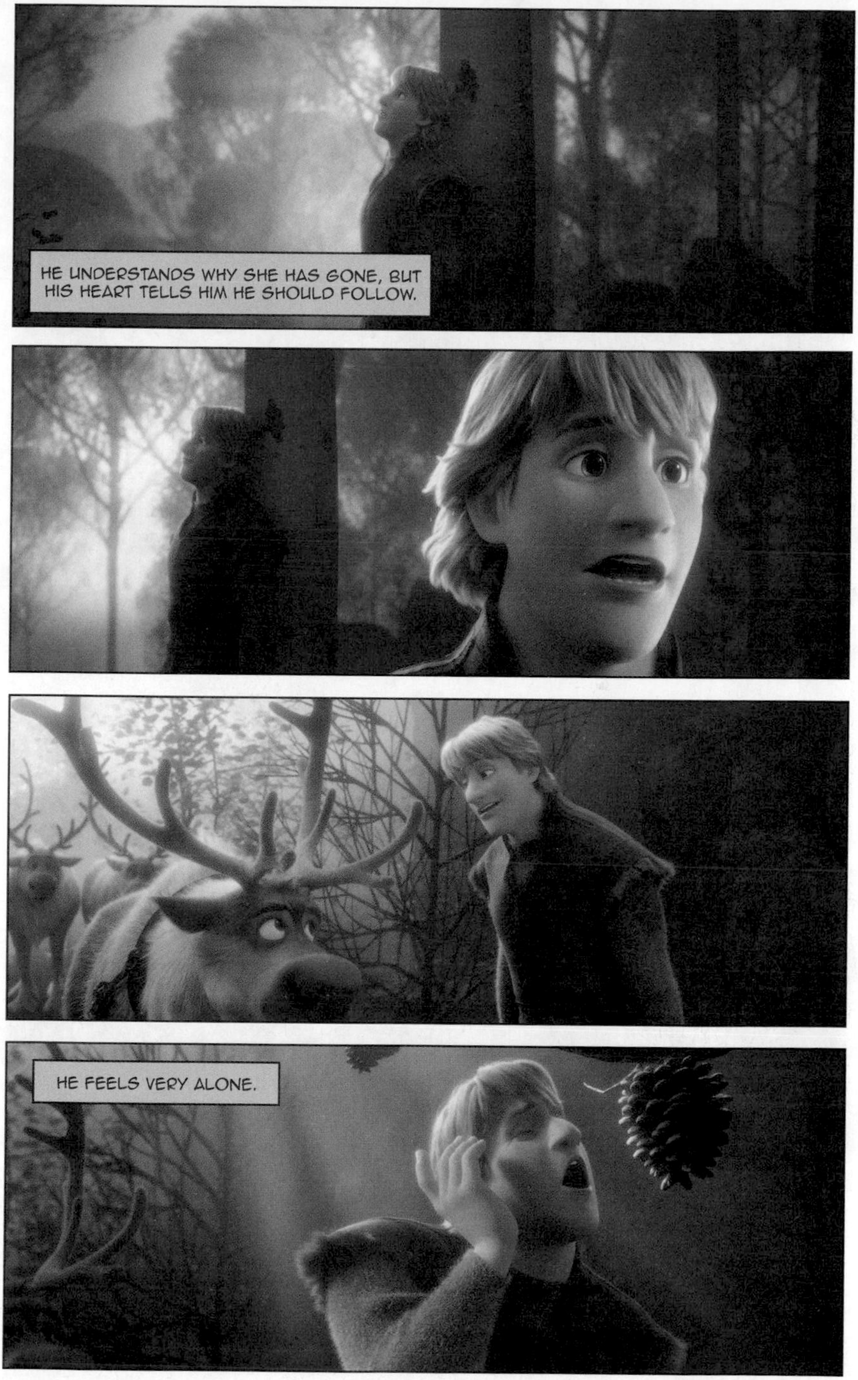
HE UNDERSTANDS WHY SHE HAS GONE, BUT HIS HEART TELLS HIM HE SHOULD FOLLOW.
HE FEELS VERY ALONE.

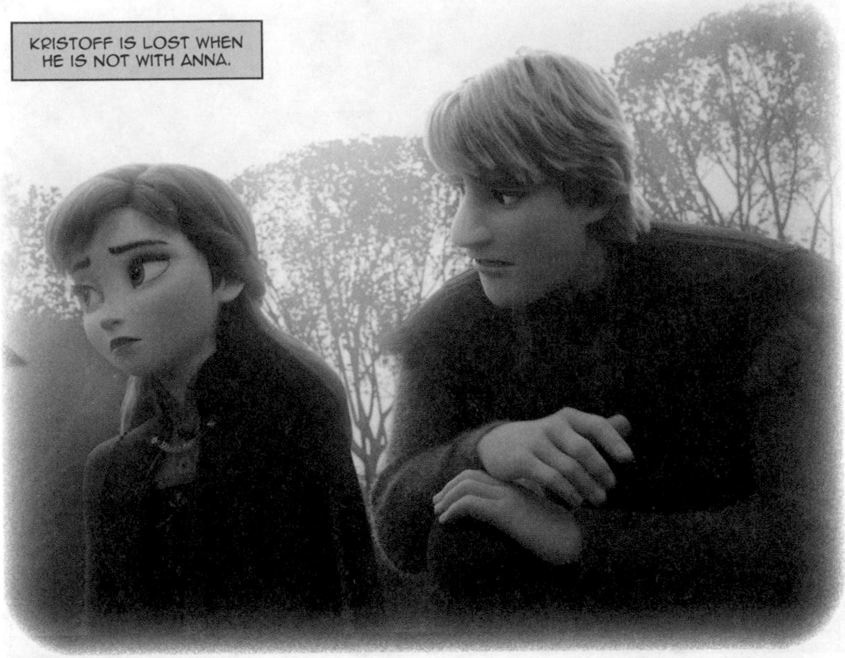
KRISTOFF IS LOST WHEN HE IS NOT WITH ANNA.

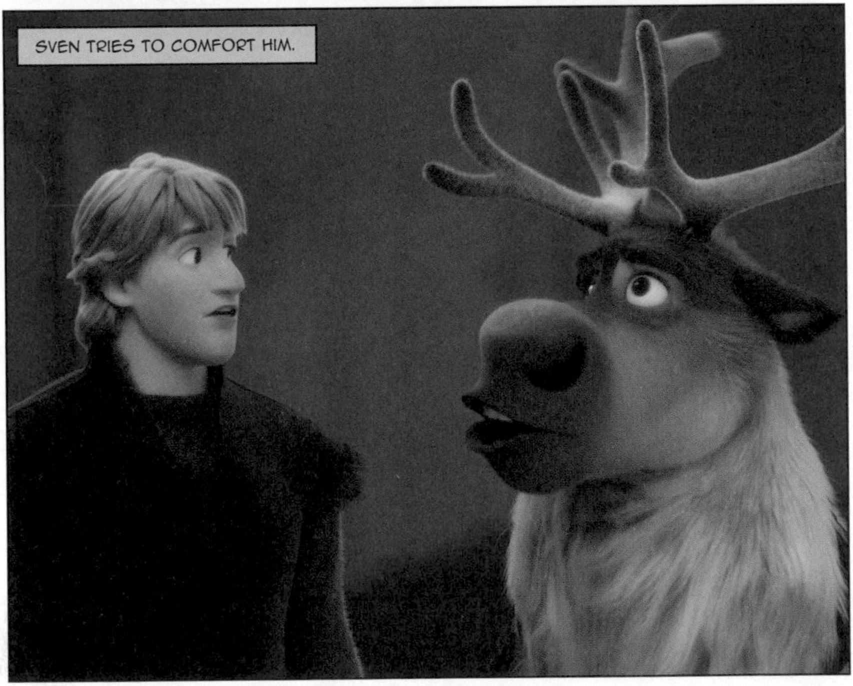
SVEN TRIES TO COMFORT HIM.

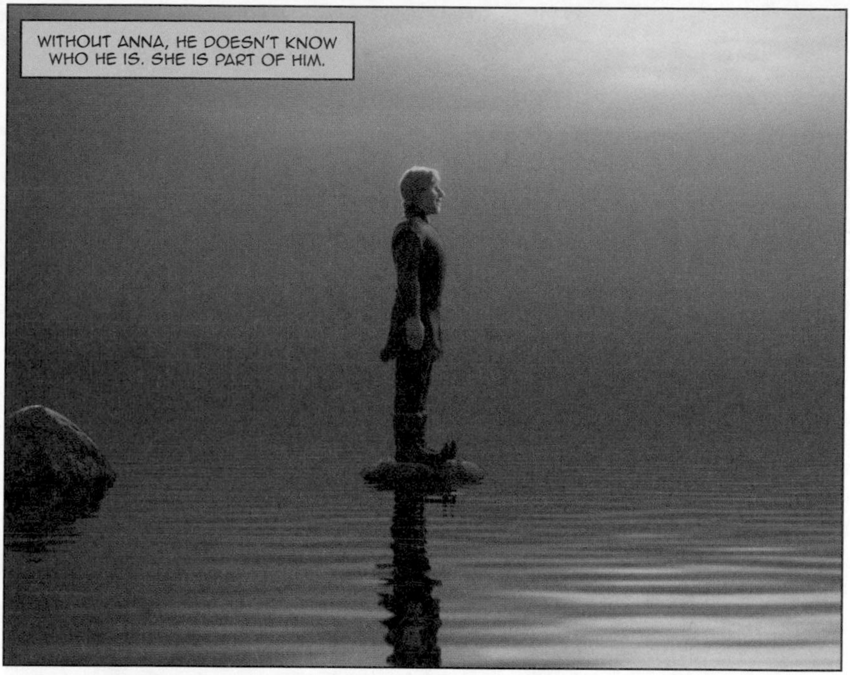
WITHOUT ANNA, HE DOESN'T KNOW WHO HE IS. SHE IS PART OF HIM.

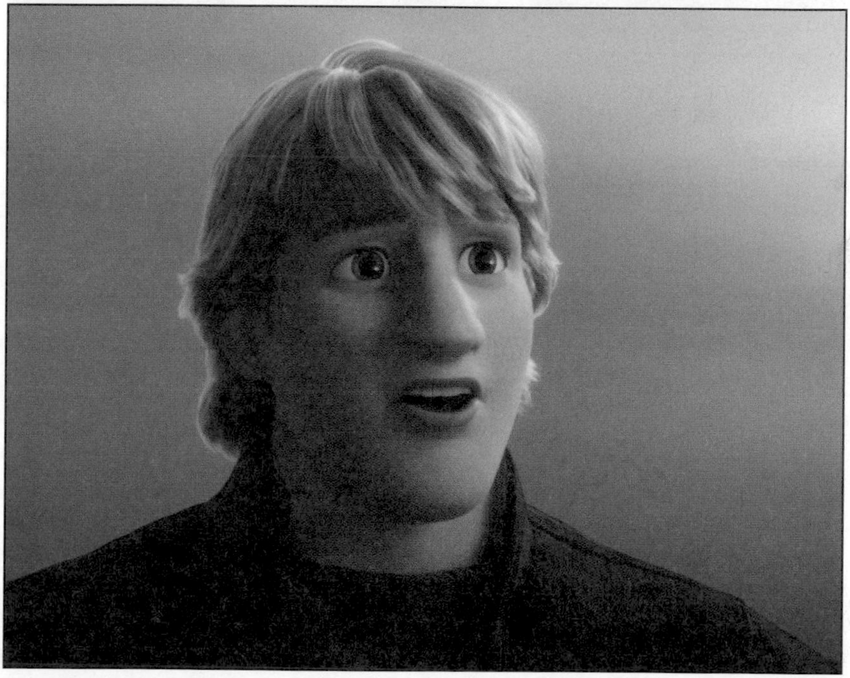

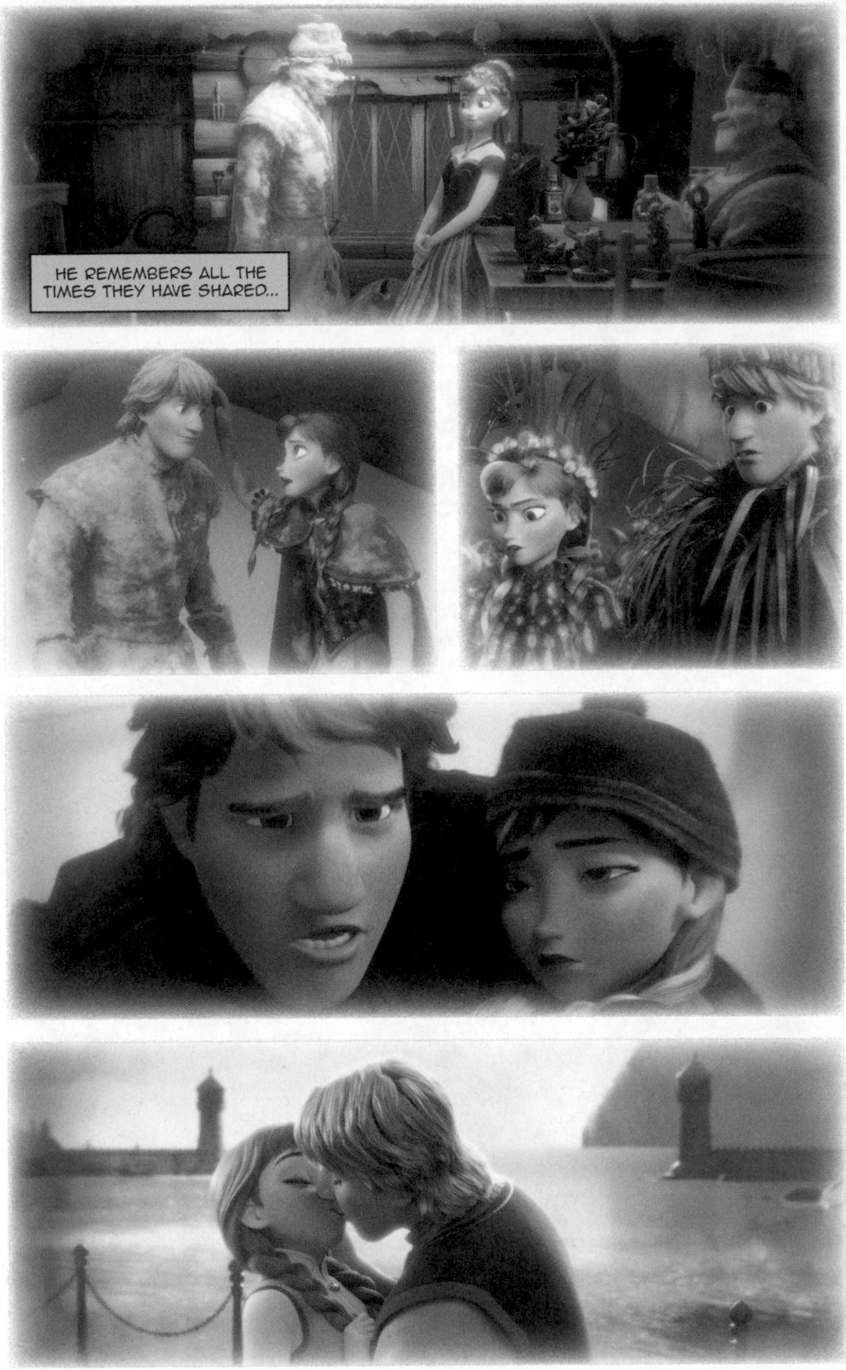
HE REMEMBERS ALL THE TIMES THEY HAVE SHARED...

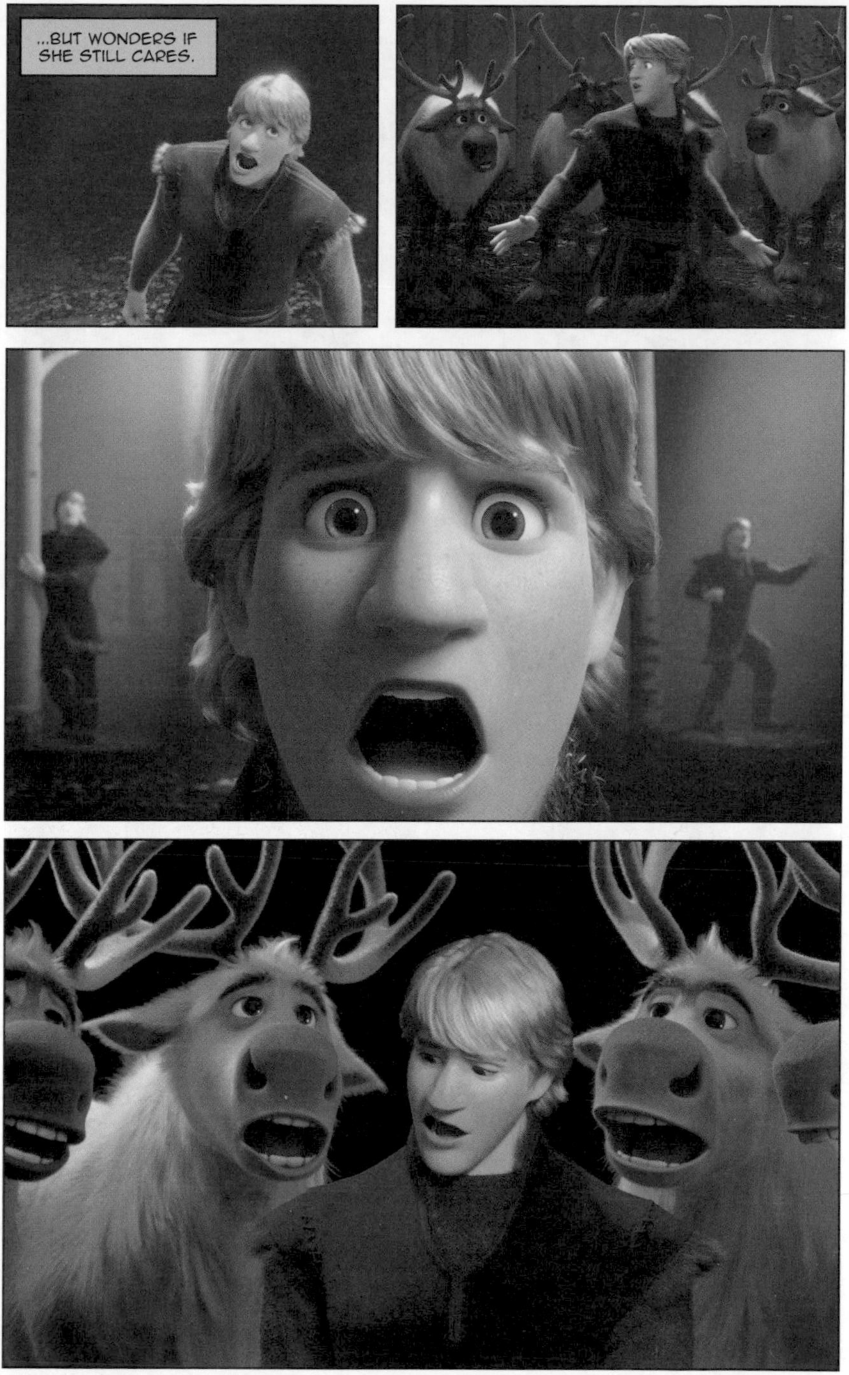
...BUT WONDERS IF SHE STILL CARES.

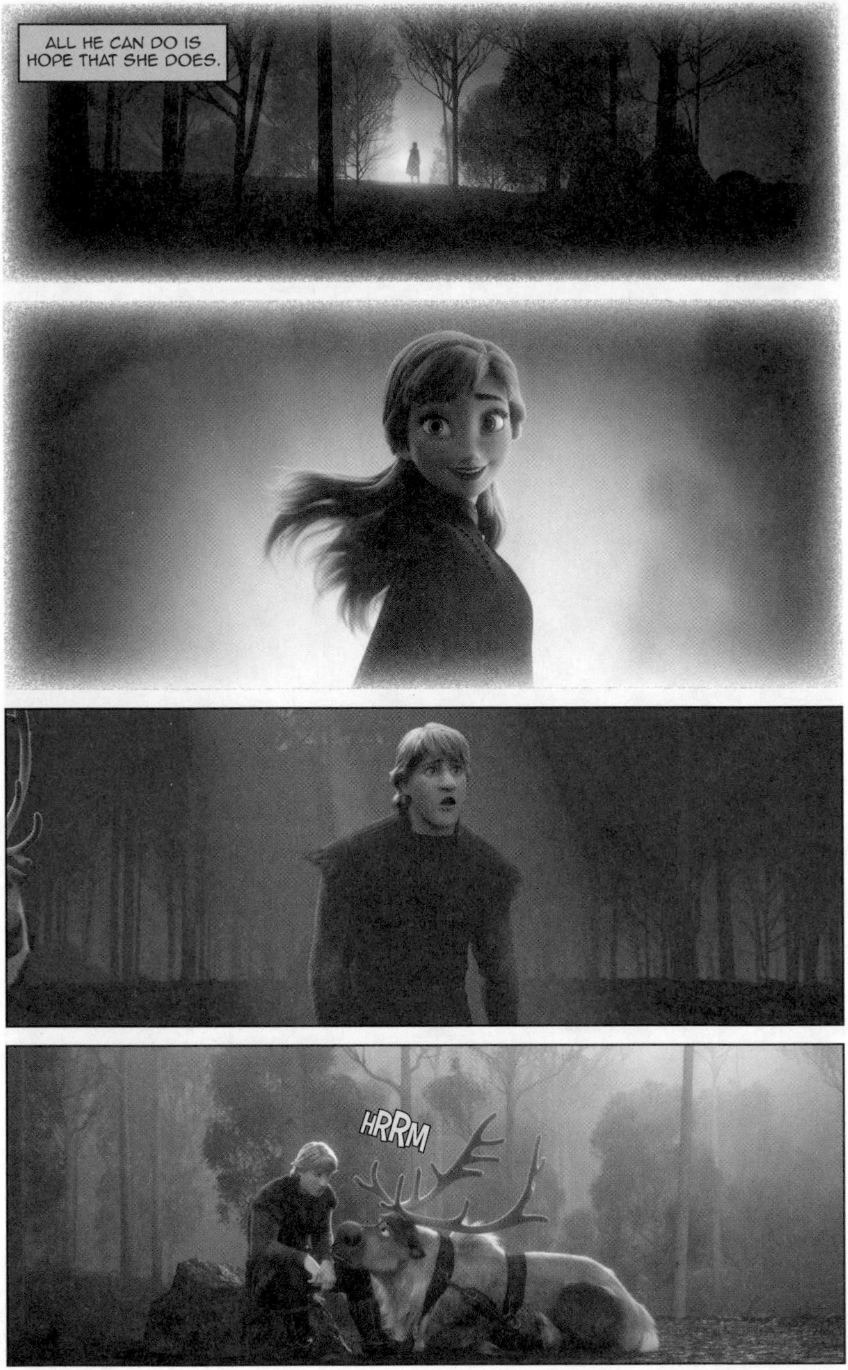
ALL HE CAN DO IS HOPE THAT SHE DOES.
HRRM

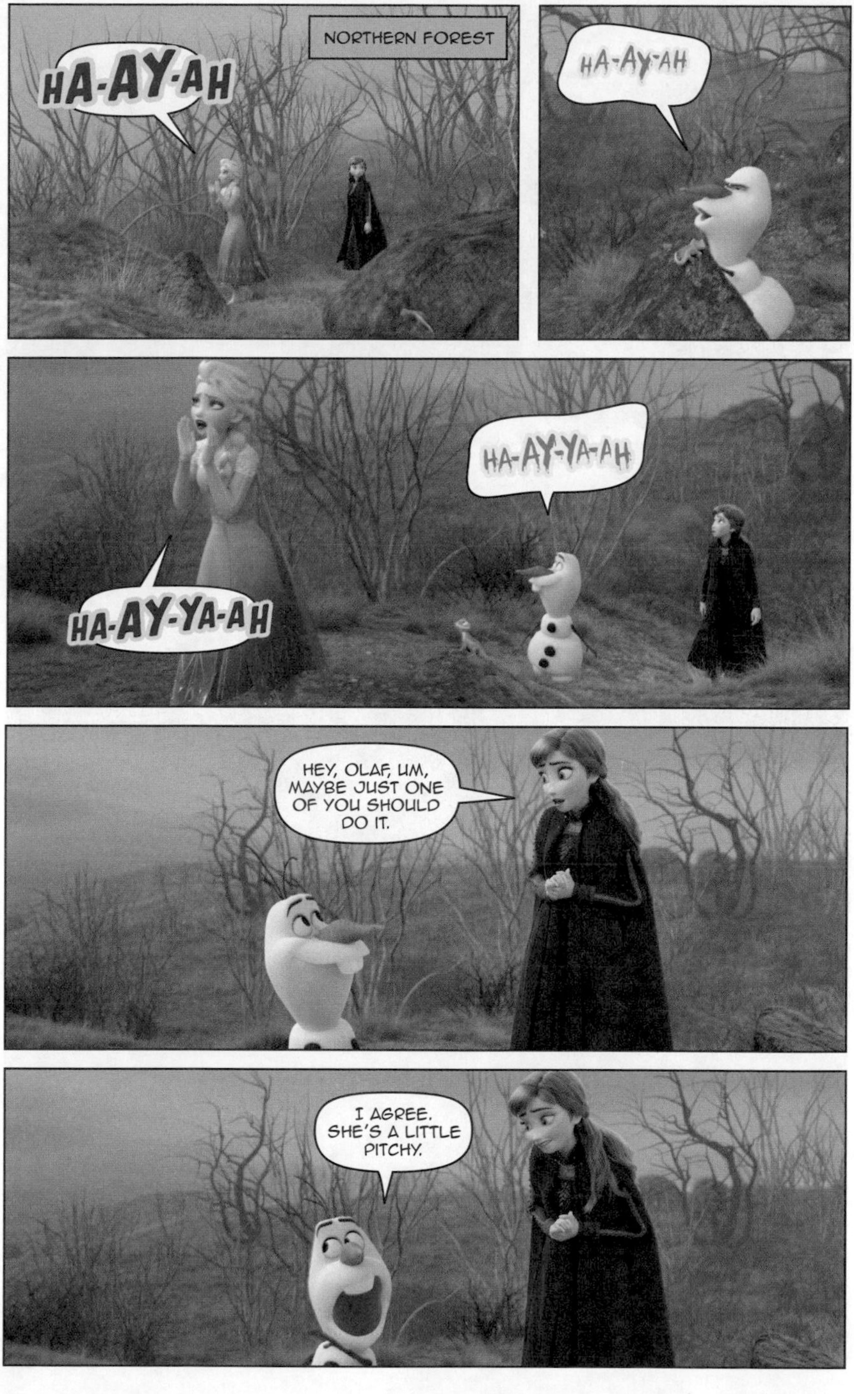
NORTHERN FOREST
HA-AY-AH
HA-AY-AH
HA-AY-YA-AH
HA-AY-YA-AH
HEY, OLAF, UM, MAYBE JUST ONE OF YOU SHOULD DO IT.
I AGREE. SHE'S A LITTLE PITCHY.

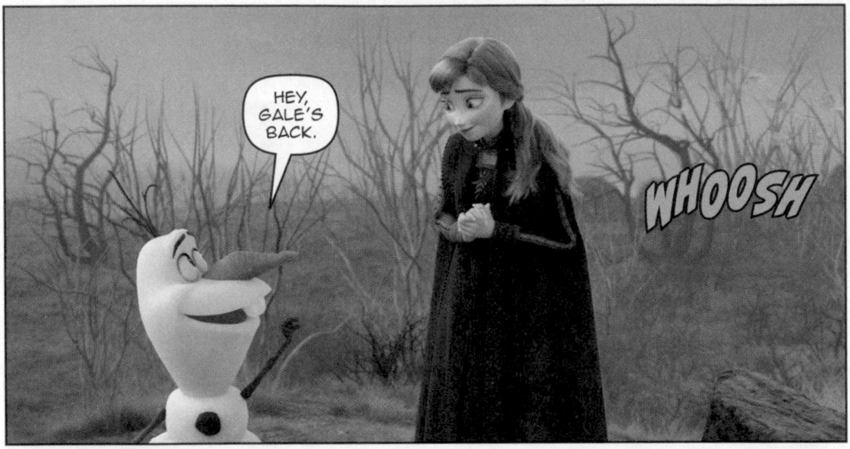
HEY, GALE'S BACK.
WHOOSH

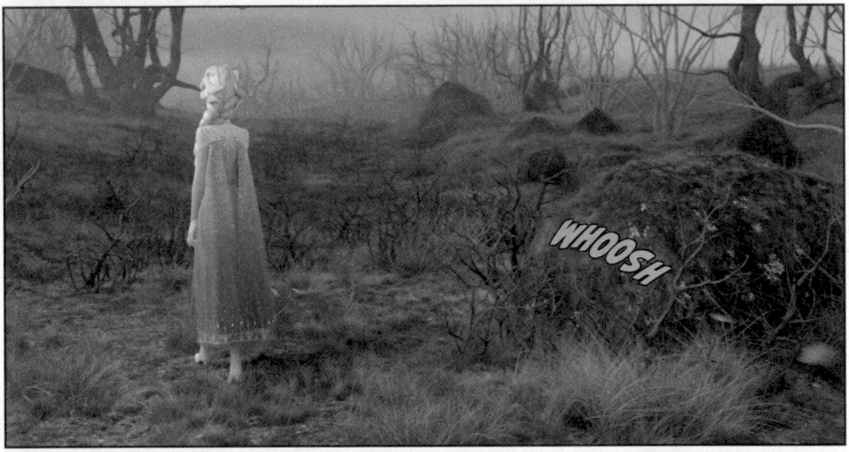
WHOOSH

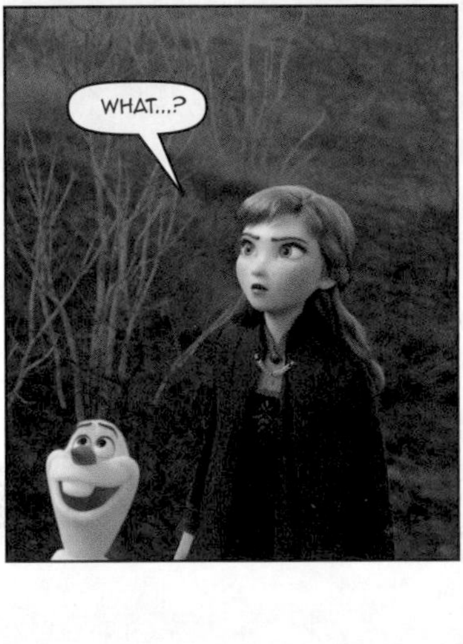
WHAT...?

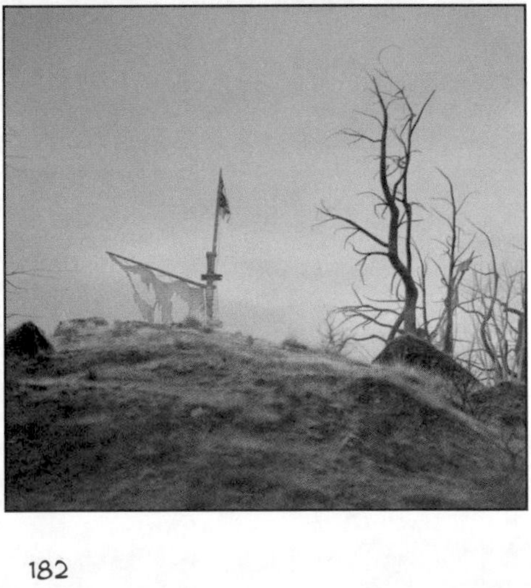

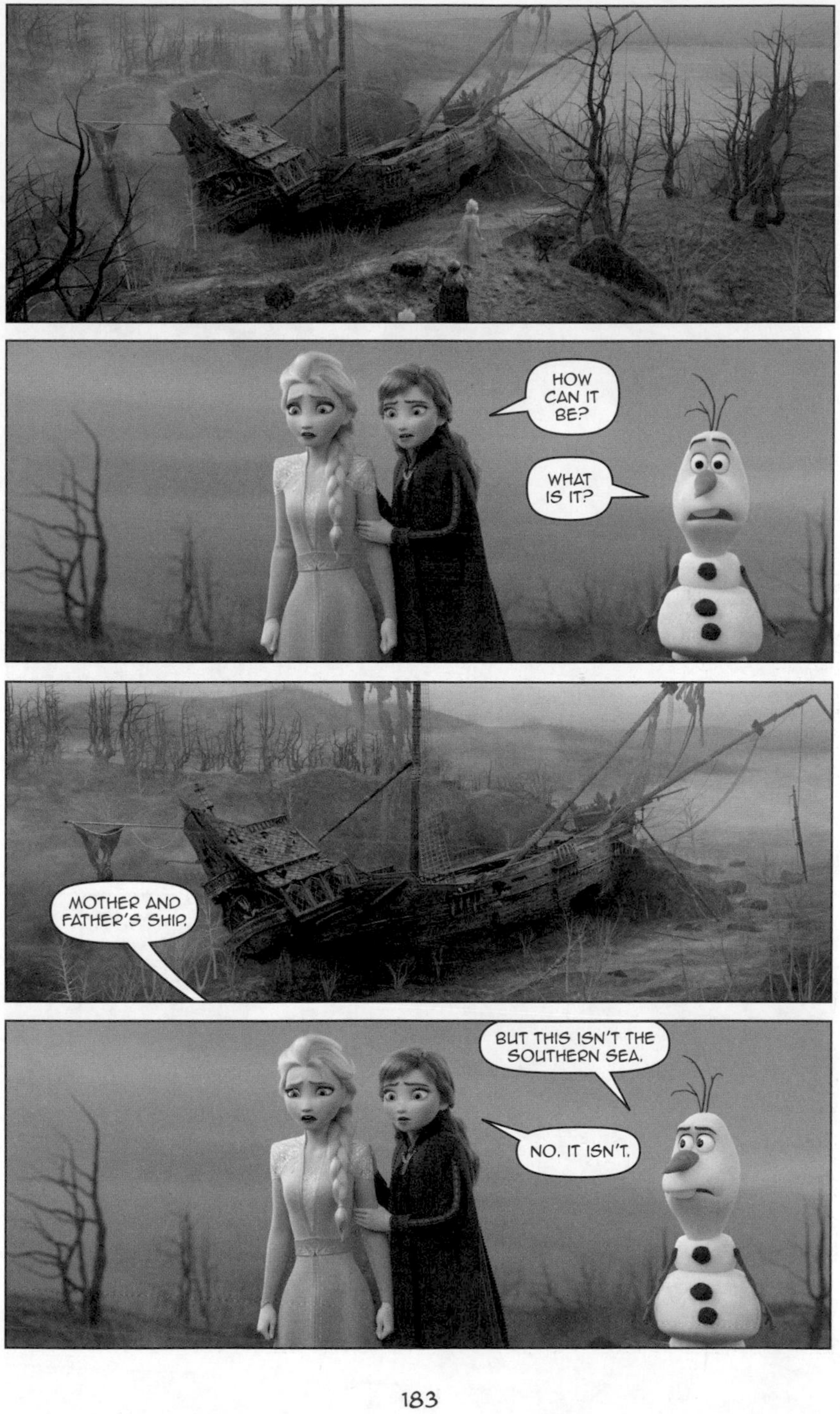
HOW CAN IT BE?
WHAT IS IT?
MOTHER AND FATHER'S SHIP.
BUT THIS ISN'T THE SOUTHERN SEA.
NO. IT ISN'T.

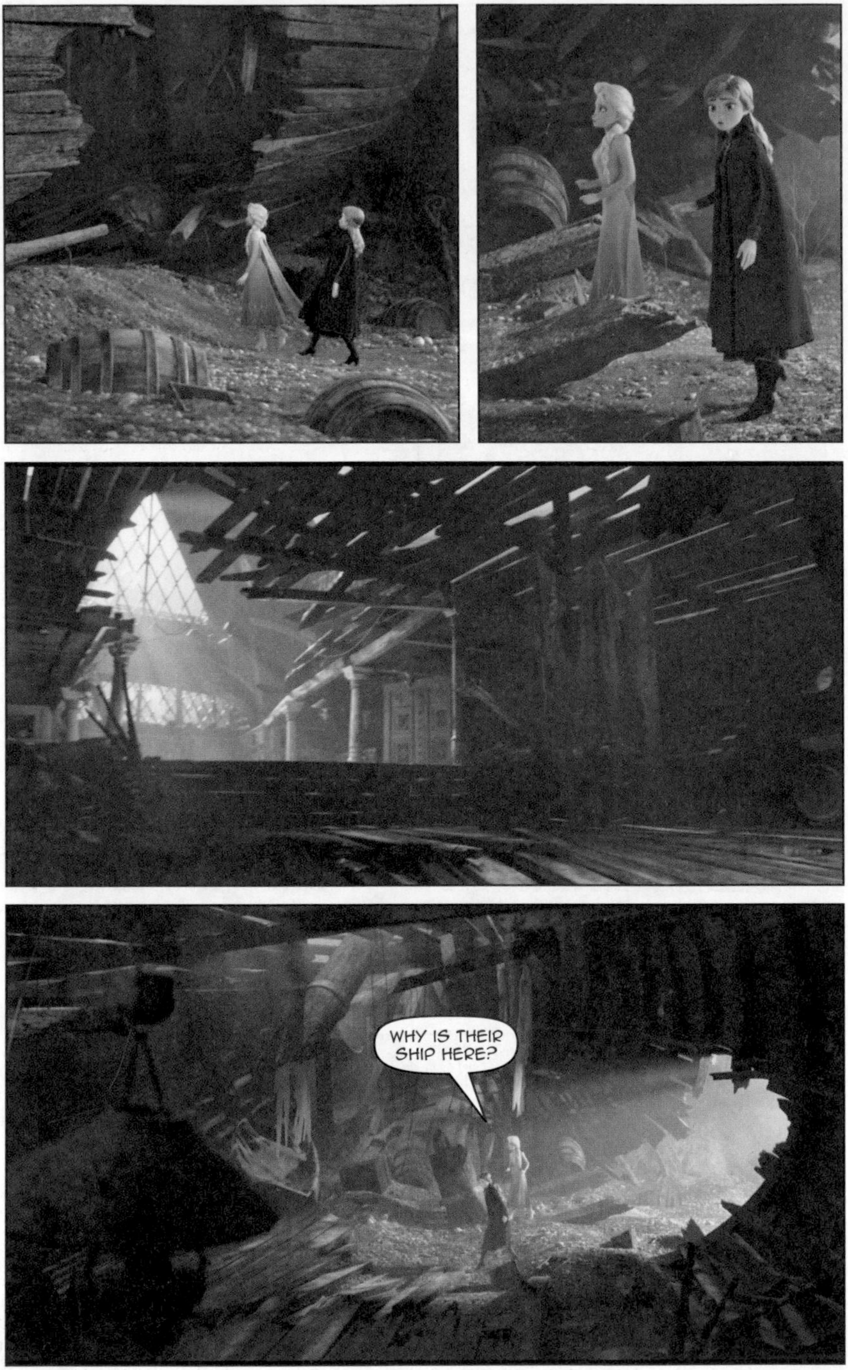
WHY IS THEIR SHIP HERE?

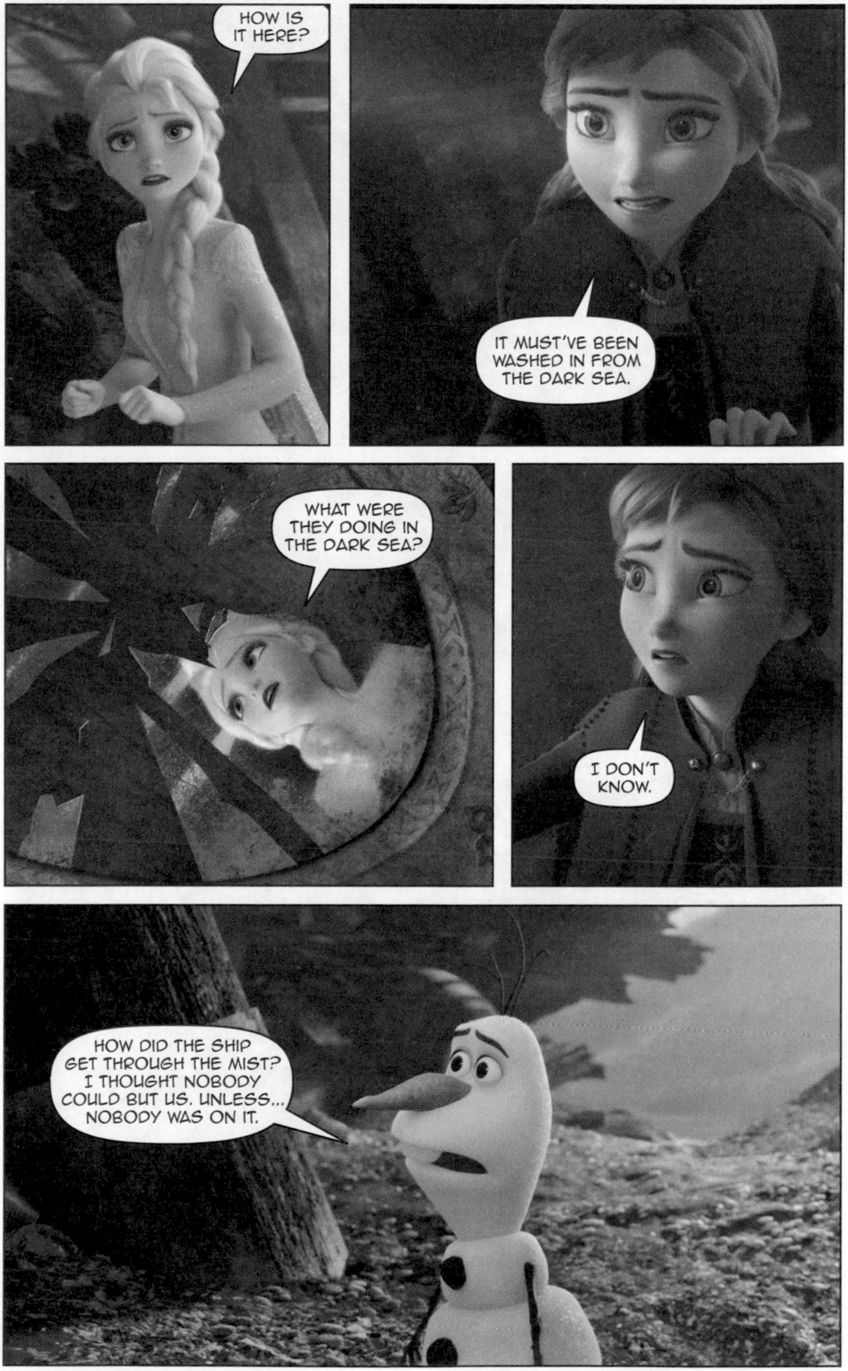
HOW IS IT HERE?
IT MUST'VE BEEN WASHED IN FROM THE DARK SEA.
WHAT WERE THEY DOING IN THE DARK SEA?
I DON'T KNOW.
HOW DID THE SHIP GET THROUGH THE MIST? I THOUGHT NOBODY COULD BUT US. UNLESS... NOBODY WAS ON IT.

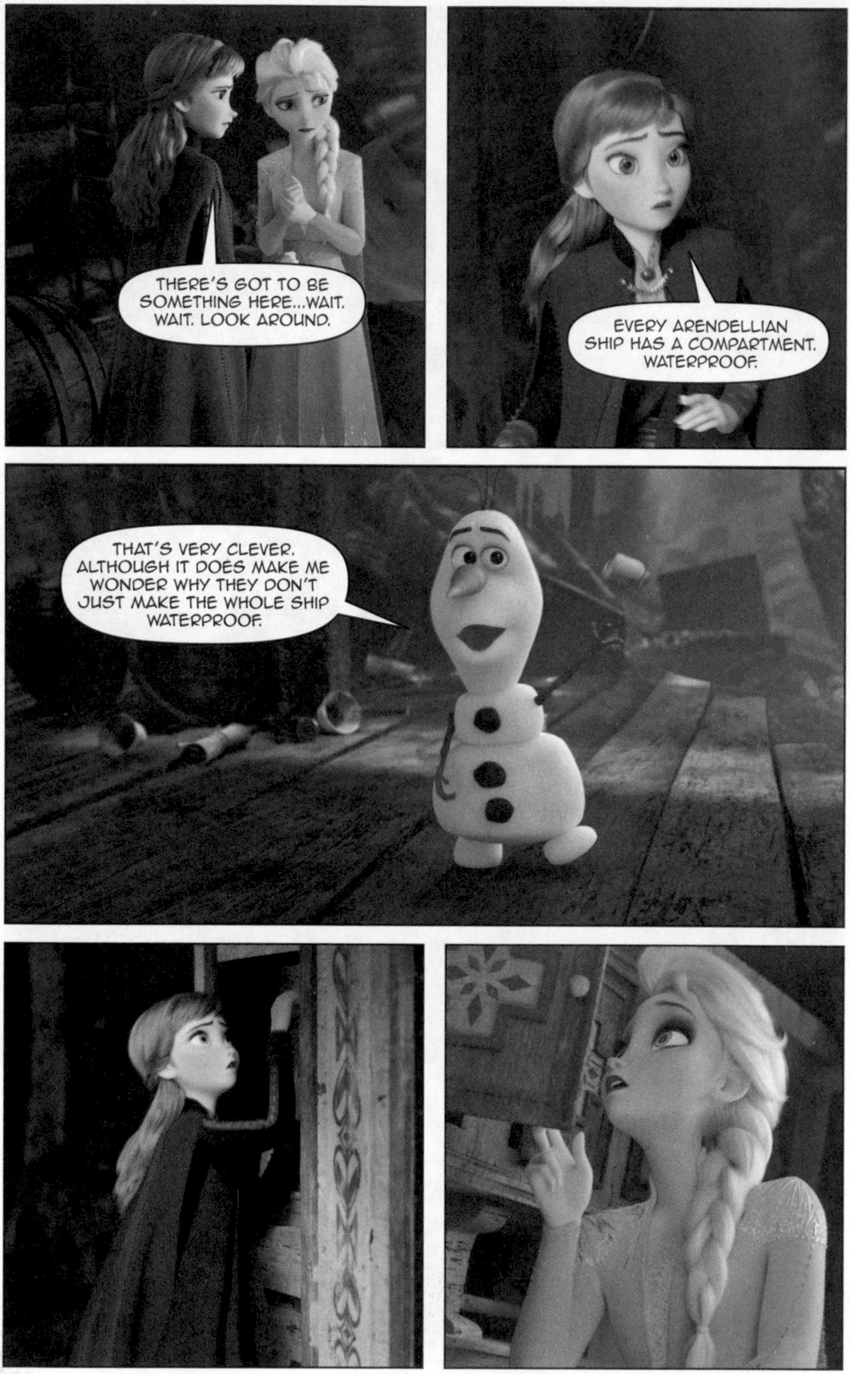
THERE'S GOT TO BE SOMETHING HERE...WAIT. WAIT. LOOK AROUND.
EVERY ARENDELLIAN SHIP HAS A COMPARTMENT. WATERPROOF.
THAT'S VERY CLEVER. ALTHOUGH IT DOES MAKE ME WONDER WHY THEY DON'T JUST MAKE THE WHOLE SHIP WATERPROOF.

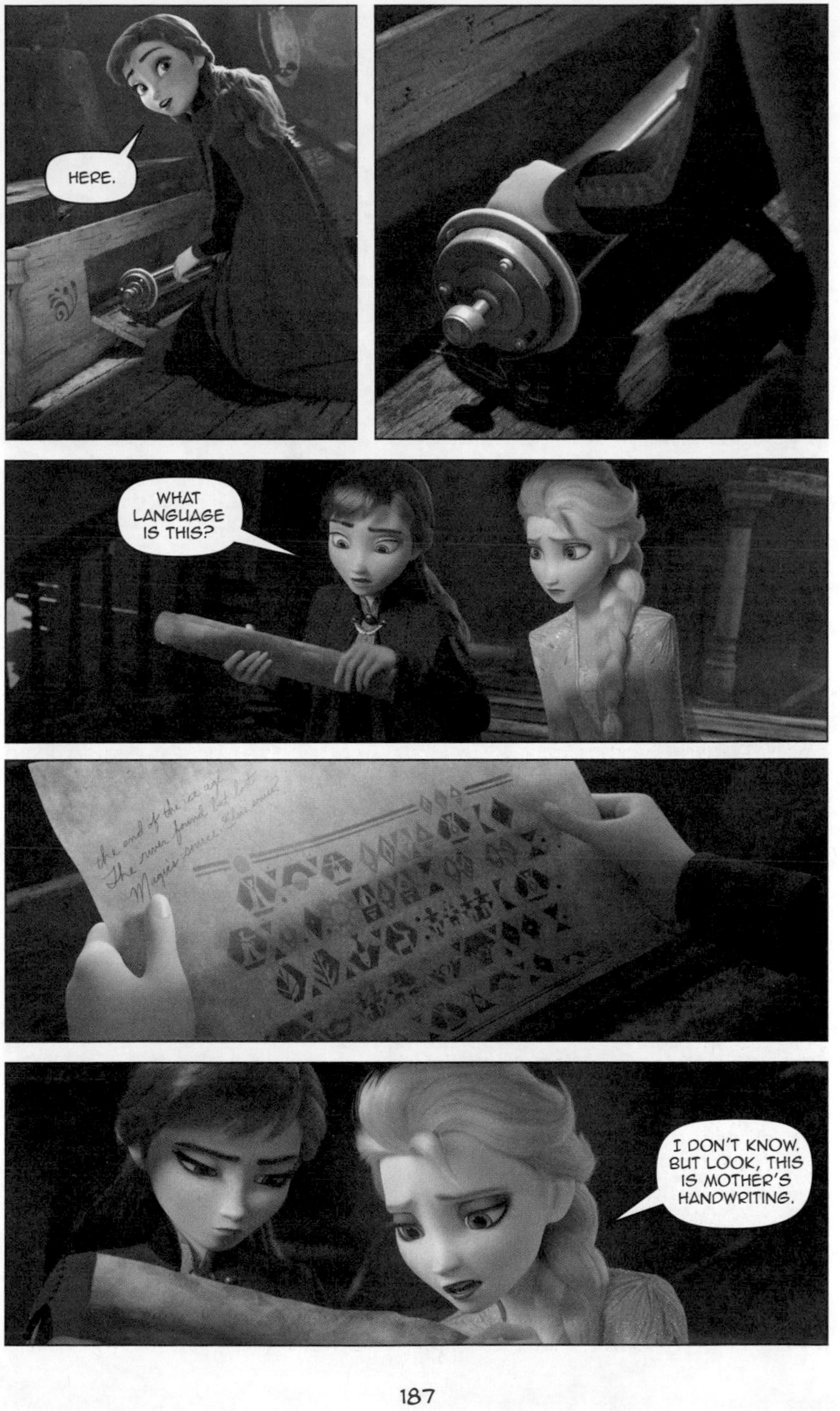
HERE.
WHAT LANGUAGE IS THIS?
I DON'T KNOW. BUT LOOK, THIS IS MOTHER'S HANDWRITING.

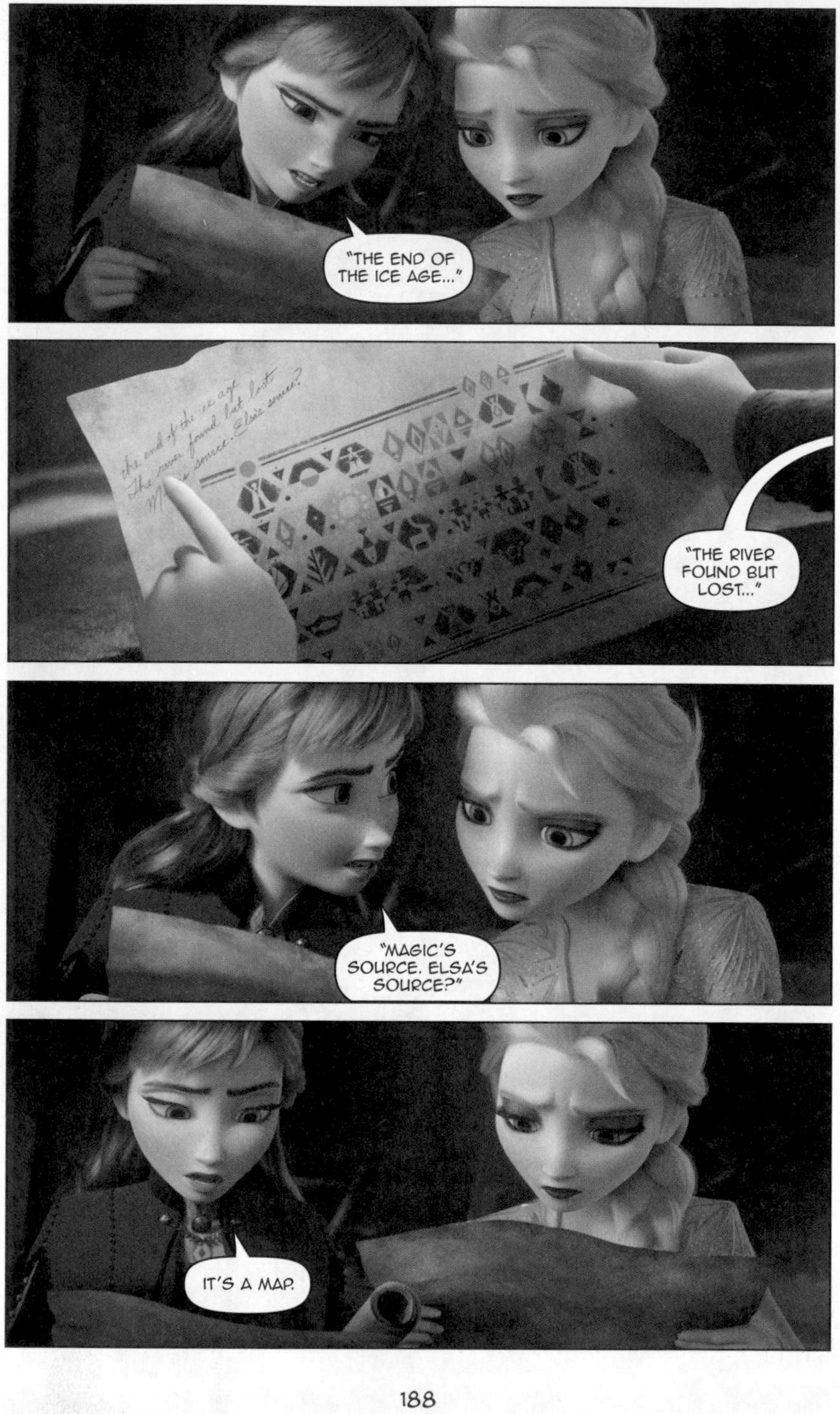

"THE END OF THE ICE AGE..."
the end of the ice age
The river found, but lost
"THE RIVER FOUND BUT LOST..."
"MAGIC'S SOURCE. ELSA'S SOURCE?"
IT'S A MAP.

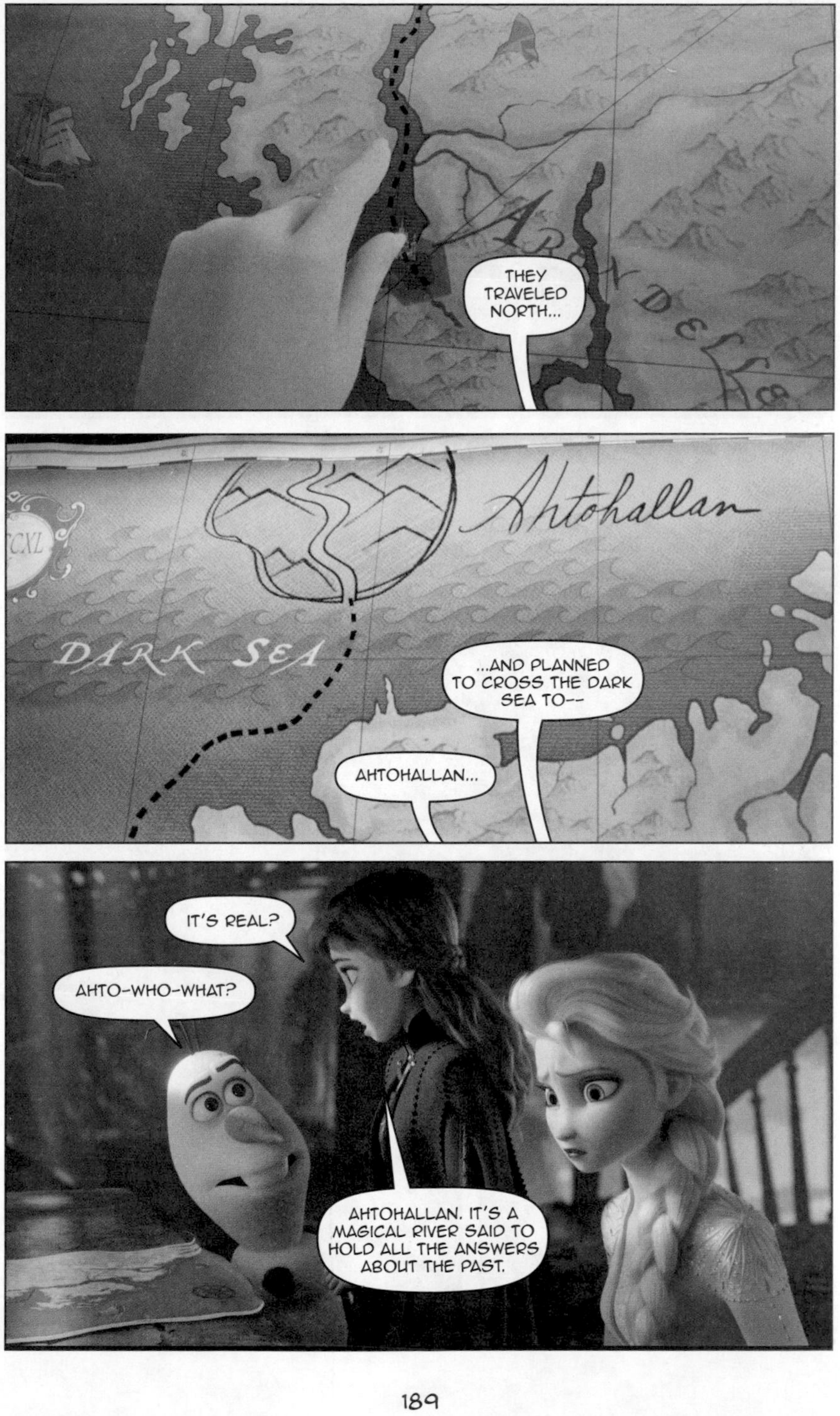
THEY TRAVELED NORTH...
Ahtohallan
DARK SEA
...AND PLANNED TO CROSS THE DARK SEA TO--
AHTOHALLAN...
IT'S REAL?
AHTO-WHO-WHAT?
AHTOHALLAN. IT'S A MAGICAL RIVER SAID TO HOLD ALL THE ANSWERS ABOUT THE PAST.

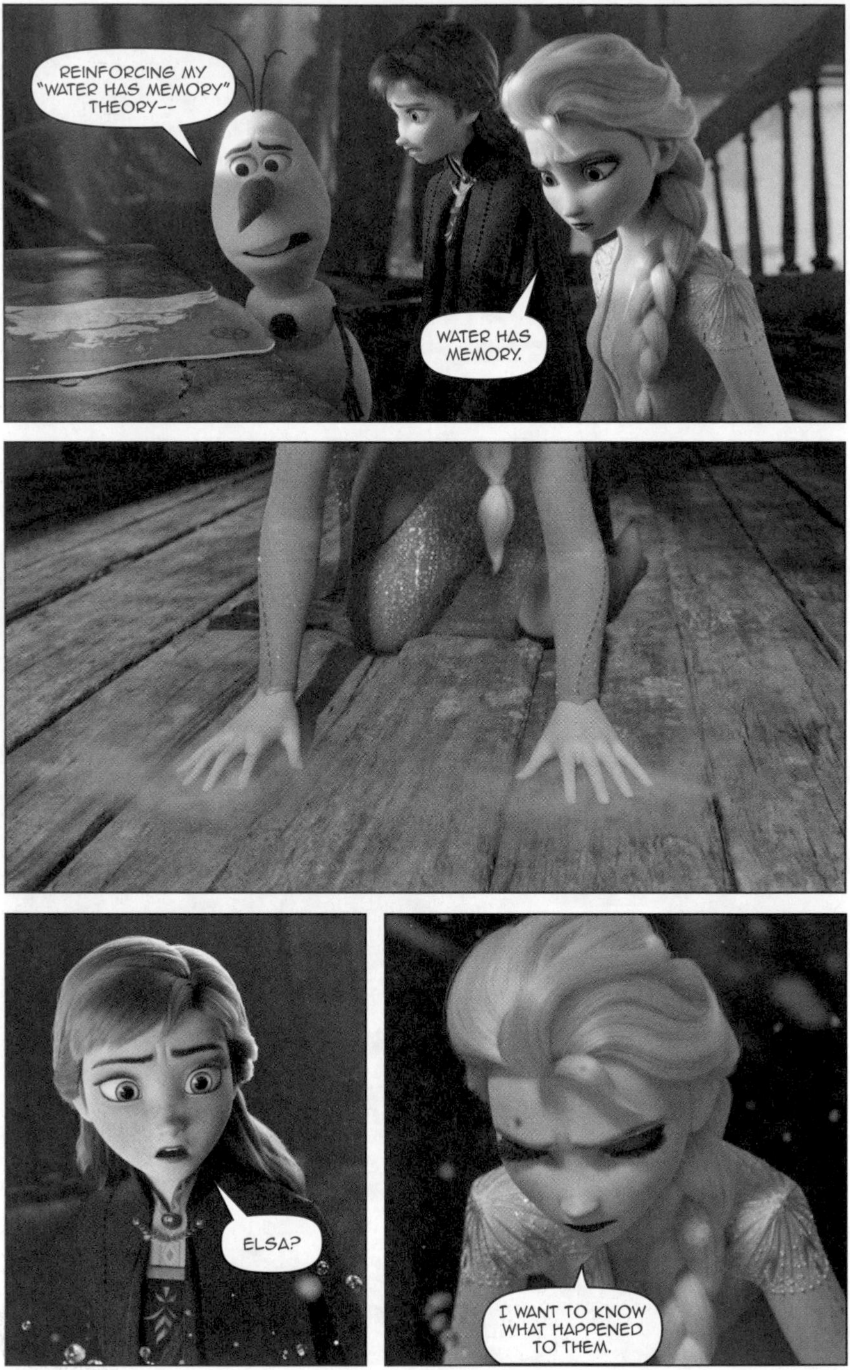
REINFORCING MY "WATER HAS MEMORY" THEORY--
WATER HAS MEMORY.
ELSA?
I WANT TO KNOW WHAT HAPPENED TO THEM.

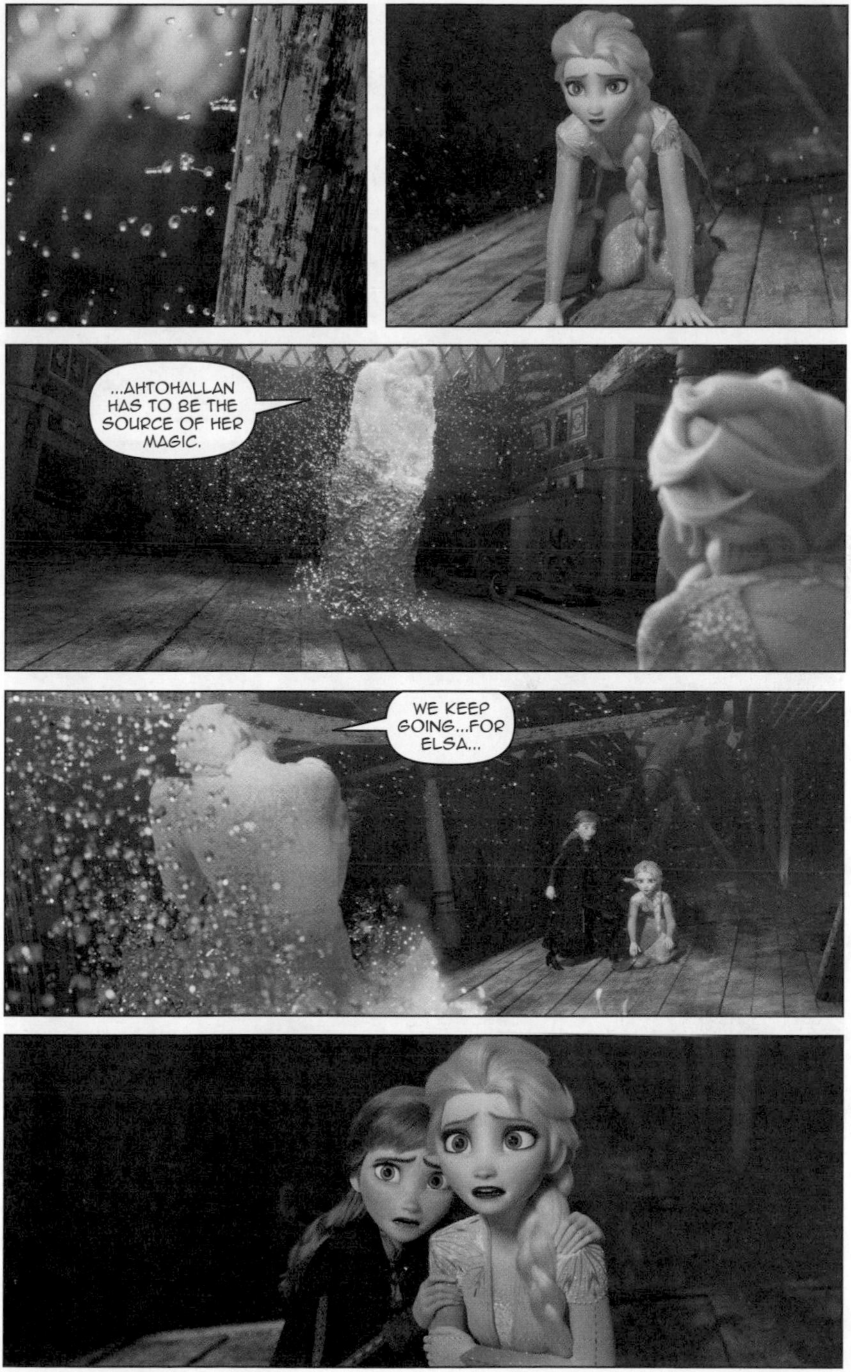
...AHTOHALLAN HAS TO BE THE SOURCE OF HER MAGIC.
WE KEEP GOING...FOR ELSA...

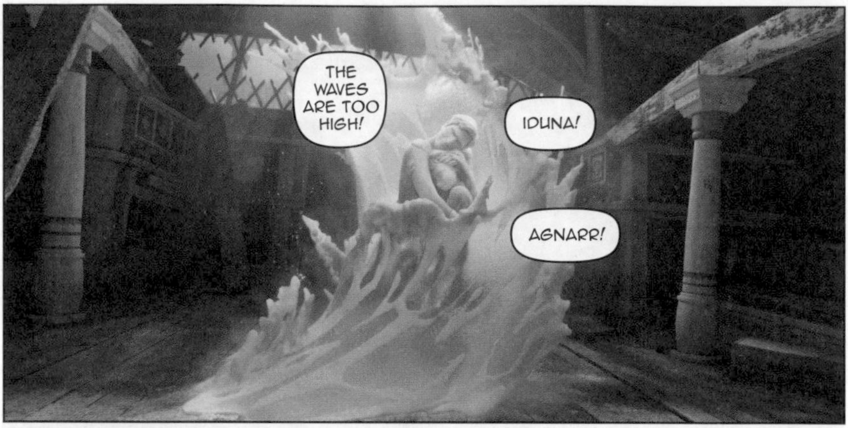
THE WAVES ARE TOO HIGH!
IDUNA!
AGNARR!
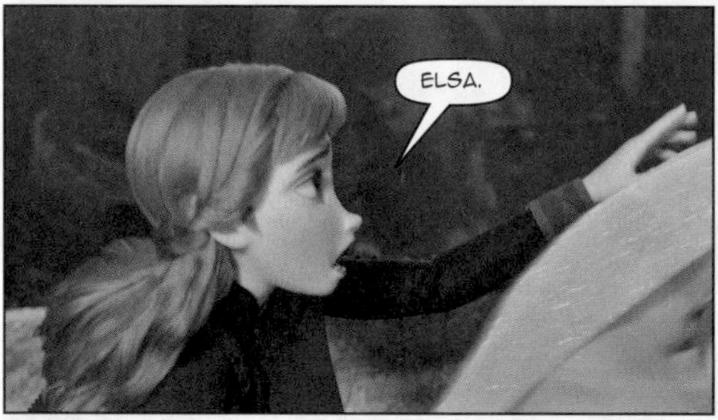
ELSA.
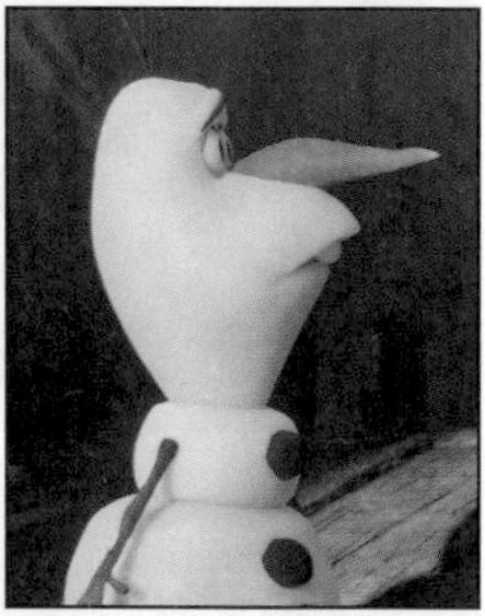
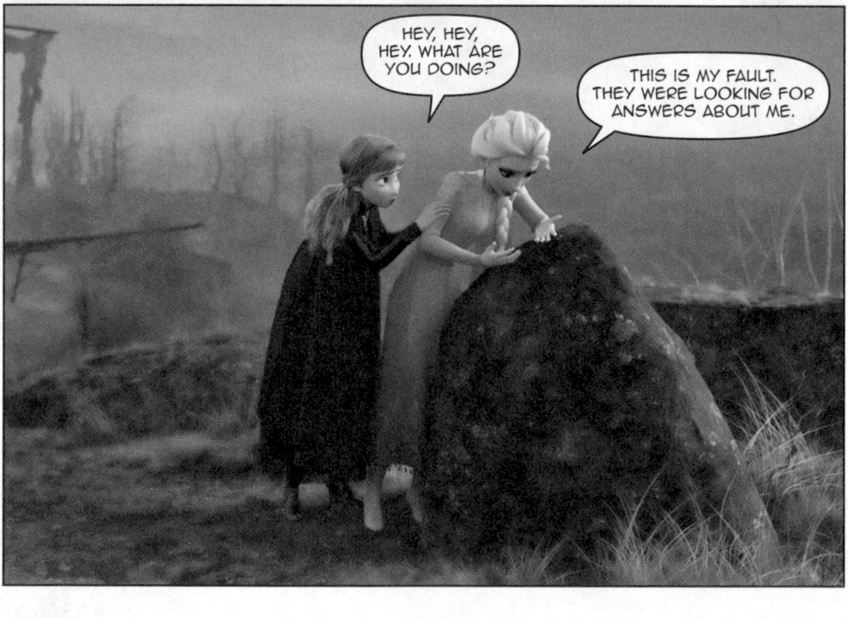
HEY, HEY, HEY. WHAT ARE YOU DOING?
THIS IS MY FAULT. THEY WERE LOOKING FOR ANSWERS ABOUT ME.

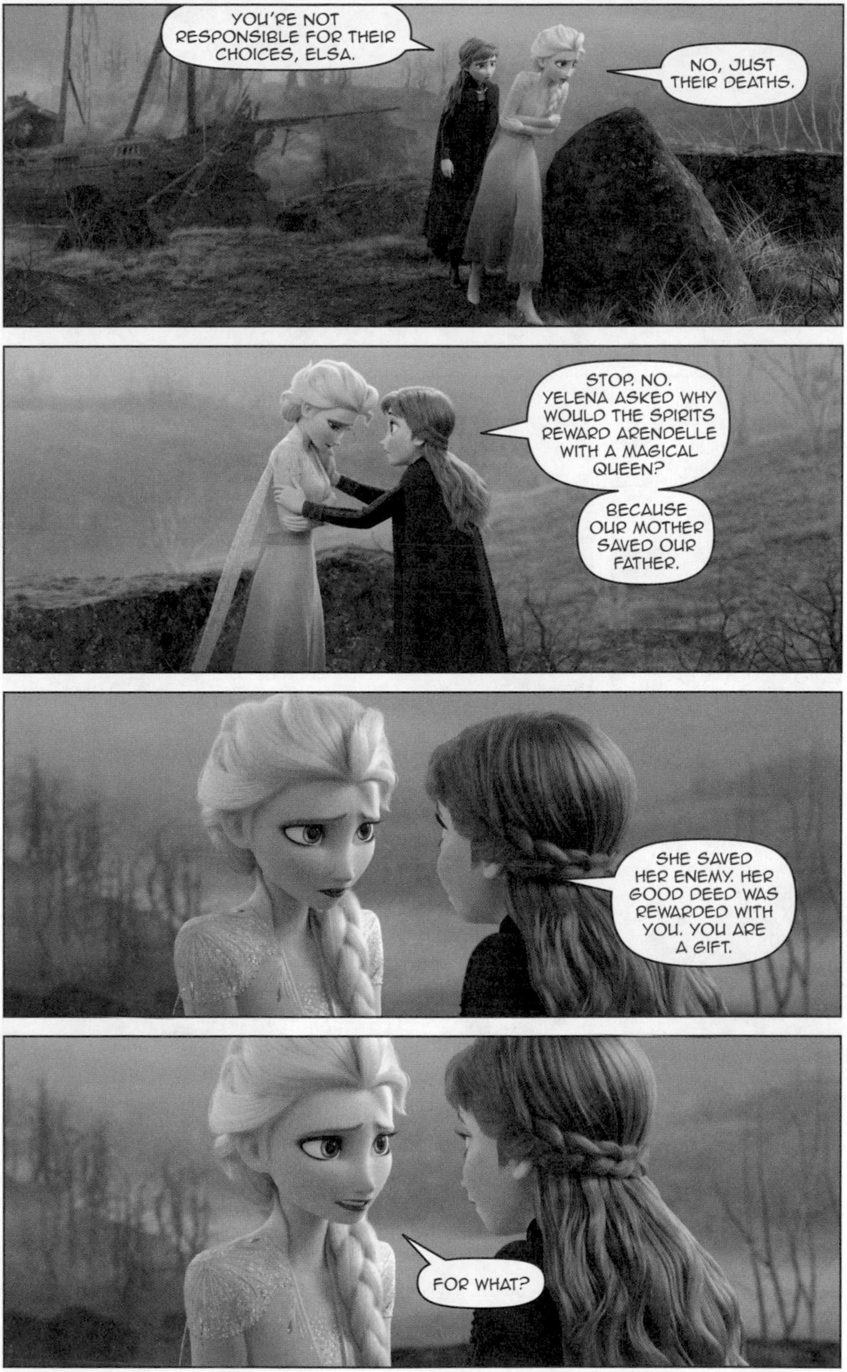
YOU'RE NOT RESPONSIBLE FOR THEIR CHOICES, ELSA.
NO, JUST THEIR DEATHS.
STOP. NO. YELENA ASKED WHY WOULD THE SPIRITS REWARD ARENDELLE WITH A MAGICAL QUEEN?
BECAUSE OUR MOTHER SAVED OUR FATHER.
SHE SAVED HER ENEMY. HER GOOD DEED WAS REWARDED WITH YOU. YOU ARE A GIFT.
FOR WHAT?

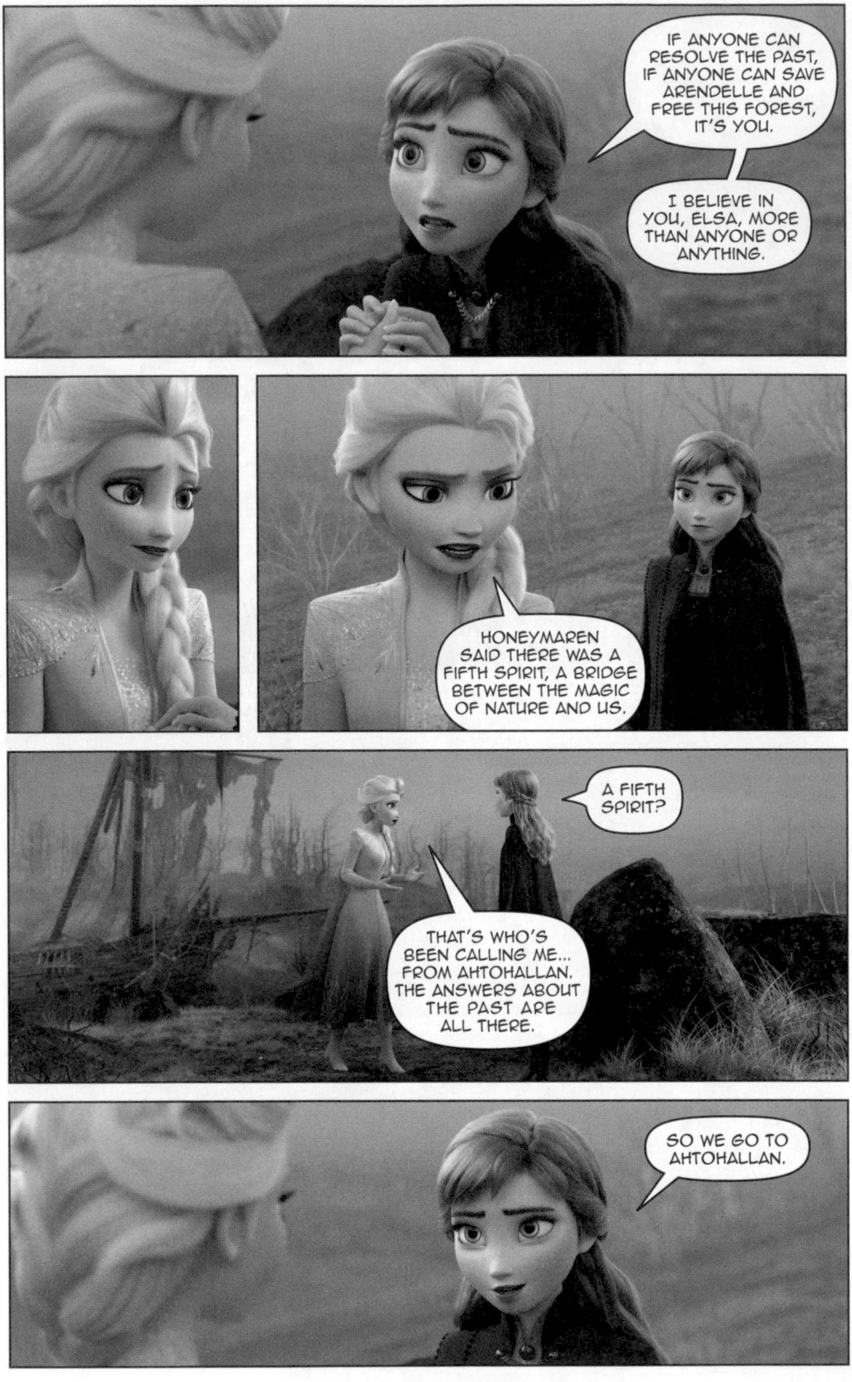
IF ANYONE CAN RESOLVE THE PAST, IF ANYONE CAN SAVE ARENDELLE AND FREE THIS FOREST, IT'S YOU.
I BELIEVE IN YOU, ELSA, MORE THAN ANYONE OR ANYTHING.
HONEYMAREN SAID THERE WAS A FIFTH SPIRIT, A BRIDGE BETWEEN THE MAGIC OF NATURE AND US.
A FIFTH SPIRIT?
THAT'S WHO'S BEEN CALLING ME... FROM AHTOHALLAN. THE ANSWERS ABOUT THE PAST ARE ALL THERE.
SO WE GO TO AHTOHALLAN.

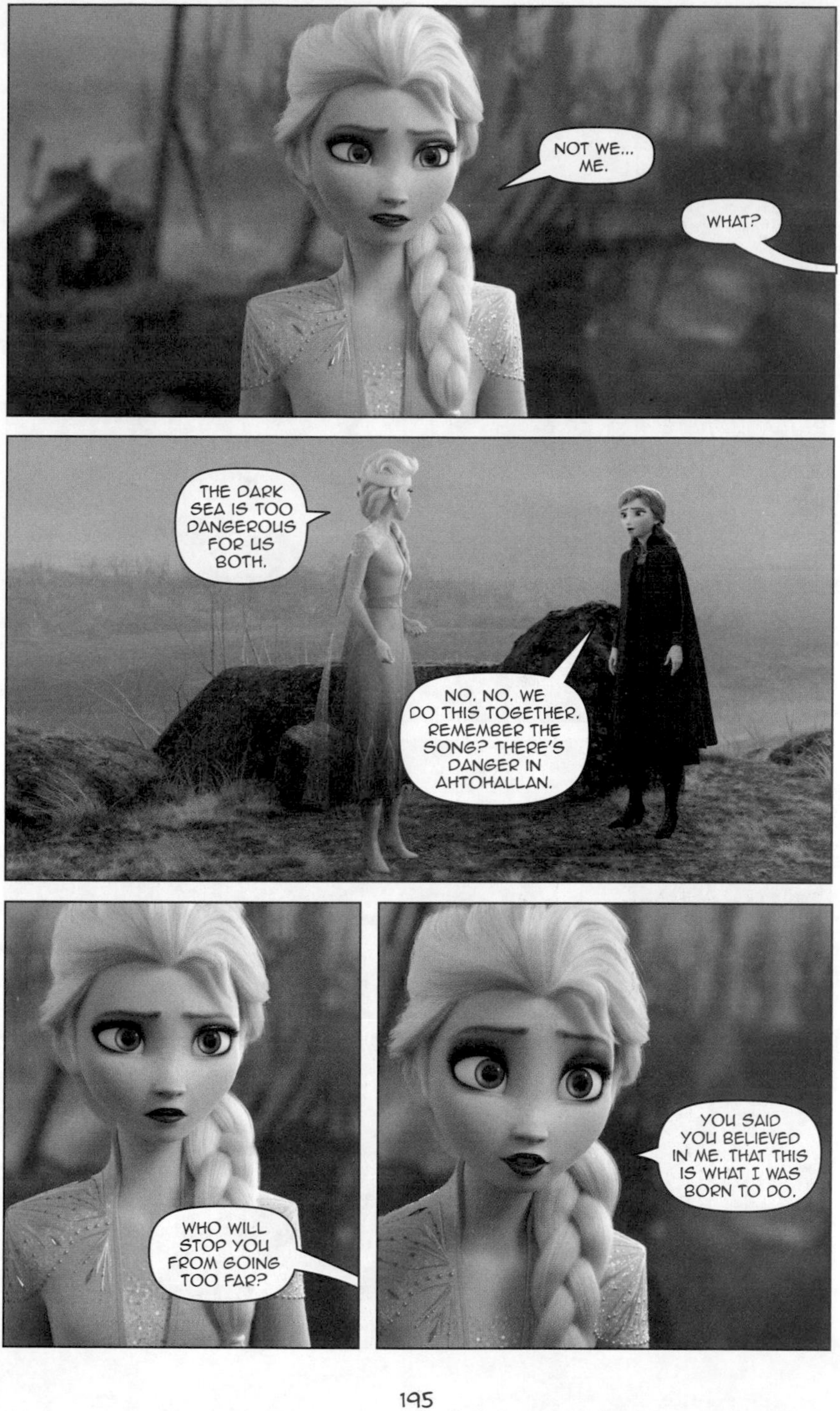
NOT WE... ME.
WHAT?
THE DARK SEA IS TOO DANGEROUS FOR US BOTH.
NO. NO. WE DO THIS TOGETHER. REMEMBER THE SONG? THERE'S DANGER IN AHTOHALLAN.
WHO WILL STOP YOU FROM GOING TOO FAR?
YOU SAID YOU BELIEVED IN ME. THAT THIS IS WHAT I WAS BORN TO DO.

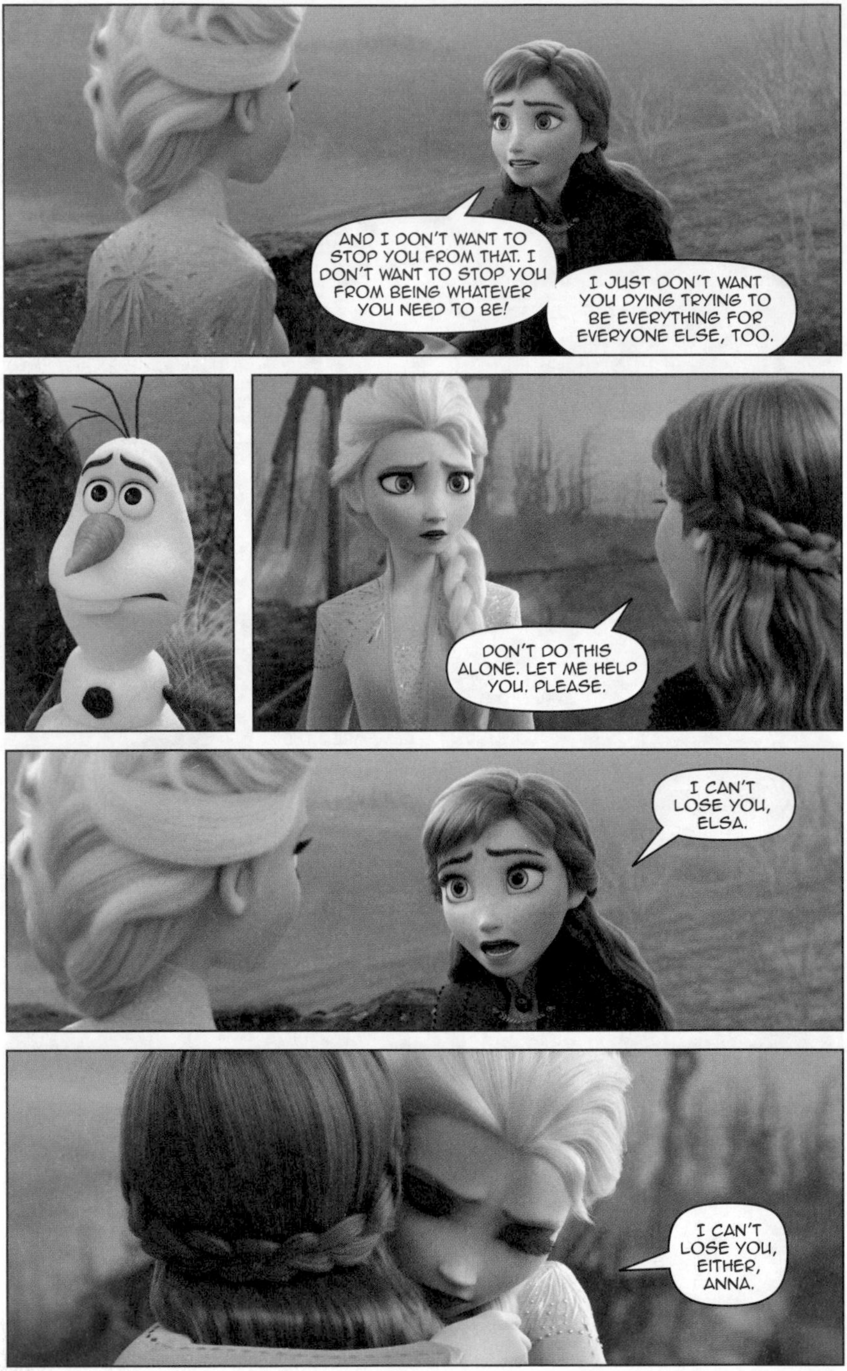
AND I DON'T WANT TO STOP YOU FROM THAT. I DON'T WANT TO STOP YOU FROM BEING WHATEVER YOU NEED TO BE!
I JUST DON'T WANT YOU DYING TRYING TO BE EVERYTHING FOR EVERYONE ELSE, TOO.
DON'T DO THIS ALONE. LET ME HELP YOU. PLEASE.
I CAN'T LOSE YOU, ELSA.
I CAN'T LOSE YOU, EITHER, ANNA.

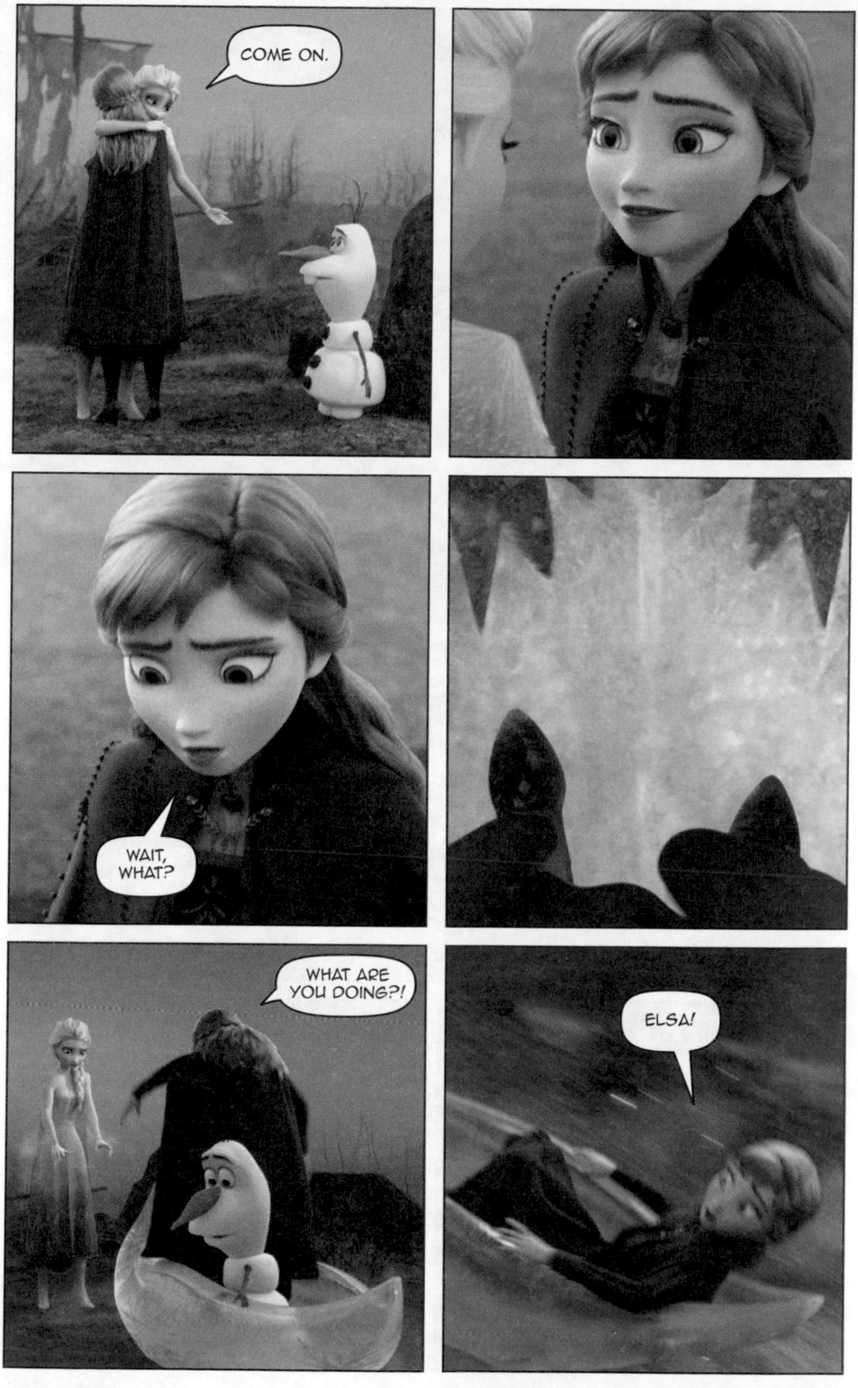
COME ON.
WAIT, WHAT?
WHAT ARE YOU DOING?!
ELSA!

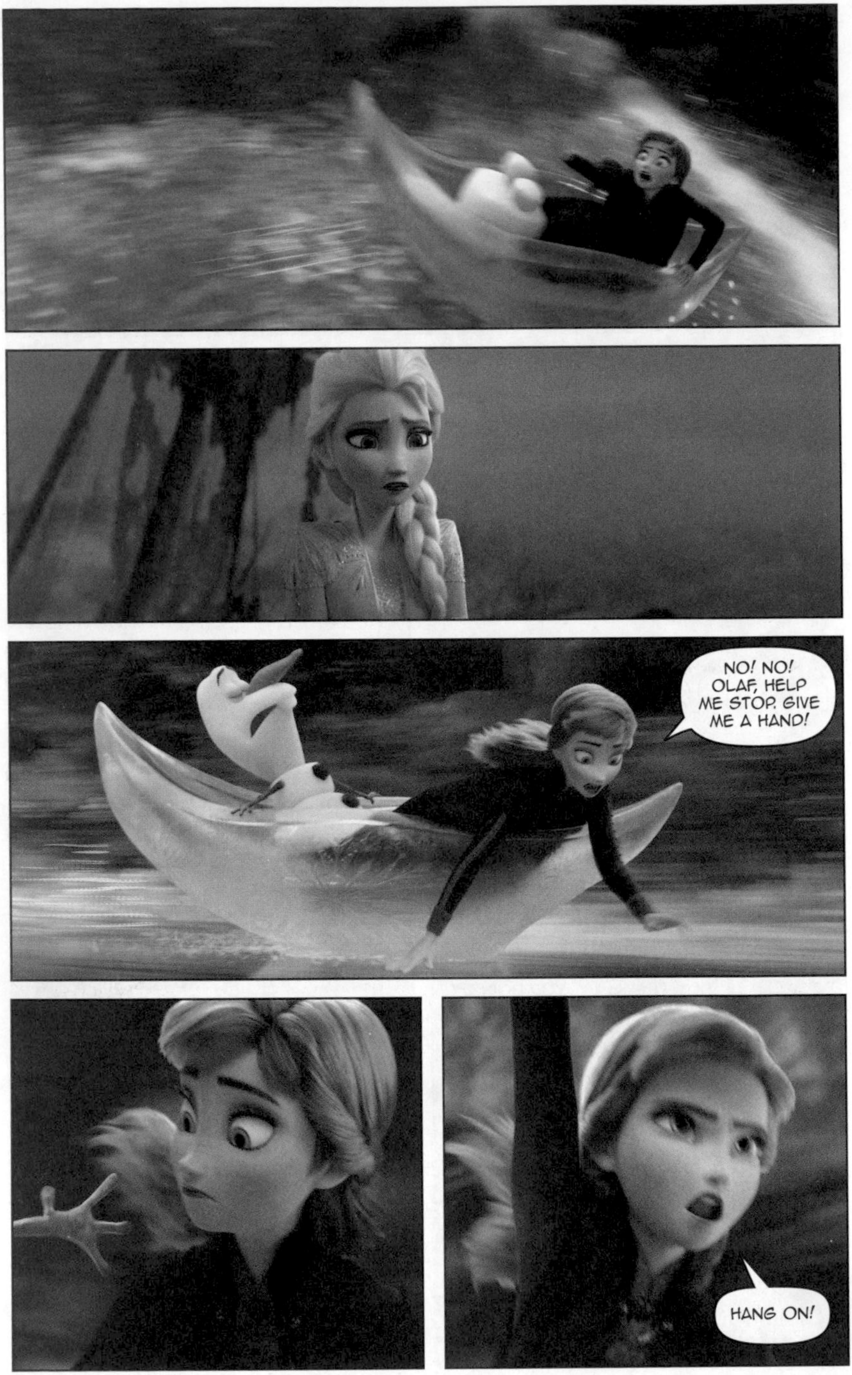
NO! NO! OLAF, HELP ME STOP. GIVE ME A HAND!
HANG ON!

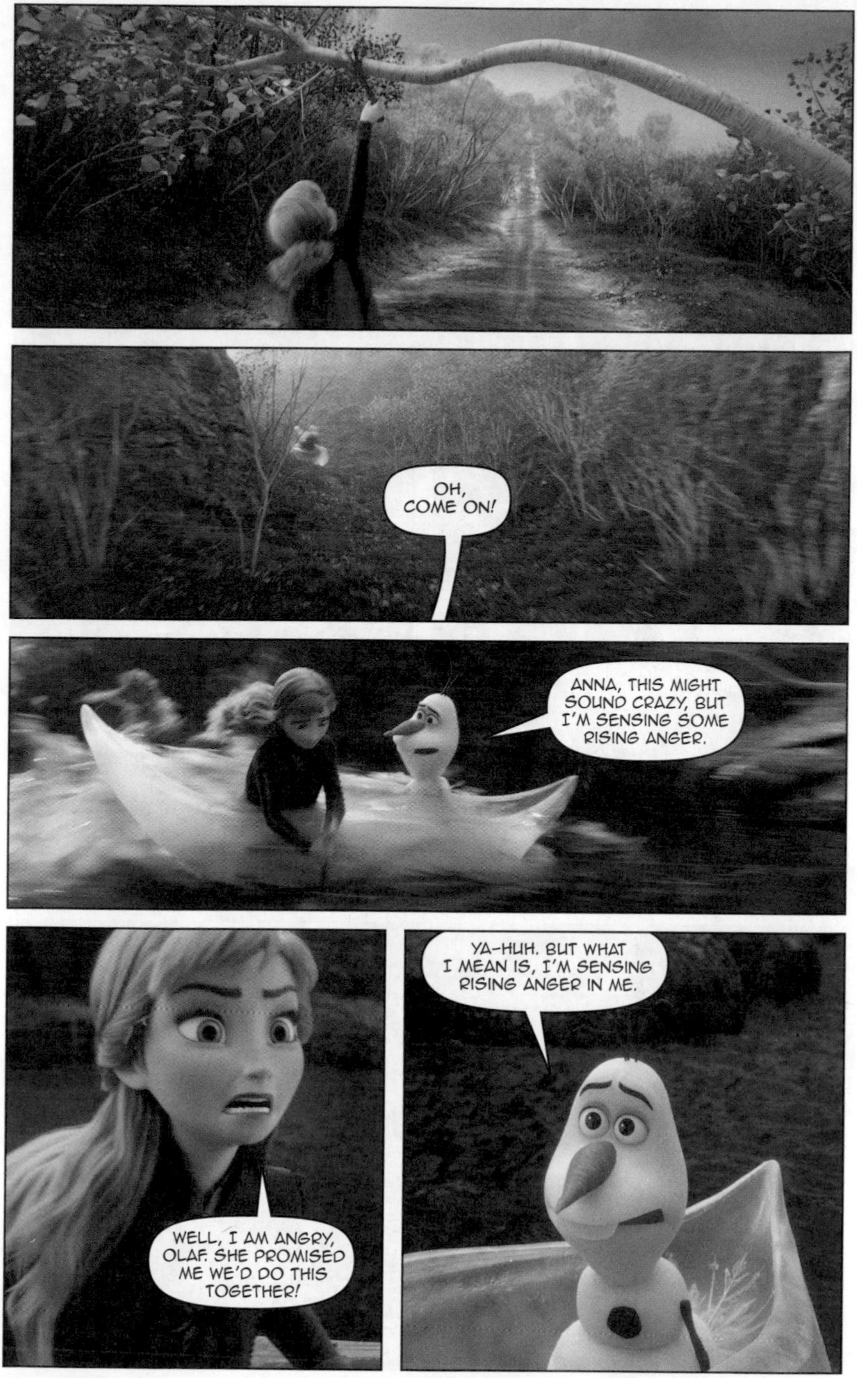
OH, COME ON!
ANNA, THIS MIGHT SOUND CRAZY, BUT I'M SENSING SOME RISING ANGER.
WELL, I AM ANGRY, OLAF. SHE PROMISED ME WE'D DO THIS TOGETHER!
YA-HUH. BUT WHAT I MEAN IS, I'M SENSING RISING ANGER IN ME.

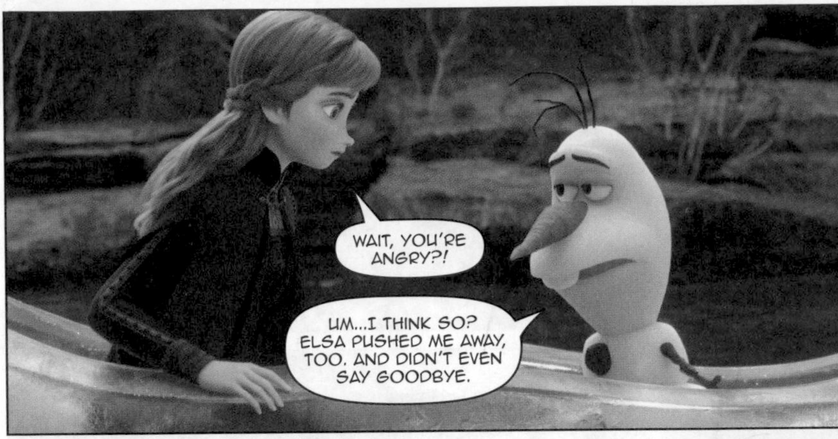
WAIT, YOU'RE ANGRY?!
UM...I THINK SO? ELSA PUSHED ME AWAY, TOO. AND DIDN'T EVEN SAY GOODBYE.
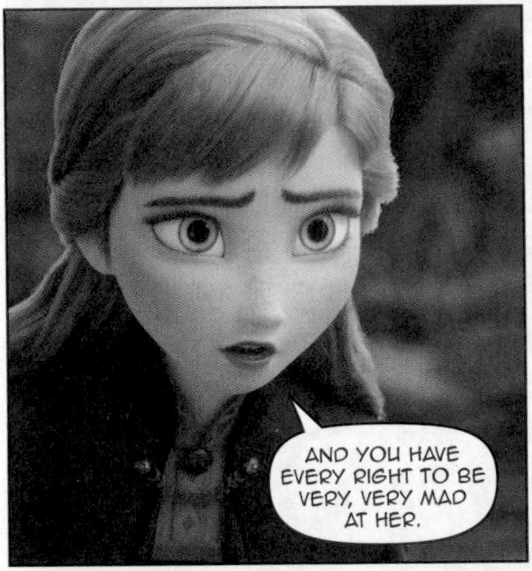
AND YOU HAVE EVERY RIGHT TO BE VERY, VERY MAD AT HER.
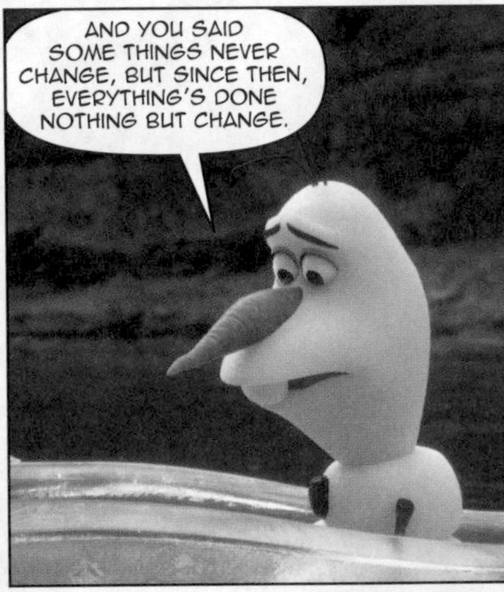
AND YOU SAID SOME THINGS NEVER CHANGE, BUT SINCE THEN, EVERYTHING'S DONE NOTHING BUT CHANGE.
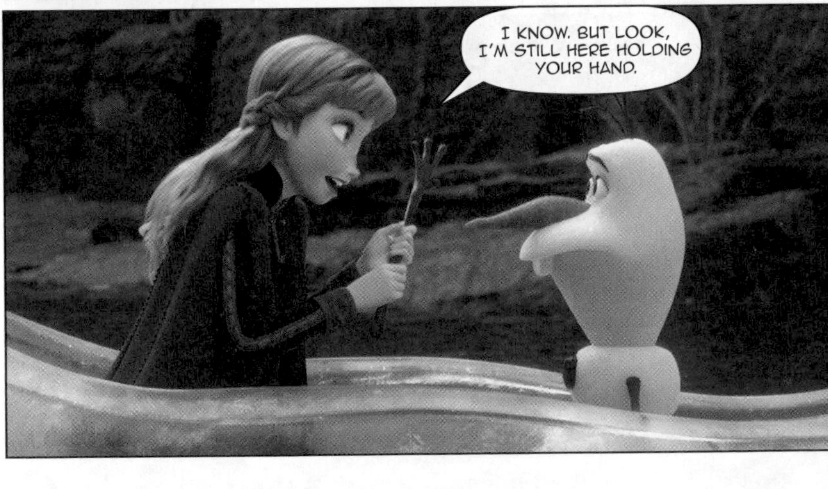
I KNOW. BUT LOOK, I'M STILL HERE HOLDING YOUR HAND.

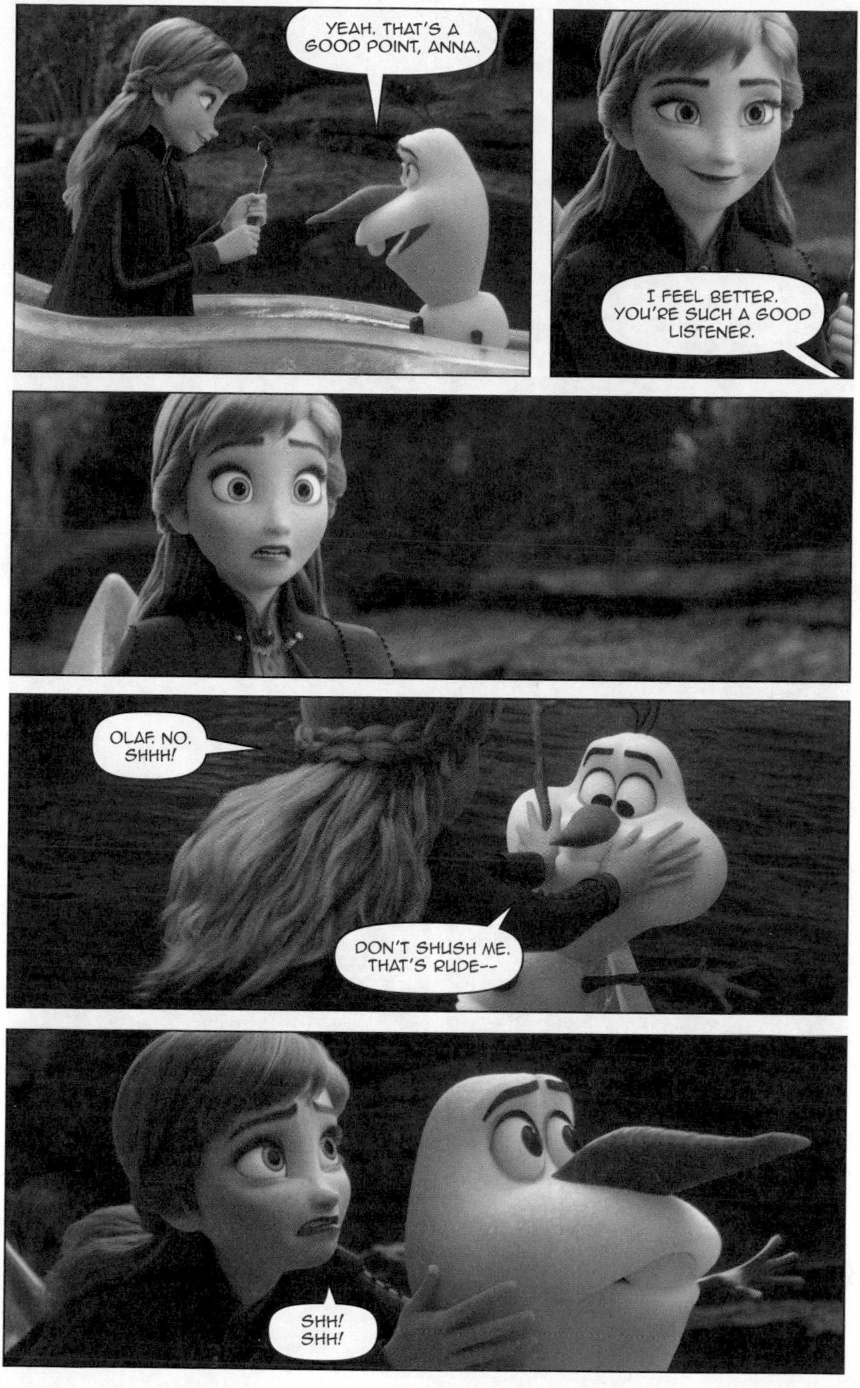
YEAH. THAT'S A GOOD POINT, ANNA.
I FEEL BETTER. YOU'RE SUCH A GOOD LISTENER.
OLAF. NO. SHHH!
DON'T SHUSH ME. THAT'S RUDE--
SHH! SHH!

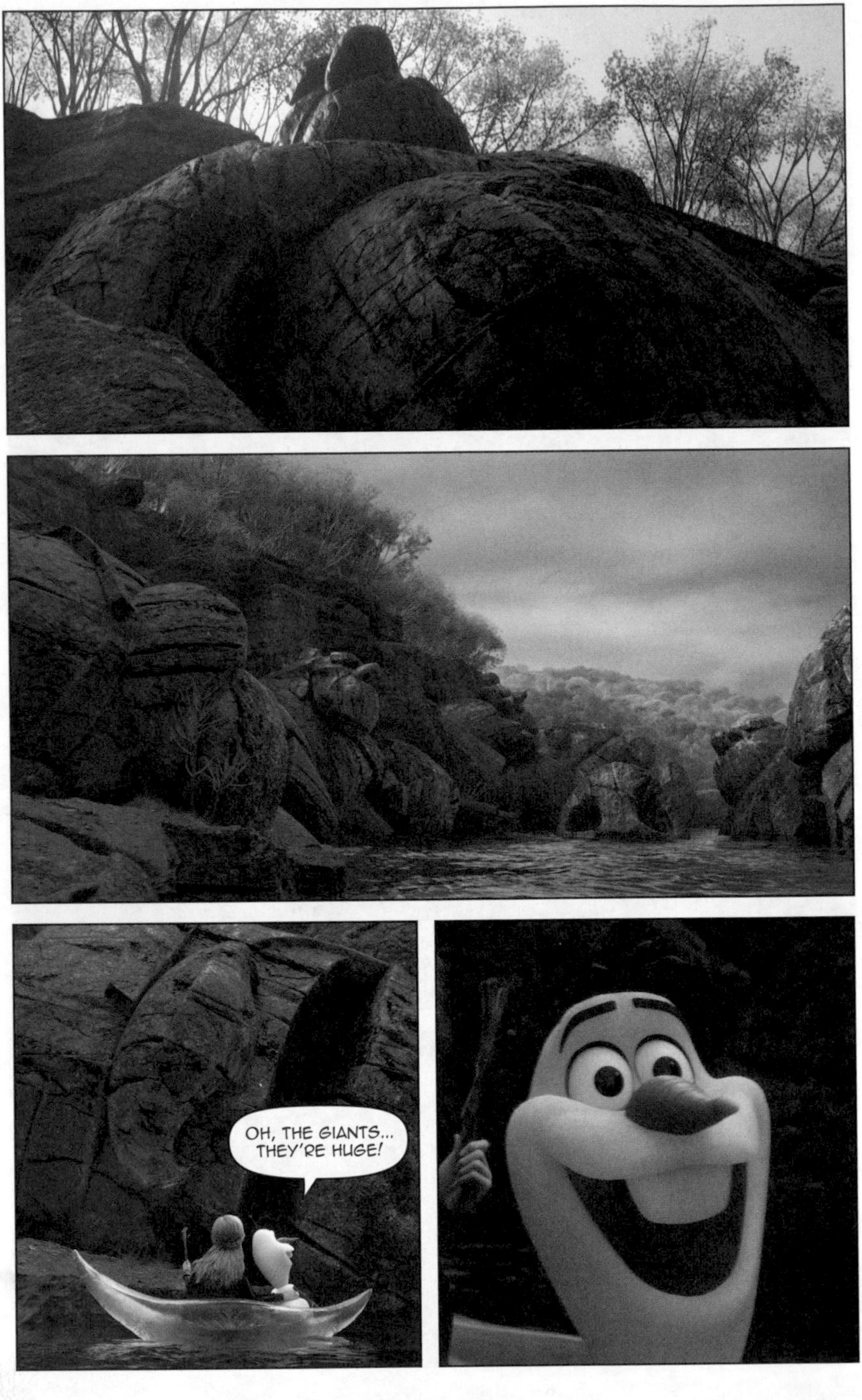
OH, THE GIANTS...
THEY'RE HUGE!

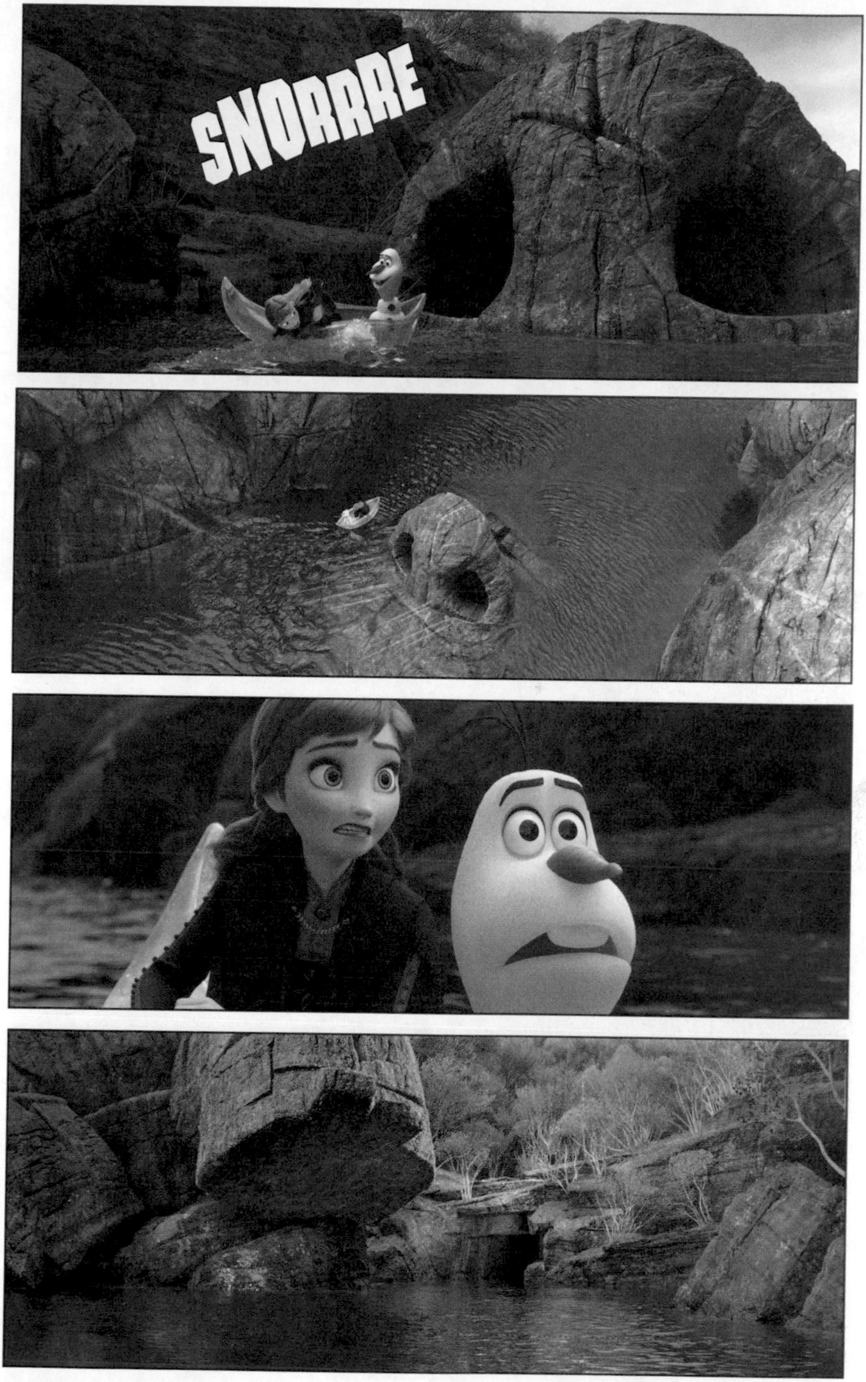
SNORRRE

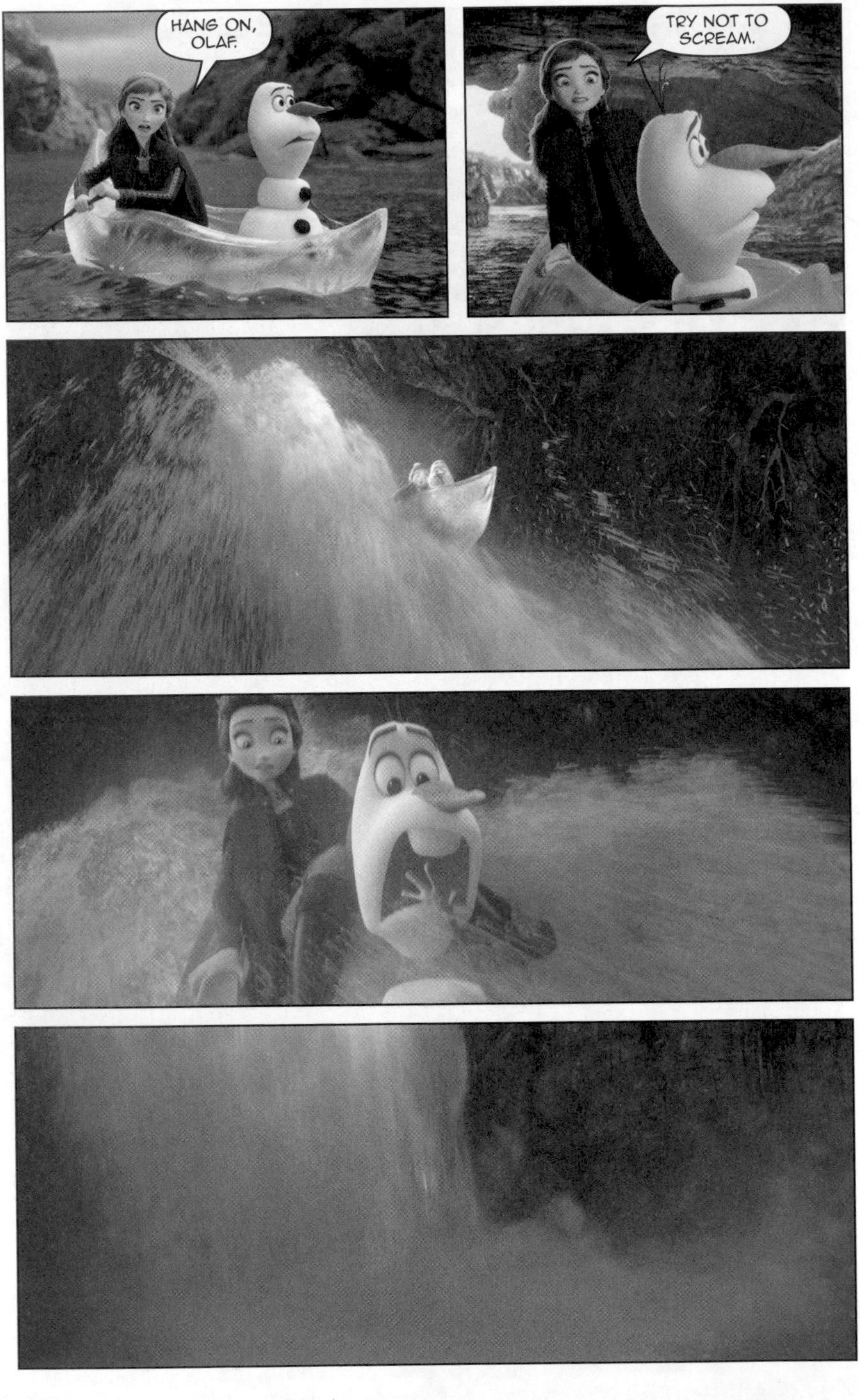
HANG ON, OLAF.
TRY NOT TO SCREAM.

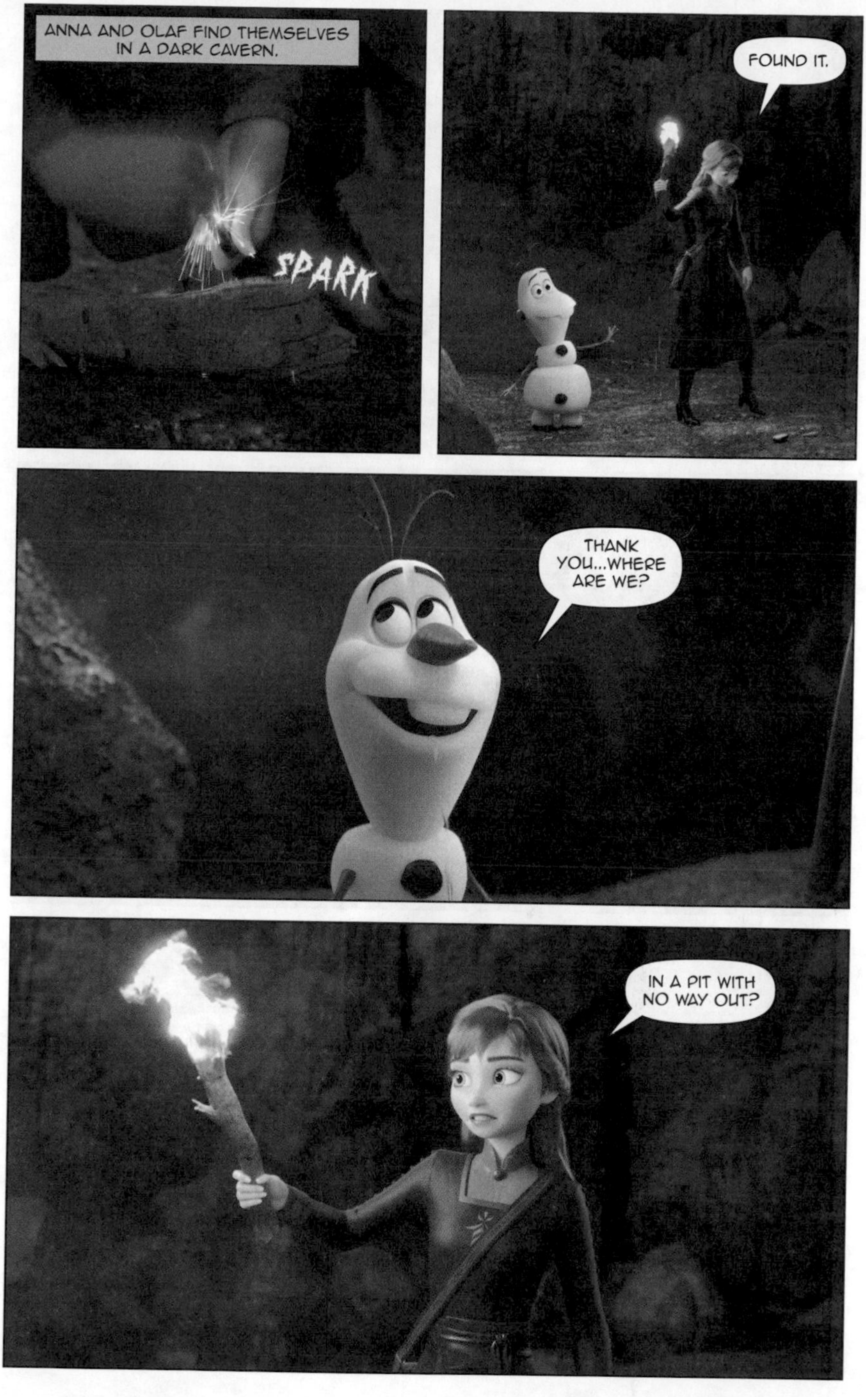
ANNA AND OLAF FIND THEMSELVES IN A DARK CAVERN.
SPARK
FOUND IT.
THANK YOU...WHERE ARE WE?
IN A PIT WITH NO WAY OUT?

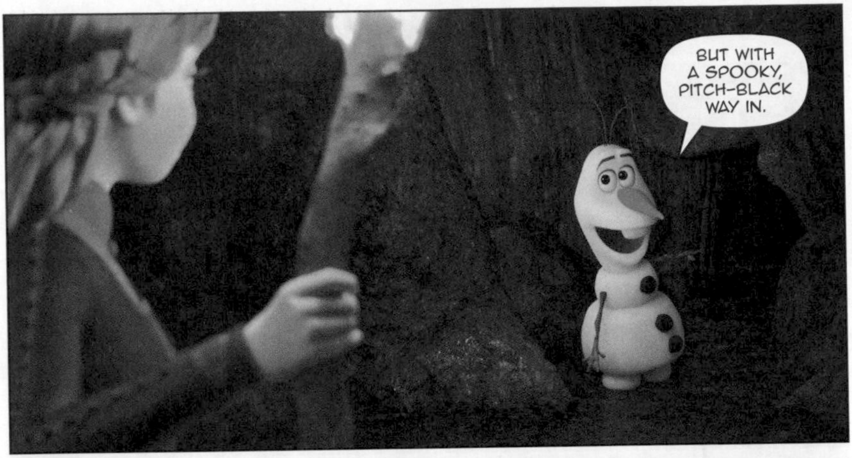
BUT WITH A SPOOKY, PITCH-BLACK WAY IN.

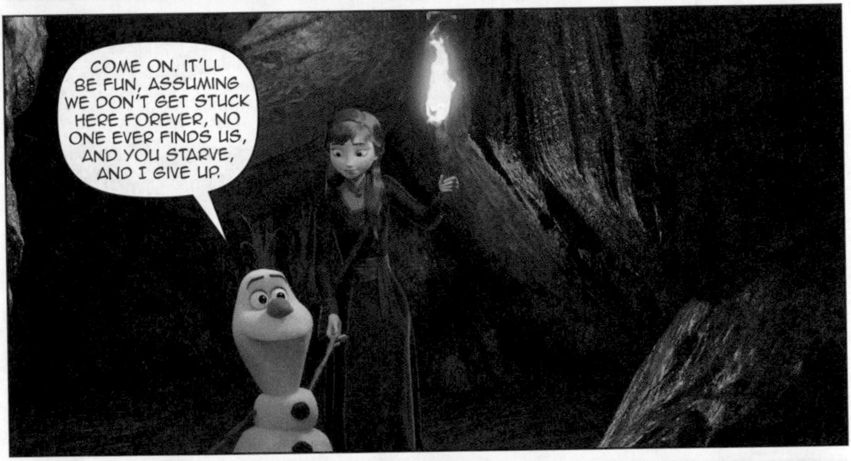
COME ON. IT'LL BE FUN, ASSUMING WE DON'T GET STUCK HERE FOREVER, NO ONE EVER FINDS US, AND YOU STARVE, AND I GIVE UP.

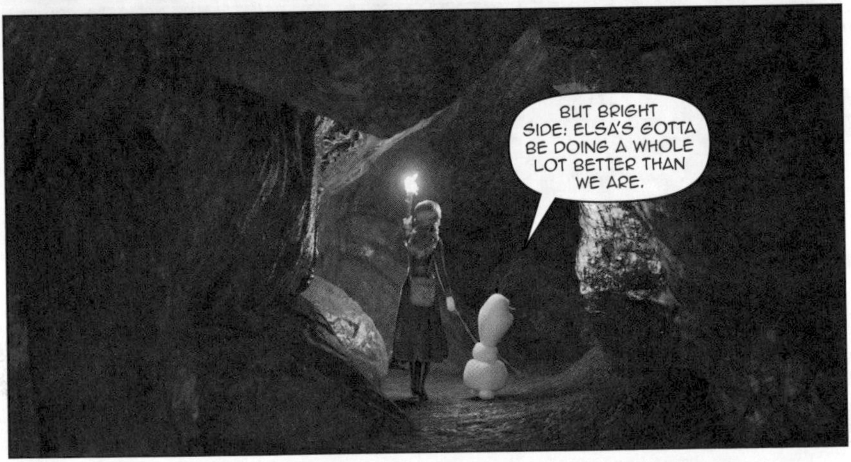
BUT BRIGHT SIDE: ELSA'S GOTTA BE DOING A WHOLE LOT BETTER THAN WE ARE.

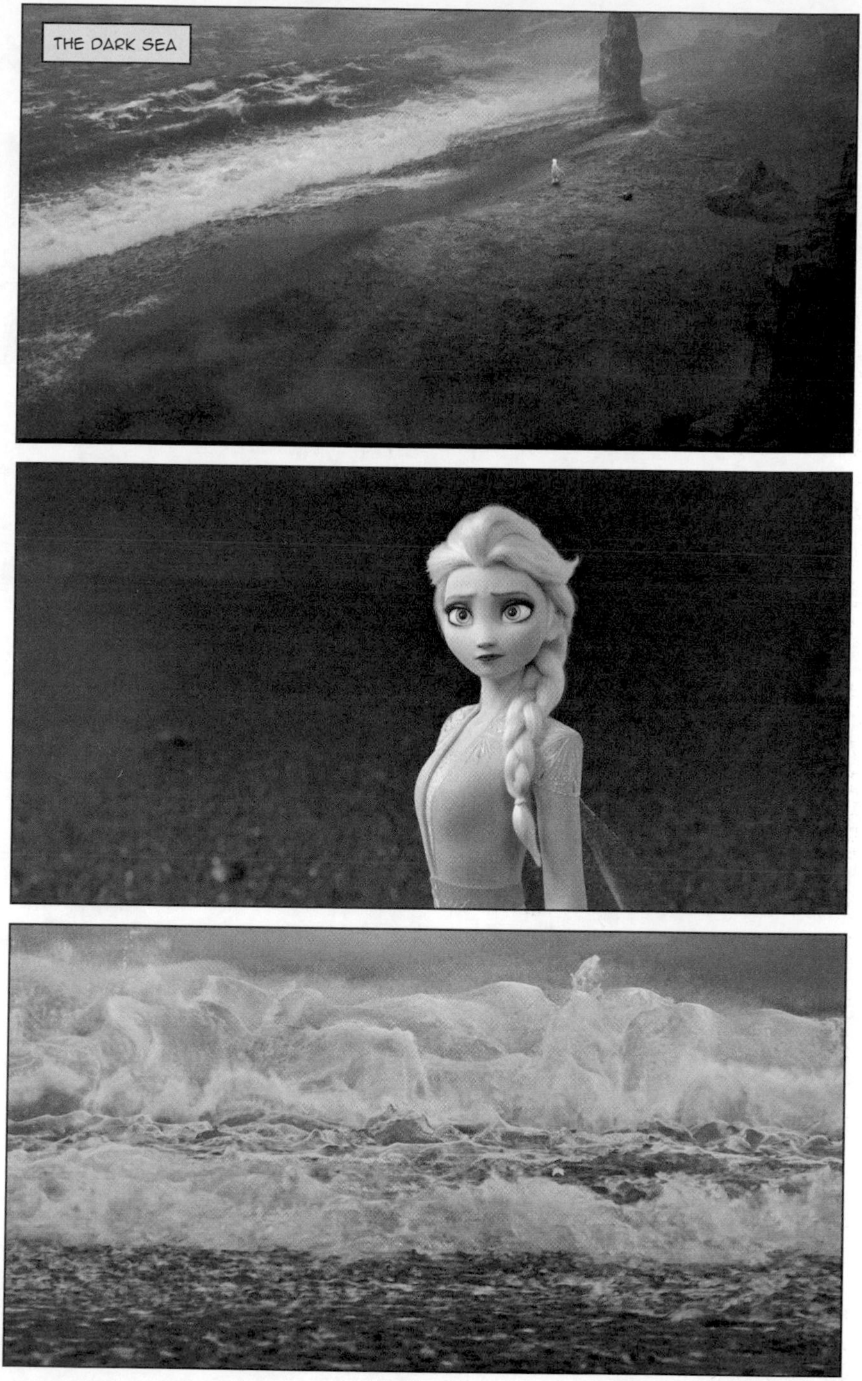
THE DARK SEA

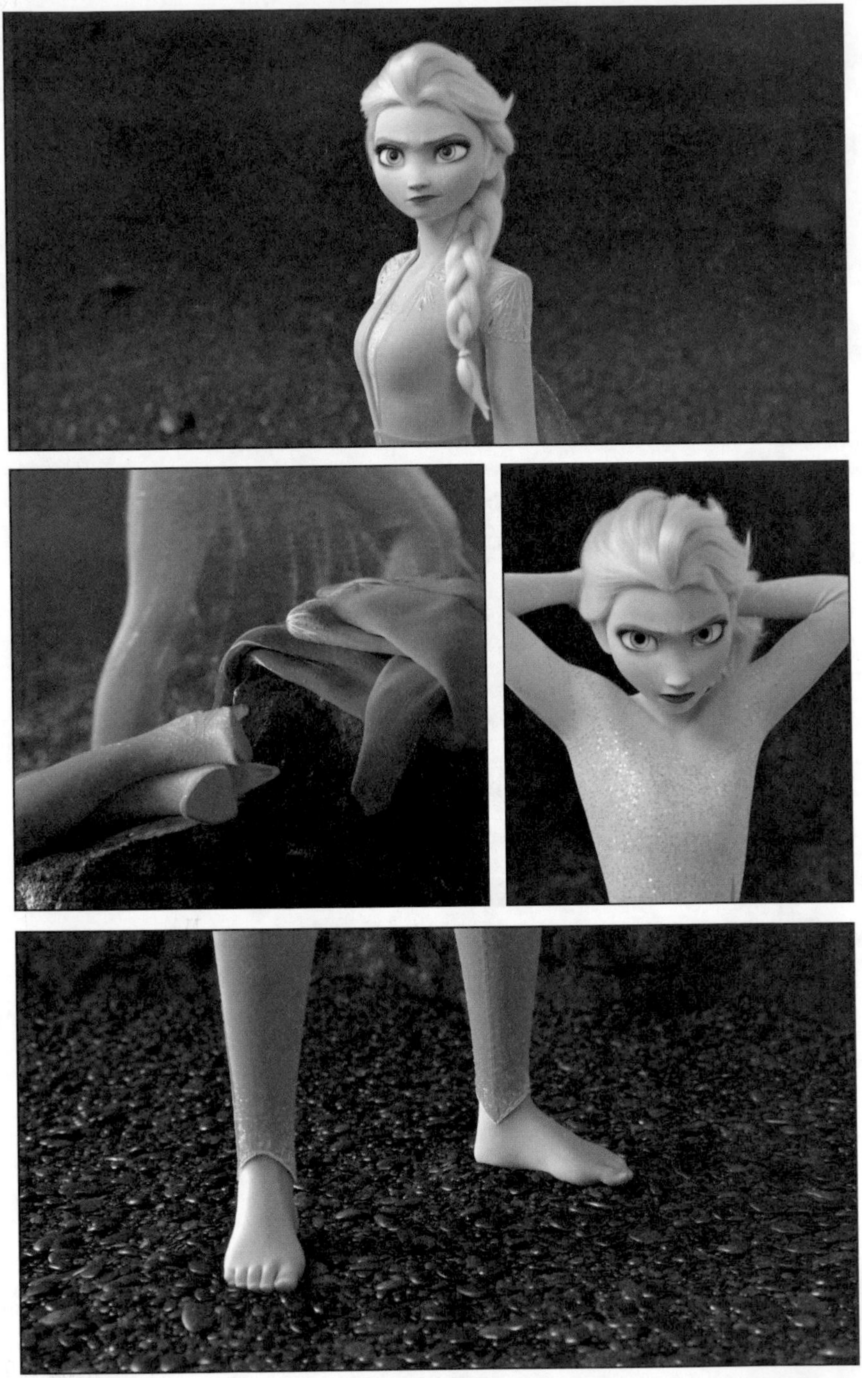

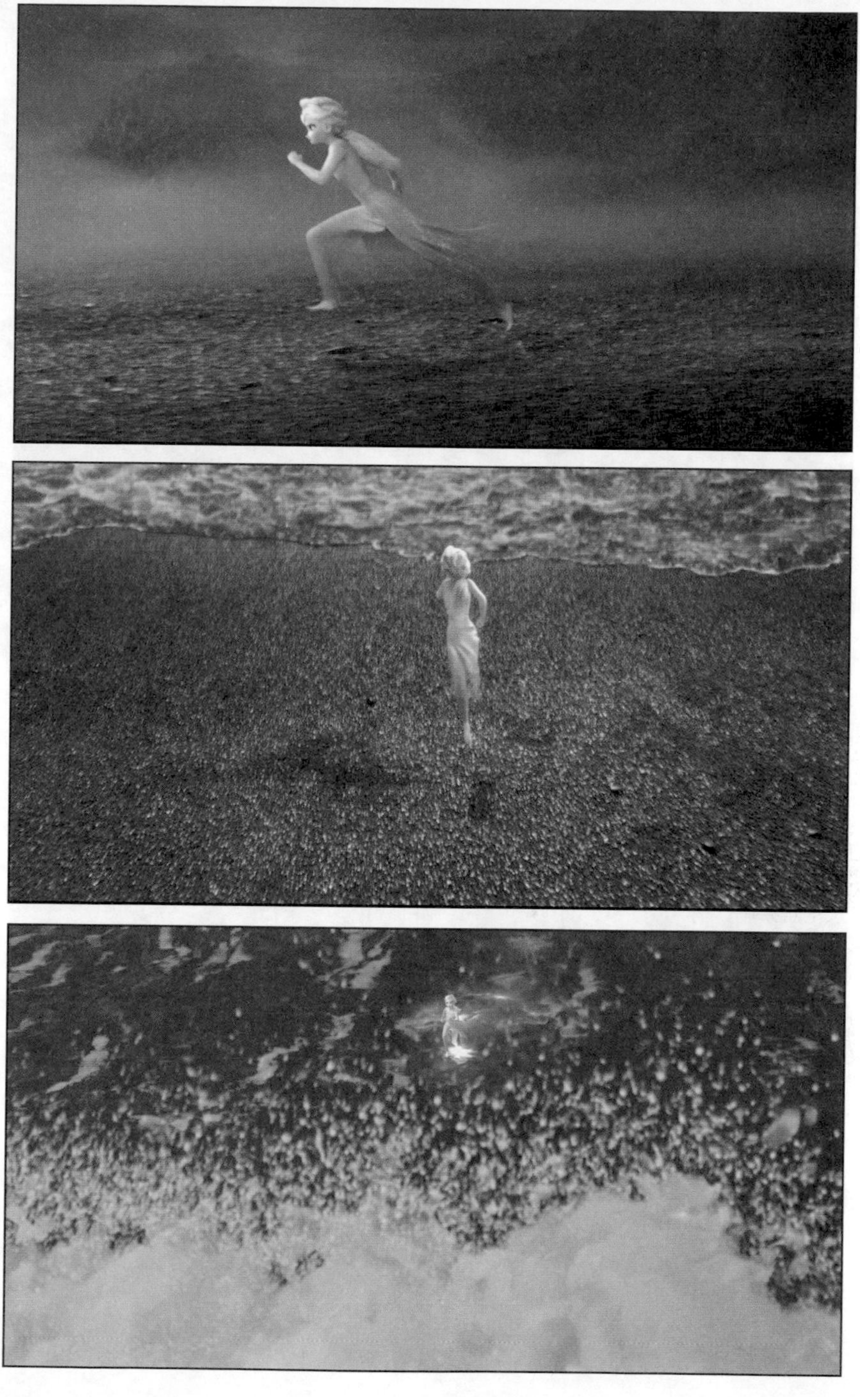

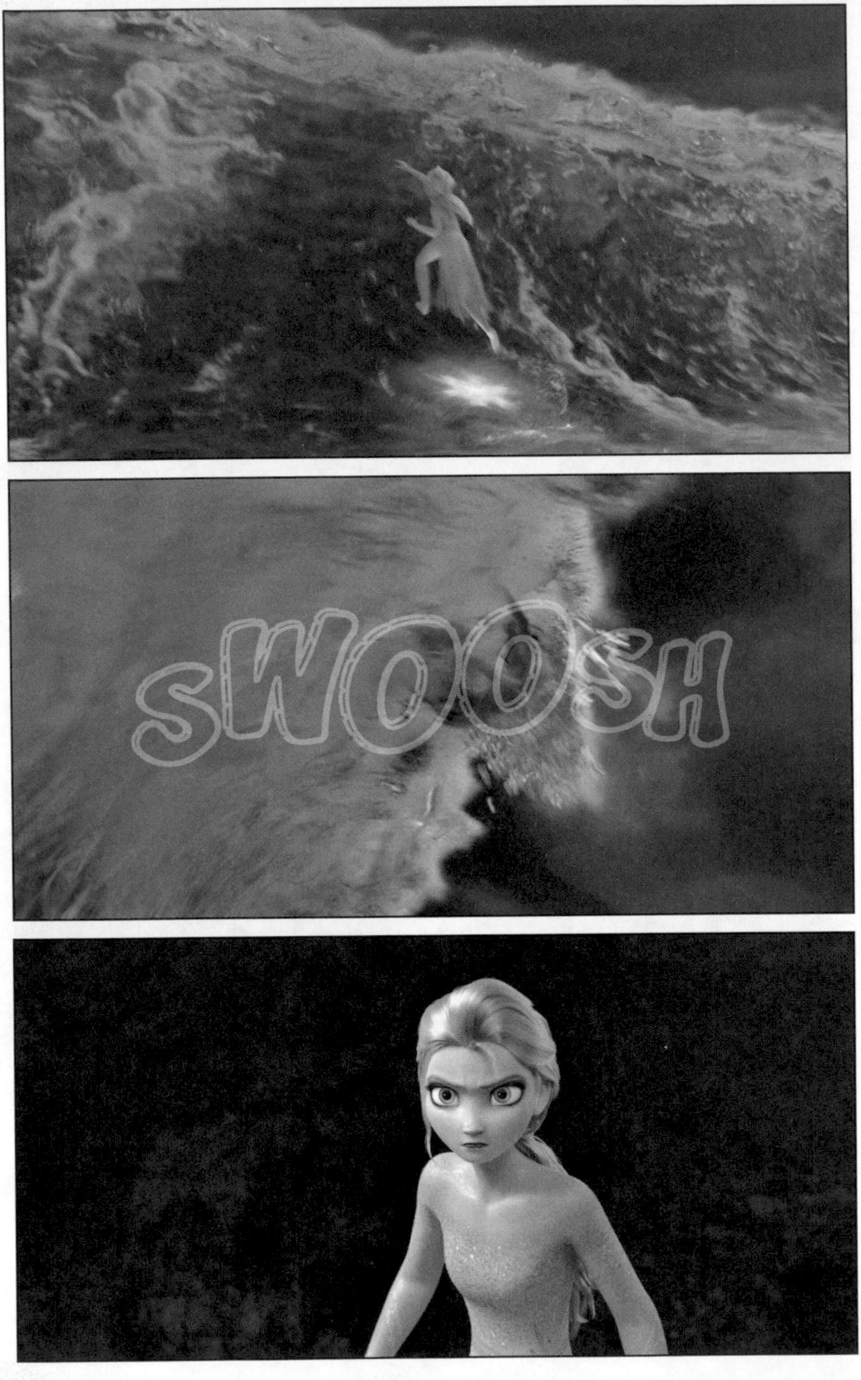
sWOOsH

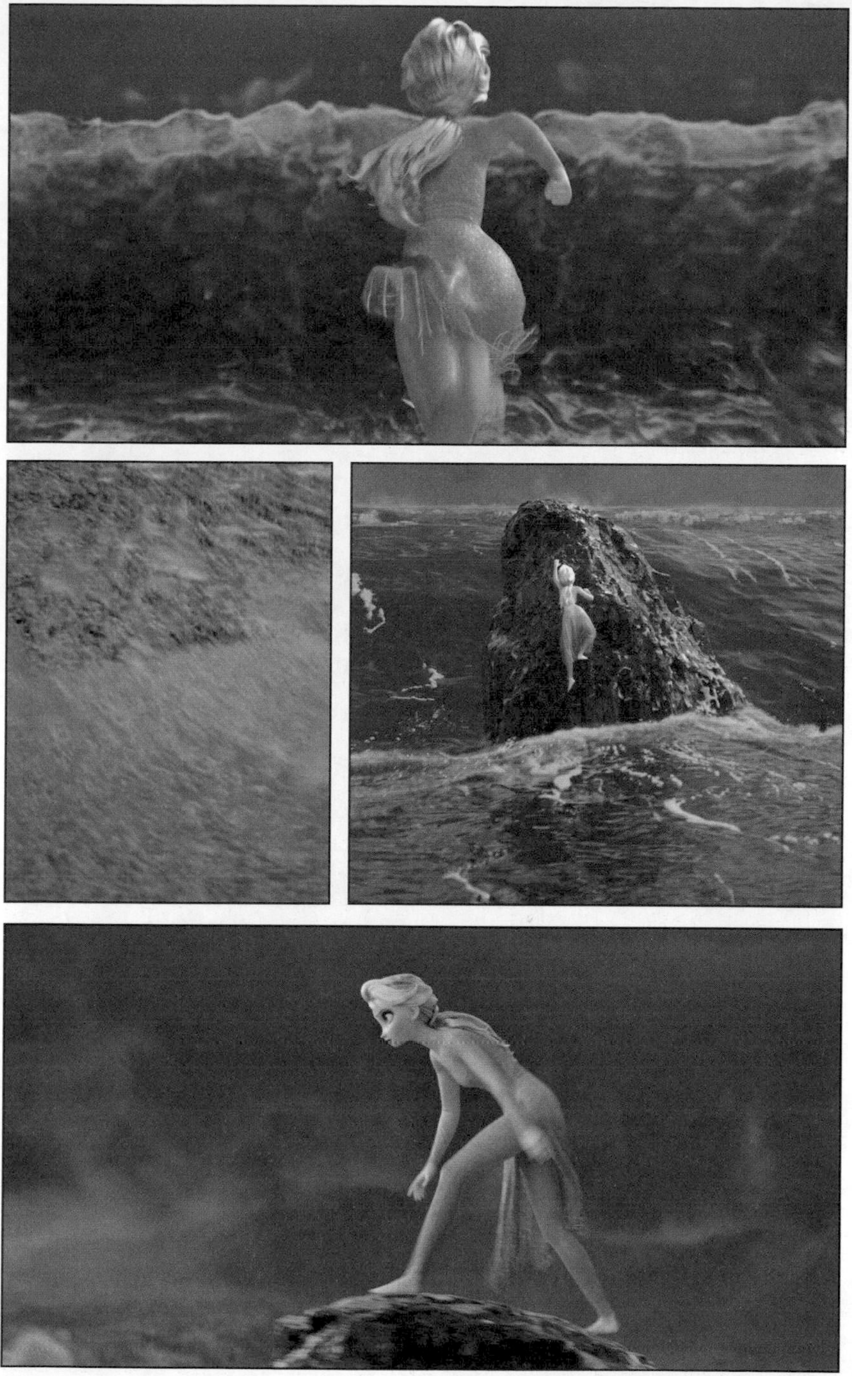

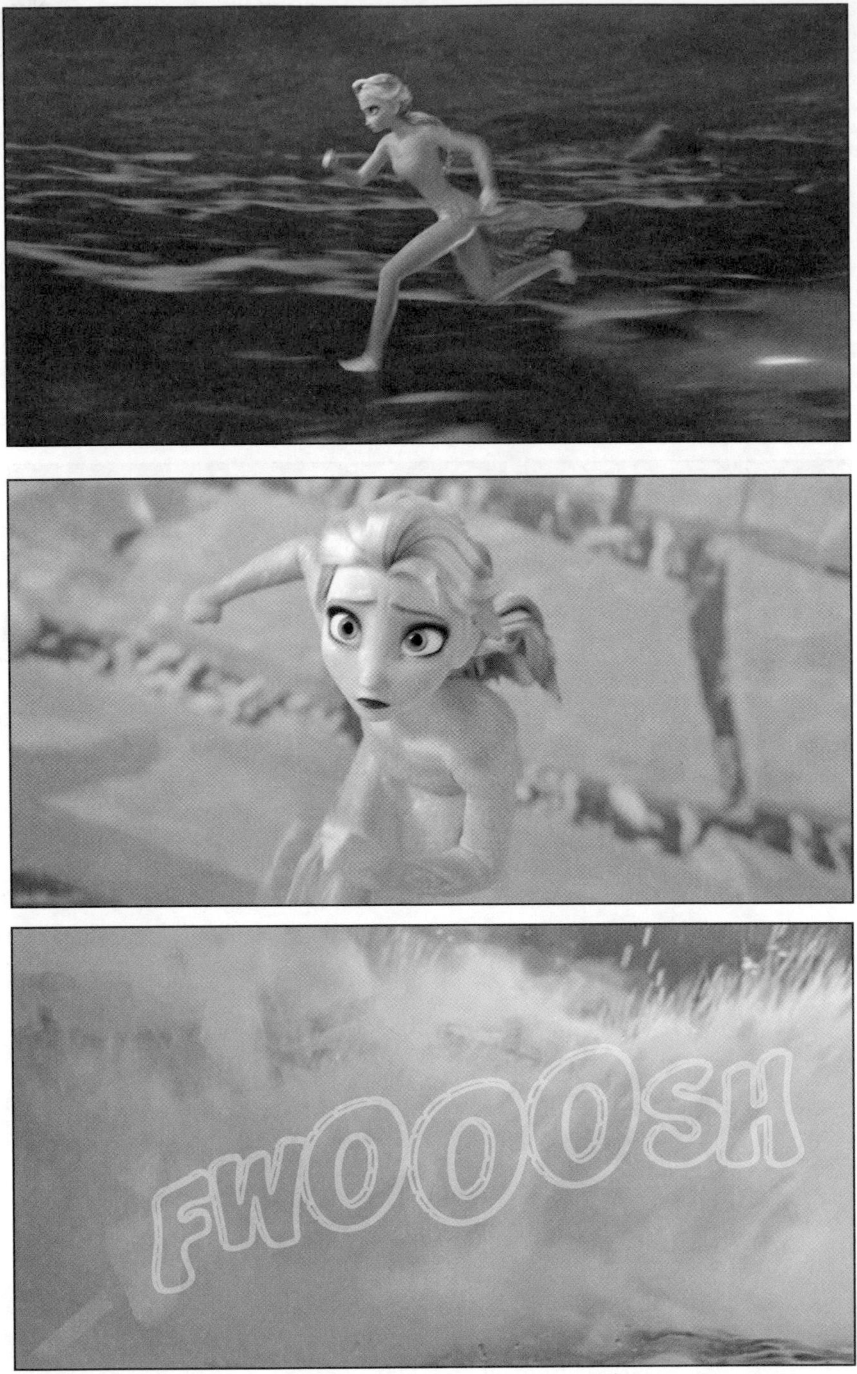
FWOOOSH

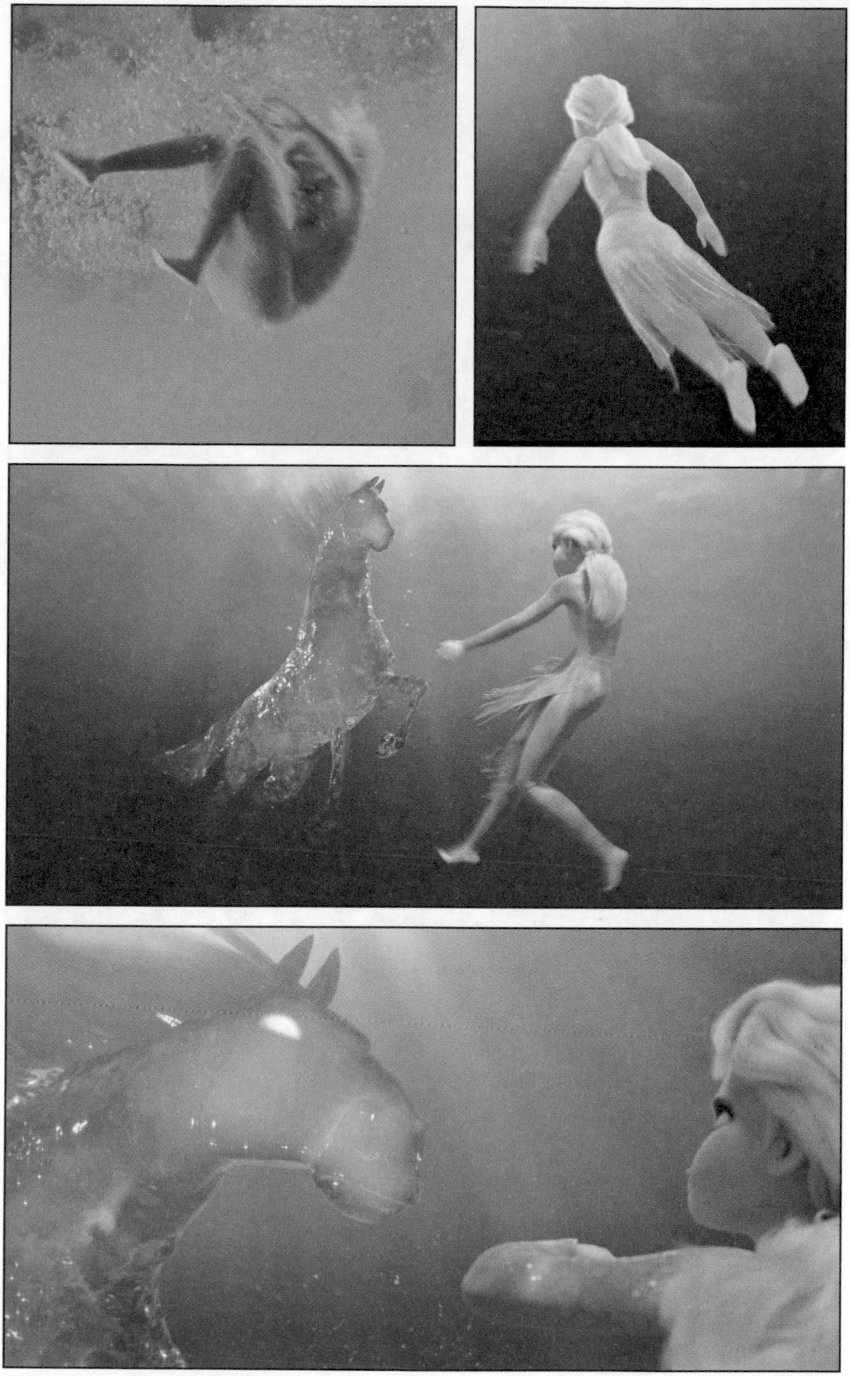

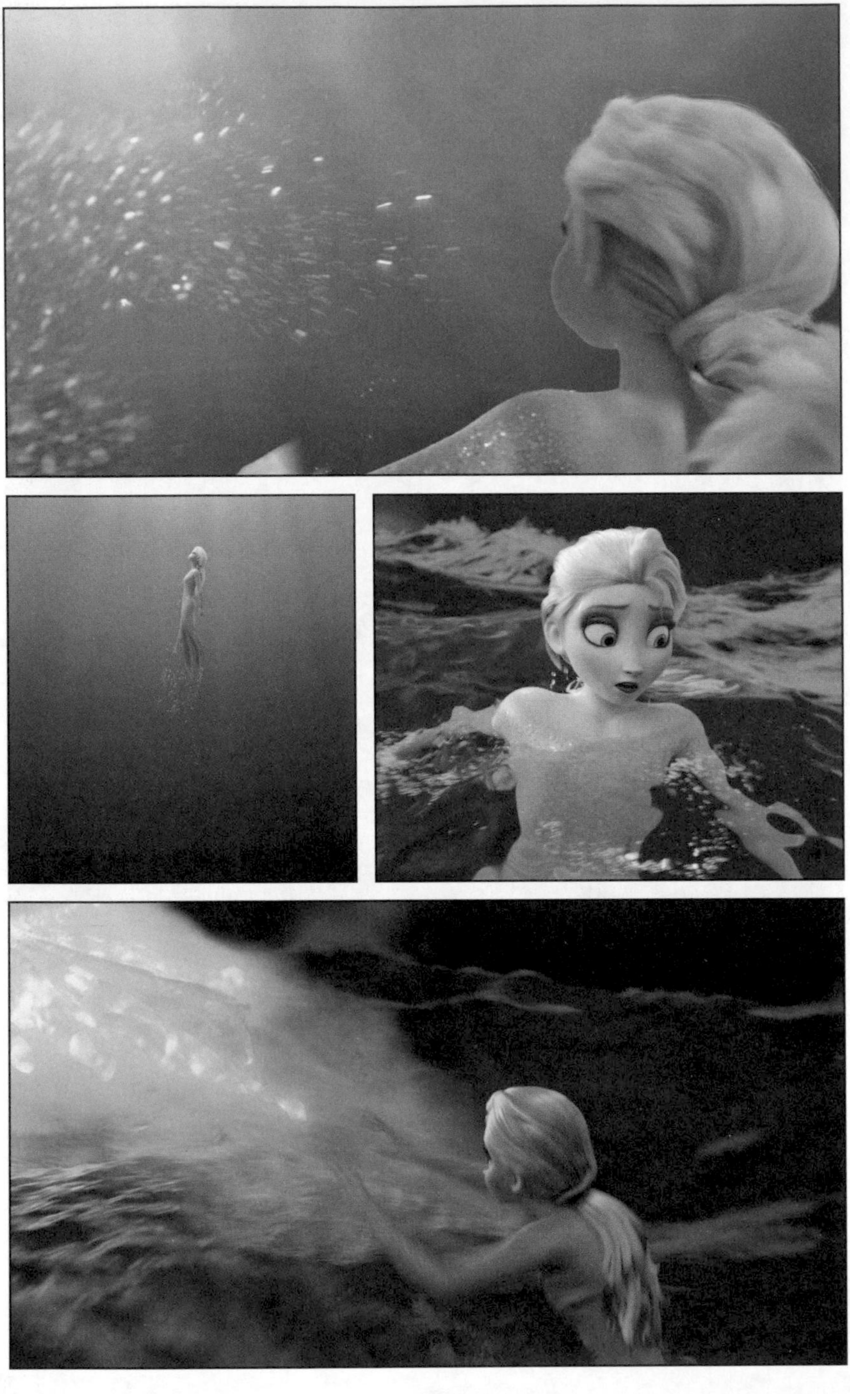

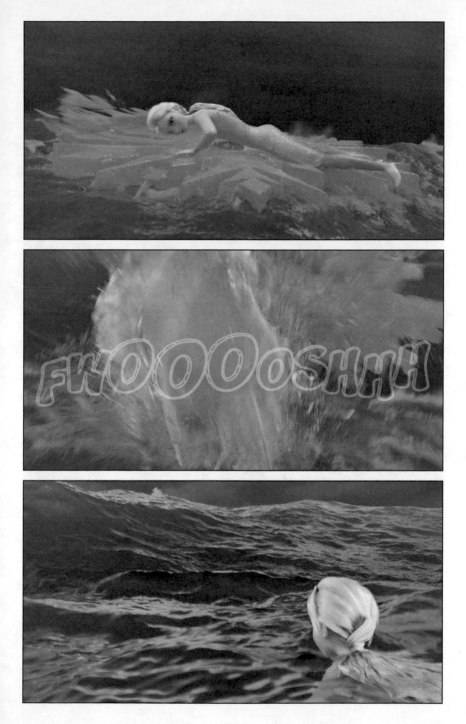

FWOOOOoSHHH

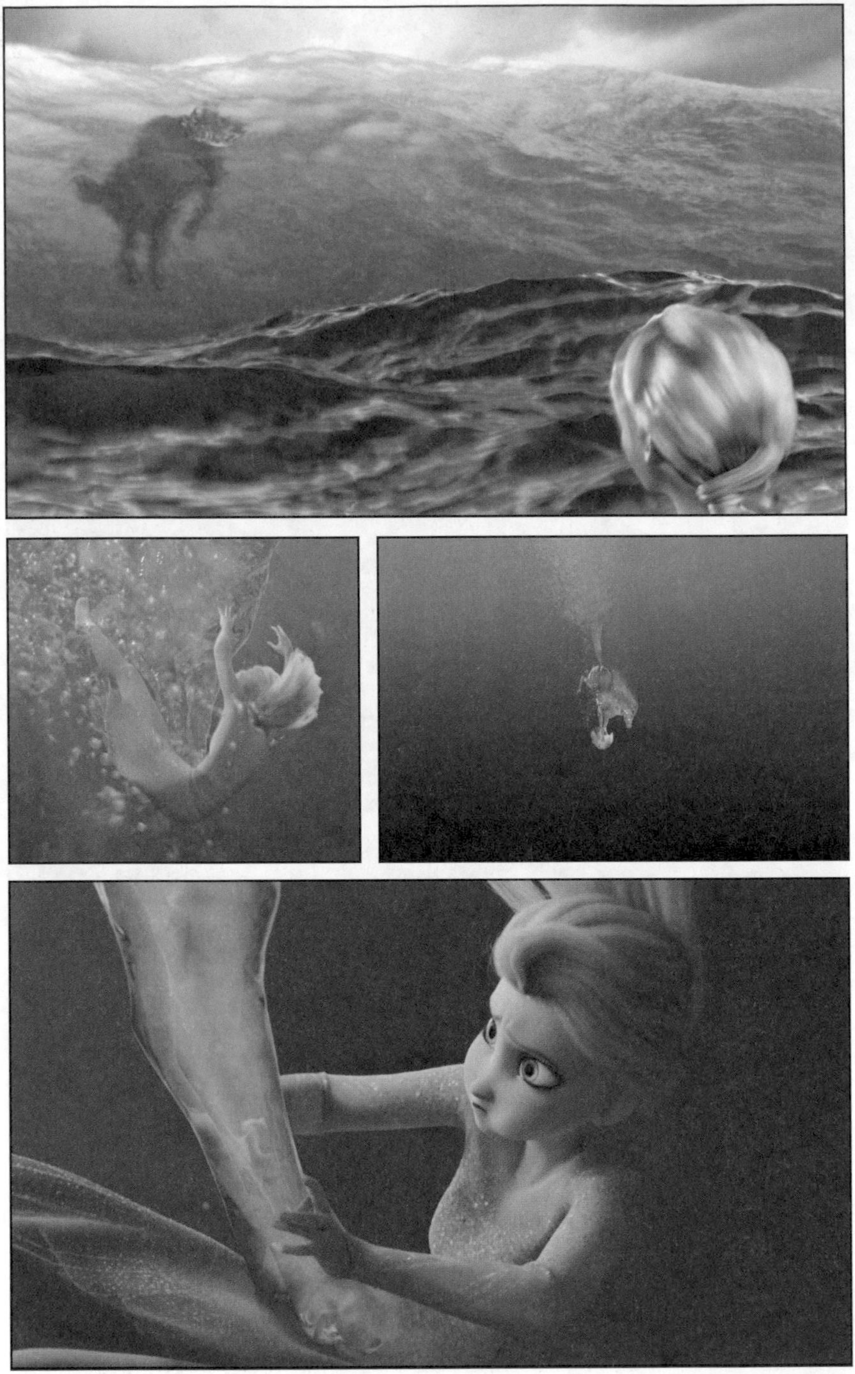

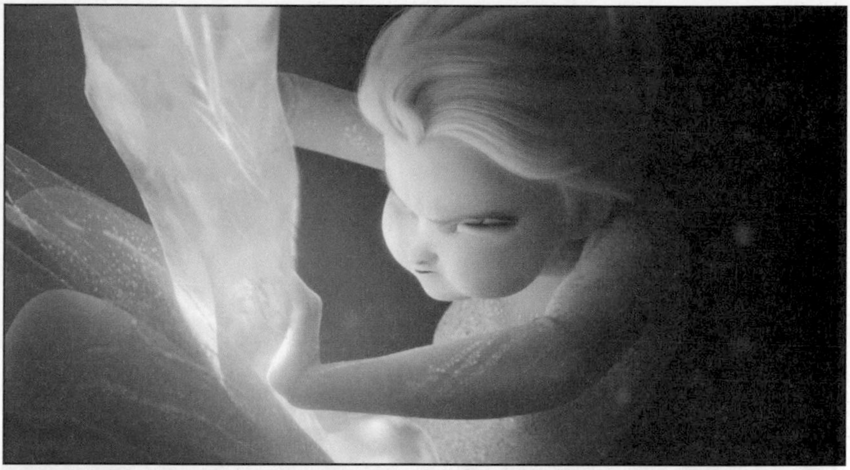

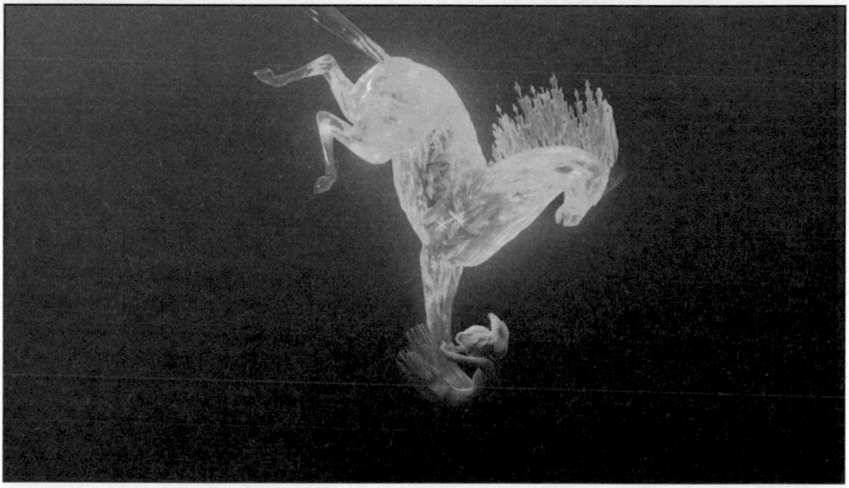

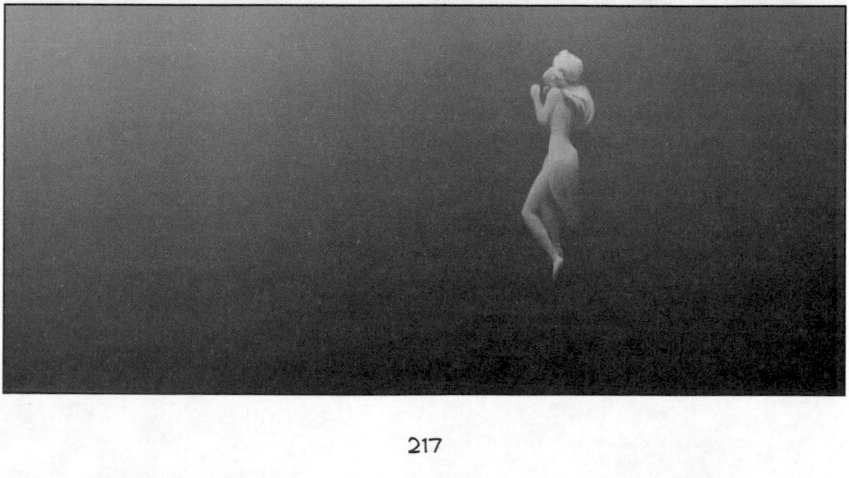

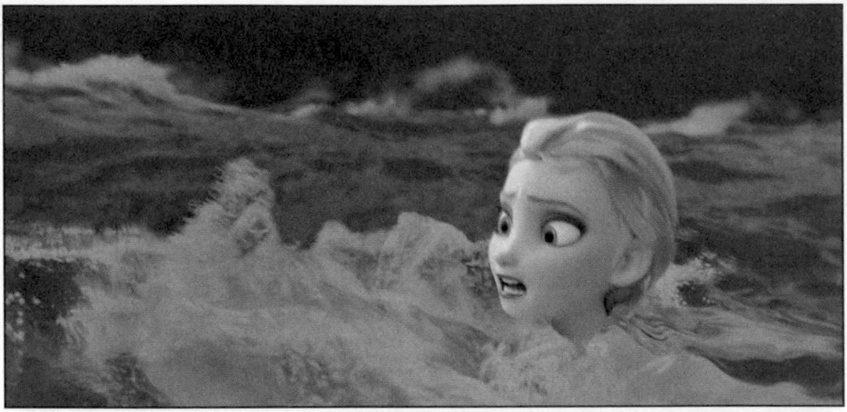

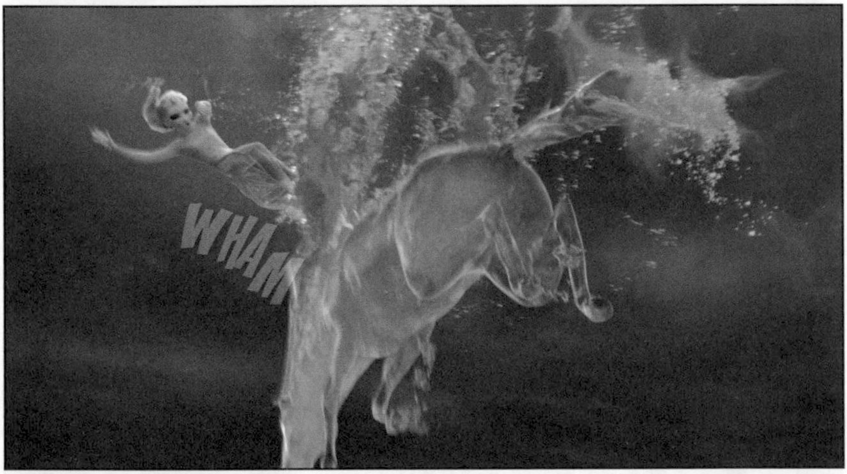
WHAM

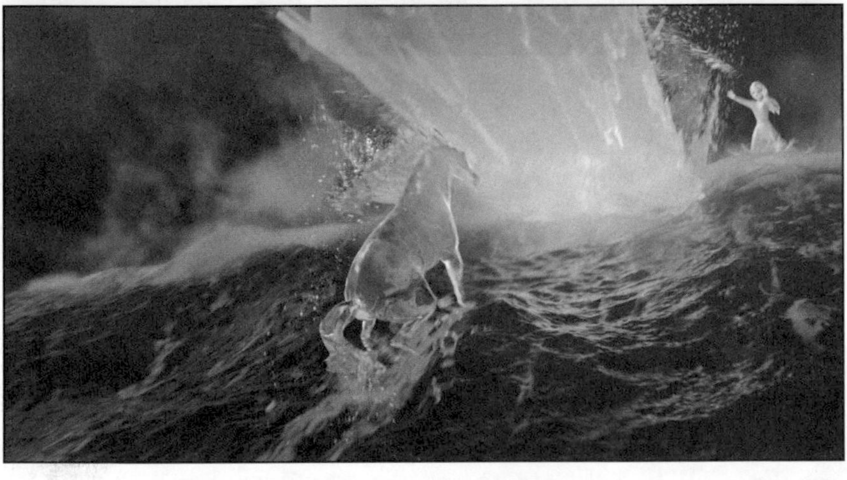

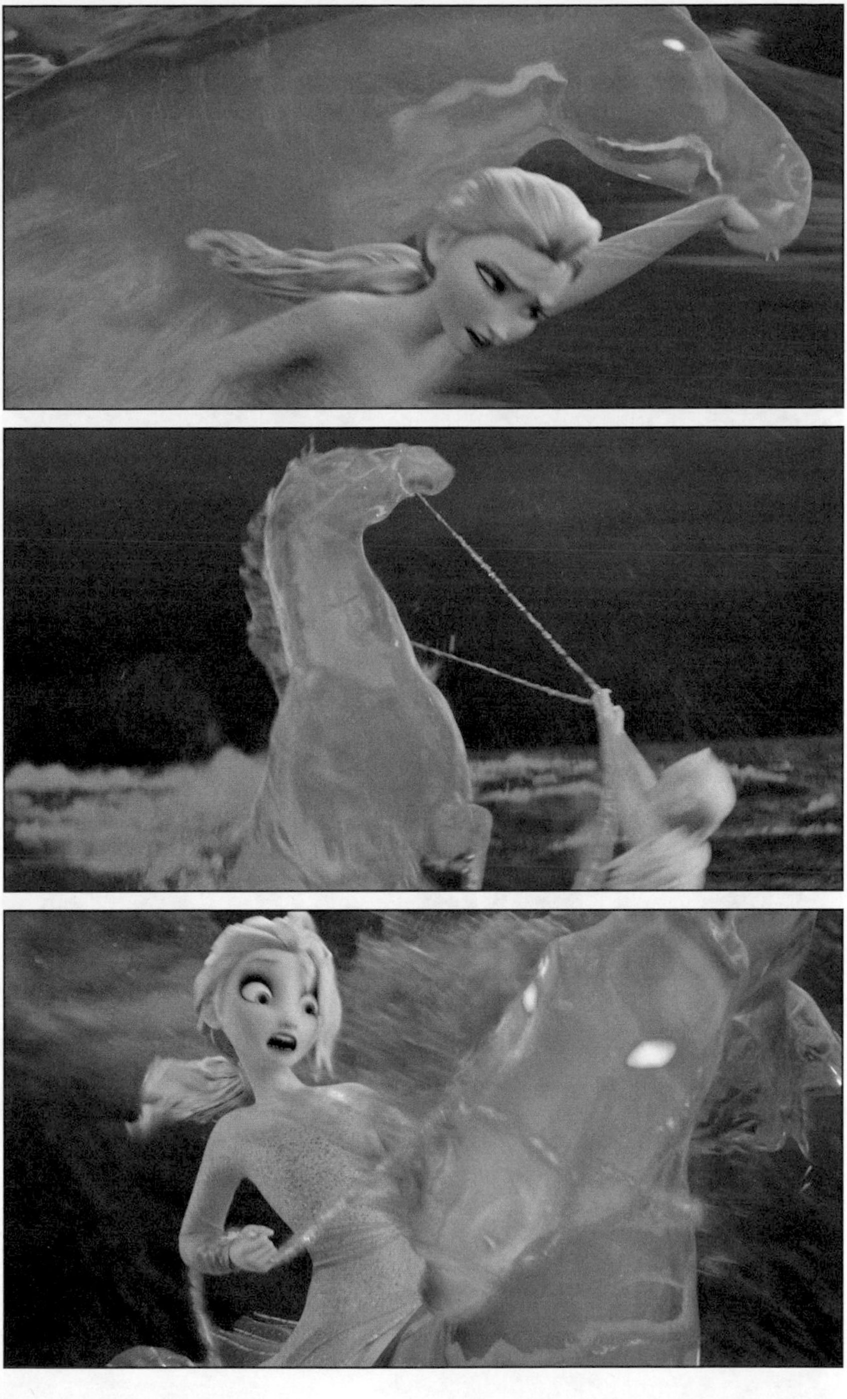

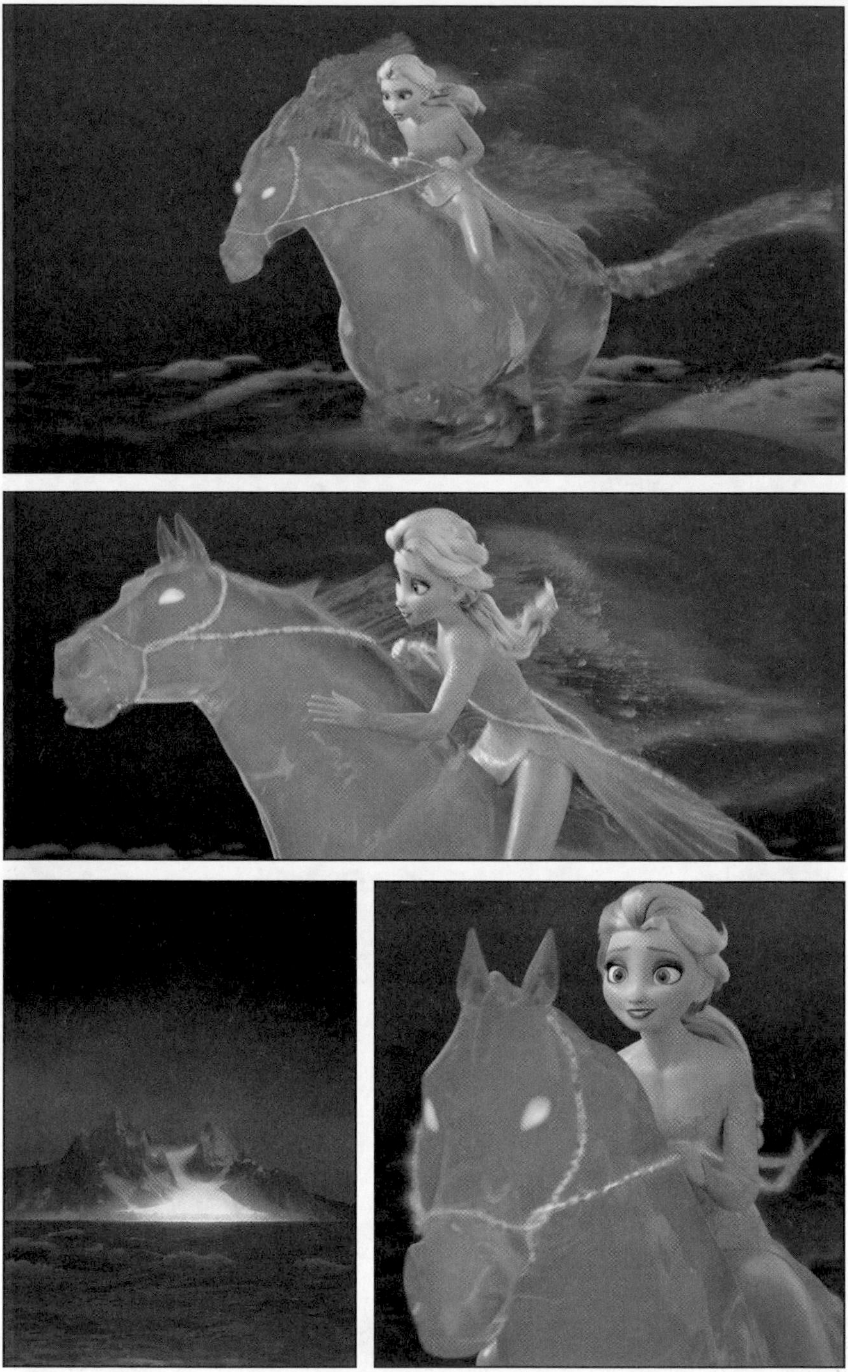

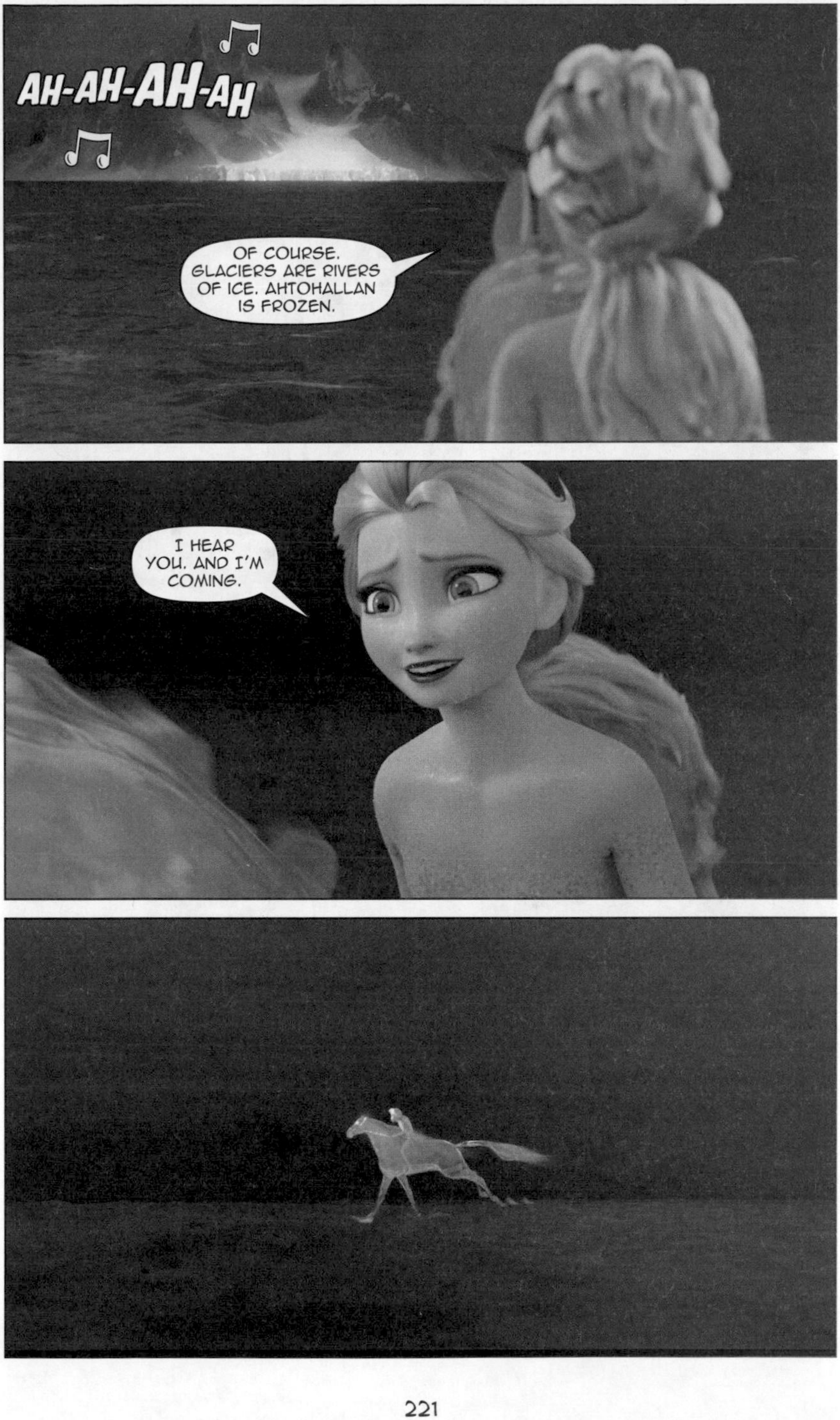
AH-AH-AH-AH
OF COURSE. GLACIERS ARE RIVERS OF ICE. AHTOHALLAN IS FROZEN.
I HEAR YOU. AND I'M COMING.

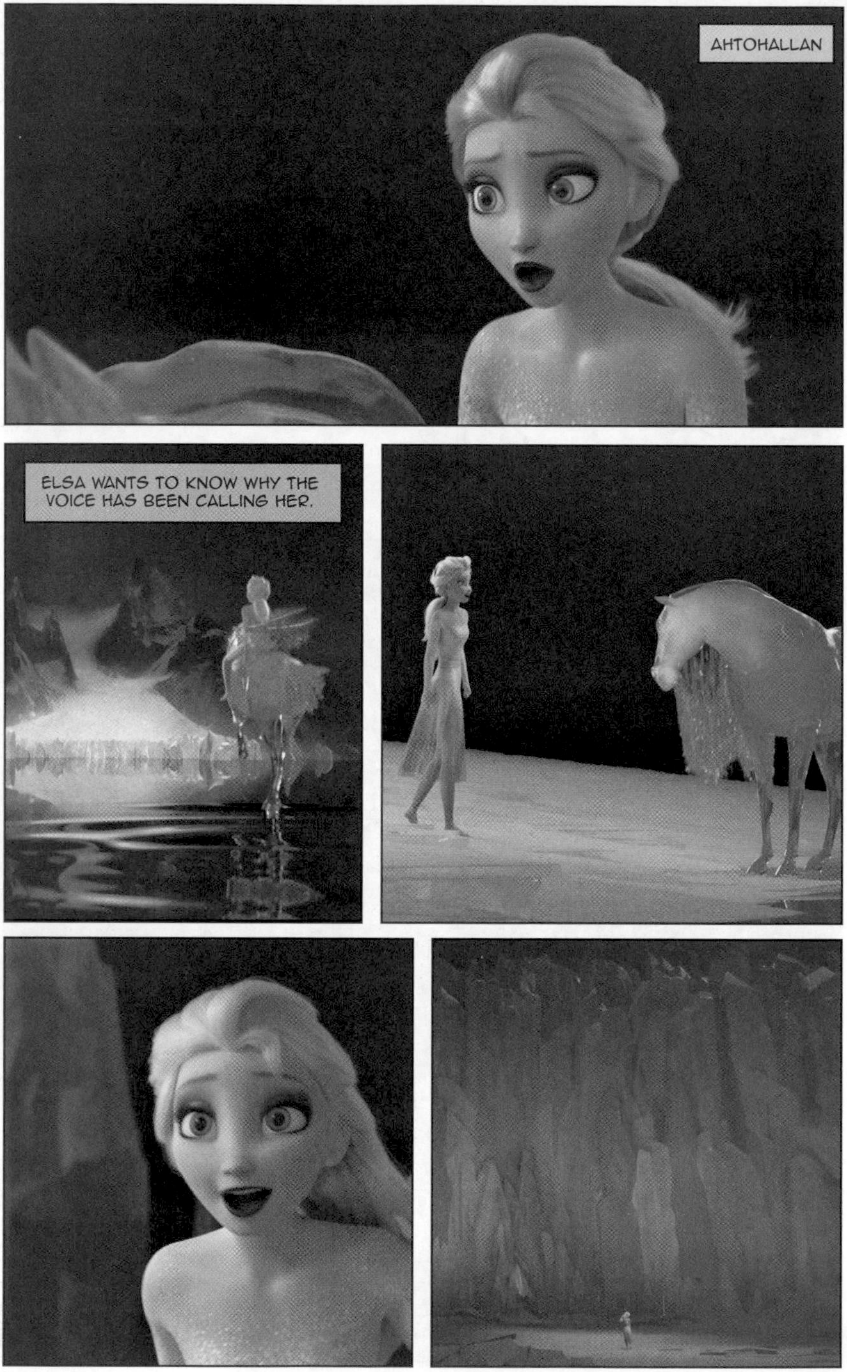
AHTOHALLAN
ELSA WANTS TO KNOW WHY THE VOICE HAS BEEN CALLING HER.

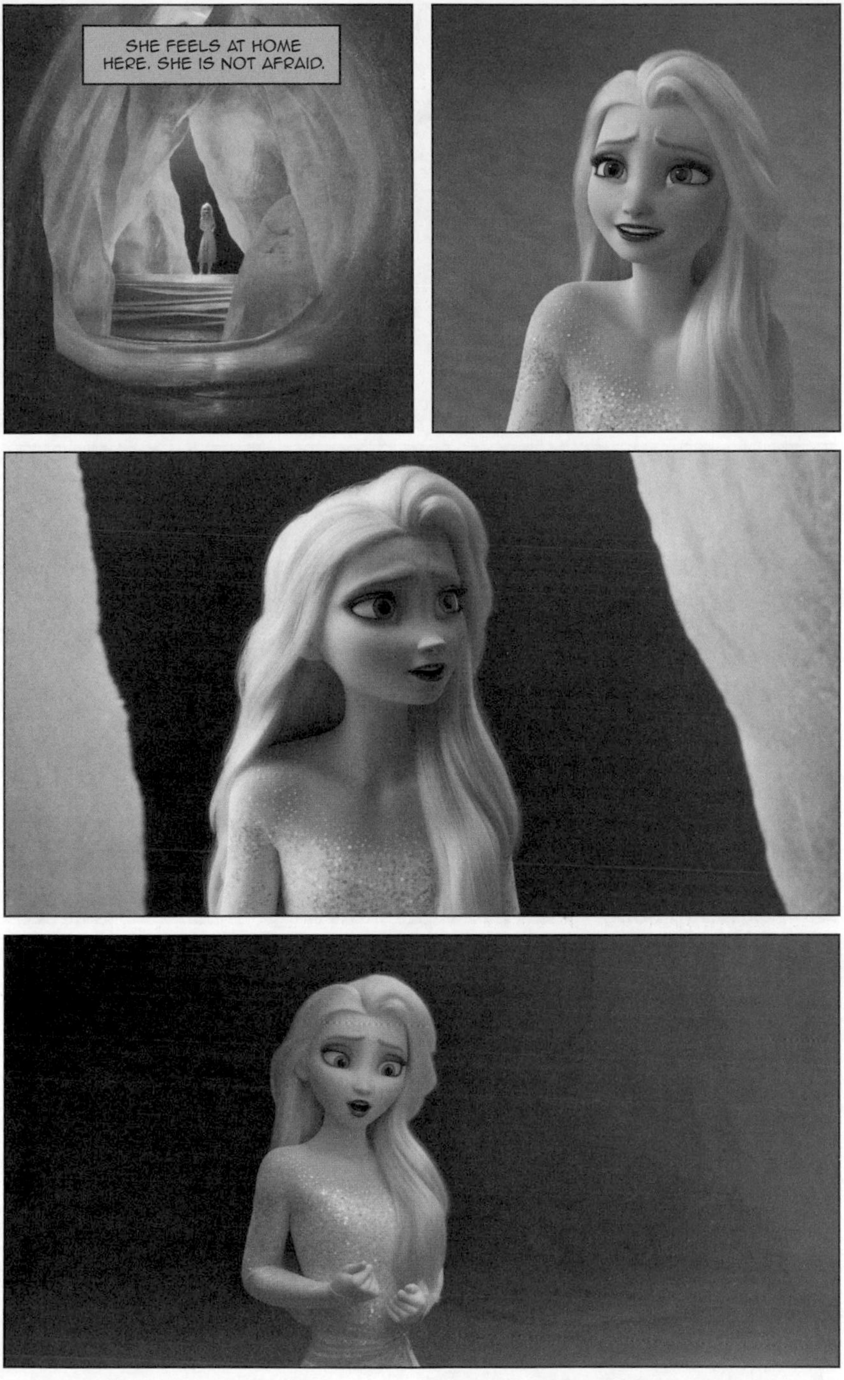
SHE FEELS AT HOME HERE. SHE IS NOT AFRAID.

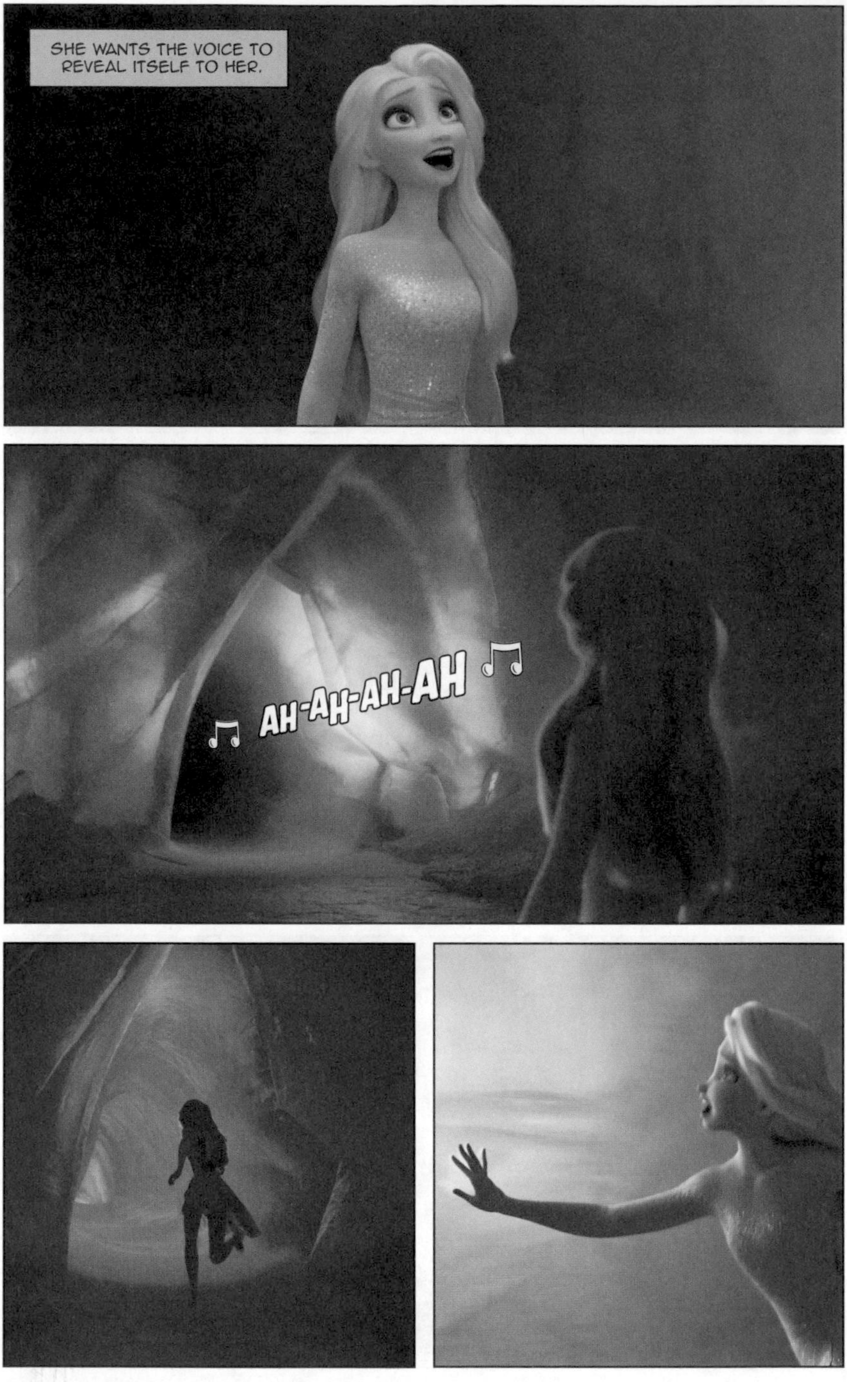
SHE WANTS THE VOICE TO REVEAL ITSELF TO HER.
♫ AH-AH-AH-AH ♫

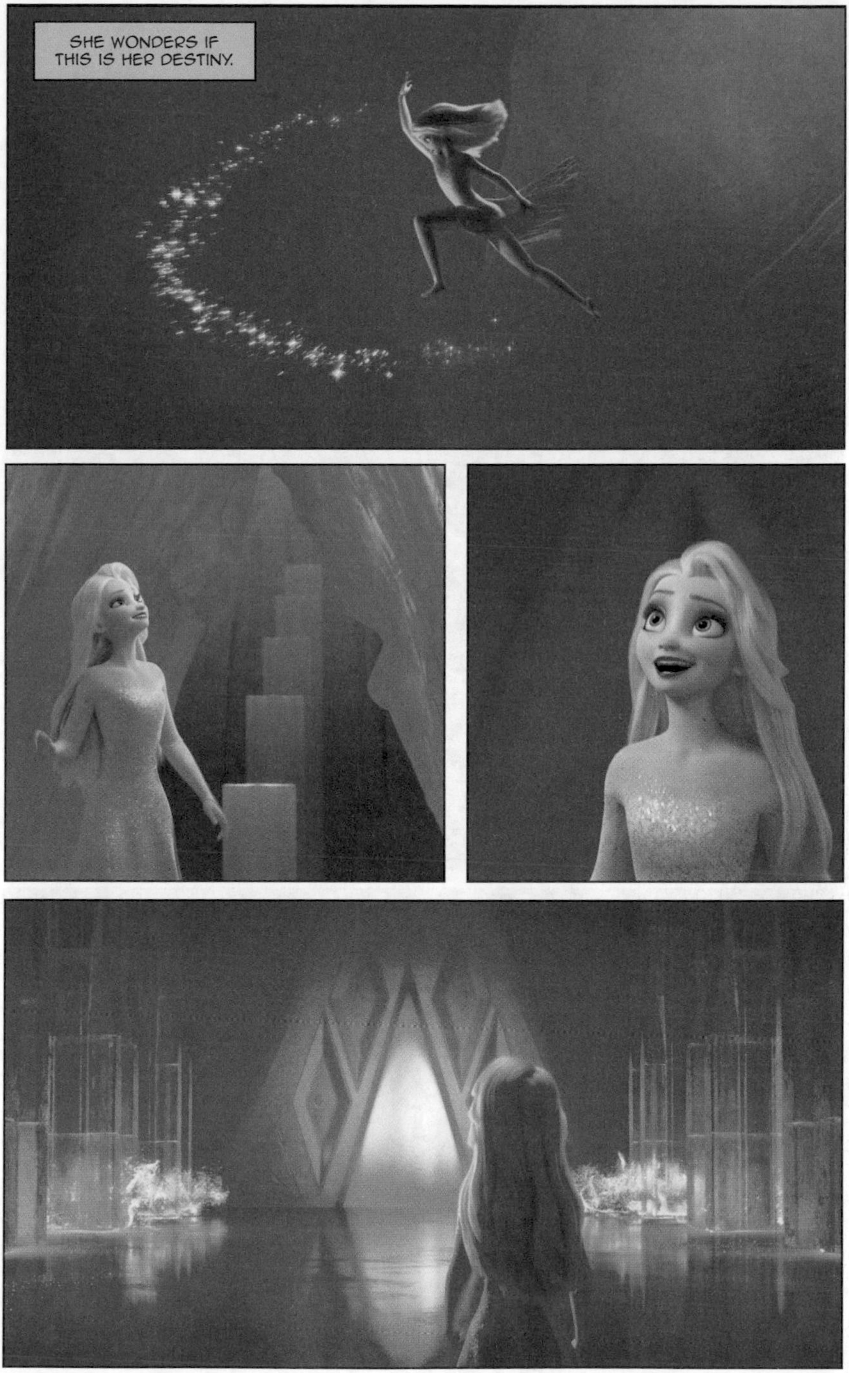
SHE WONDERS IF THIS IS HER DESTINY.

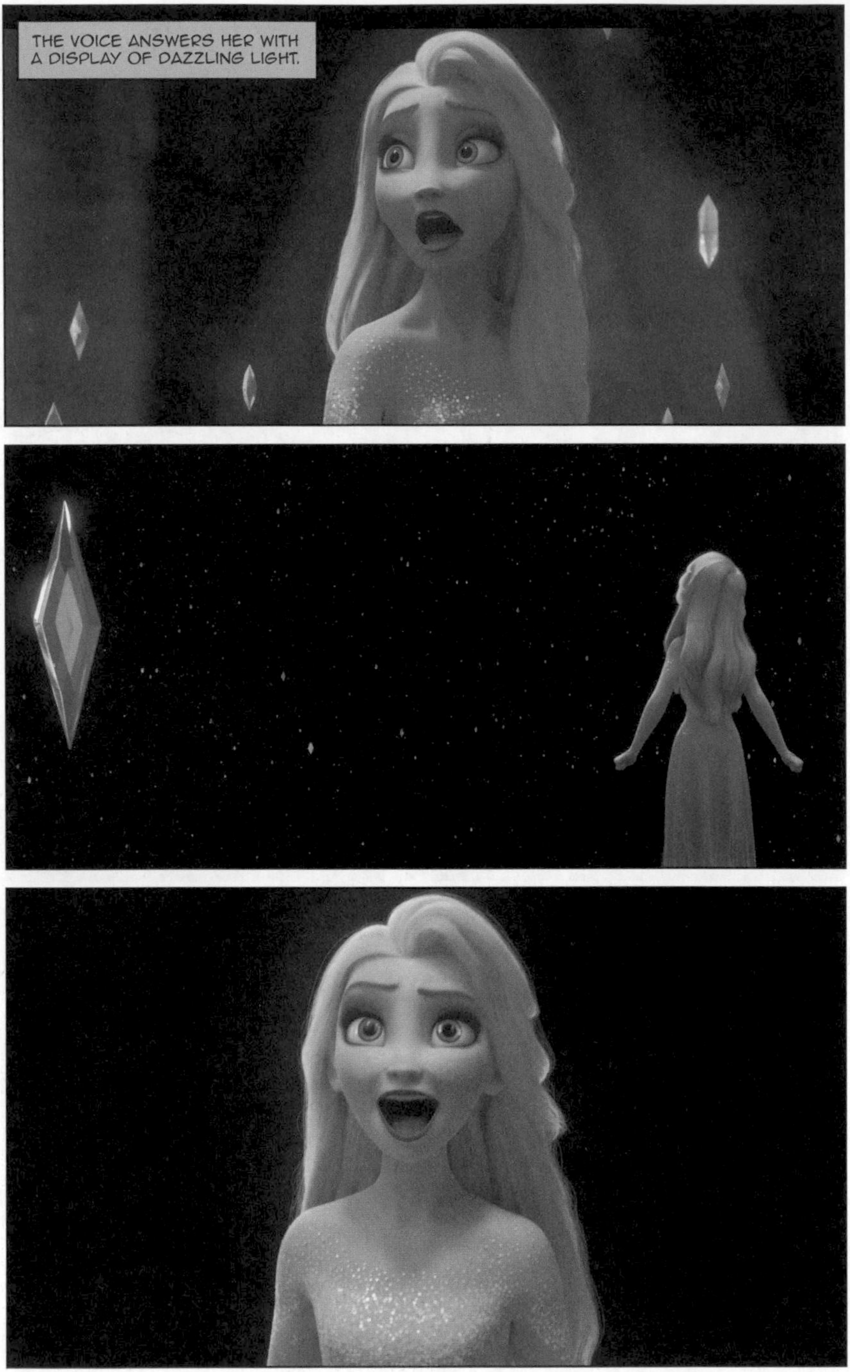
THE VOICE ANSWERS HER WITH
A DISPLAY OF DAZZLING LIGHT.

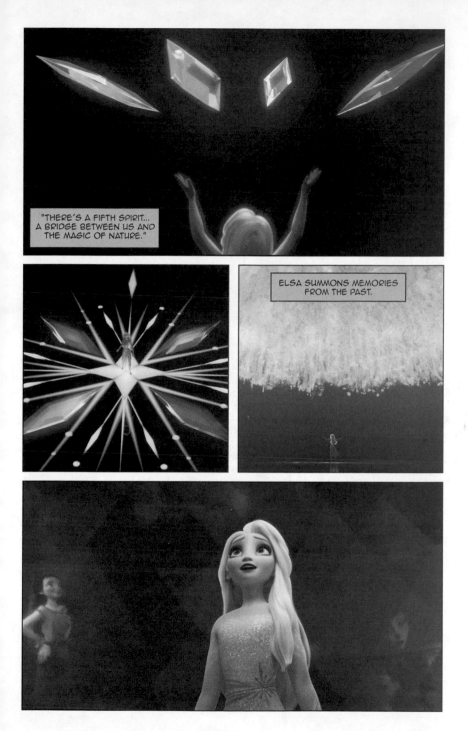

"THERE'S A FIFTH SPIRIT... A BRIDGE BETWEEN US AND THE MAGIC OF NATURE."

ELSA SUMMONS MEMORIES FROM THE PAST.

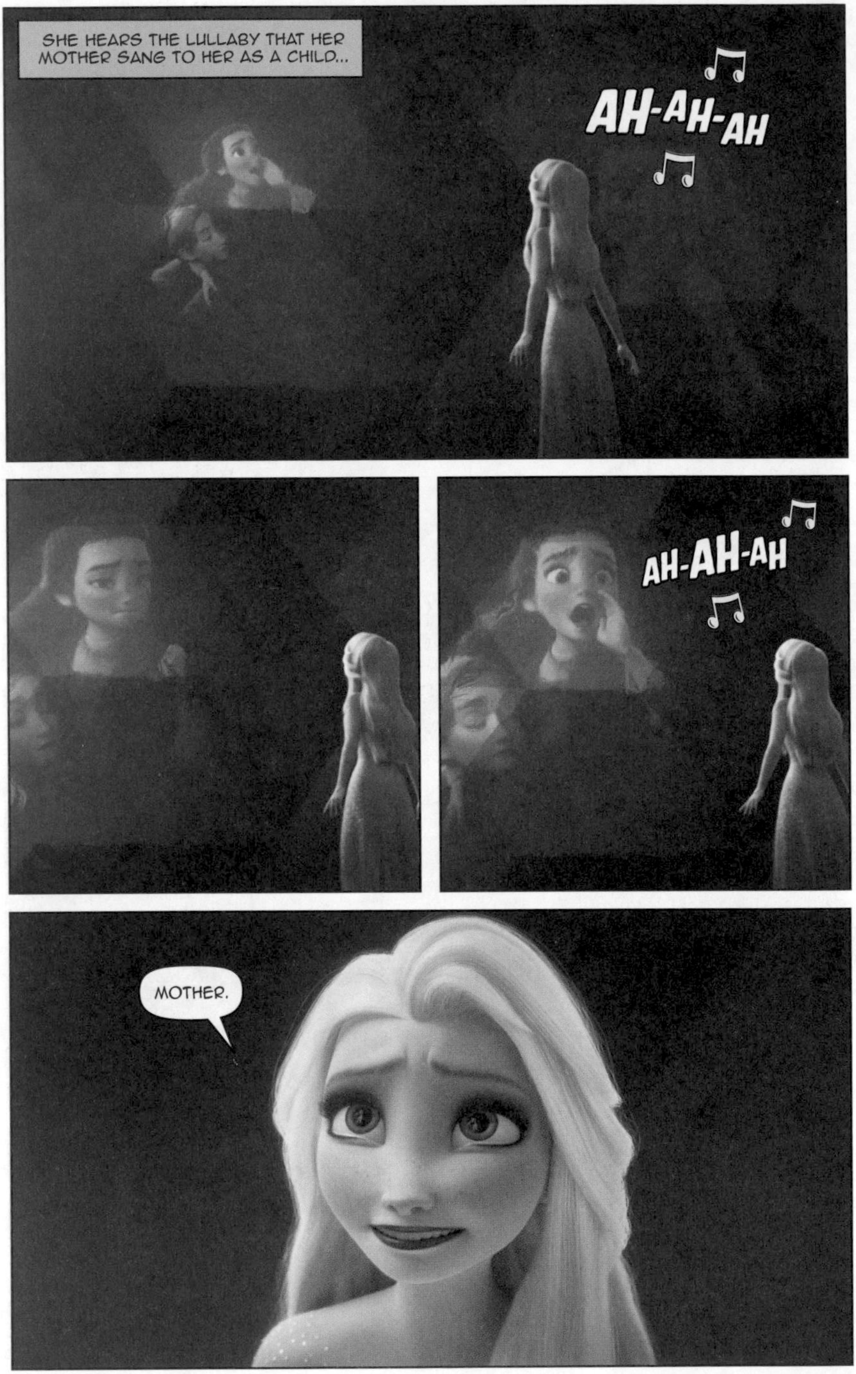
SHE HEARS THE LULLABY THAT HER MOTHER SANG TO HER AS A CHILD...
AH-AH-AH
AH-AH-AH
MOTHER.

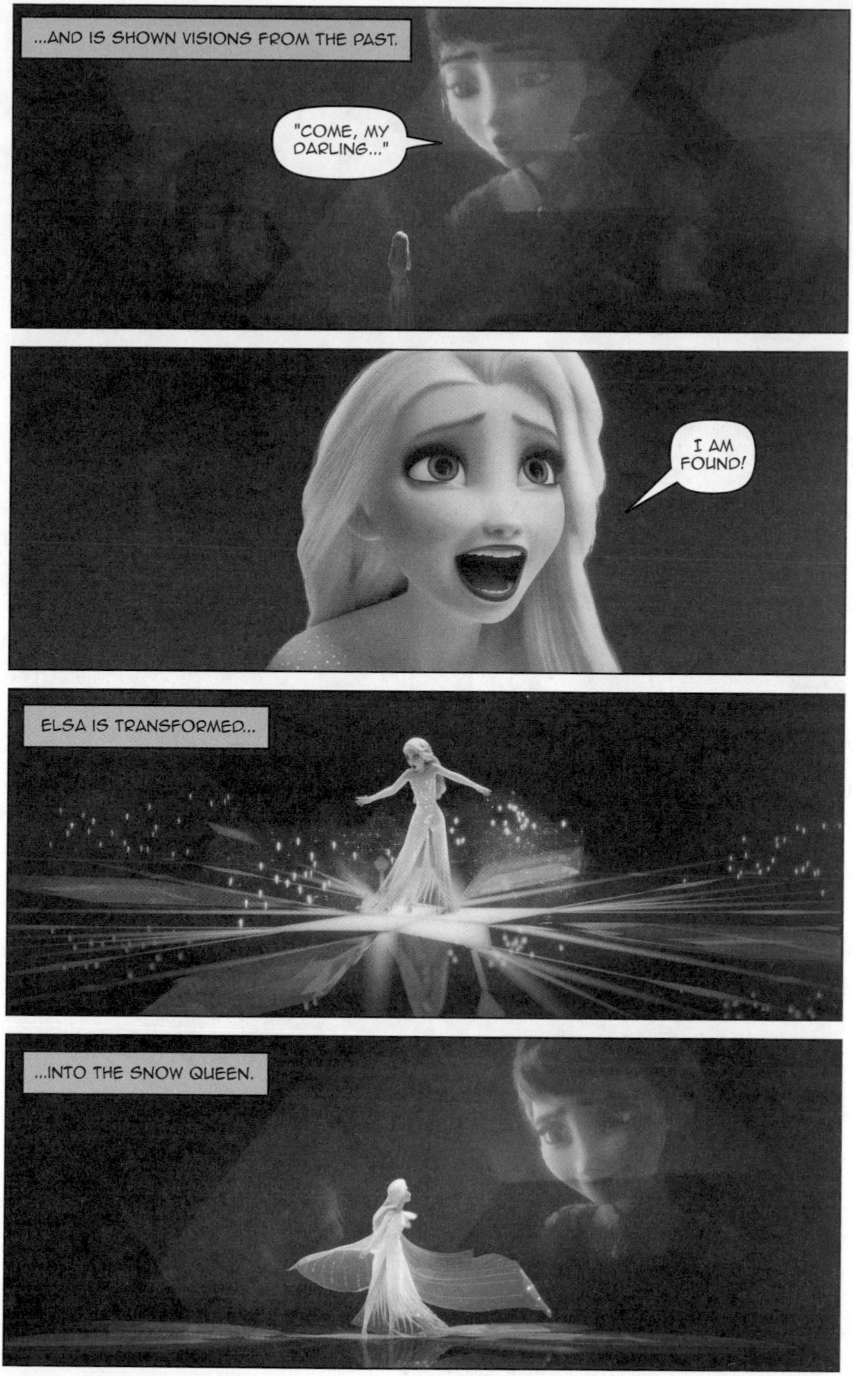
...AND IS SHOWN VISIONS FROM THE PAST.
"COME, MY DARLING..."
I AM FOUND!
ELSA IS TRANSFORMED...
...INTO THE SNOW QUEEN.

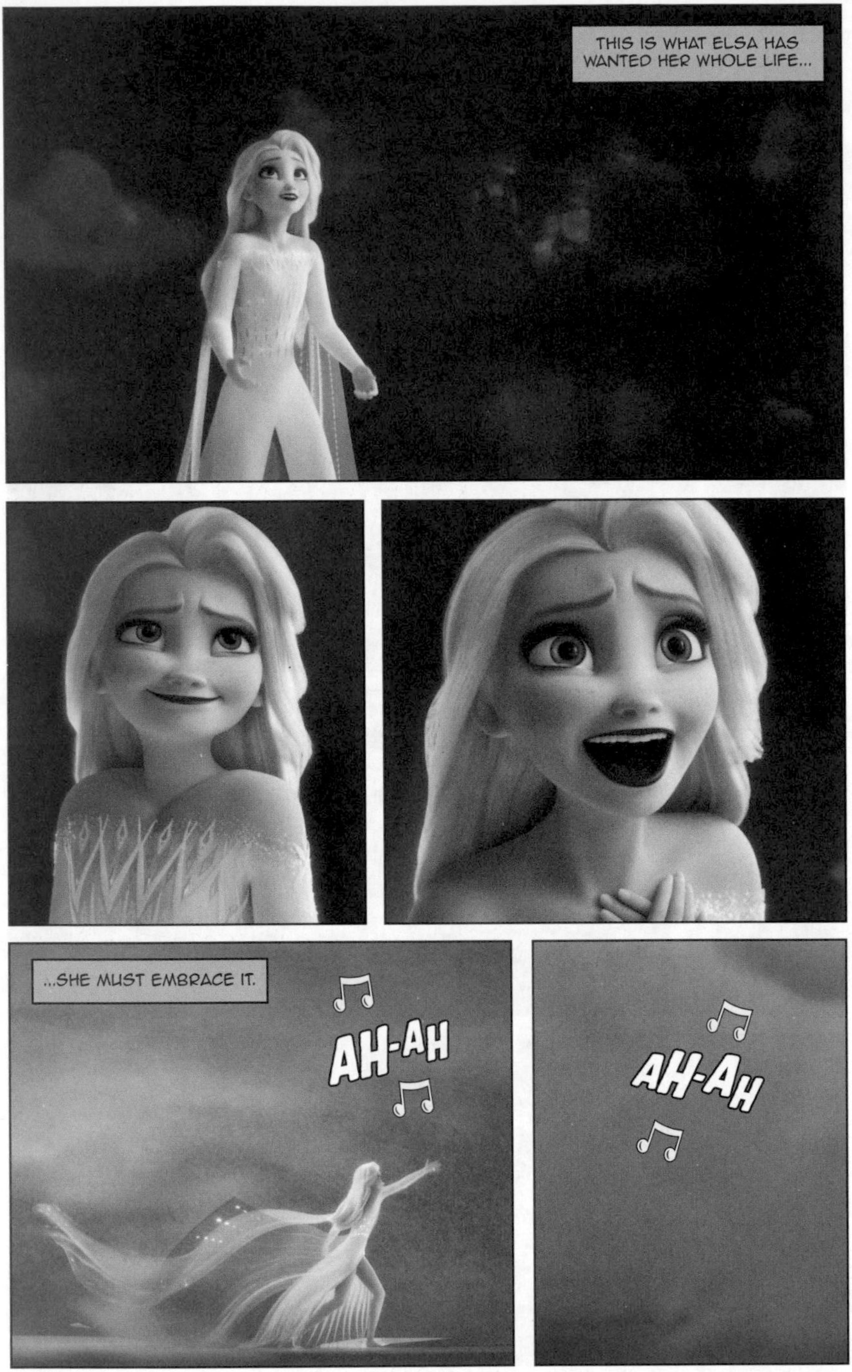
THIS IS WHAT ELSA HAS WANTED HER WHOLE LIFE...
...SHE MUST EMBRACE IT.
AH-AH
AH-AH

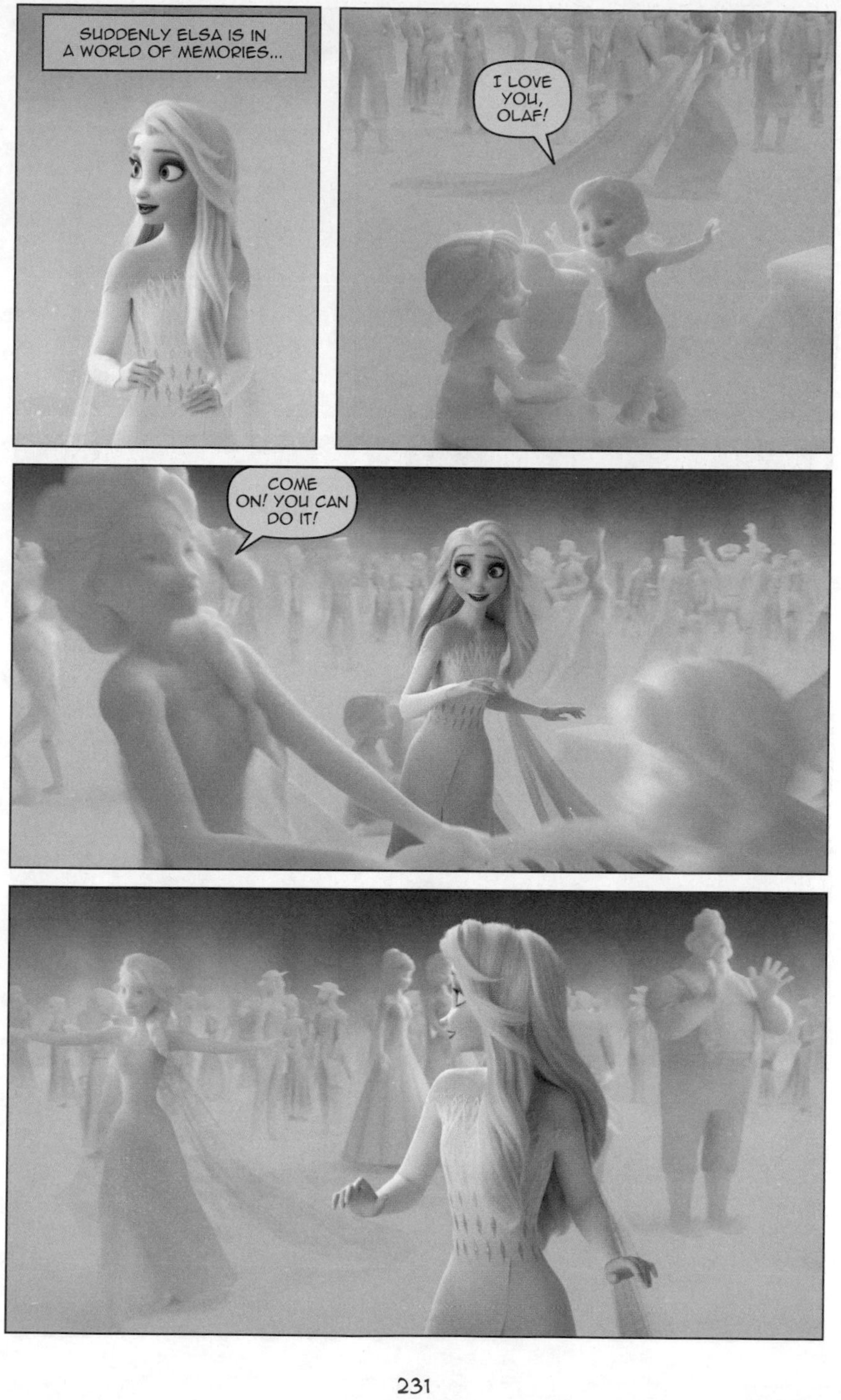
SUDDENLY ELSA IS IN A WORLD OF MEMORIES...
I LOVE YOU, OLAF!
COME ON! YOU CAN DO IT!

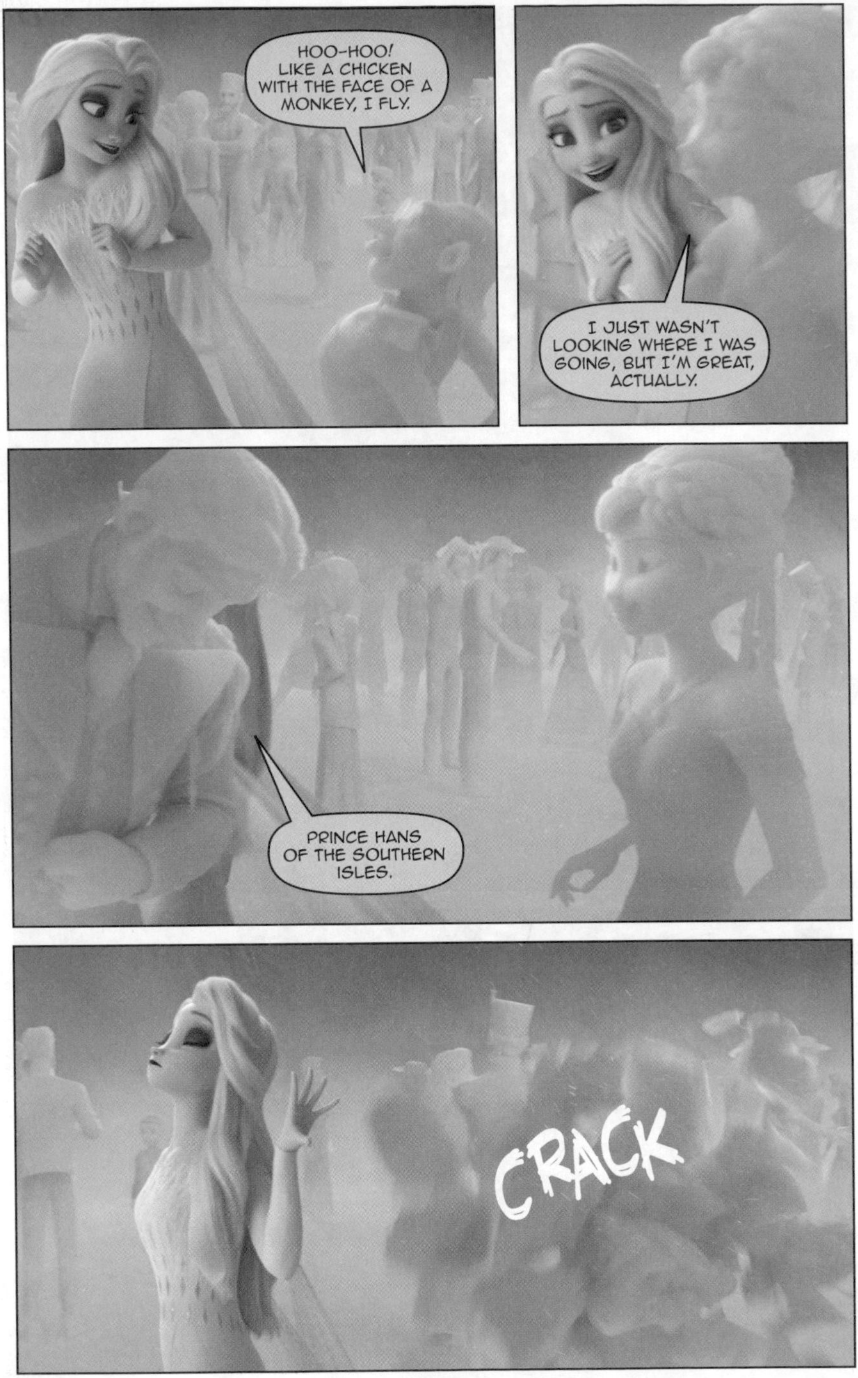
HOO-HOO! LIKE A CHICKEN WITH THE FACE OF A MONKEY, I FLY.
I JUST WASN'T LOOKING WHERE I WAS GOING, BUT I'M GREAT, ACTUALLY.
PRINCE HANS OF THE SOUTHERN ISLES.
CRACK

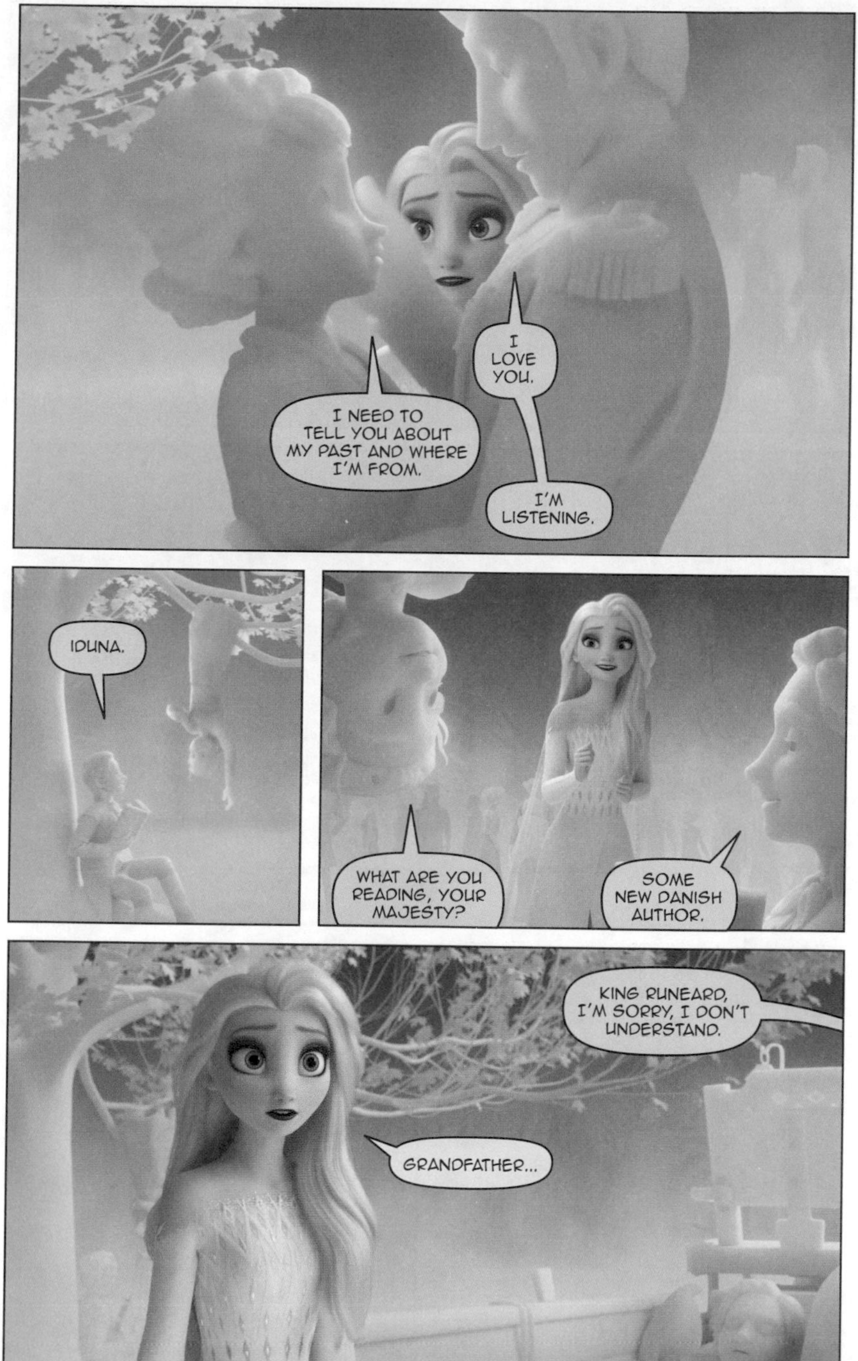
I NEED TO TELL YOU ABOUT MY PAST AND WHERE I'M FROM.
I LOVE YOU.
I'M LISTENING.
IDUNA.
WHAT ARE YOU READING, YOUR MAJESTY?
SOME NEW DANISH AUTHOR.
KING RUNEARD, I'M SORRY, I DON'T UNDERSTAND.
GRANDFATHER...

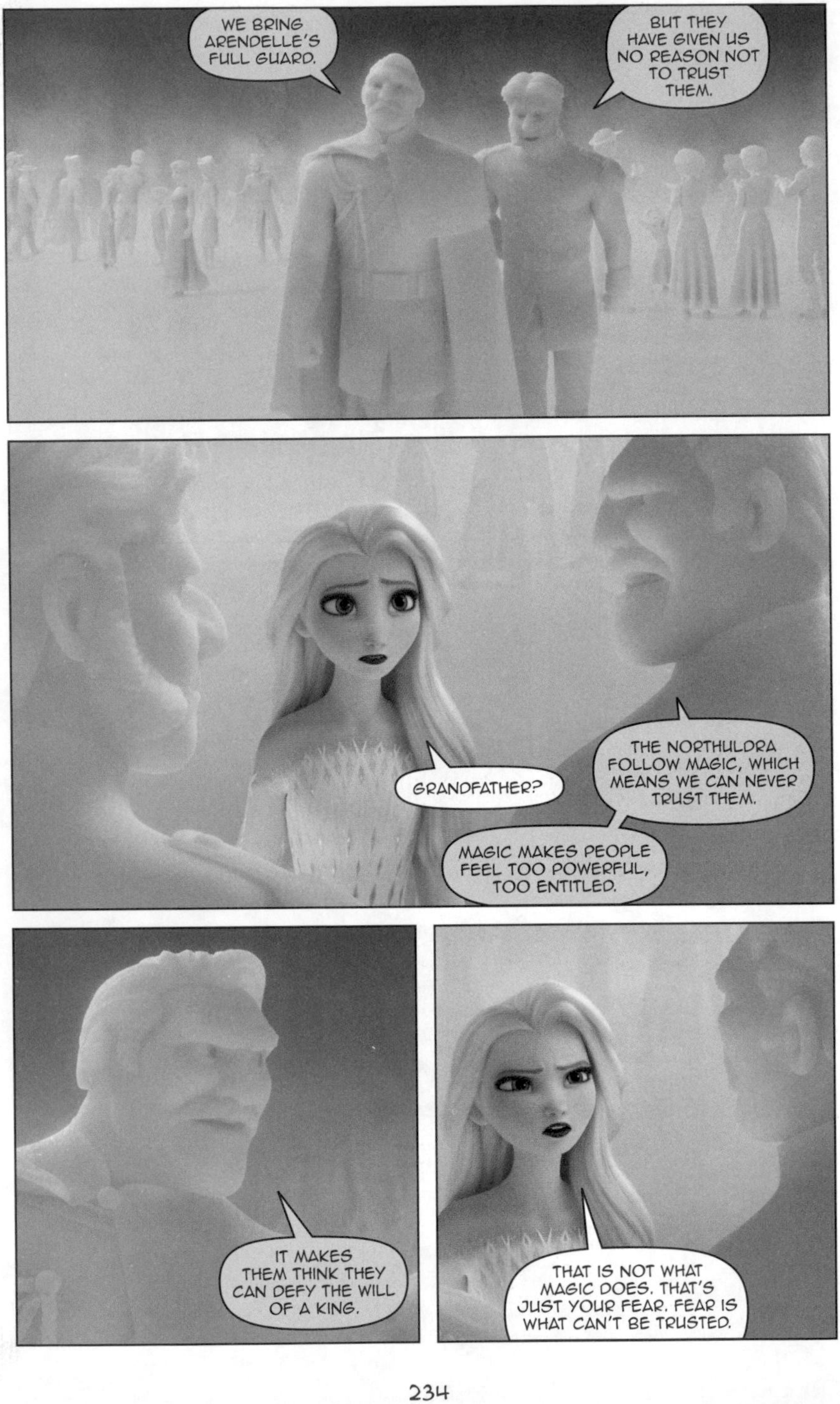
WE BRING ARENDELLE'S FULL GUARD.
BUT THEY HAVE GIVEN US NO REASON NOT TO TRUST THEM.
GRANDFATHER?
THE NORTHULDRA FOLLOW MAGIC, WHICH MEANS WE CAN NEVER TRUST THEM.
MAGIC MAKES PEOPLE FEEL TOO POWERFUL, TOO ENTITLED.
IT MAKES THEM THINK THEY CAN DEFY THE WILL OF A KING.
THAT IS NOT WHAT MAGIC DOES. THAT'S JUST YOUR FEAR. FEAR IS WHAT CAN'T BE TRUSTED.

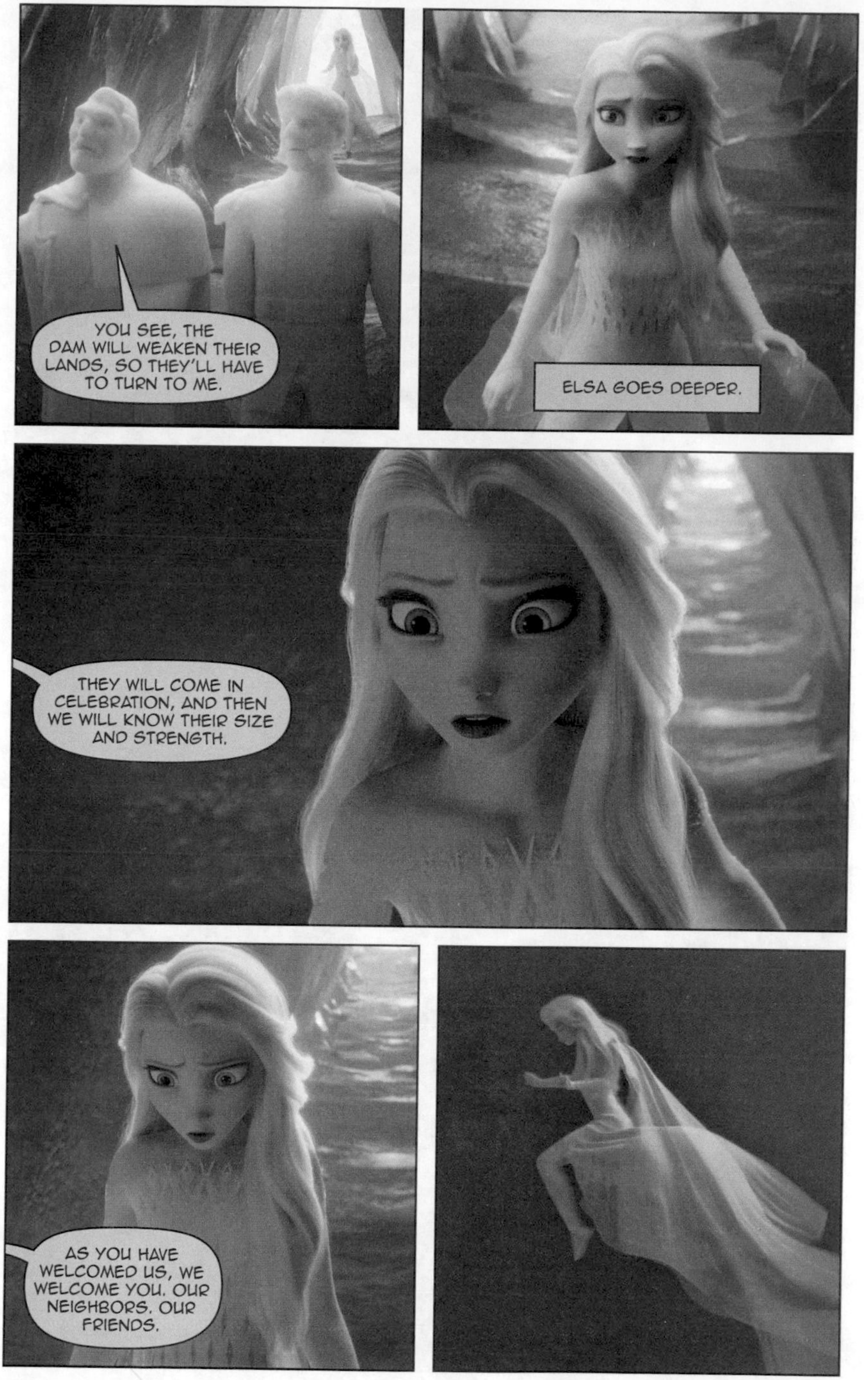
YOU SEE, THE DAM WILL WEAKEN THEIR LANDS, SO THEY'LL HAVE TO TURN TO ME.
ELSA GOES DEEPER.
THEY WILL COME IN CELEBRATION, AND THEN WE WILL KNOW THEIR SIZE AND STRENGTH.
AS YOU HAVE WELCOMED US, WE WELCOME YOU. OUR NEIGHBORS. OUR FRIENDS.

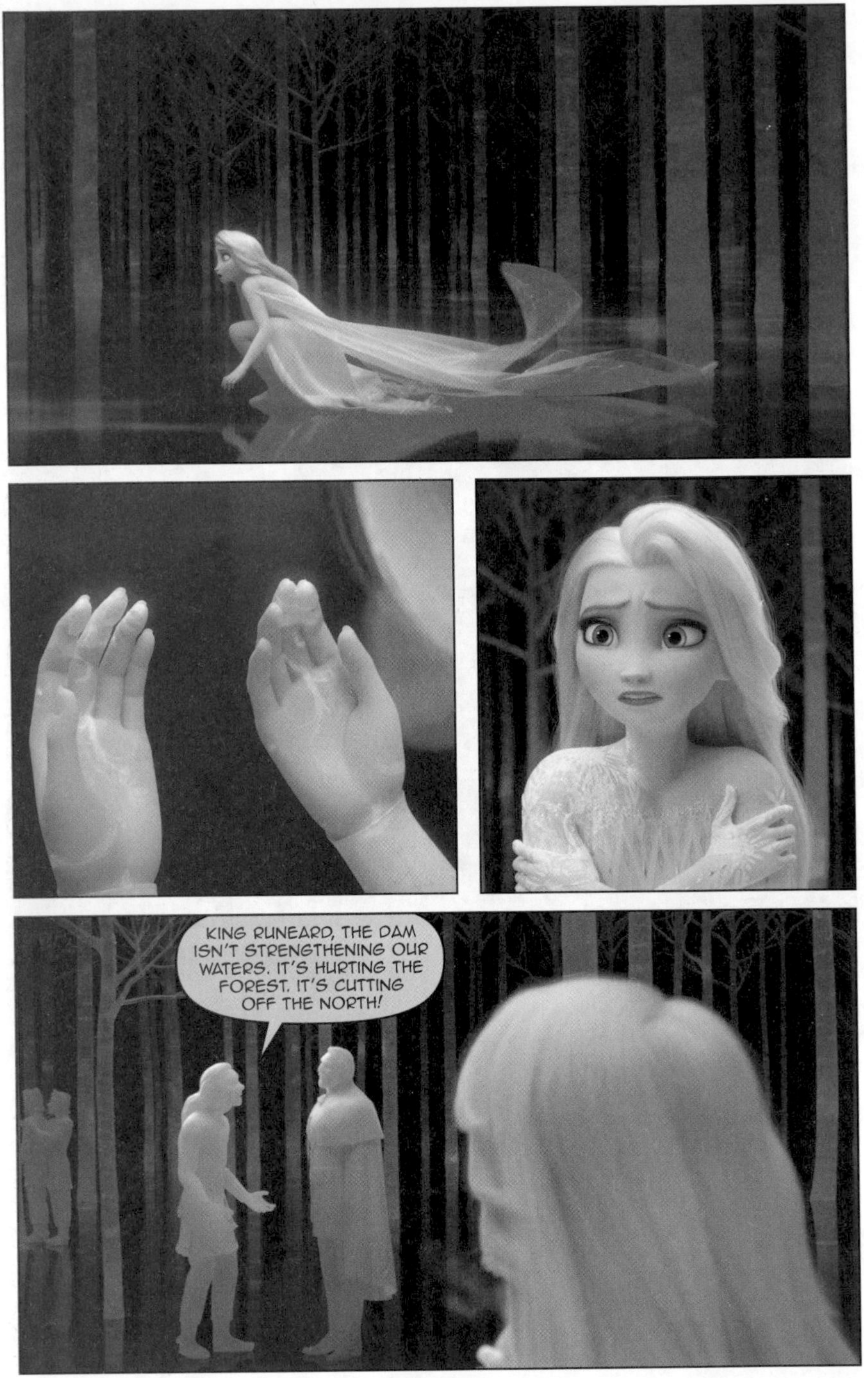
KING RUNEARD, THE DAM ISN'T STRENGTHENING OUR WATERS. IT'S HURTING THE FOREST. IT'S CUTTING OFF THE NORTH!

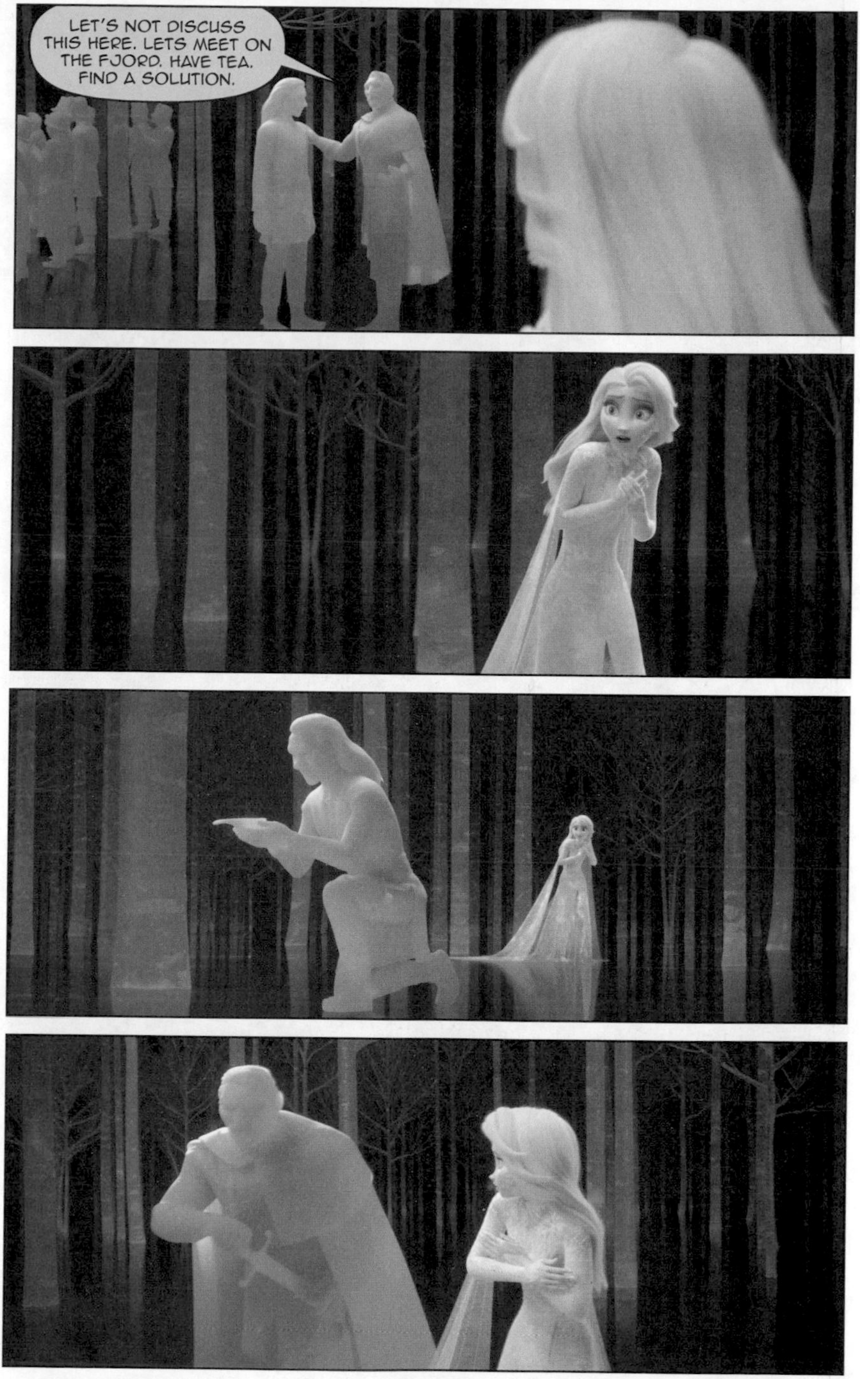
LET'S NOT DISCUSS THIS HERE. LETS MEET ON THE FJORD. HAVE TEA. FIND A SOLUTION.

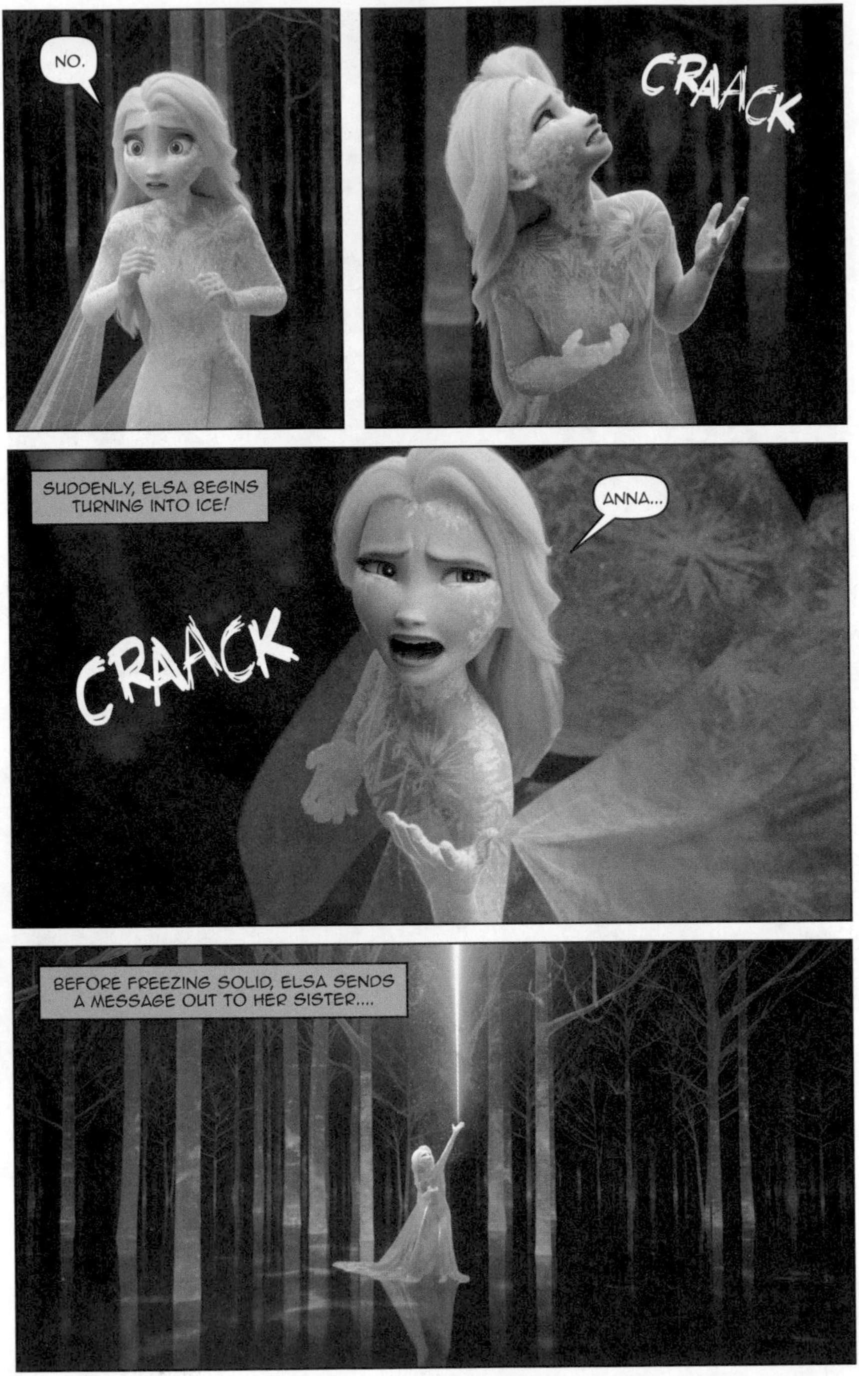
NO.
CRAACK
SUDDENLY, ELSA BEGINS TURNING INTO ICE!
ANNA...
CRAACK
BEFORE FREEZING SOLID, ELSA SENDS A MESSAGE OUT TO HER SISTER....

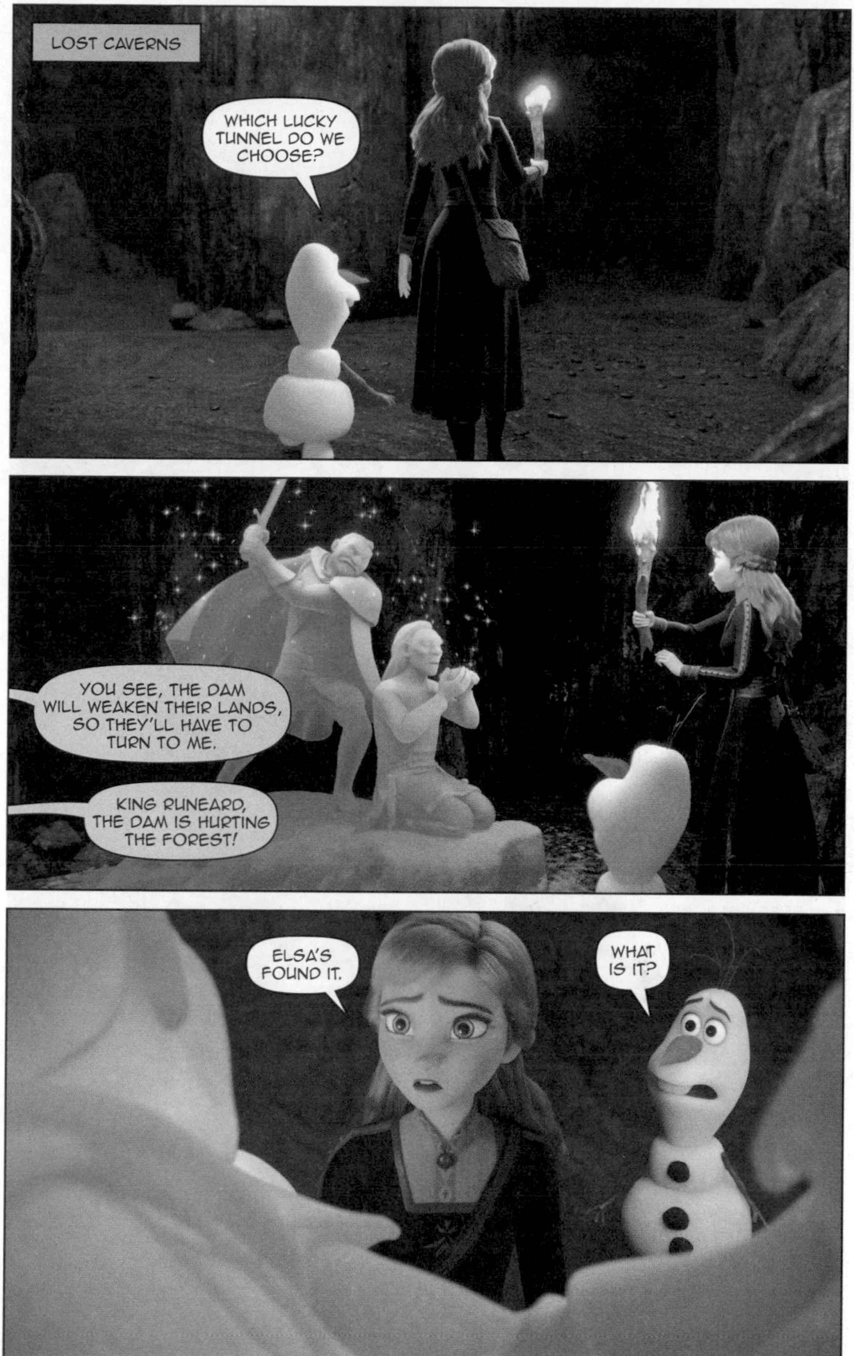
LOST CAVERNS
WHICH LUCKY TUNNEL DO WE CHOOSE?
YOU SEE, THE DAM WILL WEAKEN THEIR LANDS, SO THEY'LL HAVE TO TURN TO ME.
KING RUNEARD, THE DAM IS HURTING THE FOREST!
ELSA'S FOUND IT.
WHAT IS IT?

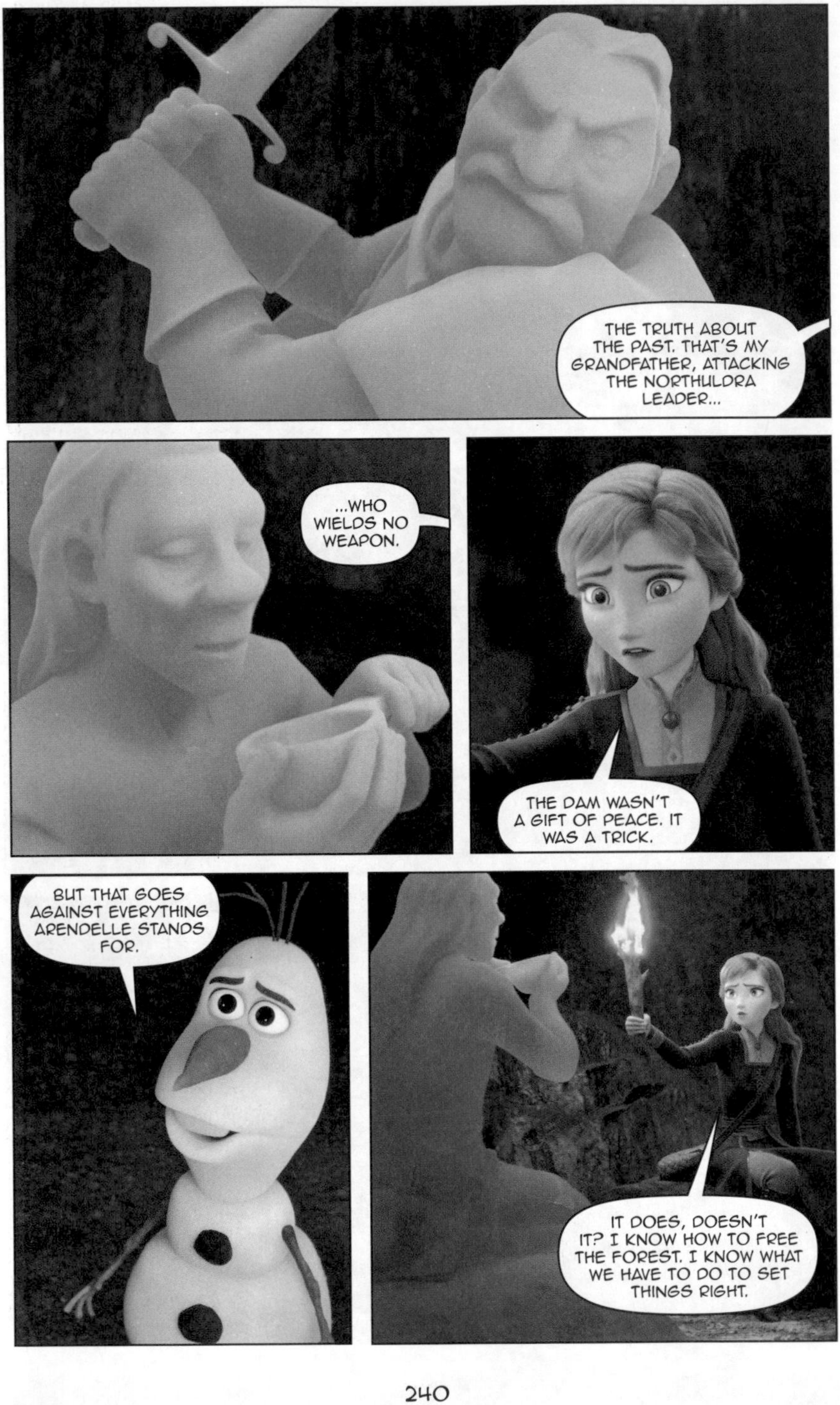
THE TRUTH ABOUT THE PAST. THAT'S MY GRANDFATHER, ATTACKING THE NORTHULDRA LEADER...
...WHO WIELDS NO WEAPON.
THE DAM WASN'T A GIFT OF PEACE. IT WAS A TRICK.
BUT THAT GOES AGAINST EVERYTHING ARENDELLE STANDS FOR.
IT DOES, DOESN'T IT? I KNOW HOW TO FREE THE FOREST. I KNOW WHAT WE HAVE TO DO TO SET THINGS RIGHT.

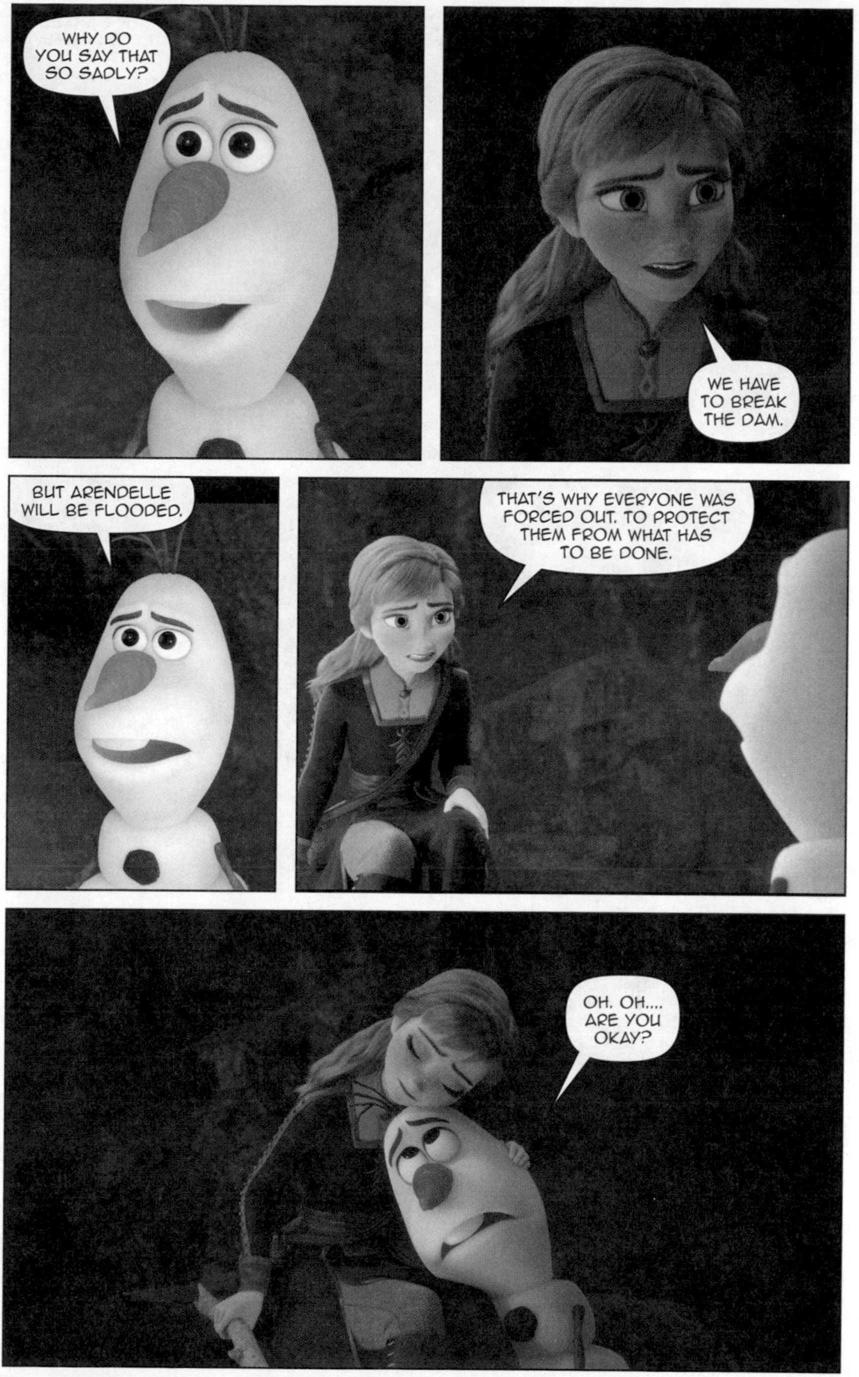
WHY DO YOU SAY THAT SO SADLY?
WE HAVE TO BREAK THE DAM.
BUT ARENDELLE WILL BE FLOODED.
THAT'S WHY EVERYONE WAS FORCED OUT. TO PROTECT THEM FROM WHAT HAS TO BE DONE.
OH. OH.... ARE YOU OKAY?

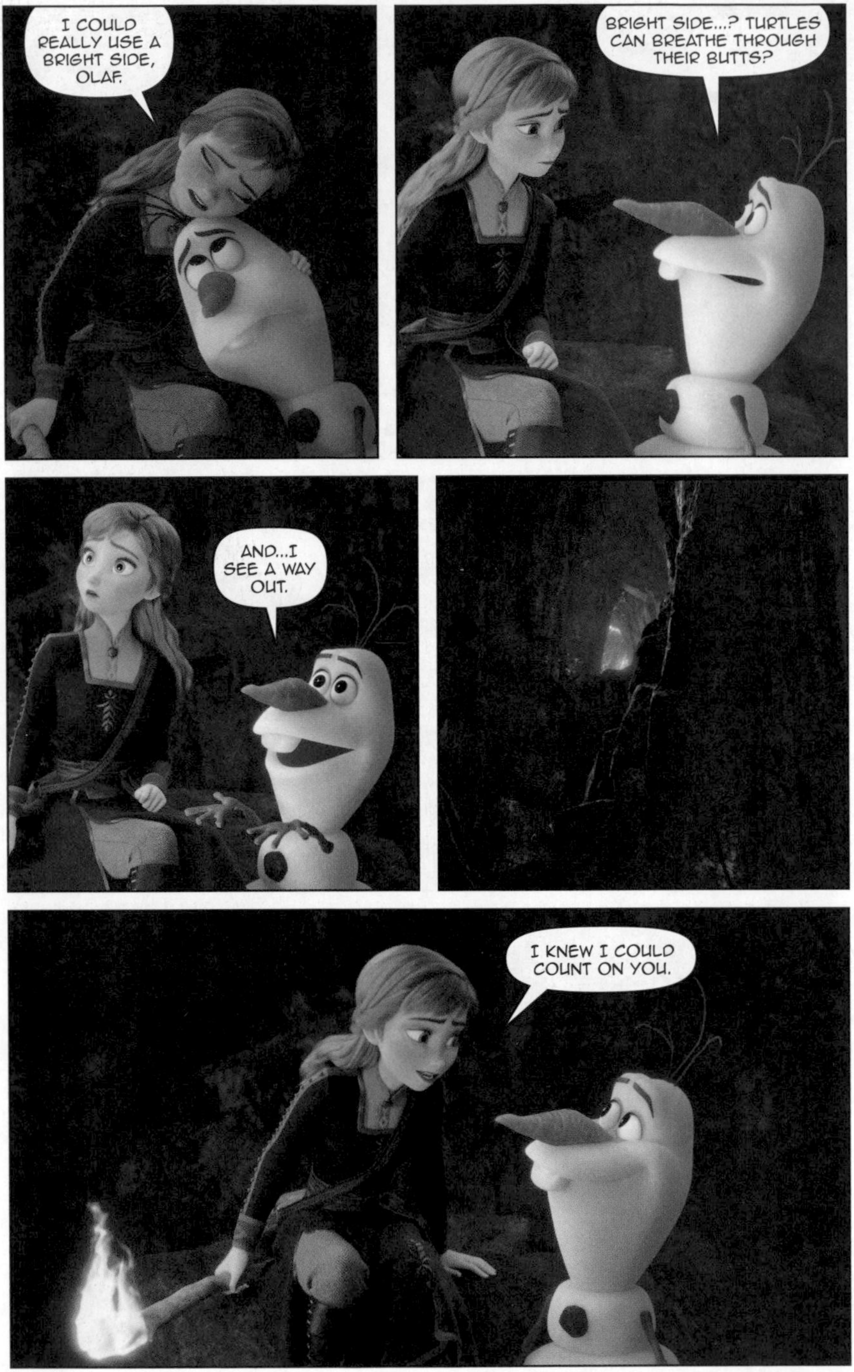
I COULD REALLY USE A BRIGHT SIDE, OLAF.
BRIGHT SIDE...? TURTLES CAN BREATHE THROUGH THEIR BUTTS?
AND...I SEE A WAY OUT.
I KNEW I COULD COUNT ON YOU.

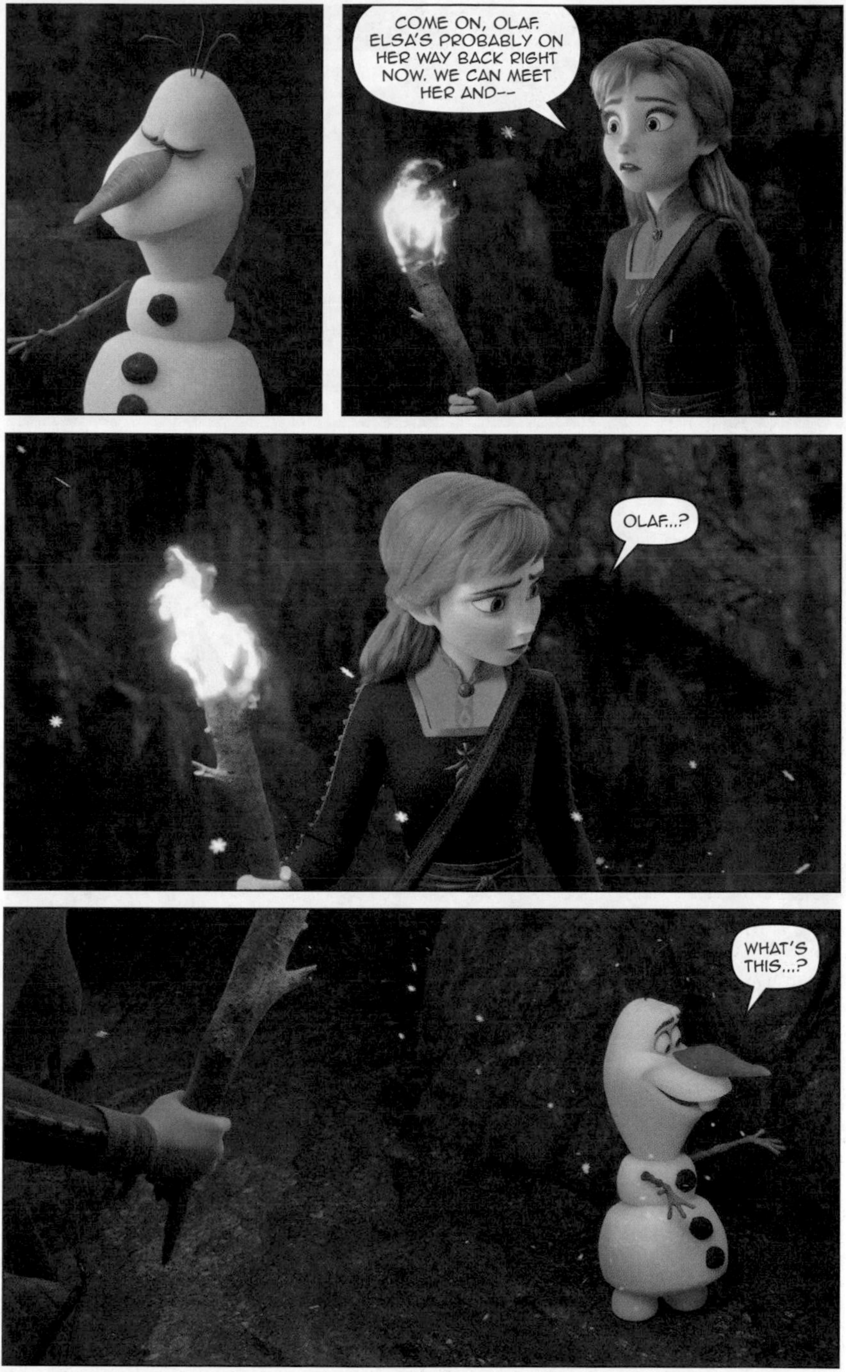
COME ON, OLAF. ELSA'S PROBABLY ON HER WAY BACK RIGHT NOW. WE CAN MEET HER AND--
OLAF...?
WHAT'S THIS...?

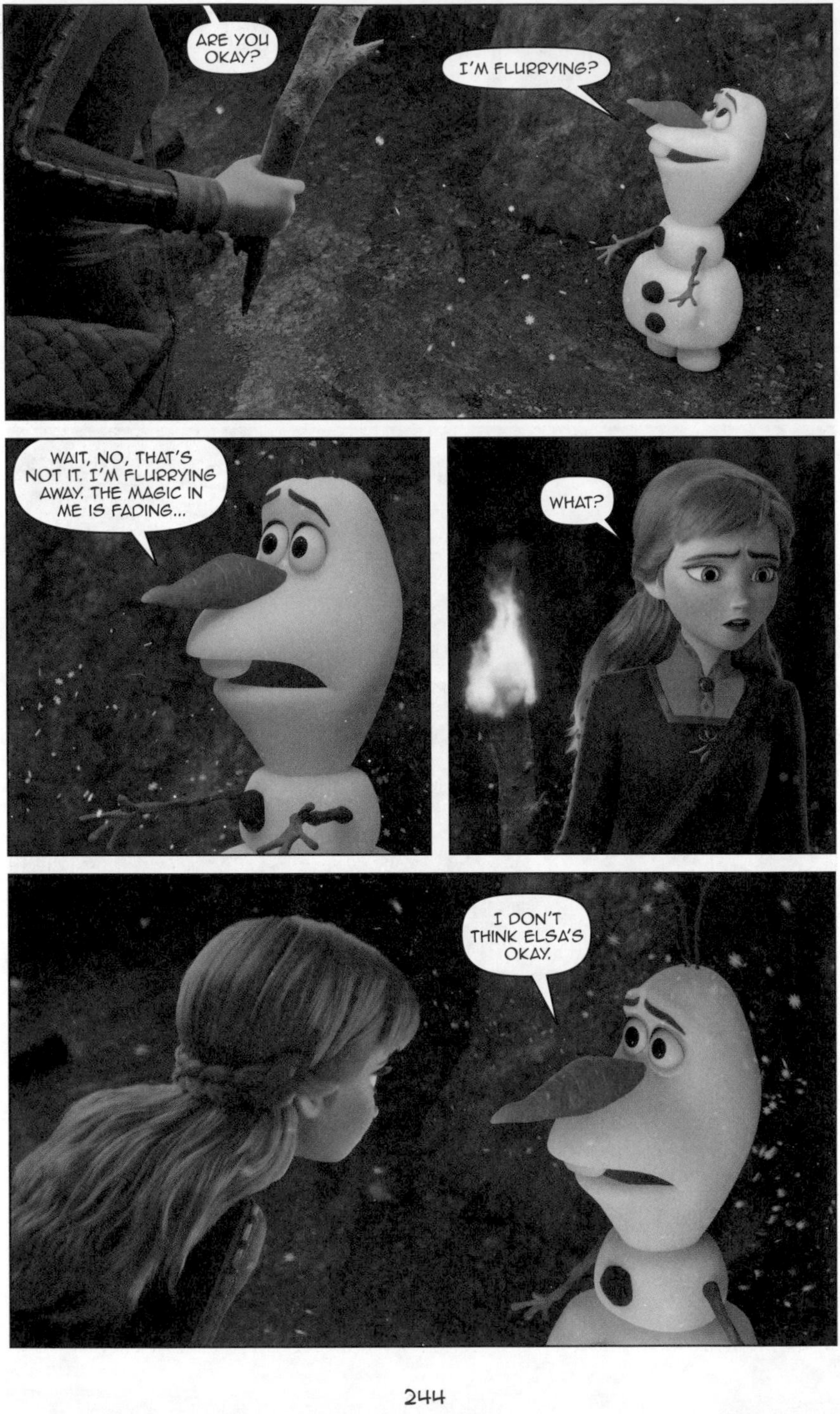
ARE YOU OKAY?
I'M FLURRYING?
WAIT, NO, THAT'S NOT IT. I'M FLURRYING AWAY. THE MAGIC IN ME IS FADING...
WHAT?
I DON'T THINK ELSA'S OKAY.

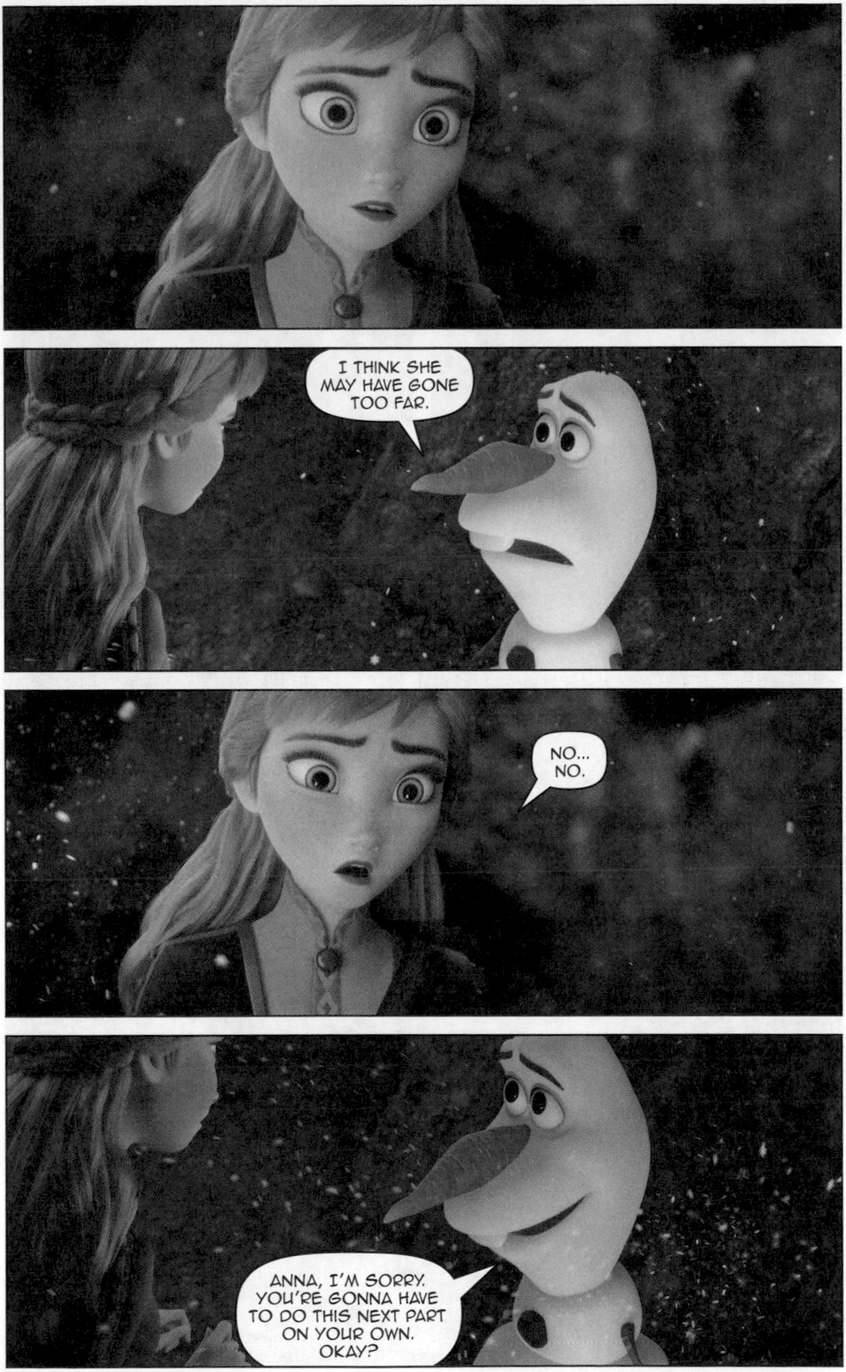
I THINK SHE MAY HAVE GONE TOO FAR.
NO... NO.
ANNA, I'M SORRY. YOU'RE GONNA HAVE TO DO THIS NEXT PART ON YOUR OWN. OKAY?

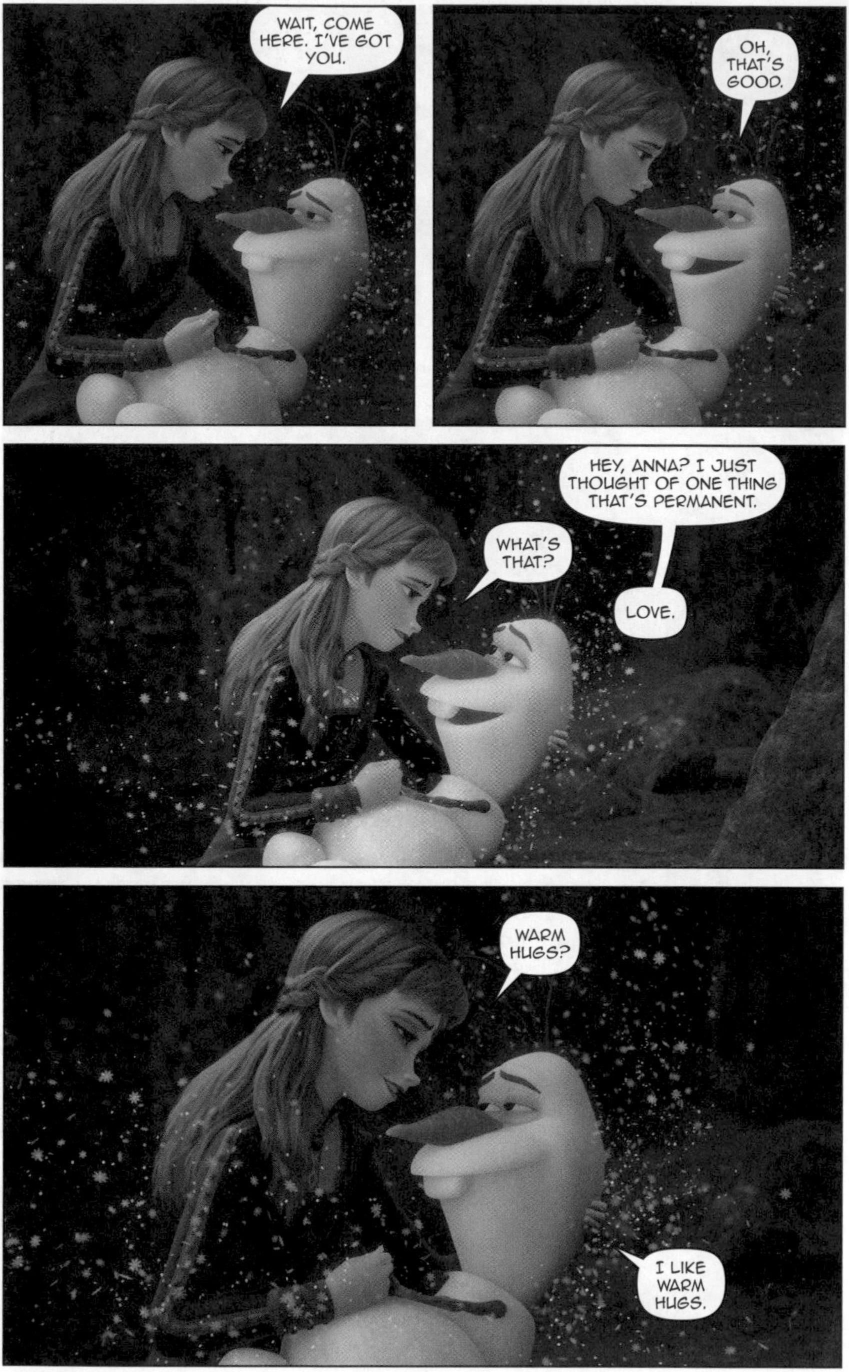
WAIT, COME HERE. I'VE GOT YOU.
OH, THAT'S GOOD.
HEY, ANNA? I JUST THOUGHT OF ONE THING THAT'S PERMANENT.
WHAT'S THAT?
LOVE.
WARM HUGS?
I LIKE WARM HUGS.

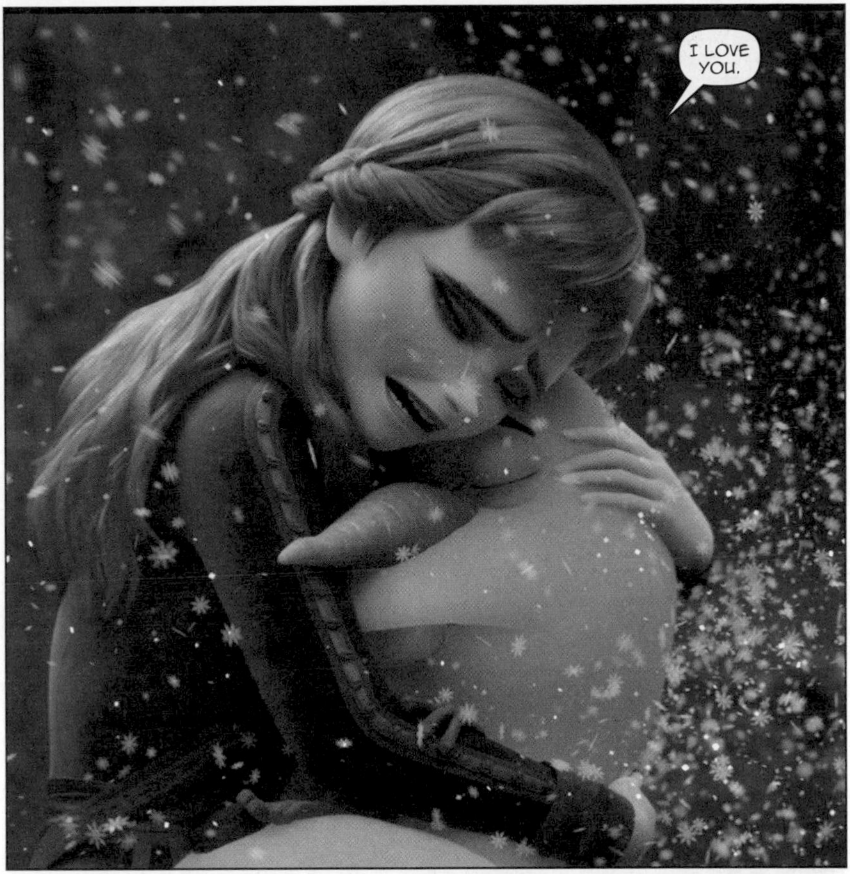
I LOVE YOU.

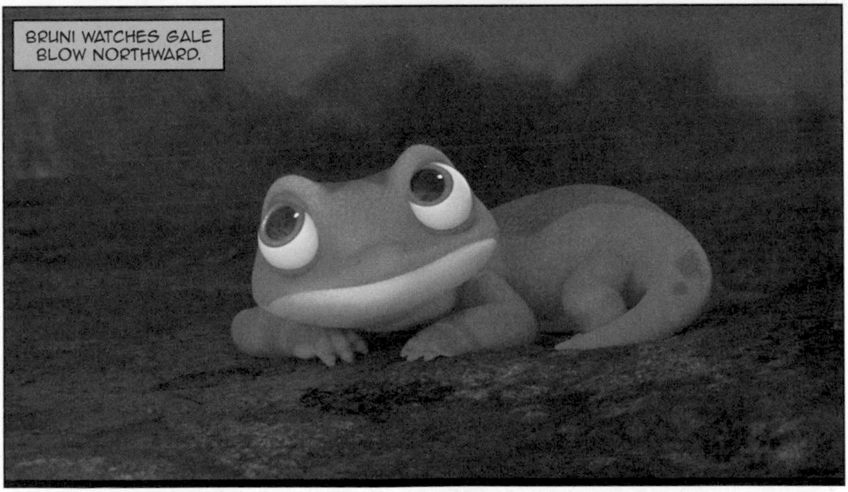
BRUNI WATCHES GALE BLOW NORTHWARD.

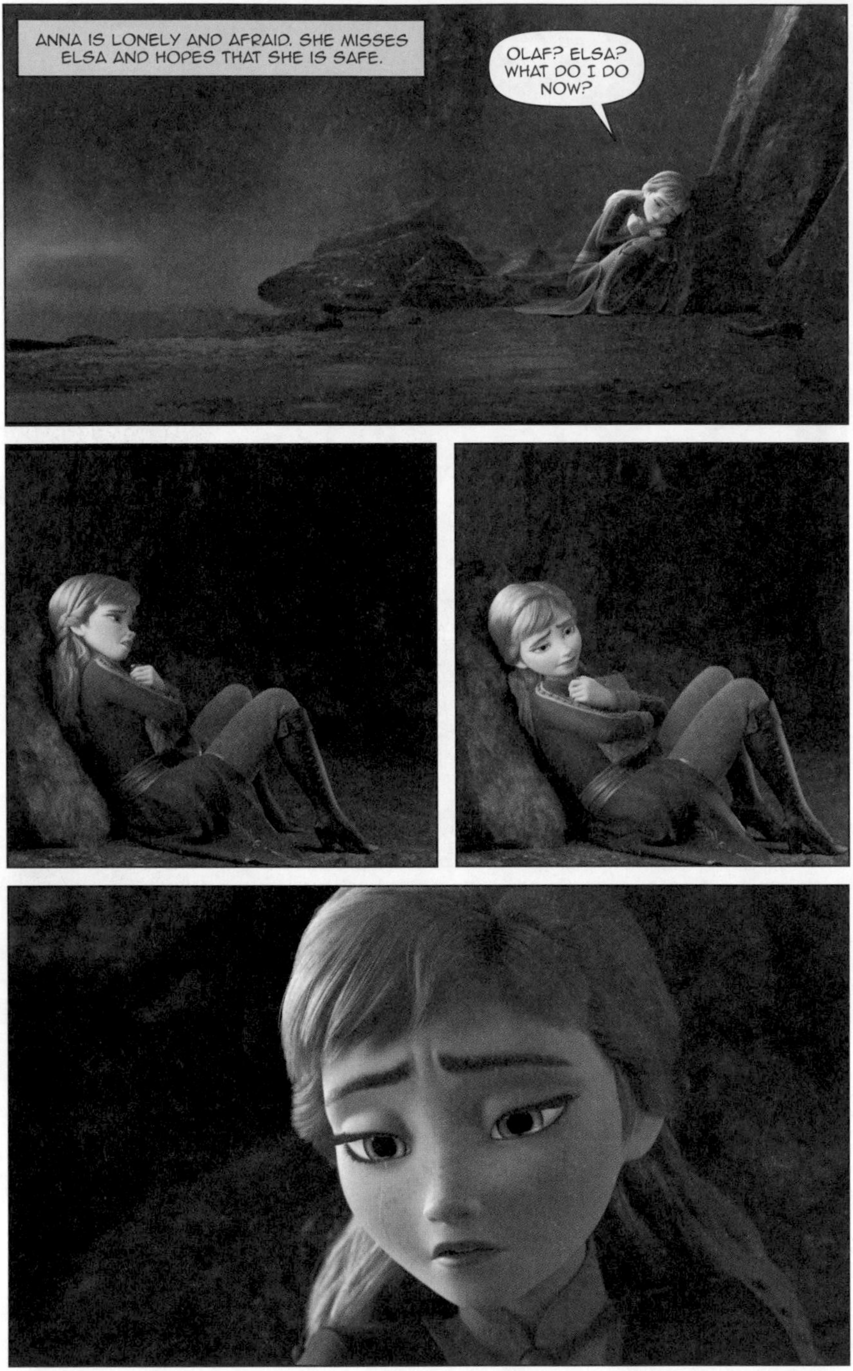
ANNA IS LONELY AND AFRAID. SHE MISSES ELSA AND HOPES THAT SHE IS SAFE.
OLAF? ELSA? WHAT DO I DO NOW?

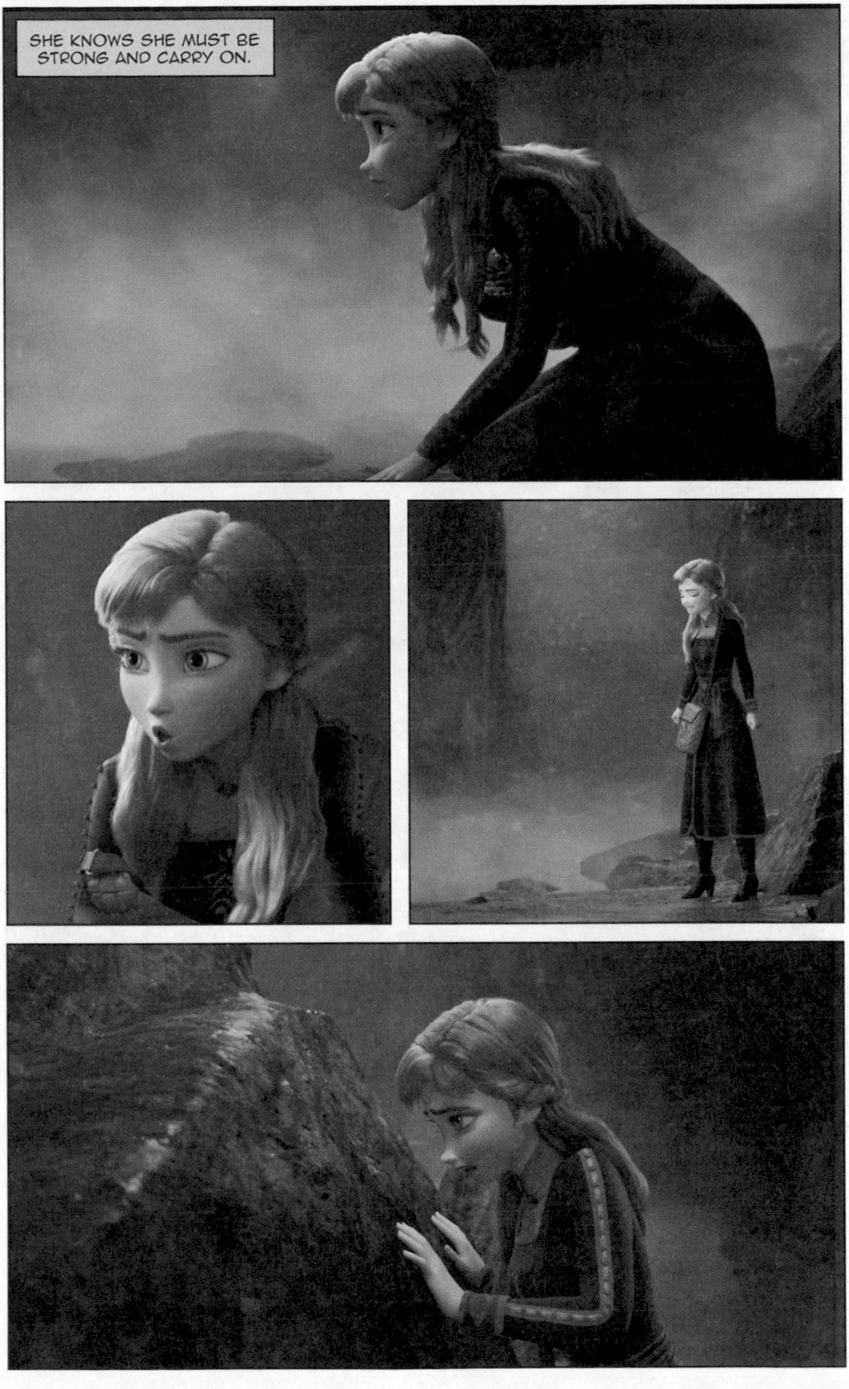
SHE KNOWS SHE MUST BE STRONG AND CARRY ON.

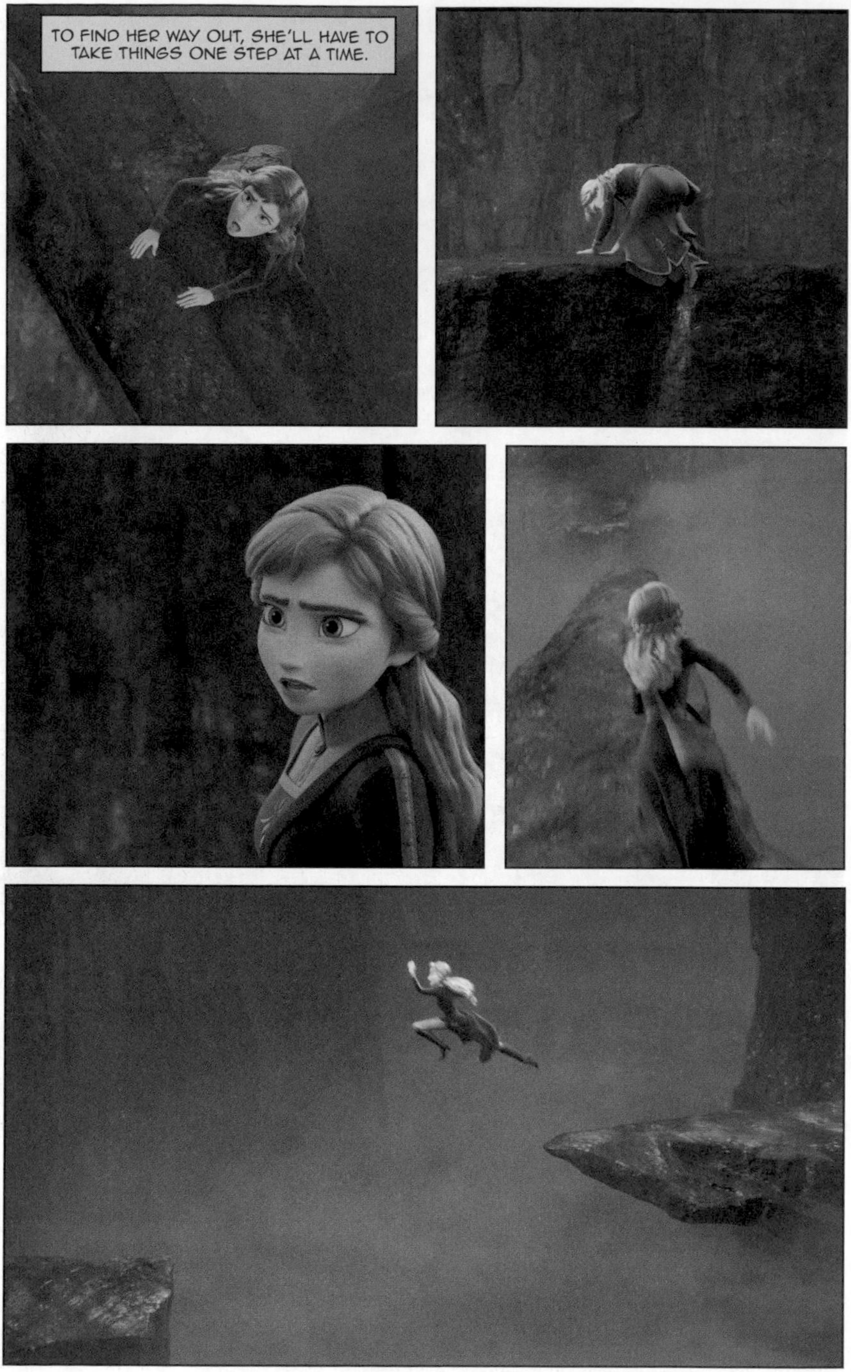
TO FIND HER WAY OUT, SHE'LL HAVE TO TAKE THINGS ONE STEP AT A TIME.

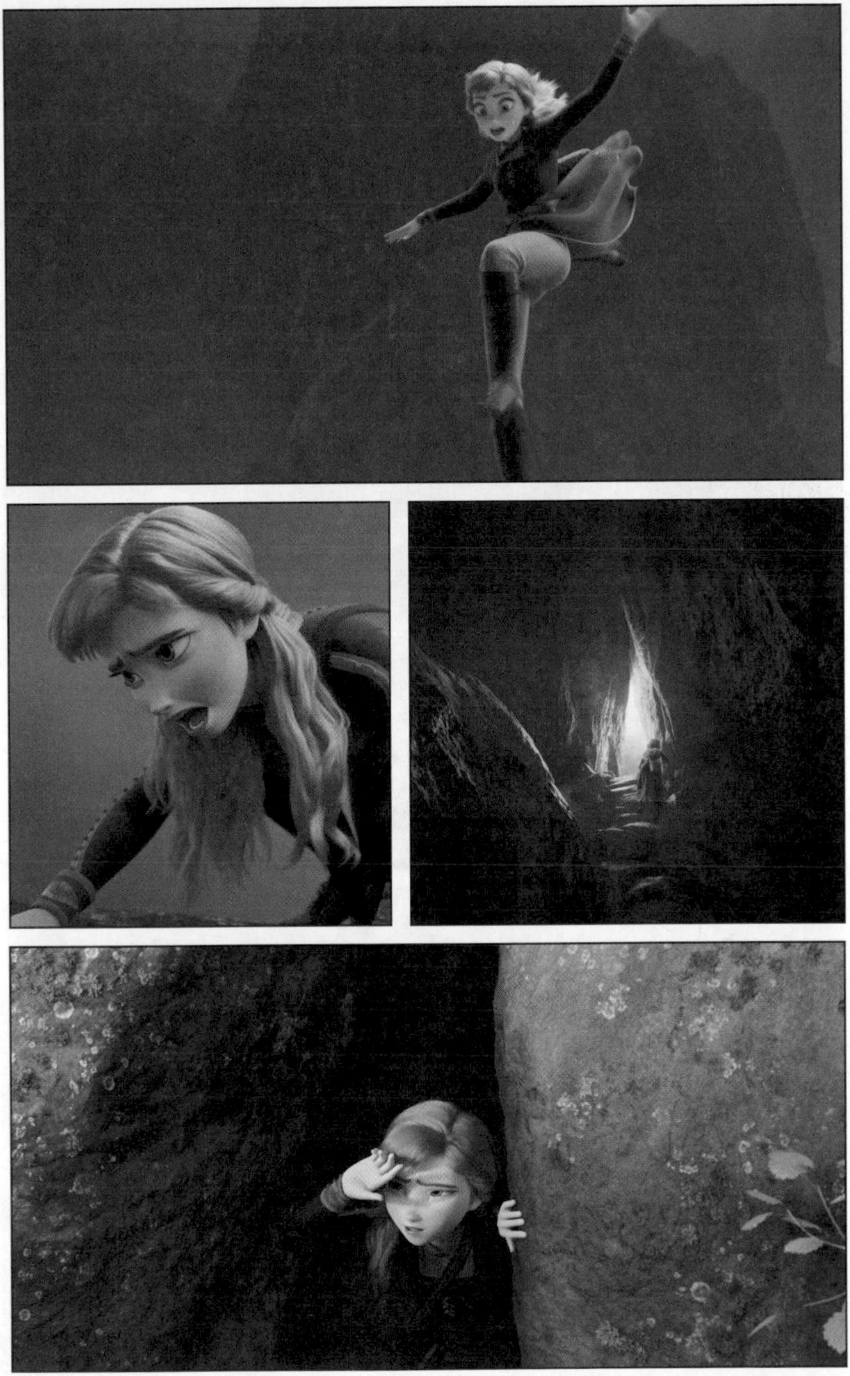

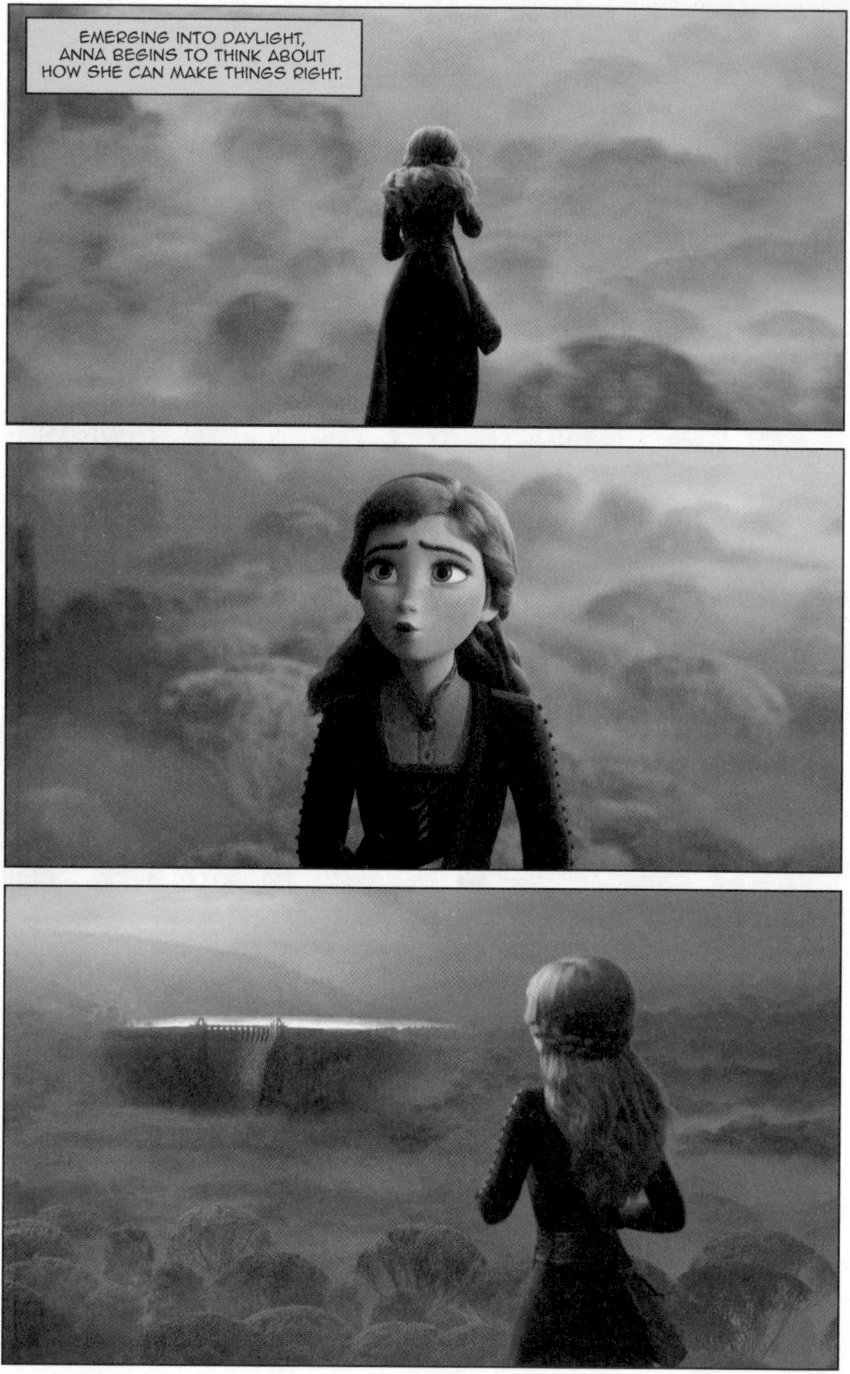
EMERGING INTO DAYLIGHT, ANNA BEGINS TO THINK ABOUT HOW SHE CAN MAKE THINGS RIGHT.

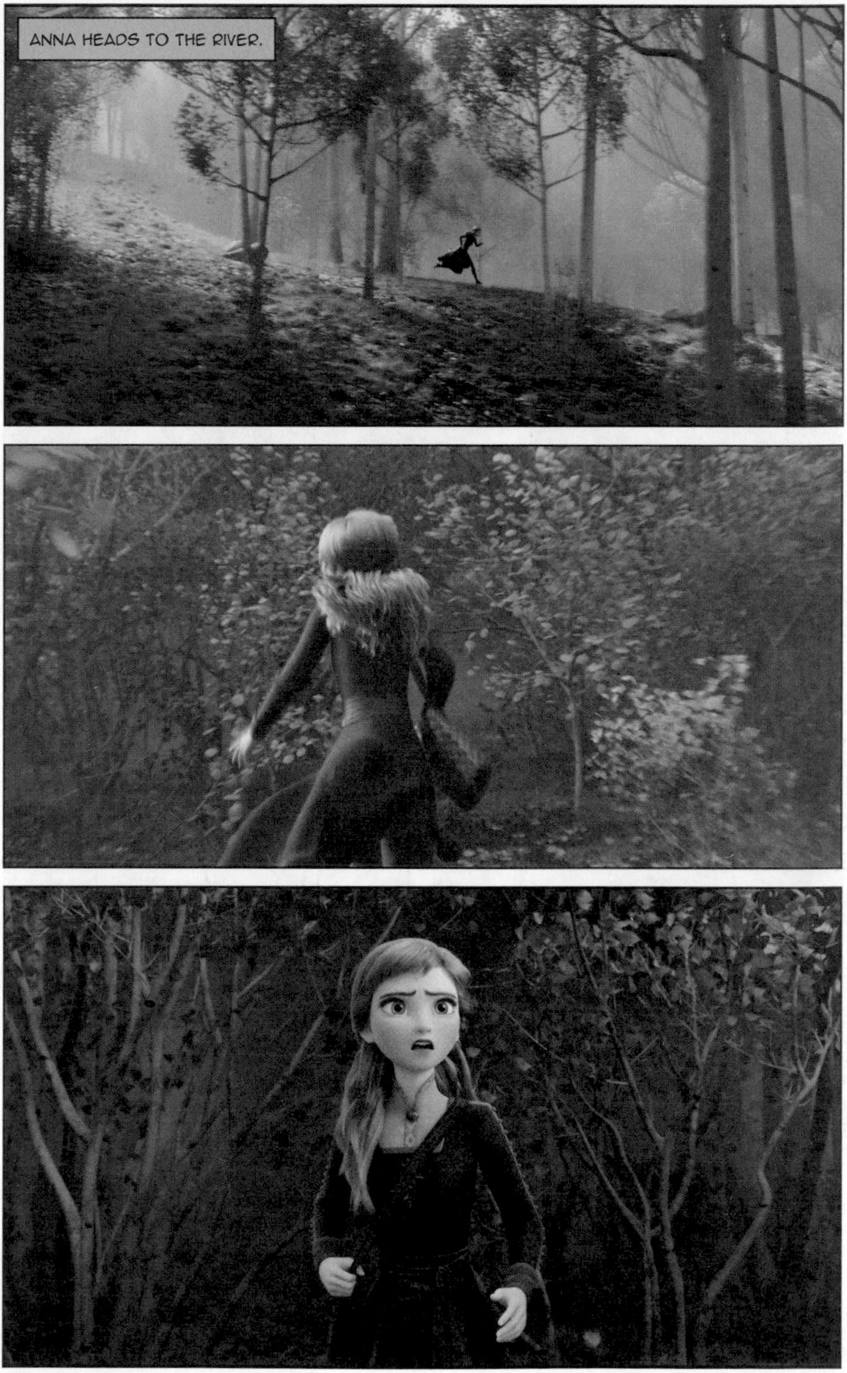
ANNA HEADS TO THE RIVER.

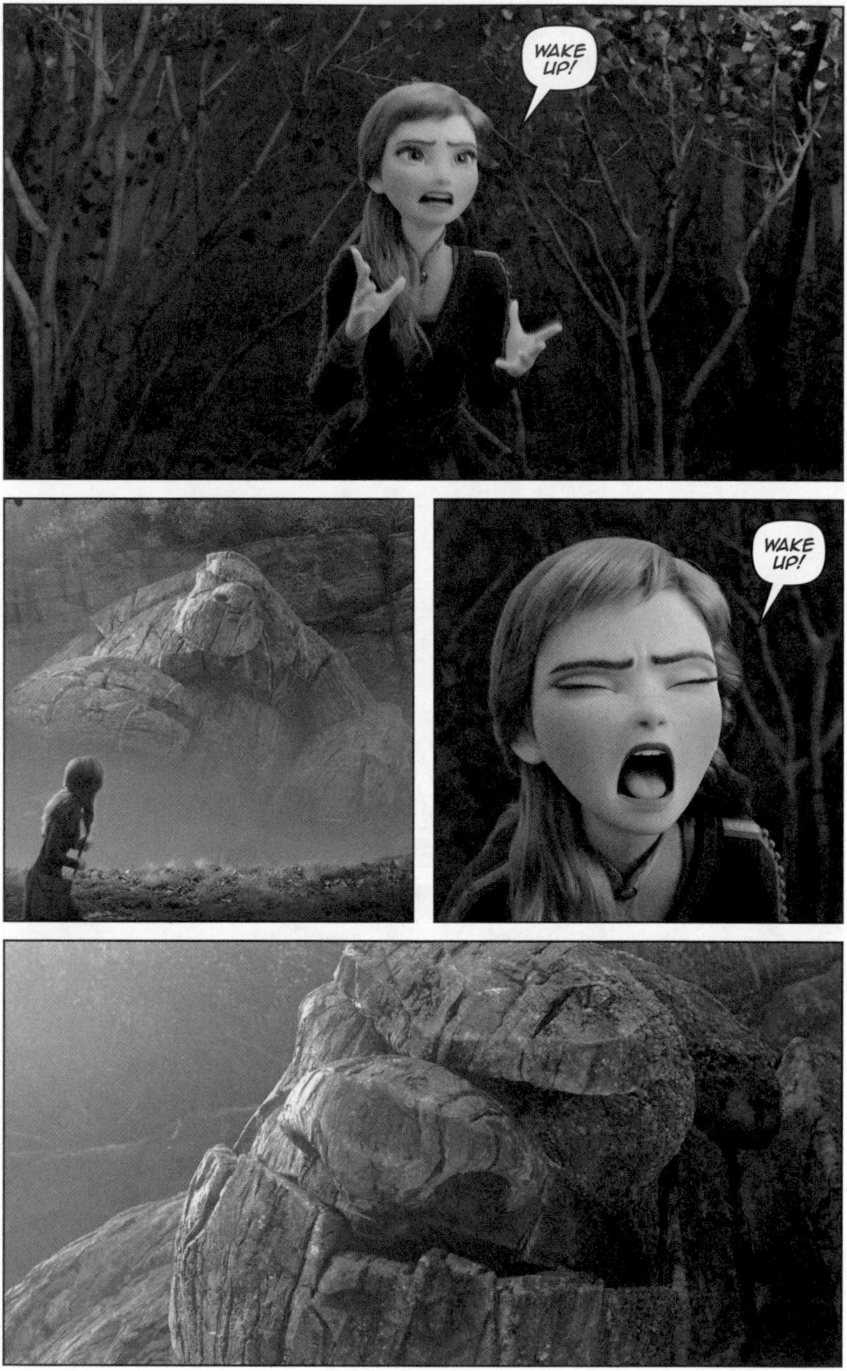
WAKE UP!
WAKE UP!

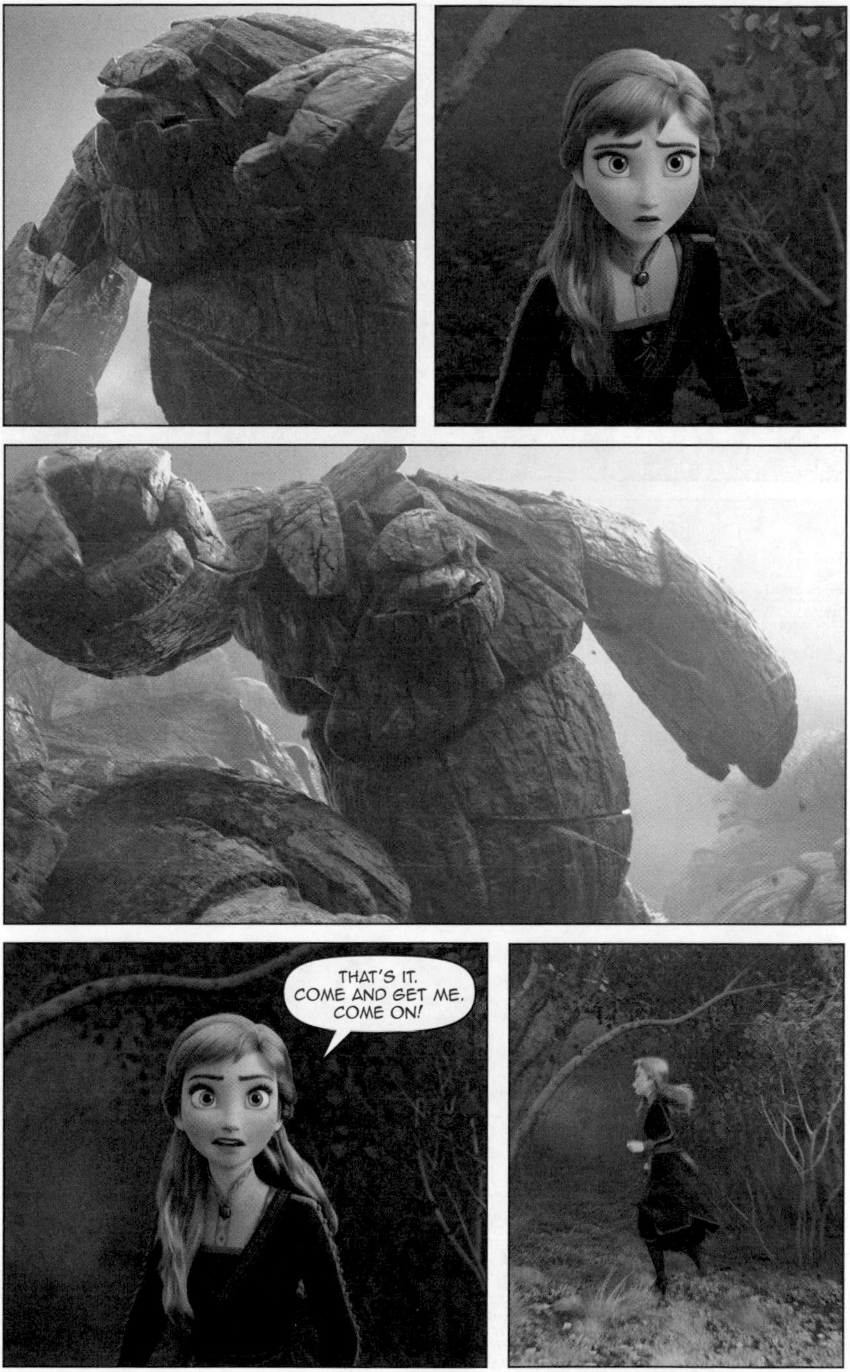
THAT'S IT.
COME AND GET ME.
COME ON!

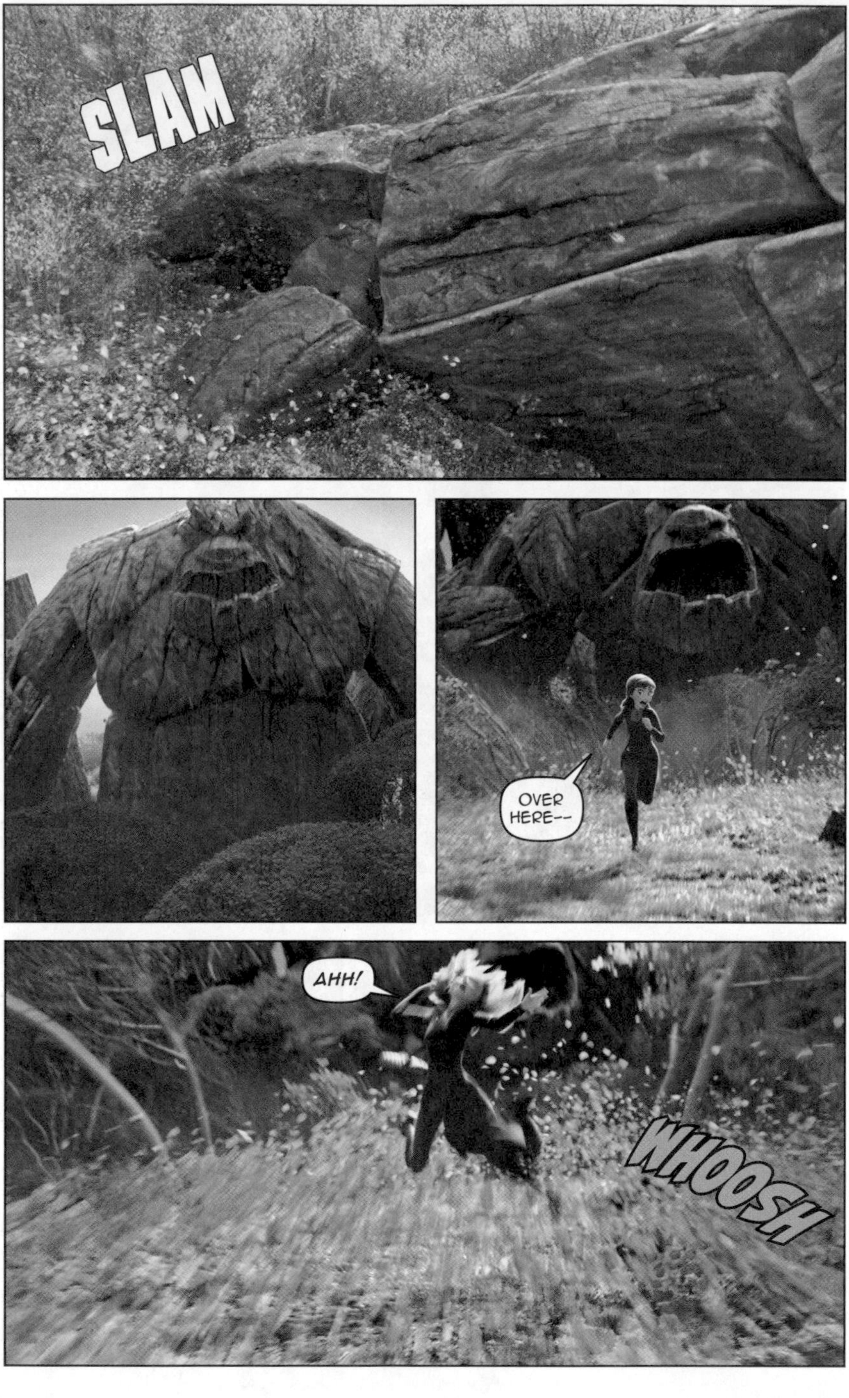
SLAM
OVER HERE--
AHH!
WHOOSH

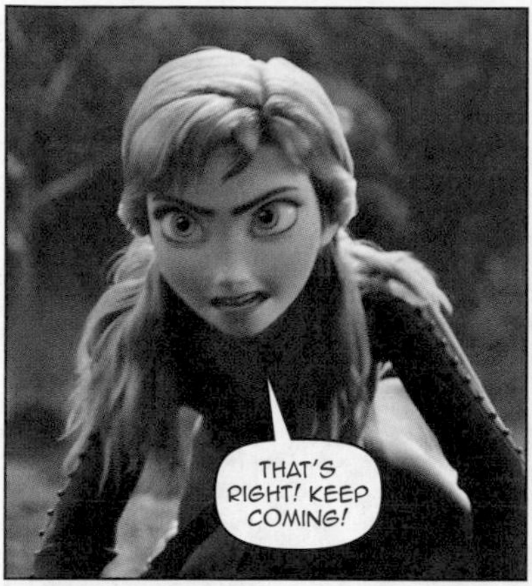
THAT'S RIGHT! KEEP COMING!

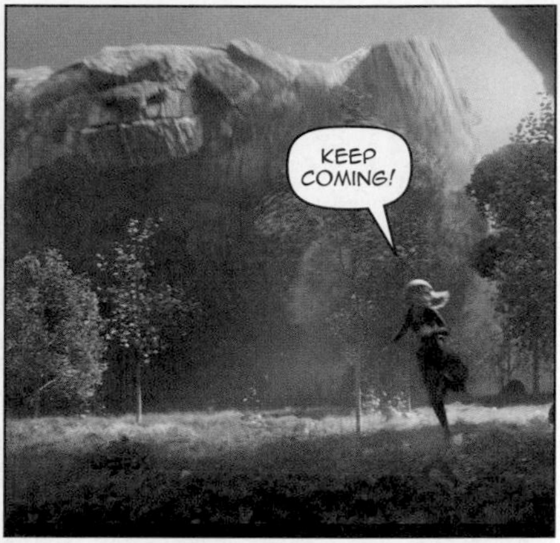
KEEP COMING!

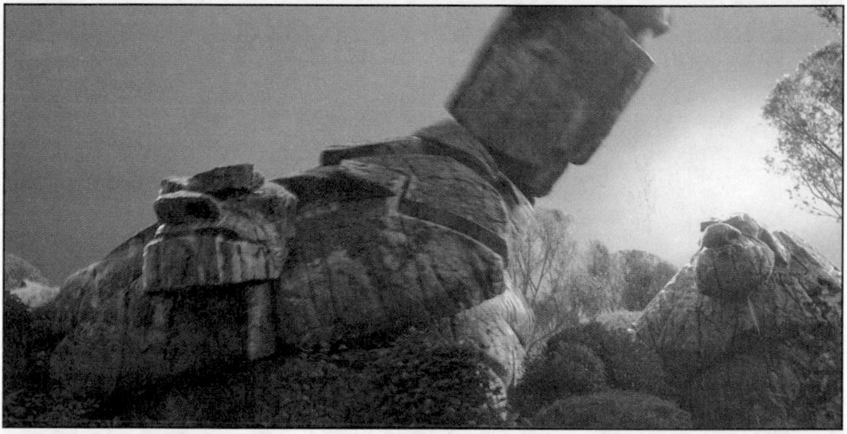

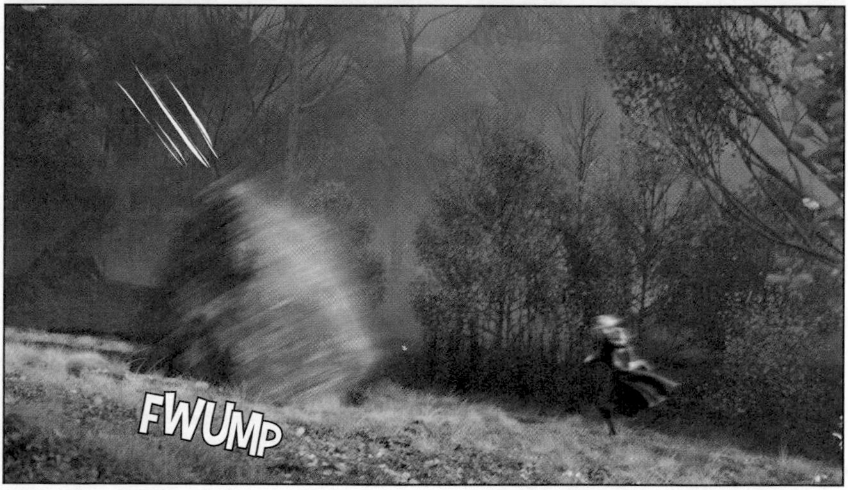
FWUMP

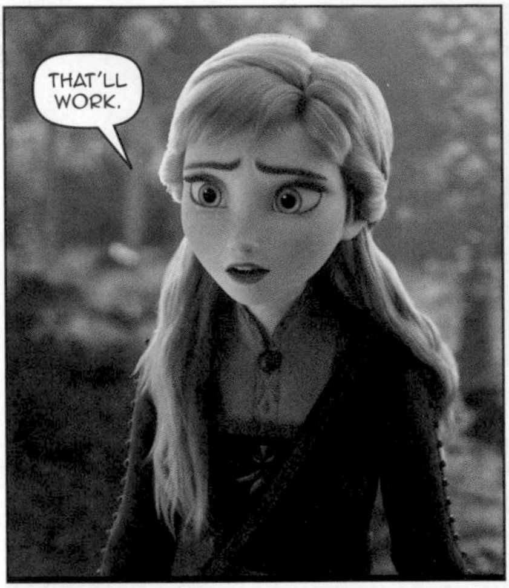
THAT'LL WORK.

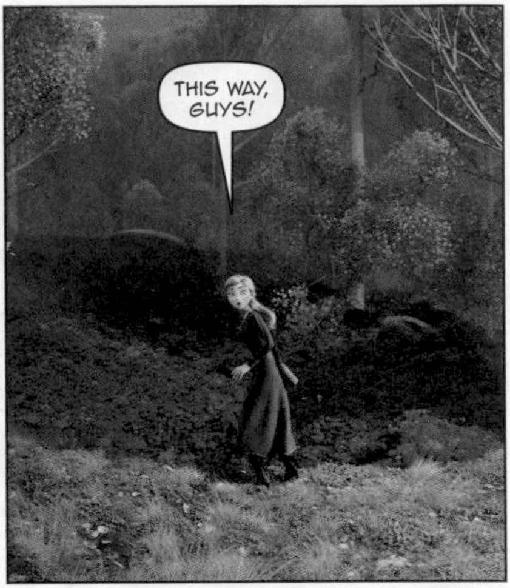
THIS WAY, GUYS!

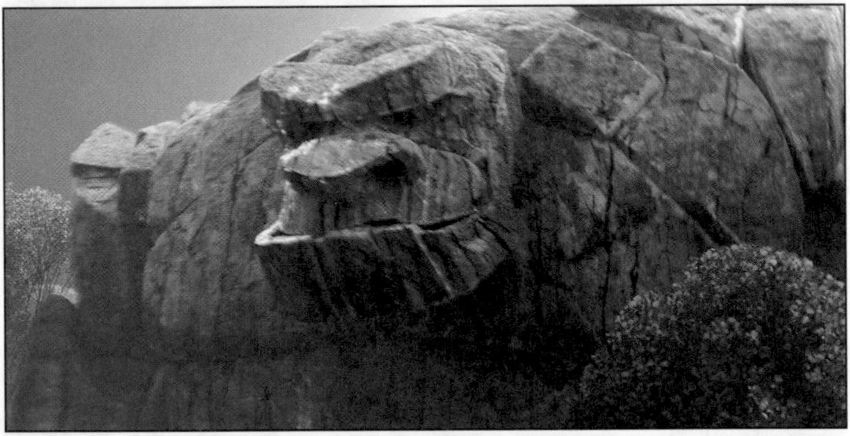

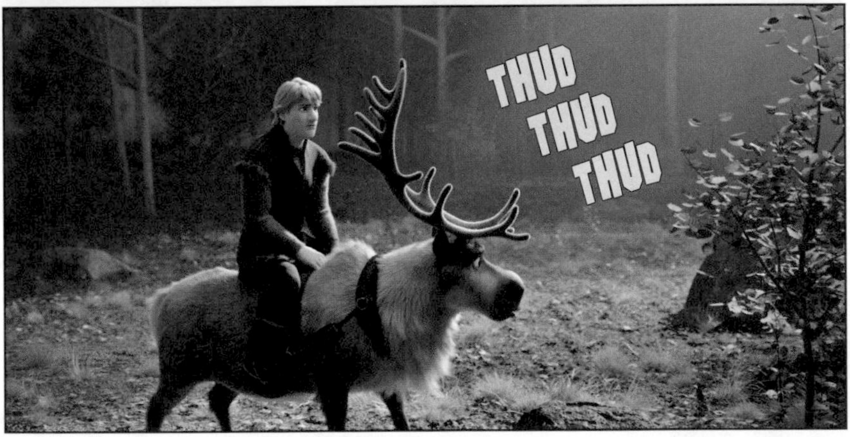
THUD
THUD
THUD

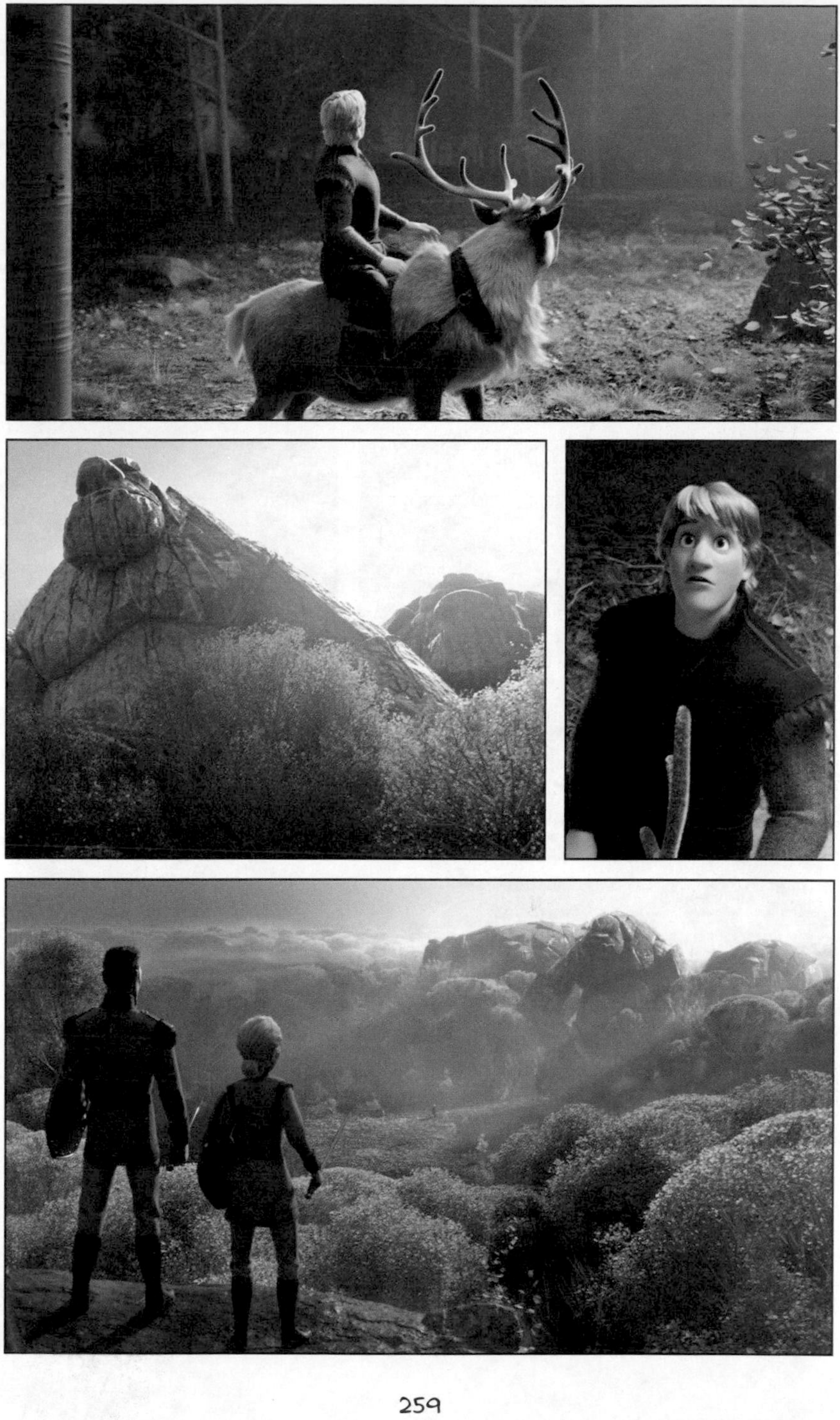

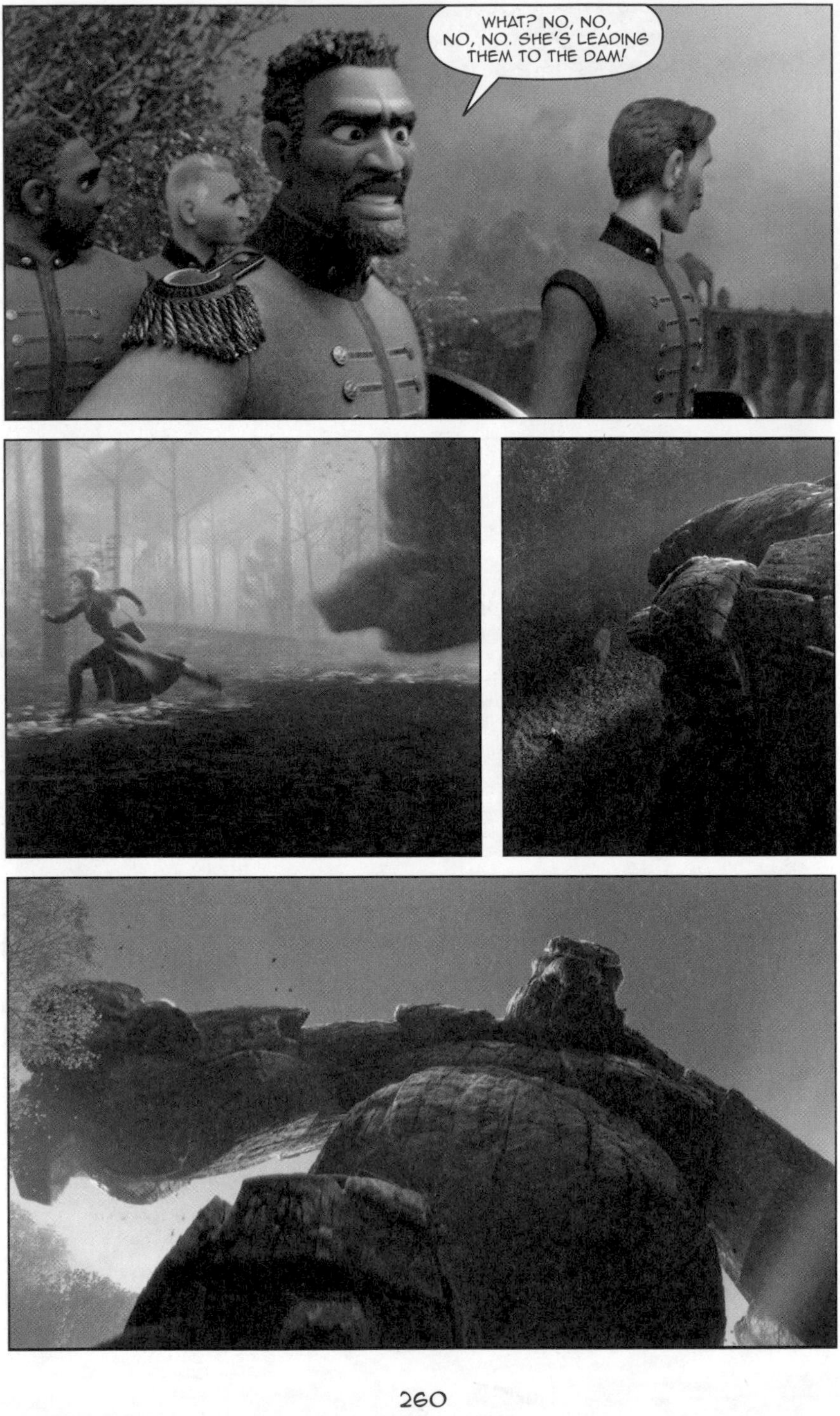
WHAT? NO, NO, NO, NO. SHE'S LEADING THEM TO THE DAM!

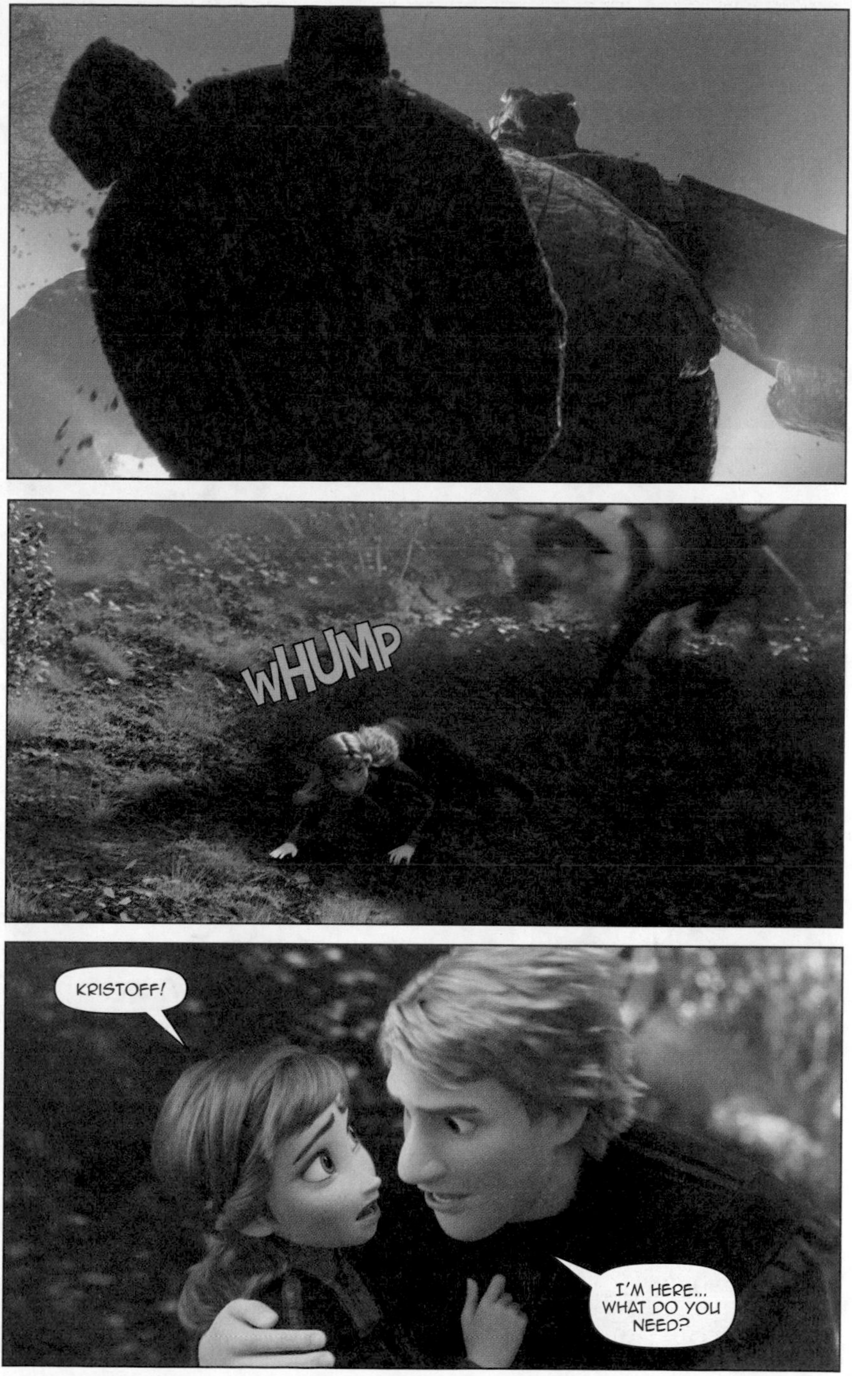
wHUMP
KRISTOFF!
I'M HERE...
WHAT DO YOU
NEED?

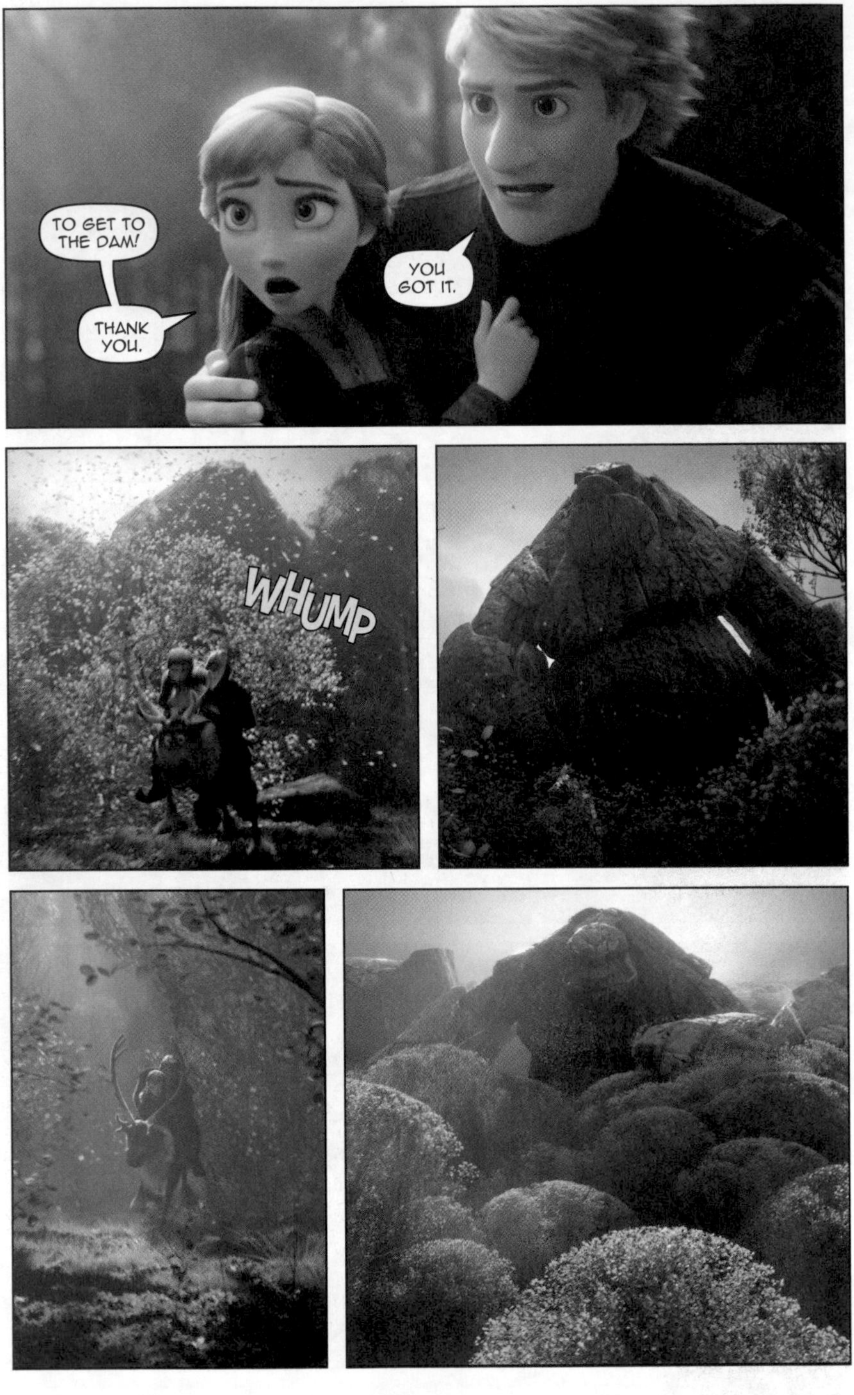
TO GET TO THE DAM!
THANK YOU.
YOU GOT IT.
WHUMP

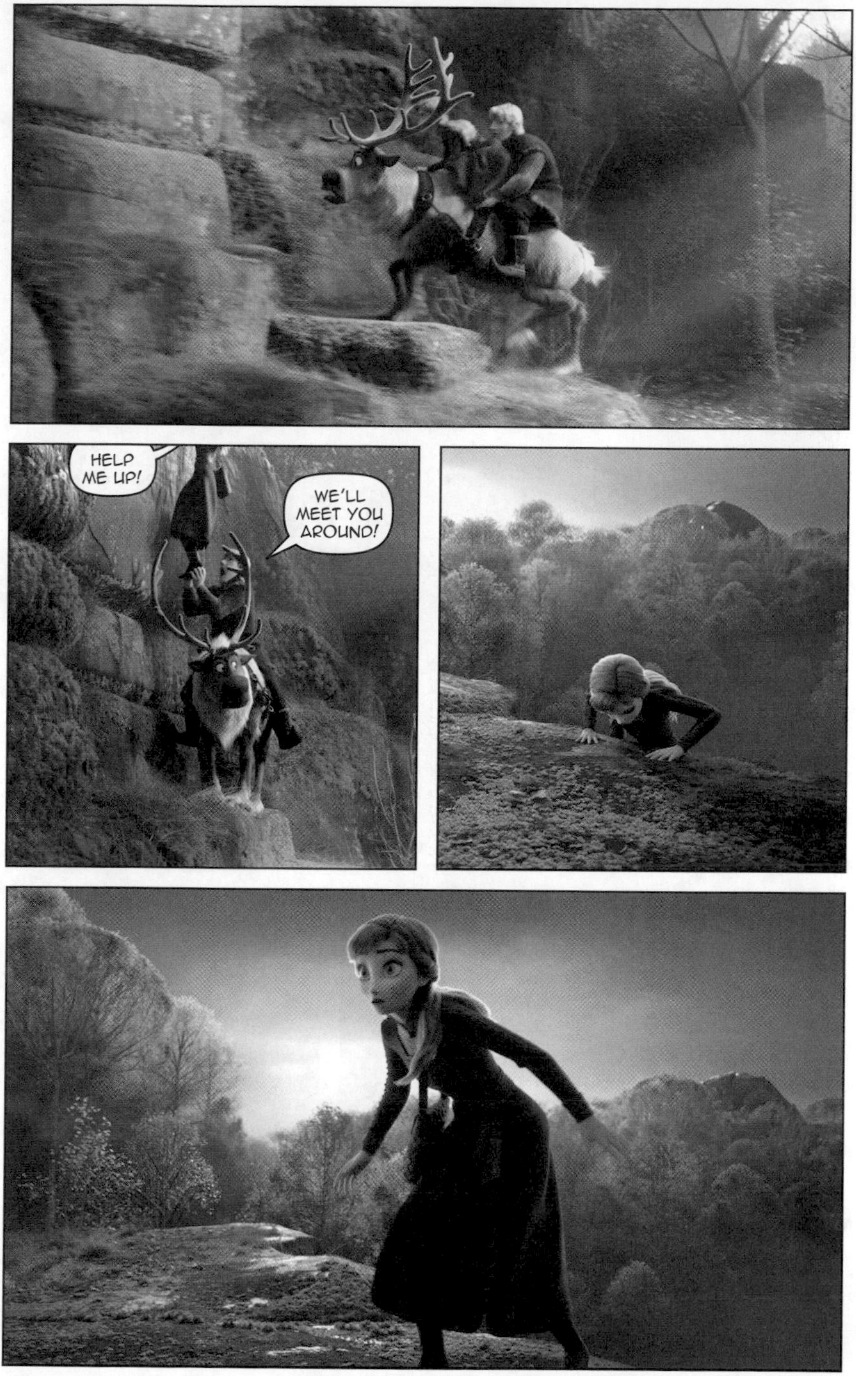
HELP ME UP!
WE'LL MEET YOU AROUND!

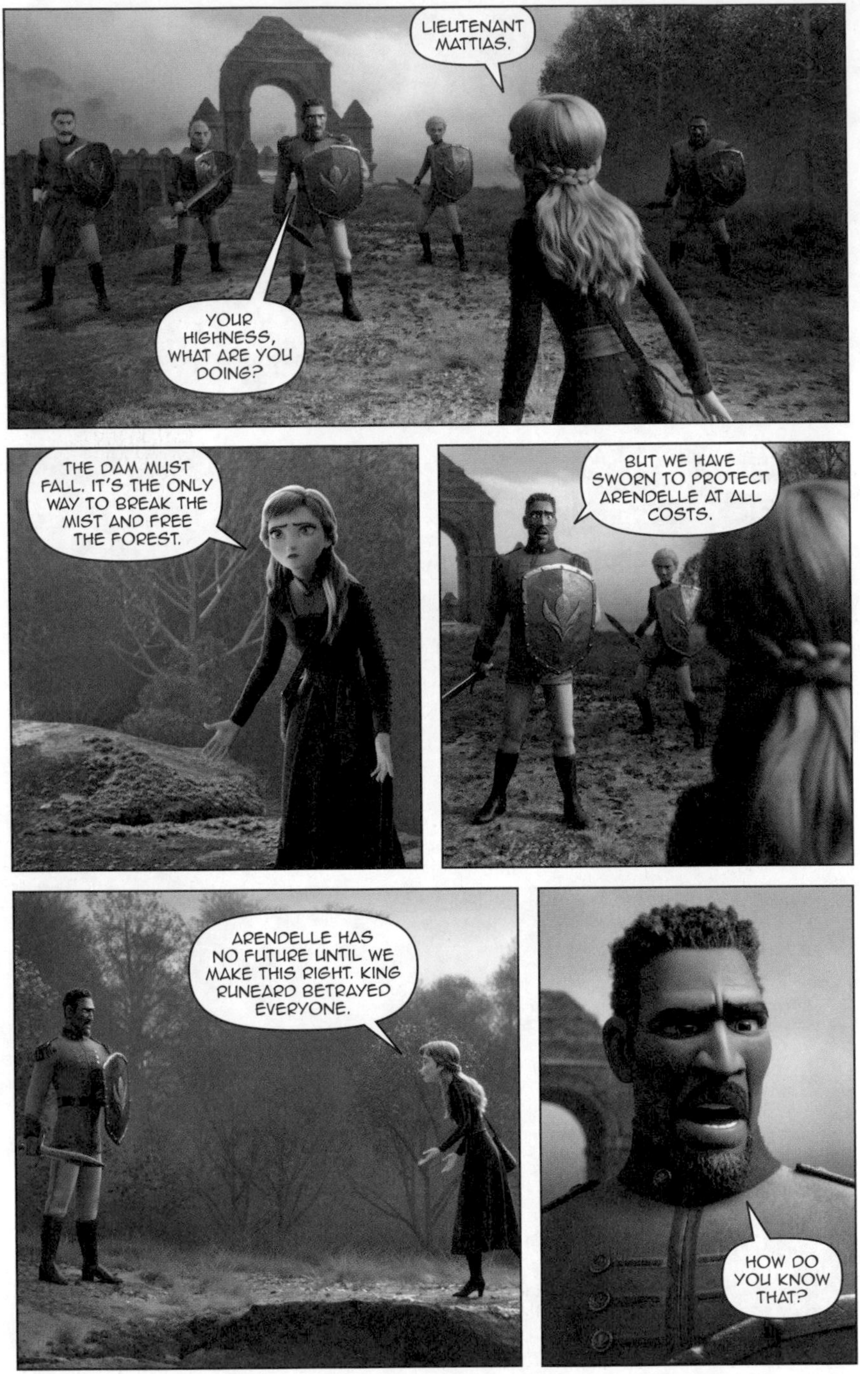
LIEUTENANT MATTIAS.
YOUR HIGHNESS, WHAT ARE YOU DOING?
THE DAM MUST FALL. IT'S THE ONLY WAY TO BREAK THE MIST AND FREE THE FOREST.
BUT WE HAVE SWORN TO PROTECT ARENDELLE AT ALL COSTS.
ARENDELLE HAS NO FUTURE UNTIL WE MAKE THIS RIGHT. KING RUNEARD BETRAYED EVERYONE.
HOW DO YOU KNOW THAT?

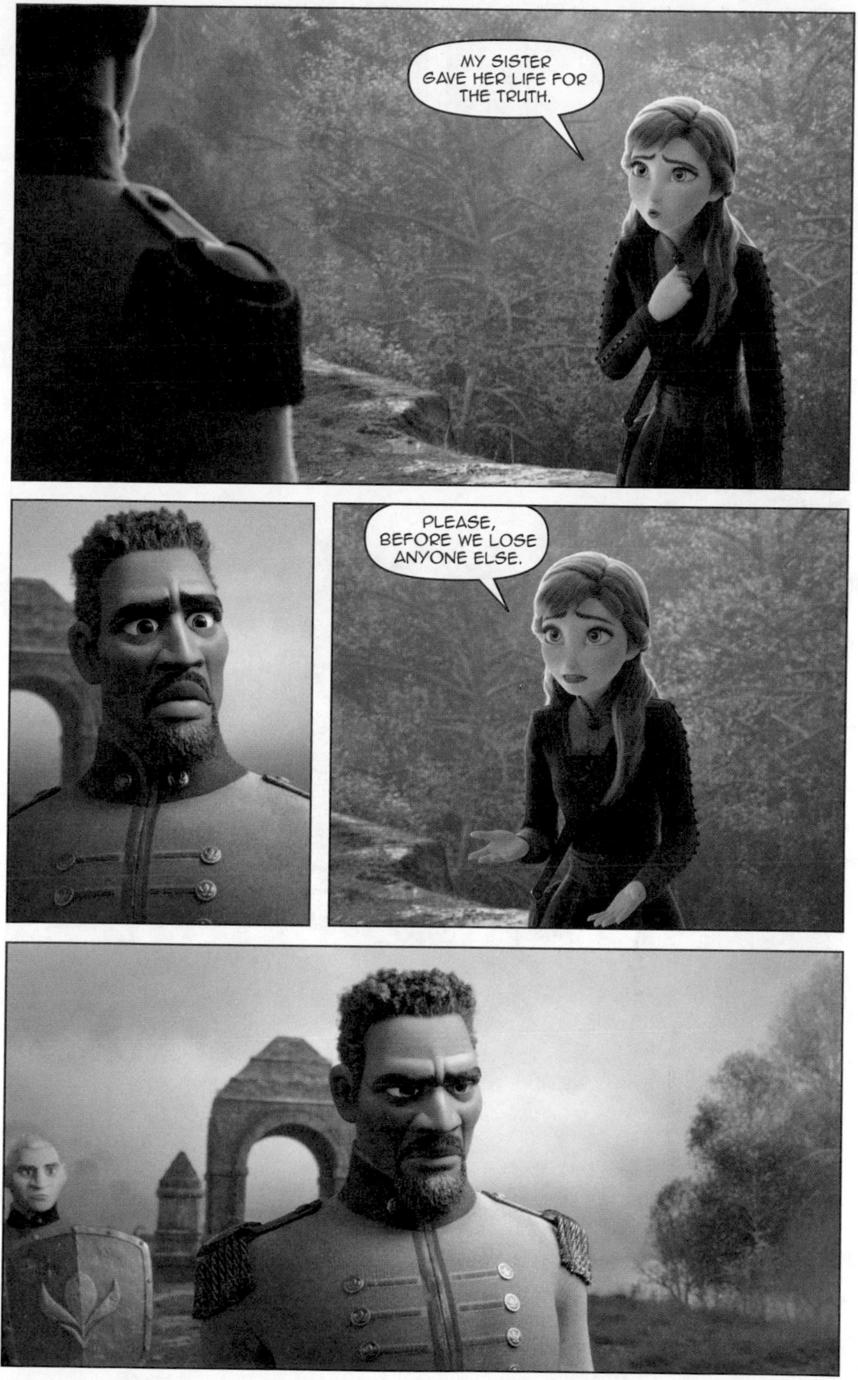
MY SISTER GAVE HER LIFE FOR THE TRUTH.
PLEASE, BEFORE WE LOSE ANYONE ELSE.

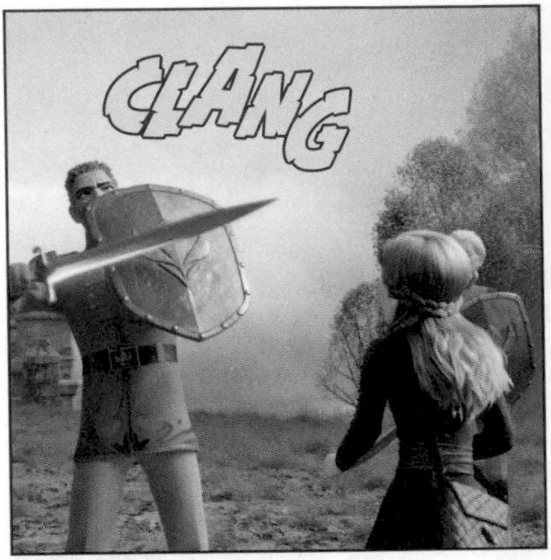
CLANG

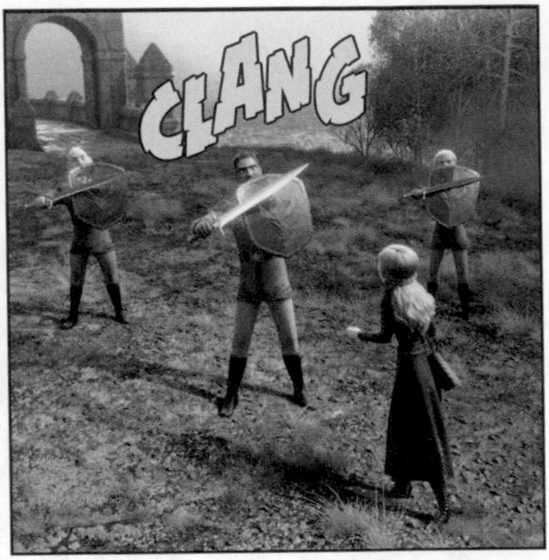
CLANG

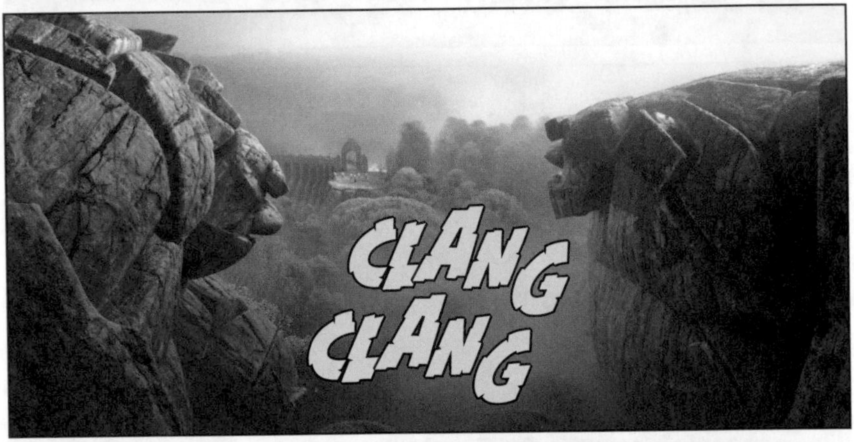
CLANG
CLANG

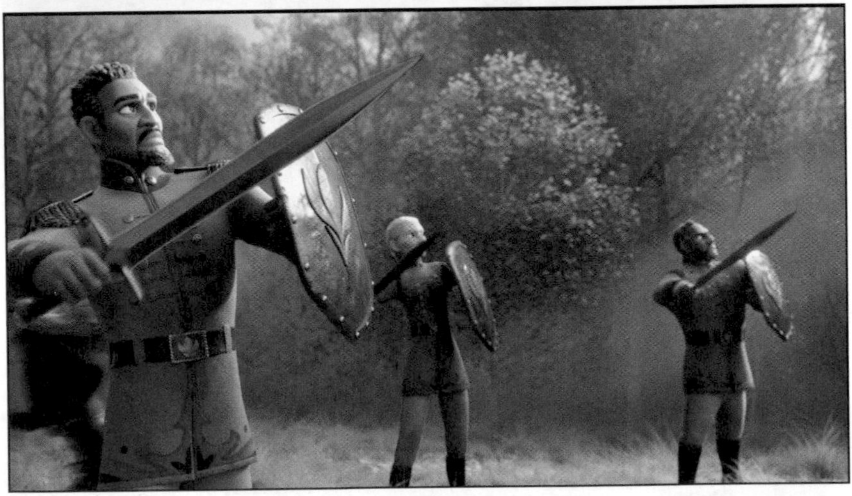

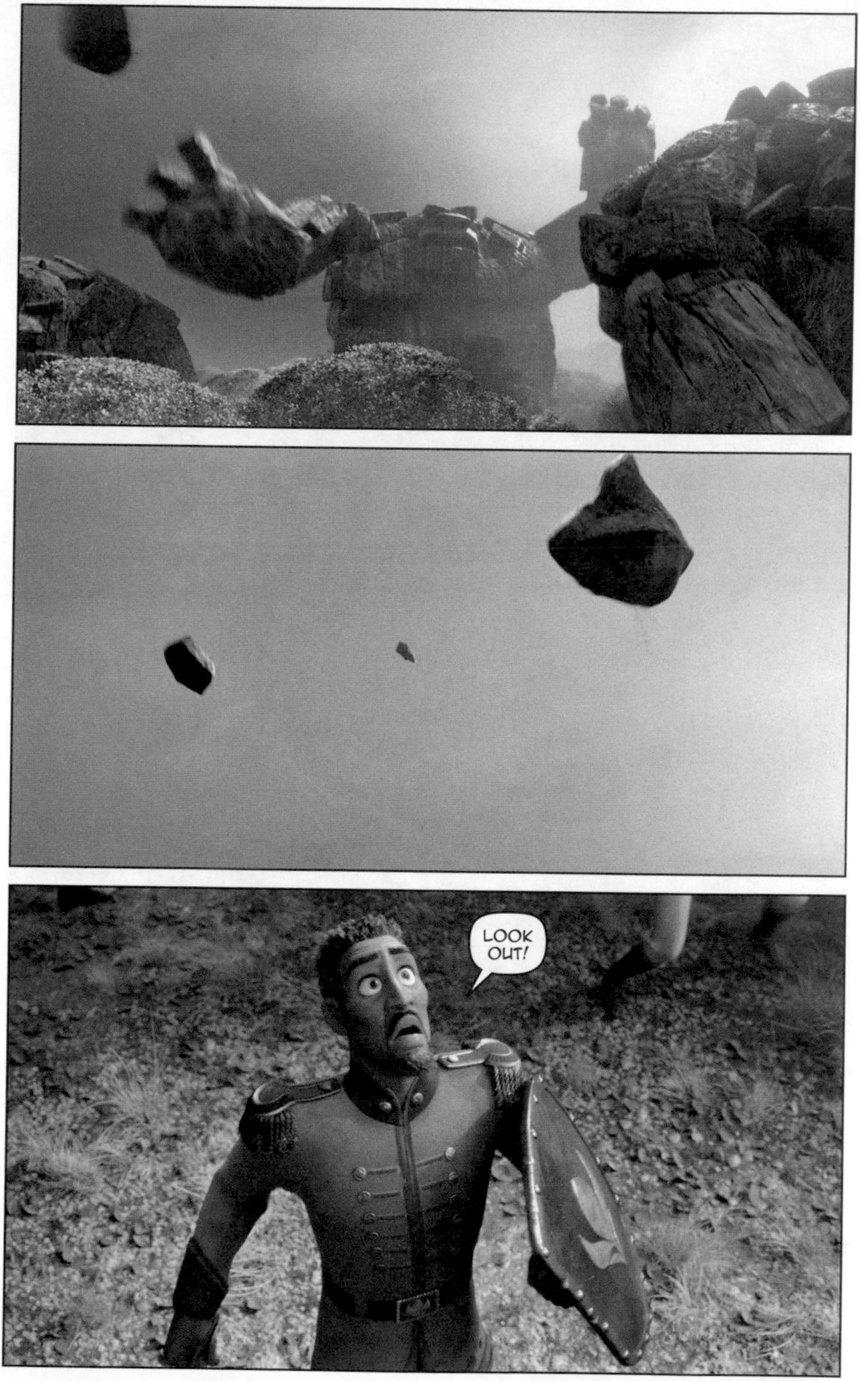
LOOK OUT!

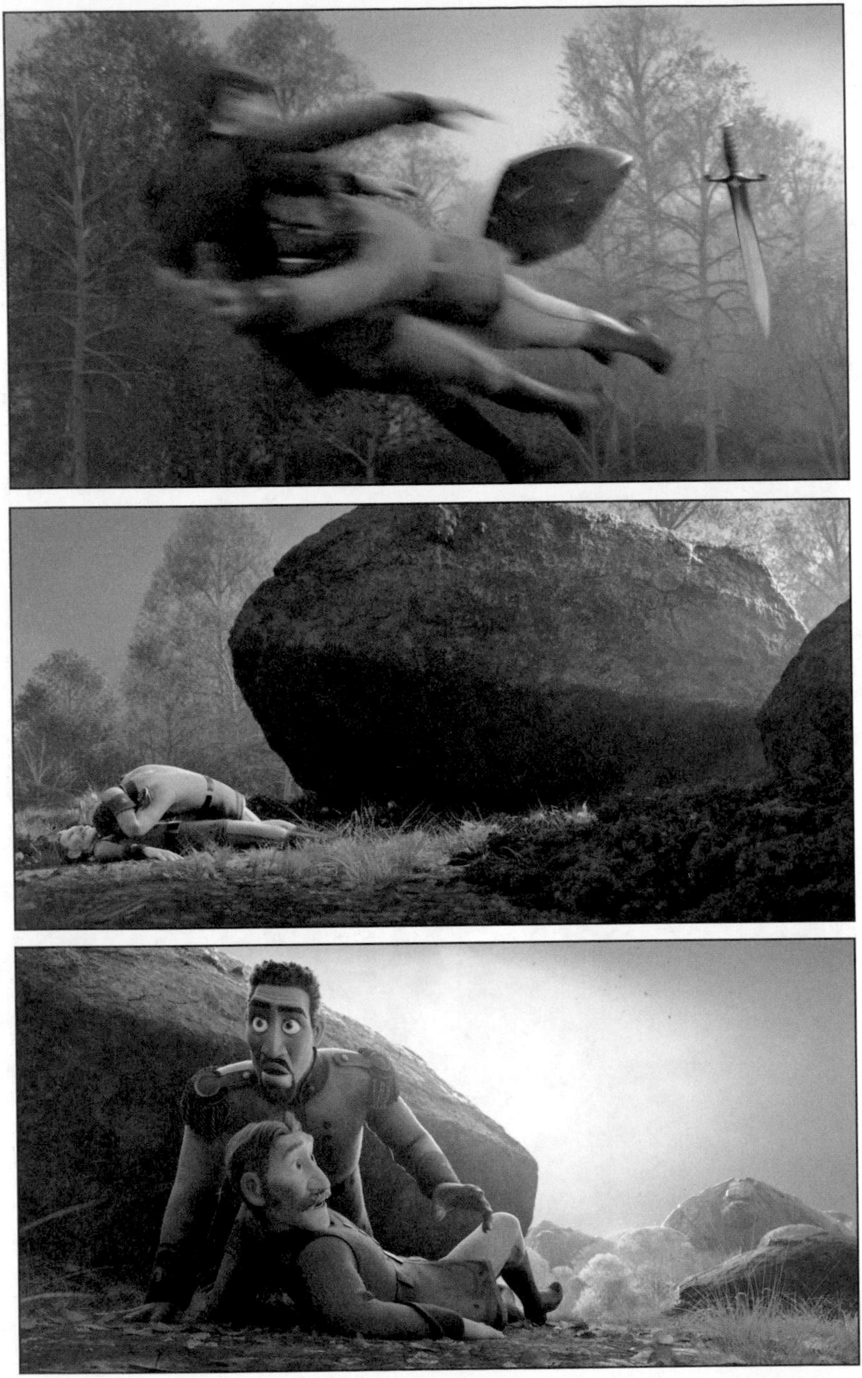

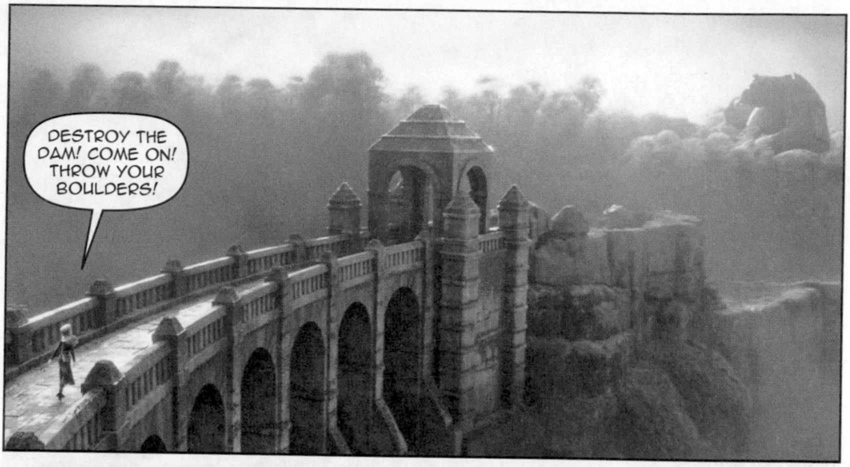
DESTROY THE DAM! COME ON! THROW YOUR BOULDERS!

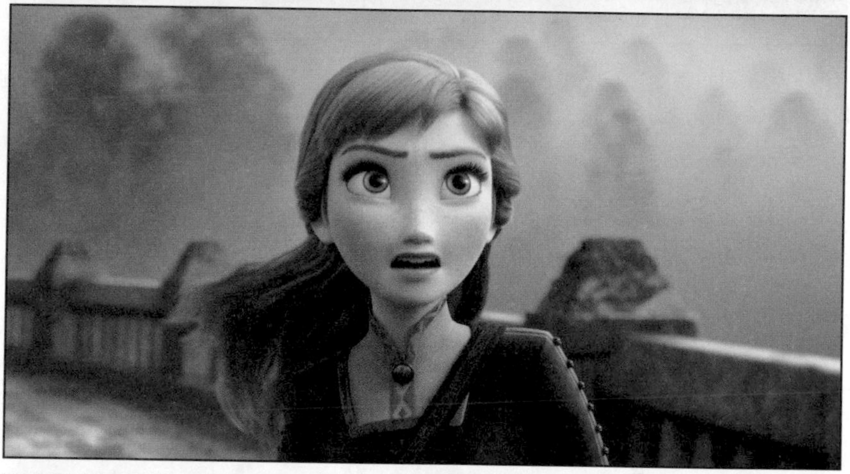

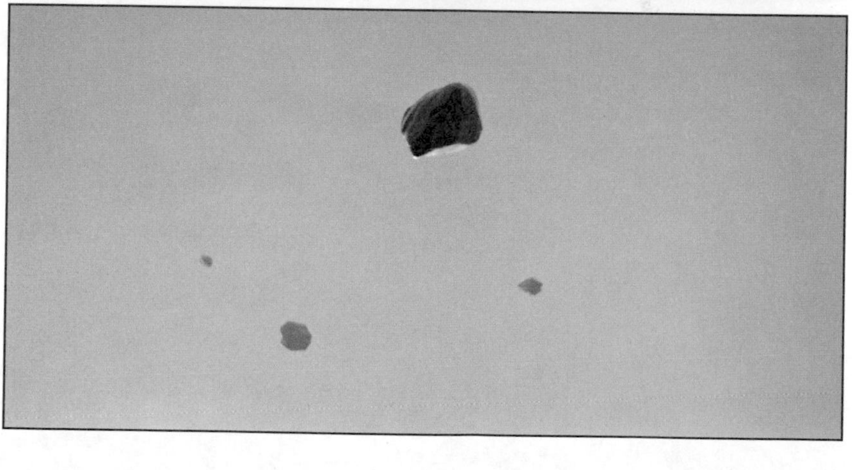

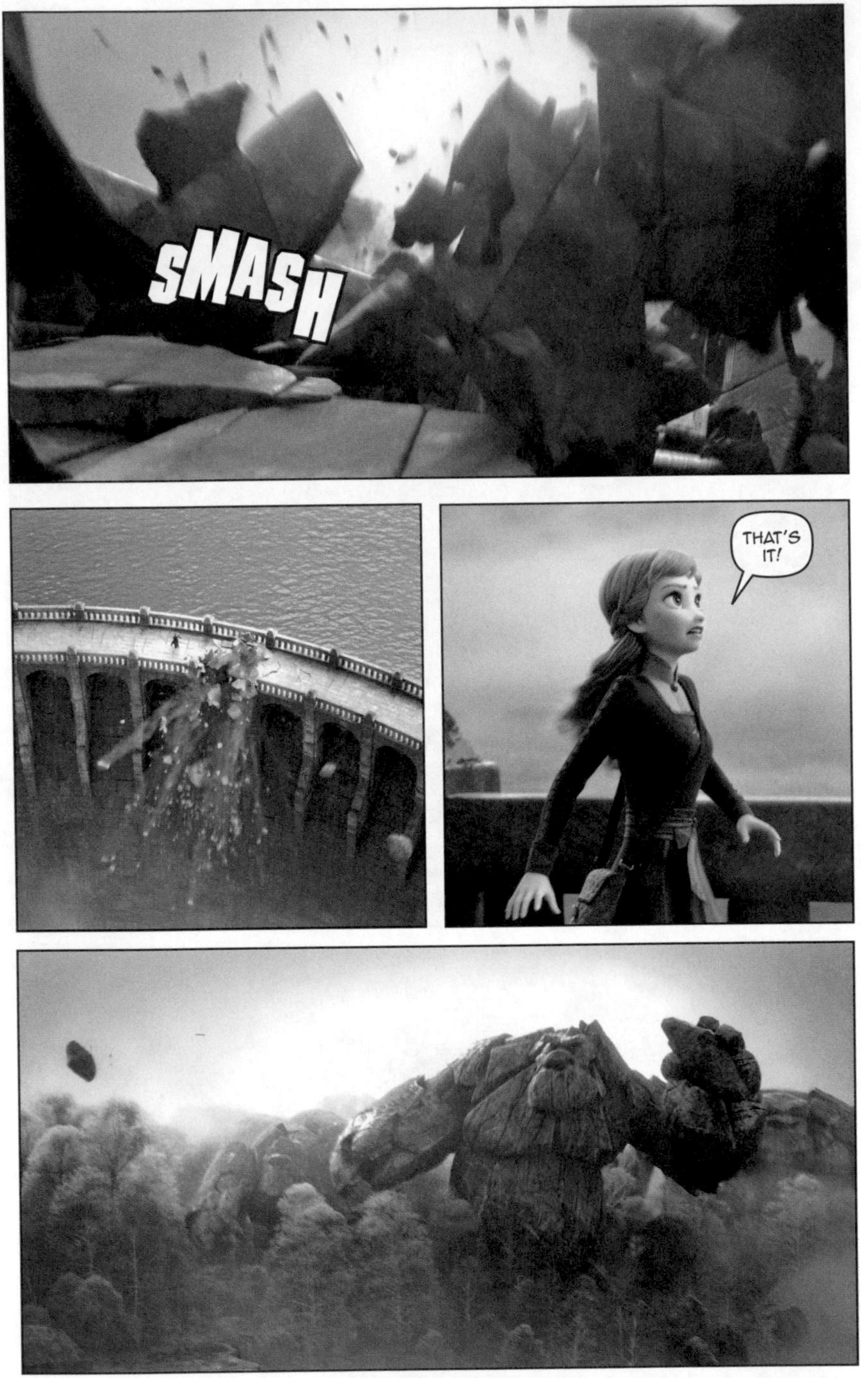
SMASH
THAT'S IT!

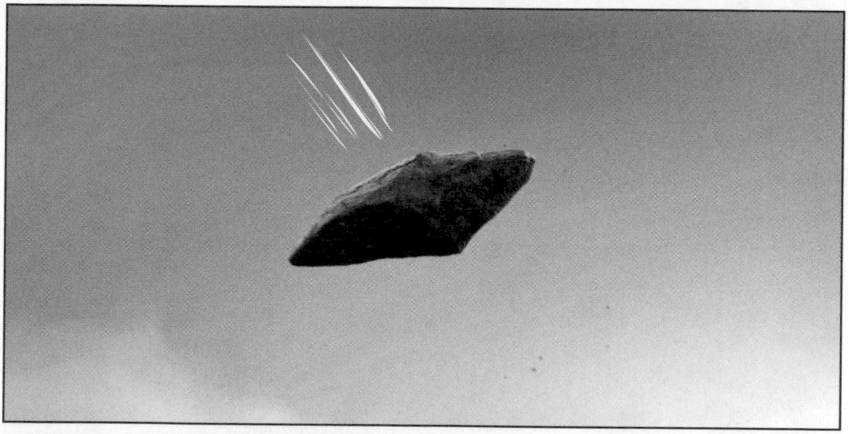

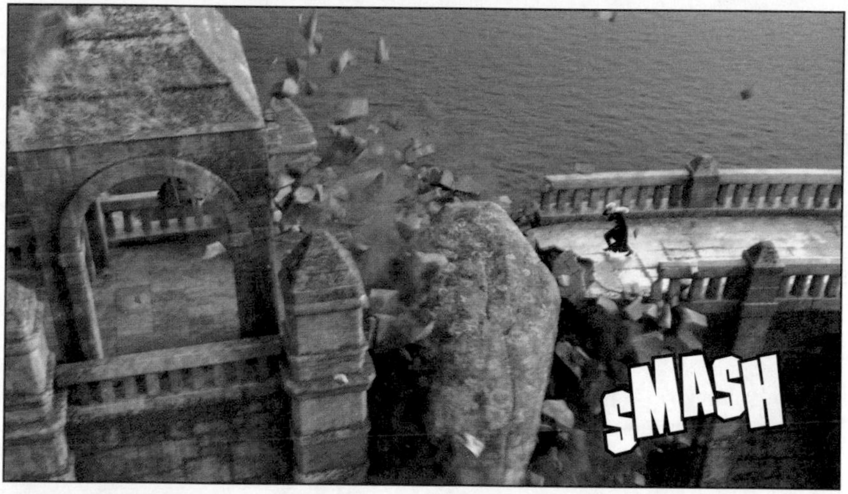
SMASH

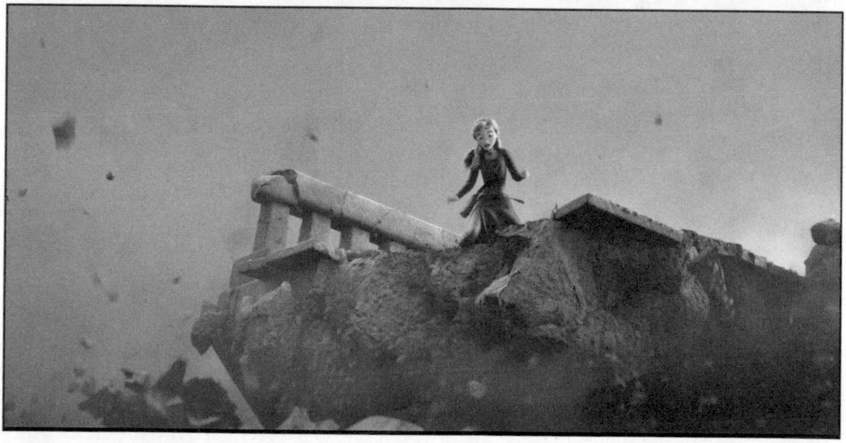

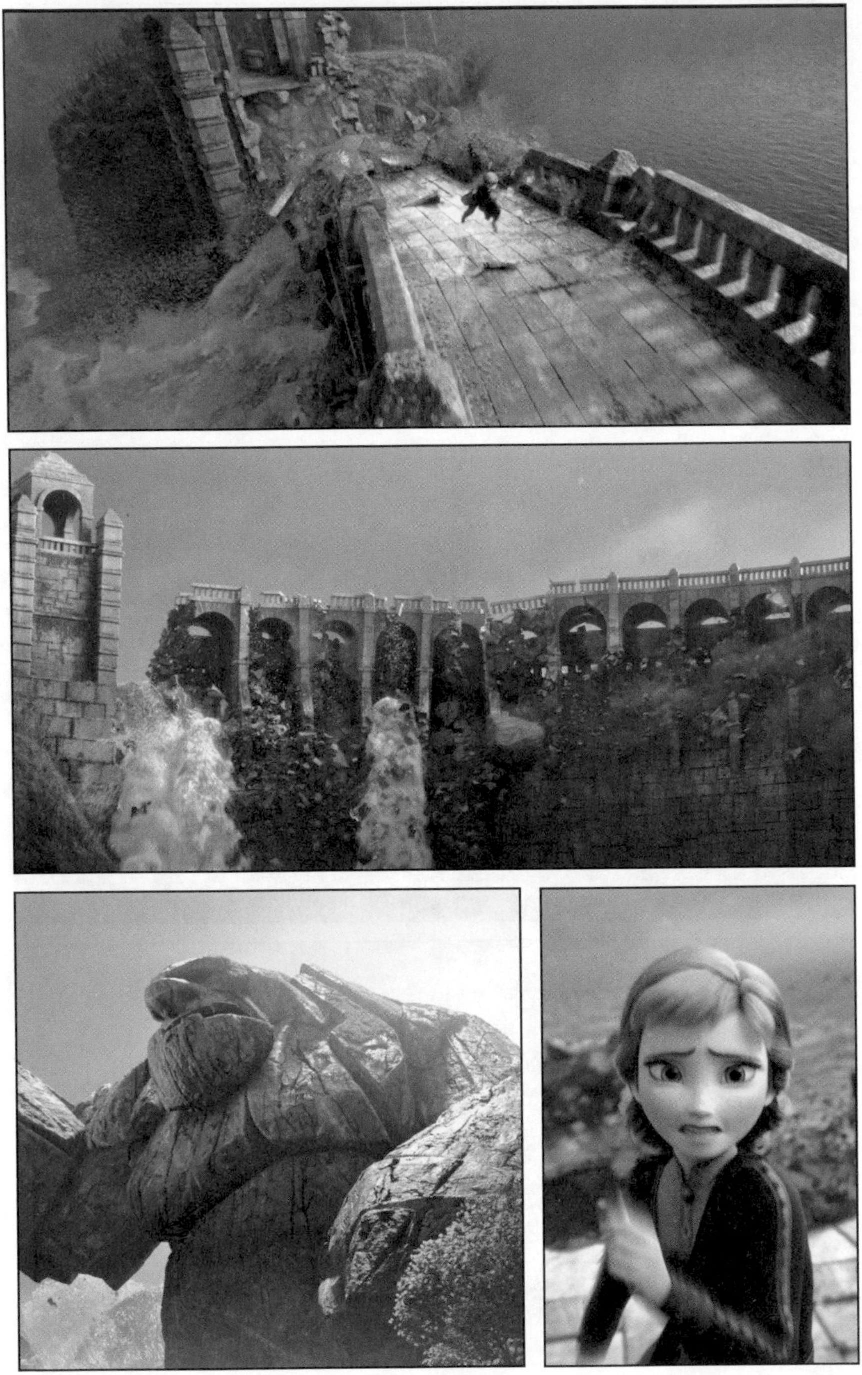

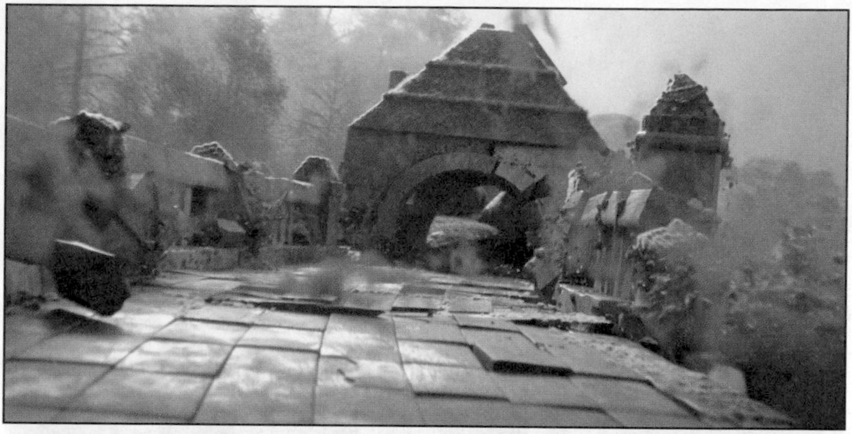

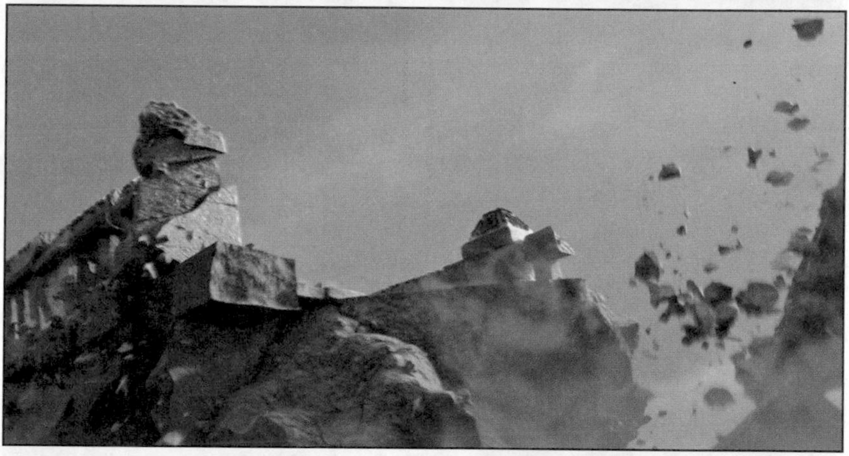

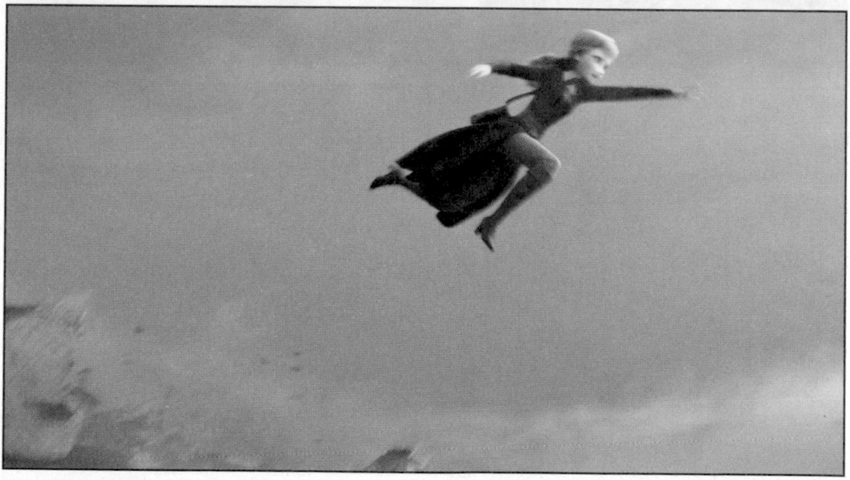

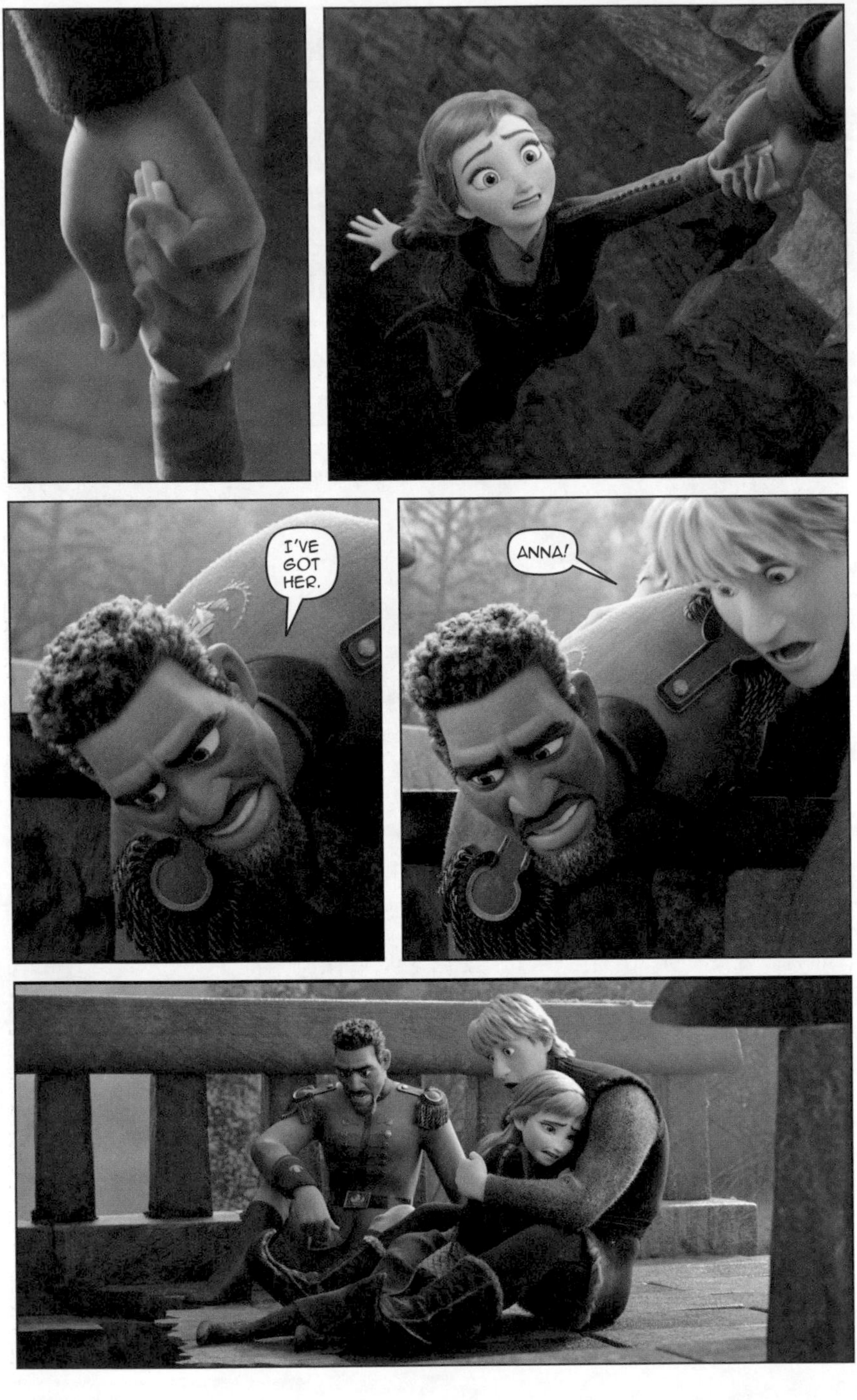
I'VE GOT HER.
ANNA!

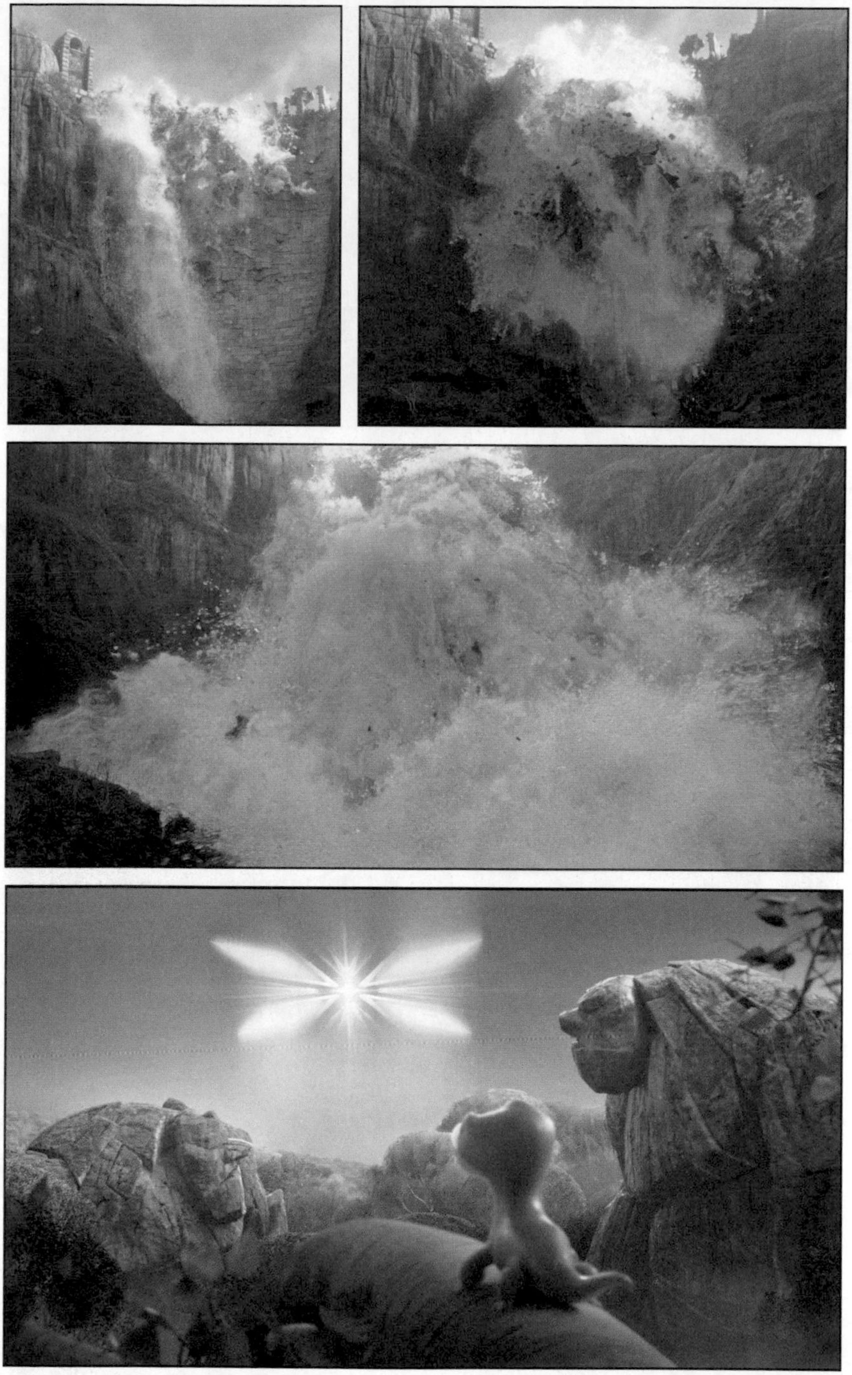

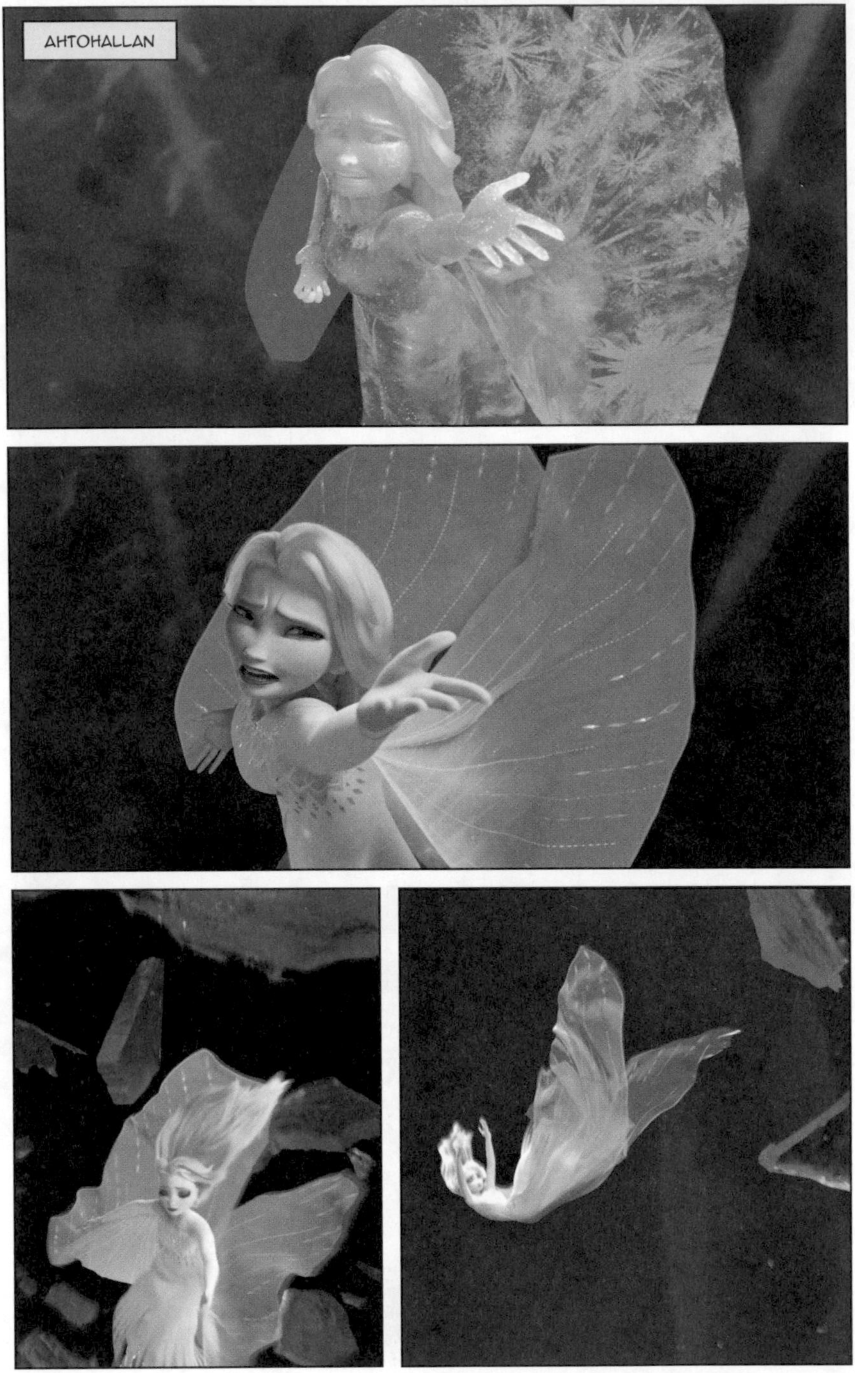
AHTOHALLAN

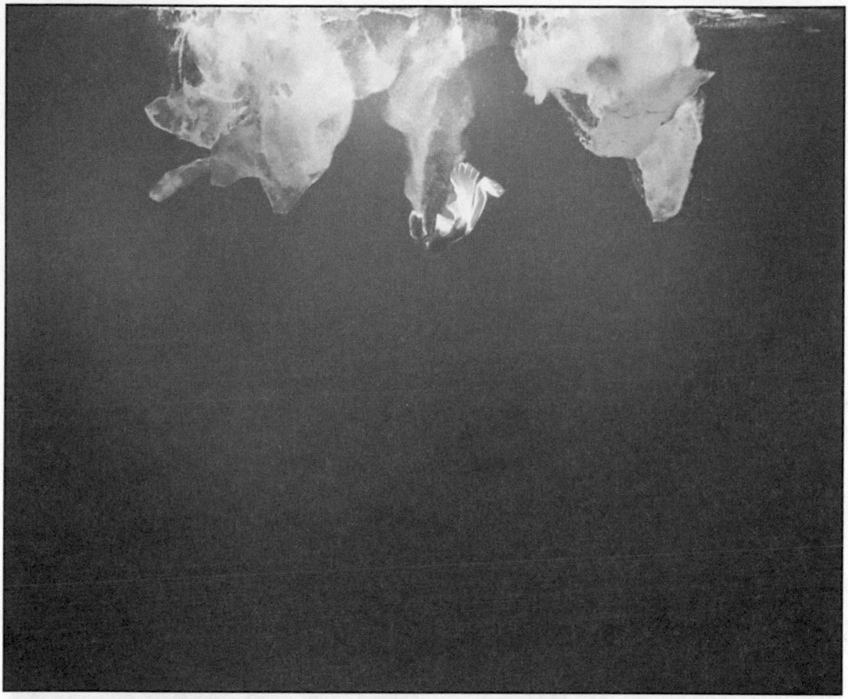

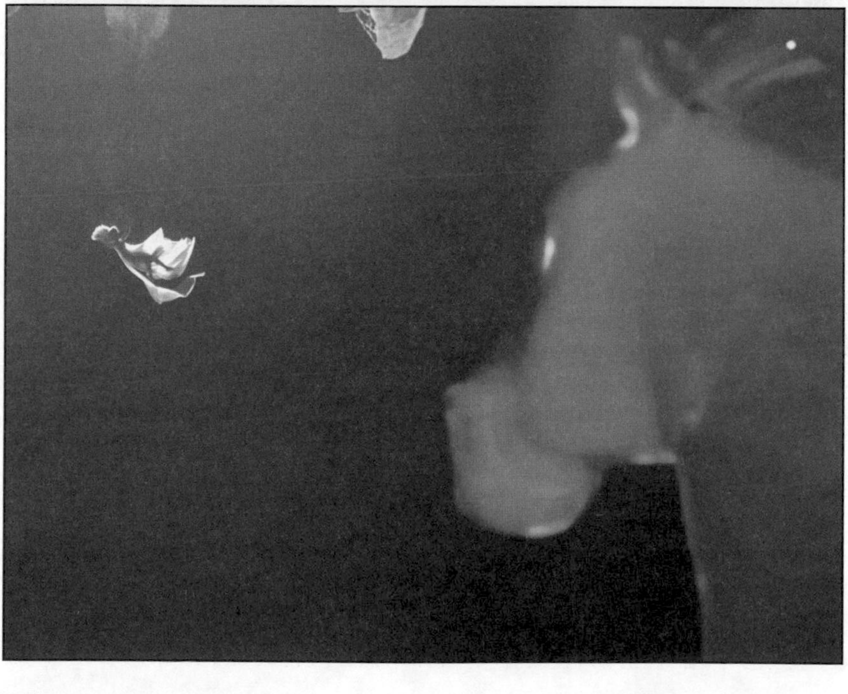

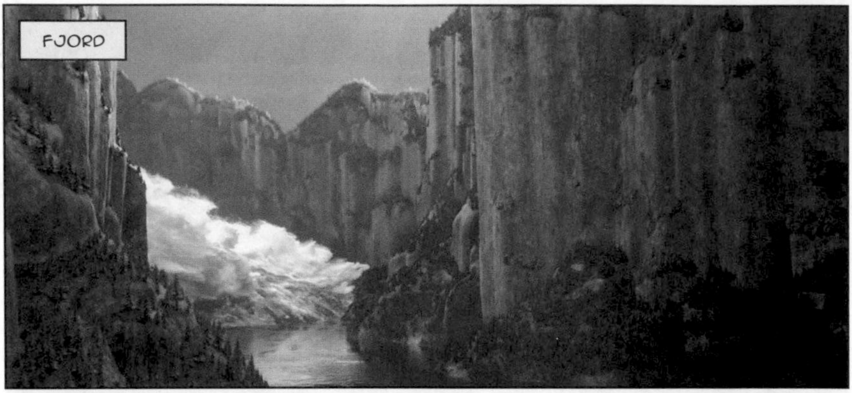
FJORD

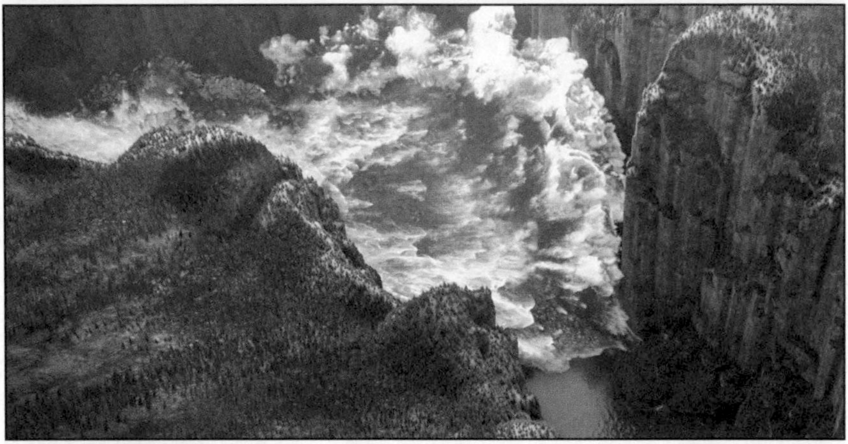

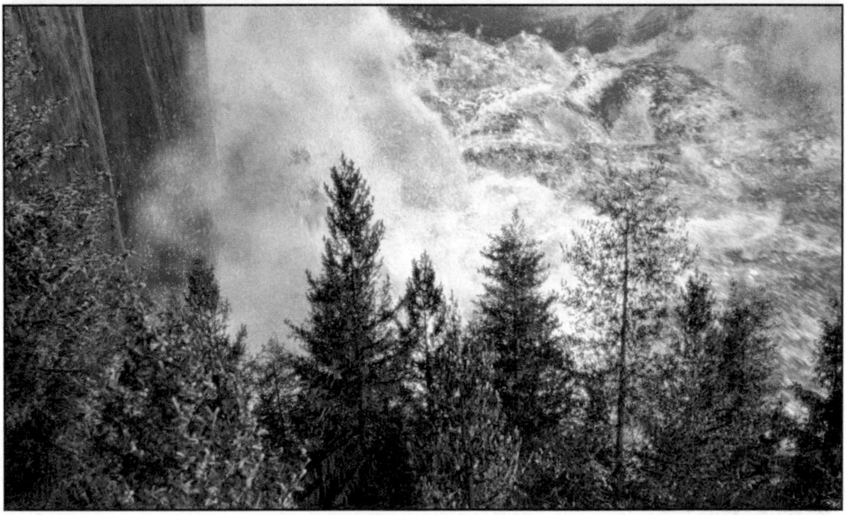

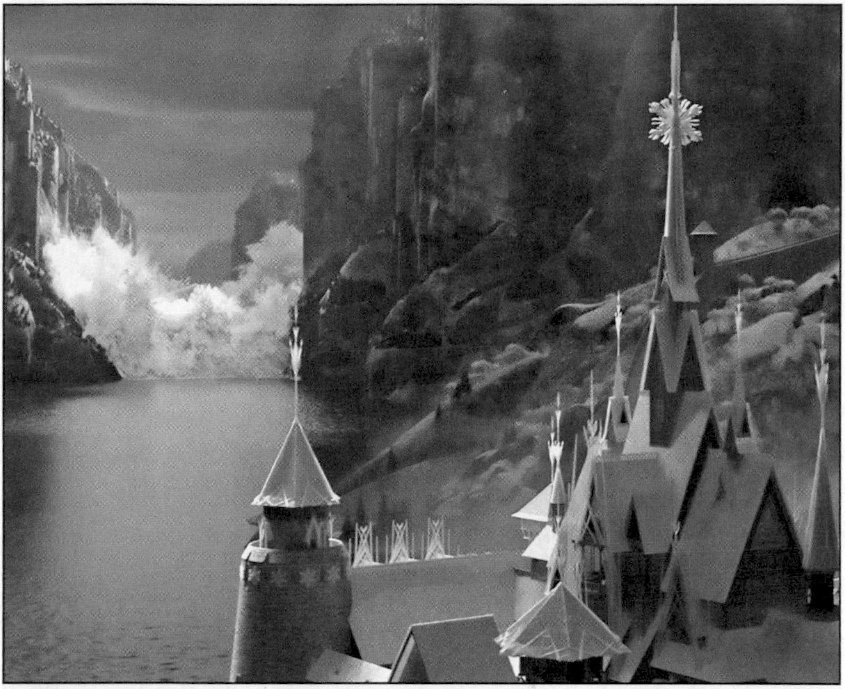

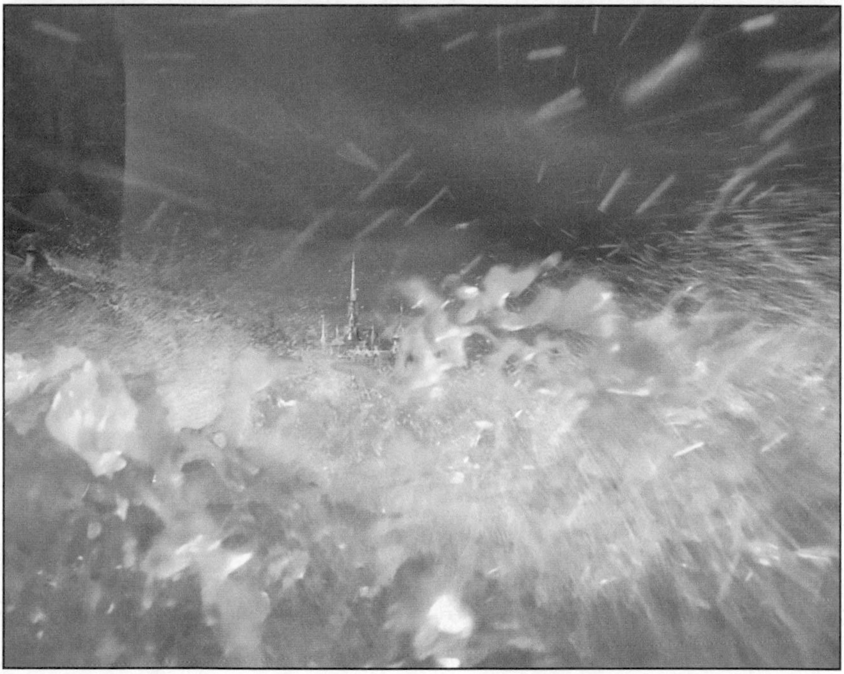

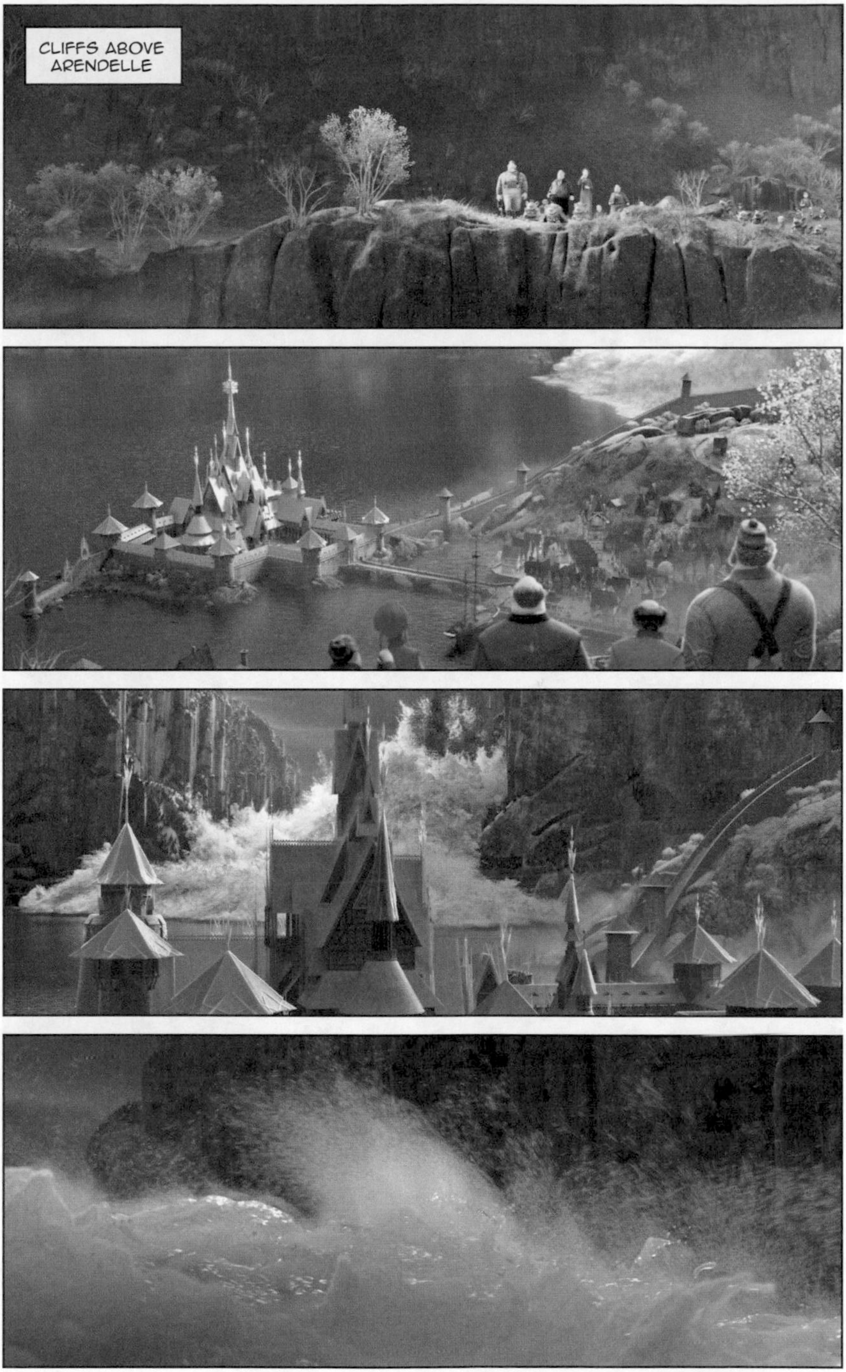
CLIFFS ABOVE
ARENDELLE

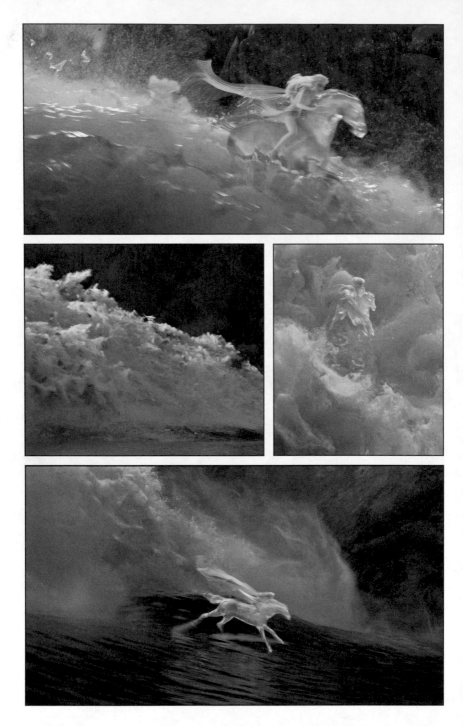

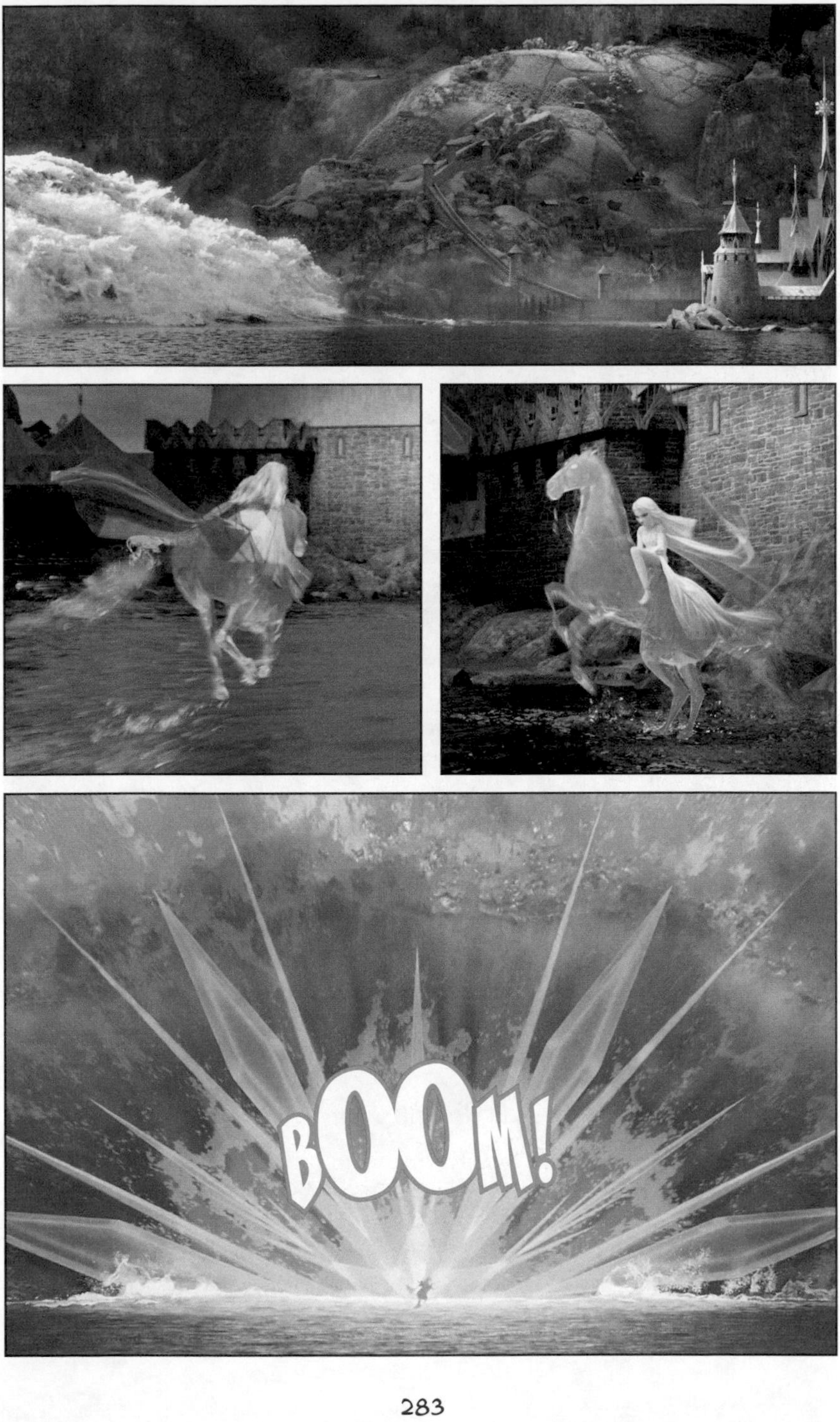
BOOM!

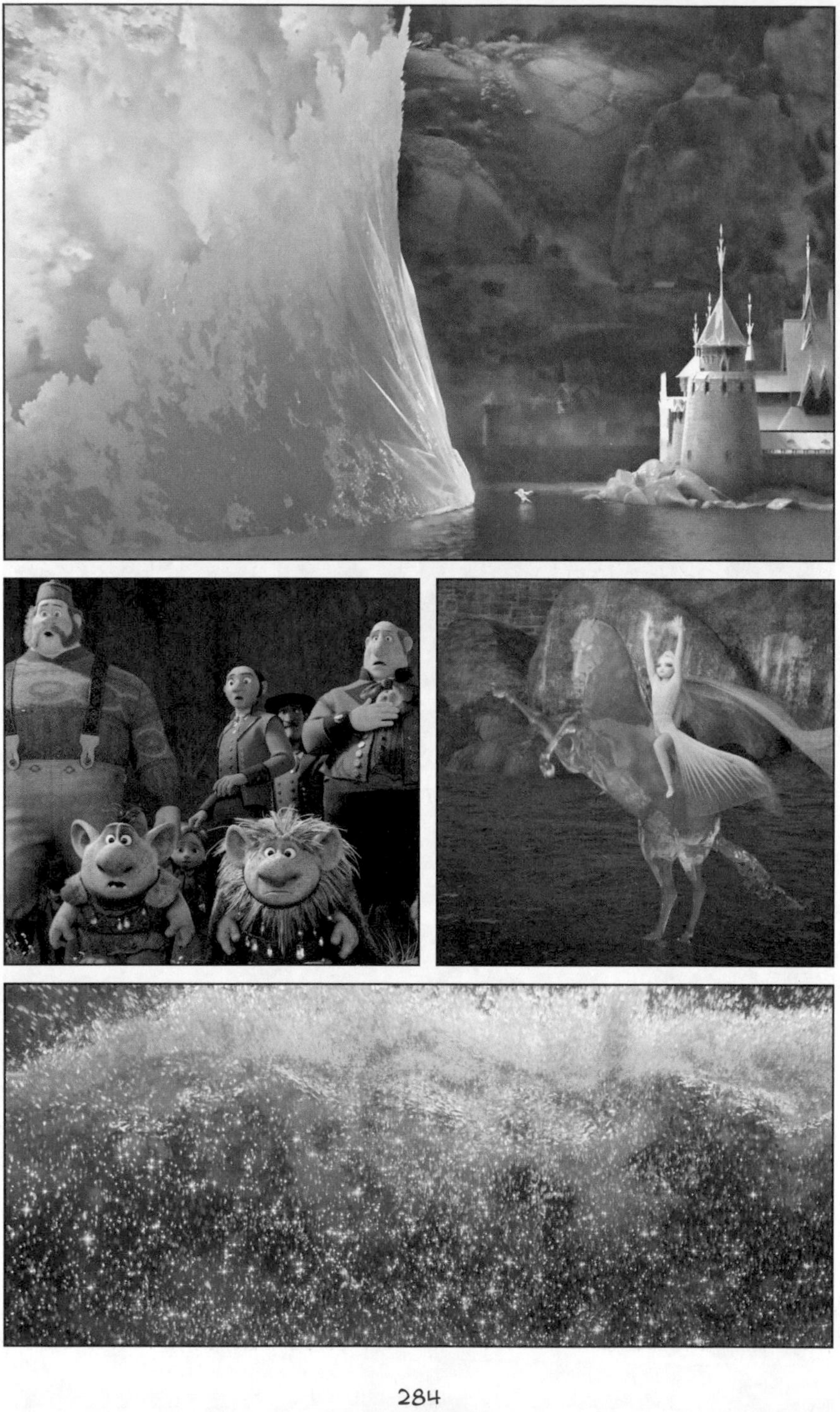

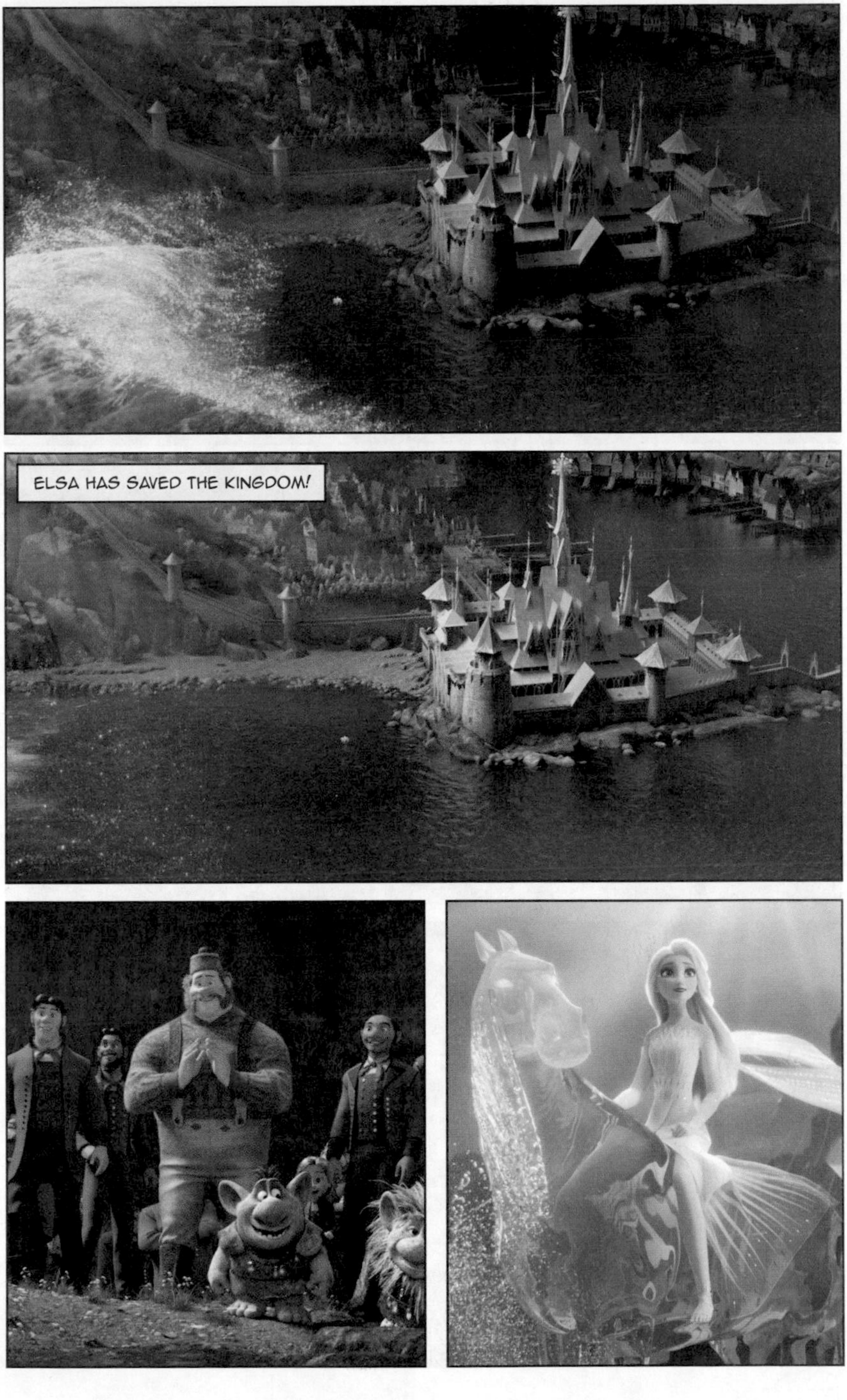
ELSA HAS SAVED THE KINGDOM!

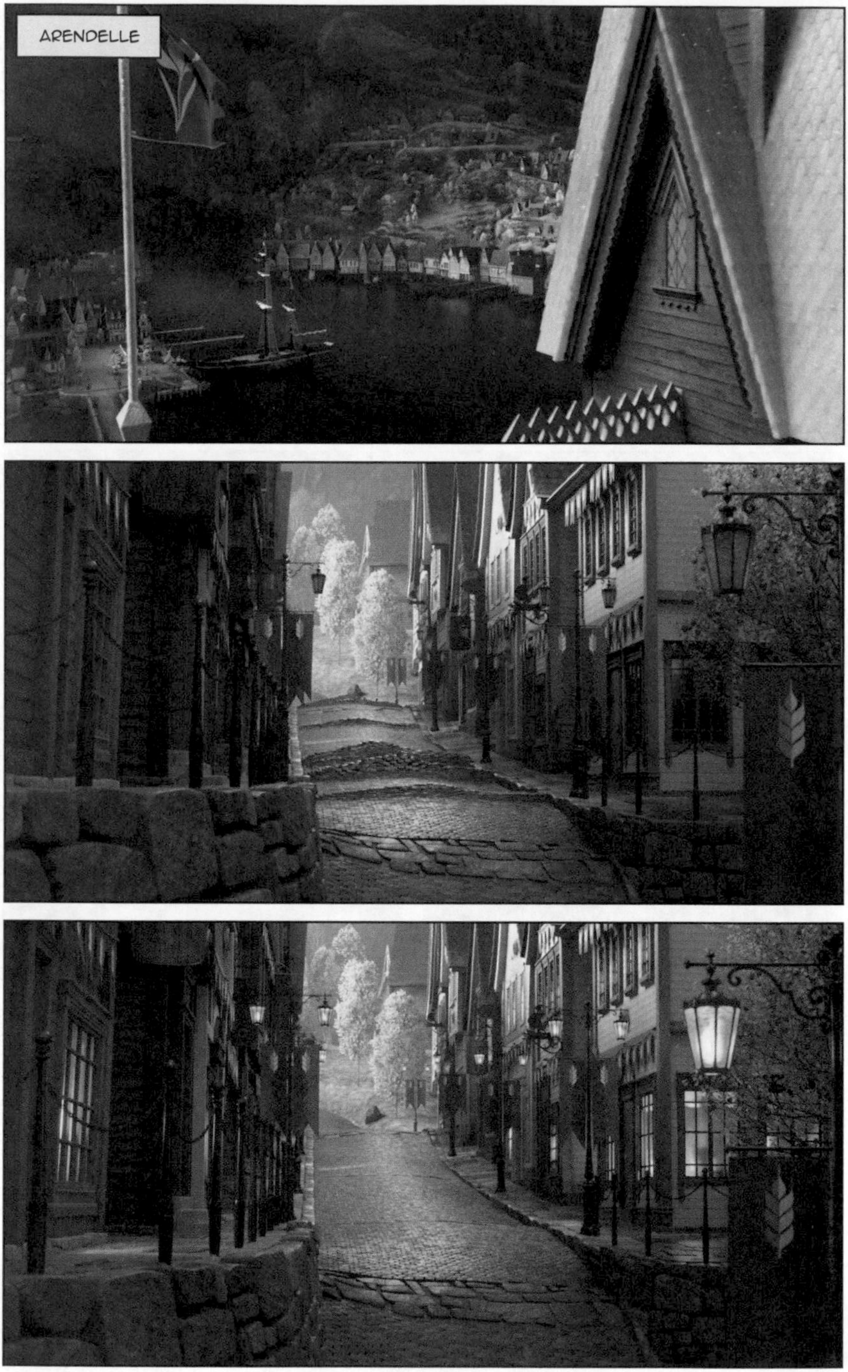
ARENDELLE

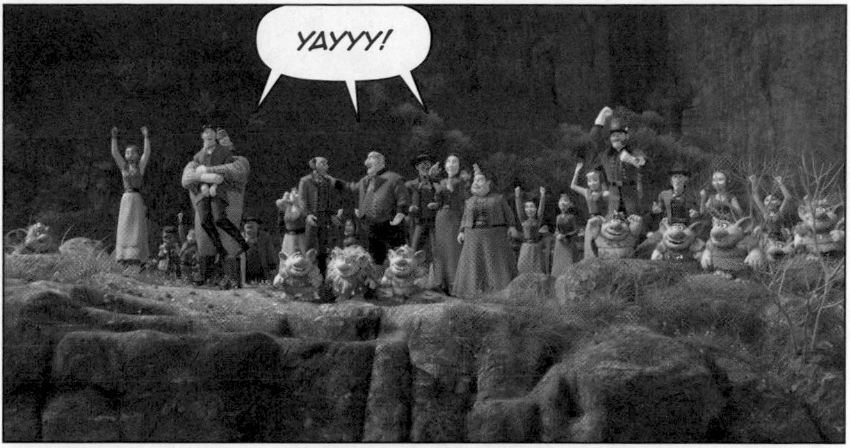
YAYYY!

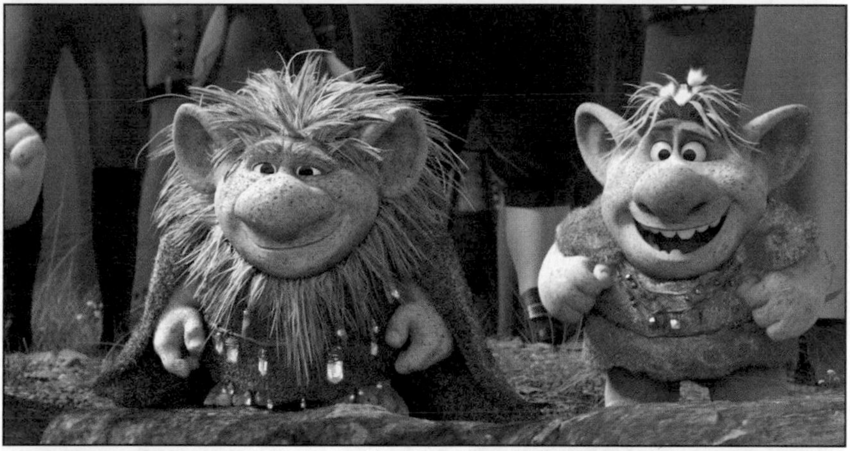

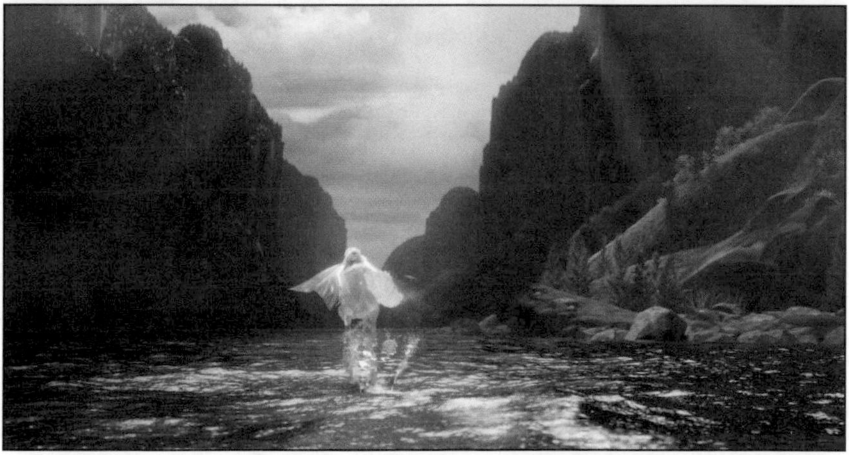

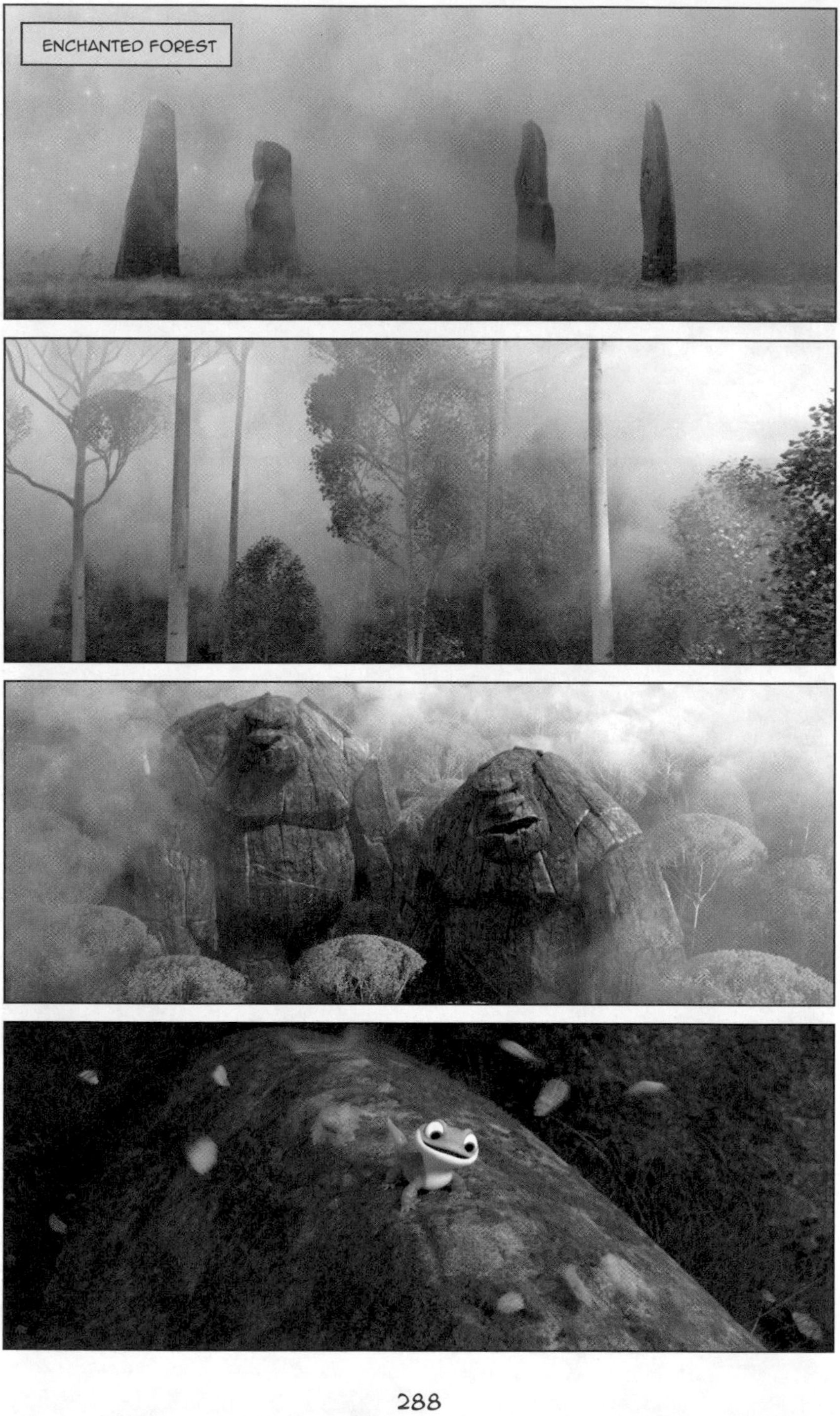
ENCHANTED FOREST

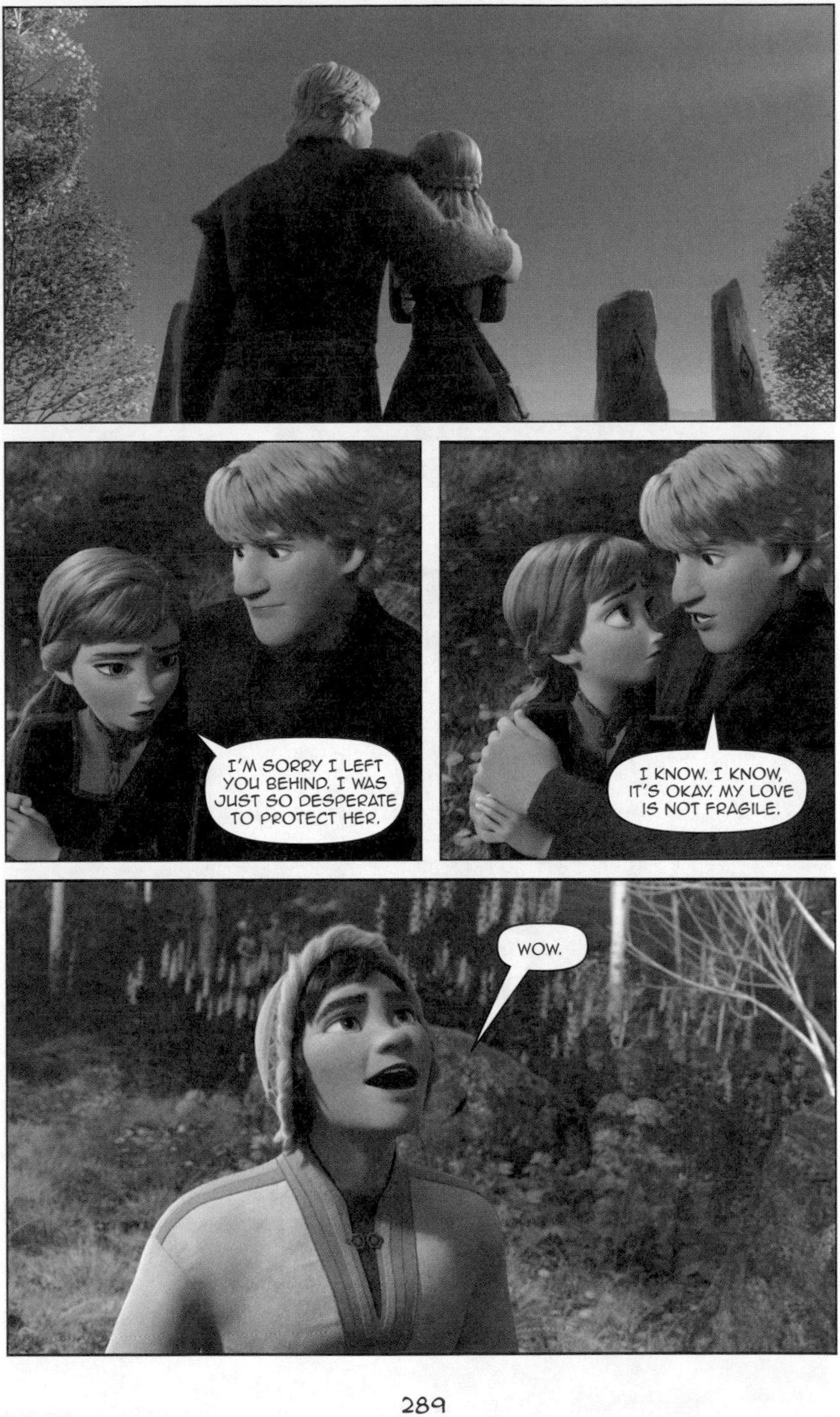
I'M SORRY I LEFT YOU BEHIND. I WAS JUST SO DESPERATE TO PROTECT HER.
I KNOW. I KNOW, IT'S OKAY. MY LOVE IS NOT FRAGILE.
WOW.

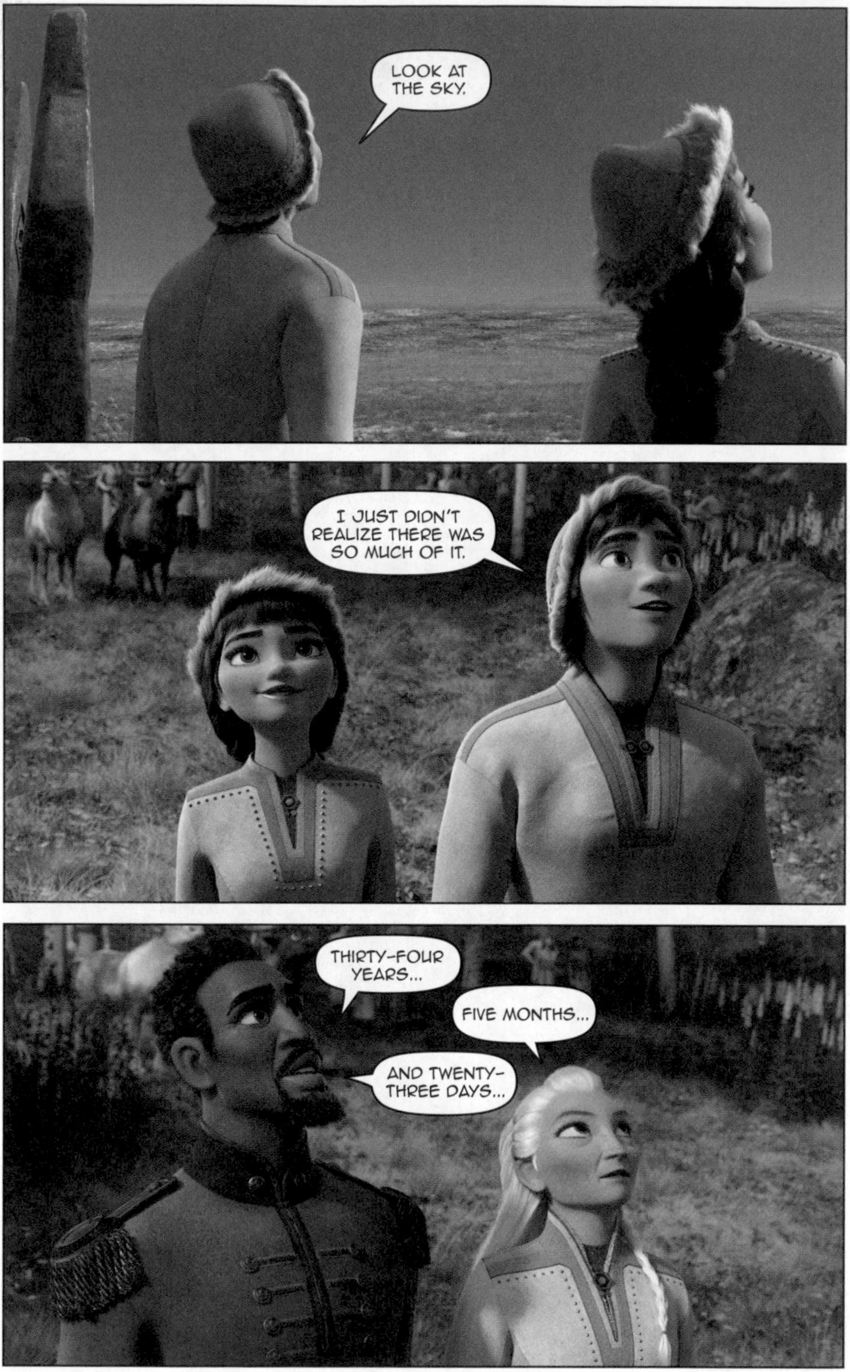
LOOK AT THE SKY.
I JUST DIDN'T REALIZE THERE WAS SO MUCH OF IT.
THIRTY-FOUR YEARS...
FIVE MONTHS...
AND TWENTY-THREE DAYS...

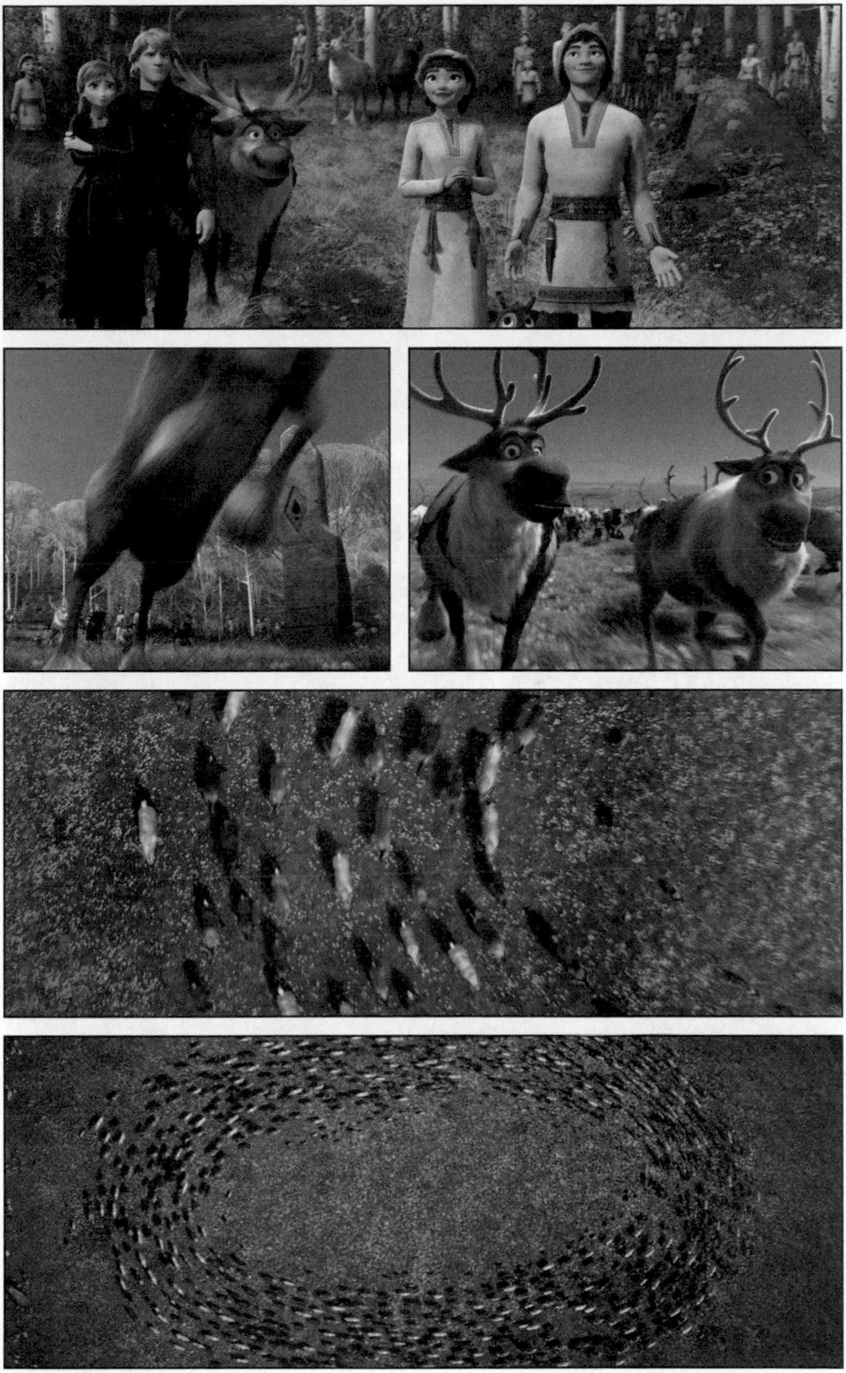

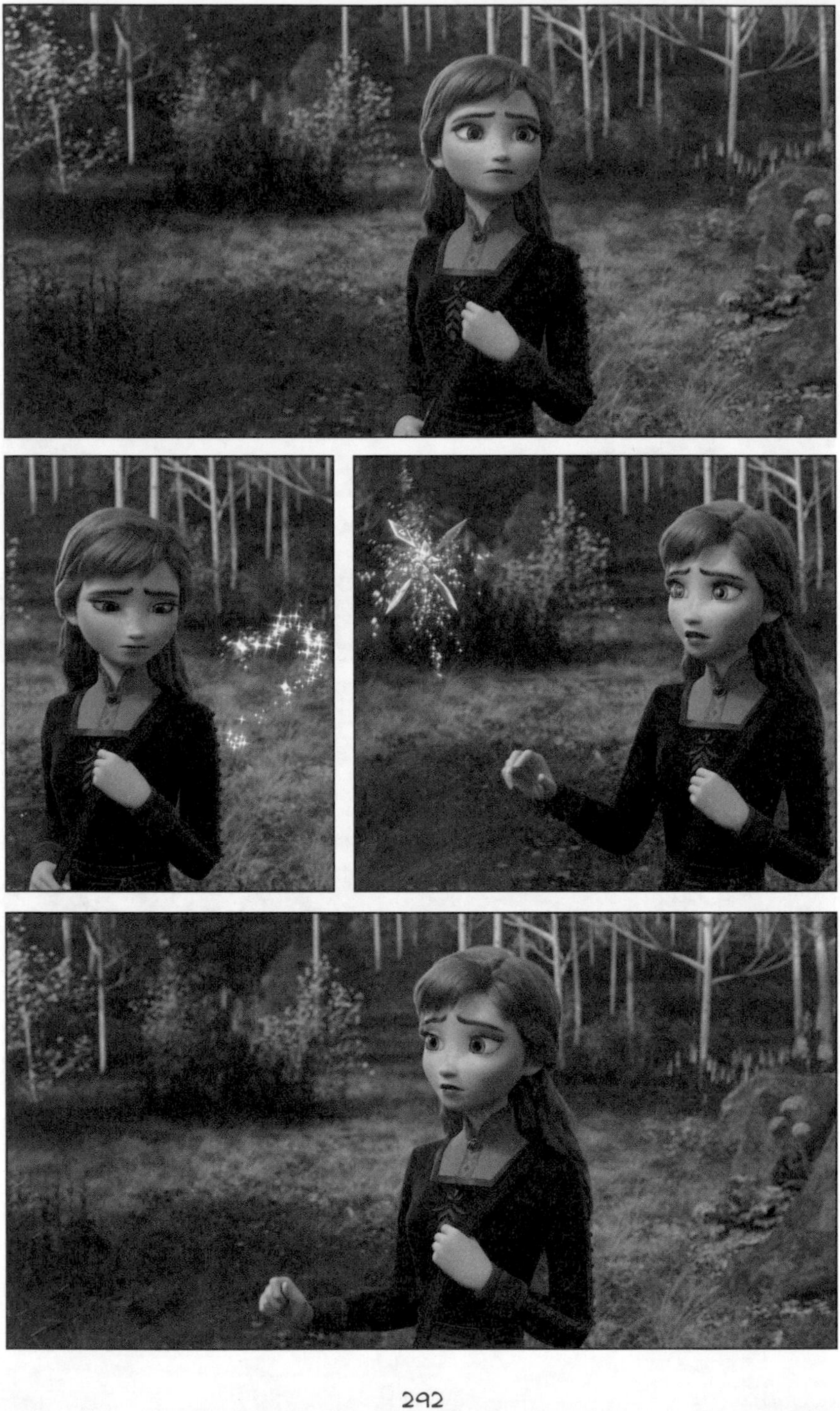

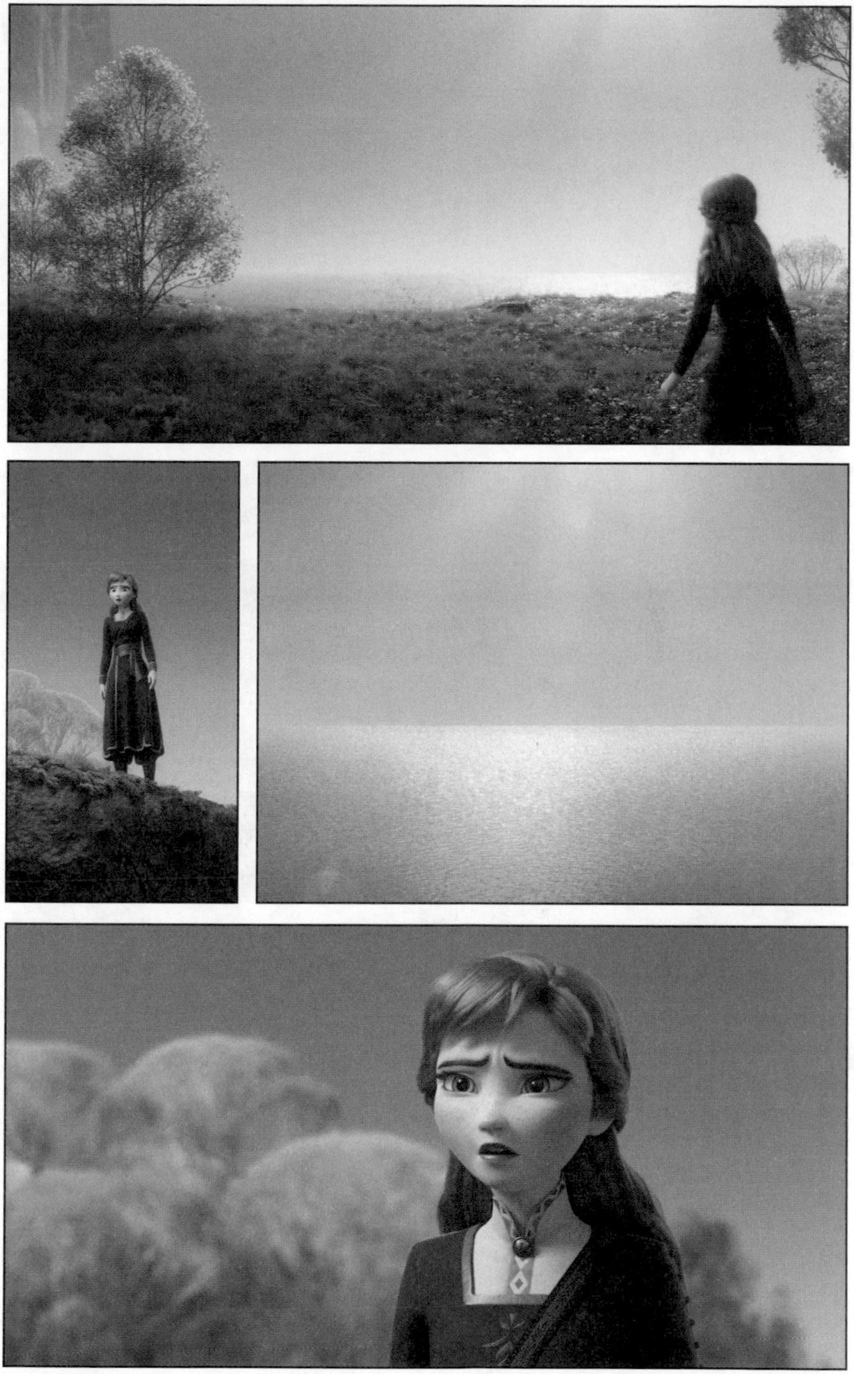

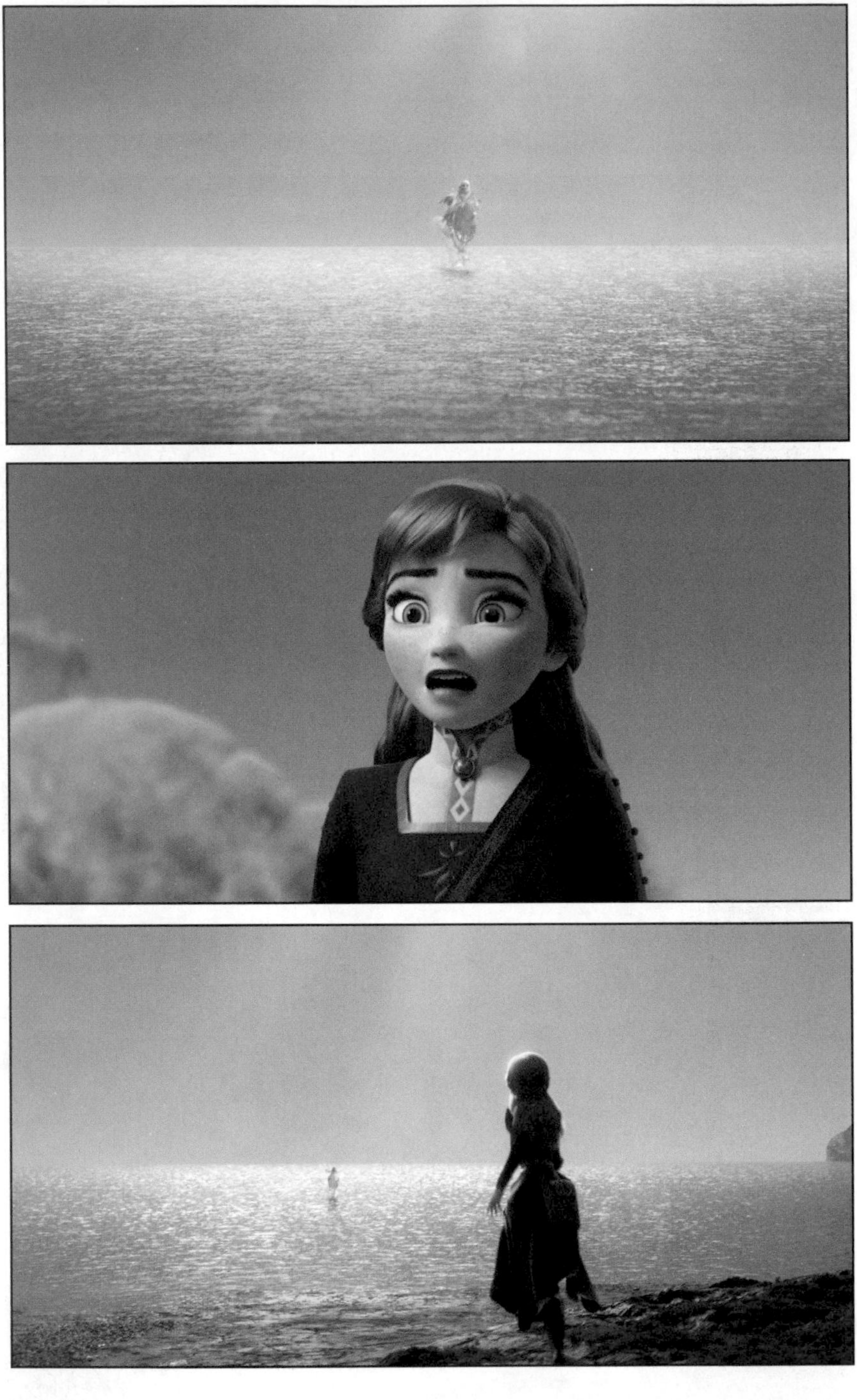

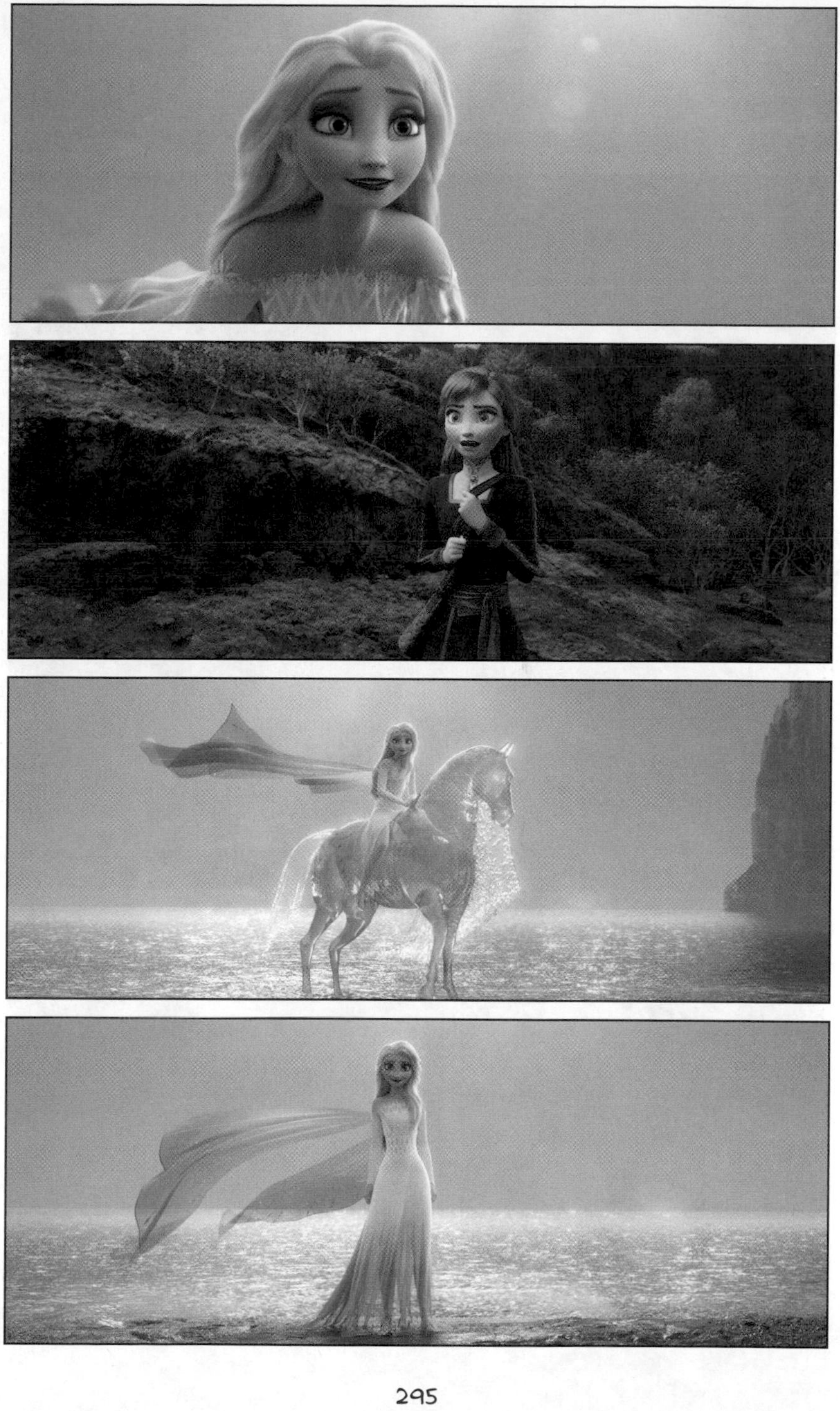

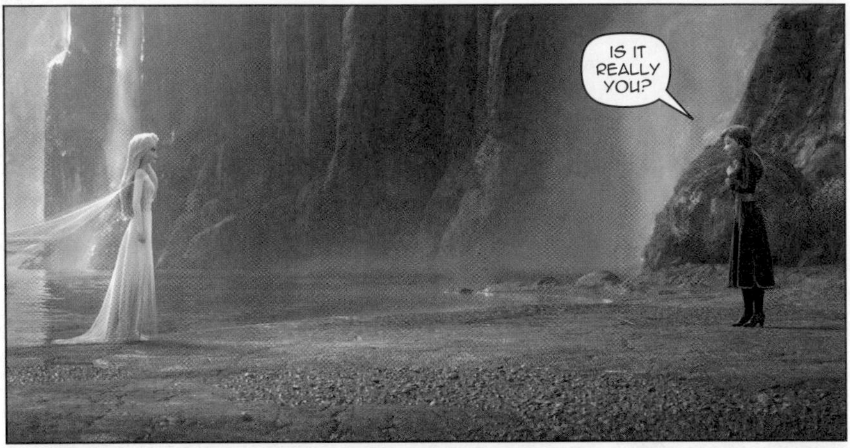
IS IT REALLY YOU?

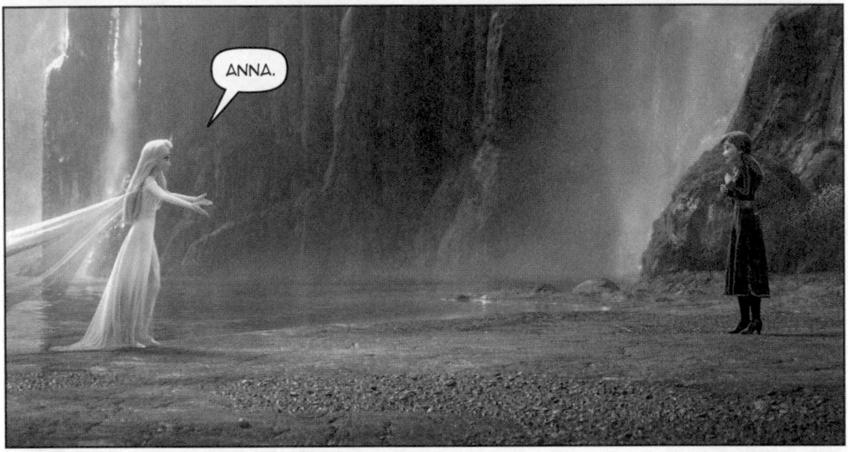
ANNA.

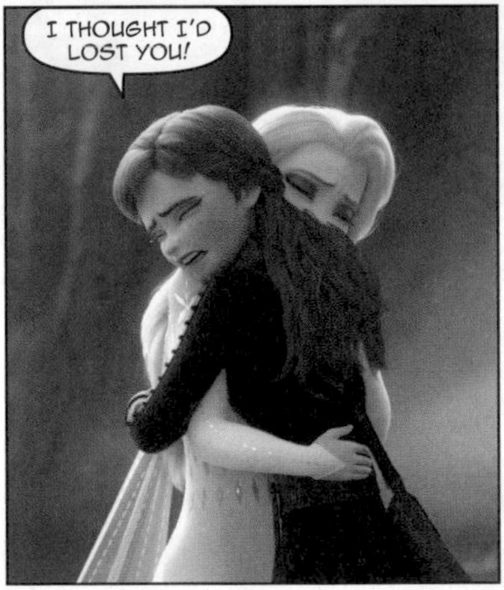
I THOUGHT I'D LOST YOU!

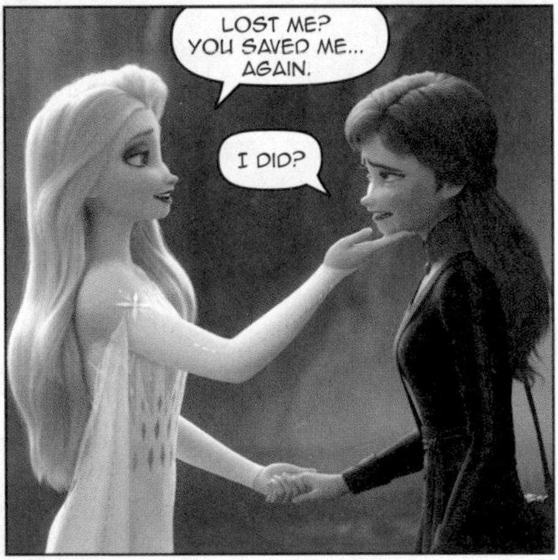
LOST ME? YOU SAVED ME... AGAIN.
I DID?

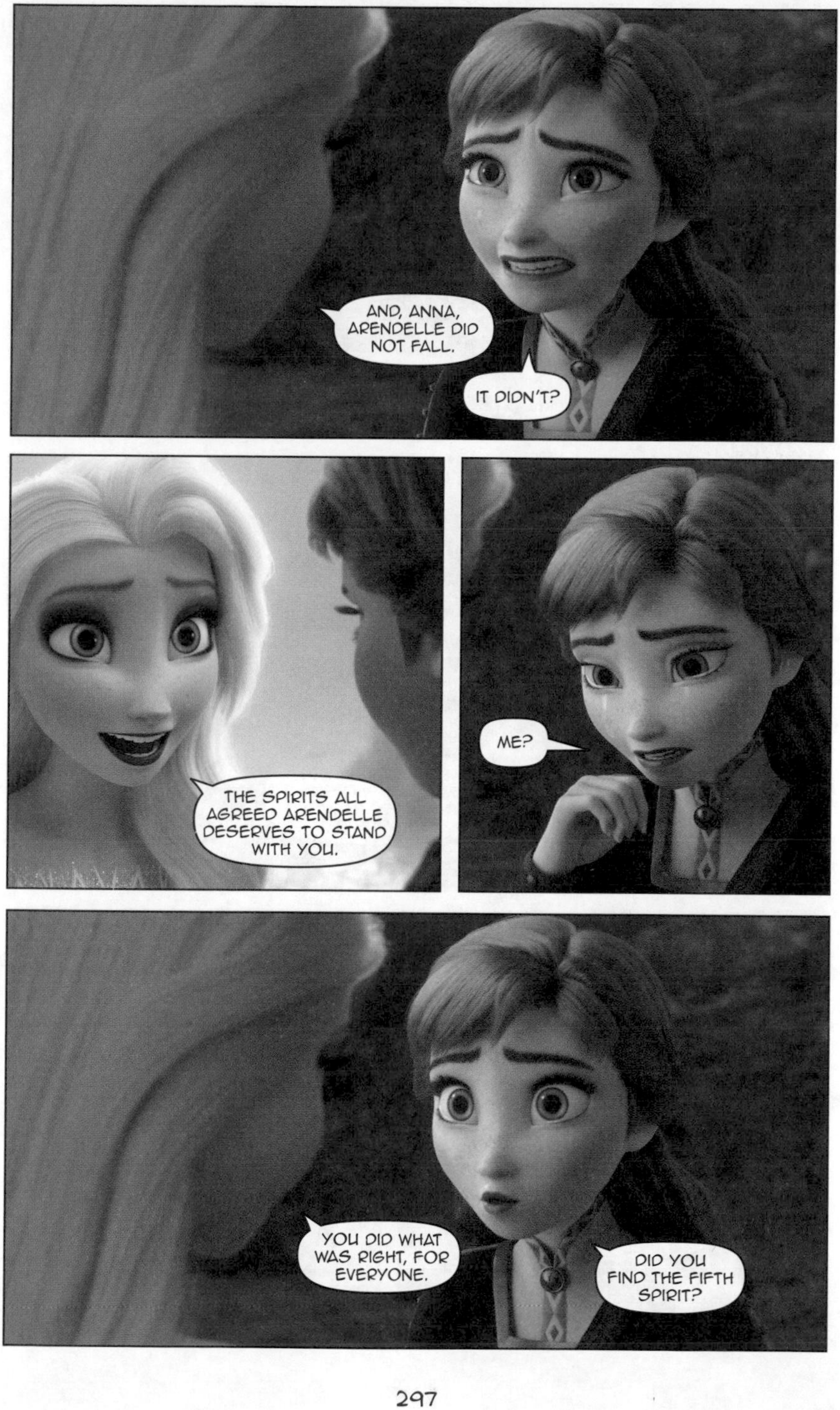
AND, ANNA, ARENDELLE DID NOT FALL.
IT DIDN'T?
THE SPIRITS ALL AGREED ARENDELLE DESERVES TO STAND WITH YOU.
ME?
YOU DID WHAT WAS RIGHT, FOR EVERYONE.
DID YOU FIND THE FIFTH SPIRIT?

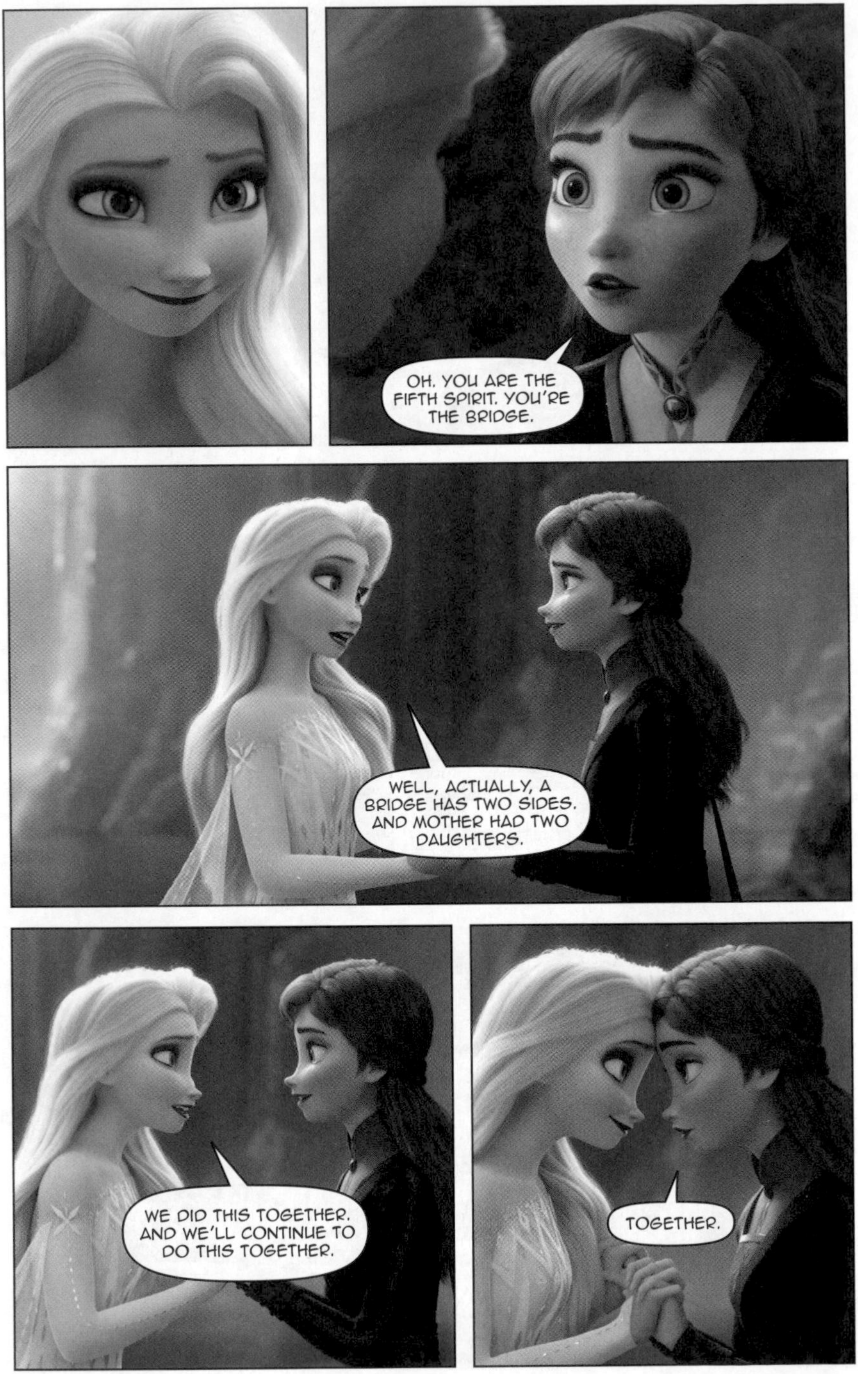
OH. YOU ARE THE FIFTH SPIRIT. YOU'RE THE BRIDGE.
WELL, ACTUALLY, A BRIDGE HAS TWO SIDES. AND MOTHER HAD TWO DAUGHTERS.
WE DID THIS TOGETHER. AND WE'LL CONTINUE TO DO THIS TOGETHER.
TOGETHER.

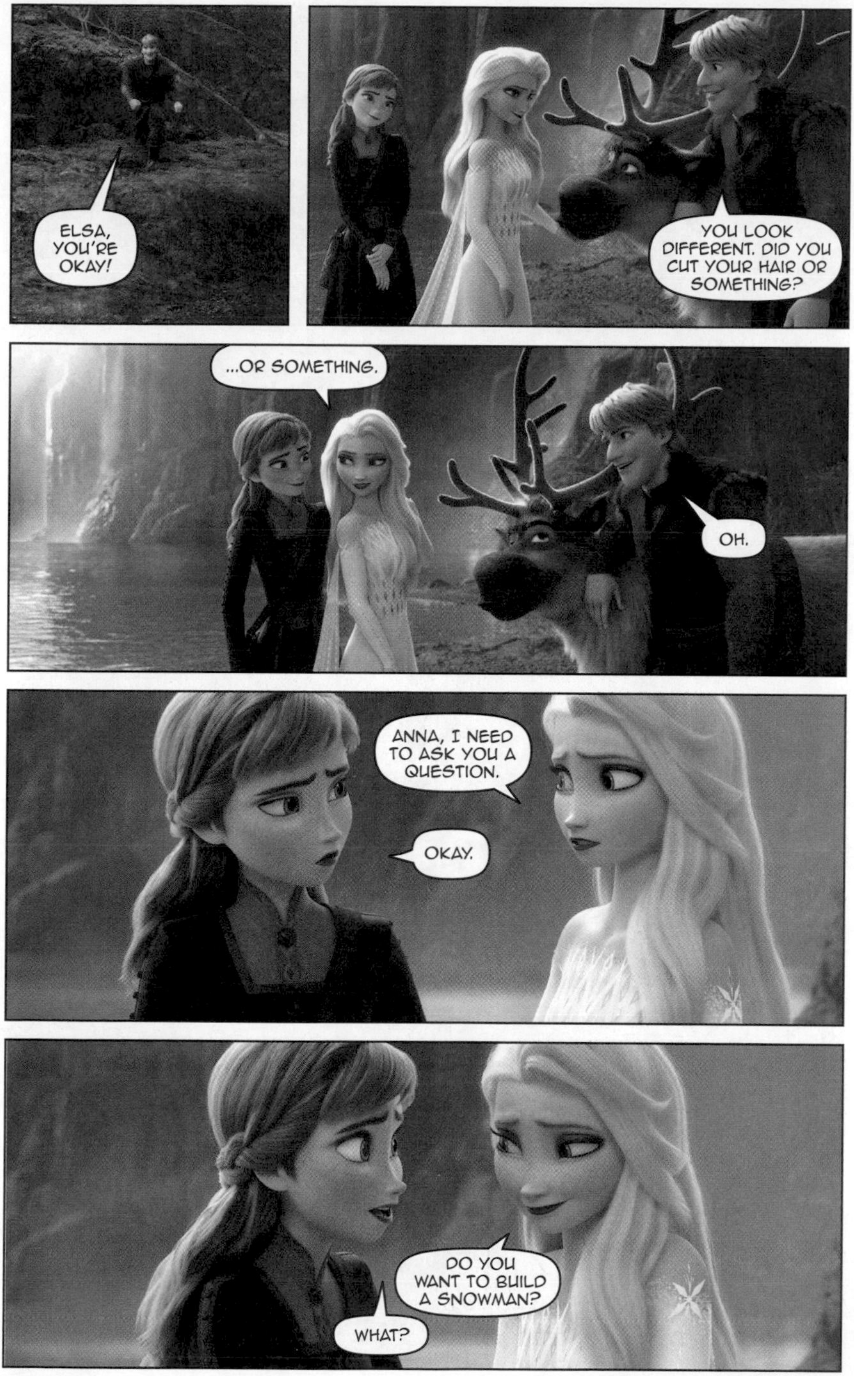
ELSA, YOU'RE OKAY!
YOU LOOK DIFFERENT. DID YOU CUT YOUR HAIR OR SOMETHING?
...OR SOMETHING.
OH.
ANNA, I NEED TO ASK YOU A QUESTION.
OKAY.
DO YOU WANT TO BUILD A SNOWMAN?
WHAT?

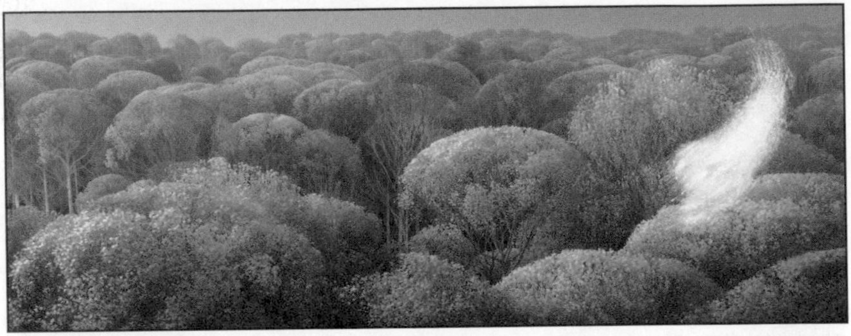

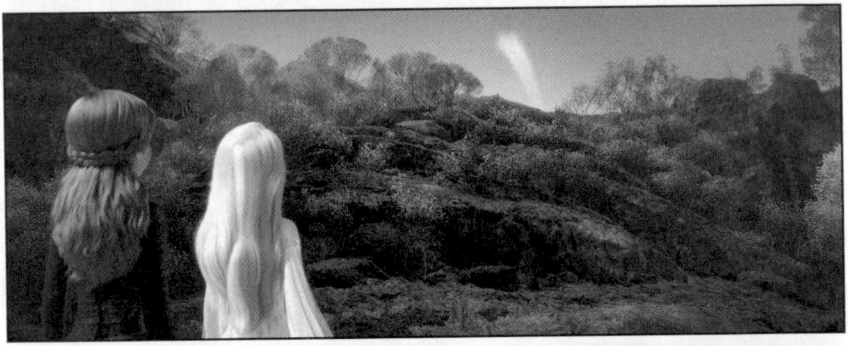

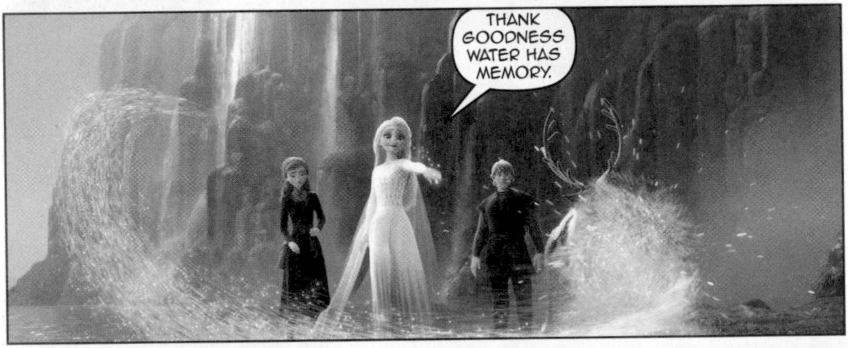
THANK GOODNESS WATER HAS MEMORY.

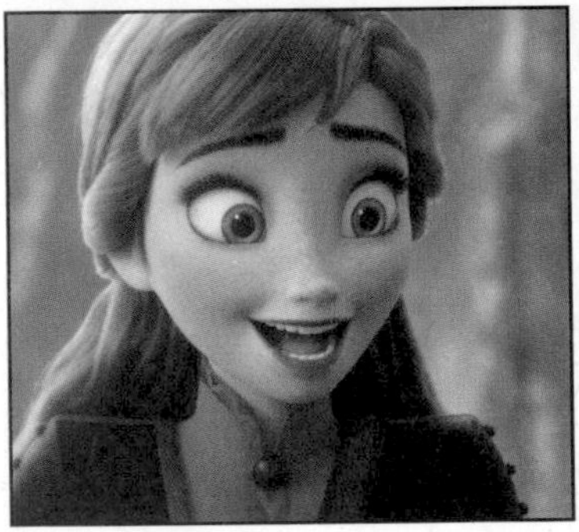

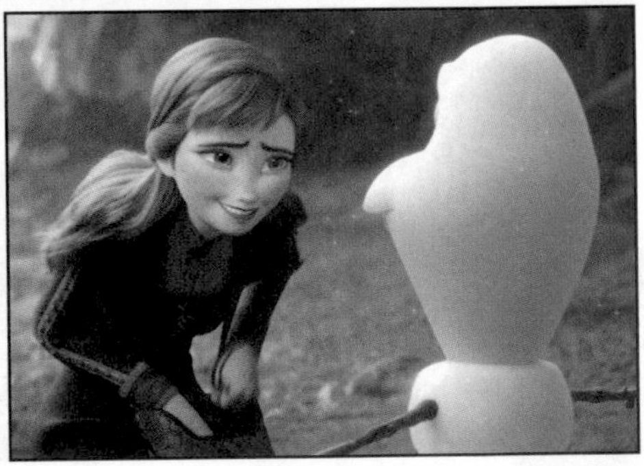

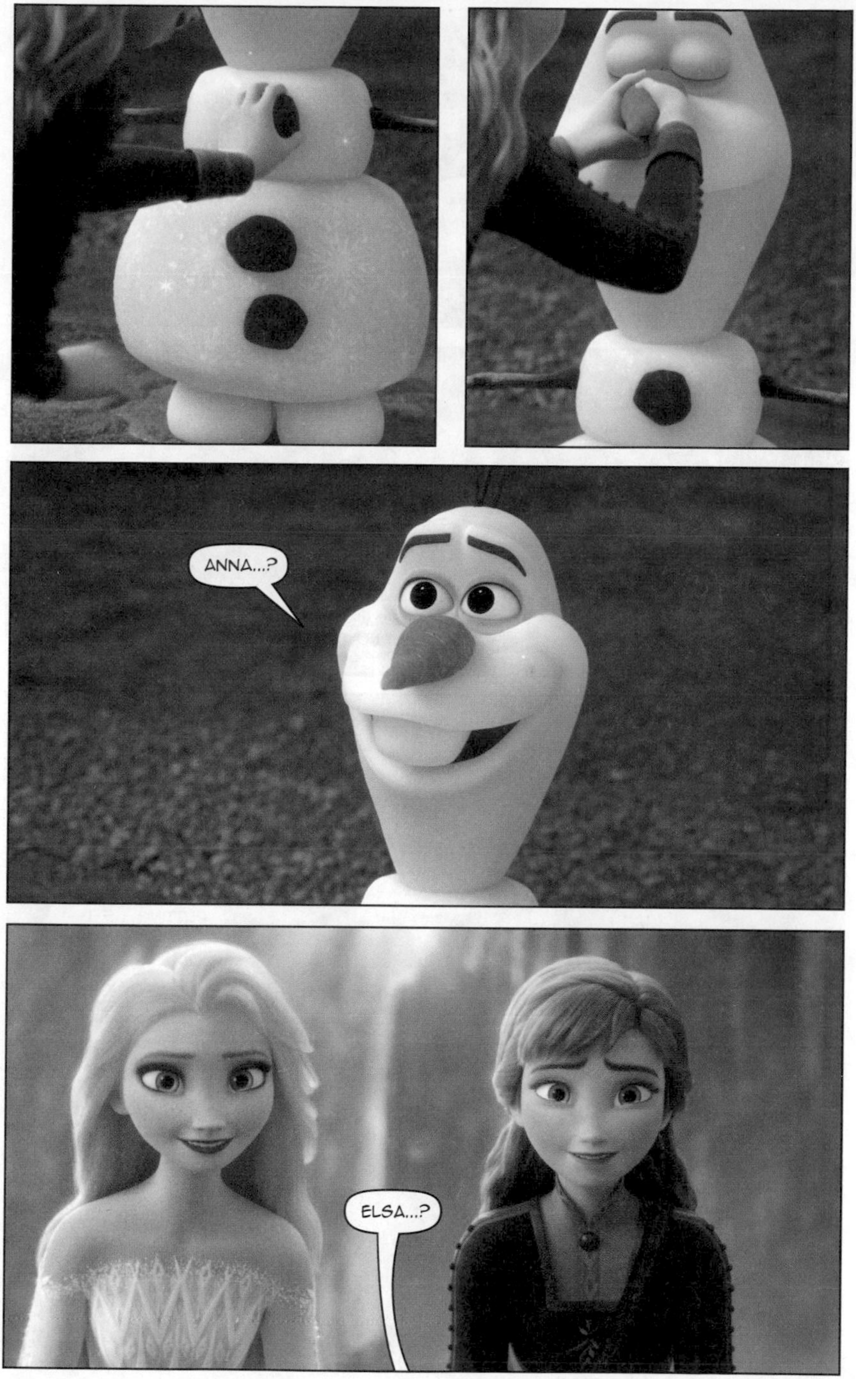
ANNA...?
ELSA...?

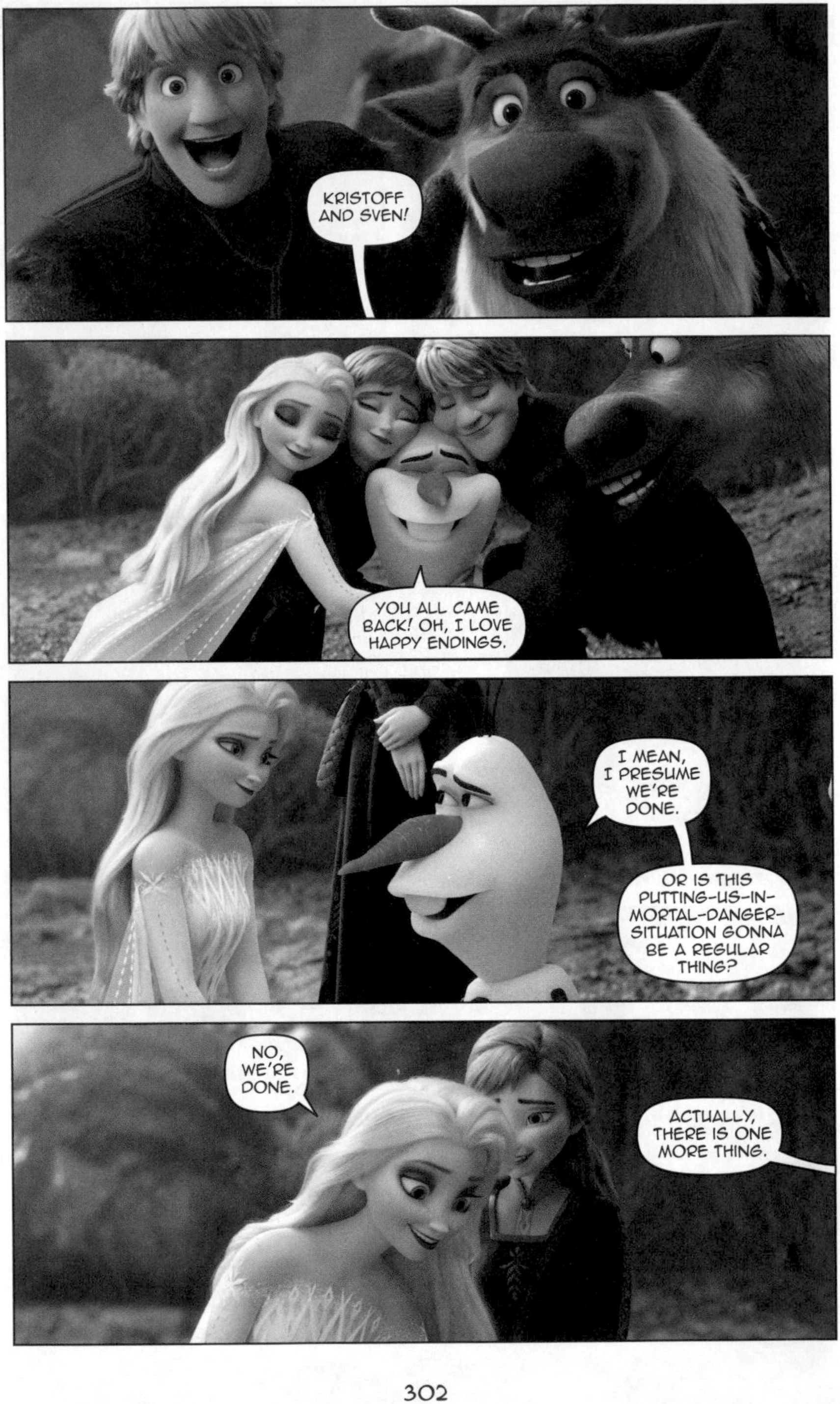
KRISTOFF AND SVEN!
YOU ALL CAME BACK! OH, I LOVE HAPPY ENDINGS.
I MEAN, I PRESUME WE'RE DONE.
OR IS THIS PUTTING-US-IN-MORTAL-DANGER-SITUATION GONNA BE A REGULAR THING?
NO, WE'RE DONE.
ACTUALLY, THERE IS ONE MORE THING.

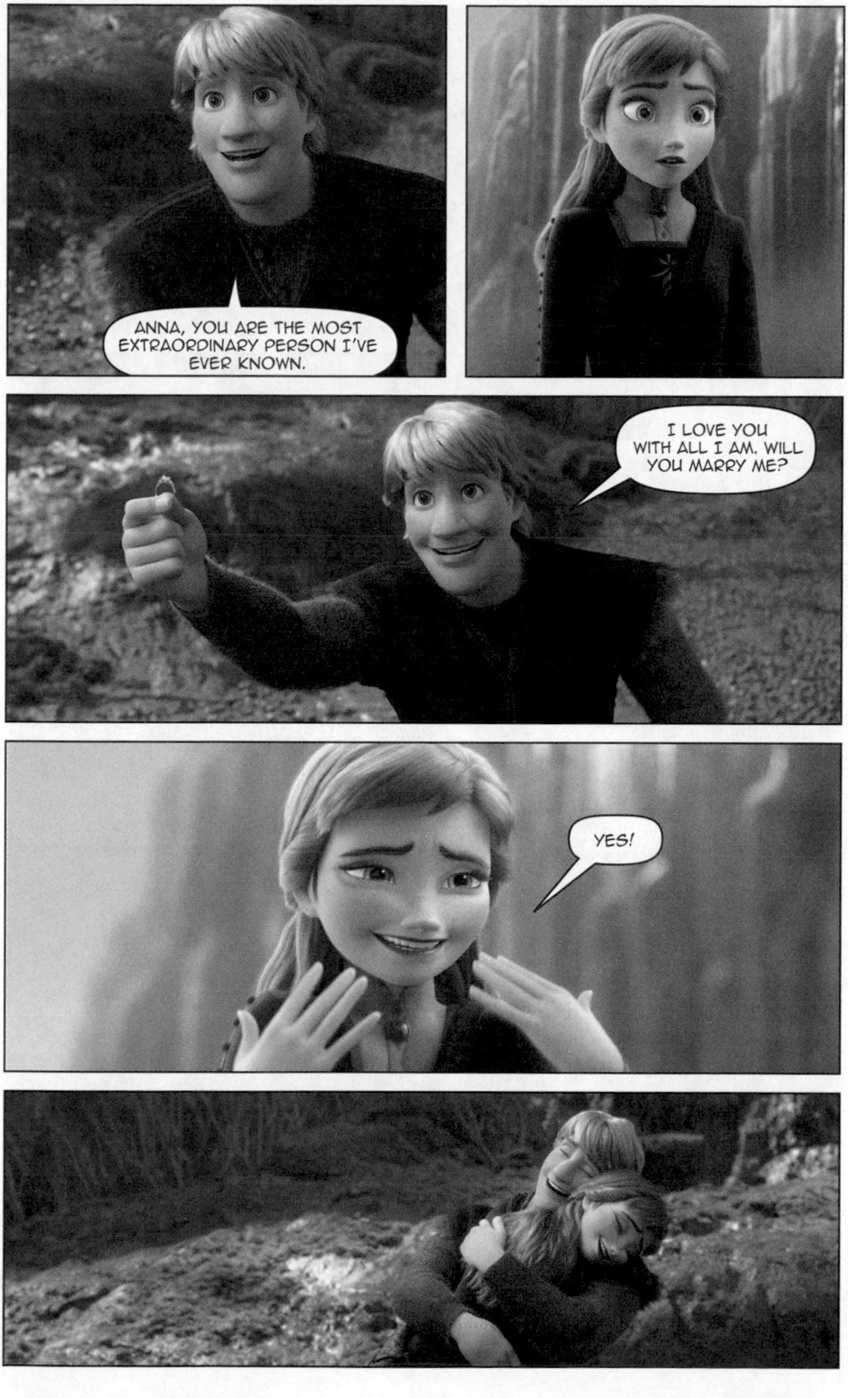
ANNA, YOU ARE THE MOST EXTRAORDINARY PERSON I'VE EVER KNOWN.
I LOVE YOU WITH ALL I AM. WILL YOU MARRY ME?
YES!

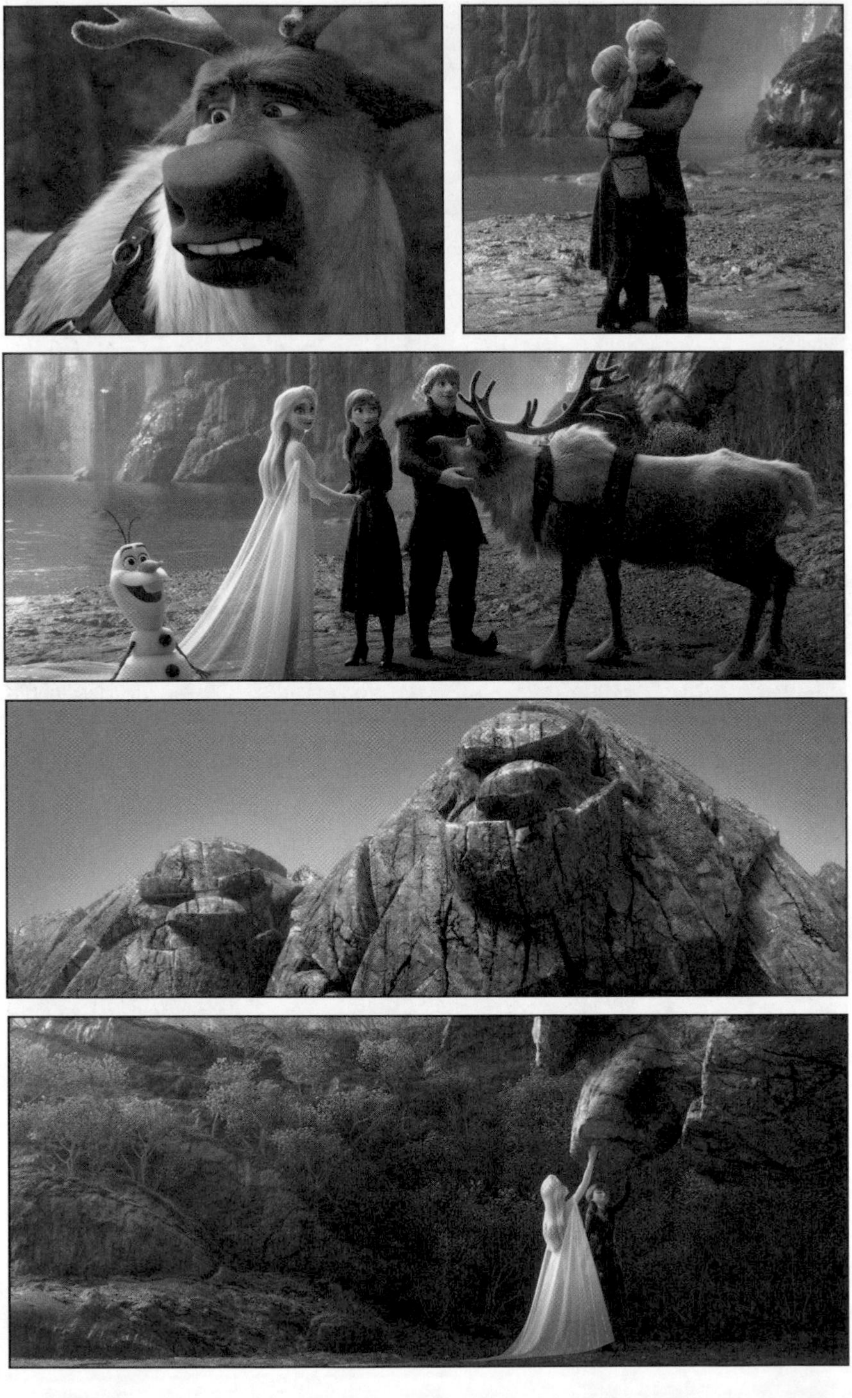

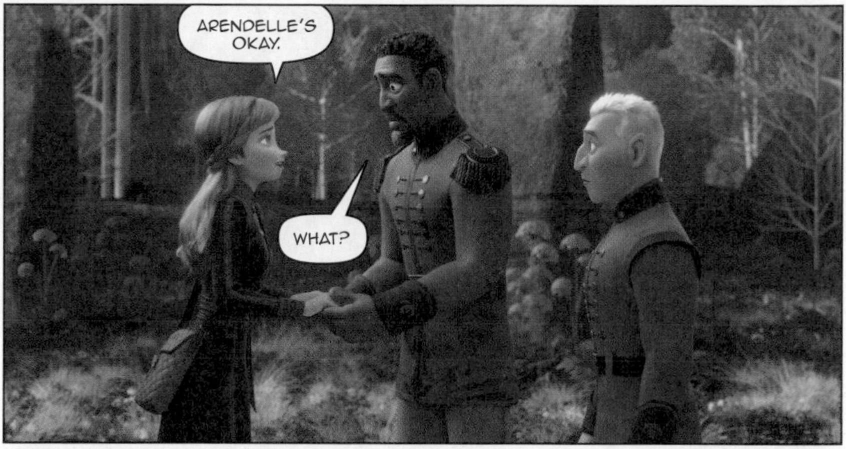
ARENDELLE'S OKAY.
WHAT?

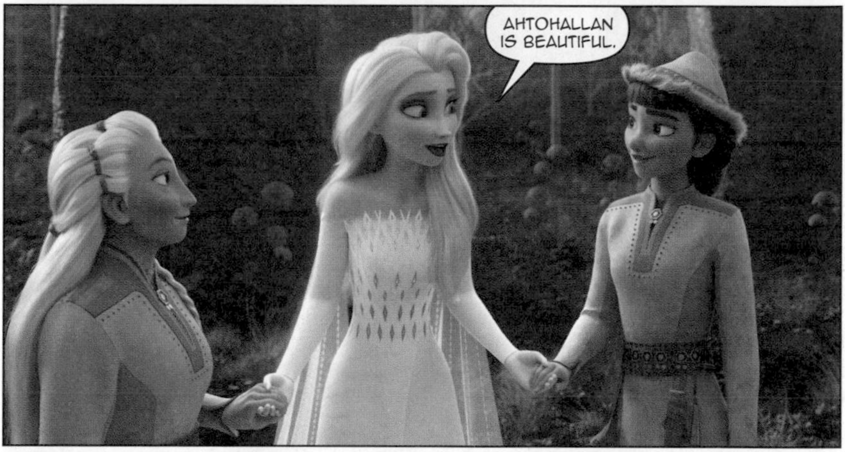
AHTOHALLAN IS BEAUTIFUL.

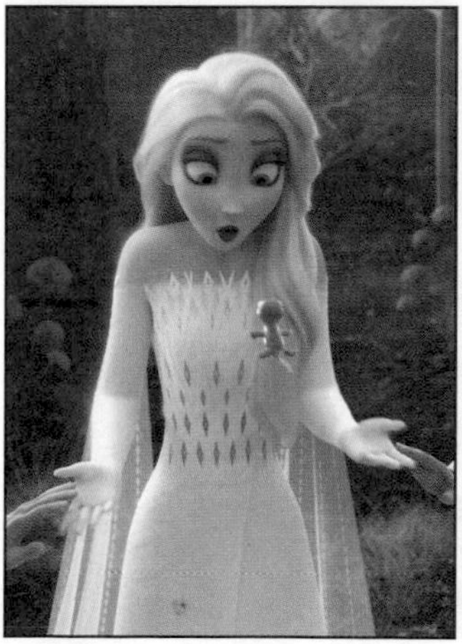

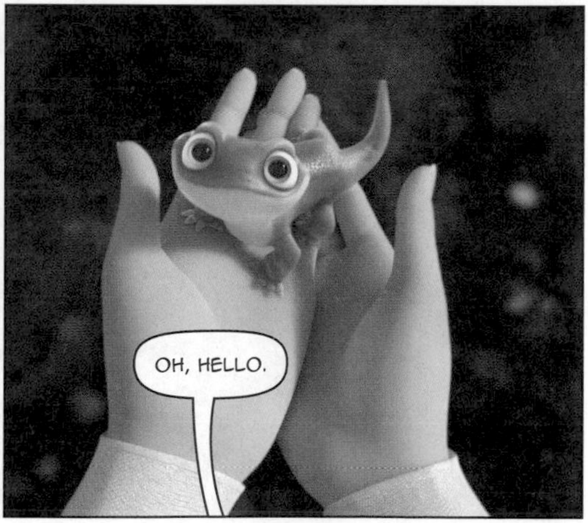
OH, HELLO.

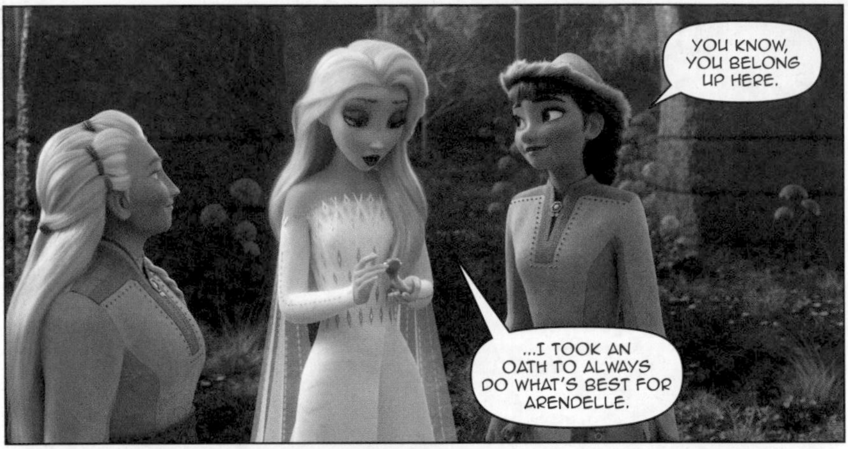
YOU KNOW, YOU BELONG UP HERE.
...I TOOK AN OATH TO ALWAYS DO WHAT'S BEST FOR ARENDELLE.

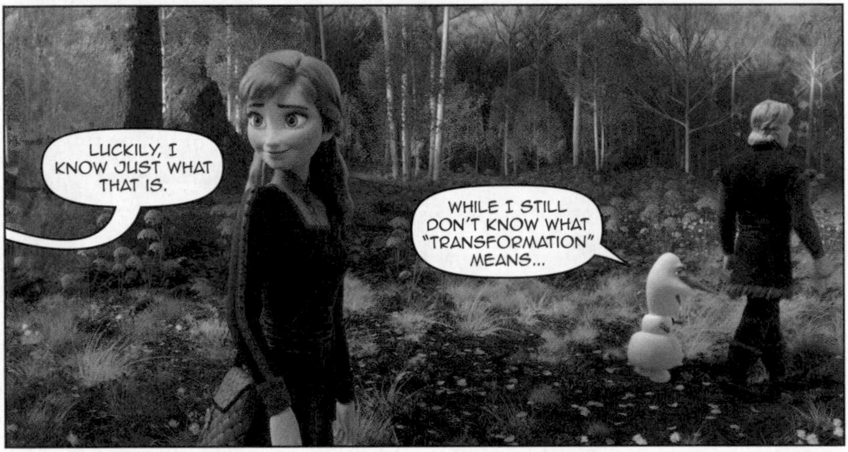
LUCKILY, I KNOW JUST WHAT THAT IS.
WHILE I STILL DON'T KNOW WHAT "TRANSFORMATION" MEANS...

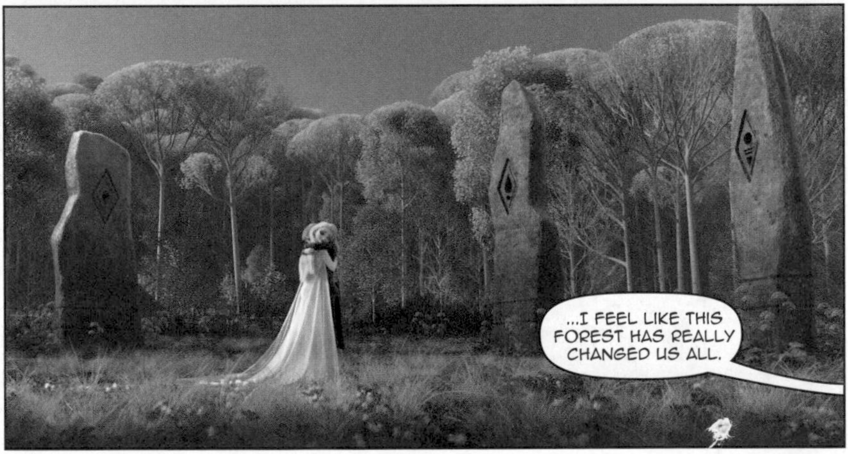
...I FEEL LIKE THIS FOREST HAS REALLY CHANGED US ALL.

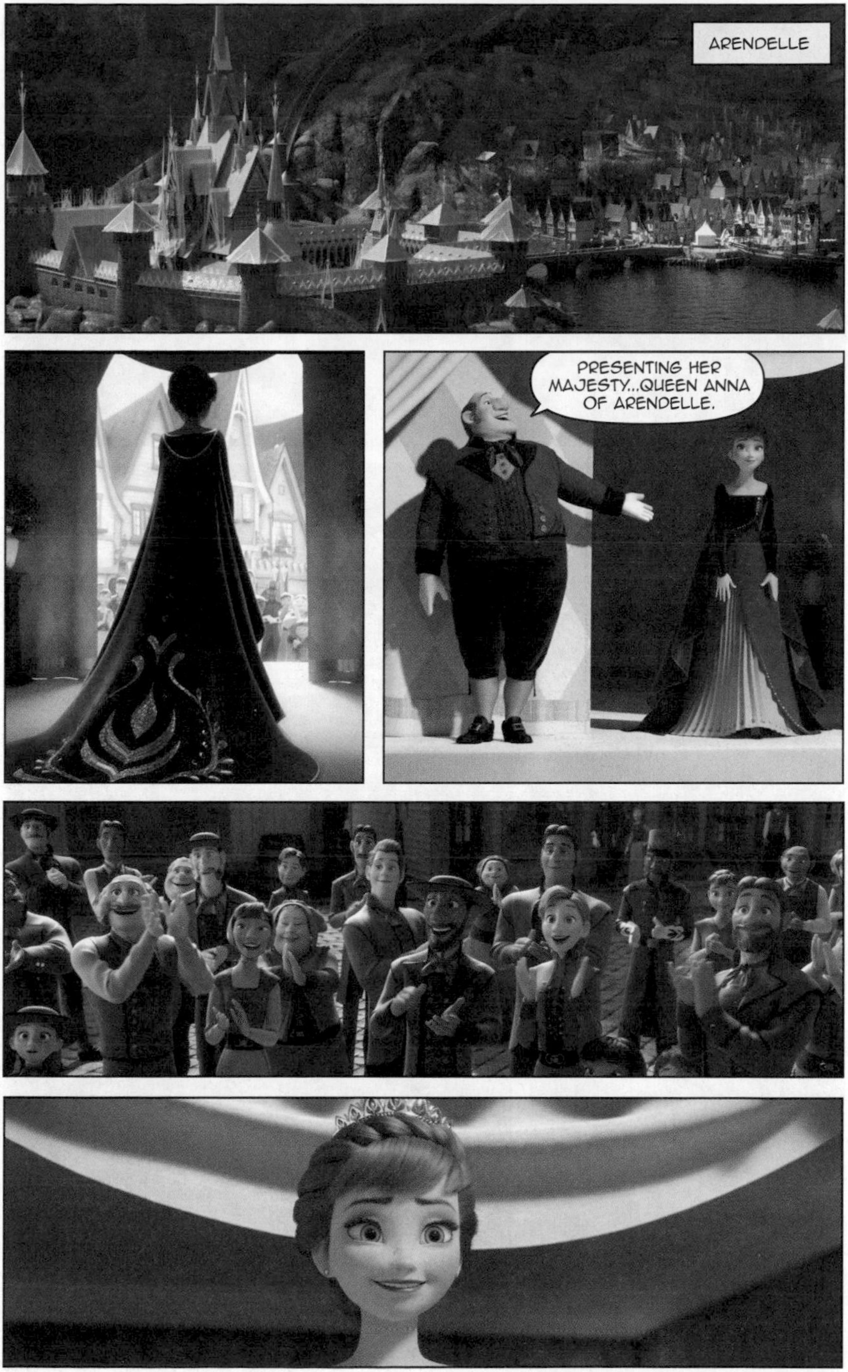
ARENDELLE
PRESENTING HER MAJESTY...QUEEN ANNA OF ARENDELLE.

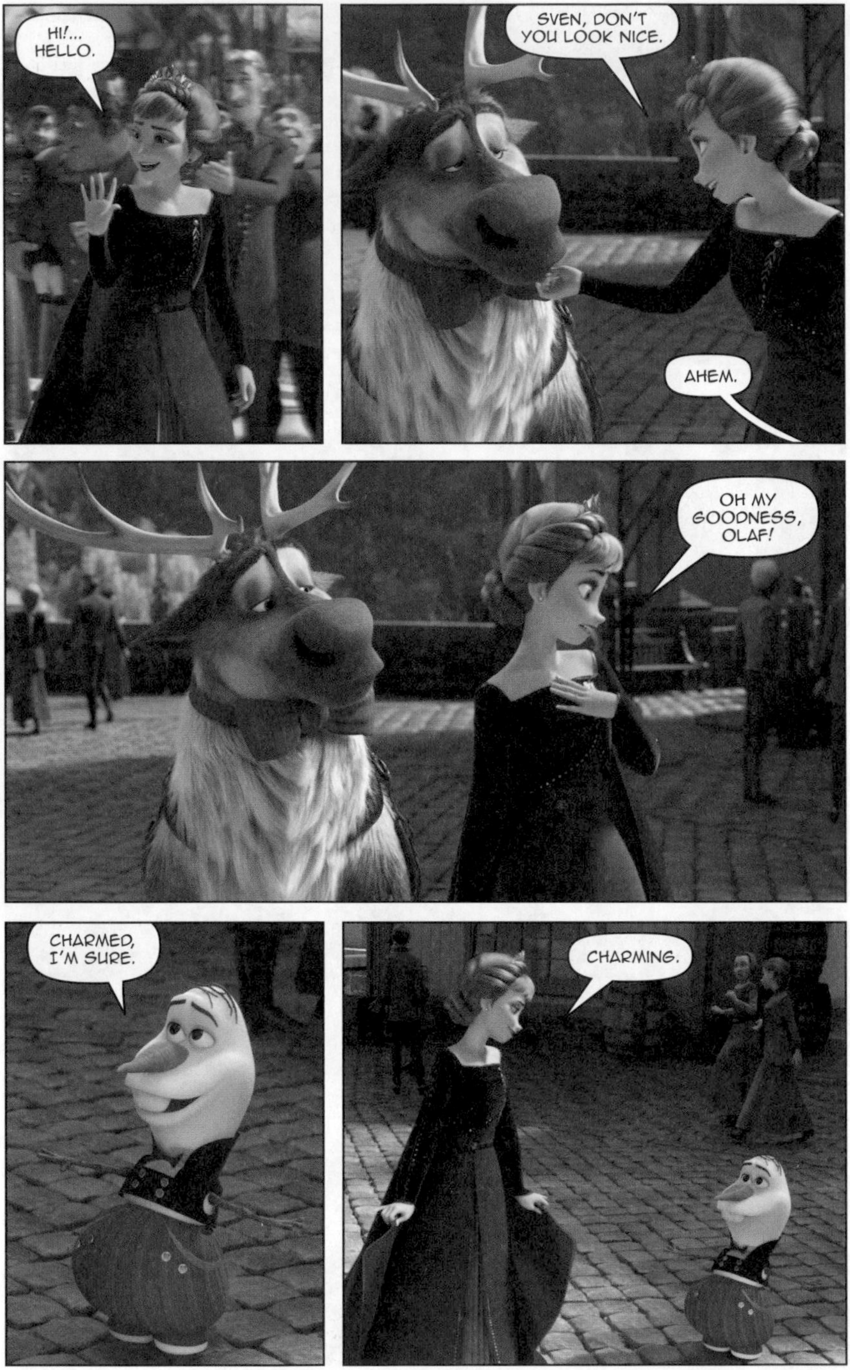
HI!...
HELLO.
SVEN, DON'T
YOU LOOK NICE.
AHEM.
OH MY
GOODNESS,
OLAF!
CHARMED,
I'M SURE.
CHARMING.

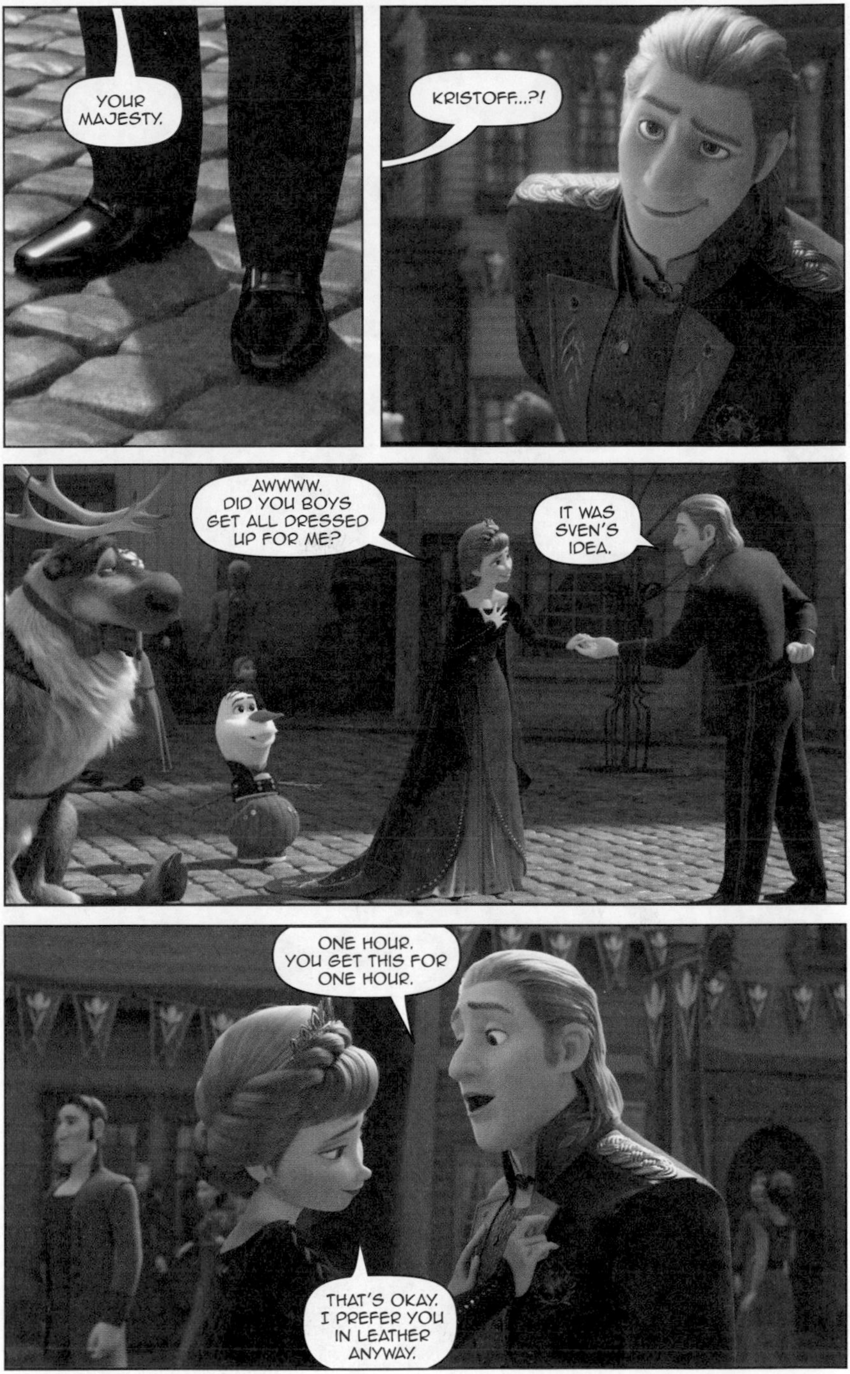
YOUR MAJESTY.
KRISTOFF...?!
AWWWW. DID YOU BOYS GET ALL DRESSED UP FOR ME?
IT WAS SVEN'S IDEA.
ONE HOUR. YOU GET THIS FOR ONE HOUR.
THAT'S OKAY. I PREFER YOU IN LEATHER ANYWAY.

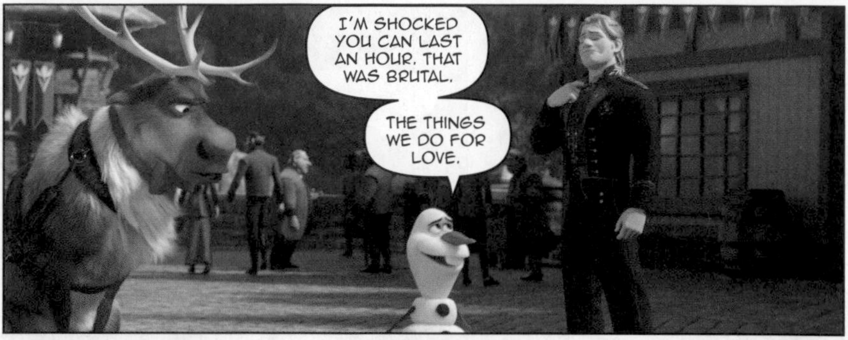
I'M SHOCKED YOU CAN LAST AN HOUR. THAT WAS BRUTAL.
THE THINGS WE DO FOR LOVE.

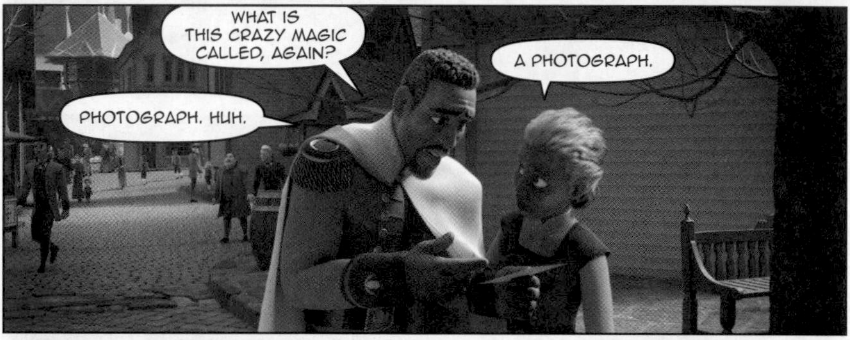
WHAT IS THIS CRAZY MAGIC CALLED, AGAIN?
A PHOTOGRAPH.
PHOTOGRAPH. HUH.

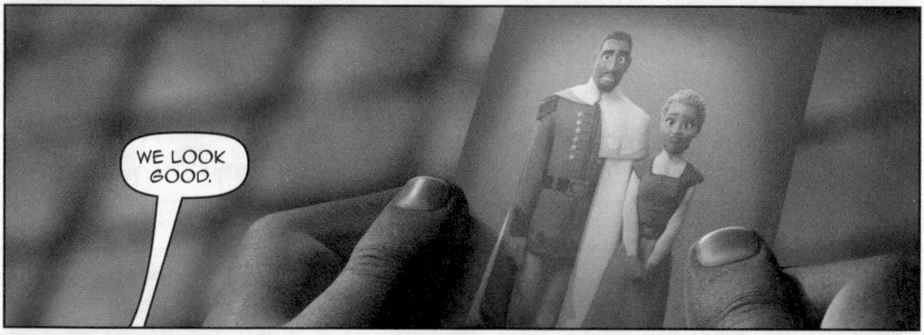
WE LOOK GOOD.

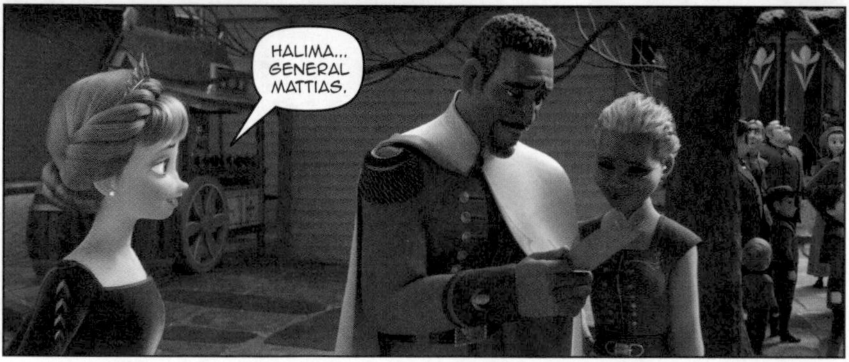
HALIMA... GENERAL MATTIAS.

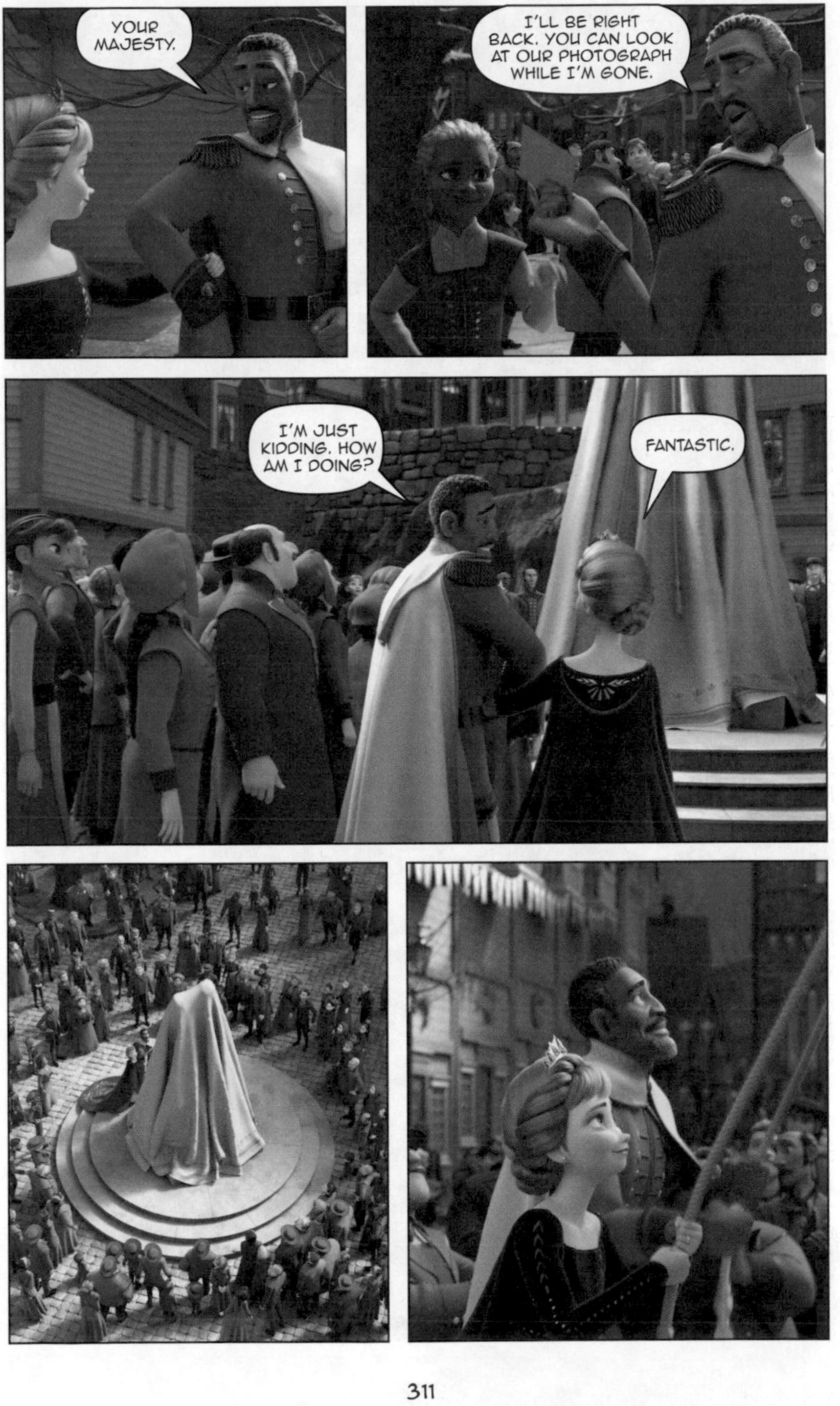
YOUR MAJESTY.
I'LL BE RIGHT BACK. YOU CAN LOOK AT OUR PHOTOGRAPH WHILE I'M GONE.
I'M JUST KIDDING. HOW AM I DOING?
FANTASTIC.

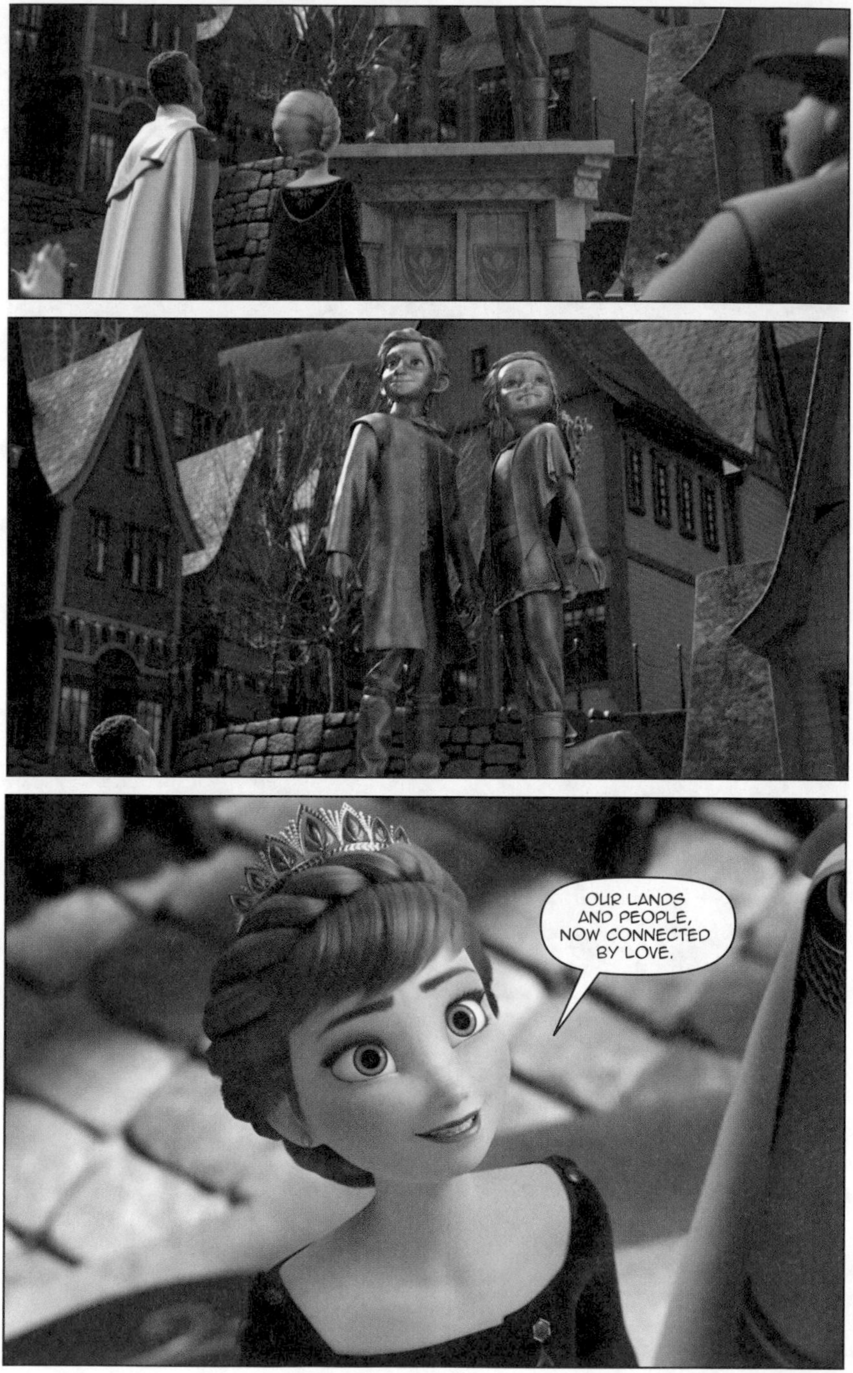
OUR LANDS AND PEOPLE, NOW CONNECTED BY LOVE.

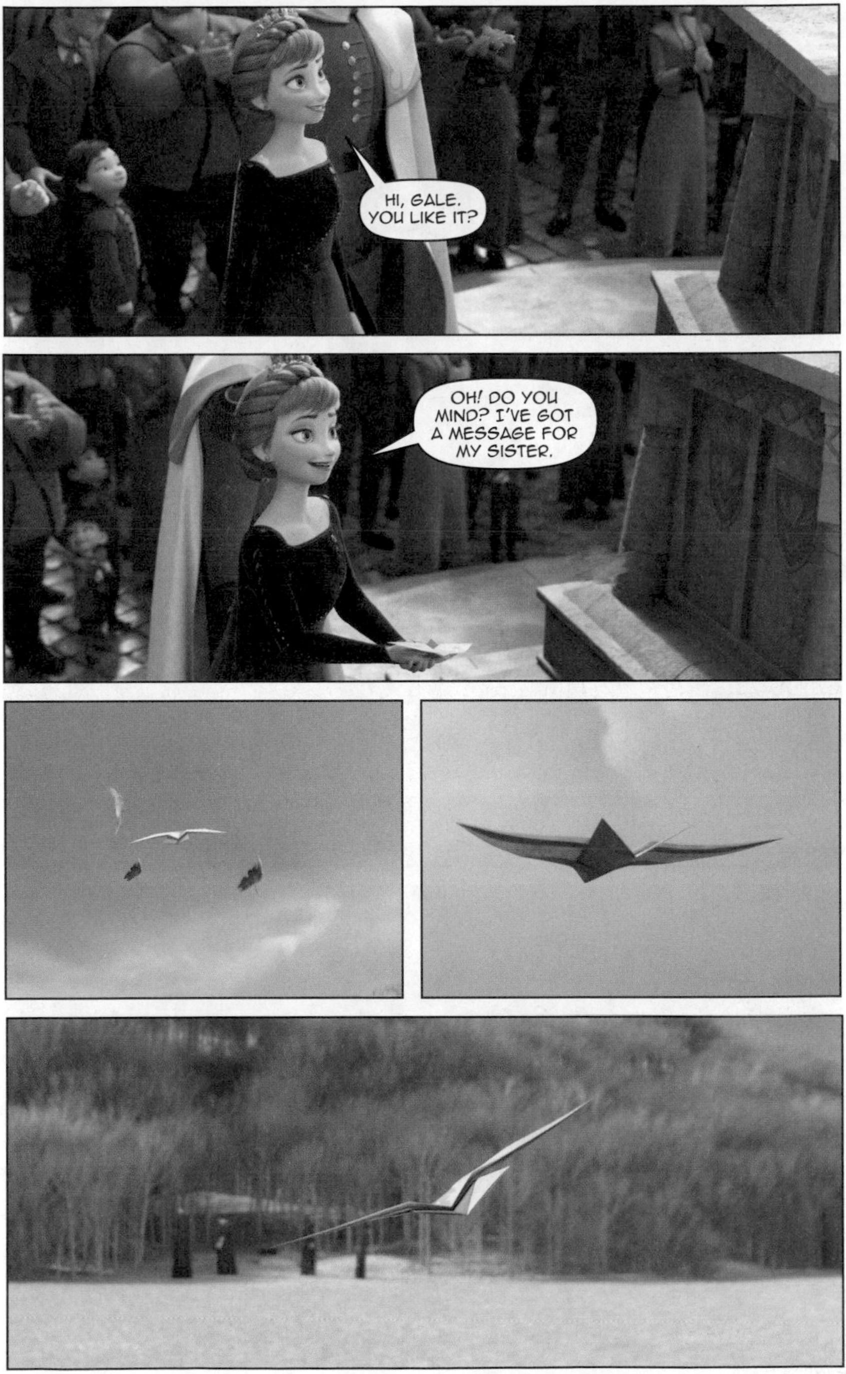
HI, GALE. YOU LIKE IT?
OH! DO YOU MIND? I'VE GOT A MESSAGE FOR MY SISTER.

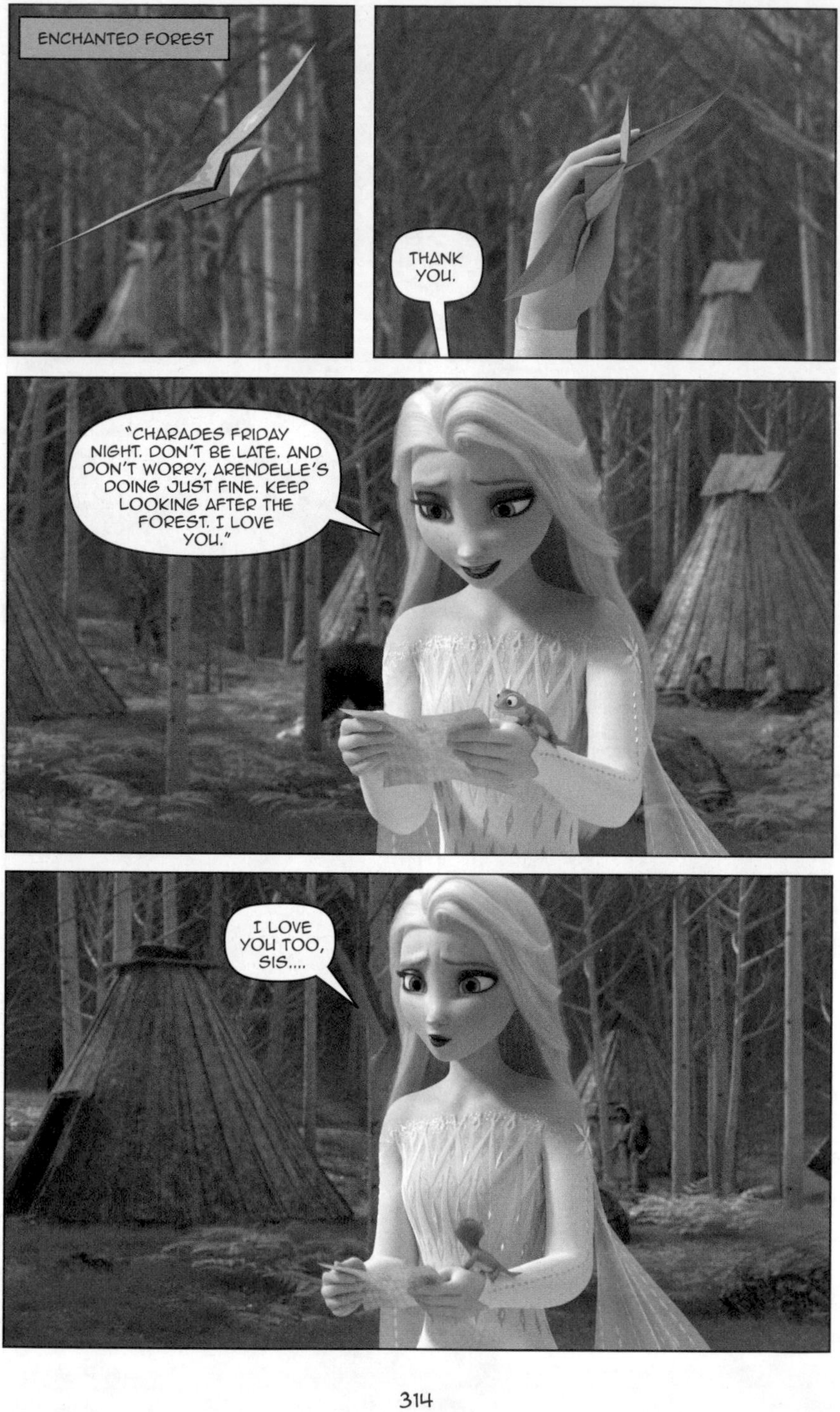
ENCHANTED FOREST
THANK YOU.
"CHARADES FRIDAY NIGHT. DON'T BE LATE. AND DON'T WORRY, ARENDELLE'S DOING JUST FINE. KEEP LOOKING AFTER THE FOREST. I LOVE YOU."
I LOVE YOU TOO, SIS....

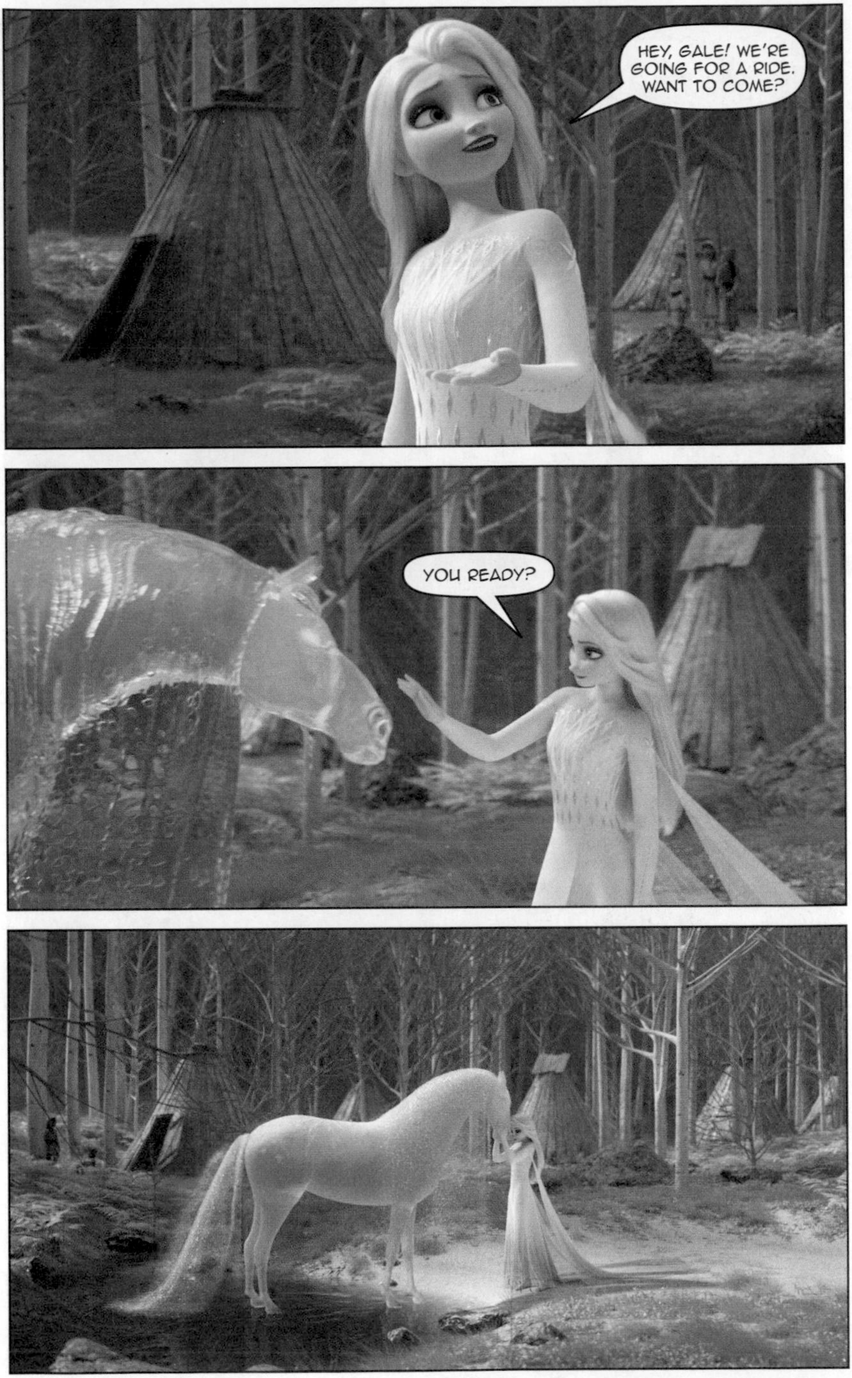
HEY, GALE! WE'RE GOING FOR A RIDE. WANT TO COME?
YOU READY?

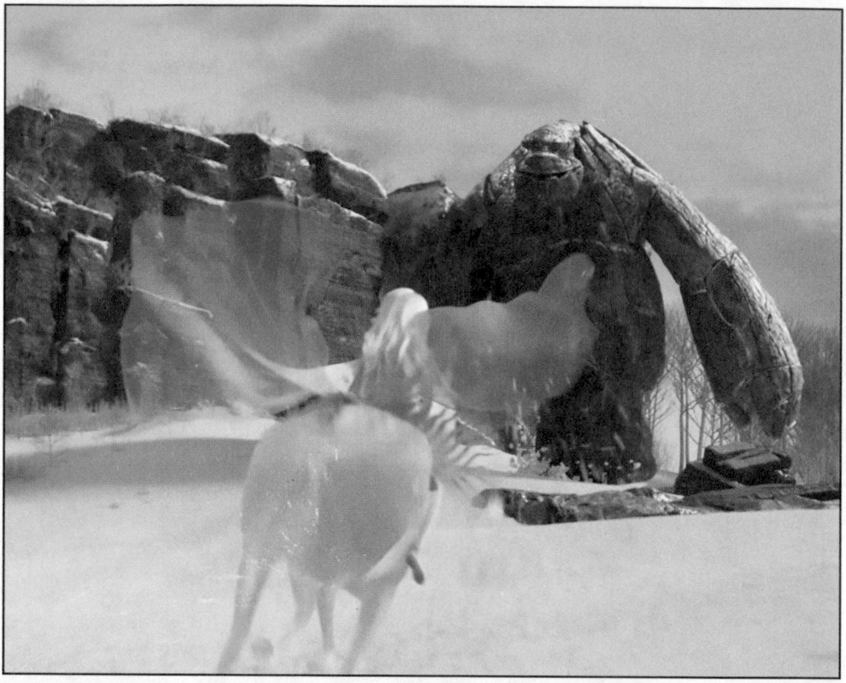

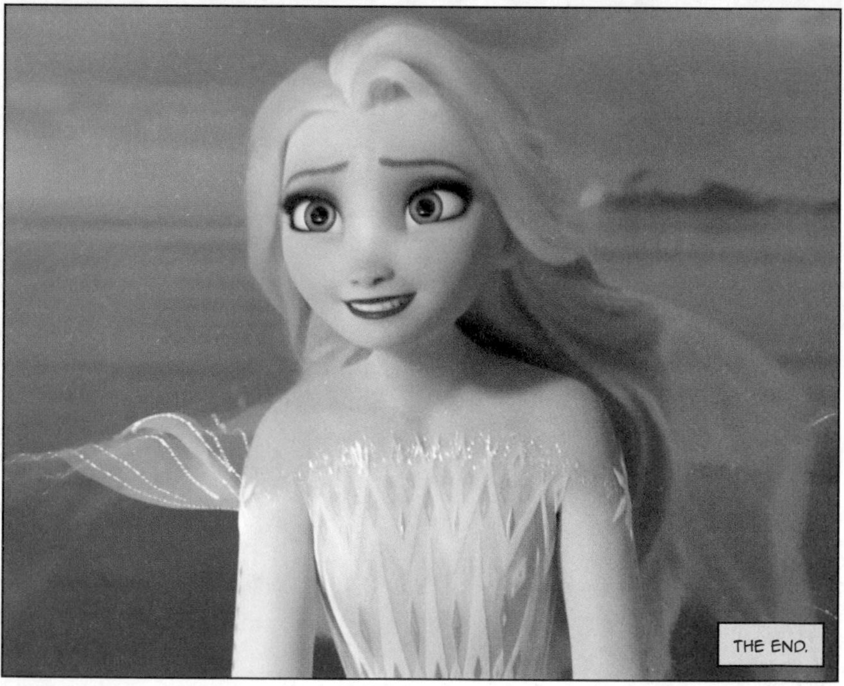
THE END.